Assassins of Kantara

Assassins of Kantara

by

James Boschert

www.penmorepress.com

Assassins of Kantara by James Boschert

ISBN-13: 978-1-942756-90-3(Paperback)
ISBN :978-1-942756-91-0 (e-book)

BISAC Subject Headings:
FIC014000FICTION / Historical
FIC032000FICTION / War & Military
FIC031020FICTION / Thrillers / Historical

Editing: Chris Wozney, Terri Carter, Danielle Boschert
Cover Illustration by Christine Horner

2nd Edition
Address all correspondence to:

Penmore Press LLC
920 N Javelina Pl
Tucson AZ 85748

Dedication

To Danielle, who is my rock of support.
And
Sophia and Eva

Acknowledgements

My sincere thanks to Christine Horner, Chris Wozney and Danielle Boschert for their tireless efforts and help.

Rubayat of Omar Khayyam;	Liber Press
Persian Miniatures	
The Legendary Cuisine of Persia	Margaret Shaida
The Valleys of the Assassins	Freya Stark
A Fool of God	E. Heron Allen
Poems of Baba Tahir	
Wikipedia	
Google	
Confucius	
Arab Seafaring	George Hourani
The Art of War	Sun Tzu

Table of Contents

Chapter	Title	Page

Middle East in 1185

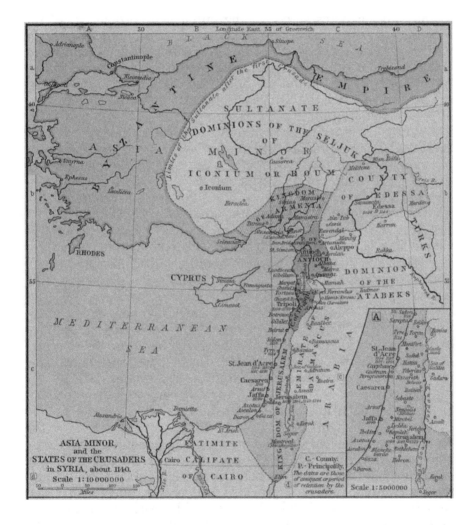

i

Knights of Christ, your ranks are broken;
Close your front, the foe is nigh;
—Robert Morris

Prologue
August 23, 1179 Jacob's Ford

Sir Guy de Veres stood on the unfinished battlements of the fortification called Chastellet and observed a host gathering on the Syrian side of the river Jordan. He knew with chilling certainty that Salah Ed Din had finally come to besiege the castle and intended to take it. Sir Guy's men and the other Templar officers gathered on the parapet to watch the Saracen army begin to cross the ford. They all looked equally grim.

"Where is the army of the King, Sir Guy?" one of them exclaimed, hammering his fist onto the newly mortared stone of the parapet. There was more than a hint of worry in his tone. He was the officer in charge of the castle, but Sir Guy was the person they all turned to, because he was the best informed and without doubt was the most capable of divining the intentions of Salah Ed Din.

"The messenger was sent a week ago," Sir Guy replied. "We should have heard something by now." He, too, was very worried.

"What are they going to do?" Another jerked his head at the horsemen splashing across the river, which was shallow after the long summer. Even the infantry would be able to walk across.

"Salah Ed Din knows this is strategically one of the most important corners of our kingdom. It is the easiest path to Jerusalem for a large army—look how easily they cross the river. He does not want this castle in place," Sir Guy responded, his tone terse. "We need to prepare for the worst as best we can."

"Then God protect us all. Go to your stations," the officer in charge ordered. "Bring the archers up here."

Deep in thought, Sir Guy walked down the steps of the battlements. As he had stated, a messenger had been sent off a week before to inform the King of the pending threat. The spies Sir Guy employed had told him of the build up of Salah Ed Din's forces, and the information they had provided had proved only too correct. Now he was trapped inside the castle with nearly seven hundred other Knights Templar and a large crew of masons, with no escape unless the King's army arrived to relieve them.

He glanced around as he walked across the courtyard to the unfinished bailey. His practiced eye took in the new masonry, which would not withstand siege weapons of the kind that Salah Ed Din could deploy; nor would the foundations be mature enough to block a determined sapping effort. Nor were the men inside the castle prepared for a lengthy siege.

Jerusalem was approximately one hundred leagues south of Chastellet. The messenger would have stopped at Tiberius before riding on, for Sir Guy wanted the Duke of Tripoli to be aware of the danger. Sir Guy had no doubt in his mind that if the king had received the message, he would have either sent an army to intercept Salah Ed Din or taken to the road in person. He hoped the former because of the king's sickness, but he knew the boy king would come himself if he could.

He became aware that the siege had begun when an arrow thudded into the dirt nearby, and shouts arose from the battlements above. He ignored the noise and walked the entire circumference of the inside of the castle wall to better understand its vulnerabilities. Unfortunately these were many, and he had no doubt that an experienced engineer on the other side could see the same.

Finally, he climbed the steps and joined a small group of armored men, who were peering over the parapet at the cavalry and infantry clustered just out of bowshot. The longbow men were taking a toll of anyone foolish enough to come within range: their accuracy was deadly at a hundred paces, and their arrows were a menace even at two hundred for any of the enemy who grouped together for too long. Their skill kept the foot soldiers away from the walls, but the enemy's mounted archers would courageously gallop their horses rapidly past the gate area and loose off their own arrows against the men on the walls. Their aim was uncanny, and unwary men had already suffered. The enemy army was also preparing some nasty contraptions called Scorpions, which could hurl a large arrow like a spear over long distances.

Sir Guy had an uneasy feeling. He left the gate area to go to the northeast corner of the castle, and what he saw there confirmed his worst fears. The enemy had already begun digging trenches. They were going to get as close as they could, and then begin a tunnel which would take them to the foundations. Once there, they would use wood and large bladders full of fat from animals to burn, creating an intense fire which would weaken the foundations of the walls and eventually bring them down. The officer in charge, Sir Edmond, joined him, and the two men watched impotently as the furious digging went on for the rest of the day. They had nothing with which to stop the sappers.

Had the message been lost? *Where was the king's army?*

In Tiberius, a town only half a day's hard ride from Jacob's Ford, the King's army sat on its hands while the lords argued. Baldwin IV, the Leper King, was in the middle of an argument with Grand Master Odo and his other lords.

"My lords," he sighed, impatiently flicking away a fly. With its broiling sun and innumerable flies, the torment of this climate could be unbearable at times. "It is almost a week since the rider came from Sir Guy at Chastellet and informed us of an approaching army. It is time to move, regardless of how small our army is. We must intercept Saladin at the river and demonstrate that we will not permit him to come and go at will."

"My Liege," Lord Joscelin responded, his tone wheedling, "our army is still preparing. There are equipment problems, and we are understrength."

"I am not always sure of Sir Guy de Veres' information," Sir Gérard de Ridefort said in a low, dismissive tone. He was one of the Templars who believed that knowledge of the ways of the Saracen was not necessary because a good charge could settle any argument with them.

Sir Arnold de Torroja, another senior Templar and well known for his hot-headed behavior, nodded agreement. Neither Templar liked the man they deemed a maverick Knight, one who was far too close to the Duke of Tripoli and the King for their liking. Sir Guy and the Duke shared a long association, and their knowledge of the Saracen bordered on the heretical. It was significant that Sir Odo de St. Armand, the current Grand Master, did not contradict Sir Gérard. He merely pulled on his long beard and looked away.

"They are only half a day away in any case, My Liege," Sir Arnold said. "We would know very quickly should there be a problem, and could deal with it swiftly enough."

Perhaps it was because Baldwin did not have sufficient energy to overrule his Lords that he failed to insist, and so the army of the King languished in Tiberius and offered no relief to a garrison that was under siege and unable to send more messengers.

One man who knew Sir Guy very well fumed at the delay. Max, Talon's friend and companion of many years, and also Sir Guy's, wanted to ride on, but Odo had forbidden him to do so, saying that the army would be leaving soon and he could accompany them.

However, the army did not leave soon, and Max raged, unable to inform Sir Guy as to his whereabouts.

It wasn't until October the 30th, almost a week after the messenger had arrived, that the army of the King of Jerusalem eventually set out.

Salah Ed Din's sappers finally managed to create sufficient heat in the tunnel to cause an explosion in the confined space, weakening the foundations of the north-eastern corner of the castle of Chastellet. The men inside the castle were worn down by the constant attacks on the gates and had devoted much effort to reinforcing them, all the while watching impotently as the sappers dug their way to the base of the walls.

They were out of food and water, and utterly exhausted by the incessant hail of arrows, and now large rocks, launched over the walls to maim and kill. A dirty and exhausted Sir Guy stared out towards the south in the vain hope that an army would appear, but it failed to do so, and as night fell on the 29th of October they heard the first sharp reports from the stressed masonry behind them.

As morning dawned on the 30th, the weary and dispirited men fought on, but later in the day Sir Guy heard what he had been dreading: the rumble of falling stones as the sapped walls collapsed. He and his closest companions rushed to defend the gaps, but the enemy charged into the openings over the rubble with great shouts of victory to overwhelm the defenders. The slaughter began.

Sir Guy and his men met them with flashing swords and stabbing spears. Theirs was the desperation of men who knew they were about to die but were determined to take down as many as they could.

Sweating and hoarse, Sir Guy and his companions fought on, faces distorted by hate and fury. He parried blows, struck and stabbed until he felt so weary he could barely stand. He parried a side swipe from an attacker, then stabbed the large man under his small shield deep into his abdomen. The man doubled over and fell aside with a groan of agony.

Sir Guy whirled to slash at another who was aiming a spear at him. He blocked the spear, but there were too many behind this one, the numbers were simply too great. Yelling enemy warriors surrounded him now, his companions having gone down one by one amid the screaming and howling of men in mortal combat; the rocks of the fallen walls were slippery with blood, making standing difficult. Roaring with battle rage, he cleared a space around himself at the top of the rubble. There was a short pause as the enemy men stopped to stare at the torn and bleeding Templar staggering and alone, on the hill of the dead and wounded; all of them were warriors who could admire a fighting man for his sheer courage, but then the yelling began again, and they surged forward. Sir Guy went down under the swords and stabbing spears of the enemy, the last obstruction to the army of Salah Ed Din's invaders at the fall of Chastellet.

Some few leagues away, Max in the vanguard of the slowly moving army stared towards the northeast and saw, to his horror, a black column of smoke rising into the sky. It was evening, and as the army approached the castle they could see, even from this distance, that the Saracen army had breached the walls. The castle was lost.

The Grand Master and his Knights were for attacking in the hope that the enemy could be caught off guard. Their first priority, however, was to keep the king safe. As the army turned to head back to Tiberius, Odo left a guard of Templars with the King, while he and the remainder of his knights rode forward to see what could be done. Max rode with Odo, desperate to see if there was any chance that Sir Guy might have lived through the battle.

They were ambushed before they could even get close, and in the growing darkness it became impossible to maintain the solid block of armed horsemen that had been so effective against the Saracens in the past. Max and several of his companions stayed close together and fought as hard as they could, but the skirmishing was haphazard, while the enemy spearmen and cavalry seemed to be everywhere.

The Templars gained no ground in their desperate push to reach the castle, which was now just a dark shadow in the distance with flames flickering against the night sky from inside. Finally, Max took charge of his embattled little group and ordered a retreat. There was no sight of Odo or the others who had charged recklessly ahead. Max was wounded, as were his companions, but eventually they managed to break off contact with the enemy in the darkness and make their way back towards Tiberius, where they arrived just as dawn was breaking.

The news they received from other stragglers was all bad. Odo had been captured, the castle taken, and over seven hundred Templar Knights slain. Sir Guy had been killed defending the gap in the collapsed walls. Others had been taken into slavery. While the army of the King of Jerusalem licked its wounds and its nobles assigned blame to everyone but themselves, Salah Ed Din proceeded to completely demolish the castle before leaving for his own lands.

Max and several of the other Knights eventually made their way back to Acre to deliver the appalling news and to recover from their wounds. Max reeled from the death of his friend and mentor, and fumed at the incompetence that had caused the loss of Jacob's Ford, but there was nothing he could do.

There was a sober and apprehensive mood in the city because of the huge losses; and yet, there was one person in Acre who was not saddened by the defeat. Brother Jonathan, still investigating witchcraft on behalf of the Bishop, heard that Sir Guy de Veres had been killed, and smiled to himself.

The last powerful protector of Sir Talon de Gilles had perished and now Brother Johnathan sensed that he was close to capturing his prey at long last. Sir Talon was wanted for witchcraft by the church.

Pass on from the name,
and look closer at the source.
The source will show you what you seek.
Leave the form behind.
—Rumi

Chapter 1
Information

High in the Alborz Mountains of northern Persia, there is a castle. The Eagle's Nest, or *Alamut* as it is known far and wide, stands on a crag overlooking the deep, narrow valley of the Alamut Rud. Alamut has been the home of the Masters of the Hashashini, or Assassins, as they were known to the Franks, going on for four generations. The names Alamut and Hashashini are synonymous and have struck fear into the hearts of men in high places, from the rugged coasts of the Mediterranean to the Hindu Kush. Vizier and Sultan alike have good reason to fear the wrath and deadly cunning of the Master and his minions. Again and again the Master has sent out his messengers of death to right a perceived wrong to his name, for revenge, or simply to shift the balance of power in another direction, and no one was safe.

The Master usually spent his winters in Alamut, which served as both his home and his refuge during the cold months, and this year had been no exception. However, spring was in the air, shifting from the bleak North Wind that froze everything in its path to a more easterly and warmer southerly wind, which melted the snow in the passes. This allowed travelers to move about from one city-state to another, or to join the huge caravans which had been halted by the winter blizzards but could now resume their journeys, either towards Tabriz in the far north, or east towards the fabled city of Samarkand and beyond.

The melting snows also permitted the passes to open and the Master's network of spies to re-circulate. Some to arrive at the gates of Alamut in small groups or as single travelers. In every instance they brought news from afar to the Master, who listened patiently and intently to every one. Slowly but surely, he built up a picture of events and incidents that had taken place while the mantle of winter isolated him. He and his shadowy people discussed situations, ranging as widely as the activities of the Crusaders in Palestine and Salah Ed Din, now in Aleppo, to the discord in Constantinople.

His interests lay not only in the clash of civilizations in and around Palestine, but also in smaller incidents occurring in remoter places. In this particular case, his messenger had come a very long way, from Oman.

Naudar, after a long and harrowing journey, had approached with trepidation the grim and forbidding fortress that glowered over the long, deep valley. He'd urged his tired horse past the villages of Gazor Khan and Chotor Khan at the base of the huge rock upon which the castle perched, and made his way up the steep path. As he'd approached the gates of the castle, he'd glanced up and inwardly shuddered. There were decaying skulls there on stakes; several were the heads of men he had known, men who had fallen afoul of the Master in one way or another. Naudar was a loyal and brave servant of the Master, but like everyone else, he always felt somewhat fearful when he came within the aura of the man who appeared to have powers far beyond those of a normal being.

Now he kneeled on the carpet with his hands on his knees, facing his Master, and waited for the man whom he worshiped to speak. The Master looked and sounded unusually impatient. His turban was made from expensive silk, and in the center was a huge emerald of deepest green. Rich robes fell about the lean man, and his eyes probed deeply into those of Naudar.

"What news do you bring me from Muscat?" he finally demanded. His tone was curt. Despite the years that had elapsed since his sister had run away from the Sultan of Shiraz, the Master was still determined to find her and inflict a terrible punishment for shaming him. Naudar had been sent to discover whether the Master's sister and her treacherous companions Reza and Talon had gone in the direction of Oman. Not a single clue had surfaced for many months as the deadly emissaries of the Master hunted far and wide, from Isfahan to Baghdad. Some had dared to come back to Alamut to tell the Master of their failure, and now their skulls adorned the archway over the great wooden gates of the castle. Others were sent out in their stead. But it was as though their quarry had simply vanished into thin air.

Naudar had moved slowly down towards the more Arab world of Yemen. He had managed to avoid the *Heyda* plague that ravaged the coastline from the tip of the Hormuz peninsular all the way down to Aden, although one of his three companions had died unexpectedly in Muscat. He had arrived in Aden, where a tiny clue had set him back towards Muscat to make an interesting discovery. An offhand remark by a horse trader indicated he had sold horses to a Frankish-looking man from Muscat, who had then sailed for India to sell the animals in that lucrative market.

Making sure that the information had been accurate, Naudar had remained in Muscat long enough to find out that indeed Talon had sailed to India, and had returned. Having verified where Talon was now living, Naudar left his second companion in the city to keep an eye on their quarry, with instructions to watch their every move until he came back. Then he had set off on the long journey to the towering mountains of the Alborz and Alamut, within which his master sat like a spider in the middle of its web.

"I found them, Master," Naudar said, with some pride in his tone. He had succeeded where many others failed. "They were there in Muscat all the time; or rather, the doctor and his wife were there. Our people missed your er ... sister because she and Reza, with the Frank called Talon, traveled far but have returned. The rumor is they brought much treasure, from India and beyond—from China." He sounded incredulous to his own ears, but the Master only nodded, as though he were well aware that ships sailed to and from China every year.

"So they have settled in Muscat?" the Master demanded.

Naudar nodded confirmation but said nothing; he waited as he had been instructed since he was a young boy. His eyes, trained to observe from under deep brows, slid around the room, noting the wealth contained therein: the richest of hand knotted carpets, gold and silver ornaments, rolls of parchment, and priceless manuscripts lying casually about on the carpets. His eyes shifted to the heavy silk drapes that kept out the cold at the openings of the narrow windows, then to the beautifully woven cushions. The sumptuous fittings of the room belied the grim exterior of the castle itself.

After a long pause the Master spoke. "You will take a team with you to Muscat, and you will bring my sister back. If at all possible, you will also bring back the two men as prisoners. I shall deal with them here, and set an example."

Naudar nodded, but felt a thin, cold chill trace itself down his back. The Master was still enraged at the affront committed against him by those two elusive former *Fid'ai*, Talon and Reza. Naudar didn't envy them, should they live to see Alamut again.

"What of the doctor, Master?"

"You will kill him and his family, if he has one. Leave no trace. No one is to be left alive other than the prisoners, whom you will bring here. Take men from the Isfahan castle. I shall provide a letter ordering Hussein to join you. Hussein will be in charge; you will be his guide."

Naudar swallowed. He had expected to be the one leading the mission, but he dared not show by gesture or word that he resented the command. He merely bowed over his hands on the floor, shuffled backwards until he reached the door, then sprang to his feet.

"Rest for two days," the Master said. "You may enjoy the women that are available, then be on your way. Go as a pilgrims. There will be many others on the roads now, and all will be going in that direction. Many pilgrims take ship to go to Mecca, so it would not be unusual for you to go via Muscat. No one is to know what you are about, not even the people in Isfahan." The Master's tone signified dismissal, but just as Naudar turned to go the Master's soft voice followed him. "Do not fail. Either die in the attempt or bring back those... people. Should you do this, you will be well rewarded."

Naudar bowed again very deeply from the waist. "It shall be as you command, Master."

After spending a happy two days availing himself of the wine and women, for the Ismaili did not forbid wine, a tired but contented Naudar mounted his horse and thankfully left the castle of Alamut behind. He turned once in his saddle to look back when he was far down the valley. Even at this distance he could feel the menace of the stronghold and shuddered. Then he turned his animal and cantered away. Two days later he crossed the high Chula pass. A track had been trodden through the snow and ice which allowed passage over the mountains to the high plateau. He spent another night with some Ismaili sympathizers in Ghazvin, after he had slipped into the city through the busy gates posing as a merchant on his way to Hamadan.

Before long he had passed through Hamadan and was well on his way to Isfahan, passing several lumbering caravans along the way. The weather improved as he moved farther south, until he rode up onto a low hill and beheld the white walls of that fabled city.

Naudar's destination was not Isfahan, but out of habit he decided to enter the city and take a measure of any local news which he could then carry with him to the remote castle in the East where his compatriots lived. Before long he was standing outside the large stone archway that led into the bazaar. No one remarked the slim, dark figure other than to take note, perhaps, of his well-bred horse, which looked as though it had been ridden hard.

After paying a man to rub his animal down and to feed it, Naudar strolled towards the entrance to the bustling bazaar, but stopped abruptly. Propped against the right hand wall of worn stone was a ghastly sight. From a distance it had looked as though a scarecrow had been left against the walls. On closer examination, it was the entire skin of a man who had been flayed, stuffed with straw to a grotesque resemblance of a man, arms and legs spread wide. It stank of corruption and was swarming with flies. From time to time one of the guards who stood nearby would brush the flies away casually with a switch. Someone in a macabre gesture had pushed two white stones into the gaping holes left by the eyes, which now glared blindly out at the crowd moving past. Pinned on the chest of the dead man was a sun-bleached piece of parchment, upon which something was written in faded ink.

Naudar edged closer among the throng of people moving past the gristly spectacle. Few looked at it, and women covered their noses, ducking their heads in disgust as they hurried past. Naudar peered at the writing, trying to make out the words. He was jolted out of his concentration by a loud voice.

"Can you not read?" one of the sentries posted at the gates demanded. Naudar cursed himself for being so obvious, but immediately adopted a pose. "I cannot read well, your grace. I am a poor merchant from Hamadan. Who is this and what was his crime?" his tone was wheedling and his manner subservient. It would most certainly not be a good idea to attract attention to himself, but he was curious.

"Why, it's the leader of those abominations who live in the mountains east of here," The guard told him gruffly.

"Who are they?" Naudar asked. Inside he was in a fearful turmoil. What had happened?

"They are the people known as the Hashashini! Their evil master lives far to the north. This is that foul creature Hussein, who was the leader of the group to the east. He was caught on the road trying to rob some merchants, but their guards managed to wound him and capture him. When they found out who he was, they brought him back to stand trial. The Sultan himself attended, and he ordered that the prisoner be flayed alive and stuffed with straw. Ha, ha! Pity he can't see himself standing there frightening all the women."

The sentry pretended to read the piece of parchment for the benefit of Naudar. "It says, 'To all who would be heretics and abominations and robbers of the innocent, know that this will be your fate.'"

Naudar shuddered theatrically, at the same time putting his hand half over his eyes as though to banish the sight from his mind. As he turned away, his mind was reeling. The sentry, however, hadn't finished with him yet. "You are not from this city. You did say you were from Hamadan, didn't you?" There was enough suspicion in the tone to make Naudar tense.

He nodded. "I was born in Tabriz, though. Far from all of this," he waved his hand in a disgusted manner at the figure in front of them. "I have heard of the Hashashini and pray to God I never meet them. I am a pilgrim on my way to Mecca and wish peace upon all men."

The sentry nodded his head; his hand relaxed its grip on his spear and he waved Naudar on. "Go with God, and may the rest of your journey be safe. You should join a caravan, then at least you will have protection. The Hashashini are ruthless."

Naudar bent at the waist and touched his forehead with the fingers of his right hand in respect. "I came south with a caravan," Naudar lied. "Insha'Allah, it will be a peaceful journey from here on."

He tore his eyes away from the macabre remains of his former companion-at-arms and joined the line of people and donkeys walking into the gloom of the bazaar.

He found a small *Chai Khane* deep inside the gloomy bazaar and sat down in a corner of the busy room, nursing a pot of tea. He was shaking with reaction to what he had seen. His destination had been the fortress of the assassins called *Qual'a Bozi*, where he had expected to convey the orders of the Master to Hussein and then head south with him. Yet here was Hussein in Isfahan: a grotesque parody displayed at the entrance to the bazaar. Eventually he calmed down long enough to make a decision. He would go to the castle and complete the first part of his mission, which would be to take some men with him to augment his own meager force in Muscat.

It took him two days to reach the hills. Along the way he passed patrols of Seljuk cavalry and was stopped several times by the horsemen who demanded aggressively what he was doing on the road. He replied that he was on his way to a village in the Zagros Mountains to bury an uncle, having come from Isfahan. He could name the village, which seemed to be enough for the Turks.

His arrival at the gates of the fortress created a stir among the subdued guardians. He was received with suspicion and had to prove who he was before anyone would allow him entrance. No sooner had he entered the fort than his instincts cried alarm. There was a palpable tension in the courtyard. Hussein had been a clever and active leader, and now there was a gap in the leadership with a dispute brewing as to who should take his place. Naudar sensed that several men wanted the role.

Naudar had no interest in any of their squabbles, but he was insistent that the master's intent be honored. He needed to take some men with him. That proved more difficult than he had imagined, for the Ismaili in the castle numbered only eighty men, and their spokesman, a sly but dangerous looking man named Firuz, informed Naudar they were facing imminent attack.

Seated on the ground around a fire in the middle of the courtyard and eating roasted lamb, Naudar realized he was on dangerous ground; but he had a mission to perform, and this setback could not be allowed to stop him.

"You should tell us all why it is that you need men to go with you to Muscat," one of the men demanded.

Naudar shook his head. "When I have the men and they are away with me I shall tell them at the right time. This is a mission that the Master will not allow me to discuss."

"Why should we give you men at all?" demanded another. "We need every man to protect ourselves from the sultan's men, who would destroy us! Curse them for what they did to Hussein."

Naudar suddenly felt the air around him become colder. They could murder him right here and no one the wiser, if they so wished. He glanced around carefully at the dark forms of the men seated all around him. The firelight played on their lean, wolfish faces and glittered in their dark, watchful eyes. Among these men were *Fid'ai*, trained killers like himself. Despite his own skill at arms he would not last a minute if they turned on him. They were frightened by what had happened to their leader and anticipated worse to come. They were sure the sultan would send a small army to besiege them in this outpost and slaughter most of them; he would flay any of them he should take alive. Naudar's intrusion was not welcome.

He took a careful breath and forced himself to sound calm.

"While I was in Isfahan I heard nothing of a planned attack on this castle," he told them. "They are pleased with themselves that they caught Hussein and might leave it at that."

One of the men lifted his head. "Hussein was betrayed," he hissed. "Someone told them he was going to be where he was at that time. Now they will come for us, that is for sure."

The reaction was immediate. "You are lying! In God's name, how could he have been betrayed?" demanded one of the men on the opposite side of the fire.

Amid shouts of anger and accusation, Firuz bellowed for silence. "No one can make an accusation like that without real proof, Mirza! You were not there, so how can you say that? I forbid anyone to make accusations like that until we know more." The men subsided into a sullen muttering.

Firuz turned to Naudar. "You should leave in the morning. I am sorry, but we cannot give you men. Go back to the Master and tell him we have lost Hussein. When he gives us a new leader, then we can help him."

Returning to Alamut unsuccessful was not an option Naudar wanted to even consider. He was quiet for a long time before he spoke again. "You know that when the Master reaches out, his arm is very long." He addressed Firuz directly as he said this. "If he hears that despite your problems you refused to help me, there will be ... consequences. No matter how long it takes for him to hear the news." He left the threat hanging in the air.

There was silence among the men clustered about the fire as the *Fid'ai* digested this threat. Finally Firuz looked up from glowering into the flames of the fire. His face was unfriendly but his eyes gave him away: he was afraid. Naudar knew he didn't want to upset the Master, even though the Master would not be able to send help, which they needed badly. He could and would send an unwelcome emissary to punish Firuz for disobedience; of that he could be sure.

Firuz scowled; he knew that Naudar was right. "You may take four men," he told Naudar with a shrug. "That is all I can spare."

Someone made to protest, but he glared at them and raised his hand for silence. "Go. Take the men with you and be gone."

Naudar relaxed a minute amount. "Give me six *Fid'ai* so I can ensure the success of my mission, after which I shall bring them back to you. It will take only a month. The Master will reward you well, that I can guarantee."

In the end, he left with five *Fid'ai*.

Three weeks later, Naudar and his five men arrived in Muscat on a dhow that had brought them from Bandar Abbas. He had told them of their objective and watched their reactions as he did so. Reza's reputation was known to all of them, so the order was received with apprehension. Most of the men, except the very youngest, had also heard of Talon, the Frank who had killed a lion, although his skills were not such a known quantity.

"This Talon has kidnapped the sister of the Master," Naudar explained, "and brought her to Muscat against her will. The Master wishes that she be returned to her family and the man Talon be punished. Unfortunately, Reza is also implicated; so he must be punished as well. They are all three to be taken alive back to Alamut."

"Reza alone makes a formidable foe. They say he is one of the most cunning of the *Fid'ai*," one of the senior men remarked.

"Then we shall have to be more cunning than he," Naudar stated.

They arrived on a hot day with little in the way of a breeze to alleviate the oppressive heat coming off the beaches and the mountains behind the town. The men were rowed ashore in a small boat, and then Naudar took them to the rented accommodation in the middle of the town, a few streets away from the bazaar. He advised them to change into clothing that resembled that of the Omani and told them to stay put while he went to find his companion.

He found him watching the discreet villa where their quarry were living. Saquib greeted him enthusiastically.

"I'm relieved you have arrived," he said as they embraced, out of sight of the walled villa. "There has been little activity, other than visits to the Mardini family, and the stables where they play Chogan. I am out of money. I hope you brought some?"

"I also brought reinforcements," Naudar stated. "Five men from Isfahan."

"Good. Did you see the Master?"

"Oh, yes. He put me in charge of the mission," Naudar lied.

Saquib went with him back to the bazaar to meet the others, and there he described what he knew of the activities of their intended victims.

"There is no point in attacking them in the street unless they are alone and at night," he stated. "But they never go anywhere alone, and I have never seen them wander about at night."

"Can we scale the walls of the villa?" Naudar asked.

"Perhaps, but any untoward noise will alert them. They post guards, and those guards stay wide awake."

Naudar gave some thought to this. "Then we must gain entry some other way," he stated. "But first you," he pointed to the men, "must see our quarry, so there is no mistaking them. We can watch

9

them for a while; there is time to do this properly. Remember, we have to capture them. That won't be possible outside of the villa."

The two men who were seated among the patrons of the teahouse when Reza and Yosef entered had been observing Reza and the men he went about with for days now. The teahouse seemed to be a favorite place. But now he was doing something odd.

Reza took from the folds of his robe two small sticks, about two-and-a-half hands long, and held them between the fingers of his right hand. It seemed to the two men that he was looking around for something.

Reza glanced at Yosef, made a face, then there was a blur of movement and Reza held a fly trapped between the two sticks. "Ah, finally," he said with a sigh. "There are too many of these in Muscat anyway," he remarked.

Yosef coughed his grunting laugh. "That seems a very impractical way to reduce their numbers, but I could certainly never do that," he said.

"It takes practice."

The two *Fid'ai* rose and departed. They did not notice the glance Reza gave them from under his brows while he pretended to focus on Yosef.

"Do you see those two men who are leaving?" he asked casually of his companion, who started to look up and around.

"Don't look up, Yosef. How am I ever going to turn you into a Companion with all the necessary skills of a *Fid'ai* if you behave like an idiot?" Reza demanded.

Yosef looked chastened. "What made you notice them?" he asked.

"First, I think I know one of them; second, they were paying far too much attention to us," Reza responded. "Come, we shall follow them. They are from Persia, I am sure of it."

He threw a coin onto the carpet and casually got to his feet; then with Yosef close behind, he followed the two men at a discreet distance as they hurried down the crowded streets of the bazaar. Their quarry left the bazaar and walked down several narrow alleys to finally come to a doorway set deep into a wall. One glanced back as they entered the doorway but he failed to see Reza and Yosef huddled in another doorway at the far end of the busy street.

When they had disappeared, Reza cautiously eased himself out of the recess and pulled Yosef after him.

"We have trouble," he said, and lead the way, hastening, with many a backward look, towards their own home and family.

"You look as though you have seen a ghost," one of Naudar's men remarked when the two assassins rejoined them.

"Perhaps we did. It was Reza," Shakil said, and went on to describe what he had seen.

"It was like a cobra striking! I have never seen anything so fast," he exclaimed, looking to his companion for corroboration. "I always knew, we have all heard how fast he is with a knife, but this?"

"I saw a fly captured between two sticks. I cannot even catch one every time with my hand!" Rashid added, his eyes wide.

"Was it something they put in your tea?" sneered one of the others. "Or maybe you brought the Hashish with you? Anyway, you should be able to catch more than one fly with your hand. You have a dozen of them flying around your head most of the time." The others laughed.

The two witnesses to Reza's feat glowered and said no more, but they looked at one another and shared the same thought. If that man could do this with a pair of sticks, how would he be with a sword?

Naudar looked at his men. He realized that if he delayed much longer they would fear their enemies, and that he could not have.

"We will move against them in a couple of days. I have found a way whereby we can surprise them no matter how fast they are."

Talon stood at the edge of the polo field, watching his son Rostam guide a pony around in circles while he tapped at a ball with his mallet.

The boy and the animal looked comfortable together. It was an experienced beast, one who listened to a good rider. Its ears flicked back and forth as Rostam asked it to canter in ever smaller circles. With almost no guidance from Rostam, who was leaning forward over its shoulder, the pony followed the ball closely, allowing the boy to continue tapping the ball every ten or so paces towards where his father and Reza were watching with critical eyes.

He brought the pony to a stop with barely any aid and grinned at them. "How did I do, Papa?" he demanded with an expectant smile.

Both boy and animal were sweating slightly in the late afternoon sun, but despite the dust Rostam looked happy and pleased with himself.

"There is work to be done, but it's coming along. You were riding one of the more docile ponies. Wait until you have a difficult one,"

Talon told him, but there was a small smile of approval on his stern, bearded face. His son had taken to Chogan with enthusiasm, and he desperately wanted to play in one of their games. He was certainly old enough now, but Talon still hesitated to introduce his son to the rough and tumble of the sport. Rostam's face dropped. He had clearly hoped for more praise, but he was getting used to the meagre compliments he received from his father.

"You could use your legs more and your hands less," Reza admonished him, "but you are coming along. You will be playing with us before long. Your father is getting old and the team needs a replacement." Reza danced out of the way of a swinging slap from Talon, who scowled, pretending to be deeply offended.

Rostam and Reza laughed at him. Reza put his arm around Talon's shoulders and together they walked the short distance to their own horses. They mounted up, and Talon led the way towards their house within the city walls.

Muscat was a large port town with a number of rich merchants—Talon now being one of them. They lived in a walled villa in a quiet neighborhood tucked away from the bustle of the town and the port, but still within easy walking distance of the bazaar and the quayside. Talon had chosen the house for its high walls and privacy, which above all he prized for his family. As they rode up the guards saluted and swung the gate open. The men were Baluchi—dark, thin and dedicated warrior mercenaries from the area of southern Persia, the dry country just across the straits from Oman. Riding through the stone archway, the three dismounted in the small yard, handed off their ponies to the syce who ran out to take them, then they strode into the building with Rostam in tow.

They found the women seated comfortably on cushions upstairs. Rav'an and Jannat greeted them with smiles, and kisses for their men. Talon always found that his breath caught in his throat at how beautiful Rav'an was. These days she glowed even more because of her pregnancy. His normally stern features softened into a smile of pure pleasure at seeing her.

"How is our boy doing at Chogan these days?" she asked him, leaning back in his arms to smile at her son.

"He will be a good player... one of these days," Talon admitted grudgingly, but he smiled at his son and she caught the expression. There was no little pride in his look.

Rostam grinned. "I love that game, Mama. It is like battle, or so Uncle Reza tells me."

"It is, young Pup. A little more work and we'll bring you onto our team," Reza responded as he released Jannat from a kneeling embrace. Jannat waved them to be seated as she began to serve tea. With a smile, she handed the first cup to Rav'an. The two women had become closest friends.

Rostam dropped to a cushion, reached for a tiny baklava cake and popped it into his mouth, savoring with relish the honeyed taste of the delicate morsel.

"Rostam! Where are your manners?" Rav'an admonished him, as she shifted the exquisite porcelain plate just out of reach. It was one they had brought back from Guan Zhou, the port in China. The cargo of porcelain had been snapped up by avid merchants within a couple of days. Some of it had gone to the palace of the Caliph of Oman, but much had gone north to Baghdad and beyond. Porcelain of this quality was rare, much in demand, and very expensive.

"I apologize, Mama," he said, without sounding in the least bit contrite, as he licked his fingers. "May I please have another one of those delicious cakes?" he asked in a mock humble tone.

"Hush, my Sister," admonished Jannat. "He is a growing boy and needs his food!" Jannat smiled at Rostam with affection.

"He *is* growing!" Reza said, observing the boy as though for the first time. "We need to start in earnest on his training, Brother. He is almost as old as we were when we began at thirteen."

"I am thirteen this year, Uncle," Rostam said, as he chewed on another cake.

"At thirteen we were in a castle called Samiran, two frightened boys who didn't know what they were going to do with us," Talon told him.

"Speak for yourself, you Frans. They brought you to that place to train or kill you, they didn't much care which," Reza laughed. "I came because, well, I was bored."

They rarely discussed this part of their lives, but slowly it was coming out in response to some persistent questions from Jannat, who had known nothing of their lives before they had rescued her, along with Rav'an, from the Sultan's harem in Shiraz.

"What did they teach you first, Papa?" Rostam asked, his eyes wide with interest. He tried to sneak another cake, but received a light slap on his hand from his mother.

"You could at least ask if your father and uncle want one before stuffing yourself, my son," she said, pretending to sound stern.

Talon took a cake from the proffered plate and popped it into his mouth, then chewed with obvious enjoyment. Finally, after a sip of tea he said, "They were only interested in teaching us how to use knives then. It was painful, as I recall, but Reza and I did well."

"We became the best of the class!" Reza stated with pride. "Our instructor used to match us up to demonstrate to the others how it should be done, and it almost always ended in a draw."

"Later we became very good at archery, and now we know much more that we can pass along to you and Dar'an and Yosef," Talon said.

"I think we should include him with those two," Reza said. "Dar'an has become proficient with the exploding devices, and Yosef can come close to matching me with his sword on occasion."

"Never!" Talon pretended to be shocked.

"How is that possible, my Reza?" Jannat teased him.

"I don't believe you, Uncle," Rostam laughed. Rav'an merely smiled.

"Well, I did say sometimes. But he is still not able to catch a fly with his chopsticks!"

"So there is still life in those old bones of yours, eh?" Talon said.

Rav'an regarded the two men with a smile. She doubted very much if any of their students could win in any match these two set their minds to.

"We have a new assistant cook," she stated to change the subject.

"What happened to Ali?" Talon asked, puzzled.

"He has taken sick and sent this man in his place while he recovers," she told him.

"Do you know anything about him?" Reza asked, suddenly cautious.

"Ali sent him along with one of his boys to introduce him. The cook says he is a distant relative," she responded. "Should I have asked more questions?" she said, looking concerned.

"We'll check up on him later," Reza told her.

A band of fierce barbarians from the hills
Rush'd like a torrent down upon the vale
Sweeping our flocks and herds. The shepherds fled.
—John Ross

Chapter 2

Assassins

Talon struggled against tight bonds, trying to find any slack which would allow him to move his hands. He heard a low groan from Reza, who was lying trussed up within a few feet of him. Talon shook his head, trying to clear the hideous ache that pounded inside. He lifted his head to look around the darkened room and noticed another body in one corner. It was quite still. He couldn't make out who it might be, but hoped that he wasn't dead.

He nudged Reza, who stirred and lifted his bruised and bloodied face to look at him. "How did this happen?" he asked groggily.

"No time to talk, Brother. They took my boots, so they found my knife. We need to get free at once!" Talon whispered.

"I have a small one on me," Reza croaked.

"Where?" Talon demanded eagerly.

"Inside... inside my pants."

"You mean... inside your... ?"

"Yes Brother, inside there."

Talon shook his head. "You are full of surprises. Very well, turn over and I'll try to get it out. What does Jannat think of that?"

"None of your business. Now will you get hold of it?"

Reza shuffled over until he was very close to Talon's back, and then even closer to where Talon's bound hands made contact.

"In there?" Talon's tone was incredulous.

"Yes, and be careful... Oooo. Not there!" Reza jerked back. "In the front, above my you know whats."

"All right! All right!" Talon grumbled. "Get closer."

Reza shuffled forward again. Talon's fingers groped and Reza flinched. "Ouch! Do you mind? Not there! Higher up... higher there, inside the belt."

"Sorry, Ah!" Talon's fingers felt the hard handle of a small knife tucked into Reza's under belt.

After much hurried fumbling they managed to loosen the small weapon, and it dropped onto the dirt floor with a soft thud. Reza rolled over and Talon pushed the blade into his fingers, then pushed himself back towards the knife, which Reza now gripped.

Within seconds the razor sharp blade had cut his bonds, then it took only a moment to free his brother.

They both scrambled to their feet, rubbing their sore wrists and ankles to get the circulation going again. The bonds had been tight.

"How did we get into this situation?" Reza whispered.

"Drugged, and I think I know by whom," Talon ground out, shaking his head. He still had a monster of a headache. He hurried over to the body lying in the corner, dreading what he was going to find. He gave a hiss when he saw that it was one of the Baluchi gate guards, quite dead. Evidently their captors had tossed him in here after they had killed him.

"Wish I had my sword," Reza commented, still rubbing his wrists, looking around him for some way out of the room. It was one of their own storerooms, one that had gone unused for a long time. Dust was everywhere, even sand, nothing in the way of equipment other than a broken harness lying on the floor in a corner.

"We have to get out of here as fast as possible and find out what is going on out there."

"I fear the worst!" Reza said, his tone dark.

Just then they heard the murmur of voices outside and the grate of a key in the lock. Metal bars were slid away with a scrape of iron on wood. Both men rushed over to stand either side of the door, flattening themselves against the mud brick walls.

The door was thrown open and men, still talking, strode into the darkened room. They stopped to peer into the gloom, looking for their prisoners, and it was then Talon and Reza struck. Talon's forehead collided with the nearest man's cheekbone, stunning him; a steel-hard hand seized the guard's sleeve and pulled as Talon whirled inside the man's sword arm and then heaved his victim off his feet to toss him, now minus his sword, into the arms of the man just behind him.

Reza had slammed his small knife backwards into the throat of the man nearest to him. As the guard fell to his knees, Reza relieved him of his sword and in one fluid motion thrust it into the chest of the man directly behind his first victim. Both Talon and Reza used their new-found weapons with savage intensity, bringing all their training in China to bear. The four guards barely had time to gasp, let alone cry out, before they were lying dead in a heap at the entrance of the storeroom.

Breathing hard, the two men paused to look down at their victims. "Just as I thought," said Reza. "I recognize these two. They are from the Master." He looked up at Talon with alarm in his eyes. "He has sent his dogs after us, Talon."

Talon nodded, his teeth bared. "Then we must find Rav'an and our family immediately. No one is safe!" He felt a hard knot form in his stomach.

They retrieved the swords of their dead opponents and then, shoeless, crept out out of the cellar and up the stairs towards the main rooms of the villa. Making no sound at all, they were able to arrive at the back entrance of the house undetected and slip inside the building. They heard a tiny scraping sound and their eyes flicked to the left towards the corridor. They saw Yosef, creeping towards the main hall where the stair went up to the second floor.

"Psst," Reza whispered. Yosef almost jumped out of his skin with surprise. His eyes wide and fearful yet determined, he froze.

Reza beckoned to him.

Relief flooded across Yosef's tense face as he slipped into the kitchen to join them.

"I came back from the ship to find the gate guards dead, so I was trying to find out what happened, Master," he whispered.

"You did well, Yosef. But where is Rostam?"

"He was just about to become a dead hero and charge up the stairs when I found him. I sent him back into the store room while I went looking for you."

"Good man. Dar'an?"

"He is down on the ship, Master Reza," Yosef responded. "Where are the ladies?" he asked.

Reza pointed upwards. "We are on our way to find out. Stay here and watch our backs. If there is anyone else, you need to hold them off until we have dealt with those upstairs. Can you do this?" Reza demanded.

Yosef nodded emphatically and turned away to stand guard, his sword held at the ready. With an approving look Talon and Reza focused on their own objective.

Both hugged the walls, trying to listen for anything that would indicate where the rest of the assassins might be. Reza pointed up and to the left.

"Someone is up there," he whispered.

Talon nodded. Reza's hearing was good and he trusted it. He leaned close. "What do you hear?"

Rav'an woke with an awful pain in her head to find herself lying on the carpet of one of the upstairs rooms. She remembered that she had stood up from the dining carpet downstairs feeling faint and had excused herself. "I... I'm not feeling very well. I think I will go upstairs and rest," she had said. Jannat had risen to her feet, pressing a hand to her head, and said, "I'll come with you."

They had both climbed the stairs slowly, Rav'an feeling woozy and wondering what had caused it. Jannat had seemed to be in the same condition. They'd reached the entrance to the first room and then must have blacked out.

Without moving, because her head threatened to fall off should she move too quickly, Rav'an glanced around and saw that she was not alone. Jannat was lying sprawled where she had fallen on her stomach, and there was a man near to the door with a sword in his hand. He was dressed in dark brown flowing robes, his face obscured by a shemagh that concealed all but his dark eyes. She felt a cold chill pass down her neck. Assassins!

The man was squatting near to the open door where he could watch her and at the same time keep a look out for anyone approaching. He carried a long sword and had a dagger hanging off his belt. There was another slimmer version of the first man crouched by the window. His bare feet were not as dark as many Omani, so she guessed that they had come to Muscat from somewhere else. She took a sharp intake of breath; he had to have come from Persia. She reached out to touch Jannat. Her fingers came into contact with her friend's ankle; it was warm, so she was at least alive.

Rav'an wondered what might have happened to Talon and Reza. She squeezed her eyes shut at the first thought that came to mind. They were probably dead. These people would not dally with either of them. Too dangerous! A tear trickled down her cheek as she contemplated the worst. Her brother had finally succeeded, curse him. She hoped death had been quick. It most certainly would not be for her, nor Jannat—and then panic struck. Where was Rostam? The servants, their retainers, Yosef and Dar'an? These murderous messengers from her brother would show them scant mercy, she was sure of that.

Jannat stirred and began to push herself up from the floor. She shook her head, causing her luxurious hair to flow around her face.

The guard by the doorway, alerted to her movements, stared at her, and even under his face covering Rav'an detected the gleam of lust as he watched the slim girl sit up and look around.

"Come over here, my Sister," Rav'an murmured.

Jannat stared at her, then complied. "What happened, Rav'an?" she asked in a frightened tone as she settled near. She had just noticed the squatting guard. "Who is he, and what is he doing here?" Jannat's eyes were wide with fear and her lower lip was quivering.

"Do not fear, my Sister. It will be all right," Rav'an whispered, although she was far from confident. She needed Jannat to be strong, not demoralized and utterly without hope.

Just then there were footsteps outside and another taller man, also barefoot and with his face covered, padded into the room. He held a sword in his right hand that was bloody, and there were darker stains on his dark brown robe.

"Ah, it seems that you are awake," he commented in Farsi.

"Who are you, and what do you want?" Rav'an managed to say, although she knew very well; her mouth was very dry and her head still pounded.

"I am here to take you back to your brother, The Master," the sinister-looking man said.

"What have you done with Talon and Reza?" she demanded. He knew who they were, so there was no point in pretense.

"They are prisoners. They succumbed to the same drug that struck you, my Lady," the man said with a smirk, and then nodded knowingly at her relieved expression.

"Oh yes, they are alive, and they come with us. The Master intends to make a very public example of them both. They are traitors and heretics. You he will deal with privately, but you will not leave Alamut alive either."

"How do you propose to take us all that distance as prisoners? Aren't you afraid we might escape... or kill you along the way?" Rav'an asked him. Her heart was beating furiously, but she was utterly determined that he should kill her here. The prospect of how they would all be executed in Alamut didn't bear thinking about. If only she could provoke these monsters to kill them quickly! Their heads would make the journey, but they wouldn't care.

"Who are you? What do you want, you pigs!" Jannat cried out before Rav'an could stop her. Her anger at their circumstances was overcoming her fear.

19

The man took two strides across the room, leaned down and struck Jannat across the face. "Be quiet! Your friend here can tell you, if you live long enough. *You* do not matter. My men will have you before we are done!" the stranger snapped as he stared down at the crouching Jannat, her hand pressed to her inflamed cheek where he had struck her.

"Leave her be, dog! She has done you no harm!" Rav'an shouted.

"Nor will she. Tell her to keep silent or I shall beat her to within an inch of her life, and the same applies to you. The Master didn't seem to be very concerned about what condition you were in when we got back," the man snarled. "We will take you to *Qual'a Bozi,* where I shall have many more men to guard you. Not even the traitor Reza will be a match for them." He paused, listening.

"Men's voices, and yes the wo—" Reza didn't finish. There was a loud slap and a cry of pain from somewhere upstairs in the main bedroom. Talon and Reza froze. It had come from Jannat. Then Rav'an shouted something. Up until now the expression on Reza's face had been tight as he concentrated on their mission; now it became suffused with rage. Talon quickly put his finger to his lips and shook his head as he held his brother's eyes. Reza took a deep breath and clamped his lips shut in a thin line, but there was now murder in his eyes.

Sliding through the kitchen towards the base of the stairs , they came across the dead servants, one of whom had been the new assistant cook. He too was dead, which told Talon just how ruthless these men were. There were to be no witnesses, nor tales told in the bazaar after the event. He wondered how many men they were up against. He heard voices again, and froze.

"Those men are taking a long time to bring up the prisoners. I can't believe how easy it was to take them down! So much for the lies and legends about Reza and Talon." The speaker laughed.

A woman's voice interrupted. "They will still stop you, dog! If they don't, I shall. You will never be able to sleep all the way back to Alamut. I shall see to that!"

"Have your say now, my lady," the man sneered. "But remember, when you get back an example will be made of you. Your brother made that quite clear."

There was silence, except for a sob from Jannat. Then the man said to another, "Mihub, I am tired of waiting. Go and hurry them along. I don't want to be here if some visitor happens by."

There was a shuffle, then a youth appeared at the top of the stairs. He scurried down and into the corridor where Talon and Reza were hiding. He noticed them too late to do more than emit a short strangled cry before Reza ran him through and Talon cut his throat for good measure. They let his twitching body down slowly to the floor, where it bled profusely, and they again listened, straining their ears for the slightest clue. There was silence above them. Talon pointed to one of the rooms across the hallway. Their bows were stored there, along with other weapons. He flitted silently across the space at the base of the stairs, watching he balcony for any movement.

He managed to retrieve their bows and their two Japanese swords. Returning to the hallway, he tossed one of the swords over to Reza, then his bow, and finally a quiver of arrows. Talon started to move to join Reza, then froze. The silence above them was ominous. Something was wrong.

Then someone spoke from above. "I see that you are better at escaping than I had imagined."

Talon glanced across at Reza, then responded. "Your sleeping drug didn't last long enough."

"What have you done to my men?" the man at the top of the stairs demanded.

'They are all dead." Talon said.

"Ah, but I have your women up here with us."

"We know that. Leave them unharmed and we will spare your life. You have my word."

"I cannot leave without the Master's sister."

"Yes you can, because if you harm a hair on her head I shall dismember you finger by finger. It won't be fun for you," Reza threatened. He swiftly drew and knocked an arrow, aiming it up the flight of stairs. Talon did the same.

"I am going to come out, and I am taking her with me. The other woman is of no importance to me, but she comes too. We shall keep her hostage upon your letting us go."

There was a scuffle, a slap and a low cry from the room, and Rav'an was pushed into view by a tall man covered from head to foot in dark clothing. He had a knife to her throat and clutched her to his chest, effectively hiding behind her. Another man shoved Jannat forward but he was not as careful; all the same he attempted to use her as a shield.

Both women looked rumpled and shaken, but Rav'an was not cowed. She regarded the two men below with wide, aware eyes. Her eyes told Talon of her relief, then flicked to the side, and he knew what she meant.

He tried one more time. "We have killed all your companions; not one is left alive. You will be next unless you let the women go."

"You know full well what will happen to me should I not bring her back to the Master!" the man responded with a jerk of his prisoner. Rav'an winced as the blade was pushed hard against the skin of her neck.

"Your head will be in a sack that goes to the Master! That's the only way you are going back there," Reza ground out between his teeth.

Rav'an blinked in an exaggerated manner, staring straight at Talon. He tightened his bow, biding his time and watching. Then Rav'an screamed, her left hand sped up to come between her captor's hand and her neck while her right fist swung down hard and backwards, at the same time she went limp in the man's arms, just as she had been taught by Talon. Surprised, off guard, and in pain from the blow to his groin, the man gasped and tried to grab for her as she dropped away, but too late; he was left with her flimsy shawl while she went down far enough to expose his upper body to the waiting archers.

Talon's bowstring twanged and the arrow flew the short distance to embed itself in the throat of the assassin, who clutched at it and then fell choking to die on the floor. But the other assassin, sensing rather than seeing what had happened to his companion, raised his knife to plunge it into Jannat. Reza shot him in the arm and yelled.

"Drop, Jannat! Drop!" She promptly went limp and fell away from the man, who howled with pain from the wound. But he was a *Fid'ai* and as quick as a whip. He dived out of sight back into the room and vanished.

Talon and Reza sped up the stairs like angry cats to reach Rav'an and Jannat, who fell into their arms, shaking with relief.

"We *must* stop him, Reza," Talon growled, as he held Rav'an briefly.

Reza nodded. Yosef, who had bounded up the stairs behind them, began to guide the weeping Jannat back down to the ground floor. Rav'an was grim and determined not to succumb to tears.

Cautiously the two men on the landing peered into the room, then relaxed. The open window told them what they needed to know.

"I know where he might have gone," Reza said. He was coldly furious.

"Then we must hurry," Talon responded, then he remembered Rostam.

"Where is Rostam?" he almost shouted.

"I'm here, Papa!" Rostam called from downstairs, looking up at the adults with tear-filled eyes. "Yosef made me hide from the men in the storeroom. I didn't know what else to do." He was weeping with relief, but also because he had been scared.

"Go to him, my Warrior," Rav'an told him. Talon let Rav'an go and ran down to embrace him. "Yosef did the right thing, Rostam. They would have surely killed you had you not. Thank God you are alive. Remember, there is a time to fight and a time to hide. You both made the right decision," he repeated, looking into the boy's eyes as he spoke.

"Where is Dar'an?" Rav'an called in alarm. They weren't at dinner with us, so where?"

"I know they were going out to the tea house in the bazaar," Jannat said through her tears. Her voice was muffled in Reza's shoulder. "But after that I don't know."

"He is safe," Reza assured her. "Dar'an went to the ship on some business or other."

"They would have killed them when they came back. Neither would have been a match for these people," Talon said, as he tore the face covering off the dead man.

"Do you recognize this man, Reza?"

"Yes, that one I do remember. He is one of the better men who serve the Master. His name is Naudar."

"Now we must go," said Talon. "Come, Reza, we will finish this off today."

The two men sped out of the compound, past the dead guards and onto the street. It was as though they were back in some normal world as they joined the throngs of traders, laborers, veiled women, and slaves on their errands. No one knew what kind of slaughter had taken place within the sanctuary.

Reza led the way at a trot. People gave way as they noticed the two intent looking warriors with their bows at the ready trotting purposefully along the street.

Soon they were moving past the tea house that Reza had frequented and were running onwards to the deeper, narrower streets of the bazaar where they hoped their quarry would have gone to ground. He would have to have his wound tended to before he left Muscat. They had no choice but to track him down.

Reza held up his hand as they came within sight of a doorway. "The last time I saw those two men, they were entering that low door down there." He pointed out a flat-roofed building to Talon, who crouched just behind him.

"You can bet that there is a back way out. We need to find it and block it off," he said.

"There will be just him," Reza said with some certainty.

"You're sure?"

They threw all they had into our capture. I doubt if there is anyone there but him, if indeed he is there."

"We need to find out. I shall go around the streets until I find a back alley; there must be something like that. I'll whistle when I get there, and then you can take the front."

"Good. I want his head."

"Be angry, but be cool, my Brother. Hot anger only gets one into trouble."

Reza nodded. "I will be fine, Brother. Go now."

Talon hastened to find a street that was parallel to the one they had been on. It was difficult. The very narrow streets of the bazaar wound in all directions except the one he wanted. Houses were so close together that the second floors almost touched, casting dense shadows that he approached warily.

Finally he figured that he might be in the right place and took careful stock of the alley and the wall where he thought the lair of the assassins might be. The street was deserted at this time, so ignoring the sun-dried wooden doorway he cautiously climbed the rough mud brickwork to peer over the wall. In front of him was a tiny yard in which was a large jar of water, some trash, and a cat sleeping on a ledge just by another door, which led into the flat-roofed building.

Talon thought about the options the assassin might have. He could either come out of the door in which case Talon had him, or he could take the flat roof and escape that way. There were plenty of avenues open to him if he decided upon that option. The door was shut and there were no windows, so Talon decided to climb the wall and place himself where he could see if his quarry decided upon the roof.

He whistled.

Reza had already gained entrance. The door had not been locked but led into another small courtyard which led off to three mud houses, all small but all connected at their walls. He had no idea which house to begin with, but a young boy was standing at the entrance to one of them.

Putting on a smile, Reza said to the shy child, "Salaam, boy. Have you seen anyone come through here last few minutes?"

All the boy did was to point. Reza nodded his thanks and glided towards the dried up doorway of the house most to his right. The planks were separated with age, but it was dark inside so he couldn't see anything.

He gently tried the door, but it was shut and fastened on the inside. Silently he took out his knife blade and slipped it into the crack to where he thought the latch might be. He pushed up very carefully. He heard a slight noise inside. Throwing caution to the wind he shoved the blade up and the latch lifted. With a thrust of his shoulder Reza slammed the door open and dived into the gloom ahead of him, stepping sideways as he did so. There was a flicker of movement ahead of him and a knife hammered into the mud wall where he had just been, then fell to the floor with a clatter, which was followed by a muttered curse.

A figure disappeared around a corner. Diving forward with his sword drawn, Reza followed. He saw the legs of the man pounding up the short steps towards the roof, a door crashed open, and he heard the sound of running feet on the roof above him. Reza also heard a whistle and knew that Talon had seen his quarry. Holding his sword ahead of him Reza bounded up the stairs and at the entrance rolled out onto the roof. A large stone flew past his head as he regained his feet and turned to find his assailant skipping over the parapet of the house towards the next roof.

The man glanced back at Reza, sending him a malevolent glare as he took off towards the neighboring house. He was still looking back at Reza when an arrow took him full in the side and knocked him over. He crashed to the surface of the roof with a cry of agony, sprawling forward onto his face. In one leap Reza was on him with the point of his sword on his back. There was no need, however, for with a shudder the assassin went limp. Reza kicked him over onto his back and stared down at him. The man, not much more than a youth, was dead.

"I know this one," he said to Talon, who had wasted no time in joining him. "He came from *Qual'a Bozi,* not far from Isfahan."

"Let's inspect the rest of the house, then we leave," Talon said.

They arrived back at their house later that afternoon to find the others already busy trying to clean up the mess.

It took some time to tidy up the house and the yard. Yosef brought Dar'an back from the ship, along with some crew members led by Tarif and Waqqas. They were shocked by what they saw, but after a brief explanation from Reza, who swore them to silence, they helped to lay out the bodies in two rows down in the cellar, the assassins in one row and the servants in another. All in all it had been a massacre, and there was much anger at the indifference displayed by the killers towards the innocent servants.

"It will be some time before news of any kind finds its way back to the Master," Talon told his family. "Reza and I checked their lair very carefully. There seem to be no others from what we can tell, and we are going to send a message which should reach the Master some time next month, by which time we must not be found here. A message does need to go back."

"My brother tried to capture us and intended to deal with us most horribly," Rav'an said. Her voice was ice cold and her face reflected her feelings. "He is no brother of mine after this."

"Reza, you know what to do, so I shall leave it to you," Talon said. "Delay as long as you can, while we plan where we can go," he went on. "I need to prepare the ship. Waqqas, come with me. We have to find the rest of the crew."

Bird in a cage
Set free
Soaring in the sky...
—Tirupathi Chanduppatla

Chapter 3
A Voyage to Somewhere

Later that night when they were in the upstairs rooms drinking tea, they talked about their options.

"I want to go back to China," Rav'an said. "We will never be safe here, now that he knows."

"I agree," Jannat said firmly. "I liked China, and Hsü would welcome us with open arms."

Reza looked thoughtful, "While I agree that China is a good option, I wonder if that is not the first place he will think of next? Remember, there are thousands of Persian and Arab people living in Guangzhou. It would take time, but eventually one of his men could arrive and we would be none the wiser. Then it would begin all over again. Talon, what do you think?"

Talon looked ill at ease. Finally, he met Rav'an's eyes and said, "Some years ago, when I was in the Kingdom of Jerusalem, I made a promise to a King."

"To a King!" she exclaimed.

"What kind of promise, Papa?" piped up Rostam, from next to his mother.

"That I would return to tell him if my mission had been successful," Talon told them, looking even more uncomfortable.

"What mission?" demanded Jannat.

"A promise to Rav'an that I would find her."

They all stared at him.

"You told a King that?" Rav'an asked him, sounding pleased. Her eyes were full of tears and a smile trembled at the corners of her mouth.

"Well, er, yes, I did," Talon said, looking embarrassed.

"You certainly took your time about it!" Reza laughed. "She was a married woman when you finally decided to come and get her."

Rav'an glared, half amused, at Reza, while Jannat snickered and slapped his arm. "But he did come back, Reza! You are so cruel. You

27

both came. Where would Rav'an and I both be had you not? So don't tease our brother here."

Reza winked at her, and Rav'an smiled at them with affection. He couldn't help it; his adoration for Jannat always gave him away.

"What did the King say, Talon?" she asked.

"He told me to come back as soon as I could, and to tell him whether I had succeeded or not."

Rav'an put her chin in her hand and pretended to consider the matter. "I think you did. But now you want to go and tell him so? Would it not be a perilous journey? Would he even be alive when you got there? It has been many years, my Prince."

"We could sail up the Red sea all the way to a place called Elat. Then it would be a few weeks, perhaps less, to Jerusalem, and on to a city known as Acre, where I have many friends. As for the King, it is true he was very ill when I left. Leprosy. But I do admire him. Despite his terrible impairment he is a true King."

There was an apprehensive look on all faces at this. Everyone knew how fearsome was that disease. No one knew any cures for leprosy.

"I have a destination in mind that is not part of the Kingdom," Talon said to reassure them. "We could disappear there and no one the wiser. I will have discharged a pressing obligation, and we can have a new life, under a different name if necessary."

"It's about honor then, Talon?" Jannat asked.

"Yes, it's about his honor, my Jannat," Reza said with a hint of resignation in his tone. "We are doomed to follow this man and his honor about."

He grinned and ducked a swipe at his head from Talon, who gave a rueful laugh. "It is true, but we can also disappear in a direction that might not be obvious."

"Will we be able to play Chogan where we are going, Papa?" Rostam asked.

"Hmm, it's possible," Talon replied with a smile.

The next day was a busy one. Dar'an was sent off to inform the doctor and Fariba about the situation. They lived in the compound attached to the Caliph's palace. It was not long before both appeared at the gates to the villa, which were now guarded by men from the ship with Yosef in charge.

A full scale conference was held after the embraces and tears of concern were over and Fariba had settled down with Rostam sitting close.

"Imagine my horror when Yosef told us the news!" Fariba said, wiping her eyes.

Doctor Haddad nodded agreement, his gray beard bobbing up and down. "They are evil men, my children. I am amazed at how you managed to get free and deal with them."

"Talon and Reza are exceptional at this kind of thing," Fariba said comfortably. She reached for Rostam and gave the boy a fierce hug. "I don't know what we would have done had they succeeded."

"You should have seen Rav'an and Jannat, Auntie," Reza said proudly. 'They stayed calm and helped us put an end to their captors. But the point is, Auntie, we have been found. If they had succeeded in taking us, there is no telling whether they would have come after you. That is part of my fear, that the Master wants to hurt all of us."

Haddad looked at Fariba, whose eyes had widened. "What do you think we should do, Talon?" she asked.

Before he could reply, Doctor Haddad interjected. "The Sultan can protect us, my children. We did him a great service during the Cholera epidemic. I even saved his youngest son's life!"

"He cannot protect us, Uncle. We were lucky this time. Very lucky, and we have to leave; but before we do I want to lay a false trail," said Talon.

"What sort of trail?" Reza asked him.

"We can put it about that we have gone to India, after first visiting the island of Lamu to pick up some African cargo. It is the time of the Monsoons again, and we are seafaring traders, after all; why would we not go off again to trade?"

"I hope the cholera is over down there, as that is where it came from. Poor Imaran did not survive because of it, and Boulos was lucky he didn't succumb," Haddad said, with a concerned glance at Talon from under his thick white eyebrows.

Haddad was referring to the two brothers of Allam Al Mardini who had sailed with Talon and his friends down to the island of Pate and Lamu on the African coast. They had bought slaves who had been infected by the Cholera, which had raged across Lamu. Subsequently, Imaran had died, along with most of his crew and all the slaves on his ship. Boulos had limped home to Muscat, only to discover that other ships had brought the disease with them to the city and people were sick and dying everywhere.

Talon and his ship had returned from China to find the population severely depleted from the epidemic, but Doctor Haddad held in very high esteem by the Caliph and his palace Vizier because he had saved many lives with his quick understanding of the situation. He had insisted upon measures to bring the spread of the disease under control, and he had nursed many afflicted people back to health, including the Caliph's son.

The aged man looked around at his family with deep affection and sighed. "I am too old to be going anywhere these days, Talon. I shall stay and pray to God that he spare me for my work here, which is important." He sent a look of appeal to Fariba, who looked back with love in her eyes. "If you stay, my husband, then I shall too. My place is by your side.

"Children!" she said sharply, as they all began to raise their voices in protest. "It is not the good doctor nor myself who face danger, it is you, and while I weep to think that you will leave us again for who knows where, you must seek safety from this vengeful man wherever you can. We are both too old to be voyaging all over the place or to start again, so we will stay and rely upon God's mercy and the protection of the Caliph, who values the Doctor. It is not open for discussion, my darling," she said to Rav'an, who was becoming tearful. Fariba placed a thin hand on her arm to comfort her.

"I lament the fact that we have to leave without informing our good friend Allam," Reza said, "but we cannot compromise him with any knowledge of our whereabouts. So it is agreed: the story we must put out is that we have gone to India after having been to Africa? India is a big place, and I do not think the Master has influence there."

"Reza has a task to perform before we leave," Talon stated. "Dar'an and Yosef will assist him."

A large jar appeared at the gates of the castle *Qual'a Bozi,* almost six weeks from the date that Talon and his extended family disappeared without a trace from Muscat. The merchant ship which Reza commissioned to transport the jar had run into a storm and the captain had put into port for safety, thereby delaying the delivery by yet another week. The container arrived on a donkey that had been led up the path by a frightened drover who knew the reputation of the inmates but not the contents of the cargo, which was very heavy. Firuz, now the leader of the pack in the castle, read a message that accompanied the jar before unsealing it.

The message read:

"You have failed. This will happen to all who you send against us. Our magic is powerful. Follow us if you dare."

With a look of growing alarm and puzzlement on his dark, angular features, he ordered the jar opened. Even he stood back in horror as its contents were revealed.

The task that Reza had insisted upon carrying out had been a gristly one. With the help of Dar'an and Yosef he had taken the heads of all the assassins and placed them in a large earthenware jar full of vinegar. This was heavily sealed with wax and covered in thick hessian padding, which was strapped closed to ensure there was no tampering.

Firus swallowed hard. He most certainly didn't want to be the deliverer of this news to the Master, but some luckless messenger had to be sent.

The tearful goodbyes had been said and the passengers were all aboard, having arrived under cover of darkness. They left in the early morning just as the first streaks of dawn appeared in eastern sky, while the city still slept.

They had abandoned much in the villa before they sealed it. Doctor Haddad had said that he would be visiting the deserted villa when they had gone. A fire might be the right thing to do he declared to Talon and Reza but would delay that event as long as he could. The crew, all trusted men who in turn trusted Talon implicitly, went to work to set sail and the steersmen guided the ship past the small island at the mouth of the harbor. No one challenged them. There were very few loiterers staring out to sea at that time of day other than a few fishing men who had risen late and were quite disinterested in the ship as they hurriedly prepared their own boats for departure.

Talon stood on the afterdeck and oversaw their departure, Rav'an and Jannat, along with their two maids Salmeh and Afari, stayed below out of sight. Talon was robed like an Omani and wore his usual loose headgear with a cloth wrapped around his lower face. His men were dressed likewise, to ensure that no one recognized them as they left.

Reza, Yosef and Dar'an were in the bows watching for any unusual signs of interest in their departure as they cleared the island, while Rostam took his place next to Talon. He was proud of his status of Navigator and intended to make his father even more proud before they were done.

Just in case anyone might be observing their ship, they tacked off to the East by Northeast. Before many hours had passed they were alone at sea. Once they were well over the horizon, Talon

31

ordered a change of course and they headed South by Southwest, their destination the entrance to the Red Sea. They would not be stopping at Aden nor any other port unless it was on the African side until they came to Elat. They had a ship full of food and would only need to put in for water from time to time.

It was an uneventful journey through the straights of Yemen. Talon, with the assistance of Rostam, kept the ship as close to the center of the long sea as they could. Most dhows sailed within sight of land and certainly did not sail at night, but that had its perils too. Sand shoals and reefs were a constant danger when sailing close to the shore, even many miles out. They could encounter other vessels, and so could only sail during the day when they could see ahead of them.

Staying out of sight of land in deeper waters, they avoided maritime traffic of the pilgrim kind, as well as the possibility of pirates. They had little fear of anyone being bold enough to take on a ship of this size; more importantly, however, they wanted no word of their passage to get back to Muscat.

The days were searingly hot, which forced them to seek shade wherever they could or remain in the cabin; but the nights were cool, which allowed them to relax on deck, rest, and discuss the future. Reza also spent time with the boys working on their training.

After two weeks of fair winds they found themselves at the entrances to two long channels, one of which went North-west, while the other appeared to go in a North-easterly direction. Talon ordered the ship to sail up the latter, and within four more days they sighted Elat, an unprepossessing harbor with many fishing boats but few of the larger sea-going vessels that one came across in Muscat. The port, once a very important harbor, was located on the edge of the desert, but most of that desert led up north towards hostile Christian lands. Moslem traders now favored the Egyptian side.

The unloading took several frustrating days, but eventually everything was off the ship and in a warehouse, where it would wait until Talon could hire a caravan of camels or join one. His preference was to hire his own camels, which would mean he and his party would be in charge of their destiny to a larger extent. Some caravan owners were not above sending out a message to the Beduin, informing them of a fat caravan on its way north. A share of the plunder went to the informer.

It took many tiresome days to bargain for animals and prepare the caravan, find reliable men, and obtain enough food for a three-week-long journey across the eastern Sinai desert. Eventually, however, all was prepared, and one evening Talon and his family stood on the shore watching the ship slip away into the night. Waqqas was taking her back to the port of Muscat with a story that would keep the Mardini family from asking too many questions. The ship would be a gift to the family, which would please Imaran, who had declared that he liked it very much. Inwardly Talon sighed; he knew Imaran would convert it quickly enough into a slave ship. But it was essential that, as far as the people of Oman were concerned, Talon and his extended family had fled to India and disappeared, perhaps even to China.

I am that wastrel called Kalandar,
I have no home, no country and no lair,
By day I wander aimless o'er the earth,
And when night falls , my pillow is a stone.
—Baba Tahir

Chapter 4
A Close Encounter

Three weeks later, Talon and Reza sat their horses and stared northwards towards a rising plume of dust. They were both dressed like Beduin, with voluminous over-cloaks of coarse, dark brown cotton, almost the color of the sun-blasted rocks around them; small, ragged turbans on their heads; and shemaghs half covering their faces. Yosef, Dar'an and Rostam were similarly dressed, as were the men guiding their twenty or so camels. The women were veiled completely, so that one could not even see their eyes behind the fine coverings.

"They are coming to investigate," Talon said, his voice slightly muffled by the shemagh. He glanced up at the nearby rugged mountains and the huge fortress of Kerak squatting on one of the steeper foothills and overlooking the road about two leagues ahead of them. It loomed over the roadway with a menacing aspect, the perfect defense against any army of invaders. It had gained a reputation that reached as far south as Elat as a haven of bandits who plundered caravans, led by a man Talon had formerly come to know as Lord Raynald de Châtillon. Caravans were looted, their women violated and then sometimes mutilated, while ransoms were demanded for any noble prisoners who were not killed outright.

"There is no way we could have slipped by at night. They appear to be too alert, and then we would have been at a disadvantage in the dark. Better this way," he said to Reza.

"I hope you are right, Brother," Reza replied, sounding doubtful. "So the knights of this castle have taken to banditry?"

"That is what the rumors at Elat told us. Better to be prepared for anything. Dar'an!" he called. Dar'an cantered forward to join the two men ahead of the camel train. "Yes, Master."

"Are you ready for my signal?"

"All is ready, Master Talon."

34

"Good. Let's hope that we do not have to resort to drastic measures," Talon said. He was unsure what kind of reception committee they faced. He intended to speak to the leaders and use persuasion. If that didn't work, there was an alternative. He noted the pennants and the dress of the riders. They were without doubt Franks, but at this distance he could not determine whether they were Knights Templar or otherwise.

"Close in the camels and guard them," he ordered Yosef, who touched his forehead and rode back, shouting orders. Now Talon could see the dull gleam of sunlight on chain armor and spear heads as the group of men that far outnumbered his small band came at the canter towards them, raising a veil of dust on the road.

"Stay back some, Brother, but be prepared for my signal," he murmured to Reza, then he rode forward to position himself even more in front of the caravan. Reza dropped back so that he was just ahead of the camels.

Talon stopped on a rise and waited. He took off his shemagh to show his face; perhaps that would help. He felt tense. Every time he had met with Franks after some time away, he reflected, it had not been a good experience. The riders were coming along the rough track that passed for a road in these parts, and now he could see clearly that they were a mixed bunch. Some wore dirty uniforms of the Crusaders, with cloth patches that passed for crosses on their tunics. He searched for the pennant of the Templars among them but could not see one. So these men were simply bandits? Who might be leading them?

He was not long in pondering that point, as the fore rider raised his hand in the air just before they were upon Talon, and they halted in a heavy cloud of dust.

Talon failed to recognize the man initially, but as soon as the leader opened his mouth and spoke, he remembered.

"You are crossing my land without permission, Saracen! I want a tithe!" the man shouted, although he was only ten paces away. Talon had halted his animal in the middle of the road, right in front of the men and in full view of his own people.

"I know you... Raynald de Châtillon. Why do you stop me?" he called back. "I am on the King's business. Are you then here to offer me hospitality?"

There was an initial shocked silence when the rough looking crew heard the man in front of them speaking French. He leaned comfortably on the pommel of his mount and regarded them with narrowed eyes.

Raynald blinked, then wiped the sweat off his florid face with a cotton rag, for under the chain mail he was sweating copiously. The sun burned in a cloudless sky and heat radiated off the desert sand and rocks all around them. But Talon gave the impression of being cool and relaxed.

"Who in hell's name are you? Saracens are not allowed to pass without my permission!" he bellowed.

Talon opened his over cloak, which had covered the tunic beneath. He too wore chain mail, but his tunic, the surcoat, displayed a red cross on his left breast. He had had all his companions dress in a similar manner to be displayed when and if needed. It seemed the appropriate moment to do so. The men in front of him goggled.

"I am Sir Talon de Gilles. Surely you remember me?" he said in a loud, clear voice that reached all the men gathered in front of him. He smiled as he observed their surprise.

Raynald was shocked, that much was clear to see, but he shook his head and bellowed back.

"Sir Talon is gone to God or Hell, take your pick, this long while back. You must be an impostor."

"No impostor, Sir," Talon responded, all the while assessing the mood of the men in front of him. They looked hot and frustrated, having just realized that the caravan was not going to be their prize.

"Why are you with this caravan?" Raynald demanded. "Why would you not be with a squadron of Templars instead?"

Talon chuckled. "You know very well that there are no Templars south of here, and while I crossed the desert I needed protection from those carrion, the Beduin," he replied.

"I want to check for myself if you are who you say you are!" Raynald blustered, and he made to move his horse past Talon. "I want to see what that caravan is carrying. Perhaps they harbor spies!" he sneered.

He found Talon barring his way. Now the two men were very close, and Talon could smell the foul breath coming from Raynald. It contrasted sharply with the hot, clean smell of the desert.

"You know I am who I say I am, Sir. You do remember who brought the Templars to the battle of Montgisard, do you not?" Talon had raised his voice.

Raynald hauled his horse in and his hand crept towards his sword. Out of the corner of his eye, Talon saw the men behind him closing in. "I would not do that if I were you, Sir Raynald. If the

King hears about this, I think he will be very upset. He might not forgive you this time."

Raynald's face had become red with frustration. There was no doubt that he recognized Talon, but the allure of pillage was very strong. Pickings must have been lean of late, Talon mused, and Raynald wanted to strike Saracens where ever he could and for no better reason than to see them in pain.

Talon's green eyes bored into Raynald's. "Do not be tempted, Sir. It would give us both pain, and that would not be good in God's eyes now, would it?"

Raynald grunted and his rheumy blue eyes shifted.

"I would be more than glad to give the King your greetings and to assure him that you are truly the guardian of the South, Sir Raynald," Talon assured him in a soft tone, but one that left no doubt that, should it not be so, then Raynald would be one of the first casualties. Raynald, sweating under his chain hauberk, leather, and heavy clothing, drew his horse back apace.

"Very well, Sir Talon. You may pass. I shall provide an escort past the castle, but then you are on your own across the hills of Jordan.

"I accept your offer, Sir Raynald. However, I want the word of a 'Nobleman' that your men will not misbehave towards anyone in the caravan. I gave my word to these people, as a Templar knight, that I would protect them once we were within Christian lands, and here we are."

Raynald grimaced, he didn't appreciate the sarcasm.

"You should not be demanding my word of me in such a manner, Sir Talon. I find that insulting; but nonetheless you have my word and you may pass. You are still spoken of in Jerusalem," Raynald said gracelessly.

Talon nodded and said, "So be it, Sir. We will continue. Please wait here and I shall inform the leaders of the caravan that we are in safe hands."

He left Raynald fuming with his restless men and turned his horse back to talk with Reza. While the earlier contact had been dangerous, the next phase might be even more perilous. Talon knew what an out of control man Raynald had been, and nothing he saw today after so many years indicated the man had changed for the better.

"We are to continue past the castle with them as escort. Be very alert, they are like jackals," he warned Reza in an undertone. "These men are bandits, not Templars, and I don't trust any of them, least of all their leader. He is the most treacherous of all."

The caravan began to lumber forward, everyone grateful that they were again in motion. The late afternoon sun burned.

Raynald wanted to have his men ride side by side with the people of the caravan, but Talon insisted that the drovers and people attached to the caravan were so afraid of the Franks that they refused to continue unless the Franks led the way.

Very reluctantly Raynald agreed, but insisted in turn that Talon ride alongside him as they approached the turn off to the castle.

"Where have you been these many years?" he asked civilly enough, as the caravan got under way again. Talon cast a sharp eye forward to where the Franks were riding as the vanguard. None of them had managed to slip past him, now he and Raynald were between them and the caravan itself, so he felt more secure. Anyone who did try and get in among the camels would come to a swift end, and that he didn't want.

"I have been exploring the lands to the East of us and have even been to the land of the silk," he responded absently.

"You must have accumulated much booty in the process, no?" Raynald asked with a sly nod of his head back towards the caravan.

"As a Templar I am unable to hold wealth, Sir. You must know that," Talon responded, his tone cool. He looked forward and up at the enormous fortress on the stony hill to his left. The immense glacis that sloped up to the walls themselves alone would deter anyone rash enough to try and storm it, he surmised. This, of course, was precisely how Châtillon managed to hold onto it. He could pick and choose his attacks on merchants and travelers who perforce had to come this way; otherwise they were routed into the deeper desert to the East where there was no water at all.

His next question was blunt. "Why do you prey upon the caravans, Sir Raynald? Is there not a truce with Salah Ed Din still in place? There was one being negotiated when I left."

"I detest the Saracen and all they stand for," Raynald snarled. "Our King is sick and not fully in control of his faculties. These people are heretics and infidels, they need to be destroyed and have no rights in our Christian world."

Talon was taken aback by the vehemence of the response. "You have not been out here all that long, so how can you decide all this?" he asked.

"I came from France with the spirit of crusade in me. I find that people who live out here are corrupted by the lures of the East. You even dress like they do, for Heaven's sake!" He flicked his fingers contemptuously at Talon's dress and at his turban.

"Tell me something, Sir. In that chain mail of yours and that iron helmet you wear upon your head, are you cool? Do you not find the weather here hot?"

"What has that got to do with it?" Raynald demanded, his tone truculent.

"I wear the clothes of this region for a reason. The one is to be less obvious, but the other is for comfort while I put my mind to things other than the discomfort of sweating. There is much we *Outremeres* have learned from these people that is worth knowing, aside from any religious differences."

"Pah! They are savages and should be put to work building our castles, nothing more."

"Can you read, Sir?"

"A soldier does not have to read. His duty is to do the work of God and destroy the infidel." Raynald stated this as though it were final. They rode on in silence for a while and the castle above them loomed larger. It was almost time to part ways.

"I was just wondering if you had read the details of the truce. That is all. How is the King these days?"

The response was short. "Sick. He will die soon. Then we shall see."

Talon didn't like the tone. "How old is his son?"

"Too young, and my guess is that the King is going to appoint the Duke of Tripoli as his guardian. Much good that will do. That scum is a friend of the infidel, hence not to be trusted at all with the future of this country."

"You have Odo still leading the Templars don't you?"

Raynald pulled up his horse and looked back at Talon. "You have been gone a long time, Sir Talon. Much has changed. Odo died in a Saracen prison four years ago." He grinned through bad teeth; it was more of a snarl.

"Here our ways part, Sir Talon. I cannot escort you beyond this point, but I am sure you know the way. Farewell." He kicked his large horse into a canter and rode off to catch up with his men who had turned off the main road and were waiting for him.

Talon watched him go with a thoughtful frown, waiting for the caravan to catch up, and when Reza rode alongside he murmured, "Rarely have I encountered a man so filled with unreasoning hate. He is as treacherous as a snake. We must be ready for anything. Bring the caravan past them, but be on your guard."

Reza grunted acknowledgement and called back orders for the drovers to hurry it along.

As her camel passed, Rav'an murmured, "They look dangerous, my Talon. Are we safe from them now?"

"They are very dangerous, my Love, and I do not think we are safe... yet."

He deliberately sat his horse on the cross roads in front of the Franks, who remained watching the caravan like wolves contemplating a good meal; but then Raynald, with an impatient flick of his fly switch, turned his mount and galloped up the road to the gates of the fortress without a backward glance. The knights followed him, but it was with reluctance. They could sense that this was not a lean caravan, and they had noticed the women.

Later that evening when they had put another ten miles between them and the castle, Talon called a halt. Dusk was settling in, and it would do them little good to be spread out along an unfamiliar road during the night.

"We should camp on the top of a knoll; that one over there will do." He pointed to one about half a league away. "There would be a good place, I think."

"Defensible, up to a point." Reza agreed, and took charge of the camp. The camels were anchored firmly to posts which they could not pull out in a panic should there be alarms.

Tents were erected and fires begun on the far side of the hill away from the distant castle. The people of the caravan were on edge. They had seen that Talon's avoidance of a clash with the unpredictable Franks had been tense. His words to them that evening, as they ate sparingly of the goat meat and drank the already brackish water, were hardly reassuring.

"We must double the guards tonight, and everyone goes to bed fully armed," he began. He sat next to Rav'an and Jannat, facing his men.

"Do you then anticipate trouble tonight, Talon?" Yosef growled, the firelight flickering on his lean, wolflike features.

"If I have judged that man rightly, the answer is yes. It is not *if*, but *when*. I suspect that a raid will be in the early hours just before dawn when they think we will be least alert."

"Then we should be ready for them." Reza said, and tossed a small bone that he had been chewing into the fire. "Check your weapons, everyone. Bows and arrows, too; we will need them. Where do you want the women to be, Talon?"

"Not here," Talon began.

"Our duty is to be beside you, my Talon. There is to be no discussion about that," Rav'an said with a sweet smile. Reza chuckled.

Talon looked at her and Jannat. "You, my Lady, are with child, Jannat also. I would be insane to put you anywhere near to danger."

"Why cannot we be near at hand with our horses to help at the right time, Master Talon?" Dar'an spoke up.

Talon shook his head, exasperated. "Very well; but you, Dar'an are with me. Your skills with the devices is needed here. Yosef, you will leave when it gets really dark and find a safe place just a few hundred paces north of here that I noticed earlier. Take five men; the women and their servants will go there and await the outcome of the attack when it comes, for surely it will." He held his hand up to prevent any discussion.

"In the event that we are overrun, you will flee and go north without being detected. Head for Jerusalem where you can go to the Templars for help. There is one Sir Guy de Veres there who will protect you."

Rav'an opened her mouth to speak, but he turned on her. "No! These men will charge straight at us, they know no other means of attack. If they break through, and there is little enough to stop them, I cannot be looking over my shoulder worrying about you, Rav'an. Do this for me, I beg of you."

Reza nodded his head in agreement. "He is right, my Sister. Take the horses and be safe. We will come for you when it is done, have no fear. Jannat, do as Talon asks; I, too, am asking this of you for your safety and my peace of mind."

There was a long silence, but then Rav'an put her hand on his arm. "Very well. I—we—shall do as you say, Talon; but I will have Rostam with me, and my bow."

He smiled at her, marveling at her beauty in the firelight. "Rostam, go with Yosef and be the protector of your mother and your aunt. Understand that this is no small responsibility for you to carry out. Obey Yosef."

Rostam made to protest, "But... Papa!"

Talon took in deep breath and was just about to snap at his son.

"Do as your father asks, my son," Rav'an told Rostam in a low voice. He subsided, glowering. Talon subsided but felt a surge of pride in his son, who was clearly not afraid of what was to come. "Everyone will have a task to perform. Your task is to protect your mother, your aunt and the womenfolk," he told Rostam.

Rostam nodded in silence and got up to prepare the horses.

The small party led their horses off around midnight. No one had slept, other than to catnap, but for Talon and Reza even that was not to be. With Dar'an to help, because he was familiar with the Chinese powder, they set up picket points half way up the small, wide knoll. All five faced the road, which was some one hundred paces to the East, and now the three men began to prepare the traps. A small barrel of powder was opened and shallow holes dug in the stony ground. The powder was poured, half covered with sand, and then rocks were placed loosely over the holes. Then a trail of powder was laid from each trap to where a stone wall in each picket was being hurriedly constructed by the nervous drovers who never stopped praying while they worked. Talon selected the sterner men who had volunteered to become his followers and distributed them among the pickets.

"We will need to have at least four good arrow bombs ready which I shall shoot from the top when I deem it time. The first explosions should happen just before that. The men are ready?"

"They are ready, although the drovers are scared silly, but they trust us and will follow when the time comes," Reza assured him.

The preparations having been carried out as best they could, they settled down to wait. Talon, to keep his mind from worrying too much, counted and named the constellations, marveling as always at the blaze of the stars against the night sky. In contrast, the low, sun-blasted, rocky desert around them and the scree-covered slopes of other hills were in complete darkness. There would be no moon tonight, for which he was glad. Light would favor the mounted enemy more than his men, whom he wanted in cover and well out of sight when the enemy came to visit.

The only sounds of the night were the distant yapping of a jackal which died out, then a light wind arrived to stir the dried out bushes and the sand, but then it too faded away, leaving the small sound of cooling desert rocks behind. A deep, almost deathly silence settled over the desert. He huddled into his cloak and shivered; it was very cold. Another hour passed before he felt Reza grip his arm.

"Something or someone is coming," he whispered, then vanished down the hill, going to his position.

Talon's eyes had adjusted well to the night, so the track of the road was clear to him. He looked further along the road to where it faded into the desert and the darkness of the distant hills. He could see a dark shape moving slowly, stealthily along the road. As the minutes passed the mass resolved and he could make out individual riders. The faint sound of creaking leather and the muffled sound of hooves came to his ears as a group of about twenty riders arrived at the point where the caravan had left the track to make camp on the knoll.

The riders stopped on the road opposite the base of the knoll, and Talon could see that they were looking up in his direction. Talon glanced down at the slightly darker shadows on his hillside, which indicated where the pickets were lying in wait behind their low rock walls, but doubted that the riders could see them. Reza was off to the left and Dar'an to the right of the path to the camp.

The riders appeared to be hesitating; there was a murmur as they talked among themselves. Abruptly a loud voice called a command, followed by the gleam of drawn swords, and the group of mounted men put spurs to their animals and charged towards the silent encampment. Talon nodded to himself; no change in tactics there.

He waited, watching from his perch on the top of the knoll as the riders galloped over the rough, rock-strewn desert towards the base of the hill. One rider went down with a yell when his horse foundered in a hole. He was pitched onto the sand, and his horse remained lying, whinnying and struggling, its leg broken. The others ignored them and reached the base, to begin whipping their horses up the gentle slope towards the ominously silent camp above them.

The riders were almost half way up the hill when a bright spark appeared just in front of them, on both sides of the path the riders were taking. The large, unearthly sparks seemed to be alive as they raced, hissing and smoking, down the hillside for ten ragged paces before just as suddenly disappearing into the ground on either side of the straining riders still charging up the slope. Suddenly there were two huge flashes, followed by a thunderous noise, and the ground erupted at their feet. The world for the riders seemed to be split apart by the huge double boom of the explosions, and then death hummed and whistled among them. Shards of stone flew in all directions, killing and maiming.

Some of the riders had hesitated with surprise, even fright, as the huge sparks came weaving down the hill towards them, but now they were stopped dead in their tracks by the two explosions that shattered the night and ripped their ranks to pieces. Horses and men went down screaming while the remainder hauled their horses to a stop and gaped in horror and unbelieving shock at what had just occurred.

They were given no respite, however, as a dark figure appeared on the top of the hill above them and loosed an arrow that glowed with fire at its point into their midst. When it struck, this fire also exploded with a fearsome bang. One of the riders seemed to disintegrate. The horrible noise of wounded and dying men and horses was unnerving.

Worse was to come, as moments later the ground on both flanks erupted with screaming, howling figures who appeared out of the ground to stab and hack at the survivors, already reduced to half their former number. The panic-stricken men and horses were easy targets for the dark, demonic figures which darted about, stabbing up at the already deafened and confused men. More went down, and those left alive simply fled in all directions, seeking to put as many leagues between themselves and this terrifying manifestation of hell as they possibly could.

Two made the mistake of heading north, where they ran into a party of riders who greeted them with a flurry of arrows, taking them both down. Two of the riders jumped off their horses and finished the wounded men off with daggers to their throats.

"You have been blooded," Yosef said to Rostam, as they stood up and retrieved their mounts. "Now you are a warrior." He clapped the boy on his shoulder. "Your father will be proud of you this night."

"My Lady is still a great archer," Yosef said to Rav'an, touching his forehead as he rode alongside her, his teeth flashing in a grin.

"My Sister also shot her arrow." Rav'an indicated Jannat, who was still staring down at the dark figures of the dead. "But I am glad you were with us, my friend. Teach my boy to be a good warrior."

"He has the makings already, my Lady. It will be an honor to help him where I can."

Three frightened men paused a league away to look back at the distant encampment. They saw a single streak of light soar into the sky, then explode in a starburst that briefly lit up the hills around.

"God protect us, for there is the Devil himself! Did you see? Fire and Brimstone! His demons came straight out of the ground!" one of the riders wailed in terror and crossed himself repeatedly.

"He is surely of the Devil's spawn, but he wears the cross of the Templars! How can that be?" Raynald de Châtillon muttered, as he fingered a gold cross he had stolen from a pilgrim some years before. They plunged on, ruthlessly spurring their lathered horses towards the relative safety of Kerak Castle.

Jerusalem behold, appeared in sight,
Jerusalem they view, they see, they spy;
Jerusalem with merry noise they greet,
With joyful shouts and acclamations sweet.
—Tusso's *Jerusalem*

Chapter 5

Audience with a King.

Talon and his men drew their horses to a halt on the Southern ridge of the valley of Jehoshaphat and stared at the magnificent city rising from among the low hills before them.

Jerusalem's light-colored stone walls shone with an almost ethereal glow in the late afternoon sun. The myriad towers, battlements and columned buildings stood out with sharp outline, making it easy for Talon to point out the various distinguishing features from the raised Temple of The Lord, the palace, and the Templar buildings in the foreground; while behind the high group of buildings were the crumbling, ancient columns that were so old none could say when they were built. From their vantage point they could just see the spires of some of the Christian churches, which were ringing their bells for Vespers.

None of his companions, other than Dar'an, had ever been near a Christian city before, let alone heard the sounds of the church bells. They sat listening in awed silence as the Holy City prepared for the evening prayers and began to settle down for the night.

"I shall go into the city tomorrow and see if I can meet with Sir Guy de Veres, my old mentor," Talon told them as they themselves settled in for the night at their encampment. All around them were other caravans. Most had come for trade from as far afield as Baghdad and Basra, and even further. Merchants were less discriminating than religious zealots when it came to trade. Talon realized that Jerusalem was still a center of commerce, perhaps not as thriving as it had been before, but over many decades it had recovered much of its former wealth.

"Will we be able to go into the city and explore?" Rostam asked, excitement in his voice.

"I shall take you with me, and then leave you to your own devices while I go and meet with Sir Guy," Talon told him.

"Perhaps Dar'an can show you where we used to live." He looked over at Dar'an. "You know this city well. I am entrusting my family to your care. You know your way around. Just stay away from the Church of the Holy Sepulcher. The monks and priests there are touchy and might object if 'Saracens' stared at them too hard. I doubt, however, there will be any trouble anywhere else; the city is full of all kinds of people," he assured them.

Rav'an looked at him. "They are not hostile here?"

"This is not the home of that bandit we encountered in the South. Here the King insists upon law and order from everyone," Talon responded. "Besides, you will have Reza and his young companions to protect you, and Dar'an will keep you away from any trouble, my Love."

"Will we see you at all once we are within the city, Talon?" Jannat asked, with a look at Rav'an.

"I hope so, but I must first deal with things that have to be done. I want to know more about how the kingdom is managing with a sick King, and I must request an audience with him, so I do not know how long I shall be," Talon said.

Later that night, with Rav'an lying in his arms as they listened to the murmurings of the encampments nearby, she raised her head and said, "I sense that you are uneasy, my Talon. What is it?"

"Perhaps it is something Châtillon said, I am not sure, but it left me concerned. Much time has passed since I entered those walls."

"What was it he said?" she asked.

"That the King was very ill and was not really in charge, at least that was the implication. I suspect I will have to seek out old friends and find out.

The next morning when Talon rode at the head of his small entourage, he was dressed in his chain mail with the cross of a Templar knight on the breast of his surcoat. He had none of the accoutrements he had departed with those many years before, but the uniform was passport enough in this city, he reflected, remembering the last time he had entered after the great battle of Montgisard. Then the ragged and wounded remnants of the Templars and the King's army had been greeted by a crowd that screamed and cheered themselves hoarse with gratitude for their deliverance from the hands of Salah Ed Din and his enormous army.

He looked over his family and companions with a critical eye as they prepared to ride into the city. A glance at the sun told him it was mid morning. The bells were ringing again. His wife and Jannat were suitably veiled, and his companions looked as though they were well-to-do traders from the north, perhaps Syria. They no longer looked like the Beduin camel caravaners they had resembled for the last month.

The gate he had chosen was David's Gate, which meant that they would have a good half an hour's ride to approach it from the West. This was one of the main gates of the city, and Talon wanted to show it off to its best effect. Once inside, Dar'an would be able to show them all they needed to know about the markets, the fruit, where to buy the best materials—which the women were eager to do —and where they could find the baths. He led the way towards the massive archway that was the entrance to the city with his surcoat uncovered. The sentries at the gate barely gave him a glance but were about to stop the others when Talon called out, "They are under the protection of the Templars. I am in charge."

The sentries stared, then reluctantly waved the group on, and then they were inside the city. Talon reined his horse to the side of the crowded main street and waited for the others to catch up. They moved out of the way of the carts and beasts of burden that filled the street. After the quiet of the desert the noise in this street was deafening. Everyone seemed to be shouting at one another or their beasts, and the air rang with the hammering of blacksmiths at work, hawkers shouting, and the sounds of people pushing and shoving, trying to get to their destinations.

"I ride in a straight line down this road and then onward to that walled place standing on the rise over there." He pointed to where the Temple of the Lord, the King's palace, and the Templar barracks were grouped.

"At the crossroads almost in the middle of the city you can go wherever you please. You may have to walk, as the streets are very narrow off this main route. Dar'an will guide you."

"When do we see you again, Talon?" Rav'an looked concerned.

"Don't worry, I shall join you later in the day at the gate of Mount Sion. Dar'an knows where it is. We shall meet when the bells are ringing for what the Christians call Vespers, just as they were last night."

They parted, and Talon joined the traffic that was moving towards the palace compound and that of the Templars. He had time to think about what he might encounter when he arrived, but soon he was at the gates that led to the Royal palace and the wide space where the Templar Knights were billeted. The sentries

47

scrutinized him casually, then allowed him to ride through the arched entrance, and he was back in a familiar place.

He turned right and dismounted. Some men who clearly worked for the Templars gave him curious looks; his horse was a handsome mottled gray Arab, quite unlike the horses Templars generally used. He noticed some high spirited Destriers, the massive animal that the Knights used for battle, being worked at the far end of the compound. A groom hurried out of the stables and took the reins of his horse. Patting the animal's neck reassuringly, he turned away to walk into the cool interior of the main Templar building.

It was just as busy as he remembered it: clerks everywhere moving about purposefully, others sitting at desks with quills scratching busily, while in another corner of the large space some knights were gathered, having a discussion. Talon didn't know any of them.

They paused to take note of him, and perhaps because he looked unsure of himself one of the men detached himself from the group with a comment that made them laugh, and came towards him.

"You look quite lost, Sir. May I be of assistance?" He was a young man, with a self-confident air. Talon estimated him to be just above twenty.

"I am looking for Sir Guy de Veres," he said.

The young knight frowned. "Did I hear you say Sir Guy de Veres?" he asked. His eyes took in the tall, strong looking man with piercing green eyes and the scarred face. He had been going to make a flippant comment, but the set of Talon's face deterred him.

"Will you wait here while I enquire on your behalf?" he said instead.

Talon nodded and watched as the young man rejoined his companions and there began a discussion. They all turned to stare at Talon; it was clear to him that they were discussing him. Finally the young man walked back towards him.

"Sir," he said, "did you not know that Sir Guy died?"

Talon was visibly shaken. "Sir Guy de Veres? Are you sure? When? When did he die?" he demanded.

"Some years back, Sir. At the siege of Jacob's Ford. Did you not know of this?" he sounded incredulous and motioned his companions to join him as though he needed support for the news he had just imparted to this strange knight.

"No," said Talon absently. He was still dealing with the shock of the news. "I didn't know. God protect his soul."

"Sir, how could you not know? Who are you?" another demanded, his tone sounded almost belligerent. They were all staring at Talon now.

"My name is Talon de Gilles," he told them. He shook his head to clear it. Sir Guy had been killed in some battle that he had not even heard of! So this was what Châtillon had meant.

"I knew of a Talon de Gilles once. But he is dead and gone these many years," the first knight stated with conviction.

Talon almost rounded on the man. "I am Talon de Gilles. I have been away for a long time," he stated, and they all knew that he was not now in the mood for disbelief.

"Then you are... you are the same Talon who brought the Templars to the battle of Montgisard!" another exclaimed.

Talon gave a wintery smile. "The very same."

"This I must tell to the Grand Master!" one of them muttered, and he departed in a hurry.

Now that they had established who he was, the three remaining knights wanted to know where he had been and why.

He was saved by the arrival of a man whom he knew, by sight at least. Lord Gérard de Ridefort strode into the room and people sat up to pay attention. Visits were rare from Sir Gérard, and already there was something of interest going on near the entrance. Gérard strode haughtily towards where Talon was standing with the growing group of curious knights and retainers. They parted at his arrival and stopped talking, leaving a small space around Talon and the Grand Master.

Gérard peered at Talon, who calmly put up with the scrutiny. Finally Gérard snapped his fingers and pointed into the air with a finger as recognition dawned. "It really is you, Sir Talon de Gilles! We thought you were dead these long years ago. Châtillon came to Jerusalem with some cock and bull story that you were alive, but I never believe half of what that man says. Where have you been?"

Talon nodded and smiled. "A long story, Sir Gérard. Are you now the Grand Master? What happened to Odo?"

Gérard frowned at Talon. "I think we need to talk. Some place more private than this. All right, get back to your work," he said to the rest of the room. "I shall deal with this from here." Taking Talon by the arm he led him off to his chambers, where he sat him down and offered him a cup of water. Talon took it gratefully and sipped. He grimaced to himself. The water was rancid to his taste. The Templars still drank unclean water.

"You are a man of many surprises, Sir Talon," Gérard remarked, as he sat down opposite him at a huge desk strewn with papers and rolls of parchment.

"The first we knew of your return was from Raynald, who claimed that you had come back and were practicing wizardry." Gérard chuckled and wiped his face with a large hand. "He claimed that he saw you ordering demons from the ground amid much fire and brimstone." Gérard laughed. "I sometimes wonder at the imagination of that man," he said. "But now here you are. I want to hear all about it."

Talon managed a wry smile at the news of Châtillon. "We did indeed meet up, Sir, but it was not quite as Sir Raynald has told it. Shall we just say he thought I was a member of a caravan that he wanted to plunder? We evaded his attempt to do so, and no harm was done."

Ridefort gave him a keen stare. "Yes," he said slowly. "That must have been it. Well, I shall welcome you home."

"Please tell me of those who are no longer here, I beg of you, Sir," Talon pleaded. "In particular, Sir Guy de Veres. What happened to him?"

"It was a tragic business, Sir Talon. I shall tell you the gist of it and later, perhaps, others can fill you in on the details," he said.

"I am listening, Sir. Please go on."

"Jacob's Ford is, as perhaps you know, a main intersection between our Kingdom and that of Syria, which as you probably also know is now ruled by Salah Ed Din. The King, on the advisement of his officers, wanted to build a castle there, which he called Chastellet. Work began, and Salah Ed Din tried to negotiate a halt to the building. He even resorted to a bribe and offered the King about sixty thousand dinars, not once but twice! And the second time I think it was one hundred thousand dinars! We all knew why. It was because at the time Salah Ed Din was fighting in the North and had no spare troops. He spends much of his time fighting his own people, does that man." Gérard's comment was dry.

"Anyway, the King refused the offer, because Sir Guy told him that Salah Ed Din was afraid that should a castle be completed at Jacob's Ford then the way to Jerusalem would be barred, and Salah Ed Din's aim is always to drive down to this city—someday, somehow. Curse him."

Talon nodded agreement at this information. "So Sir Guy was one of those who told the King it was necessary?" he asked.

"Indeed he was, and most of us saw the right of it. The King set off to protect the construction of the castle, but Salah Ed Din arrived there first and began a siege. Sir Guy was already there and was caught inside. Six days later, the castle fell and the knights inside perished, as did many others. Sir Guy died, and Odo de Saint Amand was captured in a messy skirmish. He refused a ransom and died in one of Salah Ed Din's dungeons. Salah Ed Din destroyed the castle, and Baldwin came back a broken man."

Ridefort took a swig of water and, almost as an afterthought, said, "We should have taken the money, but... men like Sir Guy always knew better."

Talon tried not to show his displeasure at this remark. Sir Guy had been one of the very few Templars who could read the minds of people like Salah Ed Din. He held in his irritation and said, "I was ordered by the King to report to him when I came back, Sir. Is there the possibility of an audience?"

Ridefort looked over the rim of his cup at Talon for a long moment. "He did, did he? Hmm, I'll have to see what can be done. Meanwhile, where are you going to be staying?"

"I have a place here in the city, Sir," Talon lied. "I will stay there for the time being."

Ridefort nodded his head in agreement, still watching Talon from under his bushy brows. "Yes, that might be a good idea, until we know what to do with you."

"I have personal business to take care of in Acre, Sir Gérard. Perhaps after that I can come back to Jerusalem and report to you?"

"First things first. I shall find out if the King will see you, Sir Talon. Report in every day at Terce and I shall let you know."

Talon took this for a dismissal and stood up. "Thank you, Grand Master," he said. "I am at your service."

At that moment an idea occurred to Talon. "Is the Duke of Tripoli in the city, Grand Master?" he asked in as offhand a manner as he could muster.

Ridefort gave him a sharp look. "Yes," he said with reluctance. "He is here in Jerusalem attending to the King. I doubt if he will have time for you, however, Sir Talon."

Talon was not so sure. Unlike Ridefort, who saw Talon as just another Templar knight with some talent, the Duke might well see otherwise.

He left the building and collected his horse in a thoughtful and somber mood. His sadness at the loss of his mentor weighed upon him very heavily. He looked about. The knights he passed were all

51

very new looking men, few of whom seemed to have been in the Kingdom for any length of time. One could always tell; the older, more experienced knights were sun weathered, their clothing patched, their chain wearing out, and they wore lighter clothing, and often a small turban wrapped over their pointed helmets—if they wore a helmet at all. He saw none of these Templars as he left the building to make his way back to the gate. For the first time he felt old.

Half an hour later, he presented himself at the gates of the Duke of Tripoli's mansion. The guards were respectful of a Templar knight and asked him to give them his name and then to wait.

He heard the Duke before he saw him.

"Where is that man? I want to see if we have an imposter! If so, I shall deal with him accordingly!" he roared from behind the closed doors, which were hurriedly opened, and there stood the one man to whom Talon could talk. He had dismounted, and he bowed as the Duke strode out to see him. Raymond halted in his tracks and stared.

"By God, it is you!" he exclaimed in a hushed, incredulous voice. "I can barely believe it. The young knight has come back to us!" Before he knew it, Talon was wrapped in a bear hug that nearly took his breath away. "By all that is wonderful, you have come back to us! Where in God's name have you been? You don't look as though you spent it in a prison!"

Talon laughed then, and it eased his grief. He was very glad to see the Duke. With a rueful smile he said, "I have just come from the Grand Master's chambers."

"Ah!" The Duke barked out a laugh, his dark, sun-lined face creasing into a grin. "Bet the stupid dog didn't even ask you where you've been, did he?"

Talon shook his head and joined in the laughter.

Raymond looked him up and down. "You look well. But I am forgetting my manners. Come in, come in, my house is your house. I, for one, want to know *all* there is about your travels. Are you going to have some wine with me? You're not too hidebound by that oath are you?"

"No, my Lord. I would welcome some wine this moment. I have just learned about Sir Guy," said Talon, as he walked into the courtyard, where a groom rushed out to take his horse.

"Bad business that," the duke said, shaking his head. "If they had left on time as the King had wanted they might have saved the castle and those within. But there are ever those who delay for no better reason than that they can, and we witnessed a tragedy."

They were soon seated on comfortable cushions in a room that Talon thought could easily pass for that of an Arab potentate. He accepted a silver cup of wine and they toasted one another.

"Now tell me, where have you been and what have you learned?" The older man asked him.

Hours later they were still talking. Talon had told him almost everything, and the Duke was looking very thoughtful.

"I have often asked myself how these beautiful earthenware plates and bowls arrive here," he mused. "The caravan leaders always say, 'From Baghdad,' or somewhere like that, but they never talk of the sea route that you describe; and yet there are many Arab and Persian traders in the China that you have talked about."

"The world is far larger than I could ever have imagined before I set out," Talon said. There was a silence for a while, as the two men became lost in their thoughts.

Abruptly the Duke asked him. "Do you want to see the King?"

Talon smiled and nodded. "He told me that I must tell him of my adventures as a condition for allowing me to depart, Lord."

"Hah! Did Ridefort say he would help?"

"He did. He seemed almost disconcerted that I had survived somehow, and wasn't that enthusiastic."

"Well he might. You were being eyed for a possible high position, as I recall."

"Sir Guy de Veres hinted at that and tried to persuade me to stay," Talon remarked.

"I miss that man," the Duke said. "And I am sure you do too. He was one of the few among us who understood the people over here. He could read their minds and it saved us from embarrassment on more than one occasion." He sighed. "Alas, the King is very ill, and there will be little to console us when he finally goes to meet with God."

"What do you mean, Lord?"

"The King, may God be kind to his soul, will die soon, Talon. After him there is only his son, a sickly boy, who will inherit. Even now we, the notables, are at odds with one another. There are two factions now. The one led by Sibylla combined with that wretched man Guy of Lusignan, remember him?"

Talon nodded recalling the haughty behavior of the knight from France who had been having a scandalous relationship with Sibylla, the eldest sister of the King.

"That's not all. Châtillon and Joscelin of Edessa, along with Roger de Moulins of the Hospitaliers, are all set against the succession."

"So there is no strong King to follow in Baldwin's steps?" Talon asked.

"Not really. Ibelin and I and precious few others want to have the throne passed to Isabella, the step-daughter of Balian of Ibelin."

"Why them, Lord?"

The Duke took a deep breath. "Because Sibylla is a woman of little morals and has married an opportunist, a weak one at that. This was the one big mistake by the King. He married her off to this gold hunter in the hope that it would sideline her. Unfortunately, it has done exactly the opposite."

"I suspect I shall be designated regent when the boy comes into his kingdom, but I am not looking forward to it at all. That palace is a nest of vipers. I shall be vilified no matter what I do."

Talon glanced out of the window. The sun was low on the foothills to the west of the city.

"My Lord, I must go," he said. "I am already late." Just as he spoke, the bells began to ring for Vespers.

Raymond looked regretful. "So soon, Sir Talon? I'd hoped to be able to provide hospitality while you were here. I have a great deal of space, as you can see."

"I have to rejoin my family, my Lord. We arrived by caravan and they will be waiting for me."

The Duke reluctantly agreed to let him go, but first made him promise to come and see him the next day.

"I shall be telling the King that you are back, Sir Talon. I am very sure he will want to see you, have no fear."

Talon thanked him and hastened to the Mount Zion gate, where he found his family and companions gathered outside waiting for him.

"We were becoming concerned, my Brother," Reza said as he came up to them. "Is everything all right?"

"I will have to wear this heavy chain mail for a few more days, and then I hope we can set out for Acre. I, for one, cannot wait to leave. I'll tell you about it tonight," he told them.

Later that night they all gathered around a fire and discussed the day.

"I find cities, with rare exceptions like Isfahan, to often be a pretty sight from a distance, more often than not foul and smelly places within," Jannat stated with a sniff.

There began an excited discussion of all they had seen. Talon was familiar with many of the places, streets and market places they described. In his mind's eye he could imagine them walking along the crowded narrow streets, the women stopping every five or six yards to examine something or other of interest, while their guards kept watch, fingered their weapons and puffed out their cheeks with impatience, or sighed and fidgeted until they moved on again.

As they talked he remembered the places where houses were almost touching at the top story, with buttresses holding them apart and an archway driven through. It was a crowded city, but unlike Acre it was constructed mostly of stone. There was not much wood to be found on the hills any more; what there was came from the olive trees, and they were not for timber.

Then they began to ask him questions.

"Who did you meet today, Talon?" Rav'an asked him.

"No one less than the Grand Master of the Templars, a man called Sir Gérard de Ridefort, and then the Duke of Tripoli. The Duke's news was not encouraging. However, he has offered to talk to the King on my behalf and obtain an audience for me." He smiled at his family and friends. "So you are doomed to stay here until then, by which time I am sure we will all be ready to leave and go to where our real home is to be."

"You don't appear to like it here very much, Talon," Reza remarked as he sipped some tea.

"It not the city itself, although I would not want to live here, it is true. It is the seething pot of politics that is currently surrounding the dying King."

"You have learned a lot in such a short time, Talon. Are people here so free with their opinions?"

Talon gave him a wry smile. "They are when they are the right people. The two great factions appear to be at each other's throats, and I do not want to be forced to take sides in this kind of dog fight, although I have a high regard for the Duke of Tripoli."

"Are you talking a civil war? Prince against Prince?" Rav'an had not yet grasped the title of 'Noble' as a rank.

"Remember that man we had our difference with down south?"

They all nodded. "How could we forget?" Reza chuckled. "But, I enjoyed myself. Didn't you, young man?" he nudged Rostam, who grinned sheepishly. There were chuckles from Yosef and Dar'an.

"Yes, but I don't think he did," Talon's tone was dry. "He carries much influence here in the heart of the kingdom, and that is a very bad thing. Even for me, as he knows full well I was involved. As soon as I have seen the King I want to leave this dangerous crowd behind."

"What about this... Duke you visited, Talon? Is he not influential? Could he not be a useful ally?" Rav'an asked him. He smiled at her, appreciating her attitude.

"He is a friend, but as to being an ally who can actually help us, I am not so sure. Make no mistake, I believe the Duke of Tripoli to be a sincere and intelligent man who knows the people of this region better than almost anyone. It is just that he is embroiled so deeply in the politics surrounding the dying King that, in comparison, I am of no significance whatsoever. I, for one, do not wish to be dragged into that pit."

"It can cost one's life if you pick the wrong side," Jannat stated with remarkable insight.

The next day, leaving the others to do as they wished, Talon once again presented himself at the entrance to the Templar stronghold. He was kept waiting for an hour and was just about to leave when a messenger came hurrying along to ask that he follow him.

Talon left with him, relieved to be out of the large chamber. He had felt like some kind of exhibit. People had been staring at him and muttering amongst themselves, clearly talking about him. The word appeared to have gone out that he had come back from some fabulous journey, but mostly what he heard was Montgisard. His name was synonymous with the battle now, he thought ruefully.

"Ah, there you are, Sir Talon," said Sir Gérard, when Talon was ushered into his chamber. He motioned Talon into a seat. "I heard late last night that the king wishes to see you at noon today," Gérard stated. He did not appear to be very pleased. "I had barely told him of your arrival when he ordered me to present you."

"Then I am honored, Sir. I shall present my self at the palace doors just before then."

"That won't be necessary. I shall be taking you myself," Gérard said. "We will go now, and then we will be in the main hall when the King calls for you."

"Calls for me?" Talon asked.

Gérard sighed, as though Talon should have known. "He is bed-ridden and almost totally blind, Sir Talon. He can, however, hear well enough." Gérard's tone was testy.

They made their way around the corner to the entrance of the palace and were admitted by the sentries at the great wooden doors.

Talon remarked the almost furtive activities going on inside the palace and the hushed tones of the people talking to one another in corners or by windows. It gave him the impression that a funeral was about to begin.

After they were announced at the door way of the great hall, Sir Gérard lead the way towards a group of men standing off to one side of the room full of knights, nobles and church people. As they walked, Talon felt all eyes upon him. Not all of them were friendly. When he passed a priest the man hissed, "Witchcraft is a sin and sinners burn." Talon frowned at the grimacing priest but said nothing. Another person, however, murmured a welcome. "We are glad to see that you are safe and back with us, Sir Talon." He glanced up but could not see who had said it. The murmurs went on all around them, and then they were standing in front of some familiar faces.

Raynald de Châtillon glowered at him and made a surreptitious sign of the cross, but Talon smiled. "I am honored to meet you again, My Lord."

Raynald muttered something and looked elsewhere. His watery blue eyes were hostile.

"Well met again, after a very long time, Sir Talon," Count Joscelin of Edessa said with what could have passed for a smile.

There was another man with them who seemed somewhat detached. He was introduced as Baldwin Ibelin, a strong man who seemed ill at ease with these other nobles. He regarded Talon with interest.

"I have heard much about you, Sir Talon, but I dare say there is still much more to know. Raynald has been talking about some magical thing you did in front of his castle to the South?"

Talon glanced at the red-faced Châtillon, who was shifting from foot to foot, fuming.

"Nothing out of the ordinary, Lord. But I am surprised, because this *thing* that I did was nowhere near his castle! Were you actually present, my Lord?" Talon turned to the angry man, his eyes boring into Raynald's. Châtillon wiped his beard with the back of his hand.

"No, I was not!" he muttered. "I merely heard rumors to that effect. Witchery of any kind is condemned by the church, as you well know, Sir Talon."

"When robbers attack a weak caravan they have to defend themselves with anything that comes to hand. Don't you agree, Lord?" Talon said with a hard edge to his tone.

The others around them shifted uncomfortably, but Ibelin grinned. "We should talk later, Sir Talon." His eyes betrayed his amusement, but also an understanding. It was common knowledge that Châtillon preyed upon caravans attempting to reach Damascus from the Red sea.

Joscelin looked up and said smoothly, "We shall have to postpone Sir Talon's story, as here comes the Duke."

Raymond of Tripoli strode up and halted in front of the group.

"Gossiping like a group of fishwives again, my Lords? I see you are here, Sir Talon." He gave the others the ghost of a bow and took Talon by the arm. "Glad you could make it today. The King is impatient to see you," he said, with a backward look at the others.

"Ibelin, please join me," he called over his shoulder.

The three of them made their way to the exit and along a silent corridor to the doorway of a chamber. "This is where you go in alone, Talon. Be aware that the King is very ill and cannot see well. Speak up, and tell him who you are. He is expecting you," the Duke said, then turned to Ibelin. "What were those snakes talking about today, my friend?"

Talon walked through the door which had been opened by a guard and looked around the room. It was an airy place with a light draft coming in through the window, lifting the almost transparent gauze curtains. He was surprised, because the Frankish physicians hated fresh air, and cleanliness was not a part of their creed, yet here was a clean smelling room with fresh air all around.

In the center of the room on a bed that more resembled a bier he saw a figure lying very still. The still young King wore a mask, even when in bed. Talon had remembered the commencement of the disfiguration, but now it seemed to be well advanced.

"Who goes there?" The voice was low and rasping.

"Sire, it is I, Talon de Gilles, My Liege. I have come as promised."

The figure on the bed had been lying very loosely but now it tensed. "I heard yesterday that you had come back, Sir Talon. My heart is glad that you have lived to see wondrous things which, alas, I never shall. Will you tell me of where you have been?"

"You exacted a promise from me before I left that, should I return, I must relate to you all my adventures, Sire. I kneel before you and will freely tell you all I can," Talon said.

The King lifted his left arm. "Come, be seated and take some wine. I know, I know, you are not supposed to, but in this one instance take some; it will relax you more. I sense that you are very tense."

Talon smiled. "I am indeed, Sire. I am not used to sitting before a King."

The figure on the bed gave a weak bark, which Talon took to be a laugh. "We have a little time and you have much to tell, so now tell me all. From the very beginning. Firstly were you successful in your quest?"

"Yes Sire, I was."

The figure on the bed sighed. "It pleases us to hear it, now ... continue Sir Talon. Tell me all."

An hour and a half or so later, Talon left the King lying still on the bed and walked out of the chamber. He could not prevent the tears from falling. With a deep sigh he dashed them away, and then noticed Ibelin, who was still there waiting by a window. Talon joined him and leaned on the sill.

"The Duke asked me to accompany you to his house. He said he was not done with you yet, Sir Talon." Ibelin said. "But you look distressed. It is very hard to see our King thus."

Talon looked up. "Were you at Montgisard, Lord?"

Ibelin gave him a sharp look. "No. Why?"

"Because there he gave us the inspiration to face impossible odds and win. I have admired him ever since and deeply mourn his condition today. It was very hard to say farewell."

"I apologize, Sir Talon. I had not known quite how you felt about our King. I, too, feel the same, as does our Duke. It is regrettable that there are others who care not for him as you, we do."

They set out, and soon they arrived at the Duke's gates and were admitted. The three men passed the rest of the day discussing the situation in their world.

At one time Talon asked about Salah Ed Din.

"Ah," said the Duke. "I wish fervently we still had Sir Guy to help us with the sort of information he excelled at gleaning, but my own information is that Aleppo and the surrounding country is slowly falling into his hands. With his back protected by that city it means that in effect he can now strike anywhere he choses into the Christian lands."

"There was a treaty, my Lord, was there not?" Talon asked.

"Yes, we do have treaties with him. The King has one that encompasses the Kingdom, and I have a separate one, as do the lords of Armenia and Antioch. It remains to be seen who will break them first," he added with a scowl.

"My bet is that Châtillon or that idiot Joscelin will break it first, and then we are in trouble," Ibelin said.

"Salah Ed Din appears to have fully recovered from the defeat at Montgisard," Talon remarked his tone was dry.

"He has indeed, and goes from one success to another, but he has a quarrelsome group of princes to manage. Nevertheless, I suspect that they, despite their internal jealousies and fickle behavior, believe in him and that," said Raymond, "is worrisome."

After more discussion the Duke asked, "What are your plans, Talon? Do you wish to remain here in Jerusalem? Has Gérard finally come to understand your unique talents and allow you to fill the role your mentor left vacant?"

"I doubt that I can fill boots as big as those of Sir Guy. I don't know yet, but I must go to Acre and take care of business there first."

Both Raymond and Ibelin shared a look and a frown.

"If you care to take my advice, Talon, it would be to take precautions when you arrive back in Acre. There have been changes, and furthermore rumor has it that the bishop is... shall we say unfriendly towards you. There is a fanatical monk there who has been investigating you for witchcraft."

Talon scowled. He remembered the bishop, and he guessed who the fanatical monk might be.

As he parted from the house, the older man said, "Come back to us one day, Sir Talon. We have need of you, even if those fools in the palace don't know it yet. I will always have a place for a man like you; there are few enough of us left here in *Outremer*."

Ivory palaces built on earth
And mansions lined with galleries—
With marble columns on inlaid floors
In spacious halls that filled with parties:
In a flash I saw them all as rubble
And weathered ruins without a soul
—Moshe Ibn Ezra

Chapter 6
Acre

The small boat bumped gently against the rocks at the base of the fortifications and Reza stepped silently onto the narrow, rocky shoreline, glanced upwards, then turned and held the boat while the others disembarked.

Standing on the wet, black rocks with ripples of the sea washing at his feet, Talon stared up at the walls of Acre, which towered above them and listened hard. It was very dark but sounds carried, even the small sounds down here on the shoreline. A gull, annoyed at having its sleep disturbed, squawked at them from a rock ten paces away. Everyone held their breath. An alert sentry might out of curiosity peer down and see the boat and the dark figures crouched against the wall. However, no dark silhouettes appeared leaning out over the battlements, and there were no alarms. Talon tapped the edge of the boat with his hand. The two men who had been rowing the boat whispered. "Go with God," then rowed the boat silently off into the darkness of the sea, heading towards a cove some distance away where they would haul it onto the beach and go back to the encampment; their work was done for this night.

No so for the men at the base of the city walls. Their objective was to get into the city and find out how things stood with the men of Talon's company. The reason Talon had not gone in through the city gates was because of something the Duke of Tripoli had told him:

"The Church is out to get you, Sir Talon. Some trumped up charge of witchery, from what I have heard. Pah! More likely the Bishop wants your wealth for himself. I would be very careful when you get to Acre."

61

Getting over the walls had not seemed too difficult when he observed them from the beach during daylight, but now, crouched under the tall stone works, he felt less sanguine. Reza, however, was all business. "I shall climb them and send down the rope. Dar'an is not experienced enough, and you are too old," he whispered with a low chuckle.

Talon grinned in the dark. He could hardly see Reza, let alone hear him over the low roar of the surf. The edge of the water where they were crouching stank of rotting fish, offal, and other unmentionable things that had been tossed over the walls for years. He wrinkled his nose and patted Reza on the shoulder. "Go!" he hissed in his friend's ear. "Before I show you how it is done."

He watched as his brother seemed to climb the wall without effort. Talon never ceased to marvel at how good Reza was at doing this. All the same, he did slip once and hung there for what seemed like an eternity, while the men below held their breath. He recovered, however, and finally made it to the top, where he paused and very cautiously checked for any unwelcome guards, then he disappeared like a cat. A few seconds later the rope was given a shake, meaning that he had secured it. It was time to move, and quickly; a patrol could come along the footway behind the battlements at any time and discover the rope.

Talon was the first to go, walking up the rope easily until he reached the top. He slid onto the footway and, following the hiss from Reza, slipped into the darkness alongside his friend. Dar'an followed close on his heels; the young man was not even out of breath as he joined the two older men. Talon looked down the length of the battlements. They had chosen a good place to enter; there was a wide gap in the number of pitch torches placed at irregular intervals along the pathway.

They quickly hauled in the rope, coiling it, and Dar'an shrugged it over his shoulder. The three men were all dressed in dark clothes with their faces concealed, leaving only their eyes visible. They were armed with their daggers and swords; after some debate they had left their bows behind.

Now it would be Talon's turn to lead the way, because he knew the inside of this city well, having prowled it often enough when he lived here. He wanted to scout out his house and meet again with his captains. He felt a keen sense of anticipation at seeing Max again after all these years.

They left the shadows and slipped quietly down the stone steps that led toward the first street. Just in time, too, as two sentries could be seen ambling along the parapet some distance away. The three men huddled in the darkness of the buildings and waited until the sentries, conversing in low tones, sauntered past, their spears casually held over their shoulders. They disappeared into the tower at the far end.

Talon led the way unerringly along the maze of filthy, stinking streets, moving from one dark shadow to another. The very few people who were on the streets were either in a hurry to go home, it being very late, or too drunk to notice the phantoms that flickered past them.

It didn't take long for the three of them to arrive at the street where Talon had formerly lived. It was very quiet here; that had been one reason he had chosen to come at this hour. There was only one dark bundle crouched against the wall, not far from the large wooden gates of his property. Bidding his friends to wait in the darkness of an alley nearby, Talon strode across the street with the aim of knocking on the door and gaining admittance. Late it might be, but he was, after all, the owner, and had every right to do so.

Just as he was about to knock, the bundle nearby grunted and sat up with a groan and noticed him. "Good Sir, can you spare a coin for a sick old man? God will bless you for your kindness." The thin, reedy voice cracked with age and despair.

It was not the words that arrested Talon and made him turn. He knew that voice! He stepped closer to examine the bundle of smelly rags. "Is that you, Simon?" he asked in disbelief.

"Who... who are you?" the figure asked him tremulously. "Please do not harm me. I only ask for a coin to live—"

Talon gasped. "It *is* you, Simon. Dear God, what has happened to you?" He leaned closer. "It is I, Talon. Do you not remember me?"

The figure on the ground shook. "Dear God almighty! Is it really you, Sir Talon? But... but you are dead these long years! Are you then his ghost come to haunt me?"

Simon waved a thin, bony hand in the air. "I cannot see well in this light, but I hear your voice. It is you! Where have you been, Sir?"

"Yes, it really is I, Simon. I am not dead. Never mind where I have been; I have now come home. You must tell me, why are you lying here? Why are you not in the house where you belong?" He squatted next to the old, ragged man. He could see, even in the starlight, that his beard was unkempt, and his gaunt features betrayed his age and his destitution.

He reached out to clutch at Talon's sleeve. "This is not your home any more, Sir Talon. The Church has taken it, these many years ago. Ever since... you left for the great battle," his voice trailed off as he seemed to forget what he was saying.

Talon looked around him in alarm. Something was terribly wrong. "Are you saying that others live here now? Who would that be, and where is Max? Where is everyone?"

Simon plucked at his sleeve. "I can tell you what I know, Sir Talon, but it should not be here. You are in danger!"

"Come," said Talon. "You are coming with me." He lifted the old man to his feet and helped his bent and shrunken frame across the street towards his companions, who emerged from the darkness to stand around them, staring at Simon. No one said anything, but their surprise was very evident.

"We must get him to some place where he can talk and where we will be safe for a little while," Talon whispered. He glanced up at Reza. "It would seem that I no longer live here," he said, his tone flat. "Come, I know a quiet place where we can at least be off the streets and where Simon—his name is Simon—can tell us more."

Talon led the way towards a derelict building they had passed while on their way to his house. It was some way back; a ruin, and the roof had fallen in, but there was enough space for five or six men to sit and lie under the beams. A couple of beggars hastened to depart when they awoke and found three dark, menacing figures standing over them. A small coin was given to each, and the frightened men shuffled off, muttering to each other. The moment the taverns opened the next morning they would be in to drink their new-found wealth away.

The newcomers crawled into the space, after having first ascertained that there were no others inside. In the darkness Simon was made comfortable, and then the questions began. Talon promised to find food in the morning, but he was frankly worried that Simon, being so frail, might not even survive the night. He forced himself to control his impatience as he drew as much information from the old man as he possibly could.

"Some time after you left," began the old man, "and Max returned to Acre, wounded from the fray at the ford, the Church sent armed men to this house and demanded entry."

"I kept them out and went to find Sir Max, but he was not there, at that time I thought he was at the Templar fortress. Henry was, though, and he came with me to the gates and demanded to know what they wanted.

Simon paused. "A skinny man, a monk, was at the head of the armed guard. He waved a parchment at us, then told us that we were all to leave at once, as this house now belonged to the Church," he sighed. "Henry, bless his heart, refused, and again demanded to know why. The monk shouted that it was because you had been accused of witchery and that all who were associated with you could be prosecuted. We were very frightened, all of us. Witchcraft is a very bad accusation, Sir Talon."

He paused again to catch his breath. Talon put a hand on his thin shoulder. "It's all right. Go on, Simon."

"Henry could not dispute this, and we were turned out. The soldiers came charging in and looted the place. They roughed up the servants and stole whatever they could before the Brother restored discipline. All of us were kicked out onto the street, told to keep our mouths shut and to stay away. Henry demanded to hear from Max, but the monk said... " Simon paused and gave a whimper, "the monk said, that Max had been stripped of his right to be a Templar and was in prison. He has been there these long years, and I fear he could not have survived the trials they would have put him through."

Talon was stunned. He squatted in the dark and ran a hand through his hair, trying to come to grips with the awful news. "What has happened, Talon? What is he saying to you?" Reza murmured to Talon after a long interval of silence. He had not understood a word.

"It would seem that I am dispossessed of everything I used to own here in Acre, Reza." Talon gave his companions a brief outline of what Simon had related. Again the silence, as they absorbed the information. They, too, were shocked, for Talon had explained that this was to be their home. Now it appeared that they were not even safe here in Acre.

Talon took some time to compose himself, then he asked Simon, "Do you know where Max would be? Is he still here in Acre?"

Simon shuffled in the dark. "I... I think he must be, Sir. He was very well respected by the Knights. They would not have allowed the Church to take him. There is little love lost there."

"So he could still be in the citadel?" Talon demanded.

"That is where the prisoners of the Knights are held. The Templars would not allow the Church to imprison him. He would be dead these long years ago, if they had. But... I do not know if he is indeed alive today. As you can see, my condition is pitiful."

Talon reached forward and gripped his old servant's shoulder gently. "You could do nothing else, Simon. Who now lives in my house?" He had a deep, sinking feeling in his gut.

"Why, I believe it is the Bishop, or some other high personage of the church who lives here at this time, but also the monk himself. He has become very powerful since he worked for the Bishop."

Talon took this in, even while he was about to ask more questions. "Why then do you spend your time outside the house in the cold and rain?"

"Because there is another monk, Brother Martin, who brings me food in the mornings. He lives there with the others but... I don't think he is a bad man. He has been very kind to me."

Talon thought about this for a minute, then asked, "Where are my captains? Where are all my men? Where are my ships?" Reza put a hand on his arm. He hadn't realized that he had raised his voice. His anger and confusion were threatening to impair his thinking. He took a deep breath and repeated the question. "My ships, Simon. Where are they?"

Simon sighed again, clearly this was tiring him. "Henry and Guy are still here in town, but their ships are idle in the harbor. They have no work and no crews. As for Nigel, I do not know where he is."

"Do you know where I can find them?" Talon asked gently.

"They sometimes can be found in their old drinking places. That at least is the same. Sometimes I go there and they give me something to eat. They have a little money, but not much."

"They cannot possibly be poor! I left them as men who had money," Talon said, startled and suddenly uneasy. What had become of his friends during his absence?

He glanced out of the opening in the ruins. A slight gray light was beginning to show. Turning to Reza he said, "This is not what I had imagined, my Brother. It will be daylight in an hour, so we must stay here out of sight until tomorrow night. I can walk around in the day, but I need to be very careful."

Reza, who had been crouching at the entrance, agreed. "We should stay with this old man and keep guard. He looks tired and sick."

"I think he does not have long in this world. He used to be a servant of mine at the house. I would give him what comfort I can before then." They were speaking Farsi in soft tones.

Simon's face lifted. "Who are these people with you, Sir? They sound like Saracens."

66

"They are with me and are my friends, Simon. They will not allow any harm to come to you. You are safe now."

Simon relaxed somewhat and appeared to doze off.

Talon addressed Reza. "Men of the Church here have taken all my possessions. They accuse me of witchery, which is punishable by death by fire. But I have friends who need my help. Tonight you should take him," he indicated Dar'an, "and go back to the encampment while I stay and try to find out more."

Reza put out a hand. "I think I speak for both of us here, Brother. We stay and help you with your problem." He lifted his hand as Talon made to speak. "We will be staying."

Talon subsided, then nodded, drawing some comfort from Reza's words. He looked at Dar'an. "We have been through much together. Perhaps we can show these people what real wizards can do!" They chuckled at that. Chinese powder was a powerful tool, all the more so because it was unknown to their enemies.

Dawn arrived, and with it the city began to stir. The early risers, the market people, both buyers and sellers, began to move about. The apprentices awoke from their slumbers and called to one another as they strode to work alongside the porters and other people doing menial work. The four men slipped into the dark recesses of the ruins and listened as the bustle of early morning started.

Finally Talon stood up, brushed himself down with his hands, and adjusted his clothing to look a little less like that of a night burglar and more like someone who had spent the night guarding a house. Universally, men—usually ex-soldiers or mercenaries—were employed for this purpose. He fit the role well; while wearing no uniform he was, nonetheless, to any casual observer just another night guard on his way home.

His intent was to find some food and drink for Simon and his companions, but also to see where he might find Henry. It was unlikely that he would find his former captain at this time of day, but he could certainly obtain food and scout out the town some more, even to watching the Bishop's new house to see what was going on.

He eased his way out of the ruins with care, watching for anyone who might be looking his way, but the rest of the city was preoccupied with waking up. He dusted off his dark brown overcoat, opened it to show a lighter shirt underneath, but not enough to show off his sword any more than just discretely, then strode purposefully towards the by now bustling market place. It was beginning to fill up with women and kitchen servants out to get the freshest food and the best bargains from the meagre supplies that had come in overnight from the hinterland.

Talon noticed that since the last time he had been here the displays of fruit and other foods seemed poorer. Did that mean that the farmers were unable to till their land as they had before? He had heard rumors, while on his way to this city, of many fields lying fallow, of derelict vineyards and the lack of livestock. What he saw now bore that out.

His face was partially covered and he wore a leather cap, so there was little likelihood that anyone other than someone who knew him very well would recognize him, but all the same he was watchful. First things first; he bought a loaf of bread, some cheese and some grapes from a small vendor who was not the least bit interested in this silent man who loomed over his stall and just pointed to what he wanted. He was just glad that he had an early customer with some good coin.

Talon took the food, along with a skin of water, back to the narrow street where the ruined house stood. He noticed that there had been a fire at some time, and it was hemmed in between some equally shabby, poorly constructed houses on either side. His main fear was that a dog or, heaven forbid, some children would discover them and alert others. This would be disastrous. He racked his mind for a safer place to hide. Finding Henry was now a very urgent matter; it seemed like his only hope at present.

Before he went hunting for his friends, however, he returned to the lair and left the food with Reza and Dar'an. A brief look at Simon told him the old man was less distressed, and some food made a wonderful difference. He did complain that the people with him did not speak his language, which worried him. Talon reassured Simon that he was safe, and left on his quest to find Henry and Guy.

Walking casually along the now busy streets, he made his way towards the center of the city and the even more densely packed areas. The stink from the offal and refuse in the street attacked his senses, and not for the first time he pondered why people lived on top of each other, moving about in each other's filth. His ears rang with the noises of people shouting, even screaming invectives at one another.

His destination was the inn where he and his former captains had often gone to relax and drink with their crews. He remembered the way, but when he drew near he stopped to scrutinize the area.

The inn was quiet this early in the day, but from where he stood he could see men still lounging around inside. Some were sprawled across tables unconscious, while others were muttering drunkenly to one another, deep into their cups.

Talon was surprised to see Guy, one of his captains, or a man who looked like Guy, seated on a bench, fast asleep and draped across a table. Nearby was a jug, which Talon assumed to be mead; the big man had always preferred mead to wine. He moved cautiously into the inn. He was ignored by the one man overseeing the morning work; the serving maids were absent, having gone to bed in the back, exhausted from their night's work both as carriers and as whores. Sidling up to the man at the table, Talon looked down at him. Sure enough it was Guy, fast asleep, snoring into his sleeve. He stank of stale alcohol and appeared not to have washed for some time, but it was his man.

Talon shook Guy gently at first, and then with more urgency. Guy reared out of his stupor with a grunt of annoyance, lifting his shaggy head to shake it, the greasy tendrils of his filthy hair whipping from side to side as he did so. He rubbed his bearded face vigorously with both calloused hands and shook his head again before looking belligerently up at Talon, who was standing beside him. "You'd better have a good reason for waking me, oaf!" he growled.

Then his eyes widened. He was about to open his mouth when Talon put one finger on his lips and shook his head. Guy was still trying to focus properly, but he got the message and comically slapped a large hand over his mouth. Surprise was written all over his normally bland features. Talon motioned him to get up and to follow him out into the busy street.

Guy got to his feet and staggered after him. An angry voice shouted from inside; it was the proprietor. "Pay up, you bastard, or I'll call the guard!"

Guy chuckled and muttered, "Their accommodation is probably better than mine." He looked down at Talon. "Talon, I've no money," he said, with a silly grin on his face.

Surprised, Talon hastily dug in his pouch for a couple of copper coins and flicked them into the gloom of the room they had just left, then grabbed Guy's sleeve just in time to prevent him from falling face down into a pile of dung as the big man tripped over his own feet.

"Where do you live, and where is Henry?"

"Aah'll show you, c'mon. Aah'll show you," he slurred.

They staggered off, with Talon half supporting the bigger man, making their way along narrow streets for a couple of hundred paces until they came to a wreck of a house made of old, poorly shaped timbers and mud which had cracked, allowing the plaster to fall away. No one paid them any attention; drunks were a common sight in Acre. Maids on their way to the market or other errands scurried by with their eyes downcast, while apprentices striding to work glanced at them with contempt. Not having two coppers to rub together, they were envious of drunks who had enough coin to spend the night carousing. There would be many more hungover drunks on the streets as the day advanced.

Guy stopped in front of the dilapidated place and waved his hand at it. "There! Our palace, mine and Henry's. Where've you been, Talon?" he asked querulously. "We've missed you!"

"Well, I'm back now, Guy, but you are a mess. Come on, let's go in and find Henry. I have urgent business to discuss." He all but hauled the heavy man off the street, kicking open the rickety door and guiding him into the dim room that encompassed the whole of the downstairs floor. It did not even have flagstones; instead there were old, shredded rushes that should have been changed years ago, as they stank of old mead, wine and piss. Not for the first time, he wrinkled his nose.

Henry was snoring loudly on a truckle bed, one of two against the far wall. Talon sat Guy down on the other bed, where he promptly rolled over and went to sleep. Talon glanced up the crude steps to the loft. There didn't seem to be anyone there, but he checked anyway. The crudely cut boards were strewn with hay and some old bits of leather and rope. He went back down the ladder and shook Henry awake, then stood back.

Henry came roaring out of his slumber, desperately reaching for his dagger. "Do you want this?" Talon grinned at him, waving the weapon. "That is not a nice way to treat a friend, Henry."

Henry gaped, sat up, and stared. "Talon! Dear God, is that really you?" he demanded and shook his head to clear the cobwebs. "Where have you been?" he shouted, as he got to his feet and reached for Talon to give him a great bear hug. "We thought... we thought you must be dead these long years." He sniffled and stood back to look at Talon, still holding onto his arms as though trying to reassure himself that it was really Talon and not a ghost. There were tears in his eyes, which he dashed away self-consciously with the back of his hand.

"No, my friend, I am not dead. I am back, and I find that all my friends are in dire straits. You and Guy here," Talon looked around the dismal room, "Max I hear is in prison, and where is Nigel?"

He dragged a stool out from under the rough table and sat on it, motioning Henry to sit with him. Henry ran his fingers through his dirty hair and pulled at the unkempt beard that had sprouted on his lined face, and shook his head sadly. Then he leaned onto the table and put his hands to his face in a gesture of utter defeat.

"Ah, Talon. It has been a disaster and a tragedy. Yes, Max is in prison, but through no fault of his own." Henry looked up and snarled, "Curse that monk to hell and worse!"

"Which monk?"

"That weasel that came with us to Constantinople, Talon. His name is Brother Jonathan, although what is brotherly about him the Lord only knows. Remember him?"

Talon leaned forward, his face close to Henry's. "You must tell me all, Henry, for a great wrong has been done here from what I can tell. I need to know if Max is alive, and also Nigel. Where is he?"

Henry nodded and took a swig of water straight from a jug. "Christ, but my mouth tastes like a Saracen slave's loin cloth!" he exclaimed. "Indeed I shall, Talon, but then you must tell me where you have been. You look well, my friend."

"Well enough," Talon said, "but you don't. You look like shit! I am distressed to find my friends almost on the street like beggars, and Simon *is* a beggar. My house is gone and Max in prison. Tell me everything you can, and tonight you have to help me bring Simon here. He is very ill."

"Agreed," said Henry. "Where to begin?" He tugged at his dirty beard.

"The last time we set eyes upon you, Talon, you were setting off with Max and Sir Guy to deal with a problem at a fort well to the north of here. Max came home wounded, but he recovered well enough. He told us that you had been kept by Sir Guy to go to Jerusalem to meet with the Grand Master of the Knights, who had expressed a wish to speak with you." Henry paused, took another swig of water, and grimaced at the taste.

"Then news came of a great battle in which we heard that you distinguished yourself. They said that you were responsible for bringing the Templars to the battle, without whom all would have been lost to the mighty army of Salah Ed Din." There was admiration in his tone as he looked at Talon. "Sir Guy brought the news back to Acre, and then it was all over the city."

Talon nodded impatiently. "Go on."

"Well, then there was nothing," Henry said. "You just disappeared. Vanished into the deserts of the East. Some rumor that you had gone after a Princess. Sir Guy was reticent about that, and Max even more so. Nothing at all after that. Max did once tell us that the Jews of the city had mentioned some kind of transaction, which meant that you had to be alive, but no other news at all."

"Then what happened here?" Talon raised his voice just a little. He was angry and frustrated. "What has Brother Jonathan got to do with all this?"

Henry stared at him. "Everything, Talon. That devil is responsible for all of it. But wait, there is more. Max recovered well enough and continued to send us three captains out on trading missions. The papers that you received from the emperor in Constantinople made a huge difference, and we did well. But then one night there was a battle at a place called Jacob's Ford.

It was a disaster of huge magnitude for the Templars. They lost their Grand Master, I forget his name, Odo, I think it was, taken prisoner; and Sir Guy de Veres was killed." Henry paused and looked at Talon with bloodshot eyes. Talon merely nodded. He had been overcome with grief at the loss of his mentor when the Duke of Tripoli had told him, but now he was quiet. He shifted on his uncomfortable stool and said, "Go on, Henry, I know about that incident. Max was not with Sir Guy, I take it?"

"He was with the Templars who came to lift the siege. They were ambushed, but he managed to escape in the darkness and made his way back to Acre with some other knights. Again he was wounded—they all were. What a sorry sight that was." Henry stopped and stared over at Guy reflectively. "That was about the time that Brother Jonathan made his move."

"What... happened!" Talon could barely contain his impatience by now.

"Why Talon, he came to your house with a patrol of armed men, and in the name of the Bishop he threw out every person in the place. Everyone! Even poor Simon, who is now a beggar, as you appear to have found out. They placed our ships under a restraint and told us that we no longer worked for the Templars. You see, Talon, your Sir Guy had enormous influence and as long as he lived we were under some kind of protection. But with him gone we lost it all. The men are gone, the ships are gone, and Nigel has not been heard of for almost two years now."

There was a long silence in the room as Talon digested this information. "How was it that Max was thrown in prison?" he finally asked.

"I hastened to find him at the citadel the very same day that cockroach took over your house, but when I asked for him at the gates they told me that he had been arrested. Something to do with witchery you were supposed to have been charged with in your homeland. Max was indicted for being associated with you!" Henry looked at Talon questioningly with bleary eyes.

"Do you know where he is, exactly?" Talon asked, ignoring the implied question.

"Pretty much. In the citadel for sure. The Knights had the balls at least to resist the church and that vindictive old bishop who clamored for his skin. He would have burned Max without a fair trial, Talon." Henry shook his head with a grimace of anger.

Talon nodded his head in agreement. The church would have tortured Max until he was insane with agony and ready to confess to anything. Then they would have mutilated him some more before putting him to the stake.

Henry continued. "The Knights might well have saved his life, but he has been in prison these long years now, and we have not seen him. Brother Martin, remember him? God bless him for his kindness. He has been to see Max from time to time and has kept us informed of his condition, which is deteriorating from the confinement."

"All the coin and wealth that was accumulated? You and Guy were well off the last time I saw you. What happened?" Talon exclaimed.

"They were after your treasure, sure enough, but Max is a canny one. Every time we brought coin back from our travels he would place it with the Jews, who hide it God knows where.

The Bishop, what a black soul he has, would love to steal from them. When the soldiers came they ransacked the entire place. They nearly set it on fire, they were so careless and frustrated. They had expected a treasure house. I also feared that they would come after me and Guy and torture us for the information. So we fled and disappeared for a long while.

"Of course they found some coin, but nowhere near as much as they had hoped. Still, all *our* money was in that house. It had seemed safe enough! One of the servants, Will the Norman, showed them the place where we kept it. He is now working for Jonathan and the Bishop as their lackey. I will cut his throat in broad daylight if I ever catch him." Henry had worked himself into a rage and pounded his fist onto the table.

That woke Guy up, and he loudly expressed surprise and delight at seeing Talon; he appeared to have forgotten that it was Talon who had brought him home to Henry in the first place. He joined them at the table and drank the rest of the water in a few gulps, grimacing at the taste, just like Henry. "God, what is this piss that old crone calls water? She must draw it from the pits!" he complained.

Talon leaned back, deep in thought. So, finally Jonathan had struck! Well, now he was back; but there was more at stake than just rescuing Max. He had to think of a plan whereby he got Max out and then all of them had to disappear... forever from the not so welcoming arms of Acre. He was stunned, but the urgency of his situation forced him to think furiously. How to do it? The vindictive Brother would not rest until he had watched Talon burn at the stake, that was sure. Talon no longer had any friends in this city.

The Knights, while they might protect Max from the stake, had still incarcerated him without a trial. Without Sir Guy to protect him, Talon was very vulnerable and could never guarantee his safety, nor that of his friends and family; not here, nor even in the Kingdom. He doubted if even the Count of Tripoli could protect him from the Bishop. No, that would not be the right place to seek refuge. Constantinople, perhaps; Byzantium somewhere? There were many places to disappear in that empire where the Latin church could not touch him. A thought occurred to him. "Did you or Max ever buy land in Cyprus?" he asked the two captains.

Henry scratched his head vigorously, his face thoughtful. "Yes, I believe he did, although where the deeds are I have no idea. It was land near to the port of Paphos, and also on the plains near a place called Nicosia where they grow sugar cane," Henry said. "I fear that the deeds, along with much coin, are now in the possession of the Bishop."

Talon had a shrewd idea that that might not be the case, but he would find out later. Perhaps they were still in the hiding place near the chimney stack of the house. The coin had been in one place, the papers in another. Max himself would be able to tell him. He had to get into the building somehow and find out.

They continued to talk for the rest of the day. Talon pumped the two men for every detail they could remember, and they were more than willing to tell him all they knew. At noon Guy was sent out for some food to be purchased with more of Talon's coin; Henry and Guy were stone broke.

By evening the two captains had told him everything that they could, including the fact that their ships were still anchored in the harbor, although there was a guard on each of them. The two men even confessed to thinking about stealing one of the ships and fleeing the city, but they had been unable to figure out how to do so.

Talon's mind was working furiously as he considered the meagre options open to him, but he was not ready to share them with his men just yet. He glanced at the gaps in the door. Light was beginning to fade. It was almost time to go and fetch Simon and his companions. He felt sick with worry. Everything he had counted on was now worthless. It was a physical effort to conceal his despair from his captains, and it sat in his gut like a huge stone. He thanked the Duke of Tripoli for his warning. Had he not, Talon was sure that he would now be in prison awaiting the pyre.

He roused himself. "We should go for Simon, my friends, but you need to know something. I have two companions with me who are guarding him. I must talk to them first to ensure your safety. They don't take kindly to surprises."

Both Henry and Guy knew a little about Talon's past, and Max had told them enough for them to know that if he had companions with him then they, too, must be dangerous people. When it was quite dark, they slipped out of the crude hovel and Talon led the way along the almost deserted streets back to the lair where Reza was waiting. A low call from Talon elicited another from the darkness of the ruined house, and someone ghosted alongside Henry, who started with surprise. It was Reza, and he had his sword at the ready; it glinted dangerously in the starlight.

"You have come, Talon," he murmured. "I was concerned. Who are these people?"

"They are my ships' captains, Reza. Has it been quiet?"

"For the most part. A few dogs came nosing around and one began to bark. I took care of that."

Talon nodded. Of course.

"We have a place, of sorts, where we can hide until I can find a better one," he told Reza. "Is Simon all right?"

"He needed food, so that helped. The old man is somewhat better."

"Then let's go to the other place. Come with me and my captains," Talon told his companions. Dar'an lifted Simon to his feet and almost carried him as they moved along the darkened streets, heading for their new destination. They avoided a night patrol that was clattering along the street, evidently to quell a brawl that they could hear going on in one of the inns in a street parallel to theirs, then they arrived at the hovel which Henry and Guy now called home.

Guy went in ahead and lit a candle, whereupon the rest hurried in, and the door was closed. Some sacking was pulled over the door to hide the light within, and the men inside regarded one another warily.

Talon gave a brief smile then said, "Henry, I want you to meet my 'Brother' Reza and Dar'an, one of my men. They have been my loyal companions for many years." He had spoken French.

Reza was staring about him with a disgusted look on his face. "Please tell me this isn't the house you have been bragging about ever since we came to this fly-infested country, Talon!" he said in mock dismay accompanied by a grimace of disgust.

Talon rolled his eyes but ignored the jibe. "Reza, these two rough-looking rogues are my ships' captains. They will help us all they can. Learn more French, my friend, because you are going to need it. They will never be able to learn your language!" he smiled at this and then said, "First there is Simon. There is space above us where he will be warm enough. Dar'an, take him up there and make him comfortable, then come down. We have some planning to do, and all of us will soon be very busy."

Turning to Henry, he said, "We need to obtain a better place than this where we can hide for more than a week. I have coin, so you and Guy must find somewhere very safe, very private, where inquisitive neighbors cannot see what is going on. A small courtyard perhaps, but high walls all around for privacy. That is urgent; we cannot continue to live in this hovel. There is work to do."

Up until this moment their faces had been etched with expressions of despair and resignation, but now they slowly brightened with hope.

"Your 'companions' look very dangerous to me, Talon," Guy said with a grin. "I am encouraged by that. Also, I recall our men used to call you the Fox. Do you have a plan?"

Talon tilted his head. "Perhaps, but much of its success will depend upon you and Henry.

We are as pieces of chess engaged in victory and defeat:
our victory and defeat is from thee,
O thou whose qualities are comely!
—Rumi

Chapter 7

Persecution

Talon woke the next day and scratched himself. Fleas! He had wondered why those two disheveled captains of his scratched themselves so much. Now he knew. Disgusting!

"I'm back in the Christian world, and it stinks!" he told himself with a rueful grimace. Getting up, he woke the others and convened a quick council of war. He had done a lot of thinking.

While the others rubbed the sleep out of their eyes and scratched themselves awake, he issued some orders.

"Dar'an, you must go back to the encampment. Go tonight, and let Rav'an know what has transpired. I'll write a letter if I can find an ink and quill. Stay there and send Yosef back to me. Reza, meet Yosef at around midnight tomorrow, at the same place where we climbed into the city. I am not yet ready to risk something going wrong at the gates. But sooner or later we are going to have to chance it, because we have to bring all the others into the city along with our possessions."

Dar'an would go down the wall where they had arrived, and the boat should be waiting for him according to a prearranged agreement that it would return every night at the same time to either deliver or receive men.

He turned to Henry and spoke French to him. "Henry, I want you and Guy here to do several things. The first and most urgent is to find a place where we can hide out until we are ready to depart."

"Why don't we go outside of the city?" Henry started to ask, but then the light dawned. He gasped. "You intend to steal one of the ships, don't you? My God, but that is really dangerous, Talon!" he exclaimed, tugging so hard at his beard Talon was afraid he would pull it out in tufts.

"Which brings me to the second task," Talon told them. "I want both ships. Not just one, so both of you are to go out there and find the crews. I want only the very best men you can find of our old crews, men who know you and know me who will swear allegiance."

Guy gaped at him, and then turned to Henry. His eyes were goggling. "He is serious, by God!" he cackled. "Well, now the Fox is back, and we have some work to do. Ha! Ha!" He slapped the table with glee.

"I doubt if it will be too hard to find them, Talon. Most of them are out of work and don't want to be pressed into the army, so they'll be glad to sign up," Henry told him.

"You must impress upon the men that this is to be done in absolute secret. Timing is the most important thing. If anyone blabs then all will be lost, including our lives I suspect," Talon admonished him. "I shall provide coin by tomorrow, which you will distribute very carefully. Withhold most of it, because I don't want that crowd of rogues who worked for you in the past to go out and get blind drunk."

Henry chuckled. "You're right, of course, Talon. I know them, but I also know that they are in desperate straights and most will come without question. This is their chance to get out of this hell hole, and they will be grateful and careful."

"What are these two ugly apes laughing about?" Reza asked Talon.

"I think they are happy that they now have something to do. Don't forget what I told you, Brother. They are captains of ships and live for the sea. I have given them some hope. We all need some of that."

Reza looked suspiciously at the two grinning Franks. He shook his head doubtfully. "What are you and I going to do?" he asked.

"First we are going to visit the Jews of this fair city, and then we are going to walk about this town until you know it all and can move around it in the dark," Talon replied. A thought struck him.

"I need robes and something else, Henry."

Henry cocked his head. "What would that be, Talon?"

"I need you and Guy here to find chain hauberks that will fit you both, and we will need... " he went on to list the things that he required within three days to the bemused captains. He finished with, "And get cleaned up. You both stink and look like out of work pirates! Go to the baths. You do know where they are don't you?"

Guy rolled his eyes. "I don't like baths," he muttered.

"You will get one if I have to drag you along by that beard of yours," Henry threatened. "Our Chief has given us an order."

A visit to the Jewish quarter by Reza and Talon took place two days later. They wore light turbans and flowing robes that blended in with the crowd that lived and worked in the Jewish quarter. Indeed, over the years of occupation many Franks who had grown up in Palestine had adopted a similar mode of dress.

Dar'an had departed with a letter for Rav'an, informing her of events and reassuring her that for the time being at least all was well. Talon had also asked for several essential things, including the bows and arrows, which he wanted immediately. In addition, Talon had directed his companions that they should be prepared to move at very short notice. He explained in detail how they were to do so, as they would be entering the city through the main gates.

Yosef had arrived up the wall on the second night, bringing with him the requested items and a letter in return for Talon. Rav'an was very worried, but Dar'an had spent some time with her and Jannat, telling them of the situation and attempting to reassure them.

Talon now carried the chits which had been provided by the Jews in Muscat, and more of the coin from the hoard that Rav'an and his men guarded in the encampment. The man they finally met was named Jacob. To all outward appearances he was just a small business Jew who sold mats, skins, inexpensive carpets, cheap ghilims, some spice, and other small household goods mainly copper pots. His place of work was deep inside the Jewish quarter and unless one knew exactly where to find him in the labyrinth of narrow streets and shops there was no point in searching.

Striding purposefully along the busy streets Talon and Reza attracted no attention whatsoever and soon arrived at the open doorway of Jacob's shop set back in a very busy part of the Jewish area. Ignoring the clang of hammers on iron and the tapping of small hammers on brass and copper in the places nearby they drifted into the quiet of Jacob's shop and were greeted by one of Jacob's relatives. They were politely asked their business and then another younger relative was sent off to find Jacob. Despite appearances Jacob was much more than a small-time merchant to Talon. He was a banker who held onto the money Talon had delivered to his care, and subsequently Max's as well. There was much coin to be handed over, but not all of it today.

Jacob was surprised and pleased to see Talon. They sipped scalding tea from small porcelain cups while seated on one of his more expensive ghilims that was spread over a wide, flat bale of wool.

"I have heard rumor after rumor about you, Sir Talon," he told him. "If half of them are true, then you are a great man."

Talon shrugged. "Great, hmm, but wealthy now, yes. Our journey to China saw to that, Jacob."

Jacob's eyes widened. "So you have indeed been to China! It was said but you know rumors they often appear like djins in the desert wind, no substance to them. So you actually went all that way? You must tell me all about it!" he exclaimed. He waved over to his brother and an uncle who had been hovering about at the back in case of trouble, and bid them be seated with them. The three men looked eagerly at Talon and Reza as though willing them to begin.

Neither Talon nor Reza saw any point in hurrying this exchange. Jacob was behaving like any other merchant, Arab, Byzantine, Turk or Jew. Gone was any reserve; they lived for gossip, and besides, it would have been unpardonably rude to act in haste and not quench some of their hosts' thirst for news outside the city of Acre. More tea arrived, and they began to tell of their adventures. It did not take long for several other members of the extended family to hover about straining their ears to hear all about the fabled China. They whispered in astonishment and hushed one another as one fantastic statement followed another from the two travelers.

Eventually the stories were told. Numerous tiny cups of tea, and sweet, honied cakes had appeared and been consumed when finally, hours later, they came to the point of the visit. Jacob and his uncle shooed the wide-eyed family away and when they had vanished he turned to Talon expectantly.

Talon reached into the folds of his robe and drew out a small bundle of narrow parchment strips. Upon each was written in Hebrew an amount of coin in either gold or silver. Jacob's eyes widened with surprise when he looked them over. As he shuffled them and began to count the amounts on his abacus, he gasped; the total amount was enormous! He showed them to his uncle and brother, who both looked shocked at the huge amount they were seeing.

"Sir Talon, we will not be able to pay all of this for a long time. There would be much time before we could bring it all to you," Jacob stammered. His normally calm demeanor had changed to one of pale-faced shock.

"You mistake my intent, Jacob," Talon hastened to reassure him. He leaned forward and said in a low tone. "I simply want to work out an arrangement with you that will ensure that what I own in Muscat that has been delivered to your cousin there will eventually come my way when I need it. Of course I do not want it all at once. I will be traveling quite a lot, but on occasion I shall send a messenger to you and ask for some payment. You, of course, will collect your usual fee. I would like to think that it will be reasonable?"

"Perhaps," said Jacob softly, "we can lower the fee, just a little, for a man like yourself. How would you like this arrangement to work?"

For the next hour he and Talon discussed the eventual transfer of his money to the Jews of Acre and how it would be moved further on whenever he asked for it.

They left well after noon to return to their new abode. Henry and Guy had had done their best to look tidier, with clean, new clothes. They had not wasted any time locating a new residence either, one discreetly placed in a back street, with escape routes to the front and back of the house should they be needed. Talon had stipulated the need for this.

It was a spacious household, although basic, and it had the advantage of being furnished. A knight had once owned it but had died in some battle, and his widow had left for France. The steward, representing the knight's lady, had remained behind to complete the liquidation of the property. He met Henry and went through the negotiations with him. If he was surprised at the condition of the men buying the house he made no comment, other than to ask if the servants should stay. Henry told him no, and, having paid for the house and not trusting the steward to make the payments to the servants, did so himself. The servants departed promptly, happy enough at the severance payment they received. The steward himself was the last to leave.

"He looks quite put out that he was not able to cheat the other servants of their coin, the thieving hound," Guy remarked with a sardonic grin to Henry as they watched him go down the street.

Henry chuckled. "I saw that. The bastard took our generous severance but still wanted more!"

Talon and Reza arrived at the house in time to see a cart being unloaded by Guy and Henry that contained some of the other items Talon had requested. They were now almost ready for the next stage of the plan.

After eating a large meal of mutton with bread and olives and drinking the horrible, vinegary stuff that Henry claimed was wine, Talon brought up the subject of Max.

"From what you have told me, Brother Martin is one of the few people outside of the citadel who knows where Max is located inside?" he asked Henry.

"I believe so, but the man who might be able to find out more is Simon." Henry cocked an eye at the now recovering old Templar servant, who looked up from his food.

Talon sent a contemplative look over at Simon. The old man had recovered some of his color and looked rested. "How many times did Martin come and see you, Simon?" he asked.

"Sometimes every day, but mostly every other day to make sure I had something to eat. He often tried to get me to an alms house, but I refused, so he would bring me some scraps from his kitchen when he could, Sir Talon," the old man rasped. "I believe Brother Jonathan lives quite well."

"I am sure he does." Talon remarked. "Would you consider going back there just one more time in rags? I want to meet Martin."

Simon nodded. "I would be glad to help, Sir Talon. But you will not hurt him?" he asked, his lined face looked apprehensive.

"May God be my witness, I will not harm Brother Martin, Simon. I just need to know where Max is. Perhaps you can pry the details out of him yourself?"

Simon nodded. "I shall try my best. You will need to know exactly where Max is held?"

"Yes. As exactly as you can get him to tell you."

The next morning, very early when there was only a glow in the east, Talon and Reza escorted Simon along the still deserted streets to the gates of Talon's old property. They both noted that there was a watchman at the gates squatting against the wall. He appeared to be asleep. They sat Simon down in his rags, and then departed to observe from several streets away. Talon wanted to make sure that Simon was going to be all right. "Observe this place very carefully, Brother," Talon told Reza. "For you and I will be paying it a visit one night very soon."

"What do you want to do, my Brother?"

"I want to leave a message," Talon muttered.

Reza smiled in the dark. He had been informed about the events leading up to the banishment of Henry and Guy from this place. It was rare that he had seen Talon so angry. Dawn arrived slowly, and once again the city awoke, rubbing its eyes or clutching its head, depending on how the night before had been spent.

The two concealed men, hooded and in the deepest shadows, listened to the noises within the property, which indicated a household waking up. There was a rasping sound as the bolts of the house gates were withdrawn. The watchman hastily clambered to his feet as the smaller door to the main doors creaked open. Someone in a monk's habit stepped out. He nodded to the watchman, who knuckled his forehead and pointed to the recumbent figure of Simon about twenty paces along the street. With an exclamation of surprise the monk grasped his lower robes and pattered along the street towards Simon. There he bent over the apparently sleeping man and gently shook him awake. Talon smiled as he watched Simon pretend surprise as he awoke and then greeted the monk. From where he was Talon was sure it was Martin. The monk would be up early. He had to go to Prayers; besides, he used to work in the scriptorium and was probably hastening to his labors.

Martin was clearly delighted to see Simon and crouched down besides him to talk. Talon had told Simon to look as worn and sick as he could to ensure that Martin was concerned, which he certainly appeared to be. They talked for some time, with Simon waving a bony hand about as he spoke, until finally Martin placed a hand on Simon's shoulder as though to reassure him and took his leave. When Martin had disappeared from view, Simon shakily got to his feet and limped along the street. He lifted his hand to the watchman, who paid him scant attention, and then Simon was walking past the place where Talon and Reza were concealed.

"Psst."

"Is that you, Sir Talon?"

"Come down this street and join us."

Glancing over his shoulder at the still disinterested watchman, Simon did as he was told and joined the two men.

"It was Martin?'

"Yes, Sir Talon. It was Brother Martin. He wanted to know where I've been. He had been very concerned. I told him that I had been frightened off by some dogs that had menaced me one night, but that I returned to the one place where I still had a friend. Then I asked him about Max. Brother Martin told me that it had been nearly two weeks since he had seen him, but he had intended to go there this week. He said that he would do it today and let me know how Max was doing."

"He didn't tell you where, then?"

Simon shook his head. "No, I am sorry, Sir Talon. But he told me that he would be back this evening to bring me food, and to tell me where Max is and his condition."

Talon was put out by this but resigned himself to obtaining the information that evening. The town was by now wide awake with people walking down the streets, hurrying to their places of work.

He and Reza didn't want to be noticed, so they walked casually back
to the house, where Simon rested until it would be time to resume
his place on the street outside the residence.

"Brother Martin told me that Max was holding up in the prison,
but that his health was poor. Some of his teeth have become
infected and this hinders his eating," Simon volunteered when they
were back.

Talon's anger at the treatment of his dear friend threatened to
overwhelm him, but he shook his head, his features tight. Time
enough for rage when the work was done.

"Is that watchman there every evening?"

"No. He sometimes comes early, but mostly he arrives late. He
has supper somewhere, then comes by much later at night."

Talon thought about that. He didn't want anyone to see what he
planned to do that night. If the guard was there he would simply
have to disappear. Reza could deal with that problem if it arose.

In the meantime, there was much else to do. Guy had already
found some men who were more than willing to work with him on
going to sea again. Guy and Henry had concocted a story whereby
they would recruit their old crews, such as were still in the city, still
in good health and willing, and tell them that there was a voyage
planned. They had impressed upon the crewmen that secrecy was of
the essence, as the city was full of Saracen spies. If news of the
impending voyage got out to the wrong people, then the ships and
their lives would be in jeopardy from pirates, with slavery or death
awaiting them just outside the harbor walls. The men they recruited
were old hands and knew this to be true.

The men who had formerly worked for the captains understood
the risks, but the lure of the coin placed in front of them, with the
promise of more, was sufficient for the moment. Almost to a man
they were broke. Some were missing. Passage on other ships had
been offered to a very few; others were dead or dying of some
sickness or other. Guy and Henry were very careful whom they
selected. They only took those who had taken care of themselves
despite their privations. As they knew every one of their men by
name it was relatively easy to put the word out to those they could
trust. Talon's name was not mentioned even once. These men would
not know he was among them until the last moment. The danger of
betrayal by stray word was too great, and Henry and Guy were well
aware of this.

Back at the dwelling, the three men discussed how they would
take the ships back. There were no servants, nor would there be any,

so cooking had been shared until Reza took over. "I cannot stand the disgusting mess those pirate friends of yours make of perfectly good vegetables and meat!" he'd exclaimed to Talon. "I shall cook, and you shall all eat what I cook and like it."

Talon had laughed and shrugged. "It cannot be worse than what Henry does."

"Your Henry is a barbarian of the worst kind with food. I just hope he is a better sailor. When I first saw them in the light of day I could have sworn that the sea had tossed them onto the beach. Their beards were like seaweed, their clothes, if they can be called that, were rags, and their eyes are as blue as the sea they appear to love so much. At this moment I have no faith in him, nor the giant." He waved dismissively at Guy, who was scowling at him. "At all!"

Reza had then set to with Yosef to prepare the food, which had improved to quite a degree. Even Henry and Guy had to admit it, although grudgingly. "That dangerous companion of Talon's knows how to cook, I'll admit it," Henry told Guy. "But there is something about him that gives me the creeps."

Guy nodded agreement. "Talon has some strange friends, but I am sure they are loyal to him."

"Dear God, but I hope so," Henry responded doubtfully.

Now the group of men sat at another table and worked on some chainmail hauberks which they were tailoring to fit Henry and Guy. Henry had worn a hauberk before, but a long time ago, and Guy never. Those were for the knights or higher Orders, such as the Templars or the Hospitaliers.

Now it was urgent to have both men, as well as Talon, dressed appropriately and correctly for the coming event. The three men, helped by the experienced Simon, fumbled with the needles and thread, unevenly stitching the cloth emblems onto the over-tunics with many a curse as a needle went into a finger or thumb instead of where intended while they went at their task. Hours later, Talon looked up and checked on the position of the sun.

"We have to go," he said. "Simon, are you ready?"

Simon nodded an affirmative, and together with Reza they set out again to meet with Brother Martin, should he come by.

It seemed hours that they waited, but it was not wasted, as Reza spent the time prowling around the area examining in minute detail how to gain access to Talon's former property. Talon had told him that there would likely be hounds at the back, which would have to be dealt with. One of the items he had asked for from Rav'an had been some powder for just such a purpose; it worked for humans and dogs alike.

Talon was just beginning to fidget with impatience when he noticed the figure of the monk walking along the by now quiet street towards the gates of the house. Even in the gloom he could see it that it was Martin. Talon nudged Reza, who was watching the other end of the street to make sure there would be not unwelcome surprises from that quarter. The watchman had not arrived yet to take up his station.

"He comes; get ready."

Martin approached Simon and stooped over him. Simon gave him a feeble wave, pretending to be weak. Talon clearly heard Martin speak.

"How are you, Simon?"

"God willing, I am alive. Blessings upon you, Brother Martin, for you are very kind," came the feeble response as Simon clutched at the half-loaf of bread the monk handed to him.

"Pray, good Brother, what news of Max?" Simon asked.

"Oh yes, that's right. I did visit him today, which is why I am a little late," Martin responded.

"Is... is he well?"

"As well as anyone could be who has been in jail for two years," Martin said, with heavy sarcasm. "At least they feed him, but his health is failing. There has been no trial and I am concerned. They will not let anyone see him except me. Not even his own friends within the Order are allowed near him for fear of contamination."

"Contamination from what?" Talon asked.

Martin lifted his head and turned slowly to face the dark figure that stood close behind him.

"I would recognize your voice in any crowd, Talon," he said, with a catch in his voice.

"I would thank you for taking care of a retainer of mine, Brother. You were always charitable in your thoughts and ways."

"It is not only my duty but also my own desire to be charitable towards those who need it most," Martin replied in an even tone.

"Am I condemned then in your eyes, too?"

Martin shook his head vehemently. "Much wrong has been done here, Talon. I know of what you did those years ago at the battle of Montgisard. Everyone knew, including... " he gestured towards the house. "They, too, knew of your courage and sacrifice, but still they continued with malice and vengeance."

"Then you agree that I am innocent of these false charges of witchcraft, and so is Max?"

Martin met Talon's gaze, eye to eye. "I am aware of the charges that were brought against you by the diocese of Albi. Yes, I read the documents, although I did not tell Jonathan; he would not have allowed it. I have never seen any evidence of this witchery of which you are accused. In my heart I cannot agree with this. Max and yourself have been wronged. But, Talon, you must know that, should they discover your presence here in Acre, you would be in mortal danger."

"Then help me to gain Max's release and I shall be gone from this rat hole," Talon grated. Then they heard the sound of someone walking towards the gates behind them.

"It is the watchman, Talon," Simon whispered.

Abruptly the sound of footsteps was replaced by a stumble, followed by faint choking sounds, then an eerie silence. All three men turned to stare down at the dark canyon of the street, but there was no further sound, and none saw any movement near to the doorway.

"That is odd. I could have sworn that I heard someone walking towards the street. Its about the time when the watch-man arrives." Martin continued to peer into the darkness.

"Martin," Talon whispered urgently, to get his attention back on the subject of Max. "I need your help to get Max out of prison. I know it will be very dangerous for you, but I am asking for your help for someone we both know is innocent. I do not care what they think of me, but Max should not be falsely accused, neither by his own Order nor the church."

Matin was silent for a very long moment, then he said."I agree, Talon. What will you ask me to do?"

"Tell me how to get to him. Where is he exactly?" There was a long pause. "Will you do this?"

Martin reached out to hold onto Talon's arm. "Yes, Talon, I shall do this; because I deem it to have been a great wrong." He went on to give Talon detailed directions where Max was interred. Finally he said, "Will I hear from you again?"

"It is in God's hands now, Martin, know this: I shall not harm you."

Martin seemed to shrink at this, but he simply said, "Very well, Talon. I must go now, as I am late getting back to the house and they will send someone out for me before long. Good night to both of you. God bless."

"God bless you, Brother," Simon said.

Talon stood back and watched Martin go, then he took Simon's hand and helped him up.

"Do you think he can be trusted?" he asked Simon.

"He is a good and pious man, Sir Talon. I don't believe he will betray you."

By the time Martin had arrived at the gates and glanced back, there was no one to be seen. Neither Talon nor Simon were where he had left them. It was as though there never had been anyone on the street. He shivered and went inside the gates. He ignored the murmured words of the guards and walked, in a pensive mood, towards the main house, passing the very bench where he and Talon had last spoken to one another those several years before. Much had changed since then.

He was now a virtual secretary to Brother Jonathan but had insisted, much to Jonathan's annoyance, that he share his time between his work for the senior monk and the hospital where the sick and the poor were housed. His work with the Hospitaliers had not gone unnoticed. Normally the Orders were wary of the church and there was no love lost between the Bishop, who endlessly insisted upon his privileges and rights as a leader of the church, and the two Orders of the Templars and the Hospitaliers in Acre, but Martin had earned their trust and respect over the years.

Now he pondered his discussion with Talon with concern. If he assisted Talon he stood to lose all of that, and possibly be accused as well. Even so, weighing the injustice done to Max, who had always been kind and courteous to him, a man of integrity and honesty, against the accusations leveled at him by Brother Jonathan, Martin had little trouble knowing on whose side he stood. Over the years he had watched as Brother Jonathan had become more intense and more cruel in his incessant hunt, not only for Talon but others who might be considered heretics.

His fanaticism unnerved Martin, who believed in right and wrong, but also the forgiveness of the sins of others, and he did not judge anyone harshly. He shook his head. He had made a decision, and for good or bad he would stick with it. He resolved to say special prayers at the church the next day.

He entered the main hall of the house, which was quiet at this time of the evening. He was hungry, so he made his way towards the main dining area where he hoped to be able to find some food. As he entered the room, he noticed the number of candles that were lit.

The room was bright with light; he wondered at the extravagance. Candles were expensive, even for the church. The smell of wax and burning candles filled the stuffy room, while shadows danced in the corners as the flames flickered. One larger, darker shadow stirred at the end of the table.

"Where have you been?" Jonathan demanded.

Martin started; he hadn't really noticed the Brother. His attention had been on the bread and other food laid out on the table. There was no one else in the room. He cleared his throat. "I was delayed. First at the hospital, and then I met Simon on the street." He had not lied, so he would not have to confess to anyone.

"Who?" Jonathan asked.

"Simon, you know, the old Templar retainer who has been on our doorstep for some years. Ever since you.... " Martin left it at that. He was not a man to seek confrontation.

"Oh, him. Why does he continue to hang around this place, I wonder? Won't they take him in at the hospital?"

"No, he refuses to go." Martin helped himself to a leg of roasted chicken and took a chunk of bread from the dishes on the table. He dipped the bread in a saucer of oil and ate thoughtfully, and nearly didn't register what Jonathan said next. "I beg pardon, Brother. What did you say?"

Jonathan sighed. "Please pay attention, Martin. I have had it on good authority that *Sir* Talon is back in this country," he spoke the word Sir derisively.

Martin had the grace to look startled. "Where... where did you hear this?" he asked through a mouthful of meat and bread. He took a sip of water to wash it down before he choked.

"He is alive, despite assumptions to the contrary. I heard this very day that he showed up in Jerusalem, but again has disappeared. Rumor has it that he joined up with the Count of Tripoli and has gone to live in Tiberius with that heretic. I shall have him too, one of these days; I swear to God." This last was delivered with such venom that Martin stared with astonishment across the table at Jonathan.

"Is there no forgiveness in you, Brother? The Count is a great and loyal noble who is close to the King, God bless his soul. By all accounts he advises him well. His knowledge of the Saracen and their world is an important asset, I would have thought."

"The Lord Raynald of Châtillon doesn't think so, nor does Lord Joscelin de Courtenay," Johnathan sneered. "The man represents the fallen, those who have gone over to the Devil. They came out

89

here and adopted the ungodly ways of the Saracen. He even dresses like them, wearing a turban and speaking their cursed language! He is a heretic and only his rank protects him. With God's aid I shall expose him and his wicked thoughts to the world."

"What are you going to do about... Talon?" Martin asked hesitantly. He tried to look and sound casual, but inside he was reeling. He had to get a message to Talon before Jonathan suspected he was in Acre.

"I will be sending a spy to Tiberius, one who knows Talon well. He once worked for the man but has repented and now works for me. When he reports back to me in a week or so, then I shall lay a trap for Talon here in Acre, for this is surely where he will come. It is where he kept his ill-gotten gains. He can then be arrested, and we will begin his trial," Jonathan said, and took a gulp of wine. Martin had the impression that Jonathan was celebrating.

"Who are you going to send?" he almost stammered.

'Why, William, of course! He would know Talon, even should he be disguised. As I recall, Talon was ever a cunning man."

Martin knew William. He had been a sly, thin man, whose eyes never readily met one's own. Now, after being raised to the dubious honor of being a spy for Jonathan, he was gaining weight, although he had not lost any of his former shiftiness.

"When does he leave?" Martin blurted out. He had not meant to be so direct, and it made Jonathan look up.

"Why? Of what interest is it to you?" he demanded.

"None, none at all. I was just curious." Martin lowered his eyes and took another piece of bread, trying to stop the shaking of his hand. His mind was in a whirl. How could he warn Talon in time?

Homeless as I am, to whom shall I apply?
A houseless wanderer, whither shall I go?
—Baba Tahir

Chapter 8

Plans for Escape

Talon woke the next day just before dawn with an uneasy feeling in his gut. He couldn't put his finger on anything, other than the fact that now Brother Martin knew he was in Acre there was the very real risk of betrayal. He told himself that he was being stupid and that Martin was trustworthy, but the awareness that Martin was too close to the enemy persisted. He rose quickly and woke Simon, who was grumpy at being woken so early; but he wanted to be helpful, so they hurried off towards the house, which was just beginning to stir when they arrived. Simon took up his usual place against the wall and settled down to wait.

Talon left him there and headed back. Despite his doubts about his ability to carry this scheme off, he knew there were precious few alternatives. It was difficult to present to his captains and even his companions, Reza in particular, a confident face when he was still in shock at the complete reversal of his fortunes.

Then the thought of Rav'an and Jannat, still outside and very vulnerable, hardened his resolve. He clamped his jaw shut and strode on, scowling and clenching his fists as he went, his anger building. Damned if he would let Jonathan win this fight! His captains and companions had much to do, and a weak looking leader was not going to help. People got out of his way; an imposing figure who strode angrily down the street.

He arrived back to find that they had almost finished modifying the hauberks and were assembling the other equipment they would need. There was a letter to forge and another to write to Rav'an. They had come to the conclusion that noon would be a good time for her and the others to enter the city, as everyone would be supine from the heat of the day and perhaps less inclined to examine the baggage. Talon, Henry, and Guy set out to verify this and to see how closely the gate was guarded. Reza was absent, doubtless still lurking around Talon's former house, keeping an eye on Simon and looking for a place to get in unobserved. Talon had described the house in detail to him, even to making a crude sketch of its layout

91

on the table with a piece of charred wood, so he knew where all the rooms were located.

While Talon and his companions worked together to complete their preparations, Rav'an and Jannat had been busy. Rostam was put to work packing panniers with gold and silver coin and bars, and then pushing cloth rolls on top of them. He was assisted by Dar'an, who would guide them into the city through the gates to where one of Talon's men, or perhaps even Talon himself, would meet them and escort them to their hideout. The plan was simple enough. They would have five heavily laden donkeys to lead and two that would carry each one of the women as well as some other possessions. Rav'an went through everything in her mind as she considered what to bring with her. Talon had been explicit.

"Bring only the treasure and yourselves, with enough clothing to see you through for a few weeks. Everything else, the tents and baggage, is to be left behind. Let Ahmed take it all. Hide the treasure and coins well so that you look like a lady of small means returning to the city. I shall have one of my captains meet you outside the gates and he will escort you in. He will be a large man dressed in chain armor and his name is Henry. Be there at noon time tomorrow."

Rav'an would not be bringing any camels with her. These she would leave behind in the care of the caravan master, who by prior arrangement would leave the area the following day as though heading further north. In fact, the men with him, who were part of the ship's crew, would return to the port of Elat on the northern tip of the Red Sea. From there they would sail back to Muscat and they would let it be known that they had come back from Aden should anyone ask. They had been well paid for their work.

Wiping the perspiration off her forehead, Rav'an sat down on a small bale of cloth to rest. The heat of the day was tiring her, and she felt her baby move.

"Be patient, my darling," she murmured as she put both hands on her growing belly. "It will be all over soon and we can rest properly. God protect us, but I hope so," she added. Everything seemed to have gone wrong since they'd arrived at Acre. She hoped Talon was not making a terrible mistake. There was a leaden feeling inside her stomach that refused to go away. Perhaps when she saw him she would feel better.

Jannat looked up from her labors at the other side of the stuffy tent. "Are you all right, my Rav'an?" she asked.

"Yes, I am fine. The baby is moving again."

Jannat smiled in sympathy. "I am not at that place just yet, but I imagine you will be pleased to get into the city and away from all the flies and sand out here."

"Very pleased, but... from what Dar'an has told me all is definitely not well inside the city either. He said that they had not found things to be as Talon expected. He told me that he had never seen Talon so... upset. I just hope that it is not as bad as it sounds."

"I try not to fret, but like you the news does not sound very good," Jannat said. She sounded fearful. "However, we can't continue to live out here like Beduin. God willing, we will be able to rest and get a bath!" she gave a nervous laugh, and so did Rav'an. "Oh, yes indeed. I am looking forward to that."

She listened to the noises coming from outside. Nothing to worry about there. Ahmed was working with the men to prepare the donkeys and explaining what they had to do next. They were well guarded. Aside from the groans from the camels and the occasional bray of a donkey, all was quiet. The well near where they were camped was used by several of the tented communities on the plain, but people kept to themselves for the most part. Rav'an and Jannat were careful to be veiled whenever they sortied from their tent.

Upon their return to the safe house, Talon discovered a very agitated Simon, who thrust a scrap of paper at him as soon as he arrived and said, "Martin is very concerned, Sir Talon. He told me there was an emergency that you needed to know about at once. I have been back here for a couple of hours already."

Talon thanked him and opened the folded paper. What he saw there made him frown. He looked up at Henry and Guy. "Martin informs me that Brother Jonathan knows I am coming to Acre, but not that I am here. He has sent one of his spies to Tiberius to find out if I am still there with the Count of Tripoli. Should I not be there, he has orders to hasten back and the city will be locked down while they await my arrival." He gave a sardonic smile as he said this.

Henry nodded his head and grinned. "So he has some idea that you are in the Kingdom, and the only person who could tell him you are already here in Acre won't."

"I believe that to be the case. I trust Martin, but the spy is none other than William the Norman. Remember him?"

"Oh yes, I certainly do," said Guy from the table. "As shifty an individual as any I have ever met."

Henry agreed. "Yes, we know him. Is there a risk that he will arrive back before we can implement the plan?"

"Not if we don't waste any more time. The others will be here at noon tomorrow, and then we have to take and load the ships and ensure that all is ready. A day or so, whereas it will take Will well over a day just to get to Tiberius and find out that I am not there, and then he will have to return."

He turned to Reza and explained the situation to him in Farsi. Reza's first reaction was to intercept the spy on his way back. "If you describe him well to me, I can take him before he ever reaches the city," he said.

"I think we can leave this one alone, Brother. There is a more important fish to deal with before we leave. Will is nothing to worry about," he turned to Guy and Henry. "I am more interested in how you two have been doing with our crew."

"We have half the crews needed for both ships, and more coming as the word goes out that we are recruiting," Henry assured him.

"We will need to pull the hour forward because of this latest news. No one knows I am here in Acre?" Talon questioned him.

"We have never mentioned you to any one of them. All they know is that we have a new commission and that it will be with our old ships. The destination is to be Jaffa, and then perhaps Sicily. To a man they welcomed the work without question."

"We have made sure the more reliable men were selected. They will come to the meeting place at very short notice when we need them," Guy told Talon, who nodded approval.

"Now we have to dress up and see what you look like in a suit of chain," he said.

When they had donned the armor he inspected his captains with their chain mail hauberks, chain leggings and helmets. "You could be mistaken for some old Templars," he remarked; he didn't sound very convincing, however.

The next day was tense for everyone. Talon went with Reza and Henry to the gates an hour ahead of the agreed time for Rav'an to arrive. Henry carried a heavy pack over his shoulder, with his armor wrapped inside. He was going to change when outside the gates; there were many places outside the city where he could find a quiet place to do so. Tents and hovels dotted the area of the plain alongside the main road.

After having a good look around at the city's main gates, they settled down to wait. Talon and Reza were very watchful, but equally careful not to attract attention. A great deal hinged on the safe arrival of Rav'an and their ability to enter the city without hindrance from the guards. Noon approached, and the traffic fell off as the heat of the sun began to bite. The guards sheltered in the shade of the gate towers and often waved the visitors through, too lazy to stop them and ask their business.

"Time to go, Henry," Talon said to his friend who nodded and hefted his pack. Henry was dressed in drab brown sacking with a hood to hide his face from the casual observer, and he drew no attention as he wandered casually out of the open gates. Only the observant would notice that he wore good boots. The guards were now eating their noonday meal. The dogs in the street were lying asleep in shady corners. Talon and Reza were squatting in the shade of an old archway, keeping a sharp eye on the entrance. Talon wished that he could be on the ramparts of the gatehouse, where he could see Rav'an and her party as they approached.

As it was, he would have to content himself with watching her arrival at the gates, unable to do much if they were stopped. He hoped Henry would be able to pull it off and convince the guards that he was the escort. The guards respected the Templars, who had a reputation for no nonsense; but one could never tell.

The sun climbed its final few degrees to arrive at high noon; the city seemed to quieten, while the guards visibly slowed down. Some were even asleep in the shade, while others, charged with watching, leaned against the walls. They relied upon the watchmen perched in the towers to warn them of any real danger.

Reza nudged Talon, who became aware of a small stir at the gate. The two guards were looking through the opening at something. Then to Talon and Reza's surprise a horse appeared with Henry seated on top. They hadn't expected to see him mounted.

Rav'an spent a restless night in the tent. Her baby moved about, and while the cool of the night helped her to rest it did little to ease her worry. Her mind would not relax and allow sleep to come for several hours after she went to bed. All that she could do had been done. Ahmed was ready to leave the moment she departed for the gates of this imposing city. He would be glad to be gone. The city was, after all, full of unbelievers and their kind. He could not fathom why Talon and his family would want to go in there and risk all; the Frans were well known for their treachery.

The risk they were about to undertake was not lost on Rav'an, and her worry had communicated itself to Rostam and Jannat. Both were wan from lack of sleep the next day as dawn lit up the eastern sky. They prepared some tea and ate sparingly, too tense to do more than nibble. Dar'an took Rostam for a short walk and explained what he was expected to do while Rav'an and Jannat tidied up the tent, although, as Jannat said, "We have no need to, as we are leaving it all behind." She picked through some pretty muslin cloths wistfully, as though she longed to take one last item with her. Rav'an, however, had been adamant. They could always buy more clothes, but the Chinese powder and the treasure they could not replace. Space had to be reserved for those items, and the animals were going to be heavily loaded as it was.

Several hours before noon Rav'an gave the order for the completion of the loading. The beasts were assembled before her tent and the remainder of the pile of baggage was hauled out and placed on the backs of the ten donkeys that were waiting. She watched as Dar'an, now a strong young man, took charge of the loading and ensured that the heavy panniers were secured. He had matured a great deal and demonstrated his ability to take charge with an easy manner that went well with the other men, some of whom had volunteered to come with her into the city. These were men that Reza had spent much time training in the arts of stealth and secrecy as they were sailing up the Red Sea. While none could match his skills, they were determined to excel and were a welcome addition to a core group of men Reza knew he would need to rely upon in the future.

Finally it was done and, then it was the turn of the camels. Ahmed had the remainder of the men take down everything except the tents and load the animals. They were forced to their knees, with much groaning and spitting, to wait for the moment when they would finally begin their long, dangerous journey down south to Elat.

Rostam, who had been sent out to watch the gates, rushed back and told Rav'an that a large Frans had left the city and was walking towards their encampment.

"That must be the man called Henry," Dar'an said. "I shall go and bring him here, My Lady."

Rav'an nodded agreement and went back into the tent. She took a deep breath. "Now we must hurry, Jannat. It is almost time; the

Frans comes. Are you all right, my dearest?" Rav'an asked, concern in her voice.

Jannat looked pale but determined. "Yes, Sister. I just feel a little unwell. It will pass." She swept back her hair and fastened it with a comb. Then she pulled her veil over her head and stood up straight. "I am ready," she said with a tight smile.

"You are very brave, my Sister," Rav'an informed her, as she did the same. "We are in God's hands now, or rather," she gave a forced laugh, "in the Frans' hands now. Come, we go to meet him."

By the time they had exited the tent, Dar'an had brought Henry to the encampment and he had changed into his hauberk. Rav'an had to admit the large Frans looked very imposing in his thick chain clothing. The effect of the helmet and its nose bar lent a sinister aspect. It was hardly surprising, she reflected, that these Frans had such a terrifying effect upon people when in battle. However, there was something wrong with the picture. Then she realized what it was.

"Dar'an, go and get one of the horses from Ahmed. Tell him I will need to take it with me. Bring it here for the Frans, Henry. He should be seated on a horse!"

Dar'an ran off, and after a quick discussion with Ahmed be came back leading one of the horses that were going to be taken south. He led the animal up to Henry, who looked oddly uncomfortable at the sight of the animal. A small crowd of curious men was beginning to form as he approached the horse and put out a tentative hand to touch its nose.

"Mount up! Get on the horse!" Dar'an ordered him in Arabic.

Henry understood from the gestures that he was to mount up. He did so very clumsily, almost falling off the other side before clutching at the pommel of the saddle and holding himself upright.

Jannat and Rav'an could not help but giggle behind their veils, while Dar'an, who could not conceive of anyone not being able to ride, looked astounded. The horse didn't seem to like its inept load either; but Henry, who had ridden a very long time ago, began to collect his wits and regained control enough to sit quietly while the donkeys were brought forward for the women.

Dar'an and Rostam assisted the women onto the saddles, where they perched on panniers loaded with their goods. Talon had told Rav'an to use light colors for their dresses and veils to make them look more like Frankish women. They were not to wear any jewelry because they were not supposed to be rich. They looked like any other merchant family of limited means coming to the city on indeterminate business.

Ahmed came forward and, holding both hands together as though in prayer, bowed obsequiously to Rav'an and said, "God protect you, my Lady. Please send my best wishes to Master Talon. Without him we would all be beggars. God protect." Tears began to flow down his grizzled face and beard, but he dashed them away and tried to smile.

Rav'an was touched. "God go with you, my friend, and with all of you. It is a long and dangerous journey for you as well." With that she urged her donkey forward and waved to Henry to take the lead, followed by Dar'an. They left with the calls of farewell from their friends ringing in their ears.

Henry somehow managed to get his horse into the lead, and the small caravan set out along the dusty road towards the great walls of Acre. As they approached the gates Rav'an felt a sense of dread. This was utterly new for her. These were Talon's people, but from what she could recall they had never been kind to him. It was still something of a mystery to her why he had wanted to come back here at all. He had pointed out that this was where much of his wealth lay, and that from here they could find refuge until he could decide upon a proper home for them. It would not be Acre, he had told her, but had volunteered little else. Now it seemed that all this had changed, but for what she could not tell. The uncertainty weighed on her.

All too soon they were in front of the massive gates, which were half open. She could see the street beyond the entrance; it was almost deserted at this hour, and the air shimmered in the sweltering heat. The guards didn't seem to be very interested in their approach until Henry rode into the gateway and stopped squarely in front of the guards.

To Talon, hidden behind a stall, it was clear that Henry was not a good horseman, but the guards didn't seem to notice. Henry clumsily drew out a parchment from his belt and flourished it at the soldiers and then waved his arm behind him.

"I am the escort for these people. They are wards of the Order. I am charged with the protection of this lady, and have been ordered to escort her into this city, then to the Citadel to be placed under the protection of the Order of Templars." Henry spoke loudly for the benefit of the guards and his hidden audience. Talon had rehearsed Henry carefully as to what he should say. Now he, along with Reza, held his breath while the guards pondered the statement among themselves.

Finally the leader nodded and waved Henry onward. Henry didn't move. Instead he gestured behind him and shouted to the caravan to come along. Slowly the first donkey walked up to the gate, led by Dar'an, followed by another of Talon's men leading the ones ridden by Rav'an. Rostam also led a donkey laden with baggage, while Jannat was perched on the last animal to arrive. It was only when she had passed through the gates that Henry began to follow. Talon and Reza both started when one of the guards said something in an undertone to another and began to walk towards Rostam and his donkey.

"What have we here?" he asked in a loud voice as he came up to the boy. "Are you with the lady?" the man asked with a sarcastic tone, jerking his thumb at Rav'an. Rostam could not understand anything of what was said, so he simply shook his head and smiled.

The man was about to reach for one of the panniers when Henry noticed what was going on. "Hey, you there!" he bellowed in his maritime voice. "Who gave you permission to look into Templar property?" he turned on the senior guard. "If any of you touches the property of this lady you will answer to the Castilian at the Citadel!" he roared, reaching for his sword.

The senior guard shrugged insolently, but seeing that Henry meant what he said he told the man to step back. The guards were surly, but obeyed their sergeant reluctantly; muttering to themselves, they stood back. Henry reached into his purse, threw some coins in a grand manner towards the guards, and waved dismissively to them before following the string of animals and their passengers as they ambled slowly along the main street of Acre.

Talon turned and grinned at Reza. "Phew, that was close. Henry is quite the actor when he wants to be. Let's show them where they have to go."

Just as he spoke, another rider galloped up to the gates. Talon clutched at Reza's arm. "Now we do have trouble! That is the messenger who was sent out by Jonathan to Tiberius. How can he have made it back so quickly?"

William the Norman walked his lathered and exhausted horse through the gates and stopped under the archway. He leaned down and spoke some words to the senior guard. Talon only just heard a couple of words. "... shut... gates. Watch for... Talon." Then he sat up and began to walk his exhausted looking horse into the city. The rider left the guards taking excitedly among themselves and looking very much more alert.

"We have to stop him! He cannot reach the house," Talon hissed to Reza.

"I shall deal with him," said Reza, and with a hard look at his intended victim he raced off down an alley to head off the messenger. He vanished into the now busy streets, while Talon hastened after Henry and his charges. While he was confident that Reza could head off William, the man's arrival had taken him by surprise. He must have had news of Talon's whereabouts to hasten so fast and return to Acre.

He caught up with the little caravan after few hundred paces and strode alongside the horseman. "I was very impressed, Henry," he said. Henry started; he hadn't noticed Talon come alongside. "I was quite worried they would want to inspect the cargo," he responded. "They were perfectly within their rights, I suspect. I have to tell you though, Talon, I prefer the sea to all this stuff and nonsense."

"The Orders have their privileges, which is exactly why you are dressed as a knight. You did very well, Henry, but now you have to get off the horse and change. If any of the real knights sees you we will have even more trouble."

Henry dismounted and began to fumble with his tunic. Talon helped him shed the surcoat with the cross emblazoned on it and shrug into a less conspicuous coat as they walked. Henry took off his helmet and hung it off the pommel. "Nice horse," he stated. "But I'll be happy to walk from now on. Not too far to go. My God, but I was sweating my balls off in that hauberk!"

Talon grinned and then strode forward to greet Rav'an and Jannat. Rostam looked back, saw him and waved, but stayed ahead when Talon signaled him to do so.

"Hello, my Love," Talon said, looking up at Rav'an who seemed tense and pale, even under her veil. "Are you all right?"

"I am so very glad to see you, my husband. I shall be very much better when this ordeal is over," she retorted, but smiled down at him nonetheless.

It was not long before they arrived at the main entrance of the property. Yosef, who had been watching for them, flung the doors open and helped to lead the donkeys inside the cramped courtyard, then shut the door before prying eyes took note of the sudden activity.

Within a few minutes the house presented its former blank face to the street. Talon had ensured that it possessed a small courtyard with three stables, none in very good condition, but it didn't matter as they did not intend to stay long. The two women and their servants were helped down, followed by embraces all round, then they were led into the relative cool of the house. Talon, after first showing them the untidy living space and the kitchens, led them up the crude wooden stairs to a bedroom which he had prepared for them.

"You will have to excuse the rude condition of the house, my Ladies. We have not had much time to prepare. The previous occupant was a mere knight, but it is adequate."

Rav'an made directly for one of the two beds and sat down with a sigh. "I have looked forward to a real bed for a long time, and this last adventure has tired me," she told him. "You have things to do, my husband, but when you are done I want to know all about this situation."

Talon leaned down and gave her a long kiss. "I shall tell you all in good time, my Love." He turned to Jannat. "How are you, Jannat?"

Jannat waved an airy hand at him as she took off her veil and stretched. "I will survive, but there was a moment back there... "

Talon laughed and said, "Yes, Reza and I were watching. Henry did well. That was a very good idea about the horse! It made all the difference."

Rav'an gave him a tired smile. "These Frankish warriors always ride horses. It seemed best to provide one, but no rider that one! He looked as though he would fall off at any minute!"

They laughed together, which helped to relieve the tension.

"Where is Reza?" Jannat asked sounding disappointed. "I thought he would be here to greet us at least."

"Er, he... er, had some business to attend to, Jannat. I am sure he will be back very soon," Talon told her. "Now I should have one of the boys bring you some cool water to drink." He got up and went downstairs to find the two captains at the table eying the newcomers warily.

First Talon greeted his men and told them of the situation and that they had to keep a very low profile for as long as they were in the house. There were the donkeys to be taken care of, and then the baggage to be placed ready for the next stage of the journey. Then he introduced Henry whom they now knew by sight, and Guy.

"These two men," he informed his men, "are captains of two ships which we are going to take from the harbor tomorrow night. I will need you to apply the skills that Reza has taught you to assist

101

with this," he told them. The six men grinned with anticipation. This was becoming an adventure.

Just at that moment, Reza slipped noiselessly into the room. Talon looked him over then asked, "How did it go?"

"There I was on this busy street when a horse shied and started bucking, then it just fell over." He picked up a grape and munched on it ruminatively. "It tossed its rider onto the street where he broke his neck! Just like that! It was chaos for a while. People running about all over the place, but this fellow was as dead as the stones he landed on. Quite the tragedy." Reza said, looked pious. "May God have mercy on his soul."

Talon gave a tiny snort of amusement but nodded solemnly. "Did he have any papers on him?"

"None that I could find," Reza replied. "I also checked his saddle bags."

"You had better go upstairs to greet your wife," he told Reza. "She has been asking for you."

"What was that all about?" Henry asked him.

"The messenger, Will, came back early. Right behind your little caravan, in fact."

Henry looked alarmed. "Saint Mary! Did he see us?"

"Nothing to worry about. Reza dealt with it."

"You mean... ?" Henry glanced at Guy, who was looking shocked.

"Reza told me that there was an accident. That's all I know," Talon replied.

"May God have mercy on his soul," both men intoned, then they crossed themselves. "But... it couldn't have happened to a nicer man." Guy grinned at Henry.

When Talon went over to the other people in the room, Guy turned to Henry. "Talon has always impressed me as dangerous, but his friend over there scares the piss out of me," he said, looking apprehensively at Reza, who was just walking up the stairs.

"I agree, but our chief is taking us out of this shit hole and giving us a chance... again. I don't really care what his friend does for a living. I want to captain a damned ship again, and if anyone can make that happen it will be Talon," Henry remarked.

Guy nodded. "Hail Mary to that. I'm with him no matter what."

Talon called over to Rostam, who was sitting talking with the men from Oman, and took him upstairs. There he met with Reza and Rav'an and explained the situation. They listened quietly until he had finished, and a long silence followed.

"So what you are saying is that your protector is dead and the church has confiscated everything you used to own?" Jannat asked him, as though to confirm she had really heard the incredible news. "So we came all this way for nothing? God protect us, but what will we do now?" She shot a look of appeal with tears in her eyes at Reza, who shook his head.

"Talon has a plan, Jannat. That is why he brought you inside the city and didn't leave you out there. If there was no plan we would be traveling back south to Elat by now."

"Then tell us of this plan of yours, Talon," Rav'an said. Her tone was skeptical but at the same time she attempted a wan smile. "You have been in tighter places than this I know, my Fox, but I am worried I have to confess."

He gave her a sober look and pulled Rostam closer with an arm over his shoulders. "Indeed we have been cheated, my Love. However, I do not intend to leave it at that. A very close friend of mine, his name is Max, is in prison here. I cannot abandon him. I will not leave this city without him."

"In prison, Papa?" Rostam twisted his neck to look up at Talon. "Where?"

"In the great citadel which you will see before long. It is the stronghold of the Order of Templars in this city," Talon told him.

"So you intend to walk up and take him away? Just like that?" Reza gasped. "Talon, I know you better than anyone, but how in God's name do you intend to do this? The Templars have a reputation for ferocity in battle and great discipline. Even I know about them!"

Talon nodded agreement. "And it is precisely what I shall use against them, Brother. Remember what the Sensei used to say while we were being beaten up by him and Qian? Use your opponent's weight against him; get him off balance and you will win."

Rostam shook his head in puzzlement. "I don't understand, Papa," he said.

Rav'an laughed, "Of course! Just as when we came into the city! You intend to do it again, Talon, only this time we will be leaving! Am I not right?" she challenged him.

Talon grinned. "Indeed and we shall do just that, my Love. *Insha'Allah.*"

They all relaxed at that, and Rostam declared himself hungry. Talon sent him down to fetch some of the food from the kitchen, where Salem was already installed, and continued to talk with the women.

He gave them a rough outline about what would occur that very night.

"There will be a diversion at some time, and then we will take the ships," he told the two women. "I am concerned about only one thing, my Love. You're condition is... well, delicate. Will you be up to this?"

"Don't worry about me, Talon. Jannat and I will be fine. Just make sure that the plan works," she responded.

He smiled, "Then I suggest that you eat supper and get some rest." He glanced out of the opening that passed for a window. "It's getting dark and we have much to do. You should both stay up here until it is time to leave; there are many men downstairs and more to come."

Later in the evening, Talon spent some time introducing people to one another. It was not very easy, because neither Henry nor Guy could speak the language of the majority. Talon became acutely aware that this could present a singular hazard to his plans unless he was meticulous about who had to do what and they all knew their respective tasks.

"Now we must go into the details of how we will take the ships."

With Talon translating for Reza and Yosef's benefit, they spent the rest of the afternoon planning. The table was used for a map with the outline of the harbor drawn with a burnt stick, and stones to represent buildings and sticks to represent the ships. Talon again impressed on everyone the need for timing.

Martin arrived at the house Brother Jonathan called home to find no trace of Simon in the street, and when he gained entry he noticed the servants were looking tense. As he passed one of the senior servants, the man pointed to the main room, where Martin could hear voices, and muttered, "Things happening in there, Brother Martin. Something bad has happened."

Martin knocked gently on the half-open door and let himself in. Once again the room was brightly lit with candles. He spied Jonathan at the far end of the room, but sitting at the table were two other men.

"Ah, there you are, Martin. Late again, I see."

Martin began to offer and explanation, but Jonathan waved him dismissively to a seat. As he sat down, Jonathan indicated the two men seated on either side of him.

"We have Sir Rufus from the Order of Templars here tonight, and Pierre d'Aix, who is the Constable of the city of Acre. I asked them come to see me because I have grave news."

Martin looked up.

"Remember the man, Will, I sent to Tiberius? Well, Pierre here tells me that he is dead."

Martin looked shocked. "How is it possible?" he gasped.

"His horse fell and threw him, breaking his neck in the process." Jonathan crossed himself piously. "May God save his soul and forgive his sins."

Martin crossed himself too. "May God forgive him his sins," he said, but he was still dazed. "Where... where did this happen?" he croaked.

The man whom Jonathan had introduced as the Constable spoke. "Just inside the city, that is why I am here. I was informed and came here once I had heard their report from the city guards, who regarded it as an accident. They think the horse shied at something, and perhaps because he was tired he fell. Hard street to fall upon; it broke his neck."

The man looked very well fed, his corpulent body was topped with a large head and bulbous nose, his big mustache looked well tended and his clothing was expensive. By contrast the other man, the Templar, was lean, heavily bearded, with severe lines etched into the corners of his mouth. His weathered features denoted a man well used to the harsh climate, hardship and the mantle of command.

"I took the opportunity of telling these gentlemen of my suspicions regarding that heretic, Talon de Gilles. I think he is on his way here to Acre, and that might well have been what Will was coming to inform me about," Jonathan told Martin.

"We will have extra guards on all the gates," Pierre said. "I am very sure that he will not be able to slip into the city without us catching him."

"I shall place extra guards on the harbor to stop and search any ship with suspicious passengers, should he try to enter the city from that direction." The Templar rasped. Jonathan seemed pleased that he was being treated as an equal by these officials. Martin watched as he almost preened at the attention.

"Then the trap is set," he said. "May I offer you more wine, gentlemen? I only take water, but you are my guests; please avail yourselves of my hospitality."

Sir Rufus stood up with a disdainful look on his face. "I do not drink wine, and I cannot stay, Bother Jonathan, but I thank you. I must go and ensure that my people are informed and take the necessary precautions. Please give my respects to the Bishop." He gave a curt bow and stamped out of the room, his cloak swirling and his sword sheath rattling against his boots.

The Constable watched him go with a sardonic smile on his face. "Those are a stiff-necked people," he observed. "No wonder few like them."

"As you well know, Pierre, there is little love lost between us, but they serve their purpose," Jonathan remarked with a smirk. "I will catch that Talon, and then I will have his friend too, despite the Templars. Both shall burn."

Martin spent several hours that night on his knees by his bed praying. He prayed for the wayward soul of the dead man; he prayed for Simon, who had disappeared he knew not where; and he prayed for himself, because he could not but think that he might have had something to do with the death of Will. He also sent a plea heavenwards for the protection of Talon.

What course of life should wretched mortals take?
In courts hard questions large contention make.
—Posidippus

Chapter 9
A Hurried Departure

Wearing dark clothing and carrying their bows and swords, Talon and Yosef left the house and slipped into the night, their destination the house where Brother Jonathan now lived. This was a mission of revenge, but also Talon needed to find out if Max had placed anything inside the hiding place near the chimney before he had been arrested.

It took little time to gain entry. The large guard dogs came rushing up as the two men were climbing over the wall, barking excitedly—until they found the fresh meat. Gulping it down, the animals continued to snarl and leap at the two shadows perched on the wall. Then they began to whine and stagger about. Moments later, both animals were fast asleep. A guard who had been alerted by the noise came running up. He gasped when he found the two inert hounds lying on the ground, but that was all he managed. A blow on the head put him to sleep alongside his animals, while Talon and Yosef ran silently towards the darkened house.

Wary of any other guards, they slipped up to the main door with great caution, and found it unlocked. Jonathan clearly considered himself safe here within his compound. By prior agreement, the two shadows split up. Yosef went towards the stables, carrying a small package wrapped in wax paper, while Talon slipped into the main dining room. The sour smells of dinner and old candle wax were strong here, but he was more interested in the stonework of the fireplace. Standing still for a long moment in the darkness, he listened for any sound of movement. There was none; the house creaked from time to time, and he could hear the squeaks and rustling of mice in the walls, but otherwise it was very quiet.

He walked up to the masonry of the fireplace. There had been no fire as it was warm at this time of year, and felt inside the cavern of the fireplace on its left side. A stone at about waist height rocked lightly. He smiled in the dark and carefully pulled the stone away from the others. Placing it gently on the flag stones at his feet, he felt inside the cavity. He gave a small sigh of relief as his fingers came into contact with the smooth surface of a wooden box, and he drew this out. It was heavy, and the contents rattled slightly when he shifted it. This was the one place where no one would think to find the papers that Max would have put aside for future use. The Jews had been adamant that Max had not given the papers to them.

Sure that he had what he wanted, he glided up the dark stairs towards the bedroom where he hoped to find his victim. This was something he would do personally. There was no mercy in his heart for Brother Jonathan. The man had destroyed Talon's world in Acre —stolen it was nearer to the truth—and had caused the imprisonment of Max, his close companion of many an ordeal, a man who had done no wrong. This time there would be no messages or warnings left behind for a man to wake and find.

He found the room where Brother Martin slept the sleep of the just and continued towards the master bedroom. Sure enough, there was a figure lying on the bed. Standing in the darkness by the door, Talon could not tell whether it was Jonathan or not, and he needed to be sure. Silently he approached the bed and stood over the figure, lying on its back asleep. It was Jonathan. As Talon leaned over Jonathan to deal the blow, his enemy must have become aware of his mortal danger, for he woke suddenly and his hand shot up to seize Talon by his wrist.

Talon was surprised, but his strength was far greater than the monk's. His left hand clamped down on Jonathan's mouth, muffling a scream, and with a twist of his wrist he broke free and his blade struck deep. Jonathan's eyes opened wide with recognition and agony just before they went vacant. Talon waited until the body was completely still, then set about preparing a fire. If he could not have the house, then neither would the Church. First, however, he set aside a large pot of water for future use. Then he went to the dark and silent kitchens and obtained a container of olive oil. It took but a moment to get a fire prepared, the center of which would be the bed. He ignited the oily cloth all around the bed and on the body with a candle.

When the flames were well started and the bed completely engulfed in fire, he strode down the corridor to Martin's room and doused the sleeping brother with the water. Then he shouted, "Fire!" and sped down the stairs to join Yosef, who was waiting for him in the courtyard,

"Everything ready?" Talon asked his friend.

"Oh yes, there will be a big noise when the time is right." Yosef's teeth gleamed in the light of the fire above them. "Come, it is time we were not here. Will your monk be all right?"

"Wet, but alive," Talon remarked, as they slipped over the wall and sped towards the harbor.

By the time they arrived at the gates to the harbor much had happened. Looking back, Talon could see a tower of fire in the city, while all along the street frightened people were running towards it, shouting. The great fear of the citizens of this city was fire. The densely packed, badly constructed houses, made of wattle, wood and mud, were as dry as tinder. A fire like this could spread like the wind and destroy much of the city unless it was controlled. Talon was satisfied that a large part of the city and its guards would be very busy for the rest of the night.

While Talon and Yosef were engaged at his former house, Reza and his men had been busy. They had no difficulty gaining entrance to the harbor. The gates were guarded by men who claimed to have once been soldiers but were completely unaware of the intruders until it was too late. Talon had asked that no one should be killed unnecessarily so Reza and his men simply crept up behind the guards and whacked them on their heads with cudgels. Talon hadn't said anything about broken heads Reza reasoned.

The unconscious guards were trussed up and gagged then tossed unceremoniously into a shed not far from the gates and then Reza and Dar'an turned their attention to the potentially more difficult task of taking the ships. The two captains and their men who had been hiding in the shadows with the donkeys and the women came running lightly onto the docks where they found cover while Reza and his men contemplated their next objective.

"Wait until we have the ships before you bring the donkeys in," Henry told his lead hands.

Reza's men split up into two teams and stole some slim row boats which were bobbing alongside the quay then rowed into the cluster of shipping anchored in the harbor pool. Henry went with Reza on the one boat and while Guy and Dar'an went with some of their crewmen on the other. Both captains knew very well indeed where their former boats were anchored.

With great care the two row boats were skulled between the dark hulls of the great Templar ships looming over them that creaked and groaned in the darkness as the boats ghosted by. In Reza's boat Henry strained his eyes for the galley that had once been his home, finally he saw it and gripped Reza by the arm and then pointed. Even in the darkness the starlight was sufficient for Reza to see the direction of his arm and then whisper to his men.

There was no sound from the galley but they could not take any chances. The oars made small creaking noises that sounded like claps of thunder to their ears as they eased their way towards the silent hull.

A man in the front of the boat grasped a rope hanging from the bows and then held their own boat off to prevent any noise as they drew alongside. With a low grunt Reza led the way up the side of the galley and stepped onto the deck. His men followed him like shadows and then sped to the corners of the ship searching for anyone on deck. He heard a snore from the steering deck and slipped like a phantom up the steps to stand over the recumbent sentry who stank of alcohol. A blow to the head and the man was unconscious. Glancing around Reza made very sure that there was no one else on deck. Leaving one of his men to gag and tied the sentry he went to the side and waved the boat around to the steps on the ship's side. The two men with him having checked the top deck carefully for more people and finding no one moved like wraiths to the gangway that led down to the lower deck and disappeared.

Henry and the rest of the men in the rowboat appeared on deck at the same time as Reza's two men reappeared and signaled that they had taken care of the other man.

"There were only two of them, Master Reza," one whispered.

"Good but make sure, search everywhere for any one else who might be sleeping somewhere below. One shout and we are lost," he told them. Turning to Henry he grinned and waved theatrically about him as though to say. "The ship is yours, Captain!"

Henry beamed at him and grabbed him into silent bearhug. Only then did Reza realize how important was this ship to the captain.

Talon and Yosef passed through open gates to the harbor less than ten minutes after leaving the burning house; apparently, someone had forgotten to shut the gates in the excitement of the distant event. It was no surprise for him to find the quayside very busy. Henry's and Guy's crewmen were busy unloading the donkeys, which had arrived some time ago.

Henry came hurrying out of the dark, whispering urgently to his men on the quayside. "Get into the boats, and hurry! There is no time to waste. Stop staring at the fire; it has nothing to do with us." He shook one of the seamen by his broad shoulders and sent him to join the men carrying loads from the donkeys to the boats waiting in the water.

Talon could see that Henry had not wasted any time. They were almost done with the cargo and just needed to ferry the remainder of the men quietly out to the ships.

"Any problems, Henry?" he asked his captain, who was again dressed in the garb of a Templar. Henry chuckled. "I am having difficulty believing this, Talon, but your plan is working. Reza and his men took both ships without even a murmur. They are ours!"

"What about the harbor officials?"

"They were asleep! Once we were all inside the gates there were only five men to deal with, and your man Reza and his evil friends took them down. They didn't kill them, just overpowered them and tied them up. They are all in that small shed over there, including the guards on the ships. There were only two on each ship." He pointed along the quayside.

"Where are the women and my son?"

"They are on my ship, Talon. Don't worry, they are safe."

"Then I must change into my uniform and join you. We'll need one of the boats."

"I have one ready. Guy will join us shortly; he is seeing to his ship. He wants to make sure it has the equipment necessary to sail out of here."

Talon nodded. That was sensible. The ships had been anchored for a long time in the harbor, and he doubted if much maintenance had been carried out since they had been impounded.

By this time the furtive bustle on the quay had been reduced to a couple of men leading the donkeys out of the way, their final loads now in the last of the boats. Reza appeared out of nowhere and confirmed that the two ships were ready and manned. Talon grinned at him. "Looks like you had a good night, Brother."

"So did you, by the look of it. Was that fire your work?"

"Yes, all has been dealt with. Yosef did well."

Just as he said that, they all heard a muted explosion, like a small clap of thunder, but the skies were clear, and the fire swelled. "Yosef did very well," Talon commented.

Talon was handed a bundle by Henry and began to get ready for the next stage. He glanced towards the city again. The fire, larger than before, would provide the best kind of diversion; he didn't want to wake up the entire garrison at the citadel. Time was becoming precious.

He heard a boat grind against the quay and a low mutter, then Guy arrived at the top of the stone steps. "Ah, there you are, Talon. I was beginning to worry," he said from behind his nose guard. He, too, was dressed like a Templar. He handed Talon a roll of parchment. "You told me to take care of this and give it to you when you arrived. Did you do that?" he jerked his head towards the flare in the sky.

"'Yosef and I started it. My old house is no more," Talon responded.

"Well, I know it is bad of me to say so, but I hope that Brother Jonathan was inside it," Henry said gruffly.

Talon said nothing except, "We must hurry." The three men hastened down the steps and climbed into the boat. Guy pushed off and they rowed silently towards the pier that led to the rear gate of the Citadel.

Martin woke, gasping with a shock. A bucket of cold water had been thrown over him! He was drenched and chilled, but the cry that followed chilled him even more. "Fire!" someone shouted.

He leapt from his bed and rubbed his face to clear the water from his eyes. Then he smelled the smoke, tendrils of which were creeping into his chamber. He struggled into his habit and snatched up his sandals, then ran barefoot to the doorway. A wave of heat from the left side made him gasp. The room where Jonathan slept was an inferno. He couldn't even see past the roaring flames.

"Jonathan!" he screamed at the top of his lungs. Instead of a human reply, the flames roared louder and the floorboards he was standing on began to smolder. The crackling and hissing of the fire was now so loud that Martin could barely hear the panicked shouts from below as the few servants who slept in the house woke up and began to realize their lives were in peril.

Martin started toward Jonathan's room, but the flames drove him back, singeing his clothing and his hair, and then following him as though intent upon devouring him. Martin put a hand over his mouth and nose and fled down the stairs to join the servants, who were clustered helplessly watching from below.

"Get out! Get out of the house! God help us! There is nothing we can do here!" Martin shouted at them, hopping about on one foot as he struggled to put on his sandals. They needed no further persuasion. Everyone jostled through the doorway into the

courtyard and the night air. Turning, Martin could see flames
greedily licking at the dry eaves of the house, then a beam fell
inwards, followed by a shower of sparks that lifted high into the
night air. All around Martin, the servants were chattering excitedly;
some of the maids were wailing, but no one attempted to put the fire
out. Indeed, as he watched the fire take hold elsewhere in the house,
Martin knew that there was little point in trying. He shook his head
and wondered about the person who must have thrown water over
him. Had he not, Martin surmised, he, too, would be trapped in the
house with Jonathan.

Then one of the servants clutched his sleeve. "Look! The stables!
They are on fire!" the boy wailed.

Martin spun around and, sure enough, he could see flames
beginning to lick at the doorway. "Save the animals!" he cried. There
were only two horses in the stables, but they were beginning to
whinny with fear. Some men rushed to release them and drag them
out of the smoking building onto the street.

"We've got to prevent it from getting to the hay and stores!"
Martin yelled, and he ran towards the well to seize a leather bucket
and pump water into it. The water seemed to take forever to splash
into the bucket, by which time a small line of men with more
buckets had formed. Martin rushed towards the stables and tossed
his load of water over some hay near the entrance, but he knew with
bitter resignation as he did so that they would not be able to save it.
Smoke was drifting off the roof-high pile of hay already. Once that
took, it would be all over. Nonetheless, with a small prayer he
rushed back towards the well, passing others with full pails as he
went.

"Its no use, we are lost," cried one of the older men. "We have to
get out of here or we will perish in the fire!"

Others joined in the call to abandon the property. Suddenly,
there was a flash and a deafening bang from the area of the hay
barn. Flaming debris from the explosion flew in all directions,
landing on neighboring houses, and the fire spread, becoming a
raging inferno.

"It is a thunderbolt from heaven!" cried one of the servants,
gaping at the streak of fire that appeared to leap into the sky. "A
sign from God!" He wailed and was joined by others who crossed
themselves; one even fell to his knees.

It had a terrifying effect upon the others. All of them dropped
what they were doing and fled for the main gate, leaving Martin

calling after them hopelessly, waving his empty bucket in the air until the heat finally drove him to the relative safety of the street.

*****

The crash of iron-bound doors slamming above him and the stamp of heavy boots echoing on the stone steps that led down to his cell woke the prisoner from a fitful slumber. Shivering under a thin blanket, Max sat up from his pallet of filthy straw and scratched at the sores on his legs. He shook his long dirty hair out of his eyes and listened, then looked up. He knew that he was one of very few prisoners in the Citadel. Other prisoners were further away in some other dungeon.

He had been in isolation for several years and still didn't know the charge against him, other than it was because of his association with Talon. Not for the first time, he wondered where his young friend might be. Dead, probably; captured by the Assassins or by Arabs. Having heard nothing for over four years, Max had given up. Talon had gone the way of Sir Guy and so many others of his comrades.

The door bolts were hauled back and the door crashed open. "Get up, prisoner. You've got guests!" the jailer called out to him. He was a rough man who did his job, but he had refrained from any cruelty, which Max appreciated. Over the years he'd had several jailers, not all of them decent people.

He got to his feet shakily and stared up at the men clustered at the head of the stairs that lead down to his barred cell. The jailer, dressed in rough homespun and a leather apron, carried a flaming torch which flickered and smoked.

"You are going to Jerusalem, my friend. Though why it should be at this time of night I have no idea, and it is not for me to dispute," the jailor told him, jerking his thumb back at the three men just behind him. In the flickering darkness it was impossible to discern their features behind the helmets and nose guards. "Orders from the Grand Master. I pity you when they have finished with you. Might have been better to let the church have you and to end it here in Acre," the man continued with a coarse laugh.

Before Max could say anything, the leader of the three stamped down the steps and stood behind the jailor. Now that he was closer, Max could see him better. To his utter astonishment, the man winked at him! Max nearly fell over, he was so surprised. It was Henry!

"I have the orders here! Come on, man, open the gate!" Henry told the jailer in a loud voice.

"I'm going as fast as I can," the jailor grumbled. "These keys are old and the lock is rusty."

"You, there, hurry up and get ready to leave." Henry growled at Max, who was standing dumbstruck. Max turned his head to stare hard at the other two and was sure that one of them was Guy. Hard to mistake that giant of a man, even when dressed like a Templar knight; but the third man wore a cowl that hid his face. There was something about him, however, that struck Max as oddly familiar, but he was too stunned, and sick, and exhausted, to do more than wonder and gape.

The key grated in the lock, then the jailor hauled open the door of the prison and stepped inside, closely followed by the three knights. Then the jailor received a hefty shove from Guy which slammed him into the wall. His head struck stone with a dull thump and he fell to the floor, semi-conscious and bleeding from his forehead. Without saying a word, the third man drew a long cord out of his robe and proceeded to completely immobilize the groaning man; he then stuffed a cloth in the jailer's mouth and bound another around his head to keep it in place. The knight stood up and Max's eyes opened wide with surprise.

"Talon?" he gasped. "Is it really you?"

"Come, Max, we're getting you out of here," Talon said with a grin. "No need to stare. Can you walk? My, but you need a bath!" He gave a low chuckle.

"I... I think I can manage. But how? Where?" Max stammered. He felt a surge of relief and hope and wondered if his heart would hold out, it was beating so fast.

"Questions later, Max. We have a boat to catch, and there is little time. Come, I will help you."

They helped Max up the stairs, and Talon locked the gate below with the keys he liberated from the jailer. When they were through the doorway, he closed it and pushed the bolts across.

"Our friend below can shout all he likes, but no one will hear him. I don't think he will be missed before dawn." Talon brandished a roll of parchment at Max. "These are your orders, Max. Where would you like to go?" he grinned.

Max managed a wan smile. "Wherever you three rascals are going, and I hope it is to sea," he croaked.

They walked up several flights of damp stone steps and along narrow cold stone corridors without running into anyone until

Talon, who was leading, paused. Guy was carrying the torch recovered from the jailer, and Talon took another one down from a sconce on the wall.

"We should now be level with the harbor pier belonging to the Knights. We will be going out that way, Max. Say nothing; just look weak and disoriented."

Max smiled weakly. "Yes, I think I can manage that." Even this short walk had left him shaking and unsteady.

"Ah, here we are. Now, this will be the most dangerous moment. Most of the knights have gone to bed, but the guards are awake." Talon strode over to the narrow, wooden door and opened it with caution. Peering out into the darkness, he scanned the area, then turned to the others. "Let's hope the piece of paper works again."

He opened the door and lifted the torch high. The guard was leaning against the iron-barred gate, staring out towards the fire that now raged in the middle of the city.

"You over there! Why are you not paying attention?" Talon said, as he strode arrogantly up to the man, who stiffened to attention. Talon thrust the parchment under his nose. "Can you read, man?" he demanded.

"Er, yes... um, no," the guard stammered.

Talon heaved an elaborate sigh of exasperation.

"Do you at least recognize the seal of the Grand Master?" His finger tapped impatiently at the big red wax seal at the bottom of the paper.

"Yes... yes, I do. That's it!" the guard told him peering at the forgery and trying to sound confident.

"Then open this gate! I have a prisoner I am taking to Jaffa and then on to Jerusalem. This is the Pope's business. Hurry, now!" Talon ordered the bewildered man, who hastened to comply. He fished out a large key from his belt and thrust it into the lock, opened the gate and then stood back, intimidated by this large man with the battle-scarred face.

Talon beckoned to the men in the doorway, and Henry and Guy strode towards the gate, dragging Max along between them. "Lift your feet, felon, or I shall beat you senseless," the guard heard one of them snarl at the prisoner.

"Poor bugger," the guard muttered as stood aside to allow them to leave.

"What did you say, soldier?" Talon put his face within an inch of the guard's as the others went by. "This man is a heretic accused of witchery." He lowered his voice to say very softly, but in a tone full

116

of menace, "Be very careful that you do not join him. Now shut the gate and lock it. I don't want to hear another word out of you!"

The sentry, who was young and inexperienced, stared and nodded. "G... Good night and God Bless you, Sir," he stammered, and he watched the three knights drag the limp body between them into the darkness. He made haste to lock the gate. He was glad to see the back of that angry man. It could have gone badly for him; the man's face was frightening with its scars and its dangerous scowl. He turned to peer into the darkness towards the end of the pier, but they seemed to have disappeared completely. He turned his attention back to the distant fire, wondering how it had started.

Guy rowed the boat silently through the dark waters of the harbor, with Henry guiding him through the tangle of shipping until the boat bumped gently against the side of the galley which would be captained by Henry. There was a whispered challenge. Henry answered it and went up the side to the deck. He spoke quietly to one of his men on deck, then he leaned over the side and offered his hand to Max, who struggled to keep his feet, but eventually managed to reach up and grasp Henry's hand. Talon pushed him from behind, and Henry swung him up and steadied him when he stepped shakily onto the wooden deck. Talon, with a quick whisper to Guy, gripped his shoulder and then climbed up to stand next to Max.

Guy's boat vanished into the darkness, heading towards the other ship.

"Come, Max, we need to get you below. We are about to sail. Rest, and then we can talk later." But Max reached over and clutched at Talon and they fell into a clumsy embrace.

"I cannot believe it, Talon! How did you know where to find me?" Max was snuffling with emotion. Talon hung onto him for a long moment, then held him gently away.

"Martin told me. Now go with Dmitri. Remember him?" Talon's voice was thick with emotion. "He will see to it that you are fed and have somewhere to rest. We have yet to get out of this harbor."

As Max was led away by Dmitri, Talon went up to the steering deck and turned to Henry. "Now we wait for the signal?" he asked his captain.

Henry nodded in the darkness. He was tense. Anything could go wrong now: some very alert sentry on the walls, the discovery of the jailer, or some curious person who observed the untoward activity on the ships and reported it. They could still be stopped if someone had the presence of mind to raise the chain at the entrance of the harbor.

"That looks like a bad fire over there," Henry remarked.

"A useful distraction, I should say," Talon replied.

The signal was not long coming. They squinted into the darkness in the direction of the other ship, and within a few minutes sighted a small glow from a lantern that gleamed on and off twice. Guy was on his ship and ready to leave.

Henry blew out his breath with relief, then reached for a lantern placed nearby and returned the signal. Then he passed an order in a whisper. Men seemed to appear from all the dark shadows and from below where they had been hiding.

Some slipped into the bow and cut the cables that held the boat to the anchor rocks. Silently, the crew pushed the long oars out of the rowlocks, then waited. Upon another whispered command from Henry, the oars were dipped with great care into the water of the harbor, the steersmen leaned on the panels, and the long, sleek vessel began to move. Henry had memorized the route he would take and muttered the occasional order to the steersmen. Fortuitously, there was a fairly good channel along which the slim vessels could be rowed without having to negotiate passage with other ships.

Only one man on the high steering deck of a huge Templar ship called across to Guy's ship as it slid by. "Ahoy there! Where are you going at this late hour?"

Talon's response was, "On the Pope's business."

There was no reply to that, and now Henry's ship was at the entrance of the harbor with the last guard tower behind them on their starboard side. Talon was amused to hear "God Speed" called across the water. He had been holding his breath. If the chain across the mouth of the harbor had been raised, they would not see it; there only warning would be the dreadful, jarring impact when the ship rammed into it. But the chain was down; the way was open.

"God protect you!" Henry called back. He chuckled and glanced back at Guy's ship, which was close behind, and called out an order. "Raise the sails, quickly now!"

There was a patter of bare feet as men rushed to haul the two sails up the masts. The ship dipped slightly as they ran out of the still waters of the harbor into the swell of the sea. Then the light wind still blowing off the land took hold and bellied the sails. They passed close by the Island of Flies with its beacon, but no one challenged them, and then they were heading out to sea. The ship gathered speed, and before long Henry ordered the rowers to stand down.

Talon had been keeping an eye on Guy's vessel and saw that he, too, had raised his sails. In the gloom it was hard to see more, but before long Talon could make out a small white bow wave on the other ship and a lantern in the bows. Henry told one of the men to place a lantern on the after rail of their ship so that Guy could follow in their wake.

Initially, Henry headed south to confuse anyone who might have been watching them from land; but within an hour of sailing he changed course to north by north-west. Talon sucked in a deep breath of sea air with great satisfaction and stared back at the dark line of the coast that was receding into the darkness. He was surprised by Henry, who came up to him and grabbed him into a bearhug and shouted, "We succeeded, Talon! By God, we succeeded! You are truly the Fox! To where do I set course?"

Ignoring the whispers of delighted surprise from the steersmen when they realized who he was, Talon replied, "Why, to Cyprus, my friend. That, I hope, is to be our new home."

Pierre d'Aix, the Constable of Acre, stood at the end of the street and stared at the destruction wrought by the horrendous fire of three days ago. He shook his head at the blackened ruins. This was only one of the streets that had been destroyed; the conflagration had devoured four whole streets in its ferocious appetite for wood and thatch.

The area was still smoking, but after a superhuman effort the population had at last managed to bring the fire under control and then douse it. The cost in property and lives was still unknown. The fire had started, according to the monk called Martin, in the house of another Brother named Jonathan. A candle had fallen, perhaps; it was not uncommon for a fire to start that way. Apparently, Brother Jonathan had been lavish with candles.

He was still staring at the ruined expanse when he heard the sound of horses and several horsemen came to a halt behind him. He was too tired to turn around. He heard one of them dismount, and then Sir Rufus was standing next to him.

"Do you still believe this was an accident?" Rufus demanded, as he contemplated the charred mess.

"I am told it began in the house of the Bishop where that unpleasant monk called Jonathan lived. The other monk says he cannot be sure how the fire started. Some are even saying that it was an act of God because they saw a lightning bolt strike the place, but he thought it was begun inside the house. According to the servants, Brother Jonathan burned candles every night, a great many of them, and always had candles in his room," Pierre replied with a tired shrug. He had been without sleep for days, it seemed. "Even the Bishop agrees. No one has seen Brother Jonathan since that night. It is thought that he died in the flames." Pierre gave a shudder. "I hate fires," he muttered.

"Well, I think I have some news for you that will change your mind," the Templar said.

Pierre spun around, surprise written all over his face. "What do you mean?" he demanded.

"I mean that the morning after the fire, two ships that used to belong to Sir Talon de Gilles disappeared from the harbor, and no one remembers even seeing them leave! The great fire took up all their attention, the imbeciles. There were donkeys standing around all over the harbor pier. No one knows how *they* got there. The gates were wide open, and the harbor guards were nowhere to be found."

Pierre gaped at him. Sir Rufus continued with what might have almost been mistaken for a hint of admiration in his tone, "They were eventually found tied up and gagged in a shed along with the guards who should have been on the ships."

"What! How in God's name did this happen? Wh—?" Pierre was speechless. He gobbled with astonishment, and then as realization struck home he became enraged. "You mean... that heretic, Talon? The one Brother Jonathan wanted to see burned for witchcraft? This is all *his* doing?"

Sir Rufus gave a bleak smile and shrugged. "Ahem, yes, it is beginning to look that way. There is more which tends to confirm it."

Pierre glared at him. "More? How could there be more? He sets half the city ablaze, steals two expensive ships... what more could he have done?"

"Remember the prisoner we had in the Citadel?" Rufus said. He looked embarrassed. Pierre blinked and nodded. "The one who was imprisoned because of his association with Talon?" he asked.

"Yes... well, he, too, is gone. They walked in as bold as brass and spirited him away. I think they took him with them on the ships."

Pierre tried to conceal his astonishment, even amusement despite his own anger. What an embarrassment! How would the haughty Sir Rufus explain that to the Grand Master in Jerusalem?

"Well, I'll be damned to hell," he said finally, with a glance at Rufus. "What you are telling me is that he was inside the city all the time!"

Sir Rufus glared at the ruins ahead of them. "It appears to be that way, and he stole a fine march on us. We will never find him now. He and his damned ships are lost to us forever."

"May he rot in hell," snarled Pierre, "In God's name, how are we going to repair all this damage?" he cried waving his hands at the wreckage before them, his voice was anguished. "It will cost the city a fortune!"

"Why don't you ask the Bishop? After all it was his house that started all this. He's wealthy enough!" Sir Rufus said, his voice dripping with sarcasm.

Wisdom is sold in the desolate market
where none come to buy
—William Blake

Part II

Chapter 10
Paphos

Paphos was a beautiful city; it rested on the southern part of the round rump of the island of Cyprus and presented a bright and enticing view to ships arriving in the ancient harbor. Talon and his family, once the ships were tied up, made haste to explore the city. The Roman ruins were extensive, in some cases built atop even more ancient Greek ruins.

The feeling of freedom and sunshine persisted as they walked the streets and explored the market place, which was a riot of color and exotic goods. Rav'an remarked that it was better than Jerusalem. Talon had heard from Max that some of the very best armorers were in Paphos and spent time watching blacksmiths at work on armor and copper smiths beating out kitchen utensils with small hammers. It reminded Talon of a smaller, prettier Cairo. He began to relax, and the hunt for a suitable accommodation began.

They had been in the city of Paphos for over a week, settling comfortably into a rented villa that came with a hot bath located on the North side of the city, before Talon sensed that something was not quite right. The harbor seemed quiet enough, sleepy even, seagulls wheeled and dived, the cormorants sat quietly on rocks awaiting an opportunity, and the somewhat scummy seawater inside the breakwater was calm. The fishermen seated on the quays and the beach mending their nets also lent an air of apparent calm, but his instincts were kicking in, leaving him unsettled.

Max, who was recovering from his ordeal in prison under the watchful eyes of Rav'an and Jannat, also noted that it was not the same place that he remembered. "When I was here last it was very busy," he told Talon. "The harbor used to be crowded with shipping, Cyprus has always been a crossroads for trade between Byzantium and the south, Palestine and Egypt. Now there are very few ships in the harbor, something seems wrong. You will need to visit a merchant with whom I did business on my last visit. Perhaps he can shed some light on the reason for this odd atmosphere."

Taking Dimitri and Reza with him, Talon strode along the harbor front, taking in the fishing boats and the few other merchant vessels in the port. There was a furtive air about the people they passed along the road. At the same time he kept a wary eye open for any of the soldiers, if they could be called that, who slouched around the town; he had not been impressed with these people. He glanced up at the castle perched on the hillside, where he assumed the sheriff of the town lived. The ancient city hugged the coastline, so it would have been very strange if the occupants had not noticed his arrival. He had paid the customs official an exorbitant amount for the privilege of anchoring his ships in the harbor, and he had expected a visit of some kind from some higher official before now.

"What is going on?" Talon asked his crewman. Dimitri, who was very happy to be out of Acre and once again in the Greek world, shook his head, looking puzzled.

"I wish I knew, Master Talon, but it will take more than just asking to find out. I can sense that, among traders and visitors from the mainland as well as the fishermen from here, something untoward is going on," he told Talon. "There is fear and apprehension. I feel it and don't like it. I think we will have to have a talk with one of the merchants in the city. Traders always have a nose for trouble. Perhaps the friend of Max can help us?"

Talon and Reza had to agree. Both had been out and about exploring the city with its maze of old streets and Greek and Roman ruins, with Dimitri in tow, seeking a good place for their family to settle permanently, but wherever they went they were met with suspicion and furtive distrust. Talon was thankful that Henry had hand-picked all the crewmen. They were rowers to a man, with huge shoulders and arms, which made them look very imposing. Henry had armed them with spears and swords and used them as bodyguards when any of the family was moving about the town. No one was going to tackle any of these tough looking men on the streets of Paphos; not unless they had an army behind them. The surly mercenaries didn't choose to accost them either which was interesting.

After a short walk, his party arrived at the house of a man named Boethius Eirenikos, located at the northern end of town where the harbor ended and the wealthy houses began. At the villa the three men were met by two suspicious guards, whom Talon rated as worthless, but who kept them waiting for a considerable time before a harassed looking secretary bustled out to greet them and asked them to follow him.

Leaving the sullen guards at the gate, they were led by the secretary up to the main building, a place of pillars, marble flags and colorful mosaics on almost every wall, denoting a wealthy household. A beautiful wisteria vine all but covered the red tiled loggia which overlooked the sea. The house had a pleasant glow in the sunshine with its lime-washed walls, colorful mosaics and bright red tiles.

They were led across a small courtyard, in the center of which a small fountain bubbled, to a large wooden door and shown inside a high-domed room where they were met by a man dressed in the Byzantine style. He wore a long, close-fitting under-tunic of patterned silk that came down to his sandals, and a blue over-robe adorned with colorful stitching which created filigree patterns down to wide-cut sleeves. His gray hair curled out from under a brown felt hat which resembled a small flat, imitation turban. His beard was trimmed in an old fashioned manner more suited to a generation of Byzantine Greeks from a previous era.

He rose courteously to greet them, dismissed the secretary, who had given their names to him in an undertone, then bowed politely and smiled with dark brown eyes, "I am glad to meet you, Sir Talon. I have heard much about you from your companion, Max the Templar. Welcome to Paphos. Is Max not with you now?"

Talon smiled back. "Thank you for asking, Sir. Max is recovering, er, shall we say from a long confinement that affected his health. I will be sure to bring him with me the next time I come to visit you."

There was no telling how speedily news could travel, and his security was still very much in question until he could find a safe place to settle. His reply had been guarded, and his host frowned slightly.

"I trust he is in good health? Please call me Boethius. I think we are able to be informal at this time."

Talon bowed in return and said, "Thank you, Boethius. Then please call me Talon. I have to compliment you on such a fine city as Paphos. It is very beautiful, the acropolis is splendid and still used I hear." They were speaking Attic Greek.

Boethius gave Talon a sharp look and then friendly smile. "I have to compliment you on your understanding of our language. You seem to know it well."

Talon shrugged depreciatingly. "I spent some time in Constantinople. I count it to have been a privilege and an honor to have served the emperor."

Boethius frowned. "I assume you are talking about the late departed Emperor Manuel, Talon?" His eyes were abruptly wary.

"Indeed I am," Talon responded, noting the tone and the look. "Who else would I be referring to, may I ask?"

Boethius relaxed visibly. "Ah, I should have known, pardon me. One has to be careful these days. I also wonder for how much longer my city will be as beautiful you just described," he said in an enigmatic voice.

Talon looked hard at Boethius and asked, "That is the reason I came today. All does not appear to be well in this city. I had hoped to be able to stay a while, as some of my men are recovering from illness. However, everywhere I go there is suspicion and... unease. I cannot put my finger on it. Perhaps you could enlighten me?"

Boethius nodded and said, "Perhaps I can, and perhaps I should, because no one is safe any more, not even visitors like yourself. I will explain. First refreshments, for you and your companions. " He called for wine, and when it had been delivered by the silent servants he told them to leave and shut the doors behind them.

They sipped the wine from silver cups in silence for a few moments. Talon nodded his head in appreciation. "You have good wine, too, Boethius. Again, my compliments."

"It is grown on the plains of Nicosia on the western slopes of the Trudos mountains, which begin right on our back door here in Paphos," Boethius remarked, then he leaned forward and began to speak in a very serious voice.

"You have clearly not heard the news about this island, Sir Talon, but it is a woeful story I must tell you. I am beginning to distrust even my own servants and doubt very much that I shall be living here by the end of this horrible year. I plan to seek another home."

He took a reflective sip of his wine and smiled ruefully at Talon's startled expression. Then he stared out of the window, as though thinking about what he should say next. He pinched the bridge of his nose between his thumb and forefinger, closing his eyes as he did so. His already lined face betrayed fatigue and worry. Finally he looked up.

"You perhaps know a little of our people, Sir Talon, having lived in Constantinople for a while. Truly we had a great empire under

John, and even Manuel didn't do too much damage, despite his unwise expedition to Myriokephalon."

"I was there on that expedition, both Max and I were at the battle." Talon interjected.

"Then I do not need to labor that point," said Boethius, and he shot Talon a look of respect. "You survived, which in itself is remarkable. But what you perhaps do not know is that when Manuel died, disaster, no horror, was visited upon our country. His son should have inherited with his mother as regent. Instead they were murdered, most cruelly put to death, and we are now ruled by Andronikos Komnenos; or rather, the mainland is ruled by that awful man.

Here in Cyprus we are now under the yoke of his unsavory great nephew, Isaac Komnenos, who is also an unspeakable barbarian. He arrived on the island this very year, around May, with an army of mercenaries. Since then he has assumed command of all the cities and ports, declaring himself emperor of the island. We in Paphos have already had a taste of his... benevolence."

Boethius sighed. "He is plundering his own 'empire', Sir Talon, and has already beggared many a rich merchant and despoiled many an aristocratic maiden since he arrived."

Talon was aghast. "So Cyprus is ruled by yet another Greek tyrant! I had thought it to be a good, safe place to live, which is why I came here!"

Boethius gave him a bitter smile. "Then you are sadly mistaken, Sir Talon. My advice is for you to leave while you can and find a better kingdom in which to settle. Isaac has been here in Paphos once, and that was devastating enough for some of the rich merchants who lived here. How I escaped his attentions I do not know, but I do not intend to remain to test my luck a second time."

"Where does he spend most of his time, if not here at Paphos? Is this not the capital of the island?"

"Not any more. Look to the north-west. The great mountains of Trudos prevents easy access to the plains, where other than trade, the wealth of Cyprus really lies. He spends most of his time now in Famagusta, where he has access to Larnaca, Nicosia and Kyrenia, and the northern coastal regions are rich pickings for him. It is very sad, Sir Talon. This was once a great, peaceful island, but now every would-be robber and mercenary is flocking to his banner like crows to carrion. I curse him and his name." Boethius shot a nervous look at the door as he finished.

They spent the next several hours talking about the recent events. "Those who opposed Isaac were executed without trial, while those who could fled to the dubious safety of the mainland. If my ship had been in port, we would not now be having this conversation, as I would have been gone," Boethius informed them.

Talon was reminded of the slovenly men who had lounged about on the quayside when he arrived. They had been insolent and unhelpful.

Boethius also told Talon something quite interesting.

"You do know that Salah Ed Din, that busy leader of the Arabs, has taken Aleppo? He is now the only real leader of the disparate and unruly tribes and petty kingdoms on the mainland."

Talon rubbed his eyes with the tips of his fingers in a tired gesture. "No, I had not heard, I have been otherwise preoccupied. It won't be long before he makes another try for Jerusalem, I should imagine."

Boethius gave him a shrewd look and nodded agreement. "We live in difficult times. I cannot see them getting better, not for a long while." He took another sip of wine before continuing.

"What you might not know is that it is rumored Isaac is friendly with Salah Ed Din." He smiled grimly as he watched the surprise flicker across Talon's face. "But there is more, and this is much more dangerous for those of us in Cyprus. He is friendly with the Norman, King William the Second of Sicily, who, although he is a man of indeterminate character, has ambitions. He wants to take the emperor's throne in Constantinople!"

"This ensures that Isaac cannot easily be unseated by Andronikos," Talon observed after he had overcome his surprise. He had heard about King William from Lord Ibelin and Tiberius, who had informed him that the King of Sicily was becoming ambitious.

"Precisely," Boethius agreed. "As long as Isaac remains here in Cyprus, Andronikos will not bother him, although he must be as angry as a nest of hornets. The loss of the revenue which used to come from this island is not insignificant."

It was a very thoughtful little group that made its way back to the villa near to the harbor that afternoon. When they arrived, Talon immediately called a council with his captains, Henry and Guy, and brought Max into the discussion. With his hair cut and beard trimmed, and having had a long bath, Max was beginning to look a lot better although he still looked emaciated. The ravages of his imprisonment were also etched deeply into his features. Rav'an and Jannat were also there, as were his small group of warriors.

Talon wanted everyone to know the facts of their situation. The truth was that he was unsure of where they could go next. His whole plan had rested upon a safe refuge in Cyprus, but with the ominous news of a tyrant running the island this no longer seemed like a practical idea.

He repeated all that he had heard from Boethius and then said, "The reason we came here is because I had made plans years ago to live on this island, which is why I'd asked Max to purchase land and find me a secure abode where we could know peace and anonymity." He paused to collect his thoughts. "This is no longer the case, and we have to rethink our future. I do not know at this time if Cyprus is where we can settle."

There followed a heated discussion in three different languages. He listened carefully to everything that was said. Some were for going back to Oman and then off to China; some were for going back to Palestine—but not many. Talon liked the idea of China, but he said, "In the first instance we will not have our former ship to sail anywhere. Before very long Ahmed will arrive in Elat and he will not waste any time. He will sail our ship back down the Red sea to Oman and we will find ourselves stranded in Elat and out of options. Perilously close to Egypt and perhaps at the mercy of the Beduin of the Sinai. They are not kind people."

"There is always Spain," Reza said tentatively.

Talon nodded. "Perhaps, but it is a very long sea voyage from here, and unlike our great ship, in these small vessels it would be perilous. Autumn is just around the corner and the Middle Sea can be dangerous at this time of year. If we had our *Baghran* it might be an option," he said, referring to his Omani ship, which made the galleys look small by comparison.

Henry and Guy looked indignant, but Talon smiled and said, "You two would be awed by the size of the ships we have seen and sailed in, my friends. Remind me to tell you about them one day."

Max spoke up then. "I have done a lot of thinking recently, Talon," he said.

"You of all people have had the time to so," Talon quipped.

Henry and Guy laughed, but it was sympathetic. "What do you have in mind, Max?" Henry asked. His own worry creases between his eyes were deeper than ever.

Max looked uncomfortable but he pressed on. "Long ago you told me of the legend of one of your Aghas fellows. I can't remember his name, but he did something very clever."

Talon stared at Max. "What did he just say?" Reza demanded.

128

"He just reminded me of Hasan e Sabah!"

"What does he know about the Master?" Reza asked, his tone skeptical.

"I know what he is going to say!" Rav'an interjected with some excitement.

"All right, Max, tell us what you are thinking," Talon sighed, with a smile at his wife.

"Did this Master not trick his way into a castle once?"

Talon slapped his side with amusement, then he translated for the benefit of the others, who looked astonished. Rav'an laughed with delight at having been right; her gray eyes, which had been very worried, now sparkled.

"What is he talking about?" Reza demanded. "A castle? Your friend Max has lost his mind, he's been in prison so long, Talon."

"Let him finish, Reza!" Jannat said impatiently. Reza subsided.

"Well, Max? There are several castles on this island. Which one should we take for ourselves?" Talon smiled at his friend.

"While you were gallivanting all over the world, I was doing what you asked of me, Talon," Max said a little stiffly. "I went all over this island, and I bought the land with the sugar cane. By the way, we have to discover whether it is still ours, and if it is still producing. I was also a visitor at a castle, north of this island, that is in a state of disrepair. The owner is a wealthy senator from Constantinople who might want to leave the island. Indeed, he probably has already. You should at least consider the option of having a castle here in Cyprus, where they do not know you, as opposed to somewhere else where there is a Latin church, where they might in time discover who you are, and then your problems will start all over again."

It was a long speech for Max and left him tired. Jannat, who had taken a liking to Max, reached for a beaker of water and handed it to him. He smiled at her and drank gratefully in the silence that followed the translation Talon offered his friends.

After a long pause, Talon gave a rueful shake of his head. "I certainly had not considered this option, Max." He turned to his friends. "What do you think?"

Reza shrugged and said, "We can at least go and look at it."

"Do people buy castles?" Rav'an asked, with an amused look at Talon.

"We have enough treasure to buy six castles if Talon and Reza wanted to," Jannat said sounding smug.

Neither Yosef or Dar'an had anything to add, but their looks told Talon that they would support him either way.

"What do you think, Henry, Guy?" Talon asked.

"We are now outlaws in Palestine, Talon. We go with you," Guy stated. He scratched his head. "I would like to discover what has happened to Nigel, but I go with you. My ship is yours, whatever you decide."

"I agree, Talon," Henry chuckled. "You fooled those bastards in Acre. Perhaps you can fool some idiot here into selling you a castle! How stupid are these Greeks anyway?"

"We only have Dimitri to judge them by," Guy said with a laugh, slapping Dimitri on the back.

"Then you should be sore afraid, my friend," Dimitri replied with a mock scowl. "For I am the brightest Greek of all, most certainly when compared to you barbaric Franks!"

"First question, Max," Talon said, after the laughter had died. "Is there a way to get to the castle by sea?"

"Oh yes. There is a very small natural harbor which serves the castle. I went down to have a look while I was there, with a small village on its rim. The castle, or what is left of it is high on a ridge. You will see what I mean if we go there."

Henry raised his hand. "From what you told us today, Talon, there is not much time. Should that whore's son Isaac come back for a taste of more in this sorry place, we ought to be long gone. No telling when he will show up again with his band of mercenaries. If he discovers you here he will stop at nothing to steal the ships and all you own."

Later that evening, Talon and Rav'an were seated on the terrace that extended from the house overlooking the harbor. The sun had set behind the huge Trudos Mountain range, but twilight lingered on. The stars were beginning to become bright in the sky to the East, Venus was low in the west hidden by the mountain, and a light breeze was blowing off the land. The sleepy seagulls sat in rows on the red tiled roofs and a flock of crows roosted in the plane trees which lined the harbor road. The birds settled in with occasional quarrelsome squawks, but other than the muted murmur of late evening pedestrians heading home there was quiet in the city. Paphos was a fishing port as well as a mercantile port; the fishermen went to bed very early, as they were up and out at sea before the dawn. Talon stared at his galleys and wondered to himself.

"You are very thoughtful tonight, Talon," Rav'an observed. She was seated comfortably on a wide, wicker chair, with cushions to support her back.

"Those two have only eyes for each other tonight," she said, with a smile and a nodded towards Reza and Jannat, who were seated further down the terrace, deep in conversation. "But you are elsewhere. Where are you, my Love?'

"I am mourning the loss of Sir Guy de Veres, and those other friends I had when I lived in Acre, my Love," he shook his head sadly. "Sir Guy was a mentor as well as a good friend. I shall miss him. Max told me of the battle and the fact that the army could have saved the men at the ford but once again Châtillon and his cronies delayed things with the King and the castle was lost along with many lives including one of their best." He was bitter with grief and worry.

Rav'an reached out to touch his sleeve in a comforting gesture. "You have lost many friends, Talon. Perhaps they are with the God of the Christians now. I am sorry," she said. Rav'an was concerned; she had noticed the tiny lines of worry at the corners of Talon's eyes. The last time she had seen those was when he had been navigating them home from China.

"We depend upon you for so much, my Prince," she told him with a tremulous smile. "I know you worry about all of us, but you have a fine band of followers with you too. Since the Acre escape, everyone of them admires you and will follow you anywhere!"

He took her hand in his and pressed it to his lips. "It is a comfort just to be with you at any time, my Rav'an, especially now when things are so uncertain," he said, then smiled at her. "I am trying to think up a plan that will allow us some peace and security. We have known very little of that in recent months. I am mulling over what Max told us."

"You are taking the idea of a castle seriously?" she asked him, with surprise in her voice.

"Well, yes. As you just said, we possess some very talented people, and I don't see why we should not take advantage of that fact," Talon finished. "But it is going to take a great deal of planning... and so much luck. I am reminded of our friend Hsü; he would most certainly have had a solution to all this." Talon was referring to his friend and mentor in China, Hsü, a man he considered to be of near infinite resourcefulness and wisdom.

"Perhaps you underrate yourself, Talon. You say he taught you much."

"You know he did, and by example even more than by words. I cannot get that game out of my mind."

"The game of Go?" Rav'an asked.

"Hmmm. First you surround your enemies, and then you dispose of them; it is your choice, not theirs. It is buzzing around in my mind at this moment."

Just then a black kitten raced onto the terrace, closely pursued by an excited Rostam, who clearly wanted to capture the tiny animal. "Kitty, come here!" he called, as he chased the frightened animal. It ran close enough to Talon for him to sweep it up into his hand and hold the tiny creature, its eyes wide with fright, in the air for inspection.

"What is its name?" he asked the boy, who beamed. "The servants call it Pan... something," Rostam told them.

"Panther," said Talon, guessing what he meant.

"Does that mean anything?" Rav'an asked him with a laugh.

"It means fierce cat. Although why anyone would call a kitten that I have no idea. It is almost invisible in the darkness, it is so black," Talon said, staring into its bright yellow eyes.

"No, Rostam," his mother said firmly, when the boy wanted to linger with them. "It is almost bed time, so take this ball of fluff and go to your room; and keep him from getting underfoot."

Rostam happily took the kitten from his father. It settled down and was soon purring against the boy's shoulder. Rostam left them to the evening. "Good night, Papa," he called.

"I shall be in later to see you," Rav'an called after him.

Later that night, as they lay together, Rav'an moved closer to Talon and caressed his chest then slowly her hand moved further down. His response brought a sound of amusement from her. "My, how quickly the magic works!" she exclaimed.

"That isn't my fault, it's all yours, woman!" he responded, pretending to sound vexed.

"Hmm, I wonder," she murmured.

He kissed her then, and she felt the wonder begin. His lips moved downward. "How beautiful you are, my Rav'an," he murmured as he kissed her breasts. "I must not hurt you; I fear I will in my passion for you."

Her nipples grew under his lips and she groaned with the pleasure of it. "I am sure of you, my knight. You will not hurt me, nor our child. Make love to me, my warrior, for I am ready." In the unhurried manner of their love-making he made sure she was absolutely ready before he entered her, and then they began to move very slowly. She held him within her as the magical spasm surged through her entire body, making her mewl into his shoulder with the intensity of it. They lay for a long while together, not wanting to move and break the spell.

And are the clods of earth so sweet to you now
that to us you prefer worms and decay?
—Hanagid

Chapter 11
A Scouting Party

Talon took Henry's ship, as it was the speedier of the two. He left Dimitri with Guy and Reza in Paphos, with the strict instructions that should there be even a whisper that Isaac was going to pay the city another unwelcome visit, they were to embark aboard Guy's ship and to sail around the island to meet up with Talon along the coast.

Unhappy that he had to be left behind, Reza fully understood that his was an important responsibility and that Talon needed to scout the location before they rushed in. They simply could not all go into an unknown situation. Talon spent some time with his captains preparing prearranged signals and studying the crude chart that Max had prepared. He took Dar'an with him and left Yosef with Reza. He also took with him two of their newly trained followers, Khuzaymah and Junayd, who had proved to be good archers and had taken immediately to the hard stealth training as administered by Reza. Talon was confident that they would be useful to have on this voyage. He left Maymun and Nasuh behind with Reza and Yosef.

"There is an inlet further east of the harbor of the castle which has fresh water from the mountains, and there a ship can spend some time without attracting attention, should you have to flee Paphos before we get back," Max informed them. He showed Guy the location on his map. Guy nodded. "It might prove useful," he agreed. "Safe voyage to you."

The following morning just before daybreak, the ship was rowed quietly out of the harbor. No one stopped them, perhaps because the men on the ship were well armed and business-like. The slovenly soldiers on the harbor front would have been no match for them in a fight. All the same, Talon had advised Guy to post guards around the clock on his ship, and to use some of them as bodyguards when moving about the town. The occupants of the villa welcomed the protection the men provided.

Henry hugged the coastline as they headed north and rounded the fat end of the island, while Max, standing on the steering deck, pointed out landmarks that he remembered. Max appeared to have aged ten years in the interval they had been apart. He was still very weak, but Talon observed that the fresh, salt air of the sea appeared to be doing him good. All the same, he took care to ensure that his old friend was well wrapped; the sea, while not rough, was choppy, and the wind was brisk.

They passed across the two wide bays of Khysokhou and then Morphou, after which they headed due north to sail around the sharp cape of Mythou. After that it was easy enough to keep off shore by a few miles. When the wind died, which it did most early evenings, Henry put the rowers to work to keep them going. The rhythmic rise and fall of the oars and the beat of the drum that helped the men keep time was good to witness. They were on a mission and the men welcomed it. They had been distressed to hear that Cyprus was not a safe haven, but their faith in their leaders was firm. Now they were being kept occupied and would have no time to dwell upon misfortune.

On the second day, Max pointed to a distant town at the base of the thin range of mountains that had replaced the bulk of the Trudos Mountains.

"Over there is Kyrenia, a popular port for the ships from Alanya on the mainland. Beyond are many inlets where we can put in at night to stay out of sight while on our journey. I don't think there are any Greek naval ships patrolling these seas, but it would be wise to keep a low profile. An encounter with a Byzantine battle ship would be a disaster."

A full three days of sailing with a good wind behind them brought them close to their destination. Max beckoned Talon to join him and Henry on the steering deck, then pointed to a range of mountains set some way back from the coast. "Kantara castle is seated on that ridge up there," Max explained. "You can just see it from the port, but it is difficult from here. The port of Kantara is small, but well protected from the open sea. I only spent a night there; Nigel was captaining the ship at the time. You will have to think of a reason to visit the castle, Talon." It was not lost upon Talon that everyone deferred to him. The escape from Acre had cemented their belief in his ability to lead them.

He stared southward at the long, thin range of mountains that stretched along the back of the narrow peninsula. According to the map Max had drawn, on the other side of the mountains in a large wide bay was the large walled city of Famagusta. What Talon could see of the castle was pleasing, because it was perched high above the narrow, northern plain.

"We should find a cove where we can anchor the ship, Henry. I don't want to advertise our presence," Talon told his captain. Max agreed. "We are within a short day's walk from the port belonging to the castle. The next inlet has a stream of fresh water flowing into it."

The crew were set to work to bring the ship into a narrow cove with high limestone walls, atop of which grew small pines and shrubs. As they pulled at the oars, with men at the bows to warn of rocks and other obstructions, Talon looked behind. They were completely hidden from the sea. It was a perfect hiding place. The waterway opened up just wide enough to provide a small sandy beach, and there was just enough room to turn the ship. Henry sighed with satisfaction. "I shall bring us about and face the sea, just in case we have to leave in a hurry," he stated.

The crew moved smartly to his orders and the anchor stones were dropped. The cove appeared to be quiet and peaceful. They listened to the silence, and small sounds of life became evident. There was the long, rasping zither of some late summer cicadas in trees, the occasional cry of a hawk, and the gentle surge and receding pull of small waves. The heat shimmered off the sand of the beach. The scent of pines was strong in the air. A few birds flitted from bush to bush, but other than that there were no signs of life, nor of human presence.

"Post sentries up there on the banks and at the entrance of the cove as soon as you can, Henry," Talon ordered. "I don't want some stray shepherd to stumble upon us and raise any alarms."

He accompanied the sentries to the top of the high banks overlooking the cove. Looking down, the ship appeared to be resting on air; the water was so clear and still. Then he saw and heard a splash as one of the more exuberant crew members jumped into the water. He was soon followed by many others. The men were clearly enjoying this part of the expedition; after sweating at the oars they deserved to cool off. Time for the hard work later, Talon decided.

He turned away and stared in a north-westerly direction. For as far as he could see, there was scrub and pine scattered along the plain; but higher up the steep mountain side, the trees became taller and more dense. The forest would provide good cover for him and his companions when they went to investigate the castle.

Talon, Henry, Dar'an and two of his men stared up at the massive walls of the castle they had come to investigate. They had made their way with care across the rough countryside, keeping to the thickets, dense scrub and clumps of forest, avoiding the open areas, which were criss-crossed with trails that meandered in every direction. There was no doubt that shepherds with their goats and sheep traversed these hills; the signs were everywhere, including the distant tinkle of small bells. Frequently, they'd had to stop and cautiously scout ahead to make sure that no one was in their path.

His alert men had found birds hanging in small snap traps in thickets along their way. Talon surmised that the goat herder boys supplemented their diet with wild birds and hares. This meant that at any time they could stumble upon a boy or herder on his way to collect the traps. They were especially careful to avoid leaving any sign of passing once they realized this.

Now Talon and his small group of men were crouched in a thick clump of young firs and shrubs, looking up at the fortress, which impressed Talon greatly. This was a formidable structure!

Kantara was perched high on a craggy rise that rose directly out of the ridge itself and overlooked a long, narrow, fertile plain to the north, which eventually ended in a primitive harbor, in which were anchored a few fishing boats. There was a deep but wide valley to the south of the ridge, which ran from southwest to northeast. The castle appeared to be inaccessible on its north side to anyone but the most determined and skilled climber. It would also be a very difficult place to attack from the valley to the south. Admiring its position, Talon decided that this castle was virtually impregnable to existing siege weaponry.

His men sat in silence behind him as he squatted on the ground, chewing on a dried stalk of grass, thoughtfully contemplating the fortification. The view from the walls was surely magnificent in every direction, in particular to the north, where a sentinel could see an enemy fleet from many leagues away and raise the alarm. Either a beacon or a messenger could send notice of danger to the citizens of Famagusta on the other side of the steep mountain range, and from there riders could alert the rest of the island long before anyone landed.

Dar'an waved away a buzzing fly from his nut-brown face and commented, "This place does not look as though it can be easily taken."

"Just so. Max told me the Byzantines built it to act as a lookout for the Arab fleets, about a hundred years ago. They seem to have added to it since then." Talon continued staring at the castle. How perfect it was, he thought to himself. If he could only take it, a tiny number of men could hold it against all comers.

It was then Talon resolved to do all it required to take this castle. Hsü, his friend and mentor, was uppermost in his mind as he came to this decision. Unless he was utterly ruthless, he might fail. Henceforth, he would give no quarter in the quest to protect his family and friends.

"It is not a small castle," Junayd stated, jerking him out of his reverie. "Wonder how many people live inside."

"That will be for us to find out," he replied. "I notice they are building on the South wall overlooking the valley. Must be making repairs."

"I can see many people swarming around it, slaves most likely," Khuzaymah noted.

"Master Talon, I see what looks like a compound down in the valley, not far from one of the villages," Dar'an murmured.

"Yes, I see it now. You've got good eyes, Dar'an," Talon said. "That could be where the slaves are kept."

"Hmm, do you think that could be useful?" Dar'an grinned at Talon as he said this.

"Our first objective has been met. We know why it cannot be stormed by any conventional means. Now we need to know how many people live inside, and then see if we cannot use their weaknesses against them." Talon spoke French for the benefit of Henry who was with them. It elicited a grunt of astonishment.

"Talon, pardon me for interrupting, but am I hearing correctly? Are you seriously thinking of taking that place?" Henry sounded incredulous as his eyes took in the forbidding walls and towers.

"Yes, we are, Henry," Dar'an said. He was still struggling with French.

Henry shook his head. The fortress on the ridge seemed to him to be quite impregnable. "Then what do you need me for, Talon?" he addressed his leader, dragging his gaze away from that of Dar'an. Talon's young servant unsettled him.

"Fear not, Henry. We will need everyone for this. I want you to find a good place from which to observe, and have your crewmen learn everything about that harbor down there." Talon waved towards the north coast. "Something has changed since Max was here. He said that the castle was in a bad state of disrepair, perhaps even deserted. I don't see any sign of that. On the contrary, why would someone repair the place if he was about to abandon it?"

He shook his head. "Someone is repairing the castle, which means an alteration to our plans. I would like to know more. We need a good, safe place to land men at night from your ship, Henry. Memorize what you can: shoals, sandbanks, and rocks in unwanted places. It's not hard to pick those out in these waters; they are so clear, you can see right to the bottom. Set your men to work observing shipping as it comes and goes. I don't see any boats other than fishing vessels there today, but that could change, and I want to know when and how often."

"Why don't we stay in the cove and march overland, Talon?" Henry asked.

Talon looked at him. "I've not known sailors to be good walkers, but if you think that would work then I am in agreement. We can split our forces in that case, and come from the land and the sea. I will want the harbor to be in our possession before we attempt to take the castle. We will need a back door."

"I agree, Talon. One of your people can lead some of my men overland, and I will come in from the sea."

"If those are slaves working on the castle, we might be able to use them, Talon," Junayd said tentatively.

Talon glanced approvingly at Junayd. His men were thinking for themselves.

"I see that you and Dar'an are of like mind," he said. "We will have to infiltrate their camp and see what can be done."

He continued. "First we will scout every approach to the castle. We will do it in daytime and at night. I want to know the behavior of the sentries and how alert they are during the different watches. I also want an accurate estimation of the numbers inside the castle. We've seen the two villages to the north." He pointed to a cluster of dwelling places at the distant end of the valley which ran parallel with the ridge where the castle was located. The valley was green with vines and crops. "That one will be inhabited by the farmers. I want to know their numbers. Junayd, and you, Khuzaymah, will scout them out. You should also note where we can best scale the walls and get into the castle itself. I will be doing the same here."

Talon sent Henry back to the ship, and then he and his remaining three men set to work to explore every inch of the area at the base of the castle and its environs. It took them two days, by which time Talon had mapped out the area of the rambling structure in his mind and had a very good idea as to where he could gain entry over the walls, despite their formidable appearance.

Extensive repairs had been completed on the walls of the castle, and presumably on the interior. The slave gang left the camp in the valley every morning well before dawn and crawled up the hill, urged on by short-tempered overseers with whips. Even from this distance the watchers could see that many of the slaves were exhausted and weakened from lack of nourishment. One died while struggling up the steep incline towards the walls of the fortress.

Talon tried to figure out who these men might be. To his surprise, some looked like Greeks, while others could have been from half a dozen different countries of the eastern seaboard. All were thin and ragged, all were shackled with chains. He counted six overseers and ten soldiers, who presumably lived in the camp at the valley base. At night the prisoners were shut into the compound and given slops, then the guards would settle down to a night of eating and drinking. Talon and his men, hiding nearby in the dark, watched as the guards drank themselves senseless every night. There were no sentries posted.

They made one interesting discovery while prowling around the valley below the north side of the castle. There were two man-made caves that showed recent excavation. They ran about fifty paces into the mountain, and there were many baskets and broken tools lying about, along with piles of rocks strewn down the hill that obviously came from the tunnels.

Then, with their food running low, Talon and his men scouted the two villages, with great care not to leave tracks or any other signs of their passage. Talon was fairly sure the inhabitants were unaware of their presence, and his men were able to go in at night and count people and houses, gaining a reasonable estimate of numbers. Then it was time to go back to the ship.

Back at the vessel, and after a good meal, Talon described to Max and Henry in detail what he had discovered.

"The castle is in new hands, Max. The people who were there before have been replaced or have fled, or even were killed, since Isaac arrived. I have to gain entry and find out who it is who owns the castle and get some measure of his character, the numbers of his men and how disciplined they are. It is impossible to tell from a distance."

Max nodded his head slowly. "It would make sense for Isaac to have this castle repaired and to install a trusted lieutenant as custodian to warn him of an invasion from his uncle Andronicus."

"Then I must get to know this person and see what options that presents me with," Talon stated. "I will go back there with Dar'an and gain entry. I shall need some rope." He paused. "There is something else we found. I believe there are mines on the land."

Max stared at him. "Could they be copper mines ?" he asked.

The island isn't called *Kupros* for nothing, Max. My coin is on copper. But no one appears to be working the caves at present."

It's possible I am pushing through solid rock
in flint-like layers, as the ore lies, alone;
—Rainer Rilke

Chapter 12

The Castle called Kantara

Two nights later, Talon and Dar'an stood at the base of the huge fortress, which loomed high over them in the dark. They were on the north-west side, the steepest and least accessible point. They had ascertained that the sentries rarely bothered patrolling the walls on this side at any time, perhaps believing that no one would be mad enough to attempt to climb them. They spent most of their time on the east side, where the main gates were located. Any visitor who came to this castle was forced to walk up a long, narrow trail on that side to gain entry to the strong barbican between two large towers.

Tonight, however, the climb for the two men was up a steep hundred paces of rugged limestone rocks upon which the castle was built. This brought them to the very base of the walls. Talon had already picked away at the limestone masonry and knew that he could climb this wall, even in the dark.

He eased his way up the slightly rounded, thirty-foot high stone wall of the tower one tenuous finger hold at a time. He took the end of a rope with him, just as Reza had done in Acre. It took fifteen minutes for him to arrive at the rampart, where he was able to hook his aching fingers over the edge. Despite the burning sensation in his arms and shoulders, he clung to the wall like a limpet and listened. He could hear people moving about in the large courtyard to the east, and the murmur of a low conversation over to his right, but there was no one on the ramparts. He eased over the top and lay motionless, listening hard and catching his breath until he was satisfied there was no one nearby to raise the alarm.

Careful not to make any sound, he secured the rope for Dar'an. Seconds later it went taut; there was a slight scuffle on the walls, and then Dar'an's turbaned head appeared. He slid over the rampart and joined Talon in the dark shadows. There was only the hint of a moon tonight towards the west, but the stars above were a blaze of light, allowing their night-accustomed eyes to see in both directions along the walkway and over to the next tower, also unattended.

The two men moved like phantoms, exploring as much of the grounds as they could in the couple of hours available and making some useful discoveries. The soldiers were quartered in the southeast in stone barracks with stout wooden doors that ran along the inside of the wall. No guards were placed at any of the entrances to the stone buildings, so they were free to move about at will. Dar'an followed Talon, taking note of the defenses and peering into the many halls that comprised the surface structures of the fortress. They stayed away from the main gate where the guards were awake, if not alert, huddled around a brazier of burning wood. The light thrown off by the flames illuminating their faces and the walls around them.

Talon and Dar'an found the aviary where the large hunting hawks were enclosed; a few ruffled their feathers in concern, but none made any other sound. Talon also noted some kennels in the far western side. The hounds smelled the intruders and became excited. Their barking brought an irritable sentry, who kicked at their enclosure and said in a sharp tone, "Shut up, you God-damned creatures, or I'll get in there and beat yer senseless."

The dogs subsided and he walked back towards the gates, muttering to himself as he passed the two men hidden in the darkness.

The sharp smell of horses guided them to the stables, but Talon shook his head when Dar'an wanted to go inside. Without doubt the horses would know they were there and might alert the stable hands, who might be more responsive than the guards had been.

They slipped from shadow to dark shadow until they came to the main keep at the center of the castle complex and eased open the great doors that led to the main bailey, which would house the lord and his family, if indeed any lord lived here. There were no guards here either which indicated that the Castilian was feeling very secure in his mountain eerie. However, Talon had noted that a guard was posted at the very top of the building, probably fulfilling the original function of lookout to sea, having seen him walking slowly back and forth earlier.

Two huge hounds got up and ambled suspiciously towards them. Talon felt a moment of panic. While he had not forgotten about the hounds, he had assumed them to be all together in the kennels, safely locked up. The Greeks kept them for hunting, as did the Franks; but in the Moslem world hounds were kept firmly away from where people ate and slept, and Talon had forgotten to allow for the differences in customs. These two must be special hounds of the Castilian he surmised, even as he wondered what might happen. The only thing he could think of was to whisper to Dar'an, "Show no fear and go down on one knee. Greet them. Just be ready for anything."

His heart pounding and his hand hovering over the handle of his knife, Talon whispered to the two huge animals that came warily towards him. One of them growled low in its throat, and Talon gripped his knife, but the other wagged its tail and approached them to sniff the hand Talon held out. It allowed him to reach forward to scratch its jaw, then moved just enough for him to scratch under it ears. Talon eased out a long breath of relief.

"Do the same with the other one," he ordered the terrified Dar'an. The other hound, seeing that its companion was unconcerned, came up to Talon and demanded to be rubbed as well. It ignored the petrified Dar'an, who remained frozen to the floor. Talon was now making much of the brindled hounds, and they wagged their tails furiously. One even pushed its nose into his chest in a friendly gesture and grunted with pleasure. Still in a state of complete disbelief, Talon patted them on their shoulders and risked murmuring endearments to the two huge creatures. Much to his relief, no one in the darkness of the hall behind the hounds woke up to come and investigate.

Rising slowly and gesturing for Dar'an to do the same, Talon—accompanied by the interested hounds—stepped warily towards a flight of stone stairs. They passed the remains of a generous meal on large wooden tables. Giving the two hounds a large bone each, then a last pat on the shoulder and bidding them stay, Talon led the way up the stairs. Then they had to get past a number of sleeping servants, huddled under blankets on the floor of the main upstairs chamber. It was a tribute to Reza's training that Dar'an never put a foot wrong and they made it all the way up to the second floor without disturbing anyone.

Making their way along a corridor, they passed several chambers where snoring indicated that the occupants were fast asleep. Eventually they arrived at the imposing entrance of what Talon took to be a large bed chamber. They could hear loud snores as they approached. A servant lay on the floor across the threshold, but he slept on as Talon eased the door open. Signaling Dar'an to keep an eye on the recumbent servant, Talon stepped over the man and found himself in a stuffy room: all the shutters were closed, and it stank of sweat and other stale, unpleasant smells, including the rank odor of the *garderobe* recess near the window.

He slipped up to the bed and drew aside the thick curtains that enclosed it. A large man was lying on his back, snoring lustily, his mouth a dark hole in his bearded face, his arms akimbo and his large belly quivering in time with each labored breath. Curled in a ball to one side was another equally large body, a woman, snoring also, though the sound was muffled. Evidently this Castilian did not share the prevalent view in Byzantium that clean, fresh air was good for one's health.

Talon inspected the room stealthily, assessing the layout of the chamber, and then he left, stepping silently over the sleeping manservant again, who snuffled by the doorway. He glanced out of a window and realized that he and Dar'an had been in the castle for over an hour; it was time to leave. Tapping Dar'an on the shoulder, he pointed downstairs. They slipped back down to the main hall and out the doors, closing them silently on the two hounds, who wanted to come and join them.

It was only a matter of moments to reach the steps leading up to the parapet. They were just about to step out of the shadows when Talon sensed someone standing on the wall ahead of them. He put out a hand and gripped Dar'an's shoulder to stop him, then signaled for him to stay where he was and remain out of sight; then he crept forward to investigate. He had been right; someone was on the parapet, and worse still, he was staring down at the rope, which was tied off against a protrusion on the wall.

The whole enterprise, which had depended upon neither of them being detected, was now in jeopardy. There was nothing Talon could do but rush in before the alarm was raised. The figure had just stood up to his full height when two strong hands wrapped themselves around his face and jerked his head violently to the right. There was a dull crack; the man's arms flailed and the body spasmed and jerked, but he made no sound; his neck was broken. Talon eased the body to the stone ground then leaned over him to check that he was dead. Dar'an joined him, shocked at what he had just witnessed. He had not known Talon possessed such killing skill.

"What do we do with him?" he whispered shakily.

"We have to get rid of him," Talon said, indicating the void below. He seized the man by the shoulders. "Quickly now, before anyone else comes."

They hastily swung the body over the wall, and seconds later heard it thud onto the rocks below. They listened as the body bounced a couple of times and slid down the steep incline, then there was absolute silence.

Talon pushed Dar'an towards the rope. "Go!" he commanded. He followed Dar'an down the rope and twitched its other end to release it from its tied-down point. As the rope fell, Dar'an was already looking for the body. He found it among a group of rocks a hundred feet down from the base of the wall. Talon glanced up at the dark walls of the fortress but could see no sign of anyone else, nor did he hear of any alarms.

Now he had a difficult decision: dare he leave the body in plain sight and hope that the residents of the castle assumed the fall was an accident, perhaps brought on by too much drinking? Or should he leave them with the mystery of the man's disappearance? Which would rouse less alarm? He shook his head; let it be the unknown, not the reminder of the unknowable.

They retrieved the body and carried it with them as they made for the forest to the south of the castle. There were no fields here where peasants might wander, so they hid the body in some dense undergrowth and then began the long trek back to the ship. Talon hoped the wild animals, most likely boar, would find the body and dispose of it before it could be discovered.

They arrived back at the cove just as dawn was streaking the eastern sky. Here they stopped, and as a test Talon sent Dar'an forward to see if he could catch unawares the guard posted on the top of the cliff overlooking their cove. Minutes later, the surprised guard stood frozen with fear as Dar'an tickled his throat with the blade of his knife, a huge grin on his face. Talon stepped forward and took the man's arm to reassure him that he was safe, then said quietly, "You must be more alert! You never know who might come by for a visit."

They then vanished down the path to the beach, leaving the bemused guard shaking. He was later to tell his mates, "I never heard a God damned thing! Not a whisper of danger, and then there was that crazy boy of Talon's grinning at me with his knife at my throat! Scared the shit out of me!"

One of the men nodded. "Sir Talon has some strange friends now. I'm just glad they are on our side."

Talon and Dar'an were greeted by a yawning Henry, who held a lantern high for them to climb aboard.

"God be praised you are safe, Talon. I was getting worried."

"We'll talk in the morning, Henry. I learned a lot. Good night."

146

Talon woke to find the ship silent. He surmised that Henry had probably told the crew to keep it quiet to let him sleep. He came out on deck, blinking in the bright sunlight, to find Henry and Max up on the steering deck talking in low tones. They both glanced up as Talon came up the stairs.

"Good morning, Talon. How did it go?" Henry asked.

"We managed to get in and look around. The place is huge! Much larger than it appears from below. I discovered that the Castilian snores very loudly, and so does the woman who shares his bed, couldn't tell if she was his wife or not!" His two astonished friends laughed.

"You were in his bedroom?" Henry asked with an incredulous chuckle.

"Oh yes, and everywhere else I could go, too. I even made friends with some hounds!"

Henry gaped at him. Max laughed knowingly.

"However, there are more men than I had calculated."

"Do you think it will be possible to take it?" Max could not resist asking.

"Yes, it is possible, Max, but... we don't have enough men with us at present. There will be only one chance! We have to go back to Paphos, pick up the rest of our crew, and then see what advantage the slaves can provide us. Those slaves are a sorry looking lot. If we could use them they might provide us with one means to entry, but we need to think about how to accomplish that very carefully. Everything has to happen at the same time, you see."

The three men became aware that there was something happening on the beach. Talon saw one of the crew talking agitatedly to another and pointing up the bank.

"There is something amiss. We need to get ashore immediately," Talon said, and rushed off to get his bow. On the way he called for Junayd and Dar'an. "Come ashore with me at once! Bring your bows!"

They were joined by Khuzaymah, and they all dropped into the small boat which was used to ferry men to and from the beach. At Talon's urging the two crewmen pulled hard.

No sooner had they landed than one of the senior crew members, with three other scouts behind him, ran down the beach towards Talon and, pointing to the slope, said, "We heard goats, Master Talon. They are approaching from the southwest."

Talon turned to his companions. "Locate them. If they do not seem to be a danger let them go by. But if they keep coming this way stop whoever it is and capture them, boy or man, and do not let anyone escape. If they flee and you cannot catch them...." He left he rest unsaid.

Junayd and Dar'an closely followed by Khuzaymah raced off along the beach and up the steep bank like hounds just released for the kill. Talon stayed behind to interrogate the scouts.

"How far away did you say they were?" he asked the men, who were gazing after the speeding boys with awe. "God save me, but I would hate to have them after me!" one muttered to his mates.

Talon repeated the question.

"I would say about three or four hundred paces away among the pine trees, Master Talon. I heard the little bells first and knew it was goats or sheep," the man nearest to him responded.

"Did you see anyone?"

"No, Sir, they were too far away; but just as Captain Henry told us to, we came to warn you. I think they are coming to the stream. If they do, they will certainly discover us!"

"You did well, men," Talon told the crewmen. "Now go back to your posts and keep out of sight. Watch for any other intruders. My boys will deal with this."

They did not have long to wait. Before much time had elapsed Dar'an and Junayd came back, holding onto a struggling boy of about nine years. As they came down the slope the boy almost escaped, but Dar'an grabbed him and slapped him hard. After that the boy subsided enough for them to drag him along the sand to where Talon stood waiting.

"How many were there?" he asked.

Dar'an jerked his head upwards. "There were two of them, Master. I had to shoot one with an arrow. We didn't see him at first, as he was behind the herd, and when he saw we had this boy he ran. He was too far for me to catch him. It was an old man." He sounded genuinely unhappy at what he'd had to do.

Talon turned his attention to the boy, who had stopped struggling and now faced him. The tear-stained face showed fear, but defiance, too. "Why are you in this area? How many of you were there with the goats?" Talon demanded in Greek.

The boy shook his head and said nothing.

Talon took a step forward. "You have two choices: to tell me everything and live, or wait until we sail again, when we will drop you overboard into the sea for the monsters to devour. Think of your family and how they will feel once they learn of your death."

"You killed my uncle!" the boy shouted, struggling again. "I hate you!" He began to cry. Tears slid down his cheeks and his nose dribbled as he dropped his head and wept.

"I am sorry for your uncle," Talon told him. "Believe me, we would prefer that he was still alive. Was he the only one with the herd, other than yourself? Answer me!" his voice cracked in the boy's ear, making him jump.

"Yes, yes, he was the only person with me," the boy whimpered. "We are a long way from home and do not come here often. Just for water after some days away from the village. Are you pirates?"

Talon looked around at the crew members still on the beach. "Take him to the ship. Tell Henry and Max what happened and let them deal with him. Do not under any circumstances let him go. If he tries to escape, you know what to do," he ordered.

The seamen men knuckled their foreheads and seized the boy, whom they dragged off towards the boat.

"What of the goats?" Dar'an asked sensibly.

"Well now, you have just become a goatherd, my lad," Talon said with a tight grin. "Come on, let's go and see how many there are. We could do with some meat, anyway. We must get rid of the old man. I want no trace of this incident to attract anyone else to the area."

The herd was not large, but they couldn't just let them wander about in this area. "Take them off southwards into the forest for several miles and leave them there, Khuzaymah. You go with him, Junayd. Sooner or later they will drift back to their home village, but by then I hope we are done with all this," he said. "We'll keep ten of them for ourselves. The crew are ready for fresh meat."

The crew had erected crude, lean-to huts on the beach. Talon had expressly forbidden wine or any other alcohol, but somehow some had been smuggled aboard. That night a couple of the men who had been playing knuckles began to drink furtively, and soon they were making a noise, which brought Henry to the scene. He was very angry and promptly arrested the two men, ordering the men on ship guard duty to take them to the ship's hold. Then he glared around in the firelight at the other sheepish looking fellows, who had clearly been prepared to join in and have a party. "Get to bed. All of you. There will be a court in the morning."

The next day, Henry convened a court. He asked Talon to preside. When the two culprits were hauled out of the hold onto the waist of the ship, the entire crew was assembled to witness. Blinking in the sunlight, their hands bound behind them, the two men were thrust in front of Henry, who stood on the steering deck overlooking the men.

"You were all warned that there was to be no liquor drunk on this voyage!" Henry said in a loud voice. "Sir Talon here was clear about the dangers of drunkenness to the successful completion of the enterprise." He paused to glare at the two prisoners, who were on their knees before him with two of the senior crew members holding them down.

"Despite this you ignored the order. You are guilty of disobedience, and for that the sentence should be most severe," Henry stated flatly. "I have turned the sentence over to Sir Talon here, to do with you as he pleases. If he stretches your sorry necks I shall not be sorry."

Henry stood back and allowed Talon to step forward. He addressed the crew at large.

"Men, you volunteered to come with me to this island. Your hopes and mine were for a better life than that in Acre. We have, however, found that Cyprus is not what we expected. We will now have to fight for what we want, and this is still possible, but only if you stay loyal and follow orders which are for the benefit of all, not just one or two.

"Our enterprise depends upon you all being alert and fully committed. Drunkenness could scupper everything. You two deserve death for that alone." He looked over the upturned faces for any signs of rebellion but saw none; then he stared balefully down at the two men, who were looking very frightened. He had the right to execute them, should he wish, but instead he said, "Twenty lashes, to be carried out immediately. For the next man who is caught drinking it will be death."

There was a collective sigh from the men. Some had expected a harsher sentence, but twenty delivered the right message. It would be a painful experience for the two delinquents. Fifty lashes could kill a man; twenty would be remembered—by everyone.

The two men were bound hand and foot to a grating, which was then lifted so that they were upright, and then the chief seaman who controlled the rowers and another designated sailor carried out the sentence. By the time the smack on flesh of the hissing cord and the screams of the two culprits had ended, both their backs were bloody, and they were semi-conscious. A bucket of sea water thrown at their backs, which revived them to cry out some more before they were cut down and taken below.

150

Henry had watched with a grim scowl on his face. When it was done he turned to Talon. "I hope the lesson is learned. The crew are volunteers to a man, but I will have discipline on my ship, Sir Talon. The punishment fit the crime."

Talon nodded agreement. "I hope so. We are very vulnerable here, and a fool could sink our enterprise. I won't have that under any circumstances." He considered their situation.

"The men are getting bored," he told Henry. "We have to move soon, or we will find ourselves with a discontented crew."

Henry agreed. "Are you ready to go back to Paphos, Talon?"

"Yes, prepare to leave. Make sure we don't leave any sign of our presence."

The castle of Kantara awoke to the call of the roosters, two of which vied for domination over the docile flock of hens that patrolled the inside of the fortress every day, looking for scraps and grass upon which to feed. The sleepy sentries who had been on duty throughout the early hours were relieved and eagerly sought their beds, while the refreshed sentries sent some of their number to the kitchens to scrounge some food.

Inside the keep, men and women servants began the day just like any other. Some prepared food and drink for the lord and his wife on the upper floor, while others set about cleaning the hall. The stable hands awoke, fed the horses and groomed them to a shine. The lord of the castle might on impulse rise from his drunken slumbers and want to go hunting. His men knew better than to wait for the command and be late. His whip was something to be avoided. So was the wrath of his wife, who bullied everyone, including his lordship.

Later in the morning, his Lordship, Cyricus Doukas, strode out of the keep and walked towards the main gates, with his two hounds trotting at his heels. He felt contented and well fed, having dined on roast pigeon, goose meat with dripping on freshly baked bread, and fresh trout, washed down by some wine from his very own vineyard in the valley below. He wiped his beard with the back of his hand and tossed a bone he had been chewing over his shoulder. The hounds dived at it, but he turned and kicked them away and shouted at the cowed animals; then he continued towards the gates, where he was met by the captain of the guard. Today the captain had a worried look on his angular, pock-marked features.

"All well, Palladius?" Cyricus demanded routinely. He was going to inspect the work on the north tower. "I want to see more progress. The work is going too slowly. I shall not only punish the slaves but you as well," he said, before the sergeant could reply to the first question.

"Everything is in order, Lord," the man said hesitantly, "but...."

"But what?" Cyricus demanded irritably, "Spit it out, man!"

"Well, all appears to be well, my Lord, except that Traianus is absent."

Cyricus shrugged. "Should I be concerned? He is one of your lot of scum, is he not? Deal with it. If he is absent he will be flogged near to death when we do find him."

"Yes, my Lord," Palladius replied. He would search everywhere again. There had been no sign of the man, and he should have reported by now. Traianus was an experienced soldier who took his duties seriously. None of the sentries had seen him leave the castle. Palladius followed Cyricus and his hounds as they climbed the steps to the other tower, from where they would be able to witness the arrival of the slaves and observe the work on the defenses.

"If the work does not progress apace, have their rations cut in half," Cyricus stated with a belch. Palladius nodded reluctantly, but inside he was disgusted. He knew that the slaves were on their last legs already. To cut their food even more was tantamount to killing them; but a command was a command, and he knew better than to disagree with this man. He would pass the order along to the overseers when the slaves arrived, which they were in the process of doing as the Lord reached the battlements.

Both men stared down at the long line of men in chains that moved slowly up the track towards the gates. The clink of their chains could be clearly heard. Palladius could see, even if his lord could not, that these people were starved already. Cutting rations was not going to improve their performance. He shrugged internally. It was not his concern. The gates were opened on a shouted command from Palladius, and the slaves shuffled through the archway into the barbican area, with the rattle of many chains. The overseers shouted at them to move along. Once inside the bailey, they waited to be released from their respective gangs before being driven to their work places with whips and curses.

Cyricus watched the goings-on in the barbican for a while, then turned to leave. One of his hounds was not quick enough to get out of the way. It received a solid kick in the side, which made it yelp with pain, tuck its tail between its legs and scamper down the steps ahead of the Lord and Master.

Cyricus had no sooner exited the tower when the unmistakable voice of his wife, Flavia, could be heard yelling from the window of the bailey. "Where are you, Cyre? I need you to help me up here, at once!"

Palladius grinned to himself and withdrew from the edge of the tower to avoid being caught watching. When the irascible wife asserted her will upon the detestable Lord of the castle, anyone with sense vanished from sight.

A new day had dawned in the castle of Kantara.

The next morning found the entire crew cleaning the ship from stem to stern under the watchful eye of one of Henry's senior crew men. Talon was amused but also pleased. The men who had been sent to observe the harbor were back with reports of a small but thriving community of fishermen and sheep herders.

"What else did you find while there?" he asked the lead crew man.

"They are a small village and would not be able to fight. We could take them in a minute if we surprised them. I saw a couple of horses, which surprised me, but I think they belonged to the two soldiers who were lounging about drinking at a small tavern," the man told him. Talon filed the horses away as useful information. "They have crops further up the road towards the castle, and I saw at least two orchards and several stands of olive trees," the man concluded.

"Are you a farmer, then, that you know this?" Henry asked him.

"Mature olive trees?" Max asked.

"Yes, Sir. I rented a land holding once, outside Acre. We near starved to death. Them Arabs killed my family." He turned to Max. "There are enough olive trees there to fill several vats when they are ready, I should think, Sir."

That pleased the listeners very much. "This valley could be self sustaining, with a little left over for trade," Henry observed. Talon liked the sound of that, should he be lucky enough to implement his plan and live to enjoy the fruits of success.

It was late in the morning when Talon finally gave his approval to the clean up of the beach. They were preparing the ship for the journey back to Paphos when one of the lookouts, who had been posted on the small headland to keep an eye out to sea, came scampering along the bank. "There is a ship coming our way, Captain!" he called breathlessly. "It looks as though they are coming right here!"

Talon dived below. By the time he come back on deck with his bow and two of the bamboo bombs in his arms, most of the crew were on board and either standing to the oars or preparing to drop sail. His own men were ready with their weapons at the bows of the ship.

"We can surprise anyone with these nasty things," he told his friends, who looked askance at the innocuous tubes.

"What do they do?" Max asked doubtfully.

"They make an awful 'bang' sound that deafens anyone nearby, if they haven't killed them first," Talon stated.

Henry and Max gaped and were about to say something more when the man posted on the top of the mast shouted down. "It is Captain Guy! I would know that ship anywhere!"

The men on the steering deck visibly relaxed. They still waited until the other ship was nosing into the cove to make quite sure, but then the figures on that ship waved and shouted greetings to them.

"Phew, I'm glad it wasn't someone else," Henry stated with obvious relief.

Talon nodded thoughtfully. Their cove could have become a trap. That was a liability he would need to reconsider, but now at least he could move ahead with his plan. The extra men he needed had just arrived.

The people on Guy's ship were excited and relieved to see Talon's ship and cheered as they drew abreast, but Henry's crew swiftly waved them to silence. As the two ships bumped together, some of them hissed, "No noise! No noise!"

He clasps the crag with crooked hands
Close to the sun in lonely lands
Ring'd with the azure world he stands
The wrinkled sea beneath him crawls;
He watches from his mountain walls
—Alfred Lord Tennyson

Chapter 13
Thunderbolt

Reza had been disappointed at being left behind in Paphos but fully understood that significant responsibility rested on his shoulders. With that in mind he spent much time with Dimitri, trying to gauge the mood in the city. What they heard and saw was not reassuring. If anything, people were even more apprehensive two days after Talon had departed.

"You know about this Komnenos who is running the country?" Dimitri asked Reza.

They were walking towards the house of Boethius Eirenikos, the merchant. Reza stopped and said, "I understand that he is a bad man and we must be careful."

"It is worse than that," Dimitri warned. "Isaac has had himself crowned Emperor of Cyprus. That means he now has absolute power here and has decided to make a complete break with his great-uncle, Emperor Andronicus Komnenos in Constantinople."

Reza was unimpressed. "I thought he had done that already," he remarked, as he observed the fishermen working on their boats in the bay. The sky was overcast, and a light but cold wind ruffled the surface of the sea, which began to take on a slate gray color. "Looks like we might have a storm coming," he remarked.

"What it means is that he is going to visit his cities, Reza, and Paphos is one of the most important," Dimitri responded. "This is a port frequented by merchants from Palestine and Constantinople. We can expect him to show up here quite soon. I hope Talon completes his business at that castle and gets back before then."

They paid their visit to Boethius, who confirmed what Dimitri had said, and then they returned to their rented villa. Both were in a thoughtful mood.

"You know he is a very worried man." Dimitri stated as they walked along the half deserted waterfront.

"Who? Boethius? How so?" asked Reza. Because of his lack of Greek he had been unable to follow much of the conversation.

"He says the emperor is at Limassol and will be marching with his army to Paphos right after he has visited Kourinn. That is only four days away. If he were in a hurry he could be here within three days."

"Do you think he might have heard that Talon is here?" Reza asked.

"I think it is possible. Boethius said there are spies everywhere ready to ingratiate themselves with Isaac. A new, wealthy looking merchant would be reported."

"That gives us two days to prepare," Reza stated. "I don't want to be here when he arrives. You should alert Captain Guy and tell him to get his crew together."

Dusk was falling and candles were being lit in a few windows of houses nearby; all seemed quiet and peaceful, but Reza, who was tuned to this kind of thing, could almost feel the tension building in the city.

Dimitri hurried off to carry out the order.

That night Reza spoke with the women and asked them to prepare to leave. Both Rav'an and Jannat knew Reza well enough to know that he was very worried.

"But where will we go, Reza?" Jannat demanded, concern in her tone.

"I think we can head northeast and find Talon along the coast. Right now that is our only good option. To stay is to court disaster," he replied.

When he had left to check on the ships, Jannat came over to Rav'an and wept.

"What was Talon thinking when he brought us here, Sister?" She wiped her eyes with her sleeve. "We are both pregnant, and all I hear from Reza is how dangerous it is here on this island. We should have gone back to China. I miss that place."

Rav'an held her close. "I agree it is worrying, my Jannat, but I am sure Talon did not expect this, or he would never have brought us here in the first place. We probably *should* have gone to China, despite that being a perilous journey. I agree with you, but we are here now and we must have faith in our men. They are trying their best to find us a home for our children, and I do not call my husband the Fox for nothing." She said the words, but her throat was dry and she was frightened. Nothing seemed to have gone Talon's way since they arrived in the land of the Frans, and now this cursed island had turned dangerous in the extreme, quite the opposite of what he had expected.

The next morning Rav'an rose early with Jannat, and they completed the preparations for a hasty departure. Fortunately they had not settled in completely, and much of their baggage was still stored on the ship. Their actions were circumspect, as they didn't want to alarm the hired help, who might also be spying on them. Dimitri had come back to the villa with Guy and had been adamant.

"We leave tonight. Trust no one, Madam, no one at all of these people. For sure they are spying on us, because they need to survive too. God help them and their daughters."

"Is it as bad as that?" Rav'an had asked him, her tone incredulous.

"I believe it to be worse, my Lady. Much worse, if the merchant is to be believed. The stories I have heard from the locals would chill your blood."

That day went by quickly as they launched themselves into their tasks.

The sky was streaked with high level clouds and a wind started up that tossed trash into the air and tugged at pedestrians' clothing. The sea became choppy, with white crests on the waves beyond the harbor sea walls. Reza stared apprehensively out to sea. If they had to leave today it might prove difficult, he thought to himself.

The same thought occurred to Guy, for he hauled in his cables and turned the ship about so that its bow was pointing directly towards the harbor mouth, then he changed his mind and docked it alongside the quayside again. It was not hard to maneuver; there were very few other ships in the harbor. There had been five, but three had disappeared in the early hours; perhaps their captains had sensed trouble.

— glanced up at the sky and, swaying to the uneasy motion of the ship, said, "At least the wind is not directly from seaward. I can sail out in this weather, but if it changes a few points we will have to rely on the rowers, Reza."

"Do what you must, Guy. I shall attend to the household." They were almost shouting by this time, the wind was blowing so hard.

"Where are those damned provisions I ordered?" Guy growled in frustration as he stamped about the deck, glancing repeatedly up at the sky.

157

The much needed water and provisions finally arrived late in the afternoon on a train of slow moving donkeys driven by sullen drovers. Rumors were flying in all directions in the town, and the drovers were anxious to deliver their goods and get away quickly.

Late that evening, back at the villa, Reza could see people fleeing into the hills behind the city. They were abandoning their homes! Trains of donkeys, driven by desperate people huddled in their cloaks, climbed the slopes of the foothills behind the town and disappeared from sight.

"They are leaving like rats from a ship," he told Rav'an. "I think that we should, too."

His misgivings were confirmed when Dimitri came rushing into the villa and called out urgently. "Reza, Madam! We must leave immediately!"

Reza ran down the steps to join him. "What is happening, Dimitri? I thought we had a couple of days before the King arrived."

"I did too, but he has sent his cavalry ahead and they will be arriving within a matter of hours. We must leave now!"

"That makes good sense," Reza muttered to himself. "He wants to secure the town so that no one can leave."

He called up in Farsi. "We leave this instant, Jannat. Find Rostam and Salem, and hurry; there is no time left."

Jannat woke Rostam, who had gone to bed earlier. He stirred grumpily. "What is the matter, Auntie? I'm tired."

"You will be able to sleep on the ship. We must go. Come, my dearest, do not waste time. Salam is downstairs with your mother."

"Where is Panther? I can't go without him!"

Jannat gave an exclamation of exasperation. "Reza says there is no time, Rostam. We must go!"

Rostam found the kitten curled up on a mat near his bed and seized it. The kitten woke, mewling and hungry, but Rostam had become aware of the tension in the air. "My bow!" he exclaimed and grabbed it up with the small quiver of arrows, then rushed with Jannat down the stairs, clutching the kitten and his prized possessions.

The house was quiet. Rav'an was waiting outside with an impatient Reza. "Come on, Rostam, for God's sake! We have to hurry!" she snapped with real urgency in her tone.

"What is happening?" Jannat asked in a frightened tone, as they hastened through the silent streets.

"Dimitri heard that the cavalry were almost at the gates of the city. They will seal the city the moment they arrive, and they will try to stop anyone leaving from the harbor. We must get to the ship and escape," Rav'an gasped as she hurried along. She could feel the baby inside her move as though protesting this frantic activity and prayed that nothing would go wrong because of it. Oh, why had they come to his benighted island so full of danger? It was no place to raise a child. Sensing her distress, Reza took her arm to help her.

Before long they came to the quayside and saw the ship drawn up alongside, armed sailors standing nearby. Guy was taking no chances. Crewmen on deck were ready with poles to push them off; others were clustered in the waist, armed with bows and spears.

Reza glanced around the waters of the inner harbor and noticed that the two other ships had already gone. The little group almost ran the hundred paces left to the boat and had just reached the ship where outstretched hands were ready to pull them aboard when they all heard a cry at the other end of the quay.

"Save us! In God's name, save us!"

Reza pushed Jannat onto the gangplank and made sure Rostam was safe aboard with Rav'an, then looked back along the quay. "Go below, Rav'an," he ordered. "It is not safe on deck."

Hurrying towards them was a group of three, two adults and one child. In the gloom it was hard to see, but he was sure he recognized the voice of Boethius Eirenikos, the merchant. The man's voice was desperate with terror. "Please take us with you!" he pleaded as he hurried towards the ship, clutching a small box in his arms and carrying a large sack over his shoulder. The woman also carried a bulky sack, and the small child was running between them, clutching at the skirts of the woman. "Dimitri! We will be killed if we stay. For the sake of my child I beg you!" His voice hit a high note in his agony of fear.

Reza hesitated.

"We have to leave at once!" Guy called from the steering deck. "Cast off!" he roared at the men in the bows and the stern.

Rav'an had not yet gone below and had seen the fugitives, "We must take them, Reza! We cannot leave them behind to that monster."

Shaking his head, Reza called out, "Yosef! Come with me!" He began to lope towards the three running figures. What he had seen behind the family drove him on. The dark figures of men on horses, some carrying flaming torches, had appeared on the harbor front. They had not yet noticed the activity at the end of the quay, nor seen the three figures, but their discovery was only to be moments away.

Reza unslung his bow as he ran and heard Yosef running along right behind him. They reached the merchant just as the horsemen caught sight of them and gave a collective whoop: they had found some victims in this nearly empty city. They began to gallop their horses along the harbor towards the turn of the quay, yelling and waving their torches.

Reza swept the child up and with the other hand dragged at the woman. "Go to the ship!" he shouted. Yosef already had his bow ready. With one swift motion he raised the bow and loosed an arrow high into the air with a 'twang' from his bowstring. It disappeared into the night, but seconds later there was a yelp of surprise from a horseman, then shouts of rage as others realized what had happened. No one toppled off a horse, but someone had been hit.

"Good shooting!" Reza gasped, as he threw the screaming child into the waiting arms of a burly seaman on deck and shoved the merchant and the woman roughly along the gangplank. "Yosef, get on board!" he shouted. "We can shoot at them from here."

Yosef needed no persuasion. He skipped onto the deck just as the crew hauled up the plank and ran with Reza up the ladder to the steering deck of the ship.

Guy was already bellowing orders at the deck crew to haul up the sail; other men were poling the ship away from the quayside and the rowers were hauling at the oars.

The rattle of hooves on the stonework added fresh urgency to everyone's actions as the mounted men galloped furiously down the quayside. One rode in front of all the others, his spurs driving into his lathered mount, and he thrashed the racing animal's rump with the flat of his sword. "Stop, in the name of the emperor!" he screamed. "Halt, or we will arrest you!"

"Let them try, by God!" Guy muttered, but he passed the word for the men to take cover. "Be prepared to shoot at them if they want to start a fight," he told them.

Reza had disappeared below deck, leaving his men with bows at the ready. There was a shouted command from the quay and men began to dismount. "I can see men with bows preparing to shoot," Nasuh said to Yosef.

"Then shoot at them now. Aim first at that man, the one doing all the shouting." Yosef pointed to the figure who seemed to be the leader. "All of you, aim at him and kill him. Perhaps that will cool their blood. Where is Reza when we need him?" he demanded, looking around the deck.

The slow-moving vessel was still only twenty paces away from shore, which was much to close for comfort. There was almost a collective cringe from the crew as everyone saw the horsemen preparing to send arrows their way.

Then Reza was back on deck, clutching a long tube. "Everyone get under cover!" he shouted, then he bent to use a flint and stone. A long stream of sparks flew and the fuse was ignited. Reza ducked behind the side of the ship just in time as a flurry of arrows came thudding into the sides and onto the deck around him—the sparks had made him the perfect target. One man cried out and was dragged hastily into better cover by his mates.

Yosef called out a command and his men popped up from behind the transom and loosed their arrows in return, all aimed at one man. Even in the dark and with the movement of the ship beneath them, with the torches of the horsemen casting weird shadows, their aim was true. The leader of the cavalry toppled off his horse, clutching his chest with three arrows protruding from it. The yells of the men on shore changed to shouts of consternation.

"Get your heads down!" Reza yelled to his men. He held in his hand the tube, which was now spluttering and hissing furiously, sending more sparks into the air. Men nearby cowered away from the terrifying sight and crossed themselves, their eyes wide with fear. With one fluid motion Reza hurled the object in a high arc towards the quay, where it fell into the massed ranks of the cavalry. The terrible, hissing object bounced and rolled. Abruptly there was a blinding flash, an enormous bang, and some small objects buzzed overhead like angry bees.

The people on the ship were momentarily blinded and deafened, but when they recovered their vision they could see the carnage on the quayside, partially obscured by dense smoke. Men and horses were down in a struggling heap of bodies, either dead or wounded. None of the survivors seemed to have any further interest in the departing ship.

"I wish no harm to the horses, but the men can go to hell," Reza said to a stunned Guy, as he joined him on the steering deck. "I do not think they will be bothering us now, Captain, but I still think we should leave."

"I think so, too. God save us, Reza, but what did you do? That was like a bolt from hell."

"In a way it was exactly that. And it has taken some of them back to hell with it," Reza laughed.

He left Guy to take the ship out into the choppy seas.

Always it is a great encouragement
to Feel and realize
That the ultimate truth
Can never, never tolerate
Human deception.
—A Sri Chinmoy

Chapter 14
Checkmate

Three days later at the castle of Kantara, a sentry came to fetch Palladius. This was soon after the slaves had been sent back down the ridge to their miserable camp in the valley. One had died and his body had been heaved over the edge of the ridge, to drop onto the rocks below on the North side. The others, having been deprived of food, were staggering with hunger and weariness as they left.

"We have visitors, Sergeant," the gawky young sentry told him.

They strolled together across the barbican towards the closed gates, and Palladius climbed the steps to the tower to get a better view. A soldier standing watch on top of the tower pointed down the track. Moving towards them was a small train of travelers. The leader was mounted on a horse, as was the person behind, but the majority were either on donkeys or on foot.

To Palladius it looked as though a merchant might be coming to visit, and he wondered why. He could make out that the leader was dressed very much like a merchant; the man did not appear to be armored other than a sword by his side. Behind him rode a woman who looked as though she might be pregnant; then came several others who had the appearance of servants, a couple of other women, and some armed men taking up the rear.

They came to a halt at the gate, at which point the rider looked around him, then up towards the battlements, where he saw Palladius staring down at him.

"Hallo up there! We come in peace," he said waving his hand behind him. "We are seeking shelter. Pray tell his Lordship Cyricus Doukas we have come from Paphos and bear tidings of His Majesty."

Palladius stared down at the group of people congregating at the gates. He counted them: twelve; most were dressed as servants in rough clothing.

They looked harmless enough, but he would still need permission to let them in.

"Wait there. I shall inform his Lordship of your arrival," he called down to the travelers, then trotted down the steps to the court yard and headed for the bailey.

Cyricus heard of the visitors just as he was about to start dinner. He lifted his shaggy, bearded head and glowered at Palladius, who bowed low and kept his head lowered. "He knows my name?" Cyricus asked.

"He gave your name and said that he brought news from Paphos, Lord."

"God's blood! I'm starving and I want to eat!" Cyricus grumbled. "Let them in and get someone to see to the servants, but bring the merchant and his woman to me."

"Stop complaining all the time, Cyr. News is scarce enough these days, with us being confined up here. It will be good to have a visitor, even one as lowly as a merchant," Flavia said testily.

"All you women want to do is to gossip about nothing," Cyricus snarled.

"All you men want to do is to compare the length of your pricks while pretending you are talking politics!" she snarled back.

Their warm-hearted chat was interrupted by the arrival of the newcomers. Palladius led the guests into the hall and past the curious retainers, of which there were not many, to present them to his Lordship and Lady seated at the high table.

"My Lord and Lady Cyricus Doukas," he called out loudly. "Sir Talon de Gilles and the Lady de Gilles."

Cyricus blinked. A Frank! Ignorant sod; probably couldn't speak a word of Greek, which meant he would have to dredge up what French he had gleaned at his tutor's table. What was the fellow doing here?

He sat up and stared at the couple in front of him. What he saw was not so much a knight as an unkempt, slightly foppish looking merchant with, it had to be admitted, a very beautiful woman at his side. The man looked muscular, his beard barely concealed a long scar, and another, smaller one that ran from just under his eye down his right cheek gave a slightly sinister aspect to his visage. The curiously unsettling green eyes that regarded Doukas seemed, however, to be free of guile; they were friendly and respectful.

163

"If I may to present my wife, Rav'an," he said in good Greek, after delivering an elaborate bow while sweeping off his hat. Cyricus barely heard him. He could hardly take his eyes off the woman and couldn't remember her name within seconds of being told. He stared rudely at the apparition in front of him who, despite being in an advanced state of pregnancy, was stunningly beautiful. The pale olive skin and almost heart-shaped face with the huge gray eyes and the full lips of a mouth that was ever so slightly too large left him speechless.

His own wife scowled at him. "Where are your manners, Cyr?" she demanded, having had enough of this ogling. "I apologize for my husband, he sometimes has lapses of attention," she said to the visitors.

"Shut your mouth, Cyr, it's drooling," she snapped in an undertone to him, then she simpered at the visitors. "Please join us for supper. You arrived just in time."

Talon bowed low again and smiled. Rav'an dropped a demure curtsey. They were shown to seats to the right of their hosts at the high table overlooking the retainers who sat below.

Cyricus managed to pull himself together and sat back, taking a long swig of wine from his silver cup. He tore his eyes away from Rav'an and glanced at Talon, who was seated at the table looking slightly amused, but who also seemed keen to talk.

"De Gilles? Isn't that a Frankish name?" Cyricus demanded in Attic Greek.

"It is indeed, Sir. You are very perceptive."

"So where do you come from, Sir Talon?"

"Originally we came by ship from Sicily. I am in the service of King William. You know him? We visited Paphos and met with the emperor—alas, very briefly; then we were on our way north."

Cyrus sat up. "King William is indeed a friend of the emperor," he stated with surprise and a touch more respect. He had not expected to be conversing with one of the barbaric Franks in Attic Greek. Perhaps this merchant knight had influence with Isaac. It could, therefore, do no harm for him to treat him civilly. "What brought you to this remote area of Cyprus, Sir Talon?"

"Thank you for asking, my Lord. Yes, yes it is remote, isn't it? It was the foul weather and God's grace. We ran into a storm while on our way north towards Rhodes, where my wife has family and I have business, and our ship sustained some damage. We were blown far off course; hence we were forced to put into the nearest place of refuge, which turned out to be your harbor. I hope you don't mind? I will willingly pay for our stay."

Cyricus shrugged his shoulders dismissively, but he was becoming interested in how much he could lever out of this bland-looking man.

Talon continued. "They have no accommodation in that small village which would be suitable for my wife and her condition. I decided to throw myself upon your mercy and kindness and beg a few nights of sanctuary in your home while repairs are underway."

Flavia had by this time turned to Rav'an and was attempting to engage her in conversation, with minimal results. Rav'an only spoke a smattering of French, and little Greek. Flavia switched to her own limited French and tried again. The results were less than satisfactory.

Talon smiled at Flavia. "You must forgive my wife for not understanding, my Lady. She is from Sicily. I am having a hard time teaching her my own language! Ha Ha!" he laughed loudly as though he had made a joke. Flavia shook her head and stared at Rav'an, who, head down, was nibbling at the roasted grouse in front of her. Cyricus joined in the laughter and slapped Talon on the shoulder. "To have a beauty like this for wife? I wouldn't care what language she spoke! Or none at all!" He glanced at his wife, who glowered, and he subsided into his cups again.

Once they were past the pleasantries Talon had no difficulty in passing along the news of Isaac's movements. Cyricus nodded his head. "He is probably meting punishment upon the merchants in that foul city, Paphos. It does not pay to be disrespectful of our new Emperor. He appointed me Castilian as a reward for helping him take Famagusta, you know."

Talon wondered what part the heavily overweight man might have played in storming a fortified town like Famagusta.

"How did you know my name?" Cyricus asked him. His voice had become slightly slurred, as he had drunk copious amounts of wine under the disapproving glare of his wife. His eyes rarely left the demure form of Rav'an, who kept her eyes downcast the entire meal. Talon had a shrewd idea what was passing through the lecherous man's mind. They would have to be very careful.

"I know of you by reputation, Lord Doukas. The people of Paphos told me of your exploits, and several told me that I should try to meet you. Fate has stepped in and allowed me that opportunity. I am honored to be here."

Cyricus beamed, then belched and took another swig. He shrugged depreciatingly, pretending modesty. "I did my part for the emperor and he rewarded me appropriately. This is a very important stronghold, and the emperor wanted only the most trusted of his people to hold it."

Talon raised his cup. "I would toast you, my host. To trusted and loyal servants of the Emperor!" he said, pretending to quaff his wine.

Cyricus chuckled and then gulped his cup down. Even Flavia, who had given up trying to converse with Rav'an, took a large swig—probably to soften the blow of not having anyone to talk to other than her pig of a husband, who was signaling for the wine bearer to refill his cup. She noticed with disgust her husband's gaze wander back to Rav'an, who now looked up and smiled innocently at him.

He nearly spilled his wine, he was so surprised.

"How... how long would you like, I mean, intend to stay?" he asked Talon, never taking his eyes off Rav'an and wiping his mustache with a gleam in his eye.

"As long as you will have us, my Lord, and the repairs are done. I was told it might even be a week," said Talon with an ingratiating smile, as though he had noticed nothing.

Darkness had fallen and servants were placing torches in sconces along the walls of the hall. Expensive candles also graced the high table, shedding a sputtering light upon the table cloth littered with small bones and spilled food. His lordship was not a tidy eater.

"Tell me more of the emperor, my Lord. I heard that he is a strong man, even a great man," Talon said, as he observed the coming and going of the servants out of the corner of his eye.

"He is a Komnenos, so of course he is brilliant. His distant uncle is also brilliant, but alas, there is no love lost between them. Isaac is a shrewd tactician. Prince William knows this and may use him to help take the empire of Byzantine away from Andronicus. I myself am a Doukas and related via his grandfather, who was the Komnenos Doukas," Cyricus said proudly, and he placed his finger alongside his nose, looking cunning. Flavia looked surprised and then nervous at this display of confidence and placed a restraining hand on his arm.

Cyricus chose to ignore her and carried on. "The way he took control of this island was a lesson to all men. Cyprus is rich—I don't know if you noticed the fertile valleys on the way here—and there is much trade between this island and Venice, as well as the mainland.

We have extensive copper mining, too. It won't be long before he strikes out and takes what is his by right."

"You mean... ?" Talon asked tentatively, his eyes wide open with feigned surprise.

"Oh yes, he intends to take for himself the Empire, and Prince William is going to help him do it."

Talon continued to sound astonished. "Indeed, I can think of no one more worthy of the right," he said.

Just at that moment Talon felt a wet nose on the end of a muzzle being thrust into his side. Turning, he saw it was one of the hounds he had met several nights ago. He fondled its ears and slipped it a morsel of chicken. Then its companion, seeing rewards were on offer, did the same and went off with a nice piece of pork between its teeth. Both seemed pleased to see him.

Rav'an looked askance at him, but he just winked at her.

"Lord Doukas also noticed. "I see you like hounds, Sir Talon," he slurred with genuine surprise in his voice.

"I have always had a soft spot for hunting hounds, My Lord," Talon responded with an easy smile.

This seemed to revive their host somewhat. He actually sat up straight in his chair and beamed. "Then while you are here we must go hunting! I have hawks and hounds for both the small and the large game, which are plentiful here," Cyricus announced.

Talon smiled again. "I look forward to that, Lord."

Later, as they were preparing for bed in a guest room at the end of the same passage as the Lord and his lady, Rav'an made sure that their door was securely closed and forced a wedge in to keep it so; then she turned to Talon with a grimace of disgust.

"You once told me that the Byzantine Greeks were civilized people, Talon. I saw no evidence of that tonight. And do those smelly hounds have to be with us all night?" she demanded, pointing to the two huge animals that had attached themselves to Talon and were now settling down on a large mat near the window.

Talon grinned in the flickering light of the candle. He couldn't resist saying, "You look enchanting and so *demure,* my Love. Who would have thought it?"

He laughed at her glare, then waved his hand at the hounds.

"Yes, they do have to stay. If they wander, who knows what they might find creeping about in the night? You are spoiled, my Love. We spent too long in China. We find everyone else is a barbarian by comparison. But... this man is not typical. He might use the fork, but he really is a pig."

"His wife isn't any better. Did you see how she shoveled the food into her mouth?" Rav'an exclaimed. "Yecch! I wonder what is living in our beds!" She went over and drew wide the curtains shrouding the bed, then pulled the bed clothes open to examine them by candlelight.

"I am making a huge sacrifice here, what with flea-ridden beds and dogs in my bedroom, my Husband. Nor shall I rest comfortably until this plan of yours is done, I swear it. How much longer will it be before you have the castle for ourselves?"

"Shhh!" He put a finger to his lips. "I hope that by midday tomorrow all will be changed," Talon said. "Come here," he whispered.

She slipped into his arms. "I hope he doesn't try to get into this chamber tonight, the lecherous old fart." She giggled and clutched at her throat theatrically with one hand as though trying to choke herself, while pretending to be sick.

"He'll never get in." Talon shook with mirth at her antics. "I'll set his own hounds on him. There's no love lost there."

He glanced out of the narrow opening in the wall that overlooked the north side. There was nothing to be seen at present. He looked up at the sky. There was a thin crescent of a moon tonight, which would help Henry and his men with the slave pens, and Guy's men who were going to secure the harbor.

Later that same night, Yosef and his men, having waited patiently for the inhabitants of the fortress to go to their beds and the candles to be extinguished, began their preparations for the next morning. Each one of them had a task to perform and he needed to be in place well before dawn.

Yosef and Junayd first walked casually past the kennels, which Talon had described to them, and some meat went into the compound. There were scuffles as the half-dozen dogs growled and fought over the scraps, which were covered with a strong powder to make them sleep. Yosef and Junayd waited in the dark shadows until there were no further sounds from the dogs, then went to the north tower and lowered ropes to the waiting men below. Guy had selected the toughest of his men to join Yosef. It didn't take long for them to climb the ropes and to gather on the deserted ramparts.

Yosef led them to various places in and around the walls, the bailey, its kitchens and storerooms where servants slept, and especially near the barracks. There they were to hide until the word was given by Talon. There was only one time when Yosef thought he might have to deal with one of the guards. The man seemed to be restless and walked around the bailey tower, peering into the night, but all that greeted him were the usual night noises of owls and the squeaks of small animals in the nearby forest below. Yosef kept an eye on the man, ready to take him out with an arrow; but eventually the fellow yawned, stretched, then returned to the barracks, closing the door behind him.

For the period of about an hour there was intense activity as the phantoms, guided by Yosef and Junayd, found their hiding places; and then Talons 'servants', augmented by crew members, settled down to await the dawn. Much now depended upon how successful Reza and Dimitri were with the slaves.

Henry and his men were waiting under cover of darkness. Dar'an, Maymun and Nasuh were in Reza's charge; their task was to first immobilize the guards and the overseers at the slave camp. Then Henry and his men would enter the compound and try to ascertain who was capable of joining with them for the uphill trek in the morning. The goal was to give the appearance of the usual movements of the slaves arriving for the day's labor.

Talon had made it clear that should the alarm be raised by some alert guard, his people inside the castle would take out the sentries and open the gates, but he would prefer their strike to be completed without excessive loss of life. As he explained it to his officers.

"Lord Hsü taught me that it preferable to surround your enemy, even as he watches you doing so, and then you have a choice of whether to annihilate his forces or take them prisoner. A pitched battle could go badly at any point, as they still outnumber us, and thus is undesirable, so control your more bloodthirsty men."

But some bloodshed was unavoidable. Talon and Reza had discussed whether to allow the camp guards to live, but finally agreed that it was far too risky. So Reza and Dar'an slipped forward in the dark to began their bloody work. The drink-sodden camp guards were killed first, and then the two assassins hunted down the overseers in their beds. It was over within minutes, and Reza appeared at Henry's side to tap him on the shoulder. Henry jerked; he had not heard a sound, but there was Reza pointing to the compound. Shaking Dimitri awake, Henry passed the word along to his waiting men. It was time to move.

Quietly, as they didn't want any noise to alert someone in the nearby village, the crew, with Henry in the lead, passed through the gates of the compound. Henry saw shadows moving swiftly about the compound: Reza and his killers making sure that no one other than the slaves inhabited the noisome place. There were three huts, more like open-walled sheds, where the prisoners were clustered in exhausted sleep.

As he stood over the pitiful groups of half-starved men, Henry shook his head. The slaves had no form of comfort, lying in their own filth, unable to go anywhere without dragging along the other men who were chained to them.

"Wake them up, do it as quietly as you can," he told his men.

Soon most of the slaves were awake, their scared, drawn faces looked up at a large group of heavily armed, bearded men who were complete strangers.

"Who speaks Greek?" Dimitri demanded.

Many raised their hands. A frightened murmuring began.

"Be quiet! We are not here to harm you!" Henry raised his voice. The murmuring quieted.

"Who are Franks?" Several others raised their arms in mute surprise.

Then Reza asked if there were any Arab speakers, and still more raised their hands.

"Well, we have quite a party here," Henry remarked. "Dimitri and Reza, will you translate what I have to say?"

They both nodded the affirmative, and Henry then explained what he wanted from the slaves. When he finished, he asked, "What time in the morning do you leave for the Castle?"

Sergeant Palladius began his rounds as always by checking that the guards at the gate were awake. It would not be the first time he had come across one of the younger, more callow youths who called themselves soldiers asleep in a corner when they should have been watching the trail below.

While he was quite confident that they could hold off an army because of the castle's perch on the ridge, Palladius knew that an enemy could always surprise the unwary and the careless. He talked briefly to the sentries, who assured him that nothing untoward had occurred during the night. Even the dogs had been quiet, which was a little unusual. The only thing of passing interest had been that one of the men had taken a walk along the North side just as a routine check in the early hours and had seen some torchlight down in the

170

slave quarters, but he had heard no alarms. The sentry only mentioned it as a point of interest in another boring night.

Palladius noted the report, but he was too busy kicking the day guards out of bed and threatening them with a flogging if they didn't show up for duty within the half hour to ponder the event. Having then dismissed the night guard and shoved the gate guards into place, he awaited the inevitable arrival of his Lord and master. He needed to compose his features into one of respect; his contempt for his master sometimes made him forget himself. Palladius was a professional mercenary who believed in good soldiering, and this was not it.

Cyricus showed up, looking dissipated and hung over. He rubbed his eyes, leaned over a trough and, groaning, splashed water over his bloated face, then glanced up to see Talon standing nearby with a friendly smile on his face. Palladius was standing impassively just across the barbican yard near the tower.

"Ah, good morning, Sir Talon. I didn't expect you to be up at this early hour. Did you have a good night?" Cyricus leered.

"Good morning, my Lord," Talon replied, ignoring the implied meaning. "It is a beautiful day, and I was just admiring your home. The view from this castle must be extraordinary! How it must warm your heart every day to see your domain spread out beneath you."

"Well, why don't you come up to the top of that tower with me and my unsociable Sergeant? We can see the view and watch the slaves on their way up to complete the repairs on the other tower." Cyricus grunted as he shook his head to dash the water from his eyes.

Talon smiled again. "Thank you, my Lord. I would like that very much." He joined Cyricus, who had begun to stride off. The two hounds came up to Talon, wagging their tails and dancing, vying with one another for his attention.

"I have never seen those two behave in this manner before," Cyricus growled. "Can't think what is the matter with them. Normally they are very suspicious of strangers."

"A merchant's lot is to travel far and wide. Perhaps they recognize some scent on me that reminds them of their former home," Talon said lightly.

They joined Palladius, who nodded respectfully to Talon and glanced at the hounds. He raised his eyebrows at the sight of their behavior; obviously he was impressed, but he said nothing. He turned and led the way into the tower. They climbed the stone steps —Palladius and Talon easily, Cyricus with huffing and wheezing—

and emerged into the soft light of dawn to stand overlooking the narrow track that led to the gates below.

Cyricus waved his arm around him in a wide arc. "Do you like the view, Sir Talon? It is all mine. Look around! This castle is impregnable from all sides," he bragged.

The view was everything that Talon had expected and hoped. Turning around he exclaimed in genuine awe at the view. "It is magnificent! You are perfectly right. No one could take this castle by frontal assault!"

He turned around completely. He could see quite clearly that there were now two ships in the distant harbor; he hoped that Guy and Henry had taken the port during the night. If it was secure, he at least had an escape route if all failed here. He felt confident that Yosef and his men had completed their tasks, as no alarms had been raised. Had there been any disturbance, this hard-bitten soldier with them would have been the one to report it, and here came the slave gang, right on time.

The three men watched as the chained slaves hobbled up the steep pathway, then turned towards the gates. The overseers where shouting and cracking their whips with enthusiasm and the men staggered along, carrying what appeared to be heavy loads for the work to be done. Neither of the men nearby evinced any sign of suspicion as the gang stumbled to a halt on a shouted command from one of the overseers. Talon, however, could recognize Henry acting as one of the noisy overseers and Reza pretending to be a slave, despite their disguises.

Palladius raised his hand in acknowledgement and shouted down to the men at the gate to open them. Cyricus simply watched through bleary eyes; his hangover was fierce this morning, so his attention was distracted. The gates began to open and the overseers were herding the first of the slaves into the courtyard when Palladius frowned and started. Then he jerked his head up and almost ran to the other side of the tower to stare down at the men in the yard.

"There is something wrong, here," he muttered to himself. "These are not the same men..." he exclaimed, but he never finished the sentence. A blow on the back of his head sent him sprawling unconscious at the feet of his master.

Cyricus stepped back in surprise and gaped down at his sergeant. He opened his mouth to shout in alarm, but stopped as he realized that the point of a curious looking sword was very close to his throat. The hand holding it was as steady as a rock. The eyes above the blade end were as cold as green ice. Gone was the avuncular behavior exhibited by his guest of the previous evening.

"I suggest that you do nothing, nothing at all, and all will be well, my Lord," Talon said, and waved his other arm high in the air as he spoke.

Suddenly all was activity in the yard below. Figures appeared, as though from within the walls themselves, and ran in several directions. The slaves suddenly were no longer chained together and were just as inexplicably armed to the teeth. The astonished guards at the gates were surrounded and disarmed before they even had a chance to put up any resistance.

Then a man, his face half obscured, bounded into sight on top of the tower. He glanced at Talon and laughed, then knelt beside the fallen Palladius to secure his hands and feet with a rope. Rising gracefully, he walked up to Cyricus while saying something to Talon, who responded with a grin and a nod. Cyricus found his own hands tied behind him and was shoved rudely down the steps by the stranger, with Talon following behind.

Cyricus who had hitherto been too surprised to do anything but gape, now came to life. "What are you doing, you rogue!" he gobbled with growing rage. "I'll see you dangle from a rope, you pirate, you thief... you, you Frank! What is the meaning of this!" he roared.

"Why, my Lord, I have just relieved you of your castle and you are now my prisoner. If you behave, you shall have payment for it. I would advise you to take the offer, as that is the best price you are going to receive from anyone," Talon responded.

Talon looked over towards the barracks to see his men preparing a fire near each doorway. The fires were lit, and Yosef tossed some powder into the flames which produced much smoke that was then wafted in through the grills of the stout doors.

"Are you setting fire to this place? You are mad!" Cyricus exclaimed, horrified.

"Oh no, but the doors are bolted on the inside. We only intend to smoke them out," Talon said, as he observed Palladius being hustled onto the yard to join the other guards. The sergeant looked dazed and confused. The dense smoke that Reza's men were fanning into the barracks had woken the guards, who choked and coughed on the acrid fumes entering their barracks. Muffled shouts from the soldiers could be heard as they clamored to be let out, but when the bolts were drawn and the guards saw the fires on the thresholds, they fell back, coughing uncontrollably.

Dimitri shouted, "If you want to live, come out with no weapons! No weapons, no knives nor swords nor spears, nothing, if you value your lives."

There was discussion within the barracks amid much coughing and retching. "Yes, yes, curse you to hell! We surrender! Let us out!" someone yelled from within before he was cut off by a fit of coughing.

"Do as I say or you will all die!" Dimitri shouted. He nodded to Yosef, now joined by Dar'an, and their men shoveled the smoking fires out of the way. Six archers, bows drawn, covered the doors, and other men stood ready with spears and swords just in case the men inside wanted to perform some heroics. The doors were dragged open and a dense smoke poured out, followed by men staggering and gasping and coughing violently, too shaken to put up any resistance. Their weapons had been left behind.

Dar'an wasted no time. His men rushed forward and began to tie the men's arms behind them, then several slipped into the barracks to see if anyone still lingered and to secure the weapons. Having satisfied himself that resistance was over in that quarter, Yosef ran up to salute Talon and report. "There is no one left in there, Master. They are our prisoners. Dimitri and Dar'an have them."

"Nice work, you two," Talon smiled. Just as he said this, there were screams and the sounds of a scuffle from within the bailey,

The lady of the house came boiling out of the main entrance to stand at the top of the steps screaming at the men who were trying to hold her still. Flavia was a stout woman whose strength seemed more than a match for the two men trying to prevent her from getting away.

"Cyr!" She screamed, "Who are these brutes? Get your slimy hands off me, you rogues!" She struggled, which made her whole body wobble and shake violently. "My husband will see you hanged for this insolence! Cyr! Help me, you worthless prick!" she screamed at Cyricus.

Then Rav'an appeared, with a couple of Reza's men in attendance. "Be quiet, Madam!" she said in a sharp, clear voice. "Be quiet or I shall stick you with this knife." She waved a slim, bright blade under Flavia's nose in a menacing manner. Flavia's small brown eyes grew wide with shock. Although she could not understand a word, the meaning was clear enough.

"You! You are part of this? God save us!" Flavia exclaimed in her own language.

"I regret to inform you that your husband no longer owns this castle," Rav'an told her, in halting French. "My husband does, and should you forget it, he will kill your 'Cyr' right in front of you. He'll probably hang him. My husband doesn't like to make a mess."

Flavia collapsed. She almost fell, but her escort held her upright with a great effort, then frog-marched her down the short flight of steps to join her husband where, after glaring at him, she sat on the ground with a thump. Leaving them under a tight guard, Talon joined Reza and Rav'an. Reza had just emerged from the bailey. "How did it go in there, Brother?" he asked.

Reza laughed. "We secured the kitchens and the servants on the top floor, but I was not prepared for this one!" he indicated Flavia. "I'm surprised I am still in one piece. We'll have to work on Khuzaymah's dragon fighting skills. She threw him across the room and was about to beat him to death with a stool before I got to her. That is one formidable woman."

"Rav'an has tamed her. She has a way with knives," Talon said, with a grin at his wife. "Are there any other places where we might meet any resistance?"

"We have scoured the entire place, Talon. I really think it is ours." Reza laughed exultantly.

Henry came up and joined them. "Good to see you are alive and well in the lion's den, Talon. Do we really own this place now?"

Talon smiled. "It might easily have been the other way around, Henry. I am glad that our ploy worked."

"Our real slaves are too weak to do any more, Talon. What should I do with them?"

"I suggest you keep them under guard until we have disposed of his Lordship and his men, then we can decide. Get some of the crew to bring food to them, Henry. You are right, they don't look in very good shape," Talon said. Henry hurried off to deal with his new charges.

"Come with me, both of you. I want to talk to the ex-Lord of the castle." Talon put his arm around Rav'an's waist as he walked.

His friends accompanied him the short distance to stand in front of Cyricus and his wife, who scrambled to her feet but was now looking very dispirited and frightened. All the fight had left her.

"Are you going to kill us?" Cyricus asked, trying to show defiance. "You know that Isaac will take this place back from you in a matter of a week. Then you will all dangle from the North walls, in pieces!"

175

"If there is to be any dangling, it will be you if you do not do as I say," Talon told him, and by his tone Cyricus finally became aware that he had very much underestimated his new enemy.

"What do you want of me?" he muttered.

Talon motioned to Nasuh, who had been hovering in the background. The young man walked up and handed over a leather bag that jingled.

"I think we should agree that you have lost this castle, Lord Doukas. While I am sure that you have made many enemies in your life who would show you no mercy, I am about to do so. Here is payment for the castle and the retainers who wish to stay on. You will leave with the clothes on your back and one chest of clothes for the Lady Flavia. Your personal servants will accompany you, as will your men at arms minus their weapons, and any of the stable hands or falconers who wish to do so. You will leave within the hour, Sir."

Cyricus was too stunned to speak, but he eyed the bag of coins with a furtive eye.

"I shall provide you and the Lady Flavia with suitable mounts," Talon continued, and then smiled. "At least, Lord Doukas, you got a fair price." Talon tossed the bag of gold at Lord Doukas's feet, where it fell with loud chinking.

Cyricus glowered and tried to shrug against his bonds. "You might have won this time, Sir Talon, but I shall be back with the full force of the empire behind me. You will pay with more than gold, I swear it!" he shouted.

Talon stepped forward till his face was very close to the former Castilian, who felt the menace emanating from his captor and shrank back. "You will do well to remember how I took this castle, my Lord. My men can find you and your family no matter where you hide. We are assassins, and we know our trade. You would do well to sleep with one eye open as long as you are still in this country.

"You will leave Cyprus on the very first ship you can find to take your worthless carcass out. I recommend you go to Famagusta and leave from there. The emperor is still in Paphos, I would imagine. I doubt that Isaac will take very kindly to you losing the castle to me in this manner. He is a vengeful man, you yourself said so." Talon spoke in a low voice, but it left Cyricus white-faced.

Talon signaled to his men and gave them directions to assemble the cowed soldiers and the servants in the yard of the barbican just in front of the main gates, which were now open.

He addressed them in Greek. "This castle now belongs to me and my people. You are free to go with all your belongings. Those of you who wish to stay may ask to do so, but it will be up to me to decide if I want you. The rest of you should leave with your Lord here."

By this time Lord Doukas was mounted on a horse, as was Flavia. Their bewildered and shaken personal servants were gathered in a small cluster around them, clutching their meagre possessions. All were warily watching the tough looking sailors and the glowering slaves who surrounded them, still unsure whether their lives were forfeit or not. Reza was on the walls with his men, making sure that there was no threat from outside during the proceedings. Talon stood on the steps overlooking the crowd with Rav'an next to him. It had come as a shock for some to hear his words, and he could hear murmured conversations, questions, even muted wailing.

Then a hand went up. "I would stay, Sir. I have your word that I will not be harmed?" a man from the stables asked, his tone apprehensive.

"You have my word as a Templar Knight," Talon stated. The murmuring grew louder at this. A Templar Knight had bested their Lord and master? Before long fifteen men and their wives were stepping forward and offering their services, including, he was pleased to see, two men he knew to be hawkers.

He smiled to himself. Lord Doukas was seething with rage, but the man had been frightened enough by Talon's words to hold his peace. The venomous look he directed at the ones who wanted to stay said it all. But there was another unwelcome surprise to come for Lord Doukas.

Palladius, having been released, was standing with the wretched-looking soldiers. Seemingly on impulse, he shouldered his way to the front of the assembly and approached Talon. Rav'an hissed a warning and his men's hands went to their swords. Talon put out a restraining hand. "Wait," he said.

Palladius stopped several paces before Talon, then went down on one knee, his head bowed. "Sir Talon, I would serve you. Will you take me? I will serve you faithfully in any capacity," he pleaded.

Lord Doukas could no longer restrain himself. "You treacherous bastard!" he roared. "Turncoat and traitor, I shall see you hang!" he spluttered in his rage.

Palladius glanced back at him with contempt. "You were never a soldier. You have murdered and raped your way to this position. The man I wish to serve is ten times your worth. I will take my chances with him." He looked up at Talon with a plea in his eyes.

"Will you take me on, Sir Talon? I will serve in the pig sties if I have to. I do not want to follow that man ever again."

Talon looked hard at him. After a small pause he said, "Yes, I will take you, Palladius. As a soldier, but," his eyes became flint-like, "your word of honor. Do not ever betray me."

"I swear upon the cross and Almighty God I shall be faithful to you to my death, Sir Talon. May he strike me now if he finds deceit in my heart." Palladius stated in a clear voice.

"Then remain here," Talon said. He then waved the Lord Doukas and his now weeping wife Flavia out towards the open gates. The sorry looking assembly turned and departed. There was, however, one last humiliation for Lord Doukas. He called to his hounds in his usual peremptory manner, but they hesitated and looked back with big eyes at Talon, who patted his thigh. They ran happily back to him, wagging their tails. "Sit," he commanded, and they settled down at his heels.

"They appear to wish to stay as well, my Lord. Safe journey, and don't forget what I said." Talon waved at the by now puce-faced Lord Doukas.

When the last one had left the castle the gates were slammed shut and the cheering began. The sailors and the slaves embraced one another, while Reza's men danced with joy on the battlements.

On the steps, Talon kissed Rav'an to more cheers from the wildly happy men who could hardly believe they had succeeded in their mission.

"I am beginning to wonder if that fat pig will survive the journey to Famagusta, Talon," Reza laughed. "He was so angry I thought he was going to have a heart attack when you kept his hounds." They both laughed.

Leaving Rav'an in charge of the bailey to organize, with the help of Dimitri, the servants who had stayed behind, Talon joined Reza on the tower to watch the Lord and his Lady depart. The dejected Lord Doukas and Flavia, trailed by their confused followers, descended the pathway of the ridge and took the path down the south-east side of the mountain towards the distant city of Famagusta.

"Send Yosef and Dar'an after them, keeping out of sight, to watch them. I want to know if they have a change of plan or direction within the next few hours," Talon said to Reza. "But I don't think he will tarry. He would not be judged kindly by Isaac."

Reza grinned. "I had my reservations about whether this was going to work, Brother, but we have possession of a castle! It is hard to believe!"

"Not just a castle, Reza. Also land to go with it that is fertile, even a mine! There is much to do, but it is a good beginning," Talon said with a wan smile. He felt as if he had been holding his breath for twelve hours. "Let's send for our friends, and then we can have a feast. I want to see Rostam, Jannat and Max safe up here. Tell Guy to come up if he can bear to leave his precious ships. Don't forget old Simon. I leave that to you, Brother."

"I will send a party to the harbor to bring them to their new home at once," Reza said. "Rav'an is right. You truly are a fox, my Brother."

Yours, Lord, is the greatness and the power and the glory
the splendor and the majesty.
Yours, Lord, is the kingdom exalted over all.
—Gibirol

Chapter 15
Emperor of Cyprus

The news reached Emperor Isaac Komnenos as he was readying to leave Larnaca for Famagusta, a journey of several hours by horse. At first he refused to believe the information his secretary presented to him. Diocles, whose official title was First Minister, was an old man whose usefulness was just about over as far as Isaac was concerned, but he had served faithfully and knew all the ins and outs of the administration, so Isaac kept him on.

"Is this some kind of joke?" the Emperor demanded, when he had finished reading for a second time the document from Famagusta. It had been sent by the governor of the city.

"N... No, my Lord," whispered Diocles, his face gray under his beard. His eyes were frightened and his hands, which he tried to conceal in his voluminous sleeves, were shaking.

Isaac read it again a third time to make sure of what he had read.

The news was unbelievable; the castle of Kantara had been taken without a fight! According to the governor, who confessed he didn't have all the facts because Lord Doukas had recently taken ship and fled the island. The castle had fallen to one Talon de Gilles who had tricked his way in and then turfed the Lord out with his entire garrison, servants and all.

By the time he read the last word, Isaac's anger had heated his blood so much it mounted to his otherwise sallow face—not a pretty sight—and he shrieked with rage.

Diocles and the other servants cowered at the storm of invective and howls of fury that followed. Isaac literally tore at his hair and gnashed his teeth he was so incensed, and all who could fled to hide until the storm abated. Those less fortunate, who had to stay and witness the terrifying display, quaked and shook. It was so bad that the aged Diocles feared he would faint. It was hours before Isaac was coherent enough to speak and to be understood.

"We leave at once!" he shouted. "Bring my horse, I shall go now! Follow as quickly as you can."

There were frantic efforts to comply. By the time the palace tent was emptied, the emperor was gone, and with him his cavalry.

As he rode, Isaac thought back on his visit to Paphos. He had arrived to find that, although the town was subdued and properly cowed, there had been an incident on the quayside. The sergeant of the squadron had reported that his commander and many others had been killed when they had tried to detain a merchant galley, one that had been leaving the city without permission. There were wild stories of ambush, and more particularly about a noisome explosion which had decimated the ranks of the cavalry. The sergeant was barely coherent as he stood in front of his emperor, trembling with fear.

"It was like a bolt of fire from heaven, Your Eminence," he stammered.

"It was Greek fire?" one of Isaac's officers offered.

"No my Lord," the poor man stuttered. " It was more like a clap of thunder, and then fire, but it killed man and horse."

"Superstitious nonsense, my Lord," sneered the senior officer. "The men are lying and they should be punished."

Isaac had agreed. Neither he nor his commanders had believed the soldier for an instant, and the protesting man had been executed for lying and cowardice.

The rest of the squadron had been deprived of their horses and sentenced to slavery, but the rumors of a flash of light and a loud blast of noise like a single clap of thunder, followed by much smoke and destruction on the quayside, somehow persisted.

Isaac had been informed that there was a man by the name of Sir Talon de Gilles, a very rich merchant, who had recently appeared in Paphos but had since disappeared. Isaac had planned to detain Sir Talon and relieve him of his wealth, then send him on his way. A single Frank was not worth cultivating in this current atmosphere of shifting alliances; his friend Salah Ed Din had little use for the Franks, either. It would have been a service to both of them to get rid of the man.

Now this Sir Talon de Gilles had by all accounts stolen a castle from him! The sheer audacity of the act almost made him choke when he thought about it. The ride to Famagusta was normally several hours long, but it was less at the breakneck speed he now rode. Along the way he was able to think. He swore he would find Lord Doukas, no matter where he had fled and hang him and his

181

entire family up by their heels for allowing such a thing to happen. Before the man died, he would tell all, because the torture he would be subjected to would be painful indeed. Doukas would be gibbering with agony before he died.

The riders arrived at the gates of Famagusta by nightfall, and the gates were thrown open to cries of, "The Emperor! Long live the Emperor!" shouted from the towers. Trumpets blared to warn the inhabitants that their lord and master had returned. Just before he rode into the city, Isaac turned his head to stare at the ridge of the mountains to the North. He thought he could see the tiny speck that was the castle high on the mountain. Was it mocking him? He would take care of that. The humiliation was almost more than he could bear.

It was too late to do much that evening, but before he retired Isaac called in his most trusted officer and gave him instructions to scour the city for anyone who had been at the castle during the takeover.

"Find Lord Doukas," he ground out through gritted teeth. "I don't care if he is related, I want him dead! I want anyone, anyone at all, man, woman, or child, who was at the castle on that day to be found and brought to me. If they try to hide, dig them out like moles! And find out who was the ship's captain who took Doukas off the island. I want his head!" This last was delivered in a high-pitched scream.

General Bourtzes was a veteran of many wars and skirmishes, having served in the Byzantine army before he decided that banditry and the pay of a mercenary was preferable to that of the Imperial army. It certainly paid better in loot and women. He and his like-minded men had helped the emperor wrest the island from the former governor, whom they had summarily executed.

Bourtzes gripped his sword, bowed his head, and left.

Isaac slowly began to calm down. He felt hungry and thirsty. Calling for his steward, he gave him instructions. "Bring food, and wine—the very best, or you shall be flogged. And hurry! Then I shall bathe, after which you will bring me one of those girls we looked at last week. On second thought, make it two of them. Tell Tamara to make sure they are bathed before I see them; the last lot were smelly."

Tamara was his favorite concubine. The girls had been kidnapped from four of the formerly wealthy merchants on the island. Two were from Famagusta; the others had come from

Episkopi and Paphos respectively. None of the girls was older than fourteen. The servant bowed, and then vanished.

For his part, Bourtzes sent out his men to do the work required, and by dawn the next day there were a number of prisoners under guard. The emperor awoke late with a pounding head after a night of wine and girls. After a leisurely breakfast of roasted quail, fruit, and oil-dipped bread washed down by more wine, he called for Bourtzes.

The general arrived, looking smart and businesslike in his burnished armor, to stand to attention in silence while the emperor finished off his meal.

"Well, did you find anyone?" Isaac demanded, as he wiped the grease off his mustache. He did not even deign to greet his senior officer, who put that down to the hangover.

"Indeed, we have a couple of dozen men, some women, and four children who were there at the time of the er... takeover, your Majesty. We are still scouring the city for others," Bourtzes stated, not looking at Isaac. Who knew what the emperor was capable of when he had not only a hangover but now this embarrassing issue to deal with?

What Bourtzes didn't add was that the city was seething with rumors. Some whispered that a magician had descended from the sky and chased the residents off with curses and threats. Others snorted and said that while there was certainly magic involved—how could there not be?—trickery and cunning were the main ingredients. Everyone was stunned by the sheer audacity of the entire business, and there were not a few who laughed under their sleeves at the emperor. He was decidedly unpopular and that was after less than a year of rule.

"Where are they?" Isaac asked pleasantly.

"Er... they are in the palace courtyard under guard, Sire." The prisoners had been brought up from the dungeons, where they had spent the night, to stand in the burning sun since dawn. It was now almost noon, and some had fainted from thirst and the heat. The children were grizzling and the women weeping.

"What did they have to say for themselves?"

"They all told the same story, Sire. They woke up to find the castle in other hands. The Lord and his lady were sent away by this man Sir Talon de Gilles and his men. There was no fighting at all. The garrison soldiers were smoked out of their barracks before they could do anything and were disarmed. Then they, too, were sent packing," Bourtzes stated respectfully. He was fully aware of the enormous humiliation to his leader and knew there would be terrible reprisals. He looked up at Isaac. "My Lord?"

"Yes, what is it?" Isaac was munching on a pomegranate. Someone had once old him they gave him vigor at night.

"With your permission, I would be honored to take an army and capture the castle from this usurper and bring his head to you."

"We'll deal with that later. First you will take the prisoners and hang every one of them just outside of the gates of the city. I shall have them punished as an example to all who would betray me!"

Bourtzes almost gaped with surprise but hesitated only a moment. "The women and children also, My Lord?"

"Are there any beauties among that lot?"

Bourtzes shook his head.

"There are too many to feed to the leopards, so hang them all and be done." Isaac turned away to admire the garden with its Arabic fountain and took a sip of wine that had been cooled with snow brought all the way from the top of Trudos Mountain.

Bourtzes bowed low and left to carry out the sentence. It took some hours to find a suitable place, but he borrowed an idea from Isaac's uncle, Andronikos Komnenos, who had recently hung over two hundred suspected traitors in a vineyard in Brusa, not far from Constantinople. It would take too long to build scaffolding for dozens of prisoners, but the tall, stout frames of a vineyard would do nicely.

Impervious to the wails, the screams and desperate pleas for mercy from the victims, he had his hardened mercenaries carried out the awful deed. The bodies were left to hang, and the horrified but gawking populace was forbidden to cut them down.

After a cursory examination of the still twitching corpses, Bourtzes reported back to Isaac and again asked permission to lead the expedition to take back the castle.

Isaac may have been a cruel and sadistic man, but he was not a fool. "You do realize why I had it fortified, don't you?" he demanded.

"Indeed, Sire. It is now almost impregnable," stated Bourtzes. "But, my Lord, I am sure my men are a match for any bunch of adventurer Franks who think they can—" he closed his mouth with a snap. He had nearly said, "make a fool of you." Fortunately, Isaac appeared not to notice.

"I have a mind to lead the expedition myself," he said. "I shall take much pleasure in feeding this upstart to the hunting leopards."

"With great respect, Sire," Bourtzes said politely, "would it not be best if you were here to keep an eye on any possibility of treachery in the city? I shall leave sufficient men behind to ensure your safety."

Isaac, however, was a Komnenos and not lacking in courage, despite his other failings.

"No, you will lead the men, but I shall be in overall command. This is a nut that I wish personally to crack." Isaac's large, dark eyes under their heavy lids swiveled to look directly at Bourtzes, giving warning that his mind was made up. "I shall take one of the leopards, Akropol. The other will stay here to guard the grounds while I am away."

The leopards were his hunting prizes, won with the rest of the island booty from his predecessor. They were fierce beasts that required tight control, as they were known to turn on their handlers and maul them. Isaac loved them, for they terrified his palace staff, and the mere threat to feed someone to them was enough to ensure their subservience.

Bourtzes sighed inwardly and bowed his acquiescence. "Yes, my Lord." He had the uneasy feeling that this man on the mountain top was not going to be an easy nut to crack, and he would have preferred that the emperor was out of harm's way. But if the fool wanted to get himself killed, that was his problem. Bourtzes' loyalty, such as it was, only went so far.

"We will bring him back alive and make an example of him to everyone on the island. I shall teach these pathetic people that it is I who am in charge, no one else," Isaac said, pursing his fleshy lips and spitting out an olive stone. It landed with an audible *plop* in a bowl of water nearby.

The army that Bourtzes assembled mustered in front of the city of Famagusta three weeks later. Diocles had arrived soon after the hangings and had been so dismayed that he'd allowed himself to complain to Bourtzes. "How on earth does the emperor hope to keep the loyalty of his subjects if he keeps plundering his own kingdom and hanging innocent peasants?" he'd wailed to the general when they were alone.

Bourtzes was sensible enough not to say anything, but his look warned Diocles not to continue in this vein. Diocles realized that he had committed a dangerous blunder and began to tremble. He was a frail old man with no wish to do harm; lately he had been so stressed he was considering asking for retirement. His big worry was whether the emperor saw retirement in the same light as he.

Bourtzes knew how valuable Diocles was at organization, although he despised him for his craven attitude towards the vicissitudes of life. He said nothing but filed away the incident for future use.

"We have spread ourselves very thin on the island, what with all the garrisons we now provide," Bourtzes said, referring to the mercenaries distributed around the major cities of the island. "We will have to conscript men from Famagusta and Larnaca, and use my men to give them a backbone. It should be a short campaign, as the castle is within a day's ride, and since even carts can cover the distance in two days, we should be able to provide for the men without difficulty."

Diocles nodded his head. "I shall see to the provisions and provide whatever siege machines are available," he said.

"We shall need scaling ladders most of all. I don't want to waste time tossing rocks at the fort. That'll take weeks, as it is well built. No, a full frontal attack is about all we will need, so make sure we have plenty of the ladders," Bourtzes replied.

Now Bourtzes sat on his horse and stared at the listless looking conscripts and wondered. "These Greeks of the island have not had to fight for anything for so long they have forgotten how!" he said to himself. There was a contemptuous curl to his lips as he watched his mercenaries shoving the five hundred conscripts into line prior to departure. Most of them had little or no armor; they carried short, badly made spears or rusty swords and knives. Their shields were a joke: one slash of his sword and he could cut one in half—including the arm that held it.

The emperor, seated on a pure white horse adorned with silver trappings from head to croup, appeared not to notice the pathetic state of his army and set out ahead of them, determined, it seemed, to lead them to glory and revenge. His extensive retinue included many servants and accoutrements designed to ensure his comfort. The hunting dogs, straining at their leashes and baying with excitement, agitated the leopard within its iron cage; it crouched, snarling. The animal handlers cast appreciative glances at the mountains looming in the distance. This was going to be an exciting expedition.

Bourtzes shouted at one of his mercenaries to keep the men moving at a brisk pace. It was already high noon; the emperor had kept the men waiting since dawn. Now he expected them to arrive at the base of the mountain before sunset. Bourtzes doubted that they would have covered five miles by then. He shook his head and cantered past the single trebuchet that was being hauled along by fourteen oxen.

It was a huge, unwieldy apparatus that ground its way along the pot-holed track that passed for a road, covering only one league in the hour; it was unlikely to arrive in three days, he surmised with a sour look at the huge engine. It was singularly unsuited for a steep mountain track, but the emperor had, as usual, dismissed the obvious and insisted. So here it was, on its way.

He came alongside the emperor's entourage before long and marveled at the extravagance. Isaac certainly liked his creature comforts. The baggage train for him alone consisted of twelve donkeys carrying everything from tents to foodstuffs to a huge, brightly polished pot that could fit a man. Bourtzes could only assume that it was a bath. He shook his head with disgust. They were not on one of the emperors' plundering tours of the island! They were going to besiege a castle, for God's sake!

However, he had learned long ago not to touch on this kind of subject, as Isaac didn't like it. His eyes would bulge, his lower lip would push forward, and the corners of his mouth turn down, then he would scream invectives at whomsoever had incurred his wrath.

The army stumbled to a stop on the southern slopes of the mountain late in the afternoon on the second day. The conscripts were tired, hot, dusty and thirsty. The supply train had not kept pace with the army, so they were hungry as well, even as the emperor's retinue prepared a lavish feast for his solitary enjoyment. Isaac was installed in a colorful tent with banners waving and servants running around doing his bidding and getting in the way of the real soldiers. Bourtzes was fed up with this nonsense, but he and his mercenaries were looking forward to one thing: the capture of the fort and the rapine and looting that would surely follow. And they had no intention of letting the miserable conscripts from the gutters of Famagusta join in that kind of festivity.

"I can't believe how useless these peasants are!" exclaimed one of his captains in a *sotto* voice. No one, not even the mercenaries, wanted to be overheard complaining and get reported to the emperor by some sneak informer. His punishments were savage and sadistic, and the leopard was always at the back of people's minds. However, the man could complain to his General; they had been together through many a scrape before they came to this pot hole of an island.

"How do you think we managed to conquer the island so easily?" Bourtzes responded. "If they were anything other than useless they would have put up a fight. So we use them as fodder; I will make them go first and bear the brunt of the usurper's defense, then when the defenders are tired out we will storm the walls."

The next day, the vanguard of the army assembled as best it could on and around the ridge upon which the castle stood. Unfortunately, the only level ground was half a mile down hill, so the trebuchet that they had hauled with such difficulty was completely useless, and the slope up to the ridge was nearly vertical in places. This caused the men to curse as they stumbled and scrambled up the steep slope, negotiating the scrub and thorns as they went. Then the captains kicked and shoved the men into place, prior to launching the first assault. Isaac on his white horse was there behind the men, dressed in his finest armor and gazing at the castle with a stern frown for the benefit of his followers. They would perform better if their leader bore a look of resolution.

He expected his men to take the castle before sunset and be done. Isaac stared balefully up at the top of the center fort and the banner flapping in the light wind. He could just make out the image of a red lion on one side of a shield with a ship on the other on a blue background. His face suffused with blood again as his anger threatened to overcome his outward regal calm.

That would soon come down, he snarled to himself. His horse shook its head as if disagreeing with him, but it was the flies bothering it, making it swish its tail and stamp. Isaac himself had to use his fly swat frequently. The flies had traveled with the army and were very aggressive, which did not improve his mood. His temper was further tried when Bourtzes approached and asked permission to go and parley before the battle.

Isaac stared at him with his slightly protruding eyes and snarled, "Why parley when I intend to gut him and hang him off the walls by his entrails before feeding him to my pet?"

"I assure you there will be a fight, Your Highness, but it will be an opportunity to see who we are up against. I want to look the man in his eyes and make him afraid."

Isaac had cursed inwardly but finally relented. "Don't waste any time. I want to be executing that bunch before dark."

He lifted his hand as a signal and Bourtzes nudged the herald next to him. "Come on," he growled. "It's time to earn your pay."

Talon stood on the ramparts of the southeast corner of the castle Kantara and stared down at the motley army assembling a quarter of a league away. He and his men had watched the dust rising from the army for two days, and now it was here below his castle. He glanced up at the small, dark clouds scudding across the azure blue sky; in the distance he could see the beginnings of a storm out to sea.

"It's as good a day as any for a fight," he murmured, then he turned to Reza and Max, who stood with him on the battlements. "It's just as well that we prepared ourselves. I hope Henry and Guy are ready." Both captains had stood off the harbor with their ships, just in case it occurred to anyone to sack the village. "If the rumors are to be believed, this emperor is the sort of man who would destroy any thing he can not have for himself."

"Those people in the villages were wise to come up here when we told them to," Reza said, nodding at the crowd of women and children huddled in the courtyard, which was protected from the barbican and the main gates by two stout walls. The men of the village had been pressed into service bringing large stones and rocks into the castle and lining the walkways of the walls with them. Now the village men and boys were crouched behind the parapets alongside the soldiers, waiting for the fight to begin.

The bleating of the village goats and sheep filled the air, making for a very noisy castle on this warm day. The animals were thirsty, for Talon rationed the water with care. The castle possessed two wells, but he didn't know how long these might provide for over two hundred souls.

"If he thinks about it, he will probably burn the villages out of spite," Max said. "Everything we have heard about this man is unpleasant. He could not have been happy to hear that you had finessed this castle out from under his control."

"Which is why he is here today," Talon said wryly. "Have the blacksmith and the carpenters finished their work yet?" he asked Reza.

"Yosef and Dimitri told me that they needed a few more minutes, and then it would be ready," Reza answered. "I will then supervise the rest. Do you really think this will work, Talon?" he asked.

"We shall see," Talon replied. He glanced up to where he could see the figures of Rav'an and Jannat watching them from the bailey. He thought he saw Rostam peeking out through one of the openings

189

in the parapet. They were safe up there, for the moment at least. "Max, are your Franks ready?"

"They are more than willing to have a fight, Talon," Max responded. He had been given command of the fifteen Frankish ex-slaves who had volunteered to stay. Although still emaciated, they were recovering, having been well-fed since their release. To a man they wanted revenge for their treatment, and now the time had arrived. Dimitri, some of the Greek ex-slaves, and a group of sailors were attached to Max's men. They, too, were eager to settle the matter.

"Ah, what is it now?" Talon muttered as he stared at the restive the army. "I do believe they are sending a herald!" he exclaimed. "Max, Reza, make sure our men do not do anything. They come under a white flag."

The men on the battlements watched as two men on horses walked their mounts towards the gates. They halted just before the entrance, and the herald lifted a trumpet to his lips and blew a few sharp notes.

"That's to awake us up from our slumbers," Max commented dryly.

Talon stood near to the parapet and called down. "What do you want?"

The second man looked up at Talon. Across this distance their eyes met, and Talon saw an implacable resolve in the dark eyes. "I am General Bourtzes, a loyal servant of Emperor Isaac Komnenos. We come in peace! With whom do I speak?" called up the rugged looking mercenary.

"I am Talon de Gilles, Knight. Pleasure to make your acquaintance, Sir Bourtzes. However, despite what you say, it doesn't look as though you come in peace from up here," Talon responded.

"I come in the name of the emperor, who offers mercy for your crimes and all who reside inside the castle. You must surrender immediately, and he shall show clemency and only crucify the ones who began this affair. The remainder of your followers will be sent into slavery."

"From what I have just heard of your 'Emperor', he is not the merciful kind," Talon called down, leaning on the parapet.

"What did he say?" Reza asked from behind.

"He wants me to give him back the castle, and his master wants to execute us all," Talon told Reza, who snorted.

190

"I can *keeill* him easily from here," he whispered, looking fierce and miming the use of his bow.

Talon smiled with amusement while Max wagged his finger at Reza."There are rules. We don't kill heralds carrying white flags, Reza," Max said, trying to sound stern.

"You'll get your chance soon enough, I suspect," Talon said, "but not now. It's very bad form to shoot the embassy, much as I'd like to. That man beside the herald is the real leader of the pack, I suspect."

He looked back down to where Bourtzes was keeping his restless horse in line. Talon hoped he was sweating in the heat of the day. Bourtzes cocked his head and called up. "Do you surrender this castle?"

"Regretfully, I cannot, Sir. Go tell your Emperor that he must take the castle if he wants it badly enough."

Bourtzes turned his horse as though he had expected this. "Then, Sir Talon de Gilles, upon your head be all the deaths that follow."

The men on the battlements watched as the two walked their horses back and halted in front of a man on a snow-white horse. They seemed to be conferring; then there was an impatient wave of the royal arm and the men of the army began to surge forward.

"They are coming, and they are carrying ladders. See?" Talon said pointing. "Get ready."

Talon remained at the main gate tower while Max hastened off to join his men, who were concealed behind battlements to the north of the twin towers which flanked the main gates of the castle. Reza went to join his men on the back wall of the barbican. Here he would carry out a special task that only he could accomplish, when Talon gave the signal. Talon sent his hounds to sit in a corner out of the way; reluctantly but obediently they settled on the flagstones next to a pile of rocks, crossed their front legs and observed their human masters with wide-eyed and unblinking interest.

Archers and spearmen were stationed in the tower to the north of the main gate, and men were hidden all around the entire perimeter of the walls, with the majority of them facing east and south towards the army. But Talon was not going to succumb to the illusion that the northwest side didn't need men to guard it. He had come in that way, and someone else might have the same idea. So Junayd and a squad of men guarded that approach, enough to provide a warning should one be necessary. He was keeping the new sergeant he had acquired, Palladius, with him to guard the southernmost of the two towers that overlooked the gates. Talon wanted to see for himself if Palladius was sincere about his loyalty when he was confronted with a fight.

Palladius's pock-marked face was tight with anticipation as he watched the army running towards the castle. "They're ragtag, Sir Talon, but they've got a backbone of mercenaries. They are quite distinct from the others, do you see? The ones with better armor and weapons, they stand out. My guess is that they number about one hundred."

Talon nodded. He agreed with the estimate; these would be the ones to take down first. He gripped his bow. He would be sniping at those men when they came within range, as would the other archers. He was already sweating in his heavy chain mail hauberk, and his pulse was rising as the prospect of a fight became imminent. One last check on his quiver hanging alongside his thigh, a tap if his fingers on the hilt of the sword, and he was ready. He looked across to the wall where Dar'an was lurking. He and his men were out of sight until the signal.

"Here they come, Sir Talon," Palladius said, hefting a javelin. He leaned out to see better, but Talon reached forward and pulled him back by his sleeve. "No need to tell them we are expecting them," he said. "Remember the element of surprise."

They could clearly hear the roar of the enemy as they charged up the narrow trail towards the castle. The emperor's men would have to run the gauntlet of the full length of the southeastern walls before they came to the gates, where they would be easy targets. Talon had prepared for this. Dar'an and his men were essential for this phase, prepared and awaiting Talon's signal. The howling crowd of Greeks ran below the apparently deserted walls to come to a bunching halt before the walls, where they began lifting the ladders. This was the moment. Talon raised his arm and waved it.

Dar'an and his men popped up all along the battlements and began to shoot arrows down at the enemy below. They also dropped big rocks on the luckless men, who began to mill about trying to evade the missiles hurtling down upon them, crushing some and maiming others. Talon had explained to Yosef and Dar'an that the architect of the castle had known what he was about, for the walls at their base angled outward so that rocks dropped from above would strike the ramp and then shoot outwards at a sharp angle, so that the missiles struck from the side and not from above, doing even more damage. There was no escape for the enemy, and when some tried to get away by jumping off the low cliff, the mercenaries who were there to stiffen their spines either killed them or beat them back into line and screamed at them to lift the ladders into place.

The raw conscripts had no choice. They struggled to lift the ladders against the walls and then began to climb them; if they hesitated they were beaten by Bourtzes' men with the backs of their swords and with whips. But they couldn't make it. The archers above shot them down, poured boiling water on them, threw buckets of human and animal waste on them, dropped rocks, and poled them off with pikes. They fell screaming, covered in shit, onto their comrades below, or even further out—a hundred or more feet to crash onto the rocks far below the walls.

Talon leaned over the parapet with his bow. He drew and shot until his neck and shoulders ached. Palladius nearby hurled javelins as fast as he could lay hands on them, and then he pointed.

"There, Sir Talon!" he yelled. His javelin had fallen short of his target, one of the better armored men who was beating a reluctant conscript while pointing up the ladder. The conscript eyed the top of the ladder and Dar'an's jeering men fearfully, but goaded by the pricking sword of the mercenary, he began to ascend the ladder, holding his shield high over his head. Talon pulled back on the string, allowed the bow to rotate itself just a little in the palm of his left hand, and tucked the knuckle of his right thumb into his cheek. The distance was just over forty paces. He paused a long moment, then released the string; the bow twanged and the arrow flew in a shallow arc past some men who were climbing another ladder and buried itself in the mercenary's neck. The man toppled over, clutching his throat to die at the base of the ladder. Talon heard Palladius suck in his breath behind him.

It had been an impressive shot, especially as only a few inches one way or the other and it would have glanced off armor. The dead man was covered seconds later by the body of the conscript, who'd had a turd thrown at close range into his eyes, then been hammered about the head with a wooden club as he struggled to remain on the ladder, and finally skewered by a spear. The men on the walls were meting out similar treatment on anyone else that managed to climb high enough to face them.

Abruptly, Palladius shoved Talon hard and the bolt from a crossbow whirred past. A crossbow man ducked back to reload his weapon. In one smooth movement, Talon sent an arrow his way and the man fell with a scream to be trampled under the feet of the army.

"I'm sorry, Sir, but I thought.... " Palladius said, sounding nervous. His eyes told Talon he was worried that he might have done something wrong.

"Thank you, Palladius," Talon said briefly. Then urgently, "Quick! One of those mercenaries has almost made it to the battlements!" He knocked another arrow, but Palladius hefted a javelin and hurled it in one smooth motion across the short distance between them and the other wall. His victim gave a strangled cry and tumbled to the ground, the spear right in the center of his back. Talon nodded his approval, and Dar'an, who had seen the incident, raised his arm in a cheery salute. They were beginning to see a marked reluctance to climb the remaining ladders on the part of the army from Famagusta. However some bold mercenaries were still determined to make a try. A group managed despite strong resistance from the men on the walls to gain a foothold where they set about the unskilled villagers with vicious effect.

Palladius and Talon noticed at the same time and wasted no time in leading the charge into the mass of milling men and boys. Talon jumped over a kneeling boy who was holding his bloody face in his hands and dived into the roiling mass of men.

He dodged a spear that had been lunged at him and stabbed its holder in the neck. Palladius was right behind him roaring and flailing with his sword and now others joined in to drive the struggling mercenaries back. There were five of them but even these skilled men were no match against the determined rush of Talon's seamen and villagers who knew they had everything to lose if they failed to drive them down.

Talon was in the forefront cutting and slashing at a large dark visaged man with long braids who wore expensive chain mail and wielded an axe which was already bloody as the bodies around him could attest to. Then another body of men with spears drove in past Talon led by Dar'an and Yosef. His former opponent fell as did the other mercenaries who were slaughtered where they stood.

Talon barely glanced at the dead. "Good work men! Get back to the walls and make sure they don't do this again," he called as he led the way back to the tower. "That was close," he remarked to Palladius who grunted agreement.

Up to this point most the fighting had been by Dar'an, Yosef, and their men, with some help from Talon, Palladius and their archers, against the enemy on the crowded pathway below, but now things changed abruptly. While the fight on the East walls had been going on, a crowd had been gathering at the base of the twin towers trying to break down the massive wooden gates with some heavy logs. The defenders on both towers put up a good fight: arrows flew; stones fell, crushing limbs; and the hum of bolts underscored the battle; but the bolts ceased flying when Talon ordered his men to eliminate the crossbow men. His men could shoot four arrows for every one of the bolts and when a cross bow man was reloading his cumbersome weapon he was very vulnerable.

The number of dead men piled along the pathway grew, and Talon could see the enemy beginning to waver. The cries of fear and distress from the wounded and dying rose higher than the battle cries that had preceded them. The shouts became more hoarse as their throats dried up.

Then abruptly there was a change of mood. An excited shout rang out in front of the gates, and the men below seemed to become re-energized. Then there were roars of excitement, and the mob of men who had only just before been almost ready to flee crowded forward. They bayed like a crazed pack of hounds smelling blood. Talon glanced down into the barbican, which was an area of space completely surrounded by high walls just inside the main gates; it was empty of anyone at all.

Palladius gasped, "God protect us now! We are done for!" Terrified, he looked over to Talon, who was leaning on the parapet almost casually, watching the event.

"Hmm. Perhaps not. Stay where you are," he told Palladius. He compressed his lips and waited.

The yelling mob, driven on by those mercenaries who had survived the terrible toll of arrows, pushed the gates wide open and surged into the yard of the barbican. At first hesitant at their change of luck, but then driven on by the mercenaries and the press from behind, the desperate conscripts poured into the confined space, believing they had won and that the castle was theirs.

Too late they realized that they had run into a trap! The gates had been unbolted by the men inside. However, now the enemy were surrounded by high walls that bristled with armed men and archers. Talon, standing on the battlements overlooking the throng below, raised his arm and brought it down hard in one sweeping motion.

Moments later there was a blinding flash in one corner of the barbican, followed instantaneously by a clap of thunder so loud that it shook the very walls, and a hail of stones and scraps of metal tore into the crowded space around the entrance way. A cloud of acrid smoke from explosion obscured the view below from the men on the battlements for a few long seconds; as it cleared it revealed the awful destruction the device had wrought on Isaac's men.

Dead and wounded lay everywhere, and the survivors limped or crawled about, dazed, bloody and deafened. They were given no respite. Talon hurled two tubes of bamboo down among the survivors, which exploded and further reduced their numbers. Meanwhile, Reza and his archers shot at any of the better-armed mercenaries who had survived the initial blast.

Talon judged the moment right and shouted a command to the men concealed in the towers. They rushed out and slammed the doors in the faces of the stunned men outside who had stopped in their tracks, rendered immobile by the hideous flashes and the smoke and thunder coming from inside.

"My God!" exclaimed Palladius. "What in God's name was that?" He shook his head from side to side, looking dazed, and both hands were clapped over his ears. Talon didn't bother answering. His attention was focussed on the enemy outside the gate. He could rely upon Max to deal with the survivors inside the barbican.

To keep the ones outside off balance, Talon ordered his men to continue hurling rocks and firing arrows down upon them, and they were subjected to two more well placed bamboo exploding tubes that Dar'an tossed down. The devices blew limbs and bodies in all directions, wounding even more. Those who could began to flee, chased by a hail of arrows and rocks and the jeers and cheers from the soldiers on top of the walls. Equally terrifying were the very small devices that hissed like snakes, then flashed and gave off a vicious little bang at the running feet of the fleeing men, who now raced as fast as their legs could carry them back to the relative safety of their own people, and this time the mercenaries did not try to stop them.

Talon turned his attention back to the carnage inside his barbican. He signaled Max, who had led his men at a charge into the once-crowded space.

"Kill all those who look like they were well armed, as they will be the mercenaries. Group the others together with their wounded until Talon comes down," Max told his gang of tall, emaciated blonde men, who brandished axes and large swords. The Franks did so with relish. None of Bourtzes' mercenaries was left alive, not even those pleading for their lives.

Half an hour later the gates were re-opened and the survivors, minus their weapons, were ejected at sword point. There were very

few. Out of over a hundred men, only a dozen shocked citizens of
Famagusta left the barbican. They were, to a man, lightly wounded
but able to limp along, and they carried some of their less fortunate
comrades. Then something happened that Talon had been hoping
for, but had not thought possible.

Palladius called to them as they left. "Go home! This is no place
for you; here you will die for nothing. This man is a magician! Go!"

Talon nodded his approval to Palladius. "You have done well
today," he told him.

Palladius looked inordinately pleased, and his rugged, pock-
marked face broke into the first smile Talon had seen on the dour
soldier. At least Talon guessed it was a smile. With his enormous
beak of a nose, deep-set eyes and cratered skin, along with his
broken and misshapen teeth, it was a frightening sight.

Many of the survivors did not return to their own lines. Instead,
they chose to scramble down onto the rocks directly below the castle
walls, and when they reached the steep hillside below they fled into
the scrub and trees, running as though the devil himself was after
them. They were not interested in fighting any more. Talon and
Palladius laughed aloud as they watched them go.

"Now that is what I wanted to see. They are deserting the
emperor and I hope more will follow and spread the word across the
island," Talon told his friends who came to join him on the tower.

"Will they be back today, Master?" asked Dar'an who joined
them beaming exultantly. He had had a good day.

Talon took a long swig of cool water from a skin that Yosef
handed him and then sprayed some on his sweating face before
handing the skin off to Palladius, who did the same. "I don't think
so, but we are not done yet... we have work to do tonight." He gave
orders for his men to rest and eat while staying near their posts.
Max and his men went to work with some of the sailors and Greek
slaves to aid the wounded and to collect weapons and armor,
especially from the dead mercenaries, as their gear was far superior
to that of the townspeople. Others began the general clean-up the
bloody mess in the barbican. Talon went down to examine his new
device.

Reza joined him, as did a very curious Palladius. "What is this
infernal device you created, Sir Talon?" he asked.

"Magic!" said Reza mischievously in Greek for the benefit of
Palladius. He had just about understood what Palladius had said.

Palladius crossed himself fearfully. He had seen Talon raise his
arm and bring it down as if casting a spell, and almost immediately

afterward the awful explosion had occurred. Perhaps this dangerous looking companion of Talon was right! Talon possessed magic of the most awful kind. Palladius, being as superstitious as anyone else, glanced at his new leader with not a little awe and fear and surreptitiously crossed himself.

Talon strode up to the remains of the Erupter, which he'd had the carpenter and the blacksmith construct according to a crude drawing he'd provided. The barrel, if it could be called that, had been made of wood, fashioned by the carpenter to resemble a long, hollow tube of thick, hardwood strips about two paces long and smooth on the inside, two hands wide in breadth and held together with bands of iron along its length.

The tube had been blocked at one end with a thick metal plug fashioned by the blacksmith, and mounted on an equally crude ramp that supported it off the ground and enabled it to be pointed at the gates. It was now split and shattered along its length. The iron bands that the blacksmith had bound around the strakes had been distorted and in several cases torn apart. The whole thing had been blown backwards against the wall behind it where it lay in a smoking ruin, having badly chipped some of the limestone blocks of the wall. It had fulfilled its purpose, however, and Talon was well pleased. He turned to Reza and spoke Farsi. "It performed just as we wanted it to, Brother. But now we must find some bronze and try to make one after the manner of the Chinese."

Max sauntered over to join them. "If this is an infernal idea you brought back with you from China, Talon, then I would be sore afraid to come against you," he said, shaking his head. "My ears are still ringing from that awful noise!" The normally imperturbable Max looked shaken by what he had seen.

"A very good thing you laid a trail up to it, Brother, and I was well out of the way when I lit it!" Reza laughed.

Talon grinned. "It doesn't pay to underestimate this Chinese powder, Brother. The making of this is something only you and I will ever know," he added. They recited the formula in Farsi: "Charcoal, sulphur and saltpeter," they said in unison, then laughed at the bewildered faces all around them.

Hearing the rumble of thunder, they all looked towards the west, where black clouds were forming out at sea. A warm wind preceded the storm, tugging at the banner on the citadel. Talon hoped Henry and Guy were heading back into the harbor.

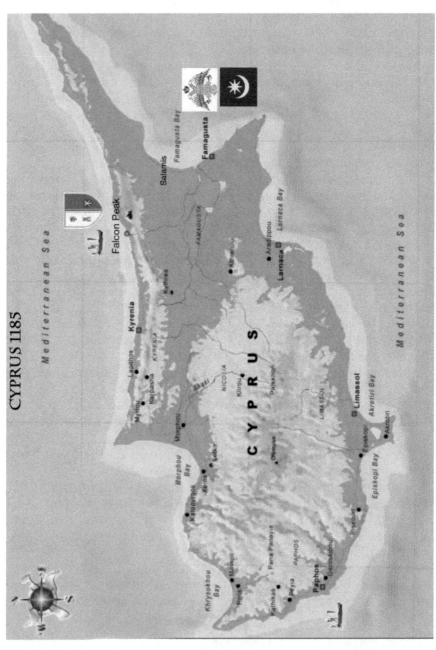

Cyprus

As the moon rises on a cloudy sky
I cry out my curse.
My feet are standing in a puddle of blood,
blood shed from the innocents
—Lucirina Telor Vivan

Chapter 16

Night Visits

From a quarter of a mile away, Isaac watched the rout of his army. He was mounted on a white horse decorated in all the finery that befitted an emperor about to conquer a castle—or a city. He had been waiting with keen anticipation for the moment that now would not come, to ride in state and claim back what was rightfully his. His face was aflame with anger and embarrassment as he watched the routed survivors straggle home, limping and bloody. Wheeling to face his advisors, he demanded to know how the men could be so defeated, and why wasn't the castle taken yet?

No one dared say anything and eyes were averted as he glared around him at his servants. No one wanted to state the obvious: they had failed ignominiously. It was now early evening and there was nothing more that could be done that terrible day, but Isaac stayed where he was, staring at the castle and the small figures lying strewn along the track that led along the path to its gates.

The banner still flew defiantly from the top of the tall Keep as though taunting him. They had all heard the roar of jubilation from the men, and a runner had breathlessly reported that the gates had been breached. But then there had been a noise like a huge clap of thunder and a cloud of yellowish smoke had climbed into the sky, followed by utter silence. Then had come more bangs, not as loud as the first, and then the terrified, running men had come back along the trail, routed and defeated. They had sped past the emperor, ignoring him and his retinue, their eyes staring, mouths gaping and faces distorted with terror, to disappear down the hill, leaving him aghast and suddenly very unsure of himself. The mutter of thunder in the distance did nothing to reassure him.

He still could not believe what had occurred, what his eyes had seen and what he had heard made no sense to him at all. It was unthinkable, incredible, that his underlings would fear anything more than his wrath.

After a very long time, a brave servant hesitantly suggested that perhaps the emperor would like some refreshment back in his tent? His senses still numbed, Isaac allowed the servant to turn the white horse and lead it towards the tented area of his army.

When he arrived, there were none of the cheers that had always attended his arrival anywhere. No one could meet his eye, and no one other than his faithful servant Diocles remained to greet him. After depositing their salvers of delicacies and drinks, the others scuttled away.

The Emperor dismounted and entered his large tent, made of heavy silk that repelled the elements, and settled onto heaped silk cushions. He wasn't sure he could stand at this time, his knees were so shaky. "Where is Bourtzes?" he demanded. He reached for an intricately inlaid cup and gulped a wine that had been made to be savoured.

"He is with the rearguard of the army, my Liege," Diocles said in a frightened tone.

"I want him here! Now!" screamed the emperor suddenly, sitting up and spraying wine and spittle everywhere. Diocles flinched and put his hand to his mouth.

"Yes, yes, Lord, at once." He fled from the tent, leaving the emperor alone but for his guards, who stood rigidly outside the tent, wearing wooden expressions. Diocles frantically gestured to servants to attend their emperor at his meal. Perhaps food would calm down his Excellency.

Komnenos, however, was only just getting started. He felt an overwhelming urge to destroy something. His foot lashed out and connected with a low, laden table. The table sailed halfway across the tent to fall hard, one leg broken. The refreshments flew in all directions: cold soup splashed onto expensive carpets, meat pattered down greasily, and jellies wobbled and disintegrated, making a slippery mess in front of him that looked like a dozen seagulls had just befouled the precious carpet. The servants cowered as his rage mounted. He screamed and yelled, and then threw himself onto his back and all but waved his feet in the air he was so mad. More howls followed, then a thorough destruction of plates, cups and jugs; more things thrown at the servants, and ferocious whippings with his horsehair fly swat.

Bourtzes arrived within half an hour and snapped to attention in front of the emperor, who was finally bringing himself under control, having exhausted himself and having satisfactorily terrorized his hapless attendants.

"You might soon wish you had died up there before the castle walls!" Isaac screamed at him.

Bourtzes blinked, then closed his eyes for a second to keep himself from answering back with the wrong tone or words. He wondered if his men would permit this sack of shit to carry out that threat. Unfortunately, they might. After all, his death would mean promotion for at least one of them.

"My Lord," he began.

"My Lord?" Isaac mimicked him. "I am your Liege, Your Emperor! You bastard, you have failed me!" he yelled. "I should have your head!" He grimaced and sneered, as though the thought appealed to him, "In fact I might still, if you don't come up with a good excuse for the mess I witnessed today and figure out how to take that dung heap of a castle back!"

Bourtzes bowed low and began again. "My Liege Lord," he said very politely, his voice dripping with patience. "I would have been here earlier, but I needed to secure our perimeter. The worthless... I mean, the citizens of Famagusta have no idea how to secure an army for the night. I had to order the posting of sentries and show the blithering idiots how to do it!" Bourtzes was thoroughly on edge, very angry, and didn't need to have this imbecile of a petty emperor to tell him what a debacle the day had been.

"About the castle, I do not rightly know what it was that caused the loss of so many lives. The weapons employed against us are of an unknown magic. They are pure evil wizardry! Witnesses say that he hurled bolts of fire and destruction upon my men, who were defenseless against him."

"So you don't have a plan, then? I should have your head for dinner!" Isaac yelled hoarsely. His throat was sore from screaming. Jellies, he realized, would be very soothing right about now.

He looked around at the appalling mess in the tent as though seeing it for the first time. "What is this mess?" he demanded. "You!" he pointed to a frightened servant, peering into the tent. "Clean it up, or I shall have you whipped within an inch of your miserable life!"

"As for you," he pointed at Bourtzes, "I shall eat my supper and you will figure out how to take the castle. You have one day, or I follow through with my promise," he snarled, his dark eyes bulging.

Bourtzes bowed and left, sweating copiously in the sweltering heat and thankful not to have had to challenge the emperor's authority. It dawned on him that the time might be coming soon. He went straight to the area where his own men were quartered. His own officers, those who had survived the carnage, greeted him with sullen looks that betrayed their bewilderment and shame. None would meet his eyes.

"Where is Radenos?" Bourtzes demanded, after looking around at the remains of his small army. There was a long silence, broken only by the flashes of lightning and the rumble of thunder out at sea, and then one of them said, "I saw him taken down by an arrow. He didn't make it back."

Bourtzes cursed. Radenos was a Frank, once a Varangian guardsman, who had been one of his best men.

He went through the roll call to identify the men who had died or were missing. He sensed that the men were feeling shaken and mutinous. They had signed up for booty, not for this kind of blood and sweat. None of them had ever encountered such a force, and it had shaken these hardened warriors to their core.

He wanted to shake them and slap a few about to straighten them up, but Bourtzes knew it was incumbent upon him to try to boost morale, yet he was at a loss. The castle was virtually impregnable; he had been right in the thick of it by the gates, seeking opportunities to exploit as any good officer should, as well as kicking and beating the cowardly conscripts as they milled about like cattle.

Only God knew how he had been spared from the massacre within the barbican. He had been about to charge in when the terrible flash of lightning, the clap of thunder, the whirr of tiny missiles like bees and the waft of evil, stinking smoke had stopped him short. And then the screams had begun. The gates had slammed shut on him and his men outside, then more of those infernal thunderbolts had been thrown down at him by the very man he had talked to during the parley. Bourtzes had fled with the remainder of his men, with those awful, noisy, hissing serpents snapping at his heels. He was sure that well-disciplined troops could have stormed the walls had there been enough of them, but he'd only had a tight knit group of mercenaries, and they on their own could not pull it off.... Or could they?

A thought occurred to him. There were men with him who could climb; why not come in by the back of the castle where the inhabitants might not be so watchful? He wondered about that. It was a daunting prospect, but they might be able to pull it off. They could toss grapples up over the parapets then climb the ropes at night. The idea appealed to him. He and his men alone could take the castle while the army and its mad emperor slept. Then he, Bourtzes, might even have a bargaining piece of his own.

He began to outline his plan. At first there was resistance.

"I'm not going back into that place," one of the men said sounding very shaken. "There is an evil magician there, and his power is too great for my taste."

Others joined in, but Bourtzes insisted that they listen to him. He pointed out that under cover of darkness they would be invisible to defenders, unexpected, unlooked-for. Furthermore, even magicians had to sleep. The mood gradually changed from near mutiny to one of cautious optimism. These men, after all, were hardened fighters who liked the idea of taking the castle for themselves. One even went so far as to say, "I'd like to take it and damned well keep it. That boss of yours is as cracked as a sea urchin, but a lot more dangerous."

"Just remember that he pays your wages, and keep your tongue quiet in that empty head of yours," Bourtzes growled. He wanted to quell all thoughts from that direction—for now anyway.

Once he was satisfied that he had them on his side, they settled down to dinner and planning. Having lost nearly thirty to the unnerving archery of the enemy, Bourtzes had only fifty men left, and he intended to use them all. Firstly, however, he needed to explore the rear side of the castle and figure out how to accomplish the assault. He and his captains would climb the hill in the dark and do some exploring. They would have to be careful of sentries posted on the walls of the castle; but his men were stealthy, experienced soldiers. They would not be seen or heard.

Bourtzes sent his best men to install themselves under the walls of the castle on the northern side, then ordered his other men to get some rest. Next, he and his four captains sped on their way up the path to the ridge.

Talon, Reza and and his men slipped out of the gates well after dark. He looked up at the sky; this was the best kind of night for what he had in mind. Oddly enough the enemy had left no one watching the gates to the castle so it was an easy matter to open them quietly to allow him, Reza and three of their new Companions as Reza was wont to dub them, to leave and then disappear into the rocks below the castle. Each man carried a bow, arrows wound around with turpentine rags, and two exploding tubes.

Talon had left Max in charge with Maymun to shadow him as his body guard, and Palladius and his men to guard the gates in case, by some extraordinary act of initiative, the enemy decided to attack at night. Talon doubted the emperor could so muster his forces, but ever present in his mind was the ease with which he himself had taken the castle. He wanted no such reversal while he was holding it.

After months of Reza's tutelage, the new Companions were well trained in stealth and concealment. Try as he might to see them below, Palladius could detect nothing. He shook his head, the hairs on his arms rising. Talon and his men scared him more than he could say. Just at that moment, Max arrived with a couple of his Franks. Max pointed down and smiled in the dark. "You will never see these people until it is too late," he said. Palladius humphed.

"They scare the shit out of me," he said.

"They should. Better you are on our side now, Palladius," Max said somberly. "It is a good night for the assassins."

The five men moved very cautiously along the ridge towards where Talon knew there to be sentries and tents. The light of several fires was indication enough that a fairly large body of men was keeping watch on the road. Here he expected men to be standing guard, or patrolling. Sure enough, just as his group approached the crossroads, they heard stealthy movement ahead. Peering into the darkness, Talon and his men watched as about twenty well armed men climbed onto the ridge road and, after answering the challenge of the alert sentries, disappeared down the other side.

Reza nudged him. "Do you think they are heading for the harbor?" he asked in a low voice.

Talon murmured back, "Have Junayd follow them to find out and report back." Reza whispered something, and the dark shadow of Junayd rose and slipped into the bushes behind them.

"Regardless of what those men are doing, we will begin to eliminate the sentries," Talon whispered. The group rose and moved silently towards the crossroads. One by one, the men who were either standing or walking about on watch were slain. A knifing here, a well placed arrow there, within half an hour the work was done. No one on the ridge was left on guard. Talon decided to leave the sleeping men to find their comrades in the morning.

"It will put the fear of God into them and further demoralize them," he told his men before they left. Satisfied that they had left no one to stop them on their way back from the enemy camp, Talon led the way down the path. About a hundred paces down the slope, he and his men encountered another group of well armed men moving purposefully up the track. They were challenged by the man leading the group.

The half-moon was obscured from time to time as dark clouds moved overhead, but it was easy enough for Bourtzes to stride up the still dry pathway. They passed two sentries whom Bourtzes had placed earlier, were challenged correctly, and allowed to pass. A wind was beginning to sough through the trees, making low moaning sounds. Bourtzes shivered and looked up at the sky; it looked as though the night might soon become very wet. They were almost at the ridge top where other sentries were posted, as this was the most vulnerable part of the trail. Beyond this point the path split: one way led to the dark, looming castle, and the other led down towards the harbor some miles away.

It was just as they were about to crest the slope and Bourtzes was expecting to be challenged that they almost ran into four men moving down the slope towards them. There was something about the dark, hooded men that made Bourtzes' instincts jangle. He had not seen nor heard the sentries where he had installed them, and now these dark strangers were walking silently towards him. He placed his hand on his sword hilt. A flash of lighting illuminated the group ahead, and his eyes narrowed. Although they didn't appear to be armed, he stopped in his path, his captains behind him, and called out a challenge. "Halt! Who goes there?"

"Friend," said a voice softly, and he heard a snick, which was the last thing Bourtzes ever heard. He recognized Talon just as his head parted ways with his body. A very sharp blade sliced into his neck and his head tumbled to the ground. The body stood upright for a moment, almost as though disputing the fact that it had just lost one of its more important parts, and then collapsed to the dust.

The other men barely had time to register what had happened before the hooded phantoms fell upon then with their swords and killed them with such speed and efficiency that no one even had the chance to cry out in alarm.

In the ensuing silence, even the owls had stopped hooting as though they were also listening and all were waiting for the storm to break. When a fox barked in the woods nearby Talon and his men left the trail and listened for any more people who might be coming up the hillside.

Then Reza, who had very sharp ears, held up his hand and hissed quietly. "Someone coming."

After a few long minutes while they waited they felt rather than saw or heard another person coming down the track. Reza grunted. Despite the wind that now tugged at their clothing he had heard something. It was Junayd. Reza stepped out and signaled the young man to join them. In an excited whisper Junayd told them what he had discovered.

The group of men had not gone to the harbor, instead they had gone off the trail and were even now circling around the castle towards the northwest side. They had stopped in among the rocks below the walls as though waiting for something or someone to tell them what to do next.

"Good. Go back to the castle and inform Max. You did well. See if you can locate the men from the top of the walls." Reza told him. Although he would rather have accompanied Talon, Junayd obediently sped off to alert the castle.

"What was it that you heard down there?" Talon whispered to Reza.

"Sounded like the growl of a large animal," Reza responded. "We know they have hounds, but this didn't sound like one of those." They all listened again but heard nothing other than the soughing of the wind in the trees as the storm approached.

Talon had two objectives in mind. One was to disable the monster trebuchet. He didn't know if Isaac had any competent engineers at his disposal. If he did, then even at that distance it could possibly hurl large rocks at the walls of his castle. Talon didn't want to find out.

His other objective took priority over even that. He led the way down the slope towards the enemy camp. Along the way the group disposed of sentries who might have raised the alarm. Their objective: the tent of the emperor, which was easy enough to identify by its size.

There was no sign of activity around the great tent, and only two sentries stood near the closed entrance. The servants, exhausted by the tantrums thrown by their master and anticipating the storm, had sought cover and were by now asleep. All the same, Talon and his men made a complete circuit. It was a good thing that they did, because they discovered something unexpected at the back.

As they were moving quietly from shadow to shadow, they all heard the growl of a large animal. Everyone stopped and eased deeper into the shadows. Ahead of them, Talon could see a cage on a wagon bed, and in the cage a dark shadow that moved. The animal was aware of them. Their very stealth might have alarmed it, because it was used to men walking openly around its location. The dark form came to the bars and stared out at them. The one thing they did not need was for the animal to roar and wake others. Its tail was beginning to lash as it watched them, and a low growl came from deep within its throat. Like phantoms the men slipped back out of its sight and settled in a dark corner near some wagons, from which vantage point they could see the sentries.

"It might stay quiet if we keep out of sight," Reza whispered. He sounded nervous.

"Reza, it's you and I who will take the guards," Talon whispered.

"How do you propose to do this?" Reza asked.

"Remember the game that Fang taught us? I hope you have been practicing?" Fang, a former bodyguard in China, had taught the two men how to draw and strike in one fluid motion.

Reza's teeth flashed in the dark. "Tell me which one is mine."

They stood up and began to walk casually along the grassy lane towards the tent where the two large guards were standing. The guards were silent, probably for fear of waking the monster within, but they were alert. They held spears, and they were well armored; but while their helmets were on their heads, the chain hoods were down. Many soldiers objected to the heat and weight of hoods, not to mention the way they occluded the wearer's field of vision. A gust of wind rattled the banners and stays of the nearby tents and tore a hole in the clouds. In the moonlight, the guards could hardly fail to notice the two men who sauntered towards them, chatting in an undertone, clearly going somewhere and just as clearly in no particular hurry. To all appearances not a threat.

As Talon and Reza drew near to them, the guards, unaware of impending danger, nodded a silent greeting, which was returned with a wave of a hand; then, as though they had decided on the spur of the moment to chat, Talon and Reza turned towards the guards and came closer. In the same instant, both men struck. Talon and Reza had practiced this maneuver so many times they moved in almost perfect unison. Their right hands reached to their left sides and—as if by magic—long, slightly curved swords appeared. The blades hissed through the air, and two heads dropped to the ground as blood sprayed the tent. The bodies fell, and it was over.

Talon and Reza, with the same swift fluidity of movement, dragged the two bodies into a dark shadow. Yosef and Dar'an assumed the positions vacated by the unfortunate victims. There had been almost no sound at all, but one of the servants in a tent nearby called out in his sleep. All five of them froze, but apparently the servant settled down again, for there was an inarticulate grumble, and then the sound of snores. A dog barked somewhere in among the tents far below them, but otherwise all was quiet.

Talon and Reza slipped silently into the tent and stood still, adjusting their eyes to the darkness within. A solitary bulge and light snoring told them what they needed to know: his eminence was sleeping alone, which suited Talon just fine. He had half expected to find the emperor surrounded by women while he slept.

While Reza stood watch, Talon walked up to the bed and nudged the sleeping person awake.

Isaac struggled up from a deep sleep to find a dark shadow standing over him. He immediately thought someone was trying to kill him and opened his mouth to scream. A hard hand came down over his mouth, silencing him, and the point of a dagger pricked his throat. A flash of lighting briefly illuminated the inside of the tent, and the clap of thunder near the mountain made Isaac, already scared half out of his wits, flinch. The presence of a second dark figure in the tent with him only added to the nightmare.

"If you value your life you will remain silent," said a voice in accented Greek. "One sound and you will die, regardless of what happens to us later, Your Highness." Isaac subsided into the silk cushions. He had begun to perspire, and it was not because of the stuffy interior of the tent.

"Let me see your hands, my Lord. I want to ensure that you don't do anything rash." Talon said.

Isaac lifted his hands in the air. "Who... who are you?" he stuttered. Talon could smell the fear emanating from the man.

"Lay your arms wide. I am Sir Talon de Gilles, Your Highness."

Isaac jerked his head up. "You!"

"Yes, I! We have to have a little talk, my Lord."

"How did you get in here? Where are my guards?" Isaac croaked. He licked his dry lips.

"You mean the ones who were guarding you, or the ones that are guarding you now?"

"What do you mean?"

"I mean that you will never really know who it is guarding you from this moment forth," Talon said quietly. "Will they be the men you think they are, or the men I placed there?"

Isaac gurgled.

"I and my people can gain access to the most secure chamber. This tent was easy, but even in your own palace back in Famagusta you will never be sure again of the men who guard you, and you will always wonder who is hiding in the shadows."

Isaac was trembling. "What do you want?" he whispered.

"I told you. We need to talk."

"You have stolen my castle!"

"You stole it first. You had no right to it, Your Highness. Your uncle would be very pleased if I killed you right now."

"I am the Emperor! I can do what I want!"

Talon gave a sigh of exasperation.

"Not in my case. I want you to leave with this rag tag army of yours and go back to Famagusta. If you do not, more men will die—and that will include you." Talon's tone was dark with intent.

Try as he might, Isaac could not discern the features of the dark shadow that leaned over him, which made the threat even more menacing.

"I have a proposal to make to you, Your Highness," Talon said in a reasonable tone.

"What would that be?" Isaac asked in a hoarse voice.

"I shall pay you a yearly tithe for the privilege of being left alone. In gold, once a year. The Assassins in Syria do this, you know. They pay the Knights Templar gold to be left alone. I am proposing a similar arrangement to you. What do you think?"

Isaac was so shaken he just nodded. For the briefest of moments he had contemplated shouting for help, but the other sinister shadow shifted near to the entrance, and he gave up all thought of resistance.

"How do I know you will keep your word?" he demanded.

"Well, it's a case of mutual distrust, Your Highness. I don't trust you, and you have to trust me. When you get back to Famagusta, your steward will tell you that a small box of gold has arrived from a place unknown to him. That is how I shall keep my word. Then you will keep yours. Leave at dawn with your entire army, and do not ever come back. I don't care much that you plunder your empire; I find it distasteful, but that is your affair. However, you will leave me and mine alone... and you will get your tithe."

"You have my promise," Isaac croaked.

"I will have more than your promise, My Lord. There will be a document with the gold inside the box, which the steward will be told is not to be opened except by you. This document, which details our agreement must find its way back to me, with your seal attached. Neither I nor anyone who is with me is to be taken or harmed in any way henceforth. Should that ever occur, should even

210

one of my household suffer harm, then your entire family will be forfeit, one by one, and last of all you will die, but I shall keep you guessing until that last moment of truth. My vengeance, or that of my people should I die due to any treachery by you, will be truly terrible. Remember the noise you heard today? I possess magic and I will not hesitate to use it should you renege on your promise." The menace was back in the tone, and Isaac gulped.

"Yes, yes I agree. It shall be so," he stammered. "I shall leave in the morning and you shall have your document."

"Good. Then there is no more to be said except for me to wish you a pleasant rest of the night," Talon said as he stood up. "Do not make a move nor call out, as my men will be here until dawn. Should you do so, they have orders to kill you, and we don't want that, do we? Good night, my Lord," he reached behind him to take a cup from Reza. Just then the first drops of rain began to fall outside.

"I nearly forgot. Please drink this, Your Highness."

Isaac did as he was so, trembling with fear. He could not be certain that his life would not end right then and there from poison, but he was so scared that he did as he was told. After a few minutes his eyelids felt so heavy he had to close them. He went to sleep to the sound of rain pattering on the fabric of the tent.

Talon and his men left the enemy camp as quietly as they had arrived. The rain made their exit easy: the exhausted men of the emperor's army needed no other excuse to huddle inside their shelters, even if they did leak. But Talon and his men now had to deal with the mercenaries who had gone around the back of the castle. Mercenaries were a real danger, as they owed no allegiance to anyone other than he who could pay them the most. Talon didn't want these men coming back to harass his people.

They returned to the castle and found Max and his men peering cautiously over the ramparts down into the darkness below. Rain was not falling on the ridge, but the lightning and thunder continued apace.

"Can you see anyone?" Talon asked the silent group.

"No, but we can hear them. They are not so good as you and your men in the dark," Max muttered. He sounded amused.

"I suspect that they are waiting for their leaders to come and guide them," Talon said. "If they realize that their leaders are not coming, they will head back to camp. We will meet them. Dar'an, you will remain here and deliver a message to the men below." Dar'an grinned. He was becoming a formidable warrior.

Talon, Reza, their archers, and some burly sailors armed with axes, long swords and pikes hurried out of the gates to the accompaniment of thunder and lightning as the storm waxed and waned over the mountains. Squalls of rain came and went; at intervals the sky would clear and the moon could be seen as the low clouds scudded past, almost at tree height. The perfect night for an ambush, Talon reflected.

They positioned themselves in a long double line of men, with the swordsmen on the wings and the pikes in the center to protect the archers, who stood back a pace behind them, and then they waited in silence. Before very long they saw small flashes from the direction of the castle walls and heard the muted sound of the crackers going off. The men who were unfamiliar with these devilish things crossed themselves and muttered prayers, casting apprehensive looks not only in the direction of the sounds, but also at the dark shadow of their leader. Sir Talon must truly be a wizard to work this kind of magic, the men reasoned.

Before long they all heard the sound of running feet scrabbling for purchase on the steep hillside. An urgent whisper from Reza and the archers drew their bows. The mercenaries were almost upon them before the command came. "Now!" shouted Talon, and he aimed his first arrow at one of the terrified enemy. After that it was chaos. The fleeing mercenaries were taken completely by surprise, and most fell wounded or dead in that first flurry of arrows. The remainder were cut down by the sailors, who ran at them with their axes and swords to deliver the final blows. The rolls of thunder and the rain that swept down the mountain damped the surprised screams of the wounded until death silenced them.

When they were certain of their kill, Talon and his men loped back up the road to the castle and closed the gates.

Dawn had barely begun to streak the eastern sky when the alarms sounded all over the camp. Horrified soldiers found their comrades with their throats cut, or with arrows protruding from their bodies. No one had heard any disruption the night before, which only added to the eeriness of the situation. Men who would otherwise have reacted in a resolute manner were terrified by what they found. Their comrades had been killed right next to them and they had not heard a thing, so they peered up at the castle looming over them, partially shrouded in early morning mist, and were filled with fear. No one, not even the emperor's steward, dared approach the blood-spattered royal tent.

So it was that Isaac awoke in solitude. He struggled to gather his wooly memories of the day and night before. He had been dreaming, having a nightmare, surely? But then his hand touched something on the bed next to him. It was a dagger, buried to the hilt in the pillow. He jerked away from it, as though it were a scorpion, and bellowed for Diocles.

With a gasp of relief, the faithful steward entered the tent and pattered over to kneel by the bedside. "My Lord, it is terrible! Dear God, it is too horrible to describe!" he wailed, wringing his hands.

"What has been going on? What is all that noise outside?" Isaac quavered.

"Ghosts, demons, and phantoms came in the night and murdered many of our people, my Lord. Your own two sentries were discovered in a wagon only half an hour ago. Oh, pity me, but their heads were separated from their bodies! Even General Bourtzes has been killed. They found his body today on the hillside."

Isaac knew then that he had not dreamed it all, nor would there be an assault on the castle this day—or any day. A cold chill ran down his back. He glanced furtively about, wondering if the phantom who had visited him last night might still be watching and listening. However, there was no sign of it, nor that it had ever been... other than the dagger. He sat up in the bed, barely listening to the babbling of his steward, while he tried to collect his jumbled thoughts.

"We are leaving," he said abruptly.

"I... I beg your pardon, my Lord."

"We are leaving! Did you not hear me the first time, you imbecile?" Isaac shouted, and began to get out of bed.

Talon had been dozing against the wall parapet when Max nudged him awake with his foot. It had been a wakeful night for everyone; Max and Palladius had been up all night keeping watch. "There is something afoot in the enemy camp, Talon," Max said. "Come and see."

Talon straightened, rubbed his eyes and hastened after Max and Palladius to the southeastern corner of the castle, the section nearest to the enemy.

Palladius pointed. "I can't figure out whether they are preparing to make an assault or preparing to leave," he told Talon.

"We should 'stand to' anyway, just in case," Talon told him. Palladius nodded approvingly and went off to roust the men.

"My bet is that they are leaving," Talon told Max.

"What did you do to make them decide that?"Max asked, looking puzzled. "True, they lost a lot of men, but there are still a great many more of them."

"Lets just say I had a word with the emperor and he was persuaded," Talon said casually. Max's eyes widened, but then men began to pour onto the battlements and he was suddenly busy deploying them to their places. If the army was readying a major offensive, they would have a long, hard day ahead defending the walls.

However, Talon seemed to be right. The cumbersome army of Isaac was indeed packing up and leaving. Talon passed the order for no cheering. Instead the men, and now women, lined the walls to watch in silence, which in itself was unnerving as the demoralized army of the emperor withdrew back down the mountain, leaving a great mess behind.

The emperor only paused when he came to his trebuchet, to find it had been sabotaged the night before by Talon and his men. The engineers had begun to prepare it for the journey back to Famagusta when the bindings and pins that should have held it together failed: Talon's men had cut through the securing ropes to leave mere threads holding the massive structure together. It began to fall apart at about the time the emperor was moving past on his horse. The machine, now in useless bits, was left where it was, a forlorn pile of timber alone in the middle of a small flat pasture.

"What I wouldn't have given to hear what the emperor said when he saw that!" Palladius said, with a fierce grin on his ravaged face.

"The miserable swine didn't even bother to spend the time burying his dead!" Max exclaimed in disgust. Talon and Palladius just shook their heads.

"When it's all clear, Sergeant," Talon said, addressing Palladius by his former rank, "I want the villagers to be put to work digging pits down by that trebuchet. I don't want to add disease to our other problems." He thought a moment, then added, "While you are at it, Sergeant, get them to bring all the pieces of that trebuchet back to the castle. I think we can reassemble it, and I have an idea as to how I might use it in the future."

His new man nodded his head in pleased acknowledgement. "It shall be done, Sir Talon," he said, and hurried off.

"You seem to have made a follower there, Talon," Max remarked, as they watched Palladius leave.

"It doesn't hurt to have a good Sergeant around, Max. You know that. I think Palladius will do well, especially with you to keep him in line." Talon clapped his old friend on the shoulder.

She lodged with the other of his concubines
Who taught her the rules she must follow all times
She never must climb in the top of his bed
But crawl beneath the sheet from his feet to his head.
—David Lewis Paget

Chapter 17
Tamura the Concubine

Isaac Komnenos, Emperor of Cyprus, might have been a sadistic tyrant and rapist, but he was also pragmatic. The chest of gold that he discovered when he eventually made it back to his palace in Famagusta certainly helped relieve some of the dreadful taste left in his mouth from the debacle on the mountain. He loathed having to sign the document that arrived with the little chest of gold, but consoled himself with the thought that it would keep him safe for the time being. He told his Chief Minister to see that the document was sent back up the mountain.

Isaac's losses had been large and embarrassing, and with the death of his faithful general Bourtzes costly; but there was still much to enjoy in life at the palace, despite the humiliation. After reluctantly issuing orders to all and sundry that the people on the mountain were to be left absolutely alone and undisturbed, he set about assuaging his greed for other indulgences besides war.

One of his occupations had not changed, and that was his peccadillo for young girls. One in particular had attracted his attention a few months previously. Tamura was fifteen, at least she thought she was, just old enough to not be totally intimidated by the emperor and his noisy behavior both in and out of the bedroom. While being, on her arrival at the palace, as frightened and confused as all the other girls, Tamura possessed some of her father's steel. Isaac liked having more than one girl at the same time; Tamura with her native intelligence and growing skills at the art of love, gradually persuaded him to have only her when the urge was upon him, which was quite frequent.

Not that she had arrived with those skills. She had been virginal when he first took her to his bed, but her fundamental instinct for survival dictated that she learn very quickly what would please her new master after she had been kidnapped. The emperor's men had stolen her from a rich merchant father, who had ended his life as a street beggar minus a foot. The emperor enjoyed destroying the rich merchant class—and occasionally maiming the merchants—for much the same reason as his great-uncle in Constantinople. They had money; he wanted it, so he took it. It never occurred to him that by plundering this source of riches he was driving his own empire towards destitution.

This left Tamura on her own, as her mother had died of a broken heart soon after they were thrown out onto the street. Tamura was very beautiful, which helped, with an innocent manner that belied the working of a keen brain. A Greek blonde, her huge gray eyes appeared to be looking at the world with a vacuous naiveté that attracted Isaac. He failed to notice the pert, slightly pointed jaw and the firm line of her lovely mouth, which she usually kept pouting prettily for him. She'd begun to figure out that she could have a life of sorts, even if it was as a concubine in his palace. What she didn't want was to be yet another girl, soon discarded, who would never be able to marry because she was tainted and end up in some brothel in Larnaca or worse, diseased and ruined. This left her with the option to become the best of his flock, to gain power, then to retain it.

Instinctively she had sought out an ally, and one appeared in the form of a eunuch—they were plentiful enough. The pogroms that Isaac's great-uncle Andronicus had set in place against the eunuch administrative caste in Constantinople had not yet reached Cyprus by the time Isaac arrived to claim his empire, so the administrators were still firmly entrenched in the system from top to bottom. One evening, not long after she had arrived at the palace, the eunuch Siranus had mentioned to her that she was doing well. Although he was a eunuch, Siranus still possessed much in the way of sexual feelings, and again instinct told Tamura that he would be interested and therefore perhaps useful. She gave him a coquettish look and pretended to be flattered.

Two days later, when she was being massaged, Siranus slipped into the chamber, motioned the not-so-skilled girl who was currently working on Tamura out of the room, and took over the work. He then began to work her back in long, sliding strokes, using oil. His fingers were strong but sensitive, and she groaned with pleasure.

"I could tell it was you at once," she told him in a muffled voice.

"How is that, my lady?" he answered.

"Because of how you use your hands. I like the touch of them. More oil on me... all over."

"Would you like me to continue, my Lady?" he asked softly.

"Oh, yes," she said, and turned over to present her front to him. She moved his hand to her lower stomach, reveling in the feeling of being touched. Isaac was inept at this form of caressing.

"Show me what you can do with those long fingers of yours," she murmured.

He moved his fingers over her oiled skin and then downward to gently move her thighs apart. She sighed deeply, and some moments later she arched her back. "Oh my God, what are you doing to me? Don't stop! Keep going!" she cried, and collapsed seconds later, gasping for breath and shaking all over.

From that day forth she would have no other eunuch touch her, nor another woman, not even for depilation. Isaac, who liked to imitate the Arab sultans, preferred his women completely hairless below the neck.

It proved simple enough to keep Siranus with her, attending to her every need—needs with which he willingly complied. The eunuchs had access to the women's quarters, where they often found girls and older women bored half to death, either discarded or neglected by their lord and master who had the sole rights to their bodies. In many small ways the eunuchs could make life miserable or pleasant for their wards, who numbered nearly twenty females in all. An ambitious and beautiful girl like Tamura was able to stand out. She made it clear to Siranus that he could partake of her favors should he wish, but there were conditions: absolute secrecy, obedience, and the awarding of privileges over and above those enjoyed by the other girls, such as much pampering, and above all, access to the emperor.

Siranus was a young dark Greek with rebellious curls and a body that had retained a likeness to Adonis, although minus one important feature. He came from the region of Cappadocia near Anatolia, and while not a native of the island of Cyprus he could blend in with the population without trouble. He had been deprived only of his testicles, so he and Tamura both enjoyed their dalliances in secrecy. Both knew that, should they be discovered, it would mean torture, mutilation and death, so they were very circumspect.

Siranus kept Tamura abreast of all the gossip going the rounds in the palace and the town of Famagusta, not forgetting what went on in the Cathedral, which was, according to Siranus, a den of iniquity. The bishop, it appeared, was as fond of young boys as Isaac was of girls. The two of them enjoyed many an afternoon laughing and recounting malicious gossip, but Siranus never forgot his position, and Tamura never took for granted her elevated position. Nevertheless, gossip is power in a palace, so Tamura became powerful.

Over the last four months of Isaac's occupation of the island she had became an absolute favorite of the emperor, whom she drove wild with her sexual antics. With her lissome body wrapped around his bulk he could forget the world. Her clever hands and mouth left him panting for breath, and often on the edge of a heart attack. And so she gained stature within the palace. Isaac never married. He didn't feel the need, as he could take any woman he pleased, so why bother? It didn't occur to him that an heir might be useful to have.

On the other hand, he might have instinctively felt that, being a Komnenos, any heir might in future challenge him for the role of emperor. It seemed to be a family trait, so any time the thought occurred to him he put the idea aside and wallowed in his power. In his selfish Komnenos way he ignored obvious realities and indulged his fantasies and whims at every opportunity. Before long he was utterly infatuated with this girl who appeared to return his affections four-fold. He never suspected that she loathed and despised him and wanted almost more than life itself to kill him, to avenge herself on him for having destroyed her family.

She became adroit at using her woman's wiles. Sometimes he would behave particularly badly, and then she would pout and punish him. Although he could have commanded her to do anything he wanted under pain of death, she managed to keep him off balance and acceding to some of her carefully chosen wishes, resulting in an increase in the respect shown to her by the ubiquitous and knowing eunuchs.

Over time, her initial desire for revenge became submerged by her growing love of intrigue, with which the palace seethed, and the power she was steadily gaining over her emperor and his followers. People began to walk carefully around Tamura, because a word from her could make life miserable and even hazardous. Marriage to the emperor had even been mooted, but she was clever enough to not seem too eager and played hard to get, while at the same time driving him insane with her skill in the bed chamber.

Their combined shouts and shrieks of ecstasy would reverberate around the labyrinthine corridors of the palace; the other concubines would chew their lips and nails, sighing with relief or weeping with hate and jealousy, while the guards would smirk knowingly to one another. The eunuchs would smile complacently to themselves, as the edge had once again been taken off the emperor's savage moods and they could get on with the task of running the country in the manner they were used to. His numerous and confusing edicts were frequently lost in the bureaucratic mire; corruption flourished, and suffocating bureaucracy oozed out of the palace like melted tar.

When Isaac came back from his misadventure on the mountain, she was solicitous.

"My Darling, my King! I am so glad that you survived the ordeal. Those monsters on the mountain used magic! How else could they have done so much damage to your magnificent army?"

Isaac was so traumatized by the whole disaster that he refused even to talk about it other than a curt, "I decided that I would go back another day. In the meantime, do not talk about it to me... ever!" he shouted the last word. As an afterthought, he called for Diocles.

"I want hostages!" he snarled. "Every one of the barons will send me hostages, or I shall burn their castles to the ground—with them inside!"

Diocles hastened off, wondering who he would be able to use as messengers.

Word sped through the palace that discussion of the debacle on the mountain was non-topic number one.

Tamura was sensible enough to keep her mouth shut, or rather, open in the right places, and focused upon keeping the emperor's mind on other things.

Thus it was that one day, Isaac, when he could get his breath back from a particularly passionate romp, said to her, "I have to go to Paphos and Limassol next week, my Jewel. Would you like to come with me?"

The excited squeak of joy from Tamura was all he needed to hear. Isaac began to take her on his trips to the other cities, ostensibly on administrative business, and a show of force, but mainly to assess which merchants were ripe for the plucking. Those who had not fled and could afford to pay the exorbitant taxes that he now demanded for their continued presence on the island would form a line to pay homage whenever he showed up with his enormous retinue; the feeding of his ravenous entourage was considered a privilege. One preferable to bankruptcy and maiming, they all agreed.

They could not help but notice that a female now often graced the chamber or tent when the emperor held court. Although she was always veiled and very circumspect, it was not lost upon the canny merchants that a very beautiful young woman was now accompanying the emperor. Was it possible that the plunderer of Cyprus was become more settled?

They soon learned that the emperor's mood might be somewhat lighter, but the avarice and cruelty was still there. Hostages had been demanded from the barons who lived in their lofty eyries in Kyrenia and Trudos, merchants were still heavily taxed, and their daughters had to be locked out of sight or sent off into the mountains for the duration of his visits.

Small groups of young men and women began to show up at the gates of the city, escorted by the emperor's mercenaries, who treated them with contempt and disrespect. These young nobles were the hostages-to-be. At first, few of them understood the meaning of being a hostage; but the mercenaries, now under the doubtful leadership of a bulky man called Skleros, took delight in informing them. The youngsters, mostly in their early teens, clutched pathetic bundles of their possessions and barely talked to one another as they stared up at the walls of the capital city of Cyprus. This was to be their home for an indefinite period of time. The mercenaries shouted to the guards on the towers, the gates rumbled open, and they were herded inside. The gates slammed shut with a sound like the crash of doom.

When Malakis, the chief information-gatherer, arrived to inspect the latest batch, he would separate the girls from the boys and send the girls to the palace, under escort, to be housed in the ladies' wing of the rambling place, while the boys were marched to a less ostentatious accommodation. The curious gawkers would disperse and the city would resume its activities, but the message was clear: the nobles had better behave themselves, unless they wanted their heirs executed.

High above the plains of Famagusta, the people of the castle set about consolidating their gains. Talon's captains had returned to the harbor, having seen the signal flags flying from the top of the castle, and Talon sent messengers to them with instructions to make their way up to the fortress for a conference. He asked Palladius to have the men of the castle, as well as the villagers, collect every arrow and item of armor left behind by the emperor's army and bring them into the castle walls. He stood for a long time on the parapet watching villagers and ex-slaves—Frank, Greek, and Arabs—picking their way over the detritus of the former camp.

He had already decided that it would take the army two full days to arrive back at Famagusta, so he had sent Yosef off with an escort by the back paths to arrive before the emperor and deliver the chest to the gates of the city with the express orders to deliver it to the emperor. Yosef was under strict orders not to tarry.

Talon, trailed by the two hounds, went into the bailey and called over to some servants, "Can someone feed these two? They have had a hard day watching the rest of us work."

The nearby servants shook their heads in amusement. This new lord was quite unlike anyone they had ever encountered before.

Talon climbed the stairs to the second floor, looking for Rav'an. He found her in the upstairs rooms overseeing the cleaning of the entire area with the able help of Jannat. All the shutters were thrown open and old bedding was being tossed out to be burned. The Greek servants who noticed him ducked their heads and presented him with nervous smiles; they appeared to be contented with their new situation. Boethius the merchant gave him a wave from the other end of the corridor. He also seemed happy as he made himself useful, acting as a translator.

"Ah, there you are, Talon," Rav'an said with a smile, as she eased her back with both hands. She looked hot and tired, but contented. Talon reflected that now his wife and Jannat had a home to take care of, they were feeling much better about the future.

"You should be resting, my Love. There are many hands to help; you and Jannat are, after all, the ladies of the castle," Talon told her with concern in his voice.

"Yes, my Talon, but first, now that you appear to have seen off the enemy, we are going to make it *our* castle and clean out the stench of the former oaf and his family. Time enough to rest later," Rav'an stated firmly. "Furthermore, Jannat and I want a garden; you will have to put someone to work preparing one for us. Fresh vegetables will be very useful in future, if we are to be subjected to this insanity again."

Talon smiled. A garden would also mean a fountain and a place to be at one with nature within the walls. He liked that idea. Simon could head up the project.

"Where is our boy?" he asked.

"Oh, he's somewhere outside," Jannat responded. She walked up to join them, wiping some perspiration off her forehead with the back of her arm. Talon looked alarmed for an instant, but she shook her head with a smile. "No, Talon, do not worry. He took his cat and Boethius' daughter to see the hawks on the North side. Dar'an will most certainly be keeping an eye on them. Panther is a big success with the girl."

"I wonder how long that cat is going to last, given the hounds we have inherited. One gulp and it will be history," Talon said.

"Then you are going to have to speak to those two dogs that follow you about like shadows and tell them the cat is off limits," Rav'an told him severely. "How I miss my two salukis," she added wistfully.

Talon cocked an eyebrow. "Hounds," he reminded her. " I too wish we still had those two animals." he was referring to the two salukis that Rav'an had possessed while living in Persia as a young girl. He had not encountered a hound as beautiful as these since. "Well, I shall visit the children later. Are you two all right otherwise?"

"Apart from feeling as though we were all on a rope bridge suspended over a ravine with the enemy about to cut the ropes at one end," Rav'an gave him a hug. "Yes, my Love. We saw most of the battle from the top of the bailey. My ears are still ringing from that enormous noise you made down in the barbican. That was cunning of you, my Fox."

"Hsü would have said that it was 'effective'," Talon grinned.

"Are we safe to move about in the area of the castle?" she asked sensibly.

"As soon as the army is far enough away, I intend to send out patrols all over the mountain to ensure that the only people on it are ours and the village people. I don't want any of those mercenaries thinking they can do what they like despite the promises of the emperor."

"I shall be glad to see the last of those herds of goats; they are making an appalling mess of our yard, and there is no peace!" Rav'an remarked. "I'm tired of their incessant bleating."

That gave Talon an idea. Why not use the goat herders as his mountain watch? He would discuss this with Reza.

What does he next prepare?
Whence will he move to attack?—
By water, earth or air?—
—Rudyard Kipling

Chapter 18
To Be a Spy

As soon as the captains arrived from the harbor, Talon called a council of war.

Present were Reza and his two lieutenants, Dar'an and Yosef; the two captains Henry and Guy; the merchant Boethius; Dimitri, Rav'an and Jannat.

They found a quiet room on the top floor of the bailey and began to discuss the future.

"We have 'inherited' a large castle with extensive lands," Talon began, "but I must ascertain whether the land is going to support all our needs." Their household had just increased five-fold or more; the question of adequate supplies was a serious one. And ever at the back of Talon's mind was the original cause of their flight from Oman. What if the Master found them again? How could he protect his family from that threat? Isaac's mercenaries were bad enough; enemy that understood stealth and patience were far less easy to detect, far more difficult to guard against. Would they never be free of that dark menace? With an effort, he directed his mind to the matter at hand.

"There is a mine, but I have no idea whether it can be productive again. There are large olive groves, and I have seen vine fields in the bottom of the valley."

"There is much livestock wandering around these hills," Reza interjected. "The villages are not poor. They were on the verge of poverty because of that stupid man Doukas, but that ended just in time."

"True, but they are small villages, which means they could support themselves on the limited land base. The question remains, can they support the castle? That is what is worrying you, isn't it, Talon?" Rav'an said.

"The harbor village has many small boats, and we saw them bring in large catches," Henry pointed out.

"Yes, we have a good supply of fish on our doorstep—more than enough to feed the crews and the castle," Guy agreed.

"Then I shall arrange to inspect the fields and the mine to discover what else we have available. We need to be able to feed ourselves, and to store food in case of another siege."

"It only lasted a day, Talon," Dimitri laughed, and he was joined by the others, who were still exhilarated by their phenomenal success.

Talon smiled at his extended family. "Access to food is a priority, but another point of concern involves you, Dimitri."

Dimitri sobered. "What do you have in mind, Talon?"

"A man called Hsü once told me that the game of life is about anticipation and making moves before your opponent is aware of what you are doing. Even more importantly, before he is aware of what *he* is going to do."

There was silence in the room as the others tried to digest the implications.

"You mean, we need spies?" Boethius said tentatively.

Reza cocked his head. "Yes, he does. It's a good idea, Talon."

"And I was hoping that you would be willing to help, Boethius," Talon said, looking directly at the merchant.

"Ah, I see. It's because Dimitri and I are Greek?"

"Yes. You can blend in with the population, whereas the rest of us are only good at night."

"I know what you do at night, Talon," Dimitri said, with some emphasis and a hard look at Reza, who grinned back at him.

"The important thing is to have ears on the ground in Famagusta and the other towns, especially in Paphos, as many ships come there from Outremer and the Empire. I don't want to be surprised by anything in the future. I want, if possible, to know what the emperor is doing before he knows himself. How will we set about this?"

"The entire population of this island is fearful of the emperor, which could be a real problem, but they also hate him, which could be to our advantage," Boethius said slowly.

"I had a mind to send you back to Paphos to rebuild your business, Boethius," Talon told him. "It will be dangerous, but if we have a good supply of spies you will know well ahead of time should Isaac be about to pay the city a visit. Your salvation, and ours, will depend upon people who hear and see everything and report it to you. Listen, both of you—I learned one thing some time ago: make the beggars your eyes and ears. Pay them to do so, they will repay you tenfold. You would be surprised at how much they see and hear, but no one pays *them* any attention."

Boethius blinked and nodded thoughtfully. "I agree, it would be dangerous to go back, but I am willing to try and see what can be done. I would ask one favor, however." He looked over to Rav'an. "My Lady, could I leave Irene in your charge until we know which way the land lies? I don't want to be worried about her safety while I am engaged upon this kind of enterprise."

Rav'an glanced up at Talon, who gave an imperceptible nod. "Of course, Boethius. We will be glad to keep her here until you send for her."

Talon smiled. "Then, Boethius Eirenikos, you are about to become a merchant again. Henry will take you back to Paphos as soon as possible to determine the state of the city, and Irene shall stay with us."

Boethius stood up and walked over to Reza. "You saved my life, and that of my daughter, Reza. I shall never forget that. Talon, I shall not disappoint you, of that you may be sure."

Reza smiled. "You will need a bodyguard. I shall give you Nasuh. His Greek is coming along very fast, you told me so yourself. I have taught him a great deal, so you can rely upon him if things get dangerous."

Talon turned to Henry. "Henry, I want you to take Boethius to Paphos, and we need to establish trade with the mainland, if possible. You must be careful; the country over there is constantly changing hands. Perhaps the islands would be a better place to start."

"Rumors are that a great fleet has sailed to Thessalonica, Talon. Have you heard anything? The seas between us and Byzantium could be very dangerous," Boethius remarked.

"A fleet from where?" Talon asked, puzzled.

"I think it comes from Sicily," Boethius told him. "William the Norman of Sicily might have finally sailed. I know nothing more."

"But the fleet is not coming here?" Talon asked.

"Unlikely, I think. The King of Sicily and Isaac are friends, for now at least. My guess is that he is going to Thessalonica, and if he wins there he will try for Constantinople."

Talon was very thoughtful at this news. He realized that there was no time to lose. "I think we have just had an example of *not* having information and being reliant upon rumor." He held up his hand to Boethius. "I don't doubt for a moment that you have heard right, my friend, but it is only rumor, and we cannot survive if we do not have accurate information." He turned to Henry.

"There is no time to lose, Henry. Take Boethius with you as soon as you can and head for Paphos. You might glean more information there than we can here. Boethius, you will need funds to help get you started. I shall provide that help, but you must seem like a merchant in all ways. And once you find out what is really going on, there is a good way to get information to us very quickly."

They all looked at him, puzzled.

"Pigeons! The Egyptians use them all the time as message carriers. They have done this forever."

Jannat sat up. "There is an old pigeon room on the North tower. I don't think there are any pigeons there now, but it could be rebuilt."

Talon smiled. "So we shall, Max, shall talk to Julian down at the village about finding some good birds, and we should hurry. Dimitri, one of the first things you must do is to set up our intelligence in Famagusta, then we must discuss how you are going to get someone into the palace. Don't forget the beggars."

There was a feast of sorts that evening. The servants who had remained worked hard to provide their new lord and his lady with a good meal.

The tables became laden with small dishes of Tzatziki—a yogurt dip made with garlic, cucumber, and olive oil. Talon particularly enjoyed the Tahini, which is a paste of crushed sesame seeds, olive oil, lemon, and garlic. Rostam made a pig of himself over the Taramasalata, a type of fish roe mixed with olive oil, lemon juice bread and onions. When his mother suggested that perhaps he should try something else he shook his head and tore off another piece of bread to dip yet again into the orange-white paste.

There was the familiar Hummus, a dish of pureed chickpea, and then chicken and goat meat kababs arrived on huge earthenware platters. Conversation was sparse as the new owners and their followers tucked into the delicious food.

Rav'an was careful to praise the cooks, who flushed with pride. They were quite unused to being complemented.

The only detractor from the meal was the wine, which Talon declared to be poor in an aside to Reza, who grimaced.

"I do not know why you even try to drink it! But I could get used to this food, which is better than that terrible stuff we had to eat in Acre, my Brother," he declared, then looked up in anticipation as yet another dish arrived.

This one consisted of baked vine leaves stuffed with minced meat and herbs, followed soon by platters of baked fish, of several types: sardines, red snapper, and tuna. The meal closed with sweet pastries laden with crushed nuts and dates, with honey poured over them.

Declaring the meal a success, Talon finally sat back and sighed. He glanced down the hall at the sailors, the ex-prisoners and his men with satisfaction. They were busy stuffing themselves as though there was to be no tomorrow.

"At last we have eaten a meal which reminds me of Isfahan and Fariba's kitchens. However, I shall have to talk to the villagers about this wine, I'm sure we can do better. Boethius told me the best vineyards are on the western slopes of Trudos; we should be able to match then before too long," Talon informed Rav'an and Jannat.

"I have not eaten a good fish in a while. That was delicious!" Jannet declared happily.

Talon allowed the others to drift off after they had eaten, but he called for Dimitri and sat him down in a small room that he had decided to make his den.

"How do you feel about acting on my behalf in the city of Famagusta, Dimitri?" he asked the Greek. His approach was blunt, because Talon was beginning to realize that time was not on his side.

Surprisingly, Dimitri responded well. "Sir Talon, you have been a companion and a leader to me. But for you I would be starving in Acre or some other useless port, drinking myself to death. I will do this, but you will need to teach me," he paused, then grinned. "You know that many of the Greek slaves whom we released want to stay here?"

"I know," Talon said. "Some of them can, but there are others who want to go home. Are any of them from Famagusta?"

"No, but, there are four who come from Limassol, which is good in a way, because they won't be recognized so easily."

"You know how dangerous this mission could be?" Talon studied the round face of his friend.

Dimitri nodded soberly. "There is excitement, and I like that. I would be bored cooped up here."

"You should also know that you will have to lie to everyone, have no close relationships, and bribery and corruption are going to be part of your life."

"Then Famagusta sounds like just the place," Dimitri chuckled. "How far into the system do you want me to go?"

"As deep as possible, but with great care and patience. It cannot happen overnight. You will have pigeons; use them well. And I shall be around from time to time. You will have your back protected by Reza's men. You will also receive some training with a knife from Reza himself. You might need it."

Dimitri recalled the brawls he had taken part in while living as a sailor and said, "I know how to use a knife, Talon."

"No, Dimitri, you don't."

Life in the castle of Kantara settled down to a comfortable routine. Talon, his family, and their followers were able to spend time exploring his new-found property. The villagers were impressed enough to send a delegation to Talon to declare their allegiance. He was invited to a feast, which he dutifully attended, bringing Max, Palladius, and Dimitri along in the hope of gleaning useful information about the castle Kantara and its environs.

Talon asked about the holes in the side of the hill on the other side of the valley. One old man, a white haired old village elder called Julian, smiled when asked. "It used to be a copper mine, Lord." They all insisted upon calling him 'Lord' now. "I remember when it was working, I was young at that time, but then there were hard times and we stopped work."

"Do you think there might still be copper?" Dimitri asked.

"Oh yes, Sir." The old man's beard wagged and his eyes twinkled. "I could smell copper then, and I can now. There is work to be done to break through a layer or two, but underneath I am sure there is copper ore. But...." The old man put a finger along his nose. "There is more than copper in there, Lord."

"What would that be?"

"I smell gold, Lord. Not much, but it is there," he told the astonished men.

"Did the previous lord of the castle know this?"

A man named John, who was the official leader of the circle of men, answered Talon. "He suspected, but when he asked us we told him that the mine was finished a very long time ago. He was a cruel man and used us as slaves. His wife was a monster, Lord."

Talon looked around at the men. "Why, what did she do?"

"They pressed our people to do many repairs on the north side in the living chambers," another replied. Talon remembered seeing mason work on the interior walls of the bailey. He nodded.

"When it was time to pay she refused to, and she had the soldiers throw our masons off the walls!"

Talon was shocked. He glared at Palladius, who looked back at him square in the eye and nodded. "I came back from a day in Famagusta to find that this had happened, Sir Talon," he said in a low voice. "It is another of the reasons I had to leave those people. They were pigs."

Talon met the eyes of the men grouped around him. "You have told me of the mines. You honor me. In return, I shall always be fair in my dealings with you. You may count upon that. In time of trouble my castle is your refuge. In good times we shall share the bounty of the land, but you must show me its potential, so that I can see that it is developed." There were murmurs of appreciation all round after that statement.

"Now about the terrible wine you send up to the castle," he continued.

To his surprise the villagers nearby began to laugh.

"What was so funny about my last remark?" he demanded of John, who smiled.

"Lord, we have a much better vintage in the valley. We just didn't want to share it with Lord Dukas."

It was Talon's turn to laugh. "I doubt if he would have appreciated it anyway. However, I think I would."

"Then, Lord, we will show you the vines and be glad to provide you with the good wine," John said, and led the way.

Talon spent some days with the villagers and visited the fishing villages clustered about the harbor. There was a sense of relief everywhere he went, but also some fear, and men crossed themselves when he was past.

He also insisted on a visit to the mine, if it could be called that. In reality it was a cave set into the mountain upon which Kantara was perched. Standing at the entrance a person could see in a straight line across the valley to the harbor with its one ship. Henry had departed with Boethius for Paphos. Julian told the villagers who had accompanied Talon to remain outside, as he wanted to show Talon the mine on his own. Some twenty paces further in, Talon stood before the blank gray wall and wondered about the usefulness of the place until Julian beckoned to him.

"See, Lord. This is not just a copper mine." He pointed to a vein of quartz that ran along one wall like an elongated, slender finger. "Inside that rock we will find gold, I can smell it. But that is for later, and others must not know. For now, listen." He tapped at the end of the shaft, which sounded hollow.

Julian called out a name, and one of the young men came running towards them with a pick in his hand. Talon's hand crept to his sword, but Julian told the boy in rapid patois to strike the wall ahead of them, which the boy did with one sharp blow. The wall crumbled and rocks fell, exposing a dark hole. Talon had to stop himself from gaping.

"We walled it up when we realized who was our new master and how cruel, Lord. He didn't deserve to gain from our work after what he did," Julian explained as the dust settled. He called his other two men to come and help, and after a few minutes of choking on dust and hauling rocks out of the way they had exposed an opening that ran deep into the mountain.

"Lord, see this?" Julian scraped on the side of the opening. "We have copper here. You have a good mine, Lord." He pointed to the wall of the mine. "Do you see the copper?"

Talon peered at the wall and noticed that there was a mottled look to it. "Is that it?" he enquired, pointing to the blue-green parts.

"Yes Lord. It is a rich vein."

But Talon had noticed something else. He drew out his knife and scraped at another part of the wall. "What is this stuff?" he asked.

"Oh that! It is just sulphur, Lord. It helps us with the smelting, but otherwise it is not much use." Talon took a deep breath to not shout out loud with glee.

"On the contrary, it is useful to me, Julian. Where did you put it when you mined it before?"

"We have a large pile of it on the path down the hill, Lord." Julian said, looking surprised and puzzled.

"Then I have some tasks for you and your people, for which I shall pay, of course," Talon told him. "I want your people to make charcoal, and I want the very purest of the sulphur to be collected and brought to the castle."

They discussed the other aspects of opening the mine and how they would extract the ore. Some basic crushing tools were needed, and smelting ovens would have to be rebuilt. Julian figured that it would take a month for the village to get the mine and the extraction process going again. Talon told him that he would pay a fair wage in coin for the work done, which seemed to please the men standing around him very much.

Talon wanted to know every detail of the farming in the valley. The tour of the fields and orchards was conducted by John with the assistance of his several sons, who proudly showed him around. The olive groves were mature trees which John assured him were still producing a plentiful crop every year.

"We need to trade. We have ships and can send the olives anywhere that is good for trade," Talon told the heavy-set villager.

"I have noticed, Lord, that you are well equipped." John's response was dry but approving; he grinned through his pepper-and-salt beard, and his blue eyes twinkled. "The ships will be a boon, as we shall save a huge amount of time. Formerly we used to send the crop overland to Famagusta and Paphos. It is a long and arduous journey, and it was difficult, sometimes impossible, to avoid the bandits that prey on travelers in the Trudos Mountains."

Having seen the rugged coastland from out at sea, Talon had to agree. "Then we can put the ships to good use; the olives are one cargo. Can we make the oil here, too?"

John nodded his head enthusiastically."Yes, indeed! But we need a better pressing system. Our tools are old and do not make good oil these days, Lord."

"Make lists of what we need in order to produce very good oil, and what we will need to be able to ship it," Talon told him.

Detail followed upon detail until his head swirled. Talon returned to the castle exhausted on more than one evening.

"You can't tell me that running a castle and its holdings is an easy task, Max," he told his friend, when they were sipping tea with the women and Reza in the smaller living room.

"I am worn out! There is no end to what has to be done. The next thing I know, I will have to adjudicate their problems for them."

"They will surely ask you to do that, Talon. I hope you are prepared for it," Max said seriously.

"Indeed you will, my Prince," Rav'an laughed. "You are the lord of these lands. You will be just and fair; that at least they should be glad of."

"I have no experience of this kind of thing," Talon replied.

"You captained the ships and held that band of cut-throats together through a difficult journey to and from China, Talon," Jannat joined in. "This should be easy for you!"

"You might not know it, but your reputation as a magician is spreading. The way the castle was defended is all they ever talk about, according to my men," Max told him. "You have become a man of many parts, Talon. You seem, well... to be comfortable with command," he added as an afterthought.

"Dear Max, he has captained a ship across vast seas and brought us all safely home. Yes, he can command men, but as you have seen, he is still a fox," Rav'an said, and she, Jannat and Max laughed together.

"Indeed he is, and I forgot to add that you have a very beautiful wife; as are you, Lady Jannat. I am glad and honored to have finally met you. You, Lady Rav'an, were always in his heart." Max bowed to Rav'an, who smiled fondly at him.

"Max, have *you* then never had a lady in your heart?" Jannat asked him.

Max reddened with embarrassment. "I cannot say I have, good Lady. My life was always bound to the Templars and my duty."

"Until they betrayed him," Talon muttered.

"Then I shall not press you, but I am sure that under different circumstances you would have taken the heart of more than one lady," Jannat told him confidently.

Max looked as though he would have liked the stones under his feet to open up and swallow him, but it was clear that he was both women's slave for ever after that.

Talon smiled to himself.

Later in their chamber, he asked Rav'an, "What women thing were you and Jannat practicing on Max this evening, my Love?"

"We were not sure if he was... well, you know, of the other persuasion," she said as she took off her shift. Her belly was very distended now, as she was in her eighth month. "He is so quiet and —how shall I put it?—self contained. He never looks at a woman. Even the servants are asking about it, because they find him very handsome. Call it mischief, too, if you like. We are very fond of your friend, you know, and would like to see him happy with something more than his duty. Hum, this little fellow is becoming uncomfortable." She sat down on the edge of the bed next to Talon, who was removing his shirt.

"You are both trouble makers," Talon smiled. "Handsome, is he? Never thought of Max in that light. I swear if he had not become a soldier for the Templars he would have become a priest. I have been lucky with my friends. He is very dear to me."

"I can see why you would not desert him, my Talon. He is a true friend."

He turned to her. "What we need is a physician for you and Jannat. I do not know of anyone within these walls who can fulfill the work needed when your time comes."

"Perhaps the villagers will have someone. They don't just drop their children like their goats."

"How do you know?" Talon asked, as he massaged her back. "They are a pretty rough crowd down there."

*****

It was not hard to persuade the people of both villages that their goat herders could have a dual function. Now that the danger had seemingly passed, the herders were out in the forests and foothills on either side of the ridge, tending their goats and sheep. Thus the boys and even the girls and old men could spend their time watching for intruders as they followed the random trails that meandered all over the land which Talon now governed.

There had been one awkward moment when the family of the old man slain by Talon's men nervously came forward along with the boy. John equally nervously nudged them all closer to where Talon was standing.

"They have suffered with the loss of the uncle, Sir Talon," he said with great respect, clearly wondering what Talon's reaction might be.

Talon recognized the boy immediately and motioned him closer.

"I regret that we had to kill your uncle, boy. There was little choice. What is your name?"

"It is Êrakas, Sir," the boy mumbled.

Talon turned to John. "Here is money to help them. Be sure that the boy gets some education, John. I am relying upon you."

John was clearly very surprised. "Sir Talon. This is too much!"

"Make sure they are cared for. I cannot undo what is done, but at least they do not have to go hungry nor cold."

One morning, a breathless boy of nine arrived at the gates of the castle and in a high-pitched voice demanded to see either the guard Sergeant or the Lord himself.

Both Talon and Reza arrived to find Sergeant Palladius standing, hands on hips, feet planted wide, listening to a gesticulating boy who was explaining with waving hands what he had seen. Palladius calmed the boy enough to get him to repeat what he had said to Talon.

"We have visitors, Sir Talon," Palladius warned.

"There are men trying to come up one of the lesser known paths to the south of the main trail, Lord," the boy panted excitedly.

"How many?" Talon asked him.

The boy showed him five fingers. Talon crouched in front of the boy.

"How far away, boy?"

"About a league, Lord. Grandpa has taken the goats and is hiding, but he is watching them."

"Are they armed?"

The boy nodded vigorously. "Heavily, Lord. They have spears and shields and swords."

Talon looked up at Palladius. "Mercenaries?" he asked.

"Seems so, Sir," Palladius nodded. "Do you want me to take some men and... ?"

"Yes, but I want you to go with Reza and his men. You will be able to understand what is being said by the mercenaries, but you do as Reza says. These mercenaries do not leave the mountain. That will be a message to whoever sent them." Talon's voice was hard. He wondered if Isaac had decided to keep the tribute and attack nevertheless? That kind of treachery was to be expected from a man like that, but they might be acting on their own. He very much wish to know which it was.

He turned to Reza and explained the situation. Reza's eyes lit up. "I'll take Yosef, Dar'an, and the others. They need some excitement." He jerked his thumb at Palladius. "He comes too?"

"Yes, but as translator and adviser under your command, Brother. He might learn something. Bring one prisoner and leave the rest; we'll take their heads later. They don't go home. Cover your faces, at all times."

Reza made an expression that meant, "Of course!" and set off. Not long after, he was leading his men out of the gates. They carried their bows and swords as they jogged off in single file; Talon saw that they had all wrapped their faces in cloth, leaving only their eyes uncovered. Within a few minutes they had disappeared among the trees along the ridge, led by the boy.

Talon watched them go thoughtfully. He needed more than an early warning line for his land. What he needed was some useful people inside the city of Famagusta who could tell him what he needed to know, before it happened. His discussions with Dimitri and Boethius had been intense. Forewarned was forearmed. It was something Hsü might have said.

He turned back to get on with the mountain of other responsibilities that had descended upon his shoulders since he had obtained a castle.

Three hours later, he was informed by a breathless Rostam that Reza and his men were back.

He hastened to the barbican with Rostam, both with their faces covered. Talon did a quick count; none of his men appeared to have been injured, and they were half-dragging a wounded prisoner.

Reza nodded to Talon. "It was as the lad told us. I am sure they were sneaking up the side of the mountain in an attempt to get at the villagers. The prisoner should be able to tell us," he said in Farsi. Talon turned to Palladius, who looked as though he had had a good day.

"We surprised them, Sir Talon. They thought they were safe because they were so far away from the castle. Reza and his archers finished most of them off before they could even reach their weapons." Palladius sounded impressed. His men forced the prisoner to his knees in front of Talon; his arms were bound behind him, and he looked frightened and exhausted.

Talon stood in front of the man. "Why did you and your companions come up the mountain?" he demanded in Greek.

The prisoner shook his head. "We were just hunting," he said. His tone was defiant.

Talon nodded. "Hunting can be a dangerous sport in this mountain. I'll ask you again, why were you here?"

"My arm hurts! I told—" the prisoner didn't finish. Palladius back-handed him across the face, snapping his head back. "You will speak respectfully to his Lordship and you will tell him the truth," he snarled.

The prisoner groaned and fell forward onto his face.

"Bind up his wound and take him down to the cells," Talon ordered. "Reza, I think I know how to make him talk."

Later that evening, he and Reza walked down the narrow stairs to the dungeons. At the far end was the place where Talon made his infernal devices, but near the entrance were two cells that he had decided to use when necessary for such an occasion as this.

"What are you planning, Talon?" Reza asked, as they descended into the cold, dark area carrying only one torch.

"Firstly, I am going to hold the torch on high and you are going to toss one of those Chinese crackers at him. Then we shall see. Make it as dramatic as you can."

Reza laughed out loud.

The prisoner was crouched in a corner nursing his bandaged arm when the door of his cell opened with the rattle of bolts and a loud creak. Standing in the doorway were two of the masked people he had come to fear. He flinched.

"Last chance. Who sent you, and for what purpose?" one of them demanded.

He shook his head; he was dead anyway. "Go to hell and burn," he croaked. He hadn't eaten nor drunk water for half the day.

"Defiant, eh? I like that, but it's no use," the taller of the two said. "This is how I punish people like you for being stupid."

The prisoner heard a loud hissing sound. The second man stepped forward and, with a great shout, pointed a long stick at the prisoner. At the same time, a hissing object appeared at the bewildered man's feet. Before he knew it, the door was slammed shut with a crash and he was plunged into a darkness that was lit by this hissing and sparking creature that seemed to dance at his feet, coming ever closer. He spun around with a scream of utter terror and tried to claw his way up the stone walls, anything to get away from this hideous creature that he was sure was about to eat him or sting him to death.

There was a flash that lit up the cell briefly, a deafening bang that blasted his ear drums, then a nasty stink, followed by complete silence except for the patter of falling pieces of some matter on the floor.

"God help me! Mercy save me! I will tell you anything! Please, I beg of you!" the prisoner wailed and gibbered into the darkness.

The door reopened and the two hooded men were once again standing there with the torch held high. The prisoner's eyes darted around, looking for the deadly creature, but there was nothing in the cell with him.

"This time you will tell the truth, or the next thunder bolt will kill you—and most painfully; it prefers go eat people from the feet up, so it is very slow," the taller one said in an icily calm voice.

The prisoner began to talk. His comrades had decided quite separately of their command to see what they could find out by raiding one of the villages. They had not told the emperor; their former leader was dead, so they had followed the impetuous plan of the next highest ranker among them. All they had wanted was some plunder and perhaps a few hostages with which to bargain. This was as Talon had suspected; he did not think Isaac would so foolishly imperil a source of tribute.

In the early hours of the next morning, a single man banged on the gates of the city of Famagusta and demanded entrance. The guards were not helpful, leaning over the parapet to peer down into the dark and demanding who was there. They could barely make out someone in ragged clothes who stood swaying with fatigue below them holding his left arm, which had been bandaged.

"Let me in," he begged. "It's Radenos. I'm wounded."

"Who? So it is, it's Radenos!" one of the brighter sentries exclaimed. "Where's the rest of you?"

"Dead!" he answered shortly, leaning his head agains the gates.

The gates creaked open and the guards peered at him as he staggered inside, minus his horse and armor.

Someone gave him a cup of water to slake his parched throat, and then they began to ask questions. "What in God's name happened? They can't be all dead!"

"The wizard found us! He knew exactly where we were and sent his devils to kill us. We had no chance at all. He hurled a deadly hissing snake at me, then made it disappear. Oh God, I was so scared I would have shat myself if I'd had anything inside," he confessed. His terror communicated itself to the wide-eyed and superstitious men gathered around him.

They crossed themselves as they stared at his disheveled and bruised face, some of them making signs to ward off a great evil. "You cannot kill demons. No amount of gold will get me back up on that cursed mountain, ever again," Radenos declared, his hand shaking. "Give me something stronger than this piss!" he yelled. "I need a real drink."

Reza walked into Talon's working chamber. His brother was working late again.

"How did it go?" Talon poured him a cup of wine.

Reza sipped it appreciatively."Hmm, this isn't as bad as it used to be," he stated. Talon rolled his eyes.

"It isn't the gut rot we were given to begin with. The villagers took me to the hidden rows where this particular wine is made."

"The cunning dogs!" Reza exclaimed with a laugh, then continued with his report.

"We salvaged what was useful from the mercenaries. In the morning we will place the heads on stakes all along the ridge as a warning to others. We told the prisoner to walk back to the city once we had taken him down the mountain. I think he might have run all the way home," he chuckled.

"I suspect that it will be some time before they are bold enough to try again," Talon said. They toasted on another. "Give it a chance; it will be very good one day," he said, referring to the wine. "Who knows, one day we might even be selling it to the emperor himself!"

James Boschert

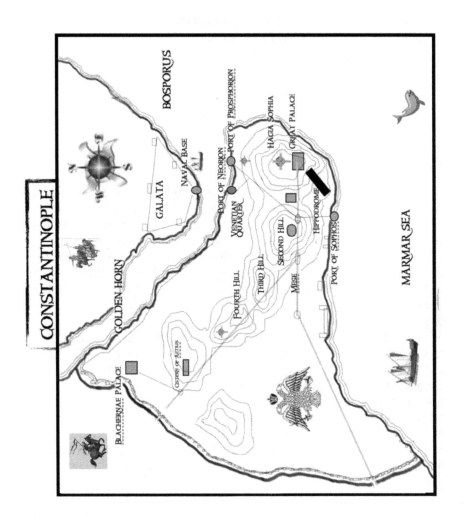

The Kings of the world are growing old,
and they shall have no inheritors.
—Rainer Rilke

Part ♭♭♭
Chapter 19
Andronicus Komnenos, Emperor. 1183 - 1185
Theodora Kalothesos

The city of Constantinople was gripped by a great fear. In the two and a half years since he had been welcomed by joyous crowds into the city, Emperor Andronicus Komnenos had made welcome changes to the glacial bureaucracy and had attacked corruption wherever he suspected it to lurk. However, he had also transformed the city and the country into a region of intrigue, treachery, and murder. Now citizens cowered in terror. The emperor had shown the other side of himself, a dark and sadistic side that had hunted the senatorial class to near extinction.

Although it was almost September, an early autumn was creeping in from the north, sending chill winds of both the natural kind and of bad news—word of the hereditary enemies of Byzantium, Bulgarians and Serbs, gathering like wolves on its northern borders, and now they had appeared its south-western borders also. A sense of impending doom pervaded the city and muted the normal sounds of a once great and thriving trading center. William the Norman of Sicily had invaded Byzantium and his army was besieging Thessalonica. He had already sacked the city of Durazzo.

Theodora half-ran the last few hundred paces to reach the gates of her father's villa, clutching her cloak about her as the cold wind threw dust spirals into the air and played with dried leaves. It was August of the year 1185 of Our Lord and unseasonably cold.

Much had changed since she was a student at the city university. Now she was an Assistant Physician and practiced at the same school where she had earned her diplomas; but, she wondered as she arrived at the gates, for how much longer?. No one appeared to be safe from the endless denunciations and killings that went unchecked. Their chill evil had reached its long fingers into the academy, and all were afraid.

241

She nodded to the old man, Angelos, who served as a guard at the entrance and petted his huge, equally old watch dog with its droopy, mournful eyes, then continued walking along the leaf-strewn pathway towards her home. She could see all the signs of neglect that went with an estate that had been unattended for a long time and was in steep decline. The gardens, once the pride of both her parents, were falling into ruin under the assault of invasive weeds and untrimmed vines. Glancing over to her left, she could see the remains of her father's once rich vineyard, the poles broken and the vines gone wild. They no longer produced grapes that could make a wine worth boasting about.

Walking up to the main entrance, she saw without really noticing the unswept steps leading up to the door and the fallen vase, blown over in a recent storm to shatter on the marble steps; the dark earth strewn about had not been swept away. The stables to her right were silent. The family no longer owned any horses; they had been sold to pay for food and fuel. Neither were there any slaves to work on the extensive grounds.

Theodora swiped a loose strand of auburn hair back over her ear, lifted the latch of the door and pushed hard to make it open. It creaked and groaned as she pushed, for the hinges were old and rusted. Then the wind seized it and would have slammed the door shut had she not held onto it and eased it closed, although she could not stop it from making some noise.

"Who is it?" called a tremulous voice from inside.

"It's only me, Mama," Theodora called back. "Is Damian with you?"

"Ah," said Joannina, her mother, "I was worried. Damian is in his bedroom playing, I imagine."

Theodora walked into the living room and tossed her satchel onto the table near the door, then kissed her mother, who was seated by one of the windows overlooking the junction of the Golden Horn and the Bosporus sea. She was wrapped up, with blankets over her shoulders and legs, but she still looked cold.

"Why has the maid let the fire go out?" Theodora demanded irritably, as she poked at the ashes with a metal rod. "I shall have to get some more wood."

"Irene is mean," said Joannina in a low tone. "I ask her to do something, she says yes, then goes off and does what she pleases."

"Then we should throw her out, Mama," Theodora said with exasperation in her voice.

Joannina took her hand and held it hard. "I neither trust her nor like her, but you know exactly what she will do, should we follow that course of action."

"Yes, Mama I know," said Theodora tiredly. "We can still be denounced to the street guards. God help us, I know!"

Joannina looked around furtively, "With your father gone and your brother in prison, we must do all we can to hold onto the land and pray for better times. Theo, I pray to God every day. We must think of your son, my grandson. I fear for us all." Her formerly beautiful features were lined with grief and worry. A tear slid down her cheek, which she wiped away with a thin hand.

So that her mother would not notice her own tear-filled eyes, Theodora busied herself with the fire. When she had some cheerful flames going she went off to find Damian, her son. She was a mother of four years, but tragedy had not been confined to her father and brother. Her husband, a former army officer, had been tried and executed along with many others in one of the infamous purges that the emperor had instigated the year before.

The ferocity of these purges had shocked and terrified the entire city. The army and the navy had all but collapsed, imperiling the very fabric of the military system. Few officers or families had escaped the horrors of the purges. The enemies of the empire were not unaware of this and had become bolder.

She was interrupted from her despondent reverie by her son, who barged out of his bedroom to rush into her arms and embrace her. "Mama, you are back early," he said, looking up at her with bright, adoring eyes.

"I am indeed, my little warrior. They sent us all home early for some reason. I have no idea why, but it is becoming a regular thing these days." She didn't mention that the principal of the university had recently disappeared—no sign of him. His wife had come to the university in tears. Wringing her hands and wailing that he was innocent of any wrongdoing, she had begged for any news of him. The senior physicians, themselves ignorant of his fate and terrified of informers, had tried to persuade her to go home and wait for news, but she had refused. Finally some stone-face guards had ejected her onto the street. Theodora sighed and squeezed her son till he gasped, "Mama, you are hurting me!"

"I'm sorry, Dami, I wasn't thinking. Come, we'll go and see if Ariadne is up to preparing supper; it's getting dark and I don't want to waste our candles."

They ate their scanty meal, a soup of vegetables gleaned from the garden, holding the bowls on their laps in the living room. The little meat or fish that they could afford was used sparingly. Theodora watched with concern as Joannina took tiny sips from her bowl and picked at the crumbs of bread on her plate. Her mother was ailing from grief, and there was no medicine her daughter could prescribe for that.

The view from the villa, located on the second hill over looking Neorian Harbor, should have been spectacular, but it was ruined by the charred remains of the area in the vicinity of the Neorian and Prosphorion harbors, both of which opened onto the Bosporus on the North side of the city. Hardly any buildings remained of the formerly bustling corner of Constantinople, where many thousands of the Latins, as the Greeks collectively called the Genoans, Venetians, and Franks, had lived and traded.

Theodora stared down at the ruins, her expression bleak. She could not get over the horror of that awful day, almost two years ago, when she had returned in a panic to her house to find her mother and father mute with horror, standing in the sloped garden watching the entire area burning furiously. They could even faintly hear the screams of the victims as the community of Latins was massacred, every man, woman, and child. They had stood in appalled silence as the looting and butchery went on throughout the night. The Varangian Guard, the palace guard, the one group of soldiers who could have prevented it or at least stopped it before it got out of hand, had done nothing while the citizens of Constantinople vented their rage and hate upon people they had come to envy and loathe. The dead emperor Manuel had favored the Venetians, the Genoans, and especially the Franks so often over his own people that it was not surprising, she'd reflected, that they would take some kind of revenge, but this was so barbaric that she was ashamed to be called a Roman. Her father, the senator, had wept with shame. He had never been the same after that.

*****

At the other end of the city, in the northwest corner of Constantinople, stood the palace of Blachernae, the primary residence of the Emperor of Byzantium. It was one of many palaces, but this one had been favored by several emperors, including the present one. It stood on the northern slopes of the Sixth Hill, hard up against the first walls of the Western side of the city overlooking the Golden Horn.

This evening within the palace there was an eerie silence. The stone-faced Varangian guards stood rigidly at their posts at the gates, the main doorways, and the entrances to all the larger rooms. The servants were either hiding or waiting apprehensively to be called, for none dared to go to their beds as long as the emperor was awake.

A single sound penetrated the darkness of the empty corridors and echoing chambers. A long continuous scream of agony came welling up from deep within the labyrinth of chambers and cells beneath the palace. Work in the dungeons was continuing apace.

Unlike the rest of the palace, the large torture chamber was a blaze of light. Candles and torches in sconces burned and flickered uneasily, as though even they were disturbed to witness the demonic figures who performed their hideous work upon their victims. The Emperor Andronicus Komnenos looked on and encouraged his demons at their task; he was enjoying his evening's entertainment.

The unfortunate wretch who was stretched out and chained onto a stone table had just passed out. Even while unconscious, his disfigured body twitched and writhed and bled. His victim's screams stilled for a time, Andronicus turned to another man who stood beside him, a tall, athletic man with wide shoulders like his own, but this man had a hideously scarred face. The right side had been burned horribly from his temple to his jaw.

He wore a wig, which amused the emperor; he couldn't care less if his grotesque servant was vain. His man in all things, Exazenos had a pathological hatred of the upper crust that matched his own, and he appeared to enjoy watching torture as much as his master. There was a smile on Exazenos' face that Andronicus could only think of as sexual ecstasy.

"You do enjoy this, don't you, my Exaz?"

"Oh ye...ss my Lord! You know I do. But I fear that we have lost this one. He is bleeding to death. Do you want me to revive him and keep him alive?" Exazenos asked. His voice had a curious sibilance. He pointed at the right leg of the victim, which was minus a foot and pulsing blood, despite applications of hot iron.

Andronicus stared at the wreckage on the table. "No, I don't think he can tell us anything more. Let him die, then toss him in the water. The fish can enjoy what's left."

He turned and walked out of the chamber, ignoring the grisly remains of other prisoners who had had the misfortune to be his entertainment that evening.

"Come, Exaz. We shall go and feast, then I shall enjoy the little present you have brought for me. You did bring her, didn't you?" he asked sharply.

"Of course, my Lord. We should talk just a little bit about those two officers I mentioned. My men have reason to believe they are conspirators."

"Arrest them, and we can deal with them tomorrow. Now I want to have a bath and prepare for the evening. No more business. I am tired of it."

"Yesss, my Lord, of course." Exazenos responded. He dismissed the two sweating jailers and followed Andronicus out of the room. They walked along dimly lit passageways, Andronicus in the lead and talking all the way.

"I have decided that the University is a bureaucratic mess. That High Principal was a corrupt and useless person, completely dysfunctional. I am sure that he was involved in a plot."

Exazenos smiled as he listened to his master rambling. It was as if he were two people, the one very efficient and concerned about how the government operated. Without doubt he had done much good in the early days, rooting out corruption and graft in the despised ranks of the eunuchs who'd had a throttle hold on the administration under the former emperor, Manuel Komnenos.

However, his methods of correction were violent and brutal. His paranoia appeared to have grown worse in the last year, but Exazenos didn't mind in the least. He had his own agenda, and it fitted very well with the emperor's. The terror that had been steadily building was as much his work as that of his master.

"I shall be hunting tomorrow, Exaz, so you are free to do as you please," the emperor told him as they parted.

Leaving the emperor in the care of his groveling servants, Exazenos took himself off to his own apartments to eat and think about events that had led up to the arrest of the High Principal of the College of Medicine.

They had targeted almost every strata of the aristocracy for offenses real and imagined—it mattered not to Exazenos. If the emperor wanted to destroy the senator class, that was fine. He himself came from that strata of society, but his hatred of the aristocrats who had destroyed him was like a deep white-hot fire. His abandonment at Myriokephalon and the shame of his father's death had fueled his hatred for his own kind. They would feel the full measure of his vengeance. It had not only been the senators; the upper ranks of the army and the navy had also been targeted at his instigation. Now it was the turn of the academic society. Exazenos' lip curled in a snarl; he'd see to it that Andronicus showed them as little mercy as he had any of the others.

As he entered his own apartments he was greeted by his henchman, Gabros, who was his most trusted aide. Together they had survived many hardships, and Gabros had saved his life on more than one occasion, including that all-important first time. He had no fear of betrayal, so he could let his guard down here.

"How did it go, Master?" Gabros asked, as he helped Exazenos off with his blood-spattered tunic, then knelt to take off his sandals. His master watched him reflectively as he did so.

"We will have to find a better reason to bring in the next person from the medical society. I know they are a snake pit of treason, but I couldn't get this one to confess to anything. It was almost as though he knew nothing," Exazenos complained.

"I am sure that the informer can be persuaded to point to someone who is involved in treachery, Master," Gabros said as he stood up. Exazenos handed him his wig, revealing a scalp that was hideously disfigured by scars.

"Your bath is prepared, Master." Gabros led the way to the pool. Later there would be a massage, followed by an exhibition of erotic dancing and copulation. Exazenos enjoyed those displays; on those rare occasions when he was highly aroused he would take the girl with cruel ferocity, impervious to her cries of pain while he strove to climax, and ignore the weeping creature as Gabros hustled her out of the room. He would then beat his fist on the pillows and grind his teeth with rage at what cruel fate had done to him. Exazenos had been castrated, and this fueled his white-hot hate of all men who were capable of normal sex.

Tonight, however, he bathed absently and ate a sparse meal. He watched the evening's entertainment with indifference, because his mind was elsewhere. He had noticed on the list of physicians a name that was familiar to him: that of the female physician Theodore Kalothesos. Very familiar, because Exazenos had been instrumental in the downfall and execution of the Senator Damianus Kalothesos and the imprisonment of his son Alexios on trumped up charges of treason.

Exazenos had appeared in Constantinople almost at the same time the emperor had been crowned in a frenzy of popular adoration, after having ensured—by a process of imprisonment and murder—that no one could by birth or force displace him. Exazenos had proved adept at ferreting out senators and officials who harbored thoughts of sedition. He had quickly established a network of spies who were faithful to him and him alone as he pursued his vengeful path to power as the emperor's fixer and procurer. As the victims were denounced, their villas were looted and he took his cut. It had astonished him to find that Theodora was still at the university and was now a well respected physician. How had she survived? Usually the families of the denounced and executed were thrown onto the streets to become beggars and prey to all manner of deprivation.

He resolved to take a look at her and see what she had become before he destroyed her and any remnants of her family. He would enjoy toying with her. It would be a most fitting revenge.

*****

The next day dawned with a stiff breeze blowing in from the northeast. Gray clouds scudded low overhead, darkening the already gloomy atmosphere of the city. Theodora rose early, bundled up with her warmest clothes, and left the house before her mother was awake, pausing only to give last minute instructions to her maid regarding Damian. The boy no longer had a tutor, so Theodora had contrived some lessons for him to complete each day.

Those who were family of someone who had been proscribed—an interesting word that dated back to ancient Rome, it meant to be denounced and executed without trial—had no rights, nor did their children who were forfeit education among other rights of the normal citizen; they could be denounced, even killed without consequences by anyone seeking a reward. The boy was often rebellious but Theodora was adamant about the homework, and Ariadne tried her best to keep the boy occupied while his mother was away. "I shall not be away long," she told Ariadne, "so tell him to behave, and we can go for a walk later."

She departed via the front gates, turned left and walked up the hill to where her street joined with the Grand Mese. In her preoccupation she failed to notice the man who left his position next to a plane tree just down the street and began to follow her at a distance. It struck her as she walked along the main street how sparse the number of street booths had become. Normally the markets were busy at this time of day, but then she saw the reason why. The Veragnian guard were out in more numbers than usual.

The tall, burly, and mostly blond, bewhiskered men from the far north were hustling people off the main streets, and none too gently. They pushed the complaining citizens off the road with the hafts of their spears, then turned and stood to attention, waiting for the parade to go by.

Theodora hurried along the side of the street, hoping to be able to get to the Medical Academy before the emperor's entourage closed the entire street down for hours. The legendary Varangian soldiers were the personal bodyguard of the emperor and enforced his will, but formerly they had had a reputation for protecting the citizens as well. This was no longer the case, and people resented it. Although they were considered virtually invincible, they were not from Byzantium, and xenophobia was strong in this city these days. People complied, but they glowered at the Saxon and Viking guards behind their backs.

Theodora had a class to teach, so she hurried along the narrow streets that ran parallel with the grand Mese, passing the enormous church known as the Hagia Sophia. Its towers and domes had always awed her, but she barely glanced at the beautiful structure today. She continued past the baths of Zeundpas, then down into the warren of old palaces and newer buildings to the college of medicine, which itself had once been a palace: the classrooms had once been bedchambers or conference rooms. For many years the Academy had been at the centre of a thriving medical community. Now classes were sparsely attended by a dwindling number of students who wanted to follow the profession of physician.

She looked around at the huddled group of students who were there to listen to her talk about sinews and bones. Theodora greeted them, then wasted no time in getting down to the subject. She left her cloak on while she talked, as the wind had found a way into the old building and created a low moaning sound as it wound its way under doors and cracks in the windows, rustling papers and chilling feet.

Here at least she could lose herself in the science of her work and forget for a short while the troubles and worries at home. All too soon it was time to leave. The students gathered up their slates, pens, ink and paper and filed out of the door, leaving her to gather up her papers before she, too, would leave for a sparse meal at one of the stalls that lined the Mese before the afternoon classes began.

Just before she left, a messenger arrived to tell her to report to the new temporary principal.

Somewhat surprised, she approached the door and knocked. A voice answered, so she opened the door and walked into the gloomy room that housed the administration area of the college. The temporary principal, one of her former professors, gave her a distracted smile as he shuffled some papers on his desk.

"Thank you for coming, Theodora," he mumbled. "I just wanted to know how you were doing?"

Theodora gave him a very slight frown. This was somewhat unusual; he had shown little interest in her activities of late. She had assumed this neglect was of a piece with the apprehension and fear that pervaded the academy. After the recent loss of the principal, everyone was looking over their shoulders and trying to keep a very low profile. Few had any doubt that he had been arrested.

Forcing herself to sound cheerful she said, "All is well, Professor. While I am not very impressed with the current batch of students, a couple will go far, I believe."

"Good, good." He nodded absently. "Do you know a man called Exazenos, by any chance?"

Theodora shook her head. "No, Professor, I do not. Who is he?"

"He sent a messenger to me today, asking for you to report to the palace of Blachernae in two days' time. You will be escorted there by the same messenger, who will come to your house to collect you with some form of transport, I presume."

"Why... why am I to go there?" Theodora demanded, a cold chill creeping down her neck.

"Ah, yes." The professor peered at a letter in his hand. "There is a problem with his vision, and you are known as a Physician, an Assistant Physician," he corrected himself pompously, "who understands eyes better than most. You are commanded to go and see what can be done about a problem this er, Exazenos has with one of his eyes." He looked up. "I would have recommended one of the other professors, but he asks for you by name."

"An optical exam of one of the senior servants of the emperor?" she asked, not fully understanding the order.

"Yes, that's right," he answered, sounding brusque, as though he wanted to drop the matter, having delivered the message. "I am sure all will be explained when you get there." He waved her dismissal.

That was the part that worried Theodora. Rumors abounded these days about the Blachernae palace being a center of debauchery and horrible tortures. No one would go there willingly, but she dared not refuse either.

It was with a heavy heart that she greeted her mother that afternoon and absently played with her son.

Two days later, the old guard came banging on the main door of the villa and told Theodora that a litter was waiting at the gates with an armed guard, of Verangians no less. She hurried after him as he limped back along the path to his station, where the old dog was barking and growling at the silent men standing outside the gates.

Theodora bade the old man goodbye and walked through the gate towards the soldiers. The leader greeted her with a gruff, "Good day, Madame Physician," in a heavy accent and saluted her. Theodora merely inclined her head. The temptation to correct the officer surfaced, then died away. What did it matter what they called her these days? Her throat was too dry to say anything. She did register that at least they were treating her decently.

She was assisted into the litter, then they set off at a trot for the palace. It took almost half an hour of being shaken and rocked in the closed, stuffy interior of the litter before they finally came to a halt. The men carrying her were puffing loudly, but she clearly heard the leader of the troop announcing them. There was a clatter of metal on metal as gates opened, and she peered out of the curtains to see that they were now entering a large cobbled courtyard where men and horses were standing about.

The litter was placed on the ground and the door opened by the troop leader. "Follow me, Madame," he said in a deep voice.

She picked up the small case that she had brought with her and stepped out onto the courtyard, then followed the tall, blond warrior as he entered the palace doors. He directed her to wait in a large anteroom with guards standing rigidly at attention before two large doors while he went off to find the right person.

Finally the blond officer returned and gestured her to come with him. They went down a maze of corridors until she was quite lost before they arrived at a door, where he stopped.

He knocked, and the door was opened by a man with hard, swarthy features who looked her over rapidly and then, without talking to the officer, beckoned her in. He dismissed the officer with a gesture, then shut the door in his face.

"You are?"

"Theodora Kalothesos," she replied using her maiden name, as she had since the death of her husband.

"Come with me, only speak when spoken to, and keep it short," the grim-looking man told her, and he turned away before she could do anything more than duck her head.

They walked into a chamber that was full of rich furnishings, from the drapes of golden silk at the windows to the ornate chairs and cushions strewn around the carpeted floors. It had been some time since Theodora had been in a room that was so luxurious, but her attention was drawn to the man standing facing her with his back to the light coming in from the window, thus making it hard to see his features clearly. She stopped and curtsied without speaking.

"Thank you, Gabros. I will speak to the lady... alone," the man said. Was there something familiar about the voice? Theodora blinked, trying to recall, but then he spoke again.

"Pleasse sit down. By that table, as I sssee you have brought your... tools," the man said. His voice had a sibilant timbre to it.

She did as she was told and sat in silence, waiting. He appeared to hesitate, but then he said. "I have a problem with my right eye. It was damaged in a fire some years ago, and sometimes it is blurred and painful. I heard that you were one of the best in the academy, which is why I sent for you. I trust you were treated well while on your way here?"

He shifted slightly, so that light from the window fell on his face briefly, and Theodora was able to see that the right side of the man's face was badly scarred. She nodded her head politely. "Very well, my Lord. Thank you."

"Pleasse... call me Exazenos," he said with a grimace that Theodora took to be a smile.

"Very well, Exazenos. Do you wish for me to examine your eye? Is this why I am here?" she asked, beginning to overcome her initial fears.

"Yess, yess, that is right. How do you want to do this?" he asked.

She looked him over. He was a strong man, well muscled; his thin robe was open at the chest as though he had only just come from bed. His pantaloons were of blue silk with a wide sash of yellow silk wrapped around his narrow waist. Subconsciously her feminine side registered that he was a good looking man, apart from the disfiguration, but her professional side took control quickly enough.

"You should sit opposite me in good light; you must face the light. Then I can check both eyes to find out what is troubling you," she stated, and stood up.

Exazenos took two chairs and moved them into the well lit area of the window, then sat facing her as she too seated herself and opened her box. He leaned forward, his face impassive and his dark eyes staring at her. Theodora had the distinct impression that he was examining her while she performed her own examination of the two eyes in front of her.

Exazenos was indeed examining the woman in front of him. For the briefest of moments before she told him to keep his eyes still he rested them on her breasts and her neck, roving over her, assessing everything. He saw an attractive woman with a slim neck and regular features, striking but not beautiful. The jaw and cheekbones were a little too strong, but the large, widely spaced eyes were full of intelligence. Her eyes were concentrating on his, so he could see deep into them, but he detected no sign of recognition. Deep inside he was disappointed, but at the same time he reveled in the thought that he would enjoy making her know who he was—eventually. Not just yet, though. She reached up with her hand and he flinched.

"It's all right," she said quietly. "I just wish to verify the condition of the area around your eye." He relaxed, and felt a cool touch on his right cheek as she moved the skin around the eye. Then she opened the lids and peered at the sclera. Her expression told him that she appeared satisfied with what she had seen.

"There was much damage to your face when you were burned. How long ago?" she asked, as she took her fingers away. Exazenos wanted them to stay where they had been.

"About six years ago, now," he muttered.

"It is clear to me that you did not have a good physician to aide your recovery," she commented dryly, as she took out a glass lens and again peered into his right eye. "Mmm, the interior is a little cloudy compared to the other; it could mean you have a cataract, er, Exazenos," she stated when she had finished.

He was close enough to be able to breathe in her clean scent; she wore none of the make up nor perfume that was common with the kind of women he knew. It was a fresh smell that he inhaled slowly into his lungs. He almost smiled and forgot to reply. Theodora repeated what she had just said.

"Ah, what would that mean?" he asked, unsure of the term.

"It means that the lens within your eye is partially covered with a cloudy substance. It can be rectified."

"You can repair it?"

"Yes, but it isn't serious, not yet. In a year or so it should be seen to. You say you have some discomfort?" she asked, sitting back and looking as though his own intense scrutiny was unsettling her now, but her eyes were steady and unafraid. He liked that.

"Enough to want someone who knows what they are doing to check it for me, yesss," he stated.

It was true, he did occasionally have blurred vision, and it annoyed him to have to rely upon one eye.

"The operation is painful, although there are drugs, such as opium, that can reduce the pain considerably; and it would have to be performed at the academy," she said. "I am not sure how much the scar tissue is affecting the movement of the eye. Not very much, it would seem."

Exazenos nodded and stood up. "Thank you, Madame... your name?" he asked, although he knew very well.

"It is Theodora Kalothesos," she said.

Later she could not be sure, but as she told him her name she noticed a look lurking deep in his eyes that was full of malice and drew back from it in surprise. But as quickly as it had appeared it vanished, and he smiled that grimace of his, displaying good teeth, then called out towards the door.

"Gabros!"

Then to her, "I wish to thank you for coming. Gabros will see you out, and he will pay you for your trouble. I shall inform you when and if I require the operation you are talking about. The officer at the main door will take you home."

He turned away and walked off into another room, leaving Theodora staring after him.

Nothing has changed.
The body is susceptible to pain,
it must eat and breathe air and sleep,
it has thin skin and blood right underneath,
an adequate stock of teeth and nails,
its bones are breakable, its joints are stretchable.
In tortures all this is taken into account.
—Wislawa Szymborska

Chapter 20

Exazenos

While Theodora was being taken home, Exazenos sat in his chambers and brooded. Something was bothering him, but he couldn't put his finger on it. Not even a glass of cool amber wine from Nicaea could stop his mind from worrying at the problem— like a dog gnawing at a piece of leather, he thought ruefully. Somehow he had been taken off balance by the woman.

Theodora had poise, and although he had detected nervousness she had contained it well under a mask of professionalism. No recognition there, but it would come in time, he promised himself.

He drained his glass and stood up. There were other issues to consider besides a snip of a woman whom he intended to destroy, along with whatever was left of her family—and that included her brother. Shaking his head, he tried to dismiss the cool eyes that had regarded him with nothing more than professional interest, but somehow he could not. To distract himself he went and looked out of the window towards the northern approaches of the Golden Gate.

Why was the emperor not more concerned about the menace threatening Thessalonica? he wondered. If that city fell then the road to Constantinople would be wide open. Those Franks from Sicily meant to destroy this city if they could, and King William would then take the entire empire for himself. Exazenos hated the senate class and wanted nothing less than their annihilation, but that didn't mean he wanted to die alongside them at the pointed end of spears wielded by Franks and other barbarians. Perhaps, he thought reluctantly, it had been... hasty to have so many officers of the army and navy executed. Now all Exazenos could do was to speculate and fume. Even he had to be careful around the emperor, who had become more paranoid than ever and trusted no one at all.

He recalled a conversation. They had been eating well, alone except for some statue-like servants against the wall, when he'd spoke of his concerns.

"My Emperor, how are the preparations going on the walls in case of a possible siege?" Exazenos knew that Andronikos had, with his usual efficiency, ordered the walls repaired. He had even ordered the demolition of houses in the vicinity of the walls to eliminate the possibility of fire. Exazenos had merely asked out of interest.

Andronikos spat out a piece of gristle, which landed on the pure white table cloth. "What siege? What are you talking about? Thessalonica perhaps, Exaz?" he demanded, mildly enough.

"No, my Lord, that siege has begun. It's too late to help them; but here, I'm talking about this city, Constantinople. Unless you intend to send an army to relieve Thessalonica?" Exazenos asked, sipping his wine.

"I have been in conference with my Generals, I have send more than one army," Andronikos snapped. "When I want advice from a psychopathic pimp of a eunuch I shall ask for it," he stated, his tone cold.

His smile frozen upon his lips, Exazenos bowed over his knees and said, "My Lord, I had not intended to offend. Merely to assk... out of interest, you understand?"

"My generals are dealing with it, so stop worrying about any of that! And don't bother me about it, either," Andronikos snapped, clearly out of sorts. "Be careful, your wig is slipping." Andronikos gave a snicker. "Why you wear one at all is a mystery to me."

"My humblesst of apologies, my Lord." Exazenos found that his hand was trembling. He had no idea how he had offended his emperor, but to continue to do so would court disaster.

"Your duty is to find traitors who are plotting against me, so get on with that and leave the generals to me," Andronikos snarled. Then with bewildering speed he switched his tone to being conciliatory. "My Exaz, you take upon yourself too much. I know what I am doing. So don't worry, and go find me some more of those pretty girls I like so much from Macedonia. I think I shall have three tonight. Don't forget to bring me the potions."

Exazenos had taken his leave soon after and gone to his rooms to recover and to think. While he had done many dreadful things in the service of this unpredictable and moody emperor: pimped, procured, denounced and much else that would have sickened a normal man, the words of Andronikos rattled about in his mind. A psychopathic pimp, was he? That stuck in his throat, but it helped to decide him upon a course of action.

If he was nothing else Exazenos was a survivor, and the thunder clouds on the horizon in the form of a vast army sent by William of Sicily to destroy the empire was warning enough for him to at least take precautions. The Serbs had already made inroads from the North, and Andronikos had done absolutely nothing about them.

He knew that the emperor, in yet another indication of his growing instability, had ordered no less than five generals to take their armies and move against the enemy who squatted before the gates of doomed Thessalonica. The appalling fact was that he had done absolutely nothing about the incursions of the Bulgars to the north.

The luckless citizens of the city of Thessalonica , which was about to fall any day now, were doomed by the ineptitude of its leader, David Komnenos. Exazenos' spies told him more than he passed along to his emperor, so he knew.

The ever-growing persecution complex of his master worried Exazenos more than anything. The unpredictability of an emperor with so much power, one who could clap him on the back one moment with sincere affection and then call him horrible names, was frightening to a man who was not frightened by very much. Death seemed to be lurking around every corner of the bloodstained palace these days. He, Exazenos, didn't intend to become another of its victims just yet.

He had one thing to do before he worked out a plan with his henchman, Gabros.

Alexios Kalothesos woke to the distant sound of keys turning in rusty locks, then iron doors being slammed open—sounds louder than the moans and cries of the other prisoners lying chained to walls and posts in dark chambers all around him, and portending a visitation. They were in a lower level of the prison within the grounds of the Blachernae palace, one reserved for traitors. The torture chambers were upstairs, and whatever went on there was clearly heard down in this rat-infested hole. Alexios painfully pulled himself up into a sitting position. By his reckoning, and that was very unreliable, it was late at night; but it was always dark in the dungeons, and the jailers were carrying flared torches held high.

Alexios listened intently. Names would be called, if a prisoner did not answer it was usually because he had died. When a prisoner did respond he would be hustled upstairs, and the screaming and shrieks of agony would commence. It did not matter how hard he pushed his hands against his ears, the sounds penetrated his skull just as they penetrated the walls of wet stone. He could feel his heart beginning to beat a trifle faster.

He was in a cell with three other prisoners, and they had all been subjected to the games above, which had left them crippled and unable to perform anything but the most basic of functions. He looked about him in the flickering light that was coming their way. His companions were sitting up, just as he was, fear and apprehension etched on every gaunt and bearded face. Their rags hung off then in streamers of filth, and they unconsciously scratched at the fleas and lice that crawled all over them.

Just as he had feared, the torches approached their cell, and then the jailor was standing in front of their door. One of the prisoners gave an involuntary moan.

"Alexios Kalothesos, stand up!" the jailor called, peering into the gloom of the cell.

His heart now beating a tattoo in his chest, Alexios stood up with a clink of his chains.

The jailor beckoned him. "Get over here," he growled. "Hurry up about it."

Alexios shuffled over towards the barred gate and stood silent. The man holding the torch on high indicated the lock to his attendant, who hurried forward to unlock the gate and swing it open.

"You're going upstairs." The jailer smirked. "Mustn't keep his lordship waiting."

"God protect you, Alex!" croaked one of his companions. There were murmurs of encouragement from the others.

"Shut your mouths, or I will come in there and stuff the torch down your throats!" bellowed the jailer. They left in silence, with the head jailor leading and his two workers hauling Alexios along with them. He could barely walk since the last time, when they had burned his feet with red-hot irons. They were not gentle as they dragged him up the stone steps to the bright lights of the torture room. The first thing that struck him as he stood, moving from one foot to the other, swaying and blinking in the bright lights, was the smell. It was the stink of blood, faeces, fear and terror, and it literally dripped off the walls. He couldn't help himself; he shuddered. Trying to put a brave face upon what he knew must come, he peered into the room.

Standing opposite him, dressed in a costume of rich silks of many colors and sandals of fine leather and gold filigree, was a man he had never seen before. They stared at one another for a long moment. Finally it was Alexios who looked away, but his eyes found no resting place to please him. The blood-bespattered table where he had been chained a month ago was still there, and from what he had heard and now saw, its recent occupant had only just departed. Probably for the deep waters of the Bosphorus.

The tools bore fresh blood that gleamed in the flickering light, and there was a dark puddle on the floor nearby. He felt his heart quail and his stomach knot at the thought of lying there yet again, unable to answer the shouted questions hurled at him for hours on end. He glanced away to look at the full chamber and was sickened to see a severed arm lying in a corner. His stomach heaved, but there was nothing in it to come out, only a small retch before he could regain control of himself.

The man before him looked vaguely familiar, Alexios realized slowly, but he was hideously scarred down one side of his face and appeared to be wearing a wig.

"Ssit down, Alexios," the man said.

The jailers behind him shoved Alexios into a heavy wooden chair with metal clasps along the arms and began to clamp him down. "Leave it alone!" the man snapped at them. "Leave us."

"But, your lordship—"

"Go!" the word cut the air like a whip. The guards scurried off like rats.

Alexios brought his attention back to the man in front of him.

"You don't recognize me do you, Alexios Kalothesos? How have they been treating you?"

"No, I don't recognize you, and they are not treating me at all well." Alexios shook his head. His long, filthy hair slapped his face as he did so; he barely noticed it.

"Yess, you do look a little thin."

"Your creatures don't go in for much in the way of food," Alexios retorted, determined upon defiance.

The man gave a grimace, like smile of amusement.

"Then let me tell you a little about mysself," he said with a slight sibilance to his voice, as he took a stool and placed it opposite Alexios and sat down. He smoothed his tunic with care, then he, too, looked around. His grotesquely distorted face registered distaste.

"Not the best of places to renew our acquaintance, but it will just have to do." He smiled, baring good teeth to Alexios.

"Who are you?" Alexios managed to croak. He was very thirsty.

As though sensing this, the man in front of him stood up and said, "You would like something to drink, perhaps? I can offer you water, or even some wine. It comes from an estate not too far from here."

"A drink of water," Alexios said huskily.

"Very well, some water," Exazenos said, and poured some into a leather cup which he handed to Alexios, who lifted it to his lips with a clink from the chains on his wrists.

"Why did you bring me here?" he asked, after he had gulped the entire contents of the mug.

Exazenos settled himself comfortably, his eyes intent on Alexios' every shift and expression. "I am going to tell you who I am, and then we will deal with the future and your place in it... or not in it, as the case may be."

Alexios did not expect to leave the dungeons alive; he wondered what this strange man could possibly have in mind. Exazenos continued in the same conversational tone he had used from the beginning.

"I am known as Exazenos by everyone here in the city, but you know me by the name Pantoleon Spartenos," said the man, and he watched the reaction from Alexios.

His eyes widened with disbelief and shock as he re-examined Pantoleon. "You can't be!" he breathed. "He died in the battle of Myriokephalon. We were all there. You're lying."

"Hmm, well, not really. You see, I did die and lived again but... as you can see, somewhat changed."

"How, how did you live?" Alexios gasped. "Where have you been all these years?" his voice still sounded as though he didn't believe what he was hearing.

"Let me tell you a little story, and then we will see if you believe me or not," said the man who called himself Exazenos—Pantoleon, the once famous charioteer.

"As you may well remember, the army was ambushed in the defile by the Turks, who rained boulders down upon us. I was up near the emperor, and if I remember rightly you were back some way with that annoying Frankish friend of yours. A boulder struck my horse and took us both down into the river. I was thrown by the animal right onto the other side of the stream, where I bashed my head and knew nothing from that moment on.

"That is, until I woke up and found that I was lying on a fire, which as you might imagine got my attention very quickly; so I did some screaming and flailing about, then found myself being dragged off this pyre by some Turkish soldiers, who tossed me back into the river to cool off."

Pantoleon grimaced at Alexios, who wore an expression of incredulous astonishment. "Yes, I had virtually died, but the fire woke me up to something... unexpected. Two days before, the Turks had gone among the wounded and the dead and scalped every one of us. Look!" he took off the wig and showed Alexios the dreadful scars on his head. His smile was a baring of teeth.

"Panto, I'm so sorry," Alexios whispered. "I had no idea."

"No, well, no one did. Our illustrious *Emperor,*" he spat out the word, "Manuel the pig ran away, didn't he? Along with his famous guard and the rest of you. You left me and many others there to die or to become slaves, which is what happened to me. I was one of the lucky ones, up to a point," Pantoleon snarled.

"The Turks didn't try very hard to keep us alive. Many died, and it was probably a relief, after the way we were treated, but I wanted to live. You see, I wanted to come home." His eyes burned as he remembered....

He woke to a terrible burning sensation on the right side of his body. Pantoleon jerked fully awake. He was in the middle of a fire, surrounded by bodies that were burning furiously. He screamed in horror and agony and struggled to roll out, thinking of all he had heard about hell, and then he felt hands seizing him and dragging him out of the fire. The agony didn't stop there; he was rolled on the grass and then tossed, still screaming, into a stream nearby. The cold of the water was almost more than he could bear, as it seemed to burn the already flayed skin off his shoulders and face. He went under and then surfaced, gasping for air.

Again hands grabbed him and hauled him onto the bank, where he lay while some Turkish men stood over him, arguing. He couldn't understand what they were saying, but he was sure it was about whether they should bother to keep him alive or not.

One grabbed him by the neck and pulled him to his knees. Pantoleon thought this was the end and closed his eyes. But a voice shouted at him and he was hauled to his feet and made to sit down under a tree beside another prisoner. He was too weak to do anything, let alone try to escape. He could see the Turks examining the bodies before they stripped them of armor, clothes, and jewelry then heaved the bodies onto a roaring fire. He wondered why they bothered. Usually a battlefield was left with its dead to rot forever; he had once ridden across an old one. Why were they burning bodies this time?

Pantoleon felt searing pain everywhere, including his crotch, which appeared to be bleeding. He looked down and cried out. His testicles were missing; where they had been was a bloody ruin. He began to weep. He was now not even half a man.

"Stop complaining," said the man on the other side of the tree. "At least you are alive and not burning in that." He gestured towards the bonfire.

"Dear God, I wish I was!" Pantoleon cried in anguish. "Where are we? Are we in hell?" he asked the world at large.

"No, but we are very close to it. You need to get over this and focus on how we get home."

"Who are you?"

"I am a soldier, or was, until this fuck up," the person replied. "My name is Gabros. Pleased to meet you, Pantoleon, charioteer."

"You know me?'

"Even through the mess you are in right now, I recognize you. You were my favorite man in the arena. I won some good bets on you."

Pantoleon groaned. "I am weak from loss of blood. I can't think."

Take a cloth; there's one, they won't miss it. Go down to the river and clean yourself up. Someone was careless: they have been cutting everything off, not just the balls. You're lucky you still have your pecker. Go on, they won't chase you unless you try to escape, and then its over." He drew his finger tips across his throat. "Stay alive, Senator boy."

"Why are they burning the bodies?" Pantoleon asked, leaning his head back against the tree with care. His entire scalp burned furiously.

"Because on this side there is a village and they want to clean up the mess so it does not spread to their homes. Wolves have already come, and worse would follow. They might make a pyre on the other side of the water later, but right now it's this side they are cleaning up."

"How do you know this?"

"Because I speak Turkish, I called out to them when they came for me and they spared me for that reason alone," he glanced meaningfully down at himself and followed with. "I spent the night in hiding and was about to rejoin the army when I was captured. I've been here ever since. I'm hungry, just like you, so stop whining and clean up, Senator boy. Your wounds will fester if you don't."

"Shut up with the Senator thing,"

Pantoleon limped down to the water's edge and began to clean himself, wincing with agony as he applied the cold water to his wounds. The Turks merely glanced at him, then returned to their gruesome work.

Half an hour later, he came back and sat down painfully next to Gabros. His wounds were excruciatingly sore, but they were cleaned now, and he wore a loincloth he had found that was clean enough.

"Why did the Turks do this to all of us?" he demanded.

"Because they nearly lost the battle and didn't want the Greeks to know who was who when our army came back down the pass on its way home. They did it to their own as well as the Greeks. A ruthless thing to do, but its aim, to demoralize the Greek army, probably worked. What would you think if you had to march back down and see all the bodies like this? I wonder how many got through before the Turks closed in and finished them off completely?"

Later that day, when Pantoleon was weak with hunger and ready to pass out, the Turkish men shouted at the two of them to get up and come with them back to the village that was perched high on one of the hills overlooking the ravine. It was a long, painful journey for Pantoleon, but Gabros who was unwounded helped him along, and he was grateful for the assistance because the Turks gave them none.

After what seemed like hours of climbing they reached the village and were greeted by curious women and children who stared, chattered among themselves, and pointed at the two prisoners. The heavily laden men shouted at the more inquisitive children to stay away and slapped those too slow to do so.

The prisoners were hustled into a low, dark, mud-walled room and left alone. They could hear an intense, shouted argument going on between the men who had brought them up the hill and an old man with a long white beard, who seemed to be angry that they had brought prisoners back with them. Gabros, his ear to the door, told Pantoleon that the old man wanted to have them killed, but one of their former captors wanted to sell them instead, claiming they could make money out of the deal.

The village quieted as dusk began to fall. The children, who had been trying to peer into the room through the splits in the wooden door, finally left; later still, the door was rattled open by one of their guards and two bowls of *mast,* a very strong yoghurt, and some flat bread were placed just inside by a veiled woman who pointed at the food and then to her mouth. Gabros and Pantoleon seized their bowls and shoveled the bitter yoghurt into their mouths, wiping the crude earthenware bowls clean with the last of the bread.

"We have to leave this place as quickly as we can," Gabros told Pantoleon. "They are going to take us east to sell us along with other prisoners. Once there we will never escape, and even if we did it would be impossible to get home across that country swarming with tribespeople."

"We would need horses, too," Pantoleon remarked from his squatting position against one of the walls. Right now he could hardly keep his eyes open, he was so exhausted.

"We should rest and think," Gabros said in the darkness. "Tomorrow might present us with an opportunity."

His words fell on deaf ears. Pantoleon was already fast asleep.

Two nights later he was woken by Gabros, who had a hand across his mouth as he shook him roughly awake. "Shhh, it is time to leave. They got careless," Gabros whispered. He had managed to pick the latch on the door and had discovered the young sentry fast asleep, along with the rest of the slumbering village.

"Can you walk and run?" he asked Pantoleon, who nodded. His wounds had scabbed over, and thanks to Gabros' intervention they were healing cleanly. He knew it was now or never, so he tried to ignore the pain in his groin and his burns and listened while Gabros explained what they were going to do. Their way out was not to try for the nearest town of Dorylaeum, which was to their east and would be the most obvious: that way was surely discovery and death. The road to that town would be full of Turkish cavalry still looking for stragglers.

"They'll still be picking over the loot abandoned by the emperor," Gabros said. "We have to go south over the mountains to Attalia. If we even survive to get away it will be a hard journey; can you make it?"

Pantoleon didn't need to be told what it was going to cost them, but to stay was to become a slave, and he didn't want that. No, he had a burning desire to get home and take his revenge on those who'd abandoned him.

Gabros proved to have some skill at the art of silent killing. The young sentry barely spasmed as he was despatched, which allowed them to make their way unhindered to the edge of the village. There were horses stabled here, not many, as the villagers were hill people, but being Turkish they kept the animals for their journeys. It was not hard to lead the animals out quietly and then to mount two, although it was painful for Pantoleon to do so. The other three they led behind them as they took a dimly lit path up the mountain, instead of heading for the road.

Going the opposite direction to the obvious might give them a couple of days grace. They were still almost naked, but the dead sentry at the door and the one who had been guarding the horses now wore less clothing than the two fugitives. The young moon assisted them to climb the steep slopes of the mountain that night. They were armed with the crude spears and knives of the dead men, but against the fury of any pursuers they would stand no chance, so they rode all night, stopping only at streams to allow themselves and the horses to drink. They had no food, but hunger was the least of their worries; they needed to put as much distance between themselves and the village as they could, because once their escape was discovered it would resemble a hornets' nest of rage.

Pantoleon had good reason to be glad of Gabros from that moment forth, as he proved to be a tough and resilient companion. He knew how to cover their tracks and to conserve their ponies, which were shaggy, tough little animals, ideal for the rugged terrain they were traversing. They stayed just below the snow line on the edge of the forests that spread down into the deep valleys below. In the very early hours they would stop and rest, huddled together near the ponies, listening to the night calls of the nocturnal creatures. Every night they heard wolves, and sometimes Pantoleon thought he could see their ghostly forms slinking between the trees not far away. The ponies would become restless and the men went without sleep, staying awake to calm the animals.

After two full days and nights of almost nonstop climbing up and over the mountain range known as the Torus Mountains, moving along ill-defined goat paths or trackless terrain, they found themselves overlooking a deep valley rich in grassland and trees, with a river running along the center. Pantoleon was weak with hunger and so exhausted he could hardly stay upright on the pony.

Gabros, although he, too, was weary, was wide awake and still alert. He took a good look at the ground and the area into which they were about to descend and stated that it looked safe enough to stop for half a day to allow the horses to feed. Pantoleon himself needed to eat but there had been nothing so far, just water from the mountain streams. Worse than the gnawing in his belly was the wound in his groin: due to the constant motion of his mount it had not healed well and was beginning to fester. He was relieved to be able to get off the pony and rest.

Gabros disappeared, leaving him sitting against a fir tree with his eyes shut and dreaming of Constantinople. Should he survive, which despite the best efforts of Gabros he doubted, he would arrive home looking grotesque and might never be able to race in the arena again. One thing he promised himself: he would avenge himself upon those who had abandoned him. This resolve was slowly becoming a white hot anger that sustained him despite the agony of his wounds, the hunger, and the sheer exhaustion that dogged him.

He must have slept, because when he awoke it was to find two shaggily dressed men sitting on equally shaggy ponies standing about twenty paces away from him. They were muttering to each other in what he took to be Turkish, gesturing towards him. He started, but then froze, his heart pounding. They had been discovered, and these men carried bows. There was no escape!

But as he stared at them in hopeless resignation one of the mounted men opened his mouth wide and threw his arms up in the air. Then, before his companion could do more than gawk, he tumbled off his pony to fall in an untidy heap on the ground, a spear protruding from his back. The next thing that Pantoleon saw was a big rock flying through the air to collide with the head of the second rider. His eyes crossed and he also tumbled to the ground, where he lay stunned. Gabros darted out of the bushes behind and, kneeling next to his victim, stabbed the man repeatedly. When he was satisfied that his victim was dead, he looked up at Pantoleon, who had not moved a muscle.

"That was close," Gabros said calmly. "You need to stay awake, Senator boy." He wiped the blade of his wicked looking knife on the dead man's thigh and stood up. Eyeing the accoutrements of the two men he said, "Good. Now we are well armed and well mounted, but first we shall eat."

"Were these two following us from the village?" Pantoleon asked. He was still shaken.

"No doubt about it, but we are in the province of Kibyrrhaiotai, which, the last time I checked, still belongs to the emperor. We've crossed the hardest part of mountains, and it's mostly down hill now. If we can make it to the coast we will be safe."

He produced a hare, which he proceeded to gut and cook over an almost smokeless fire. By the time they were finished there was very little left of the creature, and it was dusk. Pantoleon's crotch felt as though it was on fire. He went to the stream and washed carefully, but the area was red, swollen, and it was hard to urinate. He felt hot. With a sinking feeling in his gut he described the wound to Gabros, who nodded. "I was wondering when this would happen. We need to find some of our own people and get that seen to. We'll move on in the morning; meanwhile, get some rest."

While Pantoleon dozed in restless sleep Gabros went about the business of stripping the two unwelcome visitors and taking an inventory of their weapons and possessions. He muttered something when he came across a handful of gold teeth in a hide pouch. These two men had been at Myriokephalon. No Turk possessed gold teeth... in his mouth.

The next morning found them on new ponies leading the best of the other ponies, two of which they had left behind. Pantoleon was feeling ill, but he clenched his teeth and endured the painful ride. They were well armed with bows and could hold off a few enemy should any more come after them at this late stage. Gabros hoped to meet up with a patrol of soldiers from Attalia, although he was not sure how far away it was.

They crested a high rise at about noon and Gabros gave a call back to Pantoleon. "The sea! It's the sea!" He glanced back and noticed that Pantoleon was swaying in the saddle.

"Hang on there, Senator boy! We are nearly there," he called.

Just as he did so he heard a shout from off to his left. A patrol of soldiers was galloping towards them. They looked determined and ready for trouble, so he rode back to join Pantoleon and waited. Within minutes they were surrounded by grim looking men who seemed on the edge of killing them with no questions asked.

"Hold up there!" Gabros shouted for all to hear. "We are soldiers who have come from Myriokephalon! Do not harm us."

There were exclamations of surprise. "Who are you? You look more like Turks than Greeks," the commander of the patrol demanded, his tone loud and aggressive.

"We borrowed these things," Gabros stated with a disarming grin. "You are looking at two who managed to get away," he chuckled. "We survived but were taken prisoner and then escaped. Listen," he pointed to Pantoleon, "he's in a very bad way. Needs a physician urgently. His name is Exazenos."

When the patrol had overcome their shock at seeing Pantoleon's burns and head wounds they immediately made a travois and laid him on it. By this time he had a fever and was barely conscious.

While they were doing this, Gabros had a quiet word with the commander. "I would much appreciate it if this was kept very quiet," he said. "Exazenos is a very wealthy man in his own right, and I know he will reward you extremely well if you do this for him. You see... his injuries are more than just those burns and the gash on his head."

The commander stared at the recumbent figure on the travois and then looked up at Gabros with wide eyes. "We had heard something terrible that was done. Was he...? Is he...?"

Gabros put his finger to his lips and nodded.

"Ill news always travels faster than the wind," the young commander said, his voice full of sympathy now. "Rest easy, I shall swear the physician to secrecy. We must get him there before his condition gets worse."

Pantoleon spent four days in a fevered coma, while Gabros and the physician who had been found tended to him. He woke on the fifth morning feeling a lot better but very weak, and from that day forth he began to recover—physically. Inside, however, he was damaged, and while Gabros understood this he didn't discuss it with him.

Gabros explained the reason for the new name, and Pantoleon nodded his head in agreement. "Better to remain with this name," he said. Some instinct told him it would be wise to do so; besides, he was so appalled at the image he saw in the polished bronze mirror that he shuddered. He certainly did not want any of his former companions to see him like this and despise him, or worse, pity him. "We will go back to Constantinople and pick up the pieces when we get there," he told Gabros. "What are you going to do? I owe you my life several times over but cannot repay you until we get home."

Gabros looked uncertain. "If you wish to take me into your employment, I would be happy enough about that," he said.

Pantoleon looked at the man, remembering his resourcefulness and speed with weapons. A very useful man to have at his back. "Willingly," he stated. "You stay with me, and I shall be glad of it."

But disaster awaited them. When they eventually made their way back to the city, Pantoleon made a terrible discovery. His father, Senator John Spartenos, and his mother Constance were dead, their property confiscated. His father had been proscribed as a traitor after a failed attempt to depose Emperor Manuel, and all his properties were forfeit. The revolt of the Senators had been in reaction to the debacle of Myriokephalon, as many of the Families had lost sons, heirs, servants and much of their wealth in that gorge where Pantoleon had almost died. He had come back to find his disgraced and dishonored family officially no longer existed, because he was thought to be dead.

The discovery shocked him profoundly. He had slipped into the city on a Cypriot ship that docked at Neorion harbor, so no one was aware of his presence. He was now very glad of the new name given to him by Gabros. No one recognized him, but he could not stay in the city for much longer for fear of discovery. He did, however, make enquiries with Gabros' help that revealed the manner in which his parents had died and what had happened to much of their possessions.

The house had been burned to the ground, leaving a black smear in the hectare of green land surrounding it. Staring around him at the devastation and the weed-grown stables and out houses, he raged anew. The final humiliation had been when the name of a certain Frank, Talon de Gilles, surfaced as having some responsibility for the destruction of his father. Pantoleon, like all Greeks, disliked and distrusted the Latins and the Franks, but as far as he was concerned the family Kalothesos bore the main responsibility for his family's downfall. Their elder daughter had betrayed his father, and that was enough. Pantoleon cared not one whit that his father had not only been part of a plot to dethrone the emperor Manuel but had done a deal to sell out the one weapon the Byzantines possessed that could keep their enemies at bay—Greek Fire.

There was a long silence between the two men, as one remembered and the other watched the workings of his keeper's face.

"I am so terribly sorry," Alexios whispered. "I was wounded and only managed to get home because of that same man, Talon, and his companion. I had no idea that we had left you behind," he sighed. "It was a disaster, and the emperor barely made it home. So many were left on the side of the road to be killed and their bodies pillaged."

"I don't care what happened to the rest of them!" Pantoleon shouted, all his pent up fury coming out. "I was one of his *best* men, one of his most important! I was his champion charioteer! Still he left me and made no attempt to find me!"

Alexios shrank away from this rage. It took a visible effort for Pantoleon to regain his composure.

"So you see, Alexios, my good friend, I became a pirate. Many a ship has been plundered by my men and Gabros, whom you might yet meet. He is one terrific killer, that man! Myself, I am a leader, and I can boast that is I, in no small part who helped our Emperor destroy the Senators and their lackeys, their 'administrators'." He would not use the word eunuch. It was too close to home.

"Do you remember those hysterical idiots who brought him back from exile in Syria to become emperor? We already knew one another, and I had established a network of spies, both within the city and outside. He knew what value I would have for him."

Alexios stared at his former friend and rival. "So it has been you who has systematically destroyed the senatorial class?" he demanded. "My father? All those people who died horribly were denounced by *you*?

Pantoleon nodded. "The wine from your father's cellar is excellent, by the way."

"What did my father ever do to you, or your father for that matter?! He had nothing to do with the fire and your father's death, I can assure you of that!" Alexios still managed, despite his weak condition, to add bite and contempt to his words.

Pantoleon shot him a cold and bitter look. "Yes, it has been me, and I am not yet done, Alexios Kalothesos. I intend to destroy your entire family and leave no issue to continue the name."

Alexios expression must have given away the panic inside him.

"Yes, indeed I will, but in my own time, slowly. Your sister, for instance." He watched Alexios give a start of alarm. "Oh yes, I saw her; today in fact. She came to examine my right eye. There really isn't much wrong with it, but it was a good excuse to get near to her. Attractive, in an interesting sort of way." Pantoleon drew out his words for the benefit of his audience.

Had he been laid out on the table and tortured Alexios could not have imagined a more exquisite agony than this. His squeezed his eyes shut and his features crumpled with horror at what he was hearing. Tears dribbled down his filthy face to disappear into his beard.

"You must not! She is an innocent, for God's sake!" he whispered in a hoarse voice. "Are you such a monster that it means nothing to you, to destroy innocent people? Have you not done enough by destroying my father, her husband, and me?" He seemed to slump in his seat, but he would not remove his angry gaze from Pantoleon.

"We'll see." Pantoleon smiled his grotesque grimace. "If she pleases me I might spare her, but I shall enjoy her first. She smells very nice...." He lifted his head and sniffed theatrically. "So few women please me these days," he added ruminatively.

With a strangled cry of pure rage, Alexios leapt up from his chair and threw himself at Pantoleon, who, while he had been anticipating some kind of reaction, was not prepared for this arm-flailing, chain-thrashing, screaming dervish who crashed into him and tipped them both onto the filthy, blood-caked floor. It took all his considerable strength for Pantoleon to eventually subdue Alexios, who fought like a devil, pummeling with his fists, scratching and roaring as he tried to kill his tormentor, but eventually Alexios was beaten unconscious, with the help of Pantoleon's guards who came rushing in to help their master.

Pantoleon staggered to his feet and looked down upon the unconscious body of his erstwhile assailant. He wiped the cut on the side of his mouth tentatively with the back of his hand, then shook his head, breathing heavily.

"Don't kill him," he warned them, as he straightened his clothing and replaced his wig. He wasn't ready to kill Alexios, not yet. He was needed as a bargaining piece for the goodwill of his sister.

My life is far from my dream of life—
Calmly contented, serenely glad;
But, vexed and worried by daily strife,
It is always troubled, and ofttimes sad—
And the heights I had thought I should reach one day
Grow dimmer and dimmer, and farther away.
—Ella Wheeler Wilcox

Chapter 21
Flight

All the way home inside the lurching litter with its closed curtains Theodora thought about the man she had just met. Who was he? Certainly one of the emperor's highest ranking servants, he could not be otherwise living in the opulence of those chambers. How was it that in this gossip- and rumor-rife city she had never heard his name before?

She looked down at the small bag of gold she now held in her hands. It would feed them for months and keep them warm in the winter to come. The payment was more than she could ever have expected. It left her puzzled, and with an uncomfortable feeling, because the injuries to his face had not in fact wrought much damage to the eye itself and the cataract within was in its early stages. Not a very good reason for all the trouble he'd taken to find her, she surmised.

The man unsettled her, behaving almost as though he knew her, but from where? The look she had caught in the back of his eyes when she told him her name was frightening, and she shivered. She hoped that he never called upon her again, but feared that this would not be the case. Blinking back tears as she thought of her husband, brother, and father, Theodora felt very alone and vulnerable. They had been sentenced from this very palace. Could the man who called himself Exazenos be one of those monsters who worked for the emperor in his ghastly pogroms? Why else would he live like a prince in that place?

The Verangians deposited her civilly enough in front of the villa gates and left her there while they tramped off back up the hill. It was already late afternoon, so there was no point in going to the academy. Theodora walked slowly, in a very thoughtful mood, along the rough path towards the house. She didn't hear what Angelos called out to her; she just waved and walked on.

She was still wrapped up in her thoughts when she opened the door and walked into the main room to hear voices in the living area. Instantly wary she stopped, then stepped in cautiously to find her mother talking in an animated manner to a man she recognized. Giorgios, the one-time family assistant agent, was seated near to her mother, he was smiling and sipping on a cup of wine.

He jumped to his feet when he noticed Theodora standing at the doorway.

"Madame! Forgive me for the intrusion. I have just come from Rhodes and Cyprus and was in the city, so I took a chance to come and see how you were," he said.

"Giorgios, you are always welcome!" Theodora said, a smile of relief and pleasure on her face as she walked forward to take their former servant's hands in hers. "How have you been? How is your family? We are starved of news from outside the city."

Giorgios grinned with pleasure and ducked his head respectfully. "My Lady, I am well and so is my family; but alas, I see that you are not. God save us, but your mother has told me something of what has been going on. It is truly terrible." He had tears in his eyes as he spoke but Theodora would have none of it and brushed away his remonstrances.

"I see you have some wine, not such good vintage, I fear," she said. Giorgios just shrugged and smiled. "It is more important that I came to see you," he replied with genuine affection. He was a stocky man, running to a middle-aged spread and balding, but his round features were kindly. She was glad to see a friendly face.

"Hello, Mother," Theodora said, placing a kiss on her mother's forehead.

"How did it go with the visit to the palace?" Joannina asked her, with concern in her voice.

"It was strange, and I am still trying to understand what was going on. I will say one thing: the man I met was frightening. I had the impression I might know him, and I have racked my brains but cannot think where or when," Theodora told her. "He wanted me to examine his eye; he had been badly burned at one time and said that it was giving him problems. Didn't seem that way to me, but... he at least paid for the visit, so I cannot complain. But enough of this; Giorgios, you must tell us all. I want to hear of the exotic places you have visited since the last time you were here. It must have been two years!"

"Closer to three, my Lady," he answered.

"Has it been that long?" she asked, looking distracted.

They talked till dusk fell and Theodora went to get Damian to join them for supper. Giorgios made much of the boy, which brought a smile to her face. Their guest agreed to have some soup with them, as he had much to tell and his ship would be leaving in a week or so. He might be unable to come back, there was so much to do. The boat, he told them, was anchored in Neorion harbor. "You can even see it from here."

"So that is your ship?" Theodora asked him, as he pointed the vessel out to her. "I should congratulate you, you have come up in the world."

He smiled. "Well, it really belongs to Isaias, my partner in Rhodes, my Lady, but he trusts me with trade and hates sailing, so I am in charge of the ship, as it were. But I have news that might interest you," he said with a glance at the doorway, as though he didn't want to be overheard.

"Go on," Joannina said from her chair, raising her eyebrows with interest.

"Do you remember a Frank named Talon?" Giorgios asked them.

After a moment's hesitation, both women nodded. "Yes indeed, we do remember him. What a strange young man he was. We all liked him, though." Joannina said ruminatively.

Theodora actually felt her ears beginning to burn. "Yes, I remember him. What of him?" she asked, trying to sound casual. Her memories of the young Frank came rushing back. Her behavior had not, as she remembered it, been altogether circumspect towards the Frank.

Giorgios rubbed the growing patch of baldness on his receding hairline. "I was in the port of Paphos three weeks ago," he said. "The emperor of Cyprus is known to you, I believe. Isaac Komnenos?"

"Another Komnenos?" Theodora snapped. "Tell me, Giorgios, is he as bad as this one?"

Giorgios looked frightened for a moment, then he nodded his head. "Every bit as bad, I'm afraid, my Lady. One of the first things he did when he conquered the island was to seek out his former tutor, beggar him, then cut off his feet. He is just as sadistic as his great uncle."

"So what has this to do with Talon?" Joannina demanded, after making a grimace of disgust.

"Well, rumor has it that Sir Talon, who is a Templar Knight, managed to steal a castle from the emperor! And when the emperor wanted to take it back, Talon somehow, no one knows how, persuaded the emperor to let him keep it!"

"Both women had reflexively put their hands to their mouths, their eyes wide with surprise and disbelief.

"Dear God, Giorgios! Are you not joking?" Joannina asked, an expression of incredulous amusement beginning to form on her tired face.

Giorgios shook his head with a grin. "No, my Lady, no one on the island is talking about anything else! They are also laughing behind their hands, because the emperor is loathed. From what I have heard, the castle of Kantara is virtually impregnable. No one knows how he took it, but they say that Sir Talon has been to far away lands where he learned magic. He is now a wizard who makes thunderbolts fly and destroys whole armies, and his men are invisible at night." Giorgios seemed to relish the tale.

"I wonder what the emperor thought about that?" Theodora asked the room at large, her tone dry, at the same time trying and failing to stop a tiny snort of laughter. She glanced over at her mother, who seemed to be having difficulty controlling her own amusement. They were both on the edge of hysterics at this preposterous tale.

"Giorgios, you really must not tease us like this. It's too good to be true," Joannina begged him, waving her hands in the air like a happy preying mantis.

Giorgios looked hurt. "I swear it upon my honor, my Lady! All of it is true! The emperor has given orders that Talon, er, Sir Talon is to be left strictly alone and his followers too," he asserted. "It's unbelievable, but I swear it is true!"

"Are you sure this is the same Talon we know?" demanded Theodora.

"I am now very sure, because I ran into one of his captains while in Paphos harbor, a Master Henry, whom I remembered from before. We met right there on the quayside! I could not believe my eyes, but it was Henry all right; he assured me that his master had been here to Constantinople, and furthermore he remembered you. Henry was avid for news, and I had to tell him the sad state of affairs in this city. Henry assures me that Talon has a following on Cyprus who would willingly die for him."

"Where on the island is Talon living? Where is this fabled castle of his, Giorgios?" Theodora wanted to know.

"It is on the long strip of mountains that runs north of Famagusta, my Lady. There is a small harbor there. I have sailed past it on my way to Paphos from Alanya before."

Joanna nodded her head. "I am beginning to believe you, Giorgios. Talon had a friend with him, I remember."

"Yes, his name is Max, and he is there. The stories Henry told me of their adventures almost turned my hair gray!" Giorgios ran a hand through his sparse hair. "They had a man called Dimitri who helped translate for me, as I don't speak their barbaric language very well. He, like Henry, seems in awe of Sir Talon.

It is Dimitri who told me that Talon had come back from a great sea journey to lands far, far to the east where the silk is from. Dimitri told me of the time when Talon threw a thunderbolt down to the ground and many of the emperor's men perished in an instant."

"So there is much more to this story than the few words you have told us," Joannina said. She turned to her grandson, who was listening wide-eyed to the visitor. "Damian, you may stay up just this once to hear the story, but then it is straight to bed. Theo, please put another log on the fire, I am cold. We must have a good bottle of wine left *somewhere*! Giorgios, please stay; have some more of our awful wine and tell us all!"

Theodora went back to work the next day in a very thoughtful mood. Her encounter with the strange man Exazenos, combined with the news of Talon's exploits, had made for an almost sleepless night. She managed to work her way through the day and returned home, expecting to rest and relax, but she was disappointed.

The gate man, Angelos, must have been waiting for her. As soon as he spied her coming down the road he hobbled out towards her as fast as he could.

"Madame, Madame, wait!" he called, waving his arms.

Theodora stopped and allowed him to catch up.

"What is it, Angelos?" she asked the puffing old man, who bowed and said, "Madame you have a visitor."

Theodora ducked her head, acknowledging the news. "Do you know who it is?" she asked.

"Someone who has an escort of soldiers and came on a fine looking horse. He is badly scarred, what little of his face I could see, Madame."

Theodora blinked, and her heart sank. "Exazenos!"

"Thank you, Angelos. I will go to meet with him," she said, and made her way along the pathway towards the house feeling as though she had a lump of lead in her stomach. Sure enough, there was a palanquin standing on the grass and a small group of dismounted soldiers watering their horses at the old trough while talking amongst themselves. They stopped talking when they spied her walking towards them.

As she passed, she heard a muttered comment from one of the men to another. It was a crude remark that angered her, but she held her head high and pretended not to hear them. Her heart beating hard against her ribs, she made her way to the entrance, where two guards stood waiting. They nodded politely enough to her, and she passed into the main hall. The murmur of conversation from within alerted her that the visitor was talking to her mother.

As she came into the room the visitor stood up and turned to greet her. Once again there was something familiar about him that she couldn't place.

"Ah, there you are, my dear," her mother called out. "We have a visitor. Such a nice man, he has been so interesting."

"Hello, mother," Theodora said, and gave Exazenos a wary look with a question in it.

He gave her the grimace that passed as a smile and extended his hand to greet her. She gave him her hand but felt like recoiling as he held it.

"I was passing by on my way back to the palace when I decided to make a call upon you, my Lady," he said, as he bowed over her hand. She resisted snatching it away from him.

Her mind was racing. What was he doing here?

"I came because there is an emergency, my Lady. I need you to come with me to the palace. At once."

"At once?" she asked. "Surely it can wait until tomorrow. It is late and I am very tired."

"I am very sorry, my Lady, but it cannot wait. You must come with me," he voice carried iron in it that she didn't miss. She stared up at him; he was taller than she by half a hand.

"What could possibly be so urgent that I must leave tonight for the palace?" she demanded.

"I shall explain as soon as we arrive, but you must come. Please, I have brought a litter for your comfort. It will not take very long."

She turned to her mother. "I should not be too late, Mother. Please do not fret yourself."

Turning on her heel, Theodora led the way out of the house. The late afternoon sun had illuminated the Bosphorus and the land on the other side in a golden light, but she paid little attention to the momentary beauty.

They left almost immediately, with Exazenos leading his small squad of horsemen and the palanquin following as fast as the four men could carry it.

Her heart wouldn't stop its nervous pounding all the way as she endured the trip back to the Blachernae Palace. Instinctively she feared that something terrible was going to happen, despite the reassuring behavior of Exazenos, who had touched her on the arm just before he sprung onto his horse with the lithe ease of a practiced athlete. Of course they didn't have any chance of conversation along the Messe or the wide avenues that led to the palace.

When they arrived, he was there to open the door and to escort her to his quarters.

"Do you wish for any refreshment, my Lady?" he asked, as he divested himself of his travel cloak, then helped her to do the same.

"No, I am fine," she said. Her mouth was dry, but she didn't want anything but to be able to leave as soon as possible.

"Please be seated. I must first tell you something important, and then we can proceed," he told her. Turning to his man he said, "Bring me some wine and a cup of water for the Lady." Gabros nodded and disappeared, to very quickly return with a tray carrying a silver cup full of a familiar smelling wine and another containing cool water.

"You should drink something," Exazenos said in a calm tone. "You probably need it."

Theodora had to agree with him. Her throat was parched, and the cool water helped calm her nerves.

He sipped his wine and looked across the low table at her. "I shall tell you something which you must keep to yourself, my Lady," he said finally.

Theodora gave a tiny shrug. She was accustomed to keeping medical confidences. "What is it that you have to tell me?" she asked.

"Your brother, do you know where he is?"

Theodora jerked upright.

"No!" She had gone pale. "Do *you* know?"

"Oh, yesss. I can help him... and you." Exazenos spoke in a low tone.

Theodora clasped her hands together on her lap almost as though she were praying.

"Where is he? Is he then alive?" she asked, almost choking. She had tears in her eyes now, and her nails were digging into her palms as she tried to control her expression.

Exazenos sat back in his chair and regarded her speculatively. She was aware that Gabros was standing in the shadows, also watching her reaction. A cold feeling settled over her. Why did she suddenly feel like a mouse trapped between two cats?

"Oh yes, he is alive, and I can preserve his life," Exazenos replied. "But first you must know this: the emperor in his infinite wisdom has decided to execute all the prisoners in the dungeons, regardless of who they are."

Theodora thought she was going to be sick. "Why?" she whispered.

"Because he is mad, and now his paranoia is dominating his thinking. You do know that Thessalonica is about to fall? The next target for William of Sicily will be Constantinople, and His Majesty wants to... um, clean house, as it were. He is quite mad you know."

"But, but Alexios never was a traitor! Why should he be... ?" she cried. "Surely the emperor knows that?" A lump in her throat almost choked her and the lead weight in her stomach was getting so heavy she thought she might fall off the chair. With a huge effort she drew herself up and said, "What can you do then to help my brother?"

Exazenos leaned forward, and with his forefinger traced a rough pattern in the few drops of wine that had fallen on the silver tray. "Well, you see, I have the power to save his life and even yours; but that will depend very much upon what you can do for me." He didn't look up immediately. He was waiting for the words to settle in. Then he looked up straight into her bewildered eyes. "You do understand what I mean?" he asked her.

For the first time he detected a flare of fear and almost smiled. He had been waiting for that. "Your brother can be set free and even your family estates returned, but... there is a price."

Theodora sat on the edge of the chair, her back as stiff as a ramrod. "So this is why you brought me here," she breathed. Her hands were still in her lap but were now white with the grip she had on herself.

Exazenos grimaced a smile. "I could not help myself, Theodora. You are a very intelligent and beautiful woman. It came as some surprise to me to see the estate again and its condition. Wonderful view, that was always there, but to find *you* there after all this time...." He stopped. He had nearly told her. Not just yet.

"What... what do you want of me?" she whispered.

He raised his eyebrows and leaned forward again. "Why, I want you for my wife, Theodora. You must understand that from the first moment I saw you I was smitten. I can protect you, your family, and set your brother free. There is not much time, however. His Majesty is determined upon this last mad idea of his. I fear it will be carried out before too long."

Theodora cleared her throat. "How do I know you are telling me the truth?" she said slowly.

"That your brother is alive? That is easily done. I can have Gabros take you to him right now."

"Here? Here in this palace?" she cried, astonished.

"Yesss, right here," he responded. "Come, Gabros will take you to him."

She stood up shakily. He reached out to steady her, but she snatched her arm away. There was no expression on her face, but he could sense the disgust and mentally shrugged. She would soon be cured of that attitude, he promised himself.

Gabros led the way, followed by Theodora.

The walk, along echoing corridors and down steps that took them to the level where the dungeons were located, was an ordeal for her, but she quieted her pounding heart and tried desperately to stay calm. She was barely aware of the stink of fear and death that lingered in the corridors. Alexios was alive! It had been two years since he had vanished, soon after their father had died at the executioner's hand. Strangled, rumor had said.

They were walking along a dark tunnel, poorly lit by flaring torches in sconces, when Gabros turned to his right and unlocked a thick wood door. He pushed it open and stood back, then motioned her to enter. Fearing that this might be where she would be imprisoned Theodora hesitated, but he nodded reassuringly and said, "I shall come for you in a few minutes."

She couldn't at first clearly make out the dark patch in the far corner of the stone cell, but when it sat up and looked at her she gasped with shock. Barely hearing the door shut behind her, she stared at the creature who had once been her brother. She didn't realize that she was weeping as she moved towards the emaciated figure who stood up shakily to greet her.

"Alexios!"

"Theo? Is that you? Oh dear God, it is you," he whispered. She fell into his arms, ignoring the stink of his unwashed body and the slime-covered, filthy rags. They clung to one another for a full minute while she wept into his shoulder and he stroked her hair, whispering endearments.

Eventually she stood back from him to further examine him. Her horror must have shown in her expression because he shrugged and said, "They don't treat a person very well in this place, I'm afraid. I would have changed had I known you were coming." He tried to grin.

She gasped a choking laugh. Alexios still maintained his sense of humor despite his condition. His face was obscured by a long dirty beard that had gone gray well before its time. There were scabs on his cheeks and his hair was matted with something that looked suspiciously like dried blood.

"Oh God, but what have they done to you, Alex?" she wailed.

He glanced at the door and drew her closer to him with his claw -like hands. "Shhh, who brought you here?" he asked in a whisper. He spoke in Latin to her.

"A man called Exazenos. He said he could protect you, set you free and... " she responded in the same language.

Alexios stopped her with a gesture. "Do you not know who he really is?" he ground out between his broken teeth.

"I, I know he is very powerful and can help," she responded. She was not going to tell Alexios what devil's bargain she was about to strike with the man.

Alexios reached up and took her by her shoulders. His eyes, which were wild enough already, took on a new intensity. "Oh, my Theo. What have you done?" he almost choked with emotion. "That man who sent you here is Pantoleon, remember him? We all thought he had died at Myriokephalon. He didn't die, and now he is the chief spy and executioner for the emperor. The Devil curse them both!"

Theodora took a step back in shock. "You cannot mean that, Alex!" she whispered back. He nodded emphatically. "It is he, and he has a huge hatred for our entire family. He intends to destroy us all. My dearest little sister, you must escape somehow. I know what he is doing. The vile creature wants you, and I am his bargaining piece for your willing agreement. He knows that if he holds me as hostage you would do it... for me." His shoulders slumped and he looked down. "I would rather die by my own hand than permit him to lay hands on you, my Theo."

He slowly looked up at Theodora, who wore a horrified expression on her pale, tear-stained face. She said nothing for a long moment, simply looking at him with her mouth half open and tears running down her face. Then she gave a violent shake of her head. "No , no you are wrong, Alex. Its...its not like that."

"Don't lie to me!" he almost shouted. "Not now, and not about this, or you condemn me to a living hell," he retorted. "I know full well what he means to do with you. He told me himself." Alexios's gesture indicated his scabs and the matted hair. "I tried to kill him, but of course his minions prevented that.

She nodded in mute acceptance. So he had divined why she was here; despite his awful condition her brother still had a clear mind. "What else can I do? He will save your life if, if I go to him." She almost choked on the words.

He shook his head. "No! You must leave the city, somehow. Even down here in the bowels of the earth in this fearsome place we hear things. Thessalonica is falling and then the Normans will come for Andronikos and exact a fearsome revenge upon all who live here."

"But he said he would protect us and release you," she sobbed.

"You cannot possibly believe that! He is the emperor's informant and executioner! He is a sadistic and cruel man with buckets of blood on his hands! Whatever he was before, Pantoleon is now a monster as insane as the emperor himself, and as soon as he thinks he has you I shall die anyway." He took her hands in his. "You must escape, Theo! Leave this city, and my soul will at least go to my God content that you are safe from this insanity."

"I cannot do that," she whispered through her tears. "Oh, Alex, is there no hope?"

He shook his head vehemently."No, my dearest sister! There is no hope. Not for me. I want you to swear that you will leave as soon as possible. There is not much time for either you or this city. Swear it!" he demanded of her, raising his voice.

They both glanced a the closed door, which rattled as someone began to unlock it.

"Swear it! Swear to God you will flee," Alexios whispered fiercely, gripping her hands in a vice-like hold.

She nodded and sobbed, "I swear. I swear to God." He relaxed his grip, and for the first time smiled. "I love you, my beautiful sister. Go with God. You have made me very, very happy. Give Mother my eternal love, and young Damian. You must protect them first."

He could say no more, for the door swung open and Gabros strode in. "Come," was all he said, and beckoned Theodora to leave.

She embraced Alexios, and then through the wet of his tears and disregarding the filth on his face, she kissed him on his lips. "Goodbye, my wonderful brother. Go to God in peace," she whispered. She felt him slip her loose belt off her waist from under her cloak and hide it under his rags. One more lingering look and it was time.

Then she turned, and without a backward glance she hurried out of the opening. She heard the door slam, and to her ears it sounded like the crash of doom for her brother. She knew she would never see him again. Head lowered, she allowed herself to be escorted up the many stairs and along the corridors until Gabros brought her back to the room she had left only twenty minutes before.

Pantoleon stood up from his chair and gave her his by now familiar grimace. He observed her tear-stained face and knew she had met her brother.

"So you have finally seen him. Not in the best of condition, but your brother is a wild prisoner and keeps getting into trouble, hence his condition."

Theodora drew herself up. "You know perfectly well that is a lie." She had had time to do some thinking as she followed Gabros through the labyrinth. "Is it true that you are Pantoleon?" she demanded outright.

He stared at her for a long moment, then nodded. "Yess, it is I. Your brother told you, no doubt. What else did he tell you?"

That unless I come to you of my free will you will have him executed. But if I do come to you, you will set him free?"

Theodora had been a teacher and physician for long enough now to know from a person's expression or the way their eyes moved whether they were lying or not.

The information she gleaned from her patients depended upon this kind of perception. She stared directly at Pantoleon and knew without a shadow of a doubt that he lied when he said, "His freedom is contingent upon that, yes. I shall free him when you accept my offer."

The leaden feeling came back with a slam. Theodora dragged her eyes away from his and looked down. "I agree to your terms, but I will need some time to prepare. My mother and family must be made aware of the change in my circumstances. I need some time," she insisted.

Pantoleon seemed on the verge of refusing, but then he nodded reluctantly and said, "Very well, I shall give you a few days, but then I shall send for you. Be prepared. The emperor's orders of execution will not wait."

He grimaced again and said, "I am so glad that you have agreed to this, Theodora. You won't regret it, I promise you." He took her hand and leaned over to kiss it. It was all she could do not to tear it away from him and slap his disfigured face with all her strength. Her self control was now paramount if she was to leave this place alive.

The ride back with the escort was a numbed blur of tears and silent sobs. When they arrived back at the gates of the villa she stumbled along the path to the house and let herself into the darkness, trying not to make any noise. Her mother, however, had not gone to bed and heard her.

"You are back, my Darling. Where have you been?" Her tone was both concerned and somewhat plaintive, as though she felt her daughter had let her down.

In the dim light of a single candle she couldn't at first make out her daughter's features, but as Theodora slowly approached, walking like a living corpse, she gasped, "My God, Theo! You look like you have seen a ghost!"

"I have seen a ghost, Mama," she croaked.

Theodora stumbled and almost fell against her mother's chair. She knelt and placed her head on her mother's knees and wept great racking sobs that shook her slim frame and left her mother temporarily speechless. Joannina knew that it would be pointless saying anything until the storm of weeping had subsided, so she merely stroked her daughter's head and murmured words of comfort. "There, there, my Darling, cry it out, whatever it is. We can talk when you are ready."

Theodora finally came to a shuddering halt, and after a pause she lifted her head to look at her mother, who was shocked by what she saw. The tear-ravaged face and lines of grief frightened her.

"Oh, my Theo, what is it that is causing so much pain?" she asked, fear beginning to take hold of her heart.

"It is Alex, Mama. I have seen him."

Joannina jerked upright. "Alexios, our Alex?" she asked, bewildered and fearful.

"Our Alex, Mama," Theodora told her.

"My precious one, where? Dear God protect him, but he is alive?" Joannina sounded as though she was begging.

"Yes, Mother, but barely, and I know he is to die."

It was almost dawn by the time she finished telling her mother of what had happened. Remarkably, Joannina seemed resigned to the awful choice put before them.

"From everything that you have said, Pantoleon is determined to be avenged on our entire family, to destroy us utterly, my daughter," she said, looking out at the dim light coming in through the windows. To Theodora she seemed to have aged ten years within a night.

"Yes, he is, Mama. I have no doubt of that now."

"Then, my Theo, you must do as Alex told you. You must flee. Damian is the future, and he must live. Your brother always did have a clear mind." She took her daughter's hands in her thin, cold ones and gripped them firmly.

"You were very young when your sister died."

"Mama, I was there when it happened. I can remember it clearly." Theodora hadn't meant to sound sharp and instantly was contrite. "I'm sorry, Mama; I didn't mean to snap."

Joannina gave her a wan smile. "I know you were there when it happened, my love, but you never fully understood *why* it happened. I should tell you."

Theodora nodded. "Go on, Mama."

"Pantoleon's father, the senator Spartenos, was a traitor, and unfortunately our Eugenia became tangled up with a plot to assassinate Emperor Manuel." Joannina held up her hand to still Theodora's indignant reaction to the suggestion that her sister was a traitor.

"She was innocent of treason, my love. However, the senator was anything but, and he was the man who had her killed. Our Frank, Talon, was there when it happened and he took care of the assassin, as you know; but then he went on to confront the senator. All this, you must understand, came after the disaster of Myriokephalon, which triggered the revolt in the first place."

She sighed. "Whether Talon, our strange young Frank, had avenged our daughter or not, the revolt would have been discovered and the senator would have surely been denounced anyway. But Talon, Alexios thinks, took matters into his own hands and avenged Eugenia's death. The senator and his wife died under very mysterious circumstances. You might remember seeing the fire. I suspect that Pantoleon came back from wherever he had been to find that his family had perished in disgrace and their property confiscated. Without doubt he blames us for that, hence his fearsome revenge." Her mother looked up at Theodora with anguish in her eyes.

"Understand, my darling," she said, tears coursing down her cheeks, "Alexios knows of all this, and he couldn't bear to see you betrayed and used by that ruthless man. They have no honor!" she cried out in anguish. "You have only one good choice, and that is to do as Alex asks."

Theodora had been devastated when she'd witnessed the death of her sister, lying bleeding to death with a bolt in her back. She recalled also the desperate struggle in the shadows as Talon and the assassin fought to the death. She shuddered at the memory. That was when she had realized that Talon was much more than he appeared on the surface; strangely it had only added to her childish infatuation for him. She shook her head. That was all in the past now. Her situation required a level head and immediate action if they were to honor her brother's last wish.

"I shall do as he asks me," she said, desperately trying to keep her voice from cracking. "We will find a way, Mama. I want to pray for our Alexei. Can we do this now?"

Joannina bowed her head and wept yet again, but then abruptly she clutched at her upper left arm and gasped, "Oh Dear God, but I do not think I can bear it any more, the pain is so great! Dear God, be kind to his good soul." Joannina fell back against her chair with a groan. "It hurts, my Theo. Ah, but it hurts!"

Thoroughly alarmed, Theodora snatched at her mother's hand and tried to feel her pulse. It was merely a flutter. In a surge of panic she settled her mother more comfortably and called out to her. "Mama! Oh, Mama, don't leave me!" She guessed what was happening; her mother was in the throes of a heart attack.

Joannina was as pale as porcelain and her breath was coming in rasping gasps. There was very little Theodora could do, other than hold her mother's hand and rub it to try to bring some circulation back. She didn't think she could weep any more, but the tears came as she begged her mother not to leave her. She had never felt so utterly alone as she felt her mother slip away.

Damian found her a few hours later, bent over her mother, who was still and cold. He was confused and fearful, as he had not encountered death before. Now his mother was telling him between sobs that his grandmother was gone to heaven and to be brave.

Theodora realized that time was against her. Joannina was gone, and she was sure Alex would be soon. Brushing away the remnants of her tears, she stood up. It was time to be strong and to preserve the last of their family. They must leave, but first she had to give her mother a decent burial. She decided upon a patch of ground where her father had often lingered with her in the summer. It had a clear, unrestricted view of the Golden Horn.

With the help of Angelos, who provided the shovels, they dug a shallow grave and laid Joannina down at the roots of the tree. After the task was done, she stood with Damian by her side, staring down at the freshly shoveled earth and let her mind drift. Where to go? Who to turn to? Their friends were in the same predicament as she, many of them worse off or even beggared. None would take them in, of that she was sure. Besides, she dared not stay in this city any longer.

It was while she was looking down at the ground that an idea occurred to her. Perhaps Giorgios could help. She could just make out the ships in Neorion harbor. There were not many; few Latins came now, not since the massacre. He might still be there. He had said that it would be a week before he left.

Knowing the power that Pantoleon wielded in the city she knew she could not just walk down to the harbor and ask Giorgios for a ride. She had to disappear. Handing a gold coin to Angelos and telling him to go home for the rest of the day, she walked back to the house and told Damian to stay close. She gave the two maids a gold coin each and the day off also, saying that it was to be a day of mourning and she wanted to be alone. Theodora had no idea whether Irene was a spy or not, but it was too dangerous to allow herself the luxury of trust.

When the maids had gone the silence in the large house felt oppressive. Gone was the quiet voice of her mother, talking to Theodora while she attended to the tasks of keeping the fire going and preparing food. She imagined she could even hear the house sighing at the loss of so many souls.

Theodora hurried through her preparations while keeping an ear open for any footsteps at the main door. She was sure that the house would be watched, but there was another way to leave which might not be covered. There was a small door down at the bottom of the garden which opened onto a narrow alley well away from the main street.

When evening fell she had completed her preparations, and it was time to eat one last meal before they left. There was little enough: a piece of bread and some leek soup that Damian protested against. "I am tired of leak soup, Mama!" he complained.

"You will eat everything, young man," she told him firmly. "We do not know when we will eat again. Do as you are told."

The little boy, cowed by his mother's fierce expression and near to tears, did just that.

Giorgios was called to the deck by one of his night watch men just after midnight. "There is a lady on deck and she is asking for you," the sailor told him. "Good looker, too!" he grinned.

Giorgios hurried up onto the main deck, rubbing the sleep out of his eyes, and gaped when he saw a heavily cloaked figure standing on the deck holding onto the hand of a boy he recognized.

"My Lady!" he exclaimed. "What brings you here?" Looking around he realized that it might be better for her to talk in some privacy. He picked up the large leather satchel at her feet—its contents rattled—and beckoned her to follow him down to the main cabin. When they were inside he settled her on a bench, then sat down across the table from her. Theodora looked worn and exhausted, there were dark rings under her eyes, and they carried a haunted look. She cradled Damian, who was half asleep in her arms

"What has happened to bring you to my ship, my Lady?" Giorgios asked her gently.

By way of response she fumbled in her robe and brought out a small leather bag that chinked when she placed it on the table.

"That is gold, and it is all I have as payment for you to take me away as soon as you can, tonight if possible. My mother and brother are dead, and my son and I are in great danger," she said. Her large eyes were wide and pleading. "Giorgios, I beg of you, help me. I shall explain everything when we are sailing."

Giorgios looked at the gold on the table; it was worth a good deal more than the meagre cargo he had gleaned from this sad place so far. Business had dried up since the Latins had been slaughtered.

"I am desolated to hear of your loss, my Lady," he said. "Yes, I will take you, but it will be very dangerous. The Frankish ships are all over the sea south of the Hellespont because of the invasion. Where do you wish to go?"

"Anywhere! Just take me away from this awful place," she told him.

To slaughter us
Why did you need to invite us
To such an elegant party?
—Ahmad Shamlu

Chapter 22
A Royal Killing

The weather changed abruptly from being cold to becoming unusually warm for Constantinople in the year 1185 of Our Lord. The narrow streets that led off the Messe were stifling hot and airless. There was very little wind coming off the Marmara sea south of the peninsular on this particular day.

Pantoleon was not paying much attention to the weather at present. He was instead more concerned with the news from Thessalonica. His spies had just informed him that the city had fallen to the Franks, and the report was that they had sacked the city, killing a large part of the citizenry, and were busy despoiling the sacred places of worship. The emperor was as yet unaware of the catastrophe, and Pantoleon was steeling himself to go and tell him.

His instincts told him the time had come to look after his own interests. Once this appalling news arrived on the streets it would run through the city like a wild fire with God alone knew what consequences. He could feel the tension in the city, both from the ill news which seemed to be coming in from all directions exacerbated by the hot humid air and a restless and frightened population. Pantoleon's own spies within the city of Constantinople were telling him that something ugly was brewing on the streets. Gabros, who had been out and about in the last few days, arrived to tell Pantoleon about what he had observed.

"Everyone is wound up tighter than a bow string, Master," he said. "It's not just the bad news from the south...."

"So they know already," Pantoleon murmured, "Ill news travels fast. Well, what else is it? Spit it out man!" Pantoleon snapped. His own temper had not been improved by either the humid weather nor by the increasingly erratic and wild behavior of the emperor.

Gabros hesitated, but his trust in his master overcame his reticence. "There is talk of revolt, Master," he muttered, with a nervous look at the door to their apartment. Involuntarily Pantoleon glanced that way too. He was already considering whether he should find other accommodations, out of the way of the palace spies. Perhaps the villa of Kalothesos would be a good place. Somehow it had been overlooked when the proscription was handed out; it was still intact, and Theodora was living there.

"Is that what the rabble are saying? Revolt?" Pantoleon asked, a chill going down his spine. This was serious.

Gabros nodded his head. Pantoleon had never seen his man looking so ill at ease.

"Not the nobles... the senate?" They were so decimated he would have been amazed to hear they had found the courage to start an insurrection.

Gabros shook his head. "No Master. The people on the streets are murmuring. They talk about bringing back someone from the aristocracy and deposing the emperor."

Pantoleon thought furiously. Who, he wondered, would be popular enough to appeal to the scum on the street? He knew that once the mob was on the move it was almost impossible to stop until it had blown itself out. The damage done would be horrific, and he could be destroyed in the storm. His sense of self preservation demanded that he make preparations to ensure that didn't happen.

In the meantime, he would try to ingratiate himself back into the good graces of the emperor and gain some advantage for himself in the process. Their relationship had been somewhat chilly of late. He had dreadful news to deliver, and it would not be the first time that the messenger was killed for bringing ill news. He didn't relish the prospect.

"Do we have a name at all?"

"They are speaking of one Isaac Angelos, Master. There are several names, but he is the most talked about."

"Why him? He is a nobody from a small noble family, nothing more."

"A soothsayer is telling people that he will be the next emperor, Master." Gabros shuffled his feet and again glanced at the doorway.

"A soothsayer! A filthy madman is saying these things?" Pantoleon snorted, but he was aware that revolt could be right around the corner unless something was done about it. He knew that the people of Constantinople were fed up with the terror that had been unleashed upon the aristocracy and the Senate, and many, many others. The weather and the bad news were but tinder for a fire.

"I shall see the emperor right away. Where is he?"

"He is here in the palace, Master. I... I believe he is in the pool with some, er, ladies."

Pantoleon dressed carefully before he left to see the emperor. He knew he would gain access immediately, even though he had slipped somewhat in the estimation of Isaac. He was still valued for the information he could provide as the chief spy.

He found Andronikos lying on a table being kneaded carefully by one of the burly eunuch masseurs he had kept on. The eunuchs were considerably fewer in numbers these days. Pantoleon noticed that Maraptica was among the ladies by the pool and wondered cynically at the depravity of it all. She was the emperor's favorite, but she didn't seem to mind the company of the many other women who were at his beck and call. Pantoleon had "found" Maraptica in a high class brothel and had presented her to Andronikos because she was a great flautist. Also it helped that she was very beautiful, as well as skilled in the arts of love.

Pantoleon walked up to the table and murmured, "My Lord, peace be with you always. I have something important to tell you."

Andronikos looked up from his face down position on the table. He smiled. "Ah Exaz, where have you been? I have missed you!" He sat up on the table and dismissed the masseur with a wave of his hand. Andronikos was completely naked and his light brown skin shone with the oil that had been applied to his muscular body. He glanced over towards the pool where the young women were tittering to one another as they kept an eye on him. They waved and giggled some more. After eyeing them appreciatively he turned back towards Pantoleon with the smile still on his face. Pantoleon wondered if Andronikos was flaunting his manhood to annoy him, but let the thought go. The Emperor seemed to be in a fine mood and confirmed this when he laughed and pointed to the girls.

"I am like Hercules, my Exaz! I can take the lot of them and never tire! I shall soon be up to fifty, just like him! That balm you procured for me is magical!" He grinned nastily. "But you can't benefit from it, can you, my poor Exaz?"

Pantoleon seethed inwardly, but he put on a bland face and said, "I have news, my Lord, and it is urgent."

"Oh, what is it this time?" Andronikos demanded irritably.

"Thessalonica fell to the Sicilian army two days ago, my Lord."

Andronikos' head whipped around. "Tell me that again?" he snapped, his entire posture changing from one of relaxed well-being to tension. Pantoleon felt the room chill.

"Just a short while ago a messenger told me that the city has fallen and that it is being sacked even now as we speak, my Lord. Its people are being murdered and raped and our places of worship desecrated by the barbarians."

"If ever I get my hands upon that useless piece of shit, David Komnenos! He couldn't defend his virginity from a toad. He gave up the city, damn him to hell!" Andronikos snarled. "That filthy traitor, that spineless shriveled foreskin! I shall castrate him and hang him up by his heels outside our city gates!" he screamed. Pantoleon braced himself; Andronikos was just getting into his stride.

"He is weaker than a woman and more timid than a deer!" Andronikos raved. The girls in the pool hastily climbed out of the water and fled, fearful for their lives. Pantoleon stood absolutely still and endured the ravings of his master, praying silently that he would survive this hour.

Eventually Andronikos calmed down enough to ask in a completely different tone what could be done about the situation.

Taken aback, although he had witnessed these sudden changes before, Pantoleon said hesitantly.

"Your Generals should be ordered to attack at once and catch the enemy preoccupied with their barbaric looting of the city, My Lord. There is one who could do this: General Alexius Branus; but my Lord, you *must* move quickly."

But Andronikos was strangely vague about what he might decide on that matter, leaving Pantoleon feeling that in order to get the emperor's attention back he should pass along the other news.

"My spies have begun to hear talk, my Lord, that should be addressed promptly."

Andronikos sighed with impatience. To Pantoleon it seemed as though he just wanted to go back to his women. He felt an overwhelming sense of exasperation, but with a great effort he controlled it. To show impatience with this madman could spell his own demise.

"There are tangible rumors on the streets that one Isaac Angelos is fomenting a revolution, my Lord," he told his master. Passing on a mere rumor wasn't going to get his attention, Pantoleon surmised. It had to sound like a direct threat.

Andronikos stared at him. "A revolution, you say?" he asked.

Pantoleon nodded. "Yes, my Lord. A soothsayer is adding to the problem by saying that this Isaac Angelos will be emperor."

"Oh, is he now?" Andronikos said softly. Pantoleon braced himself. When his master spoke softly there was danger all around.

"Then you shall find this... Angelos and have him arrested. Bring him here, and I shall see to it that he is emperor of nothing!"

"Yes, my Lord."

"This is the work of those filthy scum, the Senators and their henchmen, the aristocracy! You will have the prisoners killed and their entire families destroyed. By the time I get back from my country estate at Melodeon I want them all gone, all dead and gone! Do I make myself clear?" he demanded.

"Yes, I shall see to it, my Lord."

"Good. Now I shall go and prepare for my holiday. I am tired of this wretched city. Let the rumors trot about, I don't care. Get out of my sight! And Exazenos... "

"Yes, my Lord?"

"Count yourself lucky that I am in a good mood. Anyone else would have had you executed for bringing all this bad news. Try to do better in future."

Pantoleon left the emperor in a cold sweat. He strode along the echoing corridors, passing the immobile guards and hurrying servants, and by the time he had returned to his quarters he had made a decision. He ordered Gabros to ready their horses quietly, and the two of them rode from the palace without escort. Once they were on the almost deserted Messe he outlined his plan to Gabros.

"I want everything in place by twelve days from today," he told his man. "You can use the villa Kalothesos for a base until I am ready to come as well, but while the emperor is away on his 'holiday' we must find this man Isaac Angelos and arrest him. Send your men all over the city and find him."

"Why don't we leave sooner?" Gabros asked him.

"Because I have to get all my wealth into a safe place before we go, idiot! The ship must be loaded and ready to leave on the instant. There will be only one chance. I was watched by that foul toad Nikoporus. He would like nothing better than to find that I am trying to leave and denounce me. That would be the end of you too, Gabros, remember that."

Gabros nodded. 'The ship will be ready, my Lord. Where do you want it to be?"

"I want it to anchor in Neorion Harbor. It has no walls and we can leave at night if need be."

"Very well, Master. We are near to the villa at present; do you want to pay the young lady a visit?"

Pantoleon thought about that. It had been almost a week since he had seen Theodora. He conjured up an image of Theodora's face, her grey eyes and her thick, reddish hair and long, slim neck. "Yes," he said. He was more than ready to see her.

They rode up to the gates of the villa Kalothesos and found them unlocked. The gate man was nowhere to be seen, and his ancient slobbering dog was absent. Gabros warily pushed the gates open with a foot from the saddle and they rode along the unkempt track that led to the villa. Looking around Pantoleon remembered what a gem this property had once been. Almost in the center of the city, it was a beautiful place, or had been. The obvious signs of neglect were everywhere. The overgrown and untended vines, the scummed pools and undergrowth where lawns had once been. The house looked equally unattended. He dismounted and strode up to the main doorway. The front door was unlocked and easily opened.

He walked into the house with a sense of foreboding. There was no one to be seen, and the feeling that the house was deserted became even stronger as he wandered around the main living room. It was as though the occupants had simply walked out of the door. The remains of a meagre supper were still lying on a low table in front of the cold fireplace. A blanket lay strewn across a low chair which he knew Theodora's invalid mother had occupied the last time he had visited. No one anywhere. He strode about the house searching for indications that Theodora might still be there.

"Go and check the outbuildings, search everywhere," he commanded Gabros.

Pantoleon wondered if in their unprotected state the house might have been attacked by robbers, but there were no signs of the violence, looting, or wreckage which would accompany such an act. There came a gnawing realization that she had fled, and a cold anger began to grow.

Gabros arrived on the main terrace and beckoned him. "I have found something, Master." He led the way out into the derelict garden and pointed to a long patch of freshly dug earth. It looked very like a grave to Pantoleon. He stared at it trying to understand what it meant; slowly he realized that Joannina must have died and Theodora had abandoned the villa. The big unanswered question was why, when he still held her brother. Returning to the house, he sought out the room where she had slept and saw that it was in disarray as though someone had packed hurriedly and just left everything else behind. There were also small signs of pilfering, as though the missing servants had taken what they could before fleeing themselves.

Pantoleon felt as though the ground had shifted seismically under his feet. He stood looking out of the window at the Golden Gates and found himself trembling. First the dreadful news of Thessalonica and the dire fate of its citizens, not that he cared one whit for the poor people being raped and killed by the barbarous Franks; he sensed, however, that it was a portent of things to come to Constantinople. Then the weird behavior of the emperor, and now the threat of revolution.

This city was like a volcano about to explode, and the emperor didn't seem to be anywhere near as concerned as he should be. He was leaving the city at just the time when he was most needed! Pantoleon felt that his life was teetering on the edge of a precipice and unless he did something about it he would be extinguished along with the others.

Turning to the silent Gabros he said, "Try to find out if she is still in the city. If she is, bring her to me, unharmed. We will use this place for our own, so bring some of our men as guards. This is where we will stay from tomorrow onwards. The emperor need not know, nor that rat Nikoporus. I'll deal with him before too long."

"What about the Kalothesos brother, Master?"

"Is he still in the cell?"

"No, he was taken back to the one he shared with those other traitors, Master."

"Leave him there for the time being. I have not given the order to kill them yet. It can wait a day or so."

With Gabros deployed on the search for Theodora and the bringing together of Pantoleon's wealth, Pantoleon planned to restore his new holding, but he had little time to enjoy the villa. With the emperor gone, he found himself in the very center of the turmoil that followed the destruction of Thessalonica, both within the palace and in the city of Constantinople. The city seethed with ugly rumors, and words of discontent were being voiced out loud and in the open.

Men from the Verangian guard who had ventured into the city alone had been found murdered. The orders went out that the guards were to stay at the palace and protect it from the marauding mobs which now roamed the streets at night.

Pantoleon stared with contempt at the frightened eunuchs and administrators who came cringing to him for directions. No one knew what to do, and as it was he who'd had the emperor's ear before, it now fell upon him to try and calm the frayed nerves of the palace staff. He had no patience with the generals and naval officers who came to him.

"Go and do your duty, you craven bastards!" he shouted at them. "Did the emperor not order you to fight? Then find out where your balls are and go fight! Don't come to me whining!"

Nikoporus, sensing an opportunity, made an effort to finesse power from him by spreading rumors that he was looking to escape. Gabros found an assassin who took care of that problem, and Nikoporus showed up drowned in the Cistern of Aetius not far from the palace. No one had any idea as to why he would be there, but people settled down after that. The familiar face of terror had been reestablished and Pantoleon was, in the absence of the emperor, the person in charge. But he couldn't do anything about the raging turmoil about to boil over within the city.

His men had eventually discovered the location of Isaac Angelos, and a small party was sent off to arrest him. Unfortunately, it did not go well for the arresting officer. The news reached the Blachernae palace late that night, when Gabros hastily ushered a panting messenger into Pantoleon's rooms.

"It is out of control, my Lord," the man said, fidgeting with his belt and sleeves with great agitation.

"Just calm down and tell me what happened," Pantoleon commanded him, and he took a deep gulp of his wine. He again felt that the ground had shifted. He exchanged a look with Gabros: this could be the moment they had anticipated.

"Isaac ran the officer through with his sword, and then before the others could react he fled on horseback to the Hagia, Saint Sophia, where he has taken refuge, Lord. A mob has shown up to support him and they are in an ugly mood. No one can stop them now."

"Anyone else of any note?" Pantoleon wanted to know the details.

"I think that his uncle, Lord John Doukas, is there, and so are many others from the senate, Lord."

"So the hyenas are congregating," Pantoleon said, almost to himself. "You may go now." The messenger almost ran out of the room. He had no sooner left than there came a banging on the door. Gabros admitted a very agitated Officer of the guard. Without ceremony the man spoke.

"Lord, I hear there are big disturbances at Saint Sophia. We need to protect the palaces there."

"What of the guards that are there already? Can't they deal with it?" Pantoleon asked reasonably.

The officer, a tall Saxon hesitated. "I received a messenger from the man in charge there, Lord. He tells me that the mob is huge and that he does not have enough men to deal with any real problems."

Pantoleon had done some very fast thinking while the Saxon talked in his halting Greek. "Yes, very well, take all the men you need and go as quickly as you can to aid your comrades," he said.

Saluting smartly, the officer ran out of the room, and they could hear him calling to his fellow Verangians in the guttural language of the Norsemen.

Pantoleon watched him leave, then in the quiet aftermath said, "Come, Gabros, it is time we left too. First we will pay the vaults a little visit. We just have time. Bring those men of yours."

That night Pantoleon and his men loaded as much of the gold and silver from the vaults as they could onto a covered wagon, which Gabros escorted out of the palace using a pass signed by Pantoleon. The wagon was headed for the villa.

Pantoleon remained for a few more hours to write a letter to the emperor informing him of the events and begging him to come home, as the city needed his leadership. The messenger was despatched with the letter in the early hours of the morning and told not to stop until he had delivered it. Not long after the messenger had departed, Pantoleon left the palace on horseback, telling the palace guards that he was on his way to St. Sophia and would be back before morning.

He made his way warily along the Messe, wanting to avoid contact with roaming mobs, only to find the streets were eerily deserted. Everyone, it seemed, had gone to St Sophia or was staying at home. He arrived at the villa not very long after the covered wagon, which had moved much more slowly than a single man on horseback could travel. Gabros had installed it in the stables and mounted a guard. It had not been hard to hire mercenaries; the city was crawling with soldiers for hire who would cut a throat for a couple of *solidari*.

Pantoleon sent Gabros and a couple of his men to judge the mood of the mob at St Sophia, while he considered his options and took stock of the contents of the villa. They came back just before dawn looking very concerned. "The man Isaac Angelos has been proclaimed *Baselius,* Master," Gabros reported. "They offered the crown to him. Someone from the mob took down the crown from above the high altar and tried to crown him, but he refused." Pantoleon lifted an eyebrow at that.

"Then his uncle John asked them to crown *him*," Gabros laughed cynically. "The crowd yelled that they were not interested in another Andronikos and they didn't like his shiny bald head, nor his forked beard!" Then Gabros sobered. "They are out to kill, Lord. It was a good thing we left the palace, as they are heading that way as I speak to you."

"Go with them, and report back to me when you can. Be careful. See if you can get hold of that man Kalothesos in the confusion," Pantoleon ordered him. "I still want him."

Gabros left, and Pantoleon went outside onto the slope overlooking the Golden Horn. It was over, that much was clear. Andronikos would never be able to put down the revolution, and even if he could manage it he, Pantoleon, had no part to play in the future of the city. Far better to cut his losses and leave while he could and find a place to start afresh. He thought he heard some kind of roar from the hill above him but wasn't sure. He imagined that the mob would be well on their way towards the Blachernae palace by now. He pondered his next destination.

*****

Alexios experienced one of his worst moments of his life when the door crashed shut behind his sister. He sat on the filthy floor on the moldy, excrement- and piss-covered straw and wept in the darkness. Later, he composed himself and knelt, praying for his mother and his sister, begging God to save them from the monster Pantoleon, whom he cursed to hell even while he was praying.

He held in his possession the long, thin strap that he had slipped off the waist of Theodora. His intent was to find one of the bars and hang himself as quickly as possible and deny Pantoleon his bargaining piece. He couldn't find anything in the darkness, however, so he slid into a corner and waited. And waited.

They came for him some days later. His jailers hauled him along by his chains to dump him unceremoniously back into the same cell that he had inhabited for months. As he lay where the jailers had left him, his companions gathered about him demanding to know what had happened. He told them very little, but it passed the time and they were content to hear that he had at least seen his sister.

Some of them had not seen anyone, let alone a relative, for as long as they had been in the stinking hell of the dungeon.

He was still determined to take his own life, and here were bars to which he could attach the belt. However, when he began quietly to inspect the bars, reaching up to then as though measuring them, one of the prisoners who had befriended him asked him what he was doing.

Alex was evasive, but it didn't fool the man, whose name was Stephan. "If you are thinking to take your own life, remember it is a sin." Stephan admonished him.

"I have nothing to live for at all any more."

"Hope is a powerful emotion. Why have you lost all hope?"

Alexios explained what had happened, omitting nothing, which he thought was ample reason for why he was desperate to die. But Stephan said, "It has been six days since that time. They might have forgotten you, in which case there is still reason to hope."

"I *hope* that my death will release my sister from damnation."

Stephan tried to persuade Alex not to go through with his plan, as did the other prisoners, but Alex would not be swayed from his aim. Finally Stephan said, "This is folly, Alexios. But you seem very determined, so I shall help you, as otherwise it is going to be a very hard death. But I shall be damned to hell for doing this awful thing."

Alex thanked him.

They planned it for the following night. The deed would be done, and several hours later the other prisoners would make a lot of noise to attract the attention of the jailers, who would then remove his body.

They were all seated on the noisome floor the next morning when they heard a disturbance at the entrance to the dungeon. They looked at each other apprehensively, and Alexios began to fear he had waited too long to carry out his desperate plan. The doors crashed open and men with torches and weapons came boiling down the stairs. The prisoners, thinking their time had come, clustered together in the corner of the cell braced for death, but the crowd of yelling and cursing men were shoving captive jailers in front of them, shouting at them to open the cell doors.

Within moments the doors were thrown open and men were hauling the dazed and bewildered prisoners to their feet and half carrying them out of their cells. Their former jailers were shoved rudely into the cells and the doors slammed shut, followed by much cursing, threats and fist waving.

Alexios found himself being carried up the stairs and into corridors filled with shouting people who cheered when the former prisoners were ushered out by an escort of helping hands. They were taken out of the palace into the front courtyard, blinking in the glare of sunlight, which none of them had seen for months, even years. Others joined them from the maze below, some weeping and others so confused they could not speak without choking on their emotions.

The crowd of people seemed to grow in size by the minute, and Alex became aware that the palace was being ransacked by the citizens of Constantinople. He looked at the mob excitedly milling about all around him. Some had items of furniture, silver utensils or paintings and carpets in their hands as they hurried away, even as others were running into the courtyard in hopes of finding their share of the spoils. There was a roar deep inside the palace when the vaults were discovered and the serious plundering of the palace treasury began.

Soon after a great shout went up and all eyes turned to the northern area of the palace, which led down to the walls overlooking the Bosphorus. "Its Andronikos!" someone yelled. "We have captured the bastard! Now we will see who is the emperor!" Alexios had no choice but to go along with the crowd, although he would have preferred to be on his way home. The crush was so heavy that in his condition he wondered if he would even survive. He felt a hand holding him upright and turned to find Stephen just behind him. "Stay on your feet, Alex, stay on your feet. I'm here," Stephan yelled at him over the roar of the crowd, which swept them along until they were looking down on the waters of the Golden Horn. He stared down the slope towards the water where several ships surrounded by many smaller boats huddled near to the beach, but standing on the beach was a small group of people who were instantly recognizable.

It was without doubt the emperor, or rather the former emperor and his ladies, but the change in Andronikos was remarkable. Gone was the arrogant emperor who stared straight through people and issued edicts without concern for consequences and surrounded himself with sycophants. Here instead stood a disheveled man in torn clothing, bound and fettered with a chain around his neck that was so heavy he was bowed down by its weight. The women with whom he had fled were relatively unharmed, although they were under guard.

The sight of the emperor excited the crowd even further. The shouts became a swelling howl of rage and venom. To Alexios' ears it was the sound of a monster giving vent to its fury. The sound reverberated off the walls of the tall buildings and the walls of the city a few hundred paces to the north.

Men reached forward to seize Andronikos, and if the guards had not pushed them aside and stood their ground he might well have been torn to pieces there and then, but word spread that Isaac Angelos wanted to confront the deposed emperor. Indeed, there at the front of the mob was Isaac, who despite his earlier refusal to accept the crown was now de facto leader of the revolution.

Andronikos was thrust before him and forced to his knees. A gradual silence settled on the crowd as they strained their ears to hear what was said. Alexios was too far away to hear anything but a murmur. Then he thought he saw the flash of a sword blade, there was a choking scream, and a huge sigh from the area near Isaac.

Then the roar began again and he could see Andronikos being hauled in the direction of the palace, which meant that he would be dragged right past him. The guards forced a pathway with their spears, dragging the prisoner in their midst. Alexios strained his neck to see his former tormenter, whose face was screwed up in an expression of agony as he moaned in pain. He was clutching at his right arm with his left hand and there was blood all over his tunic. His right hand had been severed, a crude bandage wrapped around the stump. So the preliminaries for his execution were already under way, Alexios thought to himself. The guards led their stumbling prisoner past the jeering citizens of Constantinople on their way to the dungeons, where Andronikos would spend his last hours.

Alexios could appreciate the irony. Again a hand on his shoulder, and it was Stephan.

"Do you want to go home now, Alex?" he asked. Alexios nodded, numb with the noise and exhaustion.

The chilling roar of the mob below could be heard at the villa, and the men under Gabros' command eyed one another uneasily. What if the citizens came for them? Every one of them had committed unspeakable crimes against the population, and to a man they knew the awful things that Pantoleon had done. They had witnessed it with their own eyes.

Gabros arrived with the news of the capture of the emperor and his concubine Maraptica, with a lurid description of the emperor's mutilation.

"We cannot stay here in this city, Master," he told Pantoleon urgently. "There are people who will denounce us, and then they will scour the city for you. I didn't even get close to the dungeons to retrieve Alexios. The prisoners were released almost as soon as the mob stormed the gates, then the prisoners joined the crowd."

"What is the mob doing right now?" Pantoleon asked him.

"They are looting the palaces, Master."

"That should keep them busy for the rest of today and tonight. It will leave the way clear for us to take the wagons down to the harbor and load the ship. Is everything ready to go?"

"There are now two wagons full of treasure, Master. We are ready whenever you say the word."

"Good. When it is fully dark we will leave."

Pantoleon congratulated himself on having had the foresight to not only steal treasure but to vacate the palace the night before. Had he not, he knew that he would now be in a cell along with Andronikos. That man was as good as dead, and Pantoleon had no intention of remaining any longer than necessary. It was a pity about the girl and her brother, but saving his own life was a more pressing concern right now.

After leaving the mob that was still milling around in the gardens and scrounging some food at the nearly deserted palace kitchens, Alexios and Stephan headed for his family villa. They had found some clothing strewn on the floor of the kitchen and eagerly exchanged it for their rags.

It was late after noon by the time they arrived at the street which led to the villa's gates. Alex hobbled down the street filled with anticipation at finally going home and surprising his family. But then he stopped. Walking ahead of them some distance away was someone he recognized. He snatched at Stephan's sleeve, almost tearing it, and dragged him into the recess of a gateway. He stifled the startled yell of his companion with a finger on his lips.

"What is it?" Stephan exclaimed with surprise.

"Watch that man ahead of us! I know him."

His guess was confirmed when he saw Gabros turn right and walk into the family villa. It was the man who had brought Theodora to his cell. There was no mistaking the walk and the profile. Alexios sagged against the wall, trying to think.

"Who is that?" Stephan asked him, looking confused.

"He is the man who works for Pantoleon, the sadistic monster you knew as Exazenos! They never caught him, did they?"

Stephan shook his head. "In all that confusion he must have slipped away."

"Well, now I know where he slipped away to. That is my father's villa, and he is there." Alexios turned a tortured face to his companion. "There is every likelihood that my sister is there too, a prisoner of that scab."

"There is nothing we can do without help," Stephan told him. "It is no good trying to get anyone to risk their lives to storm a property when easy pickings are to be found in the palaces tonight. We will have to wait until morning."

"Every minute we wait will be a torture for me until I have my sister back," Alexios groaned.

"Let's at least see if you are right," Stephan suggested.

Taking great care not to be seen, they were soon close enough to the gates to see that they were well guarded by men who were obviously mercenaries. The guards were alert and watchful, which forced Alexios and Stephan to keep their distance for fear of attracting attention to themselves. Even so, one of the guards did see them and shouted an alarm. They bounded to their feet and fled; Alexios had no intention of being taken prisoner a second time. When he came back it would be with a large escort, and they would storm the villa. Better to find help and a place to rest before coming back in the morning.

That night when the city had quieted, although fires still raged out of control and the looting of the palaces continued, a group of armed men escorted two heavily laden wagons out of the Kalothesos property and ground their way down the hill towards the Neorion harbor. Once there, the men hurriedly set about loading small boats with the cargo and rowing it out to a ship anchored in the still, dark waters. It took about four hours for all the cargo to be transported, and then the men themselves boarded the vessel for the last time. Gabros and Pantoleon went up to the after deck of the vessel and spoke to the captain.

"Make sail immediately, we are leaving," Gabros said.

The captain growled some orders. Soon the sail was billowing and the rowers ready. The anchor was hauled up by two crewmen, and one ran back to inform the captain.

"Anchor is up, Captain Nigel. We are free."

The ship slipped out to the middle of the Bosphorus with barely a ripple and set sail for the south. The stars and the loom of the land on either side were all Nigel needed to maintain his course and remain in the center of the Marmara sea.

"Where are we heading, Master?' he asked in his poor Greek.

"We are going to Cyprus, Captain. There is a Komnenos royal there who might have need of my services," Pantoleon told him.

Alexios didn't have much luck in finding people to help him with his cause. Interest only flickered when he described Pantoleon as the executioner of Andronikos and his right hand man in so many of the horrific crimes that had been inflicted upon the people of Constantinople.

Eventually he and Stephan managed to find about thirty men, amongst whom twenty were self appointed soldiers from Isaac's personal guard. Now that the emperor was imprisoned they were eager to find anyone else who might be implicated. The manhunts were beginning. Alexios sounded convincing, so they set off at about mid-day to arrest Pantoleon and his men.

They arrived in the afternoon to find the gates hanging open and no guards. The group of men rushed along the deserted pathway to arrive at the house in a baying pack, hoping to surprise Pantoleon, but there was no one to greet them, not even armed men. It was very quiet and all the signs were that the property was deserted. Alexios was distraught. He didn't really care where Pantoleon had gone, it was Theodora and his mother he wanted to find. He paid almost no attention as the disappointed men shouldered him aside and ran into the house, not even when some began to ransack the villa.

They blamed him for the absence of their victim and it was all Stephan could do to calm the shouting men and explain that he and Alexios had spent months in prison as the victims of the very man they sought. Eventually the leader of the mob called a halt to their behavior and told his men to leave. He turned to Alexios, who was leaning against one of the pillars, still too exhausted to do much more than protest, and said.

"I'm sorry for their behavior. I believe you were right, but he has gone now. A good thing that he has for his own sake, but don't worry—we'll find him if he is still in the city, just not today. Tomorrow that shit bag Andronikos will be brought out and tried for his crimes. You should be there to be a witness against him. He did you much harm by the look of it."

Alexios barely heard him. He slumped down on the floor in a daze. Pantoleon must have fled the city in the hours of darkness, and he would not be easily found. Stephan stayed with him when the others had left, and the silence of the house and property closed in on them.

"What am I to do, Stephan? I do not know where she is, where that animal might have taken her!" he cried to his friend, beginning to weep tears of frustration and loss.

To calm him, Stephan took him outside to the garden. Alexios gestured towards a tree on the slope of the property. "I want to go there to think," he said. "My father in his later years used to rest there. He would summon me and my mother and we would talk. He was not always an easy man to get along with."

When they arrived at the stone bench they noticed a three paces long strip of turned earth very near to the tree. With a sense of dread Alexios went to the small rise and knelt near it. There was no sign nor stone that might indicate what it was, but he was sure that it was a grave.

Stephan sat on the bench and watched him until his attention was caught by a small, narrow, earthen bottle lying nearby. He reached for it and held it up for inspection. It had not been there long; there was very little dirt on it. He broke a wax seal, took off the cork stopper and peered inside, seeing a roll of paper. "Alex!" he called. "I have found something."

Alexios climbed stiffly to his feet and came towards him.

"Here," said Stephan. "You need to read this."

Alexios peered down at the paper.

To whomever should find this: Know that the person laid to rest by this tree is my mother, Joannina. Respect her grave for the sake of her soul and yours. God will bless you.

Alexios sat down heavily on the stone bench and looked down. "It is my mother," he stated unnecessarily. "My sister buried her here, of that I am sure. Mama would have liked that; she is with Papa now." Tears came and he wept. "Oh, Mother, but I wish God had granted us some moments together before this." He put his face in his hands and sobbed.

Stephan put a hand on his shoulder to comfort him.

"Ah, Stephan, but these are terrible times. Why has God permitted such cruelty in the world?" Alexios cried.

Having no answers Stephan could only shake his head. "At least she is at peace, my friend. I pray that your sister is not with that monster."

305

The next day the entire city of Constantinople, it seemed, was on the move. It was the day Andronikos would be tried for his crimes against the people. Initially reluctant to go to the trial, Alexios was persuaded by Stephan.

"It is possible the guards will have captured Pantoleon and you will be able to find out about your sister," he told his friend.

That morning, two days after his capture and maiming, Andronikos was dragged from his prison cell, having spent the time without food or water. Besides his missing right hand, one eye had been burned from its socket.

Alexios and Stephan were witness to the barbarism of a mob gone crazy with hate and loathing. The former emperor of Byzantium was only half conscious when the guards brought him out to face the masses, mounted for some reason upon a scrawny camel. But that did not last long.

If the officials had thought they might be able to control the crowd and ensure a civilized trial they were terribly wrong and caught completely off guard. The mob surged forward baying like hounds at the kill and dragged Andronikos off his mount, then began to beat him, stab him with spikes, and hurl excrement and filth onto his prone body. A shrieking woman poured boiling water over his head which made him jerk about in agony. The screaming and howling rose in volume as they hoisted their former emperor up by his feet high enough for all to see him hanging him upside down off some railings while they continued to torment him and abuse him.

Alexios turned away in disgust, "I am revolted, Stephan, we must leave. I cannot watch this barbarism any more."

"He has died. Look, they have had their vengeance at last." Stephan pointed to the still hanging body of Andronikos Komnenos, which no longer twitched or writhed but was still being abused by the maddened people.

"How can people do this?" Alexios asked of Stephan as they pushed their way through the screaming crowd.

"He received what he handed out, Alexios. Have you forgotten already the monstrosities he committed against us and our friends? He killed so many without a second thought, and most of them were in agony themselves before they died." Stephan was angry now.

Alexios shut his mouth. What he had witnessed today would stay with him for the rest of his life; he would never forget how cruel a maddened crowd could be towards one whom they judged to have betrayed them in the manner of Andronikos.

One would think of blaming you
For hesitating so.
Who, setting his hand to knock
At a door so strange as this one,
Might not draw back?
—Rainer Maria Rilke

Chapter 23

Chinese Powder

A loud crash shook the walls of the castle, causing the women to look up from their sewing. The maids who had been cleaning the room flinched, but Rav'an smiled and called out, "Its all right, Anna, it's just the men fooling about. Nothing to worry about."

Rav'an and Jannat looked at one another with raised eyebrows. "Those two are like little boys with a new toy!" Jannat said, as she calmly threaded a needle. She lifted her embroidery to inspect it against the light. They were on the northwest side of the bailey overlooking the magnificent view of the valley and the sea beyond. There was a distant explosion, then silence.

"Let's hope they have not killed themselves while playing their games," Rav'an murmured. "Nor anyone else."

Down in the main yard of the barbican, Talon and Reza clapped each other on the back while Dar'an and Yosef danced about exultantly. "I have to say that I was not sure it would work, Brother, but it does. One more?" Reza beamed.

Talon nodded happily. "Yes, and then we should test the Scorpions. I want to mount those on the ships, but we have to make sure they work first."

With the help of a very wary Palladius and Talon's "engineers", they prepared the trebuchet, which they had reconstructed after hauling its pieces into the confines of the castle, for another swing. It took several minutes for the huge arm to be winched back down to the point where they could load its unique cargo. Talon took Rostam with him as he went up onto the battlements overlooking the gates. Rostam was beside himself with excitement.

"Does the emperor have any more of these weapons, Father?" he squeaked. His voice was breaking and was wont to embarrass him when he was excited.

"I suspect he does, but we now have the advantage," Talon informed him. Max grinned and ruffled Rostam's hair.

"Fear not, young warrior, your father and uncle know how to use these diabolical devices. Which is more than I do." They settled against the parapet overlooking the barbican to watch the demonstration below.

Gingerly, Yosef placed a small wooden barrel filled with Chinese powder in the sling. Then Reza waved everyone to step back. They needed little persuasion; men scuttled away to hide behind the walls of the barbican, but Yosef raced up to join Talon, Max and Rostam on the parapet. Only Dar'an stayed with Reza to assist.

Reza looked up to where Talon and his little group were standing with a good view of the mountain slope to the south east. Max was making a determined effort to overcome his fear of the infernal devices. He could certainly appreciate their military value. Even old Simon had taken time off from his labors in the newly built gardens to watch—from a safe distance behind the walls, along with other curious watchers. They crossed themselves as they watched the men handling the Chinese devil's powder, as most people in the castle called it.

"Ready?" Reza called.

Talon waved and called back, "Whenever you are."

Reza lifted a small flaming torch and touched it to the crude fuse sticking out of the barrel. The moment he saw it fizz and spark he stood back. Dar'an slammed a hammer against the release mechanism of the trebuchet, then they both dived for cover behind a thick wall. The giant machine jerked, the great arm seemed to hesitate for the briefest moment as though gravity refused to release it, but then it whipped up, rotating with tremendous power and speed. Its long arm slammed into the massive padded stop bar with a resounding crash that shook the ground. The sling was jerked forward and hurled the barrel high into the air, twisting and turning, leaving a small trail of dark smoke behind as it soared away into the sky.

The missile flew high over the walls hissing as it went. Everyone ducked reflexively.

"Merde," muttered Max, pulling a face. "I shall never get used to those damned things."

Talon chuckled and they all stood up to follow its trajectory. It seemed as though the barrel would stay in flight forever, but eventually it began to arc downwards, and then it fell very rapidly, becoming a small black dot. Just as it seemed about to disappear altogether there was a flash and a distant bang. It had landed very close to the flat space on the thin line of the trail that led up to the castle. Talon and Max peered down at the small dust cloud that rose on the hillside. Talon nodded to himself, satisfied. Should they ever have to fend off another attack, that was a good place for the missile to land. Right where the trebuchet used to stand.

"This is a very formidable weapon and will serve to deter any more armies the emperor might be rash enough to send our way," Max commented. Talon agreed. They were still standing there when Reza and Dar'an arrived on the ramparts.

"How did we do?" Dar'an asked breathlessly before Reza could ask the same question.

Talon pointed to the small dust cloud that had been raised far down the slope. "If we do this exactly as we did today, we will be able to kill, or at the very least terrify, men almost a league away, and there will be nothing they can do about it except run," Talon told them.

"Good," Reza said, rubbing his hands with glee.

"Let's do a test with that new arrow you have designed, Dar'an. If it works we can mount one of these Scorpions on each of the ships, or perhaps more than one. Hsü told me that in order to keep an enemy ship at bay we should be able to fire these from a goodly distance and make them explode when they strike."

"That sounds complicated," Reza remarked.

"It might be beyond our skill. I wish I had paid more attention while we were in China, but I suspect that the right fuse length would help. If we could make it strike the hull of another ship and go deep into the wood so that they couldn't pry it loose, there would be a big hole in their hull. And I want at least two for our own battlements."

"I like that idea," chortled Reza, and he went on to explain it to Palladius, who didn't fully understand the implications of this cumbersome piece of equipment. "No! It isn't for skewering rows of men all at once," Reza said patiently. "It is for making big holes in ships." He rolled his eyes at Max, who winked back. The two of them saw eye to eye on most things, but Reza found Palladius somewhat dense, even though the man tried his best, scared as he was by the devilish powder these strange people played around with.

"The ungodly stuff scares the shit out of me, Sir Max." Palladius stared gloomily at the lingering dust cloud.

"Ungodly it might be, my friend, but it will keep the emperor at bay. Remember that," Max told him. Palladius crossed himself and said nothing. As a man of war he realized that Max spoke truly. In the short time he had known this grizzled warrior he had come to respect him as a soldier. He resolved to master his fears and learn.

The group of friends continued to enjoy the rest of the morning. The Scorpions, huge cross-bow like devices with bow spans of eight feet, were manhandled to the ramparts and positioned so that they overlooked the hillside. It took some time to cock one of these, but once on the trigger, an arrow with a fused bomb tied onto its shaft could be gingerly placed in the groove along its center frame. Then the fuse was lit and the object seemed to come alive, spitting and hissing furiously as the release mechanism was hurriedly struck. With a mighty 'twang' from the bow string the 'arrow' would fly off into the distance, leaving the men by the weapon surrounded by dense, evil-smelling smoke. They had to turn away in a crouch to avoid the flying sparks. Then they popped up and eagerly gazed after its smoke trail in the air.

The arrow flew for what seemed like an impossible distance before exploding. They saw the flash and then, seconds later, heard the thud of the explosion. The men cheered, satisfied and pleased with themselves, quite unconscious of the wide berth everyone else gave them while they focused on their work. The other Greek and Frankish inhabitants crossed themselves and looked upwards, others made signs to ward off the evil eye. Meanwhile, the women in the solarium rolled their eyes at one another and focused on their embroidery. Another day at the castle was well on its way.

"If we keep this up we will run out of the powder, Reza," Talon warned him when the tests were over and they were alone on the ramparts. "Have you had the stable boys collecting the horse piss?"

"They are collecting it in troughs. We can pour it into the trench of shit you had the men prepare. Dear God but it stinks!"

Talon nodded. "Good, we need to get to work on making more powder. I have prepared one of the dungeons. I have the charcoal and the sulphur already, all we await now is the fermentation of the saltpeter. We should keep everyone out of the dungeons, as it will become very dangerous before long."

Reza agreed soberly. "I worry about that, but we need powder if we are to stay free. One of Henry's and Guy's missions should be to purchase more of the Greek Fire bombs. We are running low."

"Dimitri told me that he thought we might be able to purchase some at Anatolia on the mainland," Talon replied.

*Test them to find out where they are sufficient
and where they are lacking*
—Sun Tzu

Chapter 24

Alarms and New Arrivals

A good month after the siege, Rostam and Boethius' daughter
Irene were standing on the very top platform of the main bailey.
Rostam was chewing on a dried length of straw and gazing
thoughtfully out to sea. The view from here to the north was
stunning, and the top of the bailey was their special place. The girl
was standing on tiptoe nearby, staring out through a slit in the
parapet wall at the panorama below and enjoying the light breeze
that drifted over the ridge, ruffling her hair. It was late afternoon
and their lessons were done for the day.

Over the last months the two had been thrown together by
events, the hectic boat trip out of Paphos harbor, the hurried ride to
the castle and then the siege. They had witnessed the unfolding
events from the very top of the bailey, including the tremendous
explosion of noise followed by the subsequent departure of the
emperor's army. It had left an impression on Irene, less so on
Rostam, who was by now familiar with the hideous noises of the
devices his father and Reza set off.

"It's like being on a ship!" Rostam exclaimed, lifting his face to
the wind. He stared out over the narrow ridge that ran in a north-
easterly direction from the castle like the prow of an immense ship.
One of his favorite games was to imagine that he was the captain, or
more importantly the navigator, the mast above his head from
which fluttered his father's coat of arms being his flag of choice of
his own ship. The stone battlements were the afterdeck of the
imagined vessel. Both he and Irene had to stand on tiptoe to look
over the parapet to see forward and down to the sea in the distance.

Irene turned away from looking into the distance, slid down to
sit and leaned back against the rough warm stone of the bailey walls
and sighed. "It is peaceful now, I am happy," she said to no one in
particular.

Rostam glanced down her way. "My father said that we should
be left in peace for a while," he stated. "I want to go hunting, but
Uncle Reza told me it isn't yet safe."

311

"I'd like to go home too." Irene said. She missed her father, who had departed a month before.

"Is your mother there with him?" asked Rostam who didn't know her story in any detail.

"She died when I was born," Irene said in a low voice.

"I'm sorry, Irene," said Rostam sensing this was a difficult subject. He simply couldn't imagine life without a mother.

"You mean Paphos? That's home?" he enquired, to change the conversation.

"Yes, it is my home and I miss the city."

"Father said that nowhere on this island is safe, in particular the cities," Rostam replied in his halting Greek.

"My father is a merchant, he will manage," Irene stated firmly.

"Well, I learned Greek from him and from you, so now we can talk." Rostam tried to sound positive. He quite liked Irene. Admittedly she was a girl, and she was several years younger, but she was company when there were no other boys around with whom he could play. He missed Lin, who had been his boon companion in China. Had there been other boys present he might well have ignored her altogether, despite the fact that she seemed intelligent and didn't chatter too much.

Talon had asked that Boethius remain in the castle until it was relatively safe in Paphos and to use the time to teach his family Greek. Boethius had willingly agreed but it was a labor, as the language was hard to grasp for people unfamiliar with its complexities. Now, however, he was gone on a mission that Talon considered far more important. They could learn Greek as they went along, but Talon needed eyes and ears in Paphos.

Rostam could hear the cooing of the pigeons in the roost one floor below them. The system of carrier pigeons was now firmly established. Every once in a while one would arrive, flying in an arc around the bailey then into the window, to flutter and perch on the bar across the window of their newly constructed home.

Jannat had volunteered to become the keeper of the pigeons and appeared to enjoy the task, the gentle noises they made, petting them and attaching messages to their legs as the need arose, then sending them on their way. Rostam's father seemed well pleased with the results, and whenever a message arrived from Paphos there was always a line in the letter for Irene to cheer her up.

He looked up at the sky. "It's going to be clear night tonight, Irene. Do you want to see the constellations?"

Irene's eyes lit up. "Yes, do you know them? I only know one or two."

"Of course I do!" Rostam exclaimed. "I am a navigator! I know them all, and I shall show them to you if you want me to."

Irene nodded excitedly. "When would be the best time? How will we be able to... ?"

"I shall wake you. Don't worry, we won't have any trouble with your nurse. She will be fast asleep, snoring as always. We'll come back up here and no one will know where we are."

Irene hugged her thin knees to her chest and smiled sideways at him with her big eyes and wide mouth, the corners of which dimpled with excitement. Rostam was basking in the glow, not quite knowing why, when there was a call from down in the main yard. It was the nurse looking for Irene.

"I'd better go," Irene said reluctantly. "See you later," she added with a smile. It displayed a gap in her front teeth where two upper teeth were only half grown, which she was very self-conscious about but which only added to her pixie-like features. The light dapple of freckles, large ears and huge dark eyes of the nine-year-old added to the semblance.

"Come, Panther, we are leaving now," she called over to the black kitten that had been investigating the corners of the battlements. The cat ignored her; he could smell mice.

"I'll bring him to you when I come down," Rostam assured her.

As she scampered off on bare feet Rostam watched her go, remembering the frightened girl who had arrived on the ship, terrified of everything, especially after the awful noise on the quayside and the screams that followed. She had been too timid to speak, and it had taken some time to get her to talk to him. Eventually, the company of someone her own age had helped draw her out. He didn't mind her company at all.

His thoughts drifted to other matters. Papa had offered to take him out and show him how to use a hawk to hunt small animals—when it was safer. He longed to be out of the castle and, glancing at the glittering sea far below, wondered when he would be next on a ship. Captain Guy had offered to talk to his father about taking him some day. He couldn't wait.

He stood up again and stared across the rippled country towards the harbor. Then he tensed. Far out to sea he could discern a speck of something. He waited, blinking in the wind, staring hard, and finally he could see that it was a ship; furthermore, it was sailing straight towards their harbor!

Alarmed, he ran to the parapet overlooking the barbican where he thought he had earlier heard some activity. His father and Reza often spent time there experimenting with their warlike devices, and usually Rostam had been allowed to watch from the overlooking ramparts. Now all that stood there was the reassembled trebuchet which dominated the space like some great squatting monster; alongside were two of the nasty-looking devices that Reza called Scorpions.

Rostam glanced urgently around the rooftop. He knew of the signal rockets that his father and Reza had built for the purpose of sounding an alarm, or to send a signal to the ships in the harbor if another vessel were spotted from the lofty height of the bailey. That would give the people in the harbor time to prepare for trouble.

Three rockets were stacked in a trough-like box against the parapet, protected from the sun and rain by a rough roof made of thatch and posts. Rostam ran over to the area and looked at the devices nestled in their long holders. They could be removed easily and placed in a stand on the corner of the bailey. He looked around and found a striker and flint lying on a small shelf nearby.

He had been forbidden to go anywhere near the devices by his father and Reza, who told him how unpredictable and dangerous were these infernal devices, but now there was an emergency. What if the ship posed a threat? He ran one more time to the parapet, but the barbican, the main yard and the area below were deserted. He even called out, but the guards on the eastern walls ignored him, and no one else responded.

He would send one of these signals himself; he had watched his uncle fire one off before. All it took was a stream of sparks and the thing did all the rest. Everyone would be pleased and the harbor would be warned.

Taking up the flint he struck it to ensure it was working. Sure enough, a thin satisfying stream of sparks flew downward. But the stream of sparks ran directly down towards one of the rocket fuses. Horrified by his mistake, Rostam reached down to try and smother the sparks. Nothing seemed to happen, and for a few moments he thought that he had succeeded.

Then he saw a small glow on the fuse, followed by an angry hissing sound like a dozen snakes in a pit. It had caught, and now there was nothing he could do to prevent disaster. Too late to take it out of the box and put it in its proper launcher! He reached in to move it, but the terrifying hissing grew in volume and smoke came out of the container, obliterating the contents. Suddenly there was a flare of flame and a loud whooshing sound. Before he could dive for cover the rocket took off into the air, leaving behind a dense stream of sparks and flame that singed his face.

The situation had Panther's full attention. He was backed up with his tail straight up in the air and the size of a brush, his yellow eyes wide, and he was hissing with fright in unison with the rocket.

As the rocket tore through the flimsy roof of the shelter, it started a small fire in the thatch. Unaware of this, Rostam watched, transfixed, as the rocket hurtled high into the sky in a crazy curling fashion. Without warning a huge burst of flame ignited the box where the other two rockets were stored. Another rocket took off. Rostam was so close that it singed his clothes before he was bowled over. Both he and the cat cowered in fear. The second rocket hissed into the sky, leaving a dense cloud of smoke and flame as the whole box caught fire and began to burn in earnest.

This was too much for Panther, who scuttled for the open doorway, every hair on his body sticking straight out and his tail twice its usual size. With a yowl of terror the little black cat vanished down the stairs, leaving Rostam to face the elements on his own.

He gaped with horror at the ongoing destruction. He could do nothing other than stare helplessly at the burning wreckage where once there had been a storage place for his father's signal devices. Unfortunately it was not over yet.

The remaining rocket had fallen over, but it too ignited and shot off parallel to the roof of the bailey, bouncing off the stone walls of the parapet, spewing sparks in every direction. Then it bounced one last time. The rocket, like some malevolent fireball with a mind of its own, came directly towards an appalled Rostam.

His mouth opened in a howl of sheer terror and he threw himself backward, rolled and tried to bury his face in the wooden floor with his hands over his head, waiting for certain death. The missile hissed furiously over his back making him twitch as it showered him with sparks, then it smashed into the wall beyond to disintegrate with a splatter of flame and flying debris.

His father and Reza found him in that position when they arrived panting on the roof top of the bailey. They hesitated at the sight of the burning cover. Then Reza seized a leather bucket of water and Talon one of sand, which they used to douse the small fire. The thatch cover was gone in a smoldering mess and there remained little evidence of the rockets other than the charred and burnt-out skeleton of the third one lying against the wall where it had expired from the collision with the parapet.

315

Talon's first instinct as he took in the scene was to seize Rostam by the neck and shake him until his teeth rattled while demanding an explanation, but a snort from Reza nearby made him glance up. Reza was clutching his sides as though in great pain and slowly sat down on the floor next to Rostam who began to look up, fearful of the sure punishment that awaited him. But Talon had stopped and was looking down at his brother, who had lost all control and was rolling helplessly on the floor weeping with laughter, pointing at Rostam.

Then Talon looked harder at his son. Rostam's normally light colored hair was burned and charred, his face was black and his eyebrows were singed off. His huge eyes were dead white with two black spots in the middle in the black of his frightened countenance and his clothes were also black, burned, and even smoking. Without saying anything, because he thought he would choke, Talon knelt next to the boy and checked that there were no serious burns. He smacked at the smoldering parts to put them out, but it was hard to ignore Reza, who was making choking sounds as if he were about to die.

"Shut up, Reza!" Talon exclaimed, but he finally had to turn away with a snort of his own laughter, trying hard not to let his son see but it was no use. He couldn't help it; he too began to laugh helplessly.

"I'm sorry, Papa!" the boy said, sounding utterly miserable. "I didn't mean to do this. It was a ship, you see. One is coming in, and I wanted to send a signal." He looked forlorn and frightened as he stood and looked up at his father, who had himself stood up. Reza scrambled to his feet, for which Talon was grateful because it was totally undignified to remain rolling about on the floor.

Talon glowered at his son. "You did this, why?" he demanded, not having heard right the first time.

"A ship, Papa!" Rostam insisted. "There is a ship coming in. I wanted to raise the alarm."

"A ship? What are you talking about, Rostam? In any case, this is *not* the way it is done!" Talon roared. He glanced at Reza, who was wiping his eyes. "A ship, you say?"

"I called, but no one heard me!" Rostam said, a note of defiance creeping into his tone. His lower lip was sticking out, always a sign that he was going to stand his ground.

"Next time try not to destroy the castle when you sound the alarm."

They all went to the north side of the parapet to look. Sure enough, a ship was sailing towards the harbor. Talon could also see another ship about to sail out to greet it. The alarm had been raised and Guy had understood. The process worked!

He looked over at Reza who grinned and remarked, "He did raise the alarm, Brother."

"He could have burned us all to the ground," Talon muttered, but he was very relieved that Rostam was not badly hurt.

"Now is probably a good time to go downstairs and explain everything to your mother, although how you will manage that I have no idea," he told his son, with a gentle push to get the boy moving. "I shall deal with you later."

"Reza, we appear to have visitors," he told his grinning brother. "Will you stop laughing like a hyena?"

With the help of some men they cleaned up the roof and made it safe before going downstairs to encounter the confusion reigning below.

"What have you done to my son?" Rav'an demanded as soon as she set eyes on Talon and Reza. "He looks like you dropped him down a chimney head first! He is burned black all over! "

"He managed to do that all on his own!" Talon responded, trying not to sound defensive.

"Why are you grinning like one of those tree apes, Reza?" she snapped at him.

"I er, I er, I have to be in the barbican," Reza mumbled and hurriedly left Talon to face an irate Rav'an and an amused Jannat.

"Reza is still laughing, damn his eyes!" Talon glowered after him. "Did Rostam not tell you what happened, then?"

Jannat snorted with amusement. Talon scowled at her; this was turning into a farce!

"He muttered something about the rockets going off, but then there were tears and he ran off to his chamber. The door is locked and no one can get to him. The cat was our first warning that something was up. It ran through this room as though the hounds of hell were on its tail!"

"I'll try to persuade him to come out again soon," Jannat said, putting her hand over her mouth and giving a snort as she left. Talon could have sworn she was shaking. Rav'an, however, was tapping her foot, always a bad sign.

"There had better be a good explanation for this, Talon. Our boy looked terrible. If you are playing with that powder around him then... "

317

Talon spent the next ten minutes explaining what he thought might have happened. He couldn't control a twitch of his lips by the end of it. Even Rav'an was smiling, now that the crisis seemed to be over.

"Well, thank God he didn't get too badly hurt."

"Just his pride, I suspect. Now, my Love, I have to go and prepare for a visitor. There really was a ship coming in. Guy noticed the alarm and went out to meet it. The system works, but needs some fine tuning."

"Are you going to punish him?"

Talon tried to look stern. "It's tempting. There was a lot of damage. He nearly accomplished single-handedly what the emperor failed to do. Should I flog him within an inch of his life or just throw him off the battlements?"

"Now who's not being serious? But you said that he did raise the alarm, so in one way he did the right thing." She gave him an arch look out of the corner of her eyes.

Talon shook his head and chuckled. "I know, he did. We will have to have a talk about that and then... some training, perhaps."

"That boy is not allowed anywhere near those infernal devices of yours until I say so," she snapped, her lips tightening with resolve.

"Then how am I to train him not to destroy the castle the next time?" he countered with a grin as he kissed her on the cheek, then he went off to find Palladius, thankful that it had not been worse.

Talon was standing on the parapet of the main gate tower with his hounds nearby when the small train of travelers arrived. From here he was able to observe the people on horseback. Max, who was with him, looked him up and down disapprovingly.

"Do you not know it is good manners for the *Lord* of the castle to look more um... lordly when we have visitors, Talon? What on earth happened up there on the bailey? Most people down here being of the superstitious sort, myself included, thought the Devil had popped in to pay you a visit."

"Rostam needs a little more training with the alarm rockets," Talon told him, brushing down his coat, which made not the slightest improvement. It was burned, rent in places and smeared with black soot. He shrugged mentally; too late to change now.

Max waved and called down. "Giorgios! What are you doing here?"

Then Talon recognized the merchant. "So it is! Hey, Giorgios!" He called down. "But who is that with him?" he murmured to Max, who shrugged.

"I imagine that Giorgios will tell us," he said. "Come, perhaps he has news of Constantinople. He was going there the last time Henry and I saw him in Paphos."

They hurried down the stone steps, chased by the excited hounds, to emerge in the yard just as the riders were admitted to the castle by Palladius and his gatekeepers. Talon and Max, and now Reza, who looked as disheveled as Talon, stood off to the side with the dogs as the riders were ushered into the barbican. At a signal from Palladius, guards ran out to hold their horses.

There were only four people, one of them a very young boy. Giorgios led the group; behind him was a woman with a veil covering her face, but some loose curls of reddish hair had escaped the veil. Behind her and holding the pony upon which the boy was perched was a rough looking man; Talon assumed he was one of Giorgios's sailors.

Giorgios dismounted with evident relief and addressed the others. "We have arrived, my Lady. You will be safe here."

The lady was looking around the barbican, and despite the veil Talon had the impression that it was with some interest.

What Theodora saw were three men, one of whom dressed like a Frankish knight, who despite looking somewhat familiar wasn't Talon; the other two looked as though they had just come from cleaning a fireplace. Two large hounds were standing close by one of them. She automatically assumed these were servants and the knight's hounds. Odd for a reception committee, she thought. The next words of Giorgios startled her.

"My Lord, Sir Talon, I wish to present Lady Theodora Kalothesos from Constantinople."

Theodora was very surprised. She turned back to the three men standing in front of her and stared. Then she began to dismount, and the tall man hurried forward to assist her.

"I can manage, thank you," Theodora said in a pleasant manner and then removed her veil. Talon stood back a pace with a frown on his face. He most certainly didn't recognize this very attractive woman standing in front of him.

"Do you not recognize me, Sir Talon? Or is it my Lord Talon now?" her eyes twinkled, but they were inspecting him too.

Talon shook his head in a bemused gesture. "Indeed my Lady, I did not! Are you really so changed, Theodora?" he asked her. "You have become a... a beautiful woman," he finished as gallantly as he could.

"I didn't recognize you either Talon, you look a little um... although now of course I do," she hurried on. "Well, as you can see, I've grown up and I have a child and... here I am." There was an awkward pause.

"Er, Theo... Theodora it is good to see you," Talon almost stammered. He glanced down at his patched and scruffy overcoat, with black streaks across it, and even worse-looking boots that were charred in places. Of course she couldn't have recognized him. He looked more like a stable hand than the lord of a castle. He self-consciously tried to brush off the soot from his coat.

Max laughed next to him. "You have rendered Talon speechless, my Lady Theodora. It will pass, but it isn't often that happens. Welcome to our castle, my Lady. We are right glad to see you safe."

"Max!" she said with pleasure in her voice. "So it was you I recognized. It is so good to see you after all this time." Theo smiled as she offered her hand. Max blushed bright red and bowed his pepper and salt beard over her hand. "Deeply honored to meet with you again, my Lady. Please excuse my friends, they were just putting out a fire on the roof. It is a long story and can wait."

Talon scowled at Max and then dragged Reza forward by his sleeve. "This is my 'Brother' Reza," he told her. "Speak Greek slowly to him as he is still learning, but he is my most trusted comrade, besides Max. Max is right, my Lady. You are safe here and we all bid you welcome."

Reza smiled, his teeth showing very white against his dark features, and gave her an elaborate bow, taking her hand and passing his lips over its smooth white skin. Theo smiled.

"I am glad to meet you, Reza. I am sure we will have much to talk about, including how you and Talon met," she said with a glance Talon's way. Then she turned to the pony where her son still sat taking in the meeting with wide eyes. "This is my son Damian," she said.

Talon noted that the boy was very young. He had gray eyes, which were wide with interest and not a little apprehension. A light cool wind ruffled his reddish hair, just like that of his mother, Talon noted. So Theodora had married and had a son from the union. Had time passed so quickly, he wondered, since the visit to

Constantinople, where he knew her as a rather alarming girl of fourteen? Now here she was, a mature and poised young woman.

He strode up to the pony, lifted the boy down and gave him a gentle push so the boy ran to stand with his mother, where he hid in her long skirts as he looked up at these strangers. Theo placed a gentle hand on his head and ruffled his hair.

"I would be lying if I said this was not a surprise, my Lady," Talon said.

"Please call me Theo," she replied. "All of you. I am no longer a lady, but a woman who seeks refuge. All the rest of my family are dead, including his father." She indicated the boy pressed against her skirts.

Talon's mouth tightened at the news, while Max and Reza looked concerned. "Henry and Max told me of their meeting with Giorgios," Talon told her slowly. "We have also more recently heard terrible rumors of the events in Constantinople, the sacking of Thessalonica by the Franks from Sicily, and the defeat of the Greek armies. We have all been very worried, Theo. We had no idea how bad it was for you and your family. God be praised you escaped, with the help, it seems, of our friend Giorgios here." He smiled at her, then he realized that he was keeping everyone waiting. "But I am not being a good host at all! Please come with me and we will make you comfortable and you can meet my family."

He offered her his arm and they walked the short distance to the gate of the barbican that led to the main yard and the bailey. "What have you been doing, Talon," she murmured. "You smell like you really have been in a fire. Or is it brimstone? I am beginning to believe the wild stories Giorgios told me about you."

He chuckled. "Wait until you meet my son. He tried to set the bailey on fire. Did you see the rockets in the sky?"

"Yes! So that was an alarm system? I am very impressed, Talon. Giorgios pointed them out to me from the ship as we were coming in. No one knew what it meant and all were afraid."

"My son, Rostam, was a trifle eager," Talon said, his tone dry.

The castle yard was busy, the sound of hammering on iron down by the stables and the calls of servants who stopped what they were doing briefly to stare, then resumed their tasks after the small entourage had passed. Talon led the way towards the large entrance of the bailey, where they were met by one of the stewards who whispered something to Talon.

He turned to Theodora. "My wife is pregnant in her eighth month, and I hope you will excuse her not being able to greet us at

321

the door. We will go upstairs to the summer rooms where she and her companion await us."

Theodora smiled. "What is your wife's name?"

"Rav'an," he told her and she nodded. "So this is the woman you had to find? God is sometimes kind; you are united."

Talon smiled at her. "Indeed."

Leaving Max to entertain Giorgios, they climbed the stairs and walked down a long corridor towards the sound of low voices. Talon pulled aside the leather curtain and ushered Theodora into a wide spacious room filled with an assortment of low tables, cushions and carpets. The air smelled fresh here, as the shutters were thrown open to let in the light breeze from outside.

"Rav'an, Jannat, we have a visitor. Her name is Theodora and she has come from Constantinople," he said to the two extraordinarily beautiful women seated on piles of cushions near to the window.

The slightly older woman of the two, with large gray eyes and black lustrous hair, smiled and said in halting Greek, "Forgive me, Lady Theodora, for not rising. I am, as you see, somewhat indisposed. This," she waved to her companion, "is Jannat, the wife of Reza, whom I think you have already met," she laughed. "We are both with child, as you can see."

Theodora could not help it, she smiled back. "I am honored to meet you, Rav'an and Jannat. I hope you will forgive me for this unexpected visit but I... I had nowhere else to go," her voice became soft with grief and she dipped her head, trying to stop the tears of fatigue and worry from overwhelming her.

Rav'an said urgently, "Talon, what are you doing keeping her standing there? Bring her over here and let her sit with us. We will look after her, but call one of the maids and tell them to bring refreshments. Is she ill?" Rav'an spoke Greek out of politeness to her guest.

Theodora raised her head and smiled at her. Dashing the tears away she said, "No, there is nothing wrong with me, except I am suddenly very tired. I am a physician, so I know I don't need one; it's just relief to be somewhere safe at last."

Rav'an and Jannat exchanged startled glances. "Come over here and sit with us, Theodora," Jannat spoke for the first time. "Is this your child?" she asked.

Theodora nodded and brought Damian with her as she seated herself opposite the two women. "Please call me Theo. He is indeed my son, his name is Damian; he is four years old."

Jannat looked over at Reza and Talon who were hovering by the door. "My Reza," she said in Farsi, "Why are you still standing about? Did not Rav'an ask one of you to call a servant? Our guest is very tired. Where is her husband?"

"Er yes," Reza said and ducked his head. "I'll go at once and find someone." He disappeared.

"I think her husband is dead, Jannat," Talon said in a low tone.

Jannat gave him a sharp look, as did Rav'an. "There are many things we need to know here," Rav'an remarked in Farsi.

She called over to another person in the back of the room. "Rostam, come here and be introduced."

Rostam, somewhat cleaner and in new clothes, shuffled out of the gloom into the sunlight. He was clearly embarrassed and his eyes were downcast. Jannat had done her best to clean his hands and face, but the results of the fire were still evident on his forehead, which was speckled with spark damage, while his hair showed signs of having been scorched in patches.

"This is our son," Rav'an told Theodora in a dry tone. "He was the one who gave us warning of your arrival."

Theodora looked up at the boy and smiled, then stared at his face critically. "I see you have been burned. Is anything painful?" she asked in slow Greek. Despite the slightly burned skin and the singed eyebrows, Theodora could see the resemblance immediately. Rostam shook his head, then looked up at his father. Talon placed a hand on his boy's shoulder.

"Nothing but his pride, I suspect," he said with a grin. "But perhaps you could look him over just to make sure."

Servants bustled in and placed hot tea in front of them, and some baklava sweet cakes, grapes and apples on the table.

"First you must eat, you are our guest and you are welcome," Rav'an told her. "Tomorrow you can tell us all about your ordeal." She sent Talon a warning look that told him to save his curiosity for the next day, and then gave instructions to the servants to prepare a room for Theodora.

"Are we safe now, Mama?" Damian piped up.

"Yes, my darling, we are safe now," Theodora told him and smiled through her tears at all of them.

Not where the wounded are,
Not where the nations die,
Killed in the cleanly game of war—
That is no place for a spy!
O Princes, Thrones and Powers, your work is less than ours—
Here is no place for a spy!
—Rudyard Kipling

Chapter 25
A Clash of Spies

"I wonder what he is doing here?" Isaac, Emperor of Cyprus, asked. It could have been rhetorical, as there was no one else in the bed chamber other than Tamura, and she was otherwise occupied, but he repeated the question.

She stopped what she was doing and popped her head up to stare at her lord and master and smiled sweetly. "My Lord, I cannot answer your question and continue with what I was doing. Which is it to be?"

He looked down at her and grunted, "All right continue, my honey patch."

She bent to her task, but it was no good. There was no life where there had only a moment ago been rampant enthusiasm.

"Oh!" she exclaimed with some exasperation, "You have something else on your mind, my Lord. But it can wait," she told him. This had been happening with more frequency of late. "No matter, what is it you are so concerned about?"

He looked at her fondly as she came back into his arms. "That man Exazenos. You know, the *Lord* who arrived last week."

"Perhaps he is just passing through?" she suggested as she snuggled closer to the dark hairy royal chest.

"Perhaps, but I don't think so. My question is, why be here at all unless he is a fugitive? Uncle Andronikos is dead, we know of that. The ship that came in weeks ago confirmed it for fact. So if he is a fugitive, is he waiting for me to... give him a job?"

"What do you know about him, Lord?"

"Malakis told me that he has an extremely shadowy past. There are rumors layered upon rumors about this man. If even half of them are true then he was a very high-up official in Constantinople,

324

even perhaps as high up as Andronikos's right hand, and you know what that means."

She shifted uncomfortably. She knew Malakis all right. He was a dangerous and brutal man who had a network of spies around the island feeding the emperor information. This man Exazenos sounded even more dangerous. That boded ill for everyone. "Then he is as bad as his former master and could bring bad luck upon us too, Lord."

"Perhaps, but if he is really the person Malakis thinks he might be, then what a man to have working for me! I am glad that Andronikos is gone, no regrets there, and if William succeeds in taking Constantinople I might even have a chance at the throne!" Isaac chortled. "He as good as promised he would give it to me."

Tamura had her doubts about this but said nothing. King William wanted an empire and would most certainly not give it away the moment he acquired it.

"Our visitor will be having an audience with me next week. No harm in keeping him kicking his heels for a while. It'll show him who is in charge," Isaac chuckled again. "Think of it! I could be Emperor of a real empire instead of this piss pot of an island, and this Exazenos probably knows everything there is to know about the City. He could be invaluable!" he gave Tamura an excited kiss, which rekindled his enthusiasm for their interrupted activities.

"Beware, my Lord. This kind of man is as dangerous to his master as he is to anyone else, if all is true about him," Tamura warned. She knew of the barbaric behavior of Andronikos towards his subjects—who didn't?—and also of the manner of his death. Isaac was just as brutal and just as hated. With this man abetting him the menace to everyone on the island would increase several fold. She sighed; her lord and master was not listening.

Later she confided in Siranus while lying on the massage table enjoying his gentle hands on her shoulders and neck, which were tense with concern. "This Exazenos, what do you know of him?"

Siranus paused, "Not much, my Lady. He arrived on a ship full of dangerous looking men who behave like pirates. They swagger about the town and get into trouble with the guards." Siranus shuddered delicately. "They are barbarians! To think they come from the City! People give them a wide berth. The man himself has taken up residence in a villa on the other side of town and is rarely seen. He is badly burned on the face. None of us can decide whether he is entire or not."

"Entire?" she lifted her head. "Entire, you say? Why wouldn't he be?"

Siranus paused at what he was doing and looked down on her flawless back and pert rump. "There are things that one just knows instinctively, my Lady. All the other eunuchs have been talking about it. They are placing bets."

"They are such a bunch of gossips! Hasn't anyone ever been able to find out?" she asked with amused skepticism.

"No, my Lady. He is never seen bathing in public, preferring to keep to his expensive villa. The word on the street is that he has much treasure with him; he guards that villa with many hard-looking men," he gave another delicious shudder. "They are barbarians!" he repeated. "I think they must all come from Crete, which is where all the hairiest and nastiest ones come from."

"You need to try and find out, but also pass along the word to our *friend*," she told him in a whisper. The palace walls had ears, and neither she nor Siranus had any illusions that they had real privacy. Her enemies would like nothing better than to denounce her and her servant. Jealousy and intrigue were sustenance for some. While he worked on her in the ensuing silence her mind was busy.

Her hatred for the emperor was still as strong as ever. Perhaps this was an opportunity? She let her thoughts dwell on the idea that an alliance with Exazenos might be to her benefit. She would wait until the audience was over and then she would see. A lot depended upon whether the emperor would accept this stranger with a hideous past into his inner circle.

Siranus left his lady to rest and recuperate while he departed the palace and casually walked along the main street of the city, named appropriately enough, Emperor Street. The markets were still open but business was slowing down; it was almost noon and the pious would be attending the service in the cathedral, while the not so pious would be attending the wine shops.

He had walked out of the palace with a small bundle under his arm and watched his back to see if he was being followed. Now he slipped behind a wall and re-emerged looking like a laborer with a sack covering his curls. Any one who had trailed him from the palace would have lost him then and there. Walking with more of a shuffle, Siranus cut to his right down a narrow alley that stank of urine and muck. With one last glance back to ensure he was not being shadowed, he stepped into a hole-in-the wall that called itself a taverna.

He took a few moments to accustom his eyes to the gloom and assess the few people seated on crude benches, then crossed the small room to sit without ceremony at a table where two men slouched. One of the men watched the entrance while the other, a more bulky man, leaned over the wet surface of the able and asked, "Well, what news today?" It was Dimitri.

"Interesting news. Next week the emperor is going to have an audience with a man called Exazenos who came all the way from Constantinople."

Dimitri looked skeptical. "What is so interesting about him?"

Siranus proceeded to provide details of where the newcomer lived and what the rumors were saying about him.

As he listened, Dimitri reflected on how he had met Siranus. Following his instincts Dimitri had kept watch on anyone coming and going from the palace, which was located on the East side, within the confines of the walled city. One of his men had described a handsome youth who occasionally left the back entrance of the palace and walked the streets. Dimitri had been intrigued. He had put all his men onto the task of discovering all they could about the youth. One day, however, his men had noticed that the youth was being followed; one hurriedly notified Dimitri, and he and Maymun, sensing trouble, had in turn followed the young man as he wandered about the town. He visited an apothecary, then bought some oils from a market stall before he began to head back towards the jumble of buildings that composed the palace.

It was then that Dimitri and Maymun noticed the followers closing in. Maymun muttered something. Dimitri turned to him, "What was that?"

"They are going to do something, they mean to hurt the boy!" Maymun said, his tone had become urgent.

"What should we do?"

"What Reza would do. Stop them."

"Kill them, you mean?" Dimitri was shocked.

"Yes, and be very quick about it because they are going to kill him. Look!" The two rough looking attackers were focused on the youth, whose back was to them. They had knives out and were intent on using them.

Dimitri had swallowed hard and remembered what Talon had told him: "If you commit, then it is all the way. No half measures, no hesitation."

"Very well," he said, his voice hoarse. "You take the one with the red scarf and I'll take the other."

The market was crowded, so it was not hard to get close to the two men. Just as the one with the red cotton scarf took a step forward to plunge his knife into the youth's back, Maymun stabbed him in the kidney area. The man gasped with agony and arched his back. He was about to scream when a hand covered his mouth and all that came out was a muffled squawk.

Dimitri had been in brawls before, but this was much more deliberate and cold-blooded, and he hesitated. The other man, his intended victim, half-turned towards his companion and his eyes widened as he realized what was happening. It was now or never. Dimitri hammered his knife into the assassin's ribs from the side, he felt the blade grate on a rib, then sink in right up to the hilt. He hauled hard on the knife; already the handle was sticky with blood, it resisted, then came out with a sucking sound. The wounded man fell sideways to the ground.

The youth whirled about, having heard the unusual sounds coming from behind. Dimitri threw all his weight forward to shove him, staggering, through the crowd, moving him away from the dense group which was already forming about the two would-be assassins, who lay groaning and bleeding to death on the ground. Maymun arrived, seized the young man's arm, and between them they hustled the youth away from the consternation that was developing in the middle of the market place.

Dimitri glanced back; they needed to put some distance between them and the incident. The soldiers would be swarming soon, and it would be that much more difficult to get away.

He shook the youth, who looked about to yell for help. "Shut up! Those men were going to kill you! We saved your life. Hurry, or we will all be dead!"

Maymun led them unerringly through the alleyways until they were far enough away to stop and catch their breath.

"Who are you?" the youth had stammered.

"We are your friends, and you need to tell us why you were being followed by those two men. Does someone from the palace want to have you killed?"

And so Siranus, grateful to be still alive, had become Dimitri's contact and source of information.

*****

Talon was seated at the wide table in his working and reading chamber. The sides of the walls were already filling up with rolls of paper, and there were two shelves of books he had managed to obtain with Boethius' help. They had cost near fortune. In this day and age books were becoming even more rare than before as warfare spread. This was his den, and even Rav'an respected his privacy, although she was caustic about how untidy it had become when she made the occasional visit. In pride of place was the trophy that Reza had recovered from the island in Malaya. Talon was still astounded at what happened every time he touched it. He would hear a polo match taking place. As soon as he took his hand away, it stopped. If anything was magic in this castle, it was this enigmatic and ancient trophy.

This room allowed him a place to think, free from the constant demands of the castle administration. Here he could compose letters to his two spy masters, as he had dubbed them, Dimitri and Boethius, who appeared to be settling into their roles well. During the ensuing months he had also been able, with the help of Reza and Henry, to link up the Jewish bankers who not only held his treasure secure but also provided information about the goings on in the Kingdom of Jerusalem, supplemented by news from travelers and pigeons.

He gazed out of the window towards the sea, deep in thought, paying no attention to the stunning view on this particular autumn day. He had received a very interesting message from Dimitri in Famagusta.

Talon reflected with some satisfaction on the last visit he had paid Dimitri. It had taken a while for Dimitri to get over his initial fears and a few mistakes had been made, but none serious enough to jeopardize the venture. Talon had worked with him to provide a plausible reason for Dimitri to be in Famagusta. The ship that Guy captained was part of that cover, because Dimitri was now posing as a merchant who traded in olive oil, olives, cheese and a very modest amount of the copper ore which was now being extracted from the mine.

The commodities arrived by ship and were welcomed in the markets of the town. No one knew that the cargoes came from the castle on the mountain overlooking this very city. Commodities were becoming scarce, because of the growing piracy in the seas to the North and the depredations of the emperor himself.

From the safety of his modest villa on the south end of the walled city, Dimitri would compose a missive in tiny letters and in code to Talon. On the roof of his discretely located villa was a small pigeon coop, where he kept some five of the birds. These would be released to fly to the mountain eyrie, where they would be caught by Jannat and Rostam, the message then delivered to Talon by Rostam's own hand.

The boy had recovered from his experience on the roof and most of his hair had grown back to its former tousled mop. The penance exacted by his father had been intensive training in the use of fire crackers, not the large dangerous kind, much to the boy's disappointment, and the use of the replacement rockets. Much to the boy's delight, Uncle Reza was teaching him all the tricks of his trade; but the hardest penance was the study of Greek and the other languages. Talon pointed out that these were his tools and he would be proficient at them or else. The boy liked Irene very much, so he applied himself, and as he worshipped Theodora, who had assumed the role of teacher, studies did not prove to be too arduous a task.

From the top floor of his house in Famagusta, Dimitri could look out over the harbor and observe the comings and goings of the merchant vessels and occasional naval ships without even stepping out of his house. Talon and he had spent some time searching for just the right place, not too isolated but not too close to other houses, and surrounded by a high wall. This villa had once belonged to a rich merchant who had either fled the brutal visitations of the emperor or had succumbed and died a pauper on the streets.

The acquisition had been easily carried out with a well-placed bribe to the eunuch who dealt with such properties that had suddenly become vacant. The emperor needed the money; after all, his revenues were slowly drying up. The small sack of gold had vanished and the papers had been drawn up in Dimitri's false name. Talon's name was nowhere to be found on any papers. Dimitri had moved in with several of the former Greek slaves and Maymun, who spent much of his time teaching the others how to defend themselves, how to be invisible on the streets, and the art of archery, at which he was very good. He had been an avid student of Reza and shared his skills with enthusiasm.

Today the message was routine except for one piece of interesting news, which had been furnished by Dimitri's best informer. Talon sat back and thought about the incredible luck that had landed this person in Dimitri's lap.

He had spent some time discussing the venture with Dimitri as they walked the crowded streets of Famagusta during his stay there.

"I am sure a man like Isaac will have spies, so tread carefully and do not leave footprints if you can help it."

Dimitri appeared to have taken this to heart. He had used his men and the beggars to good effect, so before long he had people in the harbor customs, and even someone in the church's population who could tell him what the bishop was doing—better still, thinking. Dimitri told Talon that the bishop was a sycophant to Isaac and not of much importance. The man who procured boys for the bishop was now Dimitri's informant; well paid for it, too.

The eunuchs and the soldiers of the palace were often to be seen on the streets of Famagusta, either on business or taking time out from their duties. It was boring work to have them followed to see what they did with their time. The soldiers, especially the mercenaries, went to the taverns and brothels, recycling their wages with careless abandon. The eunuchs were not so easy to pin down. Very little came of these exercises, but Talon had encouraged Dimitri to continue.

Dimitri had once asked Talon where he had learned his skill as a spy. Talon's response had surprised him.

"I worked with a very interesting man in the Templar community, Sir Guy—you might even remember him. He was a gatherer of information. If that is spying then he was very effective. His downfall came because no one would listen to him. We should do better than that."

"So you are saying that every small detail is important?" Dimitri had asked.

"Yes, it is, but just as importantly you must learn to put the pieces together with great care and in their proper order to gain a true image. If they do not fit the right way then you will create an illusion or a false picture, and that could spell disaster."

Talon had spent much time with Dimitri discussing what they should look for in the royal city and had finally set their sights on the lower echelons, the cooks or the servants. Discontent provided fertile ground for Dimitri and he had had some modest successes. One of the cooks in the palace had lost a son in the debacle on the mountain. He didn't blame the new occupant of the castle, instead he blamed the emperor for his incompetence. He wanted the man dead.

Talon stared out of the window, deep in thought. This man Exazenos sounded like an enigma. Talon wondered if he was the same man whom he and Theodora had both known as Pantoleon. It was worth verifying. Old memories arose, of Pantoleon as the famous player of Chogan, the darling of Constantinople and the center of attention wherever he went.

He stood up and made his way down the steps of the tower to where Theodora had settled in. She had assumed the role of physician, as well as teacher, and she had willingly undertaken to assist Rav'an and Jannat.

Rav'an and Jannat moved about less these days, as Theodora had told them to rest more and not strain themselves climbing up and down the steps all day. The sound of laughter came to him as he made his way along the passage towards their large room. Theodora called it a Solarium. It was a large comfortable room with bright light coming in through the wide windows when the shutters were thrown open.

Theodora was reading while Rav'an and Jannat were sewing when he knocked and entered. Rav'an smiled up at him. "Ah, there you are, Talon. It has been so quiet I thought you might have gone hunting."

"No such luck, my Love. I have work to do of the writing and reading kind, and that is why I am here." He glanced at Theodora as he spoke. She closed her book and began to stand up. "I should leave you to your privacy," she said with a smile.

"Please don't go, Theo. " Talon said quickly. "This concerns you."

Theodora reseated herself. All the women were now watching him with keen interest. Talon lifted the tiny piece of paper and read it out loud.

"'There is a man who has arrived from the City of Constantinople who is about to have an audience with the emperor. The palace is abuzz with rumors that the emperor might want to employ him for certain skills which he possesses. His name is Exazenos. He—'"

Talon had been giving his full attention to the message, but the sound of Theodora's book falling with a thud to the floor made him glance up quickly.

Theodora's face was ashen. She put a trembling hand to her mouth and her eyes were wide with shock and fear. Rav'an reached out to grip her hand with a look of concern. "Theo! What is it?" she asked gently. "You look like you have seen a ghost or are going to be sick."

Theodora fumbled in her gown and pulled out a wisp of a handkerchief, which she proceeded to crush and twist. She did indeed look as though she were going to be sick. Talon took two strides and gripped her shoulder. "Are you all right?" he asked.

She lowered her head almost to her knees and whispered, "Yes, I... I'm all right now. Did you say Exazenos, Talon?"

Talon stared down at her bent head and said in a low tone. "Is it possible? Could it be the same man, Pantoleon? I am not so familiar with Greek names, so it didn't at first occur to me that it might be the same person. I wanted to know for sure, which is why I came to you."

"Does your man describe him?" she asked in a muffled tone.

"Jannat, is there some water?" Rav'an interrupted. Jannat stood up and hastened to bring a cup of water to Theo, who took it with a grateful smile and sipped. They looked at one another over Theodora's huddled frame.

"He says that those who have seen him remarked a significant feature, which is his scarred face." After a long pause Talon finally said, "So it is Pantoleon after all?"

"Remember I told you of his disfigurement?" Theo told them. They all nodded agreement. Theo had told them the full story.

"So Pantoleon survived the coup, and now he is here in Cyprus," Talon mused.

"What does it mean for us, Talon?" Rav'an asked, her voice full of concern.

"That depends upon what he finds out, and what, if anything, the emperor decides to tell him," Talon responded, but he was beginning to feel very uneasy.

"I must go to Famagusta without delay. To verify this news... and to see what can be done," he said.

In seeking wisdom, be willing
to ask and look like a fool;
But once you have it within you—
Guard it like a jewel.
—Y. Bin Ezra

Chapter 26
An Appointment

The market in the walled city of Famagusta was in full swing, it being mid-week. Many of the people streaming through the great wooden iron-studded gates had come from Larnaca and the surrounding countryside. Today was also fair day, so wealthy merchants and minor nobles arrived in their best clothes, with ringed fingers, oiled ringlets, ornate feathered caps and silk overcoats. Their veiled ladies were dressed in their best fur-trimmed mantles, displaying silk dresses underneath and riding well-bred animals while casting sidelong glances at one another, assessing each potential rival. Their escorts, who vied with one another like peacocks trying to be the most splendid, rode alongside their female charges protectively. They looked down their noses at the nearby walking peasants, who wore ragged pantaloons and coarse linen shirts; the women folk often only wore a shift of linen decorated with colored thread, carrying large baskets of vegetables from their farms.

In the square itself the rows of stalls were crowded closely together, their various wares displayed in a rainbow of color and shapes. Bread covered one table, sweet dates, figs and honeyed pastries at another, while gauze and muslin were draped around yet another. Silken bolts and linen competed with furs from the Northern countries. Clothes, robes and mantles, stamped leather work, cheap jewelry, belts, pouches and bundles of pheasant feathers were on display, along with a bewildering array of tools, weapons and tonics which the vendors assured the public were capable of ensuring long life and immunity to disease of any kind.

Carcasses of rabbits, still with their fur, chickens hanging by their feet, and wild birds culled from the central island lakes shared their respective dead smells with the fish from the sea that lay in wide wooden trays alongside octopus, sardines, shellfish of every variety, and eels from the rivers.

The most raucous were the sellers of roots and tonics for those who needed help in the bed chamber. "Buy this for your man, Ladies, and you'll have two donkeys to play with in the bed! I have lettuce in quantity for you, Master!" one particularly villainous-looking vendor shouted up to some merchant ladies riding by. "Also thistles for the donkey! Heh heh!"

The merchant raised his whip as though to strike the insolent man, who ducked, pretending to be fearful, and laughed. Few if any of these "medicines" would provide the smallest help to the needy, other than perhaps a good physic for the constipated.

"What does he mean, he has lettuce?" Talon asked Dimitri, who grinned. "You mean those?" Talon pointed at a basket of green leaves.

"Yes, those. Surely you know the powers of lettuce, Master Talon?" Dimitri smirked.

"Er... no, not really. It doesn't grow well in the places I have lived."

"Why, we Greeks consider it to be an aphrodisiac. It helps with the limp you-know-what!" Dimitri chuckled and made an obscene gesture.

"There is a saying: 'Thistles are lettuce to a donkey!' So that fellow is being doubly cheeky and the master on his horse knew it!"

Talon laughed uncertainly. "Lettuce, hum? I'll bear that in mind."

Talon and Dimitri continued to walk gingerly along the narrow passageways between the crowded stalls, which appeared to be doing good business. They finally arrived at the stall where Dimitri's man was selling olives, and the oil of olives, in large earthenware jars; the scent of the booth was pleasant. Right next to it was a booth belonging to a herbalist who sold lavender, garlic, mugwort, basil and rosemary, which added to the agreeable aroma and offset the not so nice smells emanating from the ground itself and some of the other stalls.

Talon had been asked by Theodora to buy some raspberry leaves if he could find them. Their mountain did not have them growing wild, but she had heard that they could be found in the distant foothills of Trudos. He decided to buy some lettuce seeds from the herbalist as well, "For the garden, you understand," he told the smirking Dimitri. "They look nourishing." Dimitri cackled with laughter.

The noise of the market was deafening. Donkeys brayed, dogs barked, children screamed, and vendors bellowed, while the ongoing chatter of the crowd all but drowned out normal conversation. This suited both men, who were very alert; although the market provided a good cover, there might be others watching for strangers and reporting.

Talon was dressed as a peasant, but beneath his dirty loose brown robe he carried his sword. On his head he wore a large straw hat to protect his head from the sun. It might have been late October but the sun on this day was still warm; as many others wore wide hats of straw too, he would go unremarked. Shadowing him and Dimitri were Maymun and his men, watchful for any kind of danger. There were already signs of drunkenness from the lounging soldiers, which their bodyguards noted.

"What has been the reaction to the incident on the street?" Talon asked Dimitri as they negotiated a stall full of sheep and goats.

"Initially a lot of fuss and people were pointing in all directions. I heard the soldiers came and roughed up a few people in the street, but we were long gone by then. We managed to get the boy back to the palace in one piece, and I did not hear of much from within the palace itself, but he must have told his mistress. She cheekily sent a message demanding that we assassinate one of the women in the royal harem whom she blamed for the attempt." Dimitri chuckled. "She is a piece of work, that young woman!"

"We will have to tread carefully with her," Talon agreed. "I don't want her knowing who I am for any reason, nor for whom you work. All the same, she is a prize we need to keep. When are you due to see the boy again?"

"Perhaps today. I am wondering if he is more than just a servant of the lady." Neither Dimitri nor Talon ever spoke any names while outside the villa, just in case.

As it happened, Talon was to be disappointed. Pantoleon, otherwise known as Exazenos did not show his face that day, nor the next.

"I must get back to the castle," he fretted to Dimitri. "Rav'an is due any day now, and I must be there."

Dimitri shrugged. "Don't worry; we will keep watch, and I shall inform you in detail via the pigeons."

"That's not the same as actually seeing this man. I must do that somehow," Talon responded.

The last day of Talon's stay, the watchers of the villa where Pantoleon was purported to be staying noticed much activity. The guards who had been lounging about at the gates became alert, and by late morning a small retinue of riders had left the courtyard and appeared to be riding towards the palace.

A frantic messenger arrived to tell Talon and Dimitri of the news. Without wasting a moment both men seized their swords and hurried along the busy streets. They wore over-cloaks with hoods that hid their faces and heads from the curious, but their haste drew calls of annoyance as they pushed past knots of people in the streets.

Finally they arrived at the wide avenue that fronted the palace and found a corner of a building from where they would get a good view of any new arrivals. The street before the palace was full of horses and palanquins; clearly there was something important going on. For a bad moment Talon thought they might have missed their quarry, but then they were alerted by a rising cloud of pigeons that fluttered into the sky, heralding another arrival. There followed the clatter of horses' hooves on the stones from another street. Pulling back into the cover of a pillar, Talon and Dimitri watched as the group drew up and dismounted. Servants ran down the steps to take the horses, leaving the visitors free to mount the fifteen steps to the main entrance of the palace.

Talon strained his eyes to see the four men. All wore brilliantly sewn costumes of the Byzantine fashion and swords, but their cloaks hid their faces until one of the men swung his cloak behind him with a sharp gesture and in doing so shook the hood loose from his head. Instinctively the man caught the cloth, but not before a wig he was wearing was slightly dislodged. With a gesture of irritation the man adjusted his wig and left the cloak hood lying back. Talon could see clearly that his face was badly scarred. His men waited respectfully while he adjusted the headpiece, then they all moved into the darkness of the palace entrance.

Talon turned to Dimitri. "It is he, I am sure of it. If Theodora is right we have two of the most evil men in Christianity in the palace."

They set off back to the villa, where Talon held a small council of war. Dimitri brought his closest men, including Maymun, to the meeting, which was held in one of the topmost rooms. Dimitri explained what they had ascertained, and there was a silence as they digested this information.

"If this Pantoleon, or Exazenos, escaped from Constantinople after the former emperor his sponsor was executed, why doesn't someone here turn him in, Sir Talon?" asked one of the men.

"Because he has brought with him much treasure, which I am sure he will point out to Isaac, whom he is visiting today. Also he is a skilled spy. This man could be of enormous help to the emperor, I am sure of it, and a great danger to all of us," Talon told them. "You must watch his villa at all times."

*****

Pantoleon was unaware that he had been observed as he entered the gloomy entrance of the palace. He was too preoccupied with what he would say to the emperor to notice anyone. He was all too aware that he would need to use his diplomatic skills to the full, for if his own people were to be believed this Isaac Komnenos was as fickle and dangerous as his late great uncle. Pantoleon consoled himself with the knowledge that he had survived the menaces of Andronikos unscathed; all the same, it would not do to be complacent. He would have to heed every nuance of the conversation to come.

He and his men divested themselves of their cloaks, and then he went forward alone towards the great doors of the audience chamber while his men remained near the entrance. Pantoleon was taking no chances. Should things go badly he wanted to be able to leave quickly. He had even told his ship's captain to be prepared to leave at a moment's notice.

The doors were opened by a courtier who barely deigned to bow to him, something Pantoleon duly noted for the future. As the doors swung open, he found himself looking down a long carpeted passageway lined by a thin crowd of courtiers who were all staring back at him. He squared his shoulders and walked slowly up to a cushion on the floor, about ten paces from the throne. Here he was expected to prostrate himself, then crawl on hands and knees to another cushion in front of and below the throne. Resigning himself to the unavoidable display of humility, he lowered himself to the ground. It was with some surprise that he saw the carpet he was crawling along was threadbare and dirty. This "Empire" was short of money!

Even on his knees, the finery of his clothing put everyone else in the room to shame. His under robe was of green silk, and the sleeves were patterned with gold and silver thread sewn in intricate filigreed designs right down to the tied-off cuffs. His over robe was so stiff with semi-precious stones and gold thread that it was an effort to bend into the undignified position he was forced to adopt. Before entering the chamber he had donned a small turban-like hat that was a flattering imitation of the kind the emperor favored. The material was of brown dyed silk with jewels and semi-precious stones sewn into the intricately decorated material.

Pantoleon knew by the murmurs of the nobles and court officials on either side of him that he had made a startling impression. He paid them no heed, however, as he was watching the emperor ahead of him, even as he appeared to be keeping his eyes downcast in a respectful manner. Then he heard his name announced by the courtier at the entrance, in the shrill tones of a eunuch. He had nearly forgotten—the eunuchs were still running administration on this island. Finally stopping at the second cushion, he prostrated himself again, waiting for the word to be spoken whereby he could sit back on his heels and look up.

"We are pleased to see you, Exazenos, Lord from Constantinople. Be seated," said a voice above him. The timbre of the voice sounded familiar. Pantoleon sat back on the cushion. He looked up at Emperor Isaac Komnenos and saw some resemblance to Andronikos. This face was more full, the beard was forked and graying, the eyes were darker, and the fleshy mouth was set into an expression of petulance.

"I bring a gift for Your Highness," Pantoleon said, and raised his hand.

Gabros and one other man crawled along the carpet, carrying a small chest. It appeared to be very heavy. Pantoleon waved his hand over the chest and said, "My Lord, please accept this humble gift from my poor hands."

Gabros opened the chest and Emperor Isaac Komnenos's eyes opened wide at what he saw. Inside the chest were bars of gold stacked neatly, close together. There were perhaps twenty bars, each two hands-width long, half a hand wide and two fingers deep. It was a fabulous gift. Isaac appeared to be unimpressed as he sat back, but Pantoleon, who prided himself on being an excellent judge of people, could see the naked avarice in those dark eyes as they lingered on the wealth he had just provided.

"You have brought a gift worthy of your rank, Lord Exazenos. But we wish to know why you have come to our Empire."

"Your Majesty, I am but a solitary traveller and would welcome the opportunity to stay here on this beautiful island, and perhaps to serve you in some capacity."

Isaac glanced to his left, where Pantoleon noticed a stocky, thickset man standing just behind the throne who gave an imperceptible nod. Pantoleon's eyes assessed the courtiers and officials in front of him and to either side of the emperor. He did not fail to notice a slim veiled figure standing just behind the throne. Perhaps his eyes lingered for just a moment longer than intended on this figure, because it moved and with a furtive motion the veil was dropped a fraction of an inch as though unintentionally, and he found himself staring at the very beautiful features of a young woman.

He hastily dropped his eyes and directed them to return to the old man, who was being helped by another to lift the chest and take it away. The emperor's eyes followed it as it went, even as he maintained his rigid position on the throne. So, the empire was short of treasure, Pantoleon surmised with some satisfaction. This could be dangerous if the emperor was a fool and tried to seize Pantoleon's wealth outright, but it presented an opportunity as well. Isaac seemed to make up his mind about something.

"I would talk in private with you, Lord Exazenos. We shall adjourn... to less formal surroundings." He gestured to the room at large and stood up. The courtiers bowed very low and remained in that position until Isaac had left the room, then they in turn were ushered out.

Pantoleon was approached by the old man, who introduced himself as Diocles, First Minister of the Palace.

"I am to show you to the inner chamber where His Majesty will speak with you," he said with a haughty nod to Pantoleon. "Your men may wait for you at the entrance," he added dismissively.

Pantoleon maintained an impassive face, but inwardly he was seething at the arrogance of these palace minions. However, he meekly followed the old man down a gloomy corridor to the entrance of another chamber without saying a word. His practiced eyes noted that the guards, although they were tough looking, were neither in a regular uniform nor were they very military in appearance. The emperor was in financial straits and employing mercenaries! A bad mix at the best of times, Pantoleon told himself.

He was ushered into a smaller chamber where Isaac was seated at a table covered with papers. He was picking out some grapes from a fruit bowl placed on the documents with a fine disregard for the paper and the vellum, which were being splashed with water every time he selected a grape. Pantoleon's eyes registered the threadbare furniture and cushions and the scraped and scuffed woodwork. The lime was peeling off the walls and the once exquisite frescoes were marred.

"Ah, Lord Exazenos, there you are," Isaac said, "Did you not feel humbled by the love that my subjects have for me? God is kind. I am truly beloved."

Pantoleon stared but hurriedly composed himself. "Indeed, your Highness, I felt it all around me as I entered the audience chamber!" he exclaimed.

"Be seated. I want to talk with you and find out more about you." The emperor's voice sounded pleasant enough, Pantoleon thought, as he seated himself and glanced around the room. The stocky man stood off to one side near to the emperor; lingering by a window was the woman he had seen in the audience chamber.

He smiled at the emperor and said, "I am deeply honored, your Majesty. I am happy to tell you all about myself."

"Then let's start with your pedigree, Lord Exazenos. What is your family?"

"My father was the late Senator Kalothesos, my Lord," Pantoleon lied. "He was accused of treason by the emperor's treacherous spies and quite unfairly executed, even though he had faithfully served the empire as a general for many years. Those were terrible times, my Lord."

I will never offer to make my sworn enemy
my new first lieutenant
in the presence of my current first lieutenant.
—If I Were An Evil Overlord

Chapter 27
A Byzantine Standoff

Pantoleon was spitting with rage by the time he arrived back at his villa. He held himself in with a physical effort until he had hurled the reins of his horse at a lackey and was striding up the stairs to his private rooms. He motioned Gabros to follow him as he stalked into his chamber, tossing his cloak to the floor and reaching for a jug of wine that stood on the table.

The door was closed firmly behind them by Gabros.

"Who *is* this flatulent arse who thinks he is an emperor! 'I am truly beloved of my subjects'," he mimicked, twisting his mouth. "Beloved! I'll bet my fortune he is despised and hated, more than he can imagine! The foolish and avaricious bastard," Pantoleon raged.

"Did you see his eyes light up when he saw the gold, Gabros? By God, but we need to keep this villa under constant guard. This God-forsaken little island is dead broke and he thinks it is an empire! It is a copper pot kingdom and he's a copper pot tyrant! Ha ha! That's why its called Cyprus, I suppose. Damn him! I have held more power in my left buttock than he has today, and he condescends to give me a job!" Pantoleon hissed between his teeth. His features were contorted with rage, made even more hideous by the badly healed scars, giving him the aspect of an enraged red-faced devil.

Gabros just nodded; sometimes his master really scared even him. He was, however, good at listening and looking attentive when his master fell into one of his rare tirades.

"I was introduced to his 'Gatherer of Information' as he calls his chief spy. He is called Malakis and is as dim as a rock, but cunning. Yes, he is one of those cunning toads who ingratiates himself with a fool, and now he sees me as a threat. But... there is this woman who was there with the emperor, who might be an ally if only I could get to her."

"Should I find out more about this Malakis and the lady, Lord?" Gabros offered.

"Oh yes! But be careful, right now he is the one with all the spies. But not for long. You should have seen his face when the emperor said that we would be working together. He looked like he was going to choke on his own spit! He will definitely be looking for an excuse to cut me off at the knees."

Pantoleon took a gulp of wine and reviewed the private interview with the emperor....

"Your reputation has preceded you, *Lord* Exazenos," Isaac said, with peculiar emphasis. Pantoleon darted a glance at the man standing nearby and saw him staring back in a manner he really didn't like. So they knew; well, that meant that at least they had some kind of intelligence. There was a long pregnant pause; he smelled danger all around him and prepared to move quickly. His right hand crept towards his concealed knife.

"Ah yes, I want you to meet my Gatherer of information," Isaac said. "You see, we do know who you are, from where you came and why you left."

Pantoleon smiled then, or rather grimaced, pretending to look guilty. "Indeed, my Lord, I would not lie to you, but what I said in public was for the public's ears. I used to serve your great uncle. I did so faithfully, but as you know he met an untimely death and I... well, I had to leave." He laughed and spread his hands in what he hoped looked like a disarming gesture.

There was a very long silence while the emperor's slightly bulging black eyes regarded him as though he was an insect, but then suddenly Isaac's swarthy face creased into a laugh. He held his sides and shook with laughter until there were tears in his eyes.

"Indeed you did, and you came to precisely the right place, my dear *Lord* Exazenos. How would you like to work for me?" he beamed, wiping his eyes.

Pantoleon, well used to this kind of behavior from his previous master, breathed a silent sigh of relief, and satisfaction, then said in the most ingratiating manner he could muster without choking, "I am your servant in all things, my Lord." He knew only too well that the emperor's offer was couched in a deadly threat, but he had been more or less prepared for this.

"I have some experience in obtaining information, my Lord. I will be very happy to serve you in whatever capacity you desire and where I can do the most good."

"You will build a system of spies such that I will always know what is going on in my Empire," stated Isaac. "You will have the help of my man Malakis here to get you started, but I want much more. I want an informer in every castle on this island." Pantoleon glanced again at Malakis, who looked as though he had just swallowed a large spider.

Pantoleon realized that the emperor was blithely unaware of the jealously he had just created within his own camp. He shrugged mentally; the Komnenos family seemed always to set their servants against one another. It would be up to him to be the survivor. There was certainly no room for both of them.

"Every castle, my Lord?" Pantoleon asked. There could only be about five on the entire island.

"All of them, and that includes... the Kantara Castle and that thief, *Sir* Talon." Isaac didn't elaborate, so Pantoleon decided to ask Malakis at some later date—and then the name registered. Could it be? Pantoleon's pulse began to beat a little faster. Was it possible that his quarry was here? What a delightful possibility! The fates had once again been kind to him.

His thoughts were interrupted by the emperor waving over the veiled lady, who obediently walked towards them. As she approached she touched the left side of her face and the veil slipped, as though by accident. Once again, Pantoleon found himself looking into the eyes of a very beautiful young woman who gazed back with an expression that was quite clear. She was interested in Pantoleon. He didn't display any outward show, but inside he was suddenly very interested in what she might have to say.

She quickly adjusted her veil and slipped behind the emperor, placing her slim hand on his shoulder. "My Lord?" she said in a soft tone of enquiry.

Isaac touched her hand with a display of affection and said, "We have concluded our business for today, Tamura. I will wish to eat in a short while." He turned to Pantoleon and added, "We have great hopes for you, Exazenos. I expect you to meet with Malakis and work out a strategy whereby my lords and nobles are brought to heel. We have some hostages already, but I want to be sure of these rebellious people. I want to know what they are *thinking*!" The emphasis on the last word told Pantoleon that Isaac was very unhappy with the information he was receiving thus far and that he had better perform well.

Pantoleon looked across at Gabros and said in measured tones, "What I heard was that Sir Talon de Gilles has a castle on the island. Is that true?"

Gabros looked surprised. "There is a man, a Frank, who *stole* a castle, my Lord, but I didn't know his name. The entire island is laughing about it."

"Tell me more." Pantoleon smiled and took another gulp of wine. He was beginning to feel more comfortable with his circumstances. They had teetered on the edge, but now.... The emperor needed him as much as he needed the emperor, it seemed.

Gabros recounted the tale that had already become a legend on the island. He had learned a long time ago to keep an ear to the ground wherever he landed. He could therefore inform Pantoleon fairly accurately as to what had transpired. It was a surprise to learn that his master knew of this Sir Talon.

"You mean to tell me that chinless wonder has surrendered a castle to that man, Talon?" asked Pantoleon his voice dripping with contempt.

"Not at first, but somehow overnight he decided to leave the mountain and brought his rag tag army home. After the demonstration of Talon's magical powers no one would have fought on anyway."

Gabros leaned forward to emphasize his point. "Lord, from everything I have heard, the people on that mountain ridge are led by a man we should all fear. He and his men are the spawn of dragon's teeth. He relies upon their loyalty and they would die for him, but he himself is quite without fear."

"Gabros! I cannot believe that you would fall victim to wild stories of this kind. I know this Talon, not very well it is true, but he is no magician. He is a Frank and was a Templar. I played polo with him. He wasn't so magical then," Pantoleon scoffed.

Gabros looked unconvinced. He had heard wild tales about this man in the castle. Each story added to the aura of invincibility that appeared to surround the fellow his master knew as Talon. But Pantoleon had moved on.

"I have been thinking. This ridiculous little emperor in charge of this ridiculous little island needs my help," he mused. "That we will provide but... there is going to be a high price, and it could well be more than he has bargained for."

Gabros stared at him, then slowly a smirk formed on his battle-scarred face, "You mean that perhaps... ?" he left the rest unsaid, for they both knew what Pantoleon meant. Cyprus could become "available". Gabros knew only too well to what lengths Pantoleon would go to obtain what he wanted.

"We must find out who is in command of this fine-looking 'professional' army." Pantoleon grimaced. "Gold talks."

Back in the palace there was a heated discussion taking place. Isaac, his spymaster and his paramour were talking about Pantoleon.

Malakis loathed Tamura and hated the fact that she was being drawn into the affairs of state. A woman, for God's sake, and a whore at that! Just a damned concubine, but here she was offering opinions to her master as though she were one of his most trusted advisers.

He glowered at her as she talked, willing her out of his mind; but he knew that unless he paid attention he would be outmaneuvered yet again by the cunning witch. His recent attempt at killing her slave had failed, but, he resolved, it would not be long before he got rid of them both. One of his spies, a frustrated concubine, had indicated that irregularities were taking place in the harem and implied she'd be willing to help settle a score. Perhaps he should use poison next time, instead of swords?

Tamura was indeed well on her way to becoming a trusted adviser. With one exception, Isaac's other advisers hated it, but they were wise enough not to appear to object, nor did they contradict her too vehemently, because then the emperor, like some spoiled brat, would dig in his heels and stubbornly go with her opinion—or worse, throw a tantrum. That he was totally besotted with her was not lost on the wise old Diocles, who often used the fact to maneuver the emperor into making a decision. Malakis was incapable of such subtle behavior.

With an almost physical effort Malakis shoved his poisonous thoughts into a corner of his mind and paid attention. He had already voiced his concerns and had urged the emperor to take the man down. But right now the damned witch was saying, "My Lord! I disagree with Malakis! What a prize for you! Is this not the very man who kept that unruly city Constantinople in line for the emperor? What a God-given chance it is that he came here to seek refuge."

Malakis winced, he hadn't expected her to want to keep this Exazenos fellow. On the contrary, he had expected her to try to get rid of him. The opportunity had been there, it had been a matter of touch and go for a few moments when a well placed word could have spelled the visitor's demise. He should have pointed out that if the man was so effective he should have done a better job of keeping the emperor alive. He cursed himself for not having made the play. He had been too busy considering how to eliminate Tamura to recognize the moment when it presented itself.

Realizing that he needed to backtrack quickly, he leaned forward towards the emperor and added his words. "I see what she means, Sire. In that case I agree wholeheartedly, Your Highness. You have made a brilliant decision," Malakis murmured in tones so oily that Tamura, who was looking at him, wondered how he didn't slip in it and crack his thick head. He glanced over at Tamura, who gave him a sweet smile full of venom.

"He will be a huge asset in bringing to heel those troublesome nobles in their lofty perches. In particular, that man on the mountain north of here," Malakis continued. No one ever used Talon's name in front of the emperor.

Isaac looked up at him with contempt in his dark eyes. "Good! Perhaps he will manage what you failed to do," he said nastily. "I want information, Malakis, not dead people lying around all over the place." He shuddered, remembering the threat Talon had made in the darkness of the tent. He wanted no more visitations in the night, so he would have to keep Malakis on a tight rein; the man liked nothing better than to kill and maim. That must not occur unless Isaac authorized it.

The idea of dismembering that Man on the Mountain and all his followers flickered through his mind for the briefest moment, but was quickly suppressed. Isaac was planning a quickie with his Tamura, and thoughts of the acute embarrassment he had suffered could inhibit his good mood badly, whereupon his manhood would shame him too. He grimaced; there had been these embarrassing moments more often of late.

Later, when Isaac had slaked his thirst for her and was sleeping it off, Tamura lay quietly on the bed, thinking about Exazenos. What ghastly features he had from the burns! She had not missed the hairpiece, which although well made, was clearly a wig; a woman could not be fooled by that kind of thing. He appeared to be as rich as Croesus. Could she find an ally here? she wondered. She tumbled ideas around in her head, trying to think of a strategy that would benefit her and, more importantly, rid her of the pig lying next to her. She had seen the stranger's reaction, very carefully suppressed but there nonetheless, and she drew hope from that.

He was physically in very good shape and apparently still liked women, so the rumor that he might be a eunuch seemed unfounded.

Her beauty, and now the palace power she wielded, were her two main assets. It had not been lost on her that here was a very intelligent man who came with a formidable reputation, possibly possessed of ruthless ambition too. She wanted to be a part of this somehow, anything to destroy Isaac. That at least she owed to her parents, both dead from the depredations of this monster. Whenever she visited the cathedral she always prayed for them. The problem was, how could she make contact with the stranger without being found out?

In another part of the palace, adjacent to the dungeons where he felt most at home, Malakis was seated at his rough office table, brooding. The realization that he had been outmaneuvered by Tamura yet again and that the stranger had just usurped his position as chief spy was just sinking in. Malakis liked his role and had done his best to please his bloodthirsty master, as the blood-soaked dungeons of the palace could attest. His imaginative tortures and ability to prolong the suffering of his victims had impressed the emperor such that Malakis had risen from simple torturer and jailer to chief of spies and information gatherer. He sensed, however, that he was out of his league with this newcomer.

He had done his homework as far as he could. The man was to be feared, and if he gained the ear of the emperor, as he seemed likely to do, then Malakis was doomed to no future at all. He had seen intelligence in the cold eyes of Exazenos, but what had chilled him to his bones was the calculating look of a ferocious predator.

But Malakis had earned his place alongside the emperor and would fight to remain there. What did he have to lose? Unless he did something he had *everything* to lose, he decided, smashing his fist down on the table in a savage thump that rattled the plates and cups, one of which rolled onto the floor with a tinny clang.

"Asanes! Get in here!" he shouted. Within a few moments his assistant appeared, wiping his beard and swallowing. He had been eating in the other room. "Yes, master?" he said.

"I want the villa of this man Exazenos watched night and day. I want to know when that man farts, who comes and who goes. Do you hear me?"

Asanes wiped his mouth again, shifting from foot to foot. "We'll need some more men, Master."

"You shall have them. Now get going. I want this to start now! Do not be seen, and if I do see any of your men when I go there on business I shall castrate you."

Asanes, a big burly man with arms the size of most men's thighs, grinned. "Not a problem, Master. It shall be done as you command."

Malakis nodded dismissal and went back to considering a bit of information that had come to him from one of the eunuchs. Malakis had the usual contempt for their kind, but they were useful when it came to passing along gossip, and gossip usually contained a kernel of truth. The emperor's woman, Tamura, was playing games with her favorite eunuch. At first he had disregarded this as nonsense. What woman in her position would be so stupid as to have an affair with another man, let alone a eunuch for God's sakes, especially in this seething hot bed of intrigue and slander?

Now he resolved to find out more. The woman Natalie, who was almost insane with jealousy, had actually given Malakis gold to undertake the murder of the eunuch, but the attempt had failed. Two of his best men had been killed, in broad daylight! A mystery still not solved, and one which gave Malakis cause for concern.

Who else in the city was playing games on his turf? Not Exazenos, not yet anyway, because this event had occurred before that worthy had shown up. Malakis was not going to make another attempt, despite the shrill demands from Natalie for her money's worth, until he understood the implications of that event.

Talon was preparing to leave. He and Dimitri had worked out a process whereby Dimitri could keep watch on the villa that housed Pantoleon around the clock. "It is of paramount importance that you watch his every move," Talon told Dimitri. "It would be better if you could find some way to get a man inside, but for the time being we have to rely on our watchers. I want to know the instant he leaves, either by boat or by land, and where he is going. I wish I didn't, but I have to go as soon as possible, so you are on your own."

"Don't worry, Talon. Go home and look after the Lady Rav'an. We are all thinking of her, so please wish her well and God protect her. We all wish you a son."

Talon left that afternoon on board Guy's ship. As they were leaving, with the rowers straining at their work to bring the large vessel out of the main shipping pack, they passed another vessel some distance away which Guy stared at as they passed. There were several men aboard, but his attention seemed to be riveted on the ship itself.

"What are you staring at, Guy?" Talon asked as he observed his captain's interest.

"I don't know for sure, Sir, but that ship looks very familiar. I could swear it is Nigel's old ship, but that would be impossible."

Talon gazed back at the receding ship. He doubted that he could recognize it, but Guy seemed profoundly disturbed.

"Are you sure?" he asked.

"No, Talon, I am not sure, but for a moment I thought indeed it was the ship that Nigel used to captain. It must be my imagination."

Guy returned to his duties and before long was bellowing to the crew to hoist the sails and to hurry up about it. They had to get to their haven before nightfall. Talon stood at the after rail, looking back at the town and its walls, the beacon they were just passing and the shipping clustered back in the safety of the harbor. He was worried about Dimitri and his people. The game had just become very much more dangerous and Dimitri would need all his skills to avoid running up against the emperor's new man.

Back in the harbor of Famagusta, another man watched Talon's ship leave the confines of the protected harbor and recede into the distance. Nigel had been stunned to see Guy standing on its deck and then to also see Talon, whom he recognized almost immediately.

He had dived out of sight the moment he saw the two of them, but as soon as they moved past he found a place where he could observe without being seen. After they had gone, Nigel hastened to leave the ship and hurried off up the quayside to find his new master and pass along the news.

"Are you sure you saw Talon and his ship?" Pantoleon demanded of Nigel, who had come running up to the villa to tell him. Nigel was still panting.

"I am very sure indeed, Master," he replied.

"Hmm, this ties in with what I heard today," Pantoleon said to Gabros. "But the fact that he is brazenly coming and going from this city is incredible! Well, the next time we will have him, and then the emperor will see how I operate."

He complimented Nigel on his discovery and invited him to stay the night.

Dimitri's men found out soon enough that there were others watching the villa, and he concluded quite rightly that they were from the palace and belonged to Malakis. He simply told his men to stay as far away from these people as possible and watch the villa for any activity that might indicate either a hurried departure or a trip to somewhere by land. He felt a small thrill of excitement as he realized that he and his men were now at the center of something big.

However, events were to prove dangerous within the space of two days. In the dark of night one of his men woke Dimitri unceremoniously with some unwelcome news. "What is it?" he grunted as he struggled out of a deep sleep.

"Laskaris is dead!" the man whispered in a frightened tone.

"What?" Dimitri was wide awake now. "What happened?" He pulled on his pants and boots and tried to collect his confused thoughts. Laskaris had been assigned to watch the villa that night, along with two others. They had not been clustered together, but each alone in their solitary look-out positions around the compound. Laskaris had been at the back, in a narrow alleyway that ran behind the villa walls.

"Strabo found him when he went to replace him! His body was still warm. Strabo saw men sneaking through a doorway in the wall of the villa."

"Where is the body?" Dimitri demanded.

"Er, it is still there. We did not move it."

Dimitri swore under his breath. They could have at least hidden the body. "I have to go and see for myself how he died, and we must bring him back."

They approached the darkened villa with caution. With his bow at the ready, Dimitri followed Strabo and Maymun. No lights showed anywhere, and the walls were black against a starry sky. They were far to close for comfort to the walls. On a clear night like this, anyone could peer over and see their silhouettes.

They came across the body lying in a dark recess, just off the street. Dimitri nearly gagged; the stink of effluence and other waste was very strong. In the otherwise silent alley he could hear the squeaking of rats and rustle of other creatures. He squatted down and investigated. An arrow protruded from Laskaris's back.

A a signal from Dimitri, the three of them dragged Laskaris out of the stinking gutter and turned him half over. His head lolled back, displaying a dark, gaping gash in his throat. Again Dimitri had to control an impulse to retch. Behind him he heard Strabo sob. Why would someone cut his throat, having just killed him with an arrow? Dimitri asked himself. However, they had no time to think beyond this point, as Maymun seized Dimitri by the sleeve and hissed, "Someone over there!"

Dimitri peered into the darkness further up the street. "I don't see anyone," he whispered back.

"It is man, and he runs away." Maymun was still struggling with his Greek but the meaning was clear.

"Deal with him! We can't let anyone see this!"

Maymun's bow twanged and an arrow hissed away to land with an audible thump in the back of the running man, who pitched forward onto the dirt. He cried out and jerked several times, then went still. In the ensuing silence the men held their breath, listening and barely breathing. A sentry abruptly appeared on the walls of the villa and looked down towards them—the noises must have alerted him. They all froze in place, hoping he would leave, but he leaned over the low parapet of the wall and stared straight at them as though trying to discern their shapes more clearly. Abruptly he stood back, took up a bow and knocked an arrow. He couldn't help it; Dimitri flinched. The sentry was about to loose off an arrow straight at them.

Then Dimitri heard the twang of a bowstring in his ear, again from Maymun's bow. The black silhouette on the wall gave a choking scream, fell forwards, then toppled down into the street to land with a heavy thump only a few paces from where they were hiding, to lie completely still, face down. Maymun leapt forward, kicked his victim over, broke the end off his arrow, then did the same to the first man. He rejoined them, carrying the fletched parts of both arrows, which he tucked away in his shirt.

He nodded to Dimitri. "Time to leave. He go with us?" he asked, pointing to Laskaris.

"Yes! Come on!" Dimitri whispered, frantic with worry now. They seized Laskaris by his arms and legs and rushed along the street to an intersection, down which they raced until Strabo pointed to another turn and there, well out of sight of the villa, they slowed to a walk, panting.

Behind them they could hear shouts as the alarm was raised. Someone, another sentry perhaps, had heard the scream. Dimitri hastened his men along the darkened and deserted streets, praying that they would not be discovered by the night patrol, which on rare occasions had been known to do its duty.

"No time to rest. We must hurry, for this whole town will be awake soon," Dimitri chided his men.

Gasping for breath, for Laskaris was not a lightweight, they arrived at the doorway of their own villa, and after a rapid tattoo of knocks were admitted by a very concerned group of men. His entire household was wide awake. Dimitri leaned over his knees. Only Maymun seemed to be alert and ready for anything.

"Were we followed?" he asked Maymun, after he had taken a few wheezy breaths.

"I do not think so, Dimitri," he responded. "I watch out all the way home."

"Take him into the back room. I have to think." Dimitri said. "Maymun, come with me."

They sat at the kitchen table and went over the events of the night.

"Someone knows that we are watching the villa," Dimitri said, taking a gulp of watered wine.

"Just as importantly, they don't like it and killed Laskaris because of it," Strabo interjected, as he came into the room.

"By now our other two men will have left. No one wants to be caught anywhere near that place," Strabo stated. "Not if they have any sense, that is."

Dimitri had to agree. "But that means we have no watchers in place." That bothered him, but he did not see how it could be helped. "The question is, who did it? And did the killer recognize Laskaris? Are we under suspicion?"

As though he had forecast it, there were knocks on the front door. They all froze in place, until it had been established that it was their own men arriving from the villa.

The two other watchers stumbled into the kitchen, looking worried and furtive. "Were either of you followed?" Dimitri immediately demanded.

The two men shook their heads. "We came back by round about routes. There was no point in staying there. It was like a nest of hornets had come alive!" one of them said.

"Laskaris was killed. We were trying to get his body away but someone saw us. Maymun got him, but a sentry on the wall heard something and then saw us. We had to kill him, and that raised the alarm."

His two other spies stood rooted to the floor with shock.

Remembering how casually the sentry prepared to shoot whoever he saw down in the street below, Dimitri realized that was how Laskaris had died. Not because he was suspected of spying, but because he was there when the sentry wanted some target practice! He cursed out loud.

"But that doesn't explain the cut throat!" he exclaimed outright. Maymun heard him and offered an explanation.

"Perhaps the man on the wall did not kill him immediately; from the way the arrow went in, that could be. He might have made noise and so the sentry finished the job with a knife?"

Dimitri nodded reluctant acceptance of this possibility.

"Perhaps. Well, we might have left them with a mystery of their own to solve. Oh God, what a mess! I hope it keeps the bastards awake at night, it certainly will me. We have to bury Laskaris, and it has to be now and in the garden."

A grave was dug in the garden by starlight. A prayer was muttered as the sheet-shrouded body was lowered into the deep hole and covered up.

Dimitri posted guards and sent the rest of his men to bed. He, however, had work to do. A letter had to be prepared that could be sent to Talon with the dawn by pigeon, informing him of the disaster. He was not happy to note that he had only one pigeon left.

Pantoleon had been woken by the alarm. He struggled out of his bed and hurried down to the ground floor, where he found Gabros.

"What happened?" he demanded of his man, whose features were tight in the torchlight. Pantoleon wore only a robe but he carried his sword, ready for trouble.

"Still trying to find out, Lord." Gabros's reply was curt. "Come with me. Whatever did happen occurred at the back."

They hurried along dark corridors past the occasional frightened servant, who huddled against the walls as they strode by, to arrive at the rear courtyard where the stables were located. Men were clustered on the top of the ten-foot tall walls, holding torches high and peering down into the street on the other side. The two men hurried up the stone steps and joined them. Seeing that it was Pantoleon, the men stopped their excited chatter and stood silent.

"What has happened?" he asked.

"Someone shot our man, Sir. He fell off the wall, do you see?"

Pantoleon peered down at the figure lying sprawled at the base of his wall. "Looks dead. How was he killed?"

"With an arrow, Lord," Gabros remarked. "I can see it sticking out of him. But its fletch appears to be missing."

"Go and get him. We'll find out soon enough," Pantoleon ordered the men, who hurried off to do his bidding.

While they were gone he thought about what had happened. Someone was sending a not too subtle message here, and he could guess who it might be. "It's that toad, Malakis, I'll wager," he snarled to Gabros.

"What's the message, Lord? That we better not feel too secure?"

"Just that, I think. Don't say anything, and tell the men to keep their mouths shut. I will find out one way or the other, and Malakis will discover that it does not pay to kill my men."

Nigel had been woken by the disturbance, and he arrived on the wall as Pantoleon said this.

"What seems to be the problem, Master?" he asked respectfully, looking around at the activity.

"Our unspoken truce with the 'Gatherer of information', a prick called Malakis, has just been broken. We now do things my way, and he will be swept away with the same broom that takes care of the rest of my enemies."

Nigel nodded, not fully understanding.

"You said you didn't know where the ship Talon was on might be heading?" Pantoleon asked him.

"No idea, Master," Nigel shook his head.

"Well, I have had time to think, and I suspect that I do. On the other side of the island are several harbors. Talon is in the castle Kantara, and I hear there is a harbor near there. That is where he will have gone."

He had their full attention now.

"When and not if your friend comes back to Famagusta, we will be waiting for him. I want you to go back to your ship and find out from the people who hang about the wharf what his ship was doing here in the first place. That should tell us where to begin."

"Very well, Master," Nigel said. "I shall get back there at dawn."

"Be very discreet. Malakis must not hear about this. Do I make myself clear?"

Malakis woke the next morning feeling better. He had supped well the night before and had helped himself to one of the women hangers-on who lurked in the back recesses of the palace. His thoughts drifted to the man Exazenos. He felt sure he could deal with the newcomer if he was careful.

However, when he slouched into the kitchens he saw Asanes deep in conversation with one of his spies, who was gesticulating and talking in an agitated manner, his mouth opening and shutting like a fish gasping for air. Asanes was looking very concerned. Suddenly concerned, Malakis strode forward and arrived just as Asanes dismissed the spy and turned towards him.

"Good morning, Sir," Asanes said, his eyes shifty.

"What was that all about," Malakis demanded.

"We lost a man last night, Sir. It was at the villa."

"Lost? What d'yer mean? Killed?" Malakis said, scowling.

Asanes looked very uncomfortable. "My men said so, Sir. Shot to death with an arrow."

"What!" Malakis bellowed. All activity in the kitchen ceased for a long, silent moment.

"Get back to your duties!" he snarled at the frightened cooks and maids.

"Come with me." He took Asanes by the sleeve. They left the kitchens and found a quieter place in one of the deserted alcoves.

"He was killed with an arrow. Which means, to me at least, that he was shot from the walls." Asanes said, looking belligerent. He didn't like being manhandled, even by his boss.

Malakis stood back with a puzzled expression on his face. "When did this happen? Are you sure?"

Asanes rolled his eyes. "We found him this morning. My men were concerned that he had not reported in. I know an arrow when I see one," he replied, his tone defensive.

Malakis made a mental note to discipline his man for being insubordinate. "No, you halfwit. Are you sure it came from the walls of the villa?"

"There was no one else there, Sir. Where else could it have come from?" His tone was less disrespectful now. "If I was going to kill someone on the street in the dark I'd use a knife, not a bow. It's dark and the chances of missing are great. It is better to cut the throat!"

Malakis found a stool and sat down to think. If this were true then Exazenos had sent a very clear message: "Don't hang around my villa or I shall kill your agents."

He nodded to himself. If this was not a declaration of war then he, Malakis, was not the emperor's man. "Very well, you goat's turd, war it is," he muttered. "I'll see you grovel just before I kill you myself."

"What's that? Goat's turd?" Asanes began to puff up again, having misheard. He was slightly deaf in one ear. He was constantly picking wax out of it with a finger nail.

"War!" Malakis said with a sigh of exasperation.

"War, Sir?"

"Yes, war, you great lump of a pig's breakfast! This is a declaration of war." Malakis said. He raised his voice. "*Listen carefully* to what I am about to tell you."

All we have of freedom, all we use or know—
This our fathers bought for us long and long ago.
Ancient Right unnoticed as the breath we draw—
Leave to live by no man's leave, underneath the Law.
Lance and torch and tumult, steel and grey-goose wing
Wrenched it, inch and ell and all, slowly from the King.
—Rudyard Kipling

Chapter 28
The Herb Garden and a New Addition

Talon made his way down the slope to the walled-in area that had been built between the bailey and the mews towards the newly constructed herb garden. He was in a thoughtful mood and was not relishing the discussion to come with Theodora. Simon, the old soldier who now tended the garden under her supervision, pointed him in that direction.

"She told me she is preparing some herbs for the Time, Sir Talon," Simon wheezed. He was aging fast but seemed content with the work, which was not onerous and gave him opportunities to sit in the sun.

"Thank you, Simon. How are you feeling today?"

"So so, Sir Talon. These old bones need to rest a lot more than they did," Simon said with a toothless smile. He huddled under his blanket a little more.

"You need to keep warm, Simon," Talon admonished him.

"Don't you be worrying about me, Sir," Simon croaked. "That nice lady is taking good care of me. A Godsend, she is." The old Templar retainer jerked his head towards the wall, which housed the garden. "She's in there for sure."

Talon opened the wooden picket gate, which served to keep the goats and other small animals out of the precious herb garden, and went in. The entire garden was only about twelve good paces by twenty, but between them Rav'an, Jannat and Theodora had filled it with plants that Simon tended carefully under their supervision. Even though it was now almost winter, in this gentle climate a garden could flourish year round, and there was a pleasant aroma of plants and turned soil. He caught the scent of rosemary and thyme, mingled with fennel, marjoram, oregano, and others he could not yet name. The sunlight piercing the low cloud cover illuminated the newly cut stones, softening their otherwise harsh lines, and the green, knee-high plants offered a stark contrast to the dark soil.

He saw Theodora at the far end on her knees with her back towards him, pulling weeds and checking the growth of the herbs. There was a stone bench along the east wall, upon which he sat. He rested his head against the wall. He had arrived very late the night before and was still weary.

It was curious fate, he thought to himself, that she should have come to this odd little island and to this castle. There must have been other places of refuge for the nobility of Constantinople but Giorgios, knowing of the link between Talon and the Kalothesos family, had brought her here. He shut his eyes and enjoyed the sun, in no hurry to tell her the news.

The sun went behind a cloud and he became aware that she was nearby, standing quite still and studying him. Opening his eyes, he glanced up, then stood up.

"Hello, Theo. How are you?"

She smiled. The dark rings of grief and exhaustion under her eyes had gone. She looked much better.

"I am well, Talon. I heard you had arrived, but you were busy, so I decided to come here and do some work. Simon is a great help, but he is aging and cannot bend to the task as well as he used to."

Talon grinned. "He is not above taking a little advantage of an eager worker like yourself, Theo."

"Oh how very unkind of you, Talon!" She laughed, and it transformed her normally solemn expression to one of unrestrained amusement. "He is a very nice old man, but... we have to communicate mostly by signals and gestures. I do not speak the Frankish at all well, and he has no Greek. Nevertheless, we get on somehow."

"How are *you* getting on, Theo?" Talon asked as he motioned her to be seated.

"I am treated like a sister by Rav'an and Jannat who have, as have I, been starved of female company. They are very kind and I am able to help them both, especially Rav'an. Jannat's turn will come soon enough, but right now it is Rav'an whom I am most concerned about."

"I thank you for that. You are looked upon as almost royalty by the servants and the men," Talon remarked. "Since you have been here I am sure that almost everyone has beaten a path to your apothecary room for some remedy or other. Your reputation is growing by the day."

Theodora made a depreciating gesture. "I do what I can within my skills; if I can help the people here then that is a God-given gift and I am glad of it."

"Well, Palladius for one worships you. How did you manage to take care of those horrible boils he kept getting?"

"His diet was quite terrible, he almost never ate anything green. Then there are medicines that, taken with care, can reduce that affliction to almost nothing as long as the patient does as he is told." Her tone was almost tart, but there was amusement there.

"It took Max to order the wretch to eat the right diet before he would listen, and then, my goodness! The boils went away! How extraordinary!"

Talon chuckled. "Well, we are all grateful for the change in his appearance." He paused, allowing a momentary silence to descend.

Theodora looked at him. "You found out, didn't you?"

Talon nodded. "Yes," he said slowly. "It is Pantoleon all right. Somehow he has come to roost on this island, of all places."

She paled under her new tan. The change emphasized the light drift of freckles on the top of her cheeks.

"What... what can be done ?" she asked in a very low voice. Her head drooped and she supported herself with her hands on the edge of the seat.

He loosened the hand nearest to him and held it. "Theodora, you must understand that I shall never let anything happen to you; neither will my companions, nor my men, nor will Rav'an and Jannat, who are formidable women in their own right. You are safe here within the walls of this castle."

She gripped his hand fiercely and turned towards him with tears in her eyes. "Oh, Talon, he is such a monster! He would destroy us all if he could."

He attempted to reassure her. "I have dealt with evil men before, as has Reza, my Brother. We will do so again, Theo."

She lifted her head. "You have changed so, Talon!" she exclaimed.

"How so?" he asked, puzzled.

"When I knew you we were much younger, but even then you were remote, somehow... dangerous. Mama said so, as did Alex, God rest his soul. Even Papa said there was something unreachable about you. But now you command and men obey. Not just because they have to, but because they want to. The stories I hear about you from Max and Reza! You have been to China, you are a navigator, and if half of these followers of yours are to be believed you are a magician too!" An amused twitch of her lips replaced the solemn expression. "Did you really steal this castle?"

Talon frowned, then grinned. "Well, er, yes, after a fashion. The emperor didn't like that one bit, so he came along and demanded it back."

Theodora was openly amused by now. "What did you have to say about that?"

Talon explained briefly what had happened, including the agreement with the emperor.

She leaned forward. "An agreement? With that terrible man?"

Talon nodded. "We have come to terms, but I fear that will mean nothing to Pantoleon. So we must find a way whereby we can neutralize him without jeopardizing this arrangement."

Theodora looked sober. "God protect us from that man!" she murmured.

He smiled, changing the subject. "You have changed too! Look at you, a beautiful and well-educated woman. A skilled physician no less! You have come a long way yourself, Theo."

"Well, I am not really a physician in the full sense of the title, as my teachers were often at pains to tell me, but I was almost at that point before I left," she said.

"I understand that life has not been exactly kind to you, but I don't hear you complaining," Talon said, then he grinned mischievously. "I do remember a certain incident that has remained in my mind ever since Constantinople."

"Oh Talon, no! I am so ashamed of that. You won't tell Rav'an, will you? She would never forgive me!" she begged with a look of genuine alarm. But then she noticed he was laughing.

"Strictly between the two of us, have no fear. But then, how was I to explain the scar on my middle and who bound me up and probably saved my life?"

"Stop it! I was just a girl with no sense at all," she scolded him, blushing.

"You married, and you have a child. How does that feel?" he asked, changing the subject again.

"He was a friend of Nikoporus and Antonia, do you remember them?" she asked, her large eyes regarding him now with some of the pain he had seen before.

"Yes I do remember them. I'm sorry, Theo, I didn't mean to bring up difficult things." His tone was contrite.

"It's all right, you should know. Gregaros was a kind and honest man, an officer in the Army who did not deserve the punishment that Pantoleon doled out to so many. They murdered him, along with my father and now my brother; may God judge them, for I cannot forgive them, Talon." Her hand had remained in his and now she clenched it, and her voice became hard and cold.

"I am sorry, Theo," he said. "But know this, your family will be avenged. That I promise." He glanced up at the lowering clouds. "If we do not move very quickly we will get wet!"

Even as he spoke the first drops fell with loud splashes on the leaves nearby, and then it began to rain in earnest. "Come on!" Talon called out and, still holding her hand, he ran towards the doorway of the garden. They ran through, pausing while she insisted on closing it, and then he pulled her along the path up to the bailey. They arrived breathless at the main entrance and dived out of the rain, which was pouring down in a dense shower, splashing water onto the steps where they were standing.

A flash of lightning was closely followed by a crack of thunder which ripped through the sky like a tearing sheet right overhead. With a squeak of fright Theodora buried her head in his shoulder. Talon was so surprised that his arm went around her and he held her briefly, but almost immediately she pulled away with a startled look in her eyes. "I'm sorry, Talon. I didn't mean... " she murmured.

"That was very close," he told her with a grin. "And the rain is good for the garden."

"Rav'an is due any day now, I must go to her," she answered. Her eyes wouldn't meet his. Then she was gone.

He followed her receding figure in a thoughtful mood.

Later Talon walked into the Solarium to find almost the entire family present. Rav'an and Theodora were near the fireplace, which radiated welcome warmth on this cool day. The shutters were closed tightly against the rain. Off to the side Rostam was teaching Damian and Irene the game of Go, without much success. The click of tiles came from a low table where Jannat and Reza were playing their favorite game of Chinese tiles. This was a room where the furniture was at a minimum and large cushions were strewn around on the many carpets.

Even Max was lounging on a cushion, trying to make sense of the Greek words that Theodora had given him to study. He lifted his hand in greeting as Talon emerged from the corridor, but kept studying. Everyone had been charged by Talon to learn Greek as quickly as possible.

Talon glanced around for Dar'an and Yosef, then remembered that these two were off on missions, Dar'an to patrol the border and Yosef at the harbor with Henry, whose ship had just come in from Paphos. There would be letters from Boethius, and doubtless one for Irene who, while she liked being at the castle and worshiped Rostam, clearly missed her father and the town of Paphos itself.

He waved and smiled at Rav'an and Theodora, who smiled back. They were discussing various herbs: Rav'an had enjoyed sharing her knowledge of Chinese herbalism with Theodora, who was an avid learner and very knowledgeable of the local Mediterranean plants. He walked over to where Reza and Jannat were seated and sank into a cross-legged position, just in time to hear Jannat exclaim.

"Reza, if you are cheating I shall punish you!" She held up her forefinger in a threatening manner. Reza had the grace to look guilty and dropped a tile out of his sleeve onto the table. Talon grinned. These two were always like this. Reza picked up the tile and held it up for her to see, then flicked his wrist and it vanished. "All I was doing was practicing my sleight-of-hand, my Jannat!" he said, pretending to sound aggrieved.

"Hah! But I caught you at it, so you need some more practice, my dear Reza," she responded with heavy sarcasm. Talon looked over at her with affection. Jannat was only a few weeks behind Rav'an, who was due any day now, and pregnancy seemed to have given her an extra bloom. Talon was reluctant to ask Reza to go on any visits now because of this, but he had Famagusta on his mind and wanted to talk to his brother.

Just at that moment he heard a low cry and became aware of a disturbance from the direction of Theodor and Rav'an. Jannat, with a woman's sixth sense, glanced up and immediately started to climb to her feet.

"Help me up, Reza," she commanded. "It is Rav'an's time." He leapt to obey, as did Talon, who in two long strides was kneeling at Rav'an's side.

She looked up at him from her half-lying position with wide eyes and gave a hesitant smile. "I am all right, my Love."

"Her water has broken, Talon. We must get her to the bedroom as quickly as we can," Theodora urged.

Without a word Talon picked up his wife and lifted her into his arms. Rav'an tightened her arms around his neck and whispered, "I love you." He kissed her on the forehead and strode out of the room, with Jannat leading the way to their bedroom. Placing Rav'an gently on the bed he stood back.

"Thank you, my Love," she whispered, and then winced, gritting her teeth as the first contractions began.

"Is there anything I can do?" he asked, feeling suddenly helpless.

Theodora took command and called out to Reza, who was hovering at the door. "Reza, I need boiled water, very hot, as soon as you can, and towels. Be quick!" she ordered. "Talon, please bring my satchel up here from my room, immediately."

Reza vanished to get the hot water while Talon rushed off to tell the wide-eyed maid in the corridor to find clean towels. She nodded her understanding and ran off to bring them, while he hurried off to collect Theodora's satchel. He knew it contained many useful herbal concoctions which she would need. He rushed back up the stairs to the bedroom and was about to re-enter when Jannat barred him at the doorway. "Thank you, Talon, but now this is women's work. Leave us and go take care of the children. They will be confused and frightened." He was about to protest when she said, "Fear not, Talon, Rav'an is in very good hands. Theo is very knowledgeable. Send in the maid."

Talon knew that Jannat was trying to reassure herself as much as he, so he nodded and left. He made his way down to the solarium where he found his son and Irene looking bewildered. Irene's large eyes reflected some fear. Max had stoked the fire and thrown open one of the shutters. The storm had passed, but occasional flickers of lightning over the sea could still be seen.

"Come here, you two," Talon commanded the children.

They both walked over to stand in front of him. He glanced over at Max, who stood by the fireplace. He nodded encouragement and smiled.

"I've never been in this situation before," Talon told them. "Rostam, your mother is about to have a baby and Theodora is there to make sure everything goes well."

Just at that moment Rav'an gave a yell that reverberated through the upper building. Irene flinched and Rostam looked apprehensive. Even Talon was shaken, but he understood what was happening and put on a determined face. Unfortunately his scowl must have frightened Irene, because she began to cry.

Max strode over and picked up the bawling child and held her against his chest. She accepted the old warrior's embrace and wrapped her arms around his neck, stopped crying, and leaned her head against his shoulder with a sniffle, then was quiet.

Talon, who was still kneeling in front of Rostam, gaped up at Max with surprise. Just at that moment Reza pushed aside the curtain to the room and strode in. He stopped dead at the sight of Max cradling Irene, who now clung to him.

"Max!" he said. "What a surprise! I never knew you even liked children!"

"I don't," Max growled. "Loathsome little creatures! But these two and Damian are our own loathsome little creatures, and one has to make exceptions." He glanced down at Rostam and they exchanged grins. The eager boy and the grizzled Templar had developed a rapport.

"Come on, Rostam," Max went on, "Let's take Irene down to the kitchens and see if Cook will give us some baklava to eat before bedtime." He limped out of the room, Irene still draped in his arms and Rostam skipping after him. "That's a good idea, Uncle Max," he chirped as they disappeared down the stairs.

Talon and Reza stared open-mouthed at one another. "Well I never," Reza laughed. "Uncle Max, eh? That's new."

"He might be a rough old soldier, that Max of ours," Talon said, "but we are all the family he has, and the children appear to adore him."

Another yell came filtered into the room and both men tensed.

"Dear God but I pray she will be all right," Talon groaned.

"Here, have a glass of wine. It will steady your nerves," Reza said as he handed Talon a full glass. There was another cry, and he flinched.

"This is going to be a long night," Reza muttered.

Up in the bedroom the four women were hurriedly preparing for the birth. Theodora had settled Rav'an comfortably on the bed with cushions behind her back so that she was half sitting.

"Try not to push too hard just yet," Theodora told her. "I need to see where the child's head is." Her hands swiftly moved over Rav'an and carefully probed, then she settled back with less of a frown on her face. She turned to Jannat and said, "Please bring my satchel to me. I want the raspberry leaf tea which Rav'an has been taking. Please brew some strong tea." Jannat hastened to obey, using the boiled water, which was still steaming. She brought a cup to Rav'an and said, "Come, Rav'an, drink this all down. It is going to help today."

The contractions began in earnest after that, and try as she might not to scream Rav'an could not help it. Jannat gave her a leather strap to bite down on, for which she thanked her. Theodora wore a concerned expression at one time, and gently probed the opening, then straightened up and smiled reassuringly at the two worried women. "I wanted to make sure the child's head was in the right place," she stated, and bent to her work.

"I can see the head! Now push, Rav'an, push!"

Two hours later Jannat came down to the solarium to find the men wide awake and Talon nervously pacing the floor.

"Come with me," she said with a wide smile.

The two men almost bowled her over in their rush to get to the bedroom, they stampeded into the room to find Theodora seated on the edge of the bed, the maid clearing away the towels, and an exhausted but beaming Rav'an lying in state holding a small bundle swathed in clean linen.

"You have a daughter, my husband," she told him.

Talon could barely breathe. In two strides he was over to sit where Theodora had just been to take Rav'an's hand and hold it while peering at the little creature lying against her breast, already feeding.

"We have a daughter?" he asked with an incredulous look.

"Are you pleased? A son would have been better, perhaps?" she asked with a look that was a trifle uncertain.

He snorted and exclaimed, "We have a daughter! Reza, Jannat, and you, Theo! Look what she has done!" he leaned over the baby and kissed Rav'an on the lips. "I shall teach her to ride," he told her.

After that the others cooed over the baby. Reza looked dazed, but Jannat linked arms with him and said, "Come along, Reza, it's time for bed. Rav'an is in good hands."

"What are we going to call her?" Talon asked.

"I would name her Fariba, after Aunty Fariba," Rav'an answered with a contented smile.

The next morning Rostam was up early, just as the sun cleared the horizon to the East. He crept into Irene's room and woke her with a finger on his lips and a grin, and a nod of his head towards the truckle bed where her maid was still fast asleep, snoring hard. He led Irene all the way up the stairs to the pigeon coop. The two children could hear the cooing of the birds and the occasional flutter of wings. It had become his job to clean the room on a regular basis, and Irene was only too happy to assist.

Rostam now understood the usefulness of the pigeons, and with that knowledge, the importance of their good health. The ten or so pigeons accepted their caresses and pecked at the grain in their hands with no fear. While Irene inspected them for any injuries Rostam took a broom and brushed the droppings into a pile, which one of the servants would pick up later in the day. He had been very reluctant to do this chore and to handle the pigeons before Jannat had explained their value; then his father had reinforced the idea by showing him the coded rolls that he transcribed.

To Rostam it was an exciting idea to be able to communicate with Dimitri in Famagusta and Boethius in Paphos in this manner without ever setting foot outside the castle. He yawned. He had been woken by Jannat in the middle of the night. She had been very excited and had dragged him and Irene out of their beds to meet the new family member.

He now had a little sister named Fariba after his great-auntie who lived in Muscat in Oman. Irene had cooed over the wrinkled, red-faced little creature in Rav'an's arms, but he had been just a little disappointed. He had hoped for a brother. His thoughts were interrupted by an agitated flutter on the window sill. There was a new arrival.

"Irene!" he called to her. "Look, we have a messenger, just arrived. Catch it for me?" Irene handled them better than he did, and Jannat had told him to let her do this whenever the opportunity arose to keep her interest.

Irene glided over the newly swept floor and with gentle words persuaded the new arrival to sit still, then picked the messenger up and carried it over to Rostam. "It's from Famagusta, Rostam," she told him, pointing to its coloring. While she held it firmly but gently, he worked the thin copper ring loose from its leg to release the roll of paper, and then Irene placed the bird in the cage where the Famagusta birds were housed.

It was quite late in the morning when Rostam proudly delivered the note to Talon, after his father had risen. The entire castle staff had crept about as though on eggshells for the better part of the morning so as not to wake the family.

"A message from Dimitri, Father," the boy said as he handed over the coded note.

Talon thanked Rostam with an inward smile. The boy had stopped calling him Papa recently, more or less when his training had begun. He sent him off, then took the slim piece of paper up to his study and unrolled it. After deciphering the note he sat back in his chair, deep in thought. He was still there when Reza arrived and let himself in with a light tap on the door.

"I hear from Jannat that Rav'an and the child are safe and well," Reza murmured as he sat down.

"Yes, Brother. Thank God for Theo. It might have gone badly, but she knew what to do and they are safe." Talon gave his brother a tired smile. He handed Reza the piece of paper.

Reza looked at it and said, "I am not as good as you at this code, Brother. Tell me what it says."

"It says that things have begun to get hot in Famagusta." Talon explained the details of the death of Laskaris. "Dimitri sees this as a huge disaster, but... I'm not so sure."

"How so?" Reza asked.

"Well now, suddenly everyone is killing everyone else. Reading this note, it occurred to me that the spies from the palace and Pantoleon's men might think it was each other who did the killing, if Dimitri was not detected removing Laskaris's body. Then they might go for each other's throats."

Reza smiled. "That would prove interesting. Then... they could destroy each other?"

"What's all this about killing each other?" Max had just walked into the room.

"Have a seat, Max. We have a development in Famagusta." Talon explained about the message and what he knew and guessed.

"Dimitri appears to be keeping his head at least," Max remarked.

"That's the hope, but it is imperative for me to go and find out what's really going on. He is not used to this kind of rough and tumble and must be in a panic. Also he is running out of pigeons, so we have to take some back to him. I could leave in a couple of days. I can't delay it much longer than that."

Reza and Max were staring at him.

"What is it?" he asked, looking from one to the other.

"You'll do no such thing, Talon. If you even think of leaving on any kind of trip the women will kill you, and perhaps us. Think of Rav'an, man!" Max stated, and Reza nodded emphatic agreement.

"Reza, Max, it's becoming urgent in Famagusta," Talon said, frowning and shuffling papers about on his desk in an attempt to settle his nerves. Having babies was a nerve-wracking experience, he decided; furthermore, it was exhausting. Never mind what the mother had to go through.

"Then I should go," Reza insisted. "Jannat is not yet ready to drop our child. Theodora will be here in any case should it come early. I should go."

Talon looked concerned and relieved at the same time. "Very well, Brother. That can be arranged with Guy, but only if you are very sure."

"Why don't I go, Talon?" Max offered.

"Max, you are still recovering from your holiday in Acre prison. Jannat and Rav'an would never let you leave, and Theo has told me that you have a mild inflammation in your lungs which she is still treating. Yes," he said with a smile at his old friend, "our physician tells me all, as I need to be kept informed. Besides, Reza, even if he is getting old, is somewhat more nimble and it might get nasty."

"Oye! Getting old am I, Brother?" Reza glowered, pretending to be mortally offended.

Talon responded with a grin then turned to Max with a more serious expression. "Max, there is a chance that both of us might need to go before long. I would be far more comfortable if I knew the castle was being run by you while we were away."

Reza added his argument to that of Talon. "He's right, Max. We need an experienced head here. Talon obviously can't manage on his own."

Max grunted with amusement. These two were forever bantering, but he nodded reluctant acceptance. He knew Talon was right. Theodora had taken him in hand and was giving him herbal medicines which eased the persistent aches in his knees and the cough he never seemed to be able to get rid of, which had become worse as winter drew in.

"Reza, you'd better make sure Jannat is not upset at the idea. But we need to get to Dimitri urgently and restore any fall-off in morale. The whole situation could fall apart any time, and there's no telling what Pantoleon might conjure up. You could be there and back within a week."

"At least we have Maymun in place to support Dimitri. He is a good man; good with a bow," Reza remarked.

"Dimitri implied that," Talon said in a dry tone.

"Then it is decided." Reza sat back in his chair. "I could do with a glass of wine, how about you two? There was enough excitement last night; it fair tired me out! You're a father again, Talon!" he laughed. Instead of wine Talon poured some of the local arrack, which had been presented to him by the villagers, into three small opaque glasses. It was fierce and very powerful.

They all took a deep sip and Reza pulled a face. "Ouch! That's poison!" He exclaimed. "Do you think they're trying to get rid of us?"

"It's got potential. I quite like it," Talon gasped. "Father I may be today, but you'd better be back here when Jannat gets going," he added.

Reza left on Guy's ship within two days. None of the womenfolk had been happy with the idea of his leaving, but when it was explained why Jannat had reluctantly nodded her head.

"You had better get back here for me when my time comes, my Reza," she told him with tears in her eyes. She knew the dangers that lurked in that city and was frightened for him.

A full day later, with the early evening settling in and the sun just about to disappear below the horizon, Guy conned the ship into the crowded harbor of Famagusta. As the ship glided through the clear waters within the curved arms of the sea breakers, he and Reza stood on the after deck observing the shipping. They were seeking the ship that Guy had seen before.

The rowers were put to work to turn the ship so that the prow faced seaward, then anchor stones were dropped fore and aft with satisfying splashes. They were almost alongside another three ships that were waiting to be moved alongside a quay to unload their cargo. They looked deserted; Reza assumed the crew were ashore taking advantage of the wine shops and whores. Guy had brought a medium-sized reed cage with six pigeons to replenish Dimitri's lair, and for the sake of credibility some barrels of very young wine and olives. Just enough to offer an excuse should anyone enquire.

Guy pointed towards the inner harbor. "There it is, Reza."

Reza peered at a long, sleek-looking galley. "Are you sure?" he asked.

"You're not a sailor, Reza so you wouldn't know a bireme warship from a Venetian merchant tub," Guy told him. "You were not there when we captured the ship that Nigel captained. A fast Arab fighting ship, it was. That's it over there or I am a blind man."

"Do you think this Nigel will be still on it?"

Guy shook his head. "No, I think he is dead and gone, but that's his old ship, for sure."

Reza didn't respond, but he continued to stare at the ship, assessing its points of accessibility. It might be worth a visit some time, he decided, but there was more important business at hand.

The sky darkened perceptibly, and both men became aware of a disturbance on the quayside across from their anchorage. A group of armed men strode along the stone walkway and gathered on the quay; they were staring over at Guy's ship, and one man was pointing and saying something. Then they rushed down the steps that led to the water and clambered into two boats, which they began to row rapidly across the intervening water. Reza could see two men remained on the quayside, watching.

"We have a reception committee," Guy said nervously. "It doesn't look friendly either." He started with shock. "By St. Cuthbert's balls, but that is Nigel, as I live and breathe!"

"That man is Nigel?" Reza demanded. "Which one of the two?"

"The thinner one, not so tall."

"He lives after all, but I would not say he is our friend today."

"No, Reza, this is definitely not the way one old friend greets another, and you must hide. Get out of sight. I don't like the look of this at all. I will stay and see what is going on but you *must* hide." Guy's tone brooked no argument and Reza knew he was right. Armed men making a bee-line for their ship, and this man Nigel on the wharf, pointing them out? That smacked of betrayal and great peril.

He had his sword on him but his bow and arrows were still in the cabin. Too late to collect them. *I wish I had a couple of our bamboo bombs,* he thought to himself as he clapped Guy on the shoulder. "God protect. Do what you can. We will not abandon you, neither Talon nor I."

"God bless, my friend. Go *now!*' Guy's tone was urgent. The boats were almost alongside.

Without another word Reza vanished over the side of the ship and slipped into the water. Not even Guy saw where he went, assuming that Reza had gone below to conceal himself. Very carefully, with his head only just above water, Reza paddled over to the ship Guy had pointed out and swam around to its other side, hanging onto the rough wood of the hull and peering back from behind the steering oar, He could see without being seen and observe the activity on Guy's ship. It was not long in erupting.

Men swarmed onto the vessel, rounded up the crew and drove them below, slamming the gratings and locking them. Others ran up the steps to the afterdeck where Guy stood, waiting.

They were shouting and gesticulating as they pushed Guy about and demanded loudly where the ship had come from and what Guy was doing here in Famagusta. One began to shove him hard, demanding something. It didn't take long for Guy to lose his temper. With a roar he spun on his tormentor, picked him up with both hands, ran to the starboard side and threw him overboard before his startled companions could intervene.

With a surprised yell the man flew through the air, his arms and legs flailing, to fall with a mighty splash in the water. He went under for a long moment, then surfaced, sputtering and shouting with fear. He couldn't swim. Someone threw a line to him from the waist of the ship and hauled him in, laughing all the while, and helped the half-drowned man onto the deck. He recovered enough to spit salt water onto the deck and begin cursing. He cursed all the way back up onto the after deck, where he drew his dagger and advanced on Guy, now bound and held fast, who stood bravely facing him.

"I said no killing! I want him alive!" a voice roared from the quay.

The drenched and dripping man hesitated, scowling ferociously, then sheathed his blade and slammed his fist into Guy's face. Guy, a big man, staggered back but regained his footing. A blow to the midriff doubled Guy over, but still he obstinately refused to fall.

"Stop that, you fool! Bring him ashore and get on with it!" called the man from the quay. He was obviously in charge. "In the name of the emperor, you are under arrest," he called over in a loud voice. "Get him off that ship and take him to the villa! Do it now!" Reza clearly heard what was said and tucked it away for future reference.

"Why are you arresting me? I have only just arrived and have done no wrong!" Guy bellowed at the men on his ship. He received a painful slap for his defiance.

"We are impounding this vessel. Search it for anyone hiding! Look for the man called Talon."

From his watery observation point Reza watched as Guy was bundled off the after deck. He could not see the wharf on the other side of the ship, but he could clearly hear the sounds of the rowboat transporting his companion. He wondered how the meeting with Nigel would go. From within the ship he could hear men thumping about blow decks, ransacking the quarters as they hunted for anyone hiding on board. Eventually they trickled back on deck. There was an exchange of shouts across the water and the men disembarked, leaving guards to ensure that the crew remained imprisoned below decks until someone could decide what to do about them.

Dusk settled in and the harbor quieted. The normally shrill cries of the seagulls diminished to the occasional squawk as they settled down for the night, and the activity on the quayside stopped as the workers and fishermen left for their homes. Waiting until it was quite dark, Reza swam back to Guy's ship. In a couple of minutes he was hanging onto the edge of the upper deck transom, peering over and trying to locate the guards.

It was not hard to find them. They were clustered on the main deck with their spears stacked, playing knuckles. From time to time one of the guards would peer down through the grating to make sure the crew were docile, but otherwise they seemed content to simply guard the gangway that led down to the boats.

It was easy for Reza to slip into his cabin and retrieve his weapons, but there was something very important he had to have with him when he left. The pigeons were essential, and they were in the main cabin. He was just about to slip across the passageway when he heard voices and the sound of men clumping down the stairway. Diving into the main cabin he drew his sword and waited in the dark. Two men entered the room with candles in their hands, obviously looking for loot.

"There isn't much here, no gold nor nothin' like that. I already went over it," one of them said.

"Let's have another look. Never know with these seamen. They hide stuff everywhere," the other replied. Neither had time to do more than open their mouths in shock as Reza appeared out of nowhere in front of them like some vengeful phantom. He looked like a horrifying apparition that had just risen from the deep, dripping sea water from ragged clothing, his face hidden and a wicked looking blade in his hands. The sword flickered in the candlelight as it struck with incredible speed. Two candles fell to the floor alongside the tangle of bodies, and it was over. Reza quickly retrieved one of the candles and came to a decision. It was not yet time to leave.

A low-voiced call summoned the other two guards to the after-part of the ship. Grumbling, they abandoned their game and slouched towards the dark form standing near the steps.

When they were close enough, Reza struck. The guards were too slow and shocked to react; they died with barely a sound other than the thump of their bodies on the decking. Reza casually wiped his blade on their coats while he looked around for more victims. There were none.

The crew below decks heard the grating being lifted up and Reza's voice pitch to penetrate the reaches of the hold. "Come on deck, I need you up here at once!"

Warily the rowers and sailers clambered onto the deck to find that the guards had disappeared and Reza was telling them not to worry.

"Can any of you sail this ship without Captain Guy and at night?" he asked in a whisper.

Hands went up and one man, the steering man, whispered, "I can sail it. But where is Captain Guy?"

"They took him off the ship while you were all below," Reza answered. "Now listen, this is what I want you to do." After he had explained he told them, "Clean up the mess in the after cabin and at the back only when you are well out to sea, before you arrive at our harbor. Be sure to tell Lord Talon what has happened."

Within half an hour Reza was ashore with his weapons, and the pigeons were on the ground nearby. Guy's ship was stealthily making its way out of the harbor. He expected it would be challenged, but the guards here were so slack that there were no calls. He watched until he could no longer distinguish its dark form out at sea, then picked up the crate and began the walk to the darkened city.

Dimitri was woken again at another unearthly hour by one of his guards. "Wake up, wake up, Dimitri. Someone is here to see you!" the guard chanted. Exhausted with worry and bleary-eyed from lack of sleep, Dimitri staggered out of bed and followed the guard. Then he gasped with surprise. He had never been so happy to see Reza in his life. After embracing him with great emotion he said, "I have been worried! My men reported the arrest of Captain Guy and there was nothing we could do about it! We thought Talon might have been on board with Guy. The beggars told me the bastards were looking for another man."

"I came instead, and yes, they were searching for me but I avoided them," Reza grinned. He now wore dry clothes, having changed before he left the ship. "Do you know where they might have taken Guy? The palace dungeons, perhaps? We must waste no time getting him back. They will certainly torture him."

"Oh yes, but not to the palace dungeons. Those were Pantoleon's men and they will have taken Guy to his villa," Dimitri said confidently.

"You have a new supply of messengers," Reza informed him. "The ship is on its way home, and the sailors will tell Talon what has happened. He will know what to do."

373

Dimitri gaped. "How in God's name is that possible?" he demanded. "The ship was seized! Didn't they post guards?"

"Well, yes they did, but if you can see your way to feeding me some sardines with some good bread, olives, a little cheese perhaps and some *decent* wine, I shall tell you, my friend. I am very hungry."

"Your will be done!" Dimitri beamed.

Treacherous time has put me in prison
Where I've chirped away like a bird in a snare.
How pure and fine my inspiration
Is and was and will be there.
—Todros Abulafia

Chapter 29
Prison

All during the row over the water Guy struggled against his bonds, and he raged when he was brought before Nigel. "Nigel! What in God's name are you doing here? What is the meaning of this?" he shouted at his former friend.

Nigel, looking very uncomfortable, shrugged and stepped aside without a word as Guy was dragged off.

"You traitor! Nigel! If I ever get my hands on you I'll break you in two!"

Guy roared abuse at his captors and fought as they wrestled him off the boat. In the end one of them clouted him with a cudgel that dazed him enough so that they could throw a flour sack over his head and drag him off the pier.

Upon arrival at the villa he was bundled down the back stairs to a makeshift cell and shoved none too gently into the bare room. The thick wooden door was slammed and he was left in the dark with the sack still over his head. He tried to work his bonds loose but they had been well tied. All Guy could do was to blunder into the walls. Finally he sat down and contemplated his situation.

So it had been Nigel, and he worked for either the emperor or for the fellow that Talon called Pantoleon. Guy didn't know which, but he was beginning to think that it might be the latter, as this kidnapping had been furtive. He leaned back against the wall, wondering if Reza had escaped and reached Dimitri. Guy had no idea where Dimitri lived, so even if he did escape, which seemed unlikely, he wouldn't know where to go. He finally managed to work the sack off his head and stared around him in the dark. As his eyes became accustomed to the gloom he began to see more. It was windowless, and there was not even a bed on the earthen floor. There was nothing he could do, so he settled back against the cool stone wall and tried to rest.

On being informed that the captain of the ship had been captured but there had been no sign of any man matching Talon's description, Pantoleon was coldly angry. "Did you search the boat from top to bottom? Are you sure there was no one else?" he demanded of Gabros. "Why would the captain come on his own?"

Gabros shook his head. "I cannot say, Master. Nigel pointed out the boat and we went over and arrested this man. Nigel calls him Guy, and he is certainly one of Talon's captains. They knew each other well before—"

"Yes, yes I know," Pantoleon snarled. He was livid. His chance of proving to the emperor that he had better intelligence and could act on it was lost. Talon had either anticipated him, which he doubted, or had simply decided not to come on this particular trip. That left Pantoleon with only half of what he wanted.

He felt the prickle of a premonition. Was this Talon prescient after all? Had he somehow known and not come? He shook his head. No, there had to be another explanation.

"Go and get the prisoner and bring him to me. Better still, we will pay him a visit," he said.

Gabros nodded vigorously. "Right away, Master."

Pantoleon led the way down to the cellar. The guards slammed the door open and rushed in to seize Guy by the arms. They hauled him to his feet and dragged him towards the doorway, where they forced him to his knees. It wasn't easy; Guy resisted all the way, earning himself more bruises from blows and kicks. Finally he was kneeling before Pantoleon, who filled the doorway.

"Why did you come to Famagusta? Who was with you and where is he now?" Pantoleon demanded.

"Why don't you go and eat goat shit?" Guy responded.

Gabros hammered his ribs with a thick stick, then smacked him on his forehead, breaking his nose.

"More respect from you!" he said to Guy, who was now lying on the floor, bleeding from mouth and nose and grunting with pain. They hauled him upright to his knees again.

"I shall repeat the question," Pantoleon said, his tone calm. "We have, after all, much time to become acquainted."

"Who came with you to Famagusta?"

"My crew, of course. How else could I get here?" Guy mumbled through a badly bruised jaw.

There was no further conversation for a few very long moments while they beat Guy almost senseless. The only sound in the room were the thuds of the clubs and his gasps and grunts of pain. By the time they had finished he was lying on his side.

"You should really consider your predicament, Captain Guy. No one knows where you are, and no one can help you now. Tell me what I need to know and I can allow you to go free," Pantoleon informed him gently. "Give him some water," he commanded.

Guy, who was barely conscious, didn't respond. Water being dashed over his bloody face woke him up. He groaned and shook his head, then spat out some blood and a tooth. He didn't try to sit up, he doubted if he could. He opened his eyes to see Pantoleon's face close to his.

"Someone came with you to Famagusta. A passenger. Who was it? Was it Talon?" Pantoleon insisted.

"Tal... Talon didn't come this time. Sent me alone to deliver oil," Guy muttered, and then passed out.

Pantoleon crouched next to Guy, staring down at him in disgust.

"Does he really expect me to believe that nonsense? We are going to have to be more refined, I think," he told Gabros.

Just at that moment Nigel came hurrying down the steps to the cellars. "Master, there is a messenger at the door demanding to see you," he said.

Pantoleon stood up. "Very well, leave him." He nudged Guy with his foot. "We'll deal with him later. There is time."

He paid no attention to the shocked look on Nigel's face when he saw the condition of his erstwhile friend. Gabros led the way out of the cellar to the main living area, where a servant in gaudy clothes from the palace waited impatiently.

The man looked down his huge nose at the arrivals and said, "My Lord his Majesty requires your presence without delay." There was no mistaking his haughty tone and condescending attitude. Pantoleon was tempted to beat the man to death there and then. However, he controlled his anger and said evenly, "Take us there now." Turning to Gabros he said, "We'll get back to that ship's captain tomorrow. He can stew while he waits."

Pantoleon was admitted by the same surly guards who had been at the palace before. He surrendered his sword to a servant at the door and was kept waiting a long time. "So much for 'without delay,'" he fumed to himself. At last the old man called Diocles appeared and, after a perfunctory greeting, led Pantoleon down long corridors into the depths of the meandering palace. Pantoleon followed, ever watchful, as the old man shuffled up to the same doorway where he had been before; there were guards standing outside. They opened the doors and admitted the courtier and the spy.

The emperor was standing by his table, which was still strewn with papers. Nothing much appeared to have been moved since the last visit. Pantoleon prostrated himself.

"Ah, Exazenos. No more need for that! Get up and come over here," the emperor said from near the window.

Pantoleon stood up, brushed off his coat and walked carefully over to join the emperor and his Gatherer of Information, who stood off to the side, glowering at him. Pantoleon gave Malakis a cold stare. "Your time will come," he thought, as he tilted his head respectfully to the emperor.

"Your Majesty sent for me?" he said in tones of deepest respect.

Isaac beamed at him, clearly in a good mood this afternoon. "I am going to Paphos tomorrow, and I want you to come with me."

Pantoleon blinked. "What, may I ask, is the purpose of this visit, Your Majesty?"

"Why, to check in on my cities of course, to make sure the nobles are behaving and to whip them into line if they are even contemplating sedition!" Isaac laughed. "You will be able to see each of the cities as we visit them. It will take about two weeks, and then we come home."

"This is... very short notice, Your Majesty, but I shall leave the palace at once and prepare," Pantoleon said, bowing his head and thinking furiously.

"Surely you knew that you would have to visit the towns sooner or later?" Isaac asked him with some asperity in his tone.

"Of course, your Majesty. I was preparing for this honor but it came upon me sooner than even I expected. Is there a problem in one of the cities?" Pantoleon wanted to divert the emperor off this particular track.

Isaac looked at him. "You are perceptive, Exazenos. As a matter of fact, there is a problem. Some Arab pirates decided to make a nuisance of themselves off the coast near the town of Limassol. We will be going there with some cavalry. My second in command Julian is somewhat new to the job. His predecessor got himself killed not long ago. Careless of him, but now Julian is coming along nicely and I want to support him."

"I see, Majesty. May I ask if Malakis will be accompanying us?"

"No. You are dismissed, Exazenos. At first light we leave. Be ready."

"Yes, your Majesty."

He bowed himself out. As Diocles was about to follow, Isaac called out, "Let Exazenos go, old man. I need to talk to you. The Lady—"

Pantoleon didn't hear any more, as the guards shut the doors. He slowly retraced his steps towards the main entrance. At some point along the gloomy corridors he became aware of a woman standing in the corridor ahead of him. It was Tamura, veiled and cloaked.

He paused and looked behind him. There was no apparent danger, so he continued to walk slowly towards where she stood in shadow.

"My Lady," he murmured as he drew close.

"My Lord," she responded. "Come, I must talk to you." She beckoned him to follow. With his hand on his hidden dagger Pantoleon allowed himself to be drawn into a small darkened room with closed shutters.

She shut the door behind them, then sighed as though deeply distressed.

Alert for any danger but also intrigued by this stealthy behavior, Pantoleon allowed her to come closer.

"My Lady, what is the matter? You sound unhappy." He kept his voice down.

Another sigh, and now she was very close to him. He was keenly aware of her scent of rose petals, but still wary. What was she doing?

"I need help, Exazenos. I need the strength of a real man who can save me from my fate," she whispered, her breath on his cheek. He did not flinch, knowing that to do so would destroy a fragile form of trust she was offering him.

"If there is anything I can do for my Lady, you have but to ask," he whispered back.

"It's... it's the emperor." She leaned in and kissed him.

At first Pantoleon feared her actions might be part of a trap, but then he remembered the look of malevolence he had seen Malakis direct at the veiled lady. As her soft lips remained on his he leaned into the kiss and returned it. For a long moment there was silence, other than their breathing and the eager workings of her tongue, but then she stepped back and whispered.

"I am but a woman, but he, that loathsome man.... "

He stared at her. So this was how it was!

"I sense," she whispered hesitantly as though not sure if she could trust him, "I sense in you a man who is strong and wise and... capable of, of ruling," she said, almost so quietly that he was barely sure of what he heard.

Pantoleon was frantically adjusting to the situation. His thoughts flashed back to the two times she had dropped her veil to let him see her face.

"My Lady, I am here to serve you, in any way I can," he whispered back, beginning to feel an interesting stirring.

He leaned forward to take another kiss as though to seal their pact. Instead she came into his arms and pressed her hips against him. Pantoleon was aroused, and there was no doubt that she could feel him pressed against her. He heard her sigh into his shoulder as though satisfied, or with pleasure, he could not tell. She kissed him hard, her tongue seeking his, and then her hand reached down to take him. Pantoleon almost panicked. He swiftly reached down and took her wrist and prevented it from moving.

"I want you, I want you now, my Exazenos!" she whispered fiercely.

"All in good time, my Lady. Here is not a good place, nor is it the time right. There will be a more propitious occasion when I return, and we shall enjoy it all the more for waiting."

"Oh yes, you are accompanying my master to Limassol and the other cities." She nodded in the gloom. "I asked if I could stay behind this time. Then it is goodbye for now. We can talk more when you come back. Word is that your people arrested someone today. Is it true?" Another kiss burned on his throat.

Pantoleon was surprised. Rumors certainly traveled fast. "Yes, he is one of the captains belonging to that man on the mountain the emperor appears to hate so much."

"Indeed he does!" she whispered. "My, but you don't waste time!" she exclaimed, and she was gone.

Pantoleon dabbed at the sweat that had formed on his forehead and eased himself out of the room. Glancing up and down the corridor, he hastened to leave the palace.

Unbeknownst to him, one of the servants who worked at the palace noticed him leaving the room just after the Lady Tamura and reported it to Malakis.

Pantoleon arrived back at the villa in a high state of excitement and called for Gabros, who clumped in and waited expectantly.

"I am ordered by the emperor to attend his visit to Paphos. That means you will be in charge here while I am gone. I want you to find out more from that captain, and bring some of the crew in for questioning. Perhaps they will be more willing to talk," he told his man. "Don't waste time with niceties, get anything you can from them."

Gabros nodded. "I'll go myself to the ship in the morning, Master."

"Good, and make sure that Nigel is present so that they know he is with us. It might help them to remember," Pantoleon said. "One last thing, Gabros."

"Yes Master?"

"The emperor is leaving his *master of spies* behind." Pantoleon's tone was sarcastic. "Be careful. I don't trust that dog turd at all. Remember what it iss that we have to protect."

"Fear not, Master. We will be vigilant," Gabros assured him.

"I am going to find out more about Isaac's other resources. Have you been able to assess his men at arms yet?"

"Yes, they are a miserable bunch of misfits and thugs with one or two halfway decent soldiers among them. I do not think they will present too much trouble, Master."

"Good. Who do we have who can get into the palace without being caught?"

"Nesto is a born assassin. He comes from the same group that used to work for your father. Very good at what he does."

"He had better be," Pantoleon said between his teeth. "I don't want any hint of suspicion of our presence," he said. "I want him to find out where the ladies' rooms are and where Malakis lives in the palace. Have him do so before I get back."

Dismissing Gabros, Pantoleon tool stock of events. He certainly had not expected the woman to seek him out so directly, but now that she had, he pondered how he could take advantage of it. His words had been.suggestive at more than one level.

Back at the palace Tamura was also thinking hard. She had been astonished at how free Exazenos had been with his information. She decided it must have been the shock of her coming on to him in the manner she had. It had worked sufficiently for her to glean information for her shadowy spy in the city.

She still didn't know names, but by now she was sure the spy worked for the strange man on the mountain who had humiliated Isaac. If that was indeed the case then she was happy to pass along anything useful. He could do with it as he willed. Siranus was despatched post haste to a pre-arranged meeting place where a beggar was always lurking about.

Once word reached them at the villa, Dimitri and Reza debated the news and their options. They had been desperately trying to figure out how to gain access to Guy, but so far had come up with no solutions.

"They have probably started on Guy and even now might be torturing him," Giorgios told Reza, who nodded agreement. The discovery of the absent ship in the morning would only make things worse. Guy would be in peril of his life.

"We will go in tomorrow when we see the emperor has left. Speed and surprise might do the trick," Reza decided.

"We are missing something." Dimitri said, scratching the top of his head.

"What is it?" Reza asked. He was impatient to get on with the planning.

"The Spymaster, Malakis, is going to stay behind. I wonder why? Is the emperor trying to divide those two? He cannot be such an imbecile... can he? If so, what can we do to help that situation along?" Then he slapped the table with his hand. It made even Reza jump. "What?" he demanded.

Dimitri leaned forward with an excited gleam in his eye. "Reza, could we not pretend to be soldiers sent from the palace?"

Reza looked skeptical. "I think you are leaving your senses," he said.

"Think on it, Reza," Dimitri urged. "Pantoleon took matters into his own hands, and if Malakis heard about it then he is not likely to be pleased. In his shoes I might want the prisoner for myself."

Reza laughed. "My God, Dimitri, but you are beginning to think like Talon!" he considered. "The timing has to be exactly right. After Pantoleon has left but before the alarm can be raised about the absence of the ship, but... it might just be possible."

"We will need written orders," Dimitri said. "I'll have to forge letters, just enough to get us in and out again."

"We will have to spirit Guy out of the city somehow," Reza said.

They worked half the night and made sure that their men were fully aware of the objective. Five of the men who were to go were nervous, but the stoical example of Maymun helped steady them, and Reza reassured them that as long as they maintained their calm the operation could work. Even so, they made contingency plans for the eventuality of a disaster. If it went badly, the men were to flee and hide wherever they could; none were to come back to the villa for at least two days. Reza forbade Dimitri to attend the operation because if he were seen it could compromise all future work. Dimitri reluctantly agreed, so Strabo was carefully rehearsed for the role of Guard commander.

"You must remember to be an arrogant son of a bitch and demand everything. Don't take no for an answer from anyone at all," Dimitri coached him, as he used softened wax to extend his nose into an impressive hook and painted on a larger mustache.

So it was that at dawn the emperor, on time for a change, departed the city of Famagusta with a cohort of cavalry and Pantoleon in attendance. Gabros, having seen his master off, returned to the villa for a leisurely breakfast and then left for the harbor.

A pigeon arrived on the window sill of the coop at the castle. Rostam was there with Irene; Jannat was slower to rise due to her condition. The message was delivered to an owlish looking Talon, who rubbed the sleep out of his eyes and then blinked them wide open as he read the note.

At the same time Talon was reacting to his message, a contingent of palace guards stamped along the cobbled streets in hobnailed sandals to arrived at the entrance of the villa recently vacated by Gabros and demanded entrance. The surly and puzzled mercenaries moved to prevent them from getting to the doors. A hook-nosed captain with a huge mustache read out an official looking document that ordered the prisoner, known as Guy, to be released into their custody.

"You can wait for our leader to come back. He will be here soon," one of the bolder guards informed them with a rude shrug.

"I shall do no such thing!" bellowed the officer in his loudest and harshest tones. "You will produce the prisoner or you will find yourselves guests of the emperor. *In his dungeons!* It is on the orders of Master Malakis who is in charge while the emperor is away that I am here, and by God and the Emperor I shall have the prisoner! Do not dare to disobey!"

The loud discussion had drawn a couple of the other men from inside the villa, but there was also a crowd beginning to form and they murmured among themselves as they watched this display of wills; clearly they didn't like the occupants of the villa, but neither were the palace guards popular either.

The mercenaries looked stubborn, putting their hands to the hilts of their swords, but the palace guards leveled their spears at them and one of the slimmer men of the squad stared straight at the man who had spoken up. The mercenary saw a smile on the man's lips and knew what it meant. This one, at least, could kill him in the blink of an eye and enjoy it too. He quailed.

The confused men looked at one another, utterly bewildered; there was no one to lead them and make a decision. They tried desperately to delay things further in order to wait for Gabros to get back. One even left at the run to find him. "We cannot give you the prisoner. He is ill," another told Strabo, who sneered and shouted a command to his men, who stamped their hobnailed sandals menacingly forward another pace, their spears leveled. The guards retreated.

"You dare to disobey the emperor? Then your days here are numbered!" Strabo screamed at them. "Stand aside. I shall take him for myself and you will be crucified in the square. How dare you insult the Emperor! Long live the Emperor!" he bellowed, putting his hand to his wax nose extension, which was beginning to melt under all the strain.

The small crowd roared back, "Long Live the Emperor!" Someone snickered and received a haughty glare from Strabo, who was by now well into his act. "Get out of here, you scum, before I set my men on you!" he shouted.

A more reckless wag among the crowd called back, pretending to be frightened. "Ooo, ahhh, I'm so scared! Bet you weren't so brave on the mountain, were you!" The crowd laughed outright at this.

Strabo and his men pretended to ignore them. "Sounds like the word has spread," Reza muttered to Strabo out of the corner of his mouth, trying not to grin.

A few minutes later two men came to the door, staggering under the weight of Guy, who could barely walk. At a sharp motion of his hand from Strabo, Reza stepped forward with one of the other men and took possession of the prisoner. They half carried him to the squad, which closed ranks around them.

Strabo glared up at the confused and unhappy thugs on the steps. "Just in time, you louse-ridden scum! You have saved your worthless lives. Now get out of my sight!" he roared.

Needing no further encouragement the mercenaries vanished behind the doors of the villa, which slammed shut.

"Go on go home, there's nothing here for you!" Strabo called out to the mob, putting his hand up to his nose just in time to catch his wax extension, which had finally slipped off.

The crowd lost interest and began to go about their business, while Strabo and his men marched off in the direction of the palace. No sooner were they well out of sight of the villa than they changed direction and hurried their semi-conscious friend back to Dimitri's villa. They hustled Guy into the building and sat him down on a chair, where he lolled back. He was in poor shape and both Dimitri and Reza looked at him with concern.

"Jesu, but I didn't think we would get away with it!" Strabo grunted, as he sat mopping his brow and picking off the last of the wax. Then he rubbed off the false parts of the mustache with a grunt of pain. "Ouch! Even the crowd was fooled!" he chortled happily.

"You were magnificent!" Reza told him, clapping him on the back. "You should have seen him, Dimitri! He had them scared witless."

"I think it was you who had them scared, Reza. I was watching the one nearest you. He was shitting himself," Strabo sniggered.

"No matter. You succeeded, by God. But now we have to take care of Guy," Dimitri said, after a cursory examination. "I don't think he will be able to ride."

"He must!" Reza snapped. "It is the only way and there is no time to lose. Once they discover what has happened they will close the gates and hunt for him all over this town. We cannot be discovered with him here. You will have to make sure that you and your men lie low for a while. It will be like a hornet's nest overturned."

"Guy! Guy! Can you hear me?" Dimitri demanded as he dabbed at Guy's battered face with a wet cloth.

Guy shook his head groggily and lifted it to peer through swollen eyes and cheekbones at the men gathered around him. "Where am I?" he asked.

"You are safe... for the moment," Reza told him.

"Reza? Dimitri? What, what happened?"

"Later, Guy. You must leave the city as soon as possible. Can you ride?"

"Bedder at sea," Guy mumbled through swollen lips. "How'd I get here?"

Reza ignored him and turned to Dimitri. "Where are the horses?"

"They are being held by Maymun outside the gates."

"I'll need help, I'll take Maymun with me. Guy is going to be difficult to keep on a horse."

"Yes, all right. God help us, but we must get him going now!"

"Put him in a cart and we will try to leave with him under something. They don't care much what goes out, more about what comes in," Strabo suggested. "Food comes in but shit goes out, if you get my meaning." He chuckled at his own wit.

They left through the city gates with Guy buried under a pile of horse manure, with a space made for him to breathe, with Reza and Maymun on horseback leading a pack animal. One of the natives of Famagusta drove the cart. He would be returning later in the day with an empty cart. The guards at the gates barely gave them a glance, turning away from the odious stink as the cart trundled by.

They drove without appearing to hurry towards a copse of woods about a league from the city, where they stopped. Guy was hauled out of the pile, bundled onto the largest horse and tied onto the saddle, after which they set off for the castle at a canter, Guy swaying in the saddle as they went.

The empty cart was driving back through the city gates as a highly agitated Gabros was leaving the harbor, livid with rage that the ship had disappeared overnight, along with all its crew and the men who should have been guarding it. No one could tell him what had happened; the ship had vanished as though by magic. This spoke of witchcraft, and he was beginning to guess whence that came. He shook his head. Pantoleon should not have underestimated that Talon.

He arrived back at the villa to find his men milling about in the house unable to coherently inform him of what had happened earlier that morning. He grabbed one of the men by his front and lifted him off his feet, he was so angry, and shouted, "Tell me this is not true! You allowed the Emperor's men to take the damned prisoner away?"

They nodded, dumb with fear. Gabros was not a man to anger quickly, but when he did it was a fearsome sight to behold. "You stupid, *stupid* cowardly fools!" he ranted, and threw the man backwards against the wall, reaching for his knife. Just at that moment they all heard a shouted order outside on the street and another of his men came running into the front room.

"They are back!" he said, his voice shaking with nervous tension. "Those crazy palace guards are back!" he sounded incredulous.

In a few swift strides Gabros was at the front door staring down the steps at the group of armed men gathered at the base. The leader, a scruffy hulk of a man with a huge nose, shouted up at him.

"Orders to pick up the prisoner and take him to the palace! Where is he? Bring him out, in the name of the emperor!"

Gabros and his men gaped. Recovering himself enough to shake his head and glare at the man, Gabros called back, "Your men have been here already and taken him."

"No we haven't, you piss pot. We've only just got here. Bring out the prisoner or I'll come and get him."

Gabros by now was thoroughly confused and angry. The loss of both the ship and his prisoner made him reckless.

"I have already told you, you mindless turd! You came for him earlier and we gave him to you! Now piss off and leave us alone."

"Don't you tell me to piss off! I'm not a... whatever turd either!" Asanes shouted back, deeply offended by the insult. "I'm here in the name of the Emperor and by the orders of Malakis," he bellowed. Gabros had seen Asanes before lurking about in the palace, which gave credence to his mission, but there was still the puzzle as to who had taken the prisoner earlier. To make matters worse, a curious crowd was beginning to gather.

"Wot happened? Did you lose the prisoner on the way home?" came a voice from behind the gathering.

Asanes glared at the speaker. "Take names, we will arrest them when we are done here," he snarled.

Someone overheard him and the crowd rapidly dispersed.

Asanes and Gabros were almost nose to nose at this point, their bearded faces infused with blood and distorted with anger. "I told you, we don't have him. I swear to God that we gave him over to *your* men earlier, so don't come here and tell me that your left hand doesn't know what the damned right hand is doing!" Gabros snarled. Then realization began to dawn.

"You really don't have him, do you? Oh my God, this cannot be right!" he muttered and slipped out of range of Asanes' huge hands reaching for him. Gabros whipped out his dagger and was now pointing it at his antagonist.

"Stop! Stop!" he yelled at Asanes. "Don't you see? We've been tricked!"

"The bastards tricked us," he repeated, stamping around in fury. "You must believe me when I tell you before God that we *did* hand the prisoner over to some men. They said they were from the palace. You don't know anything about that?"

Asanes, being somewhat slow, was still hung up on being called a mindless turd, but even he began to realize that all was not as it should be and that this offensive man was trying to tell him something.

"You have to shut the gates and stop anyone from leaving the city!" Gabros shouted urgently at him.

"Why?"

Gabros rolled his eyes. "Because they have escaped and are taking him to the castle on the mountain, that's why!" he snapped. "I'm going to see for myself if he is here or not!" Asanes glared stubbornly at Gabros.

Gabros threw his hands in the air and groaned. Who *was* this great oaf? "Oh very well. Come on in. Just you. I'll prove it to you and then you must listen to me."

Asanes told his men to wait and followed Gabros up the stairs and into the house, past the sullen mercenaries and frightened servants, down the stairs to the basement.

Gabros kicked the door to Guy's former cell open with a booted foot and said, "There! I told you he was gone. Now will you listen to me? Have the gates shut now, before it's too late. For the sake of Saint James's holy bollocks, do it now!"

The sense of the order percolated through the dense mass of Asanes' skull; there was something very wrong, and the least he could do was to shut the city gates.

He returned to his men, who were facing off against Gabros's men, fingering their sword hilts and spears and sneering at one another, ready for a brawl.

"Go and tell the sentries to shut the gates and stop anyone from leaving. Hurry up about it, or I'll have your hides!" he shouted at them. "I'll clear it with Malakis. He won't be pleased," he warned Gabros with an ominous glare.

Gabros couldn't think of anyone who was going to be pleased, but somehow he had to redeem himself. First the ship and then its captain spirited away right under his nose. How was he going to explain this to Pantoleon when he came back?

Asanes threw an insult at him and hurried off with his men, seeing no point in staying any longer, leaving the mercenaries to stew. Gabros stood on the steps, thinking furiously. Then he decided to go to the gates himself and find out if anyone suspicious had already left. The way things were going, it wouldn't surprise him one bit if the fugitive had just walked out of the gates in broad daylight.

Except, he thought with some satisfaction, the man was hardly in any condition to walk anywhere.

"Mount up!" he called to his men, then ran towards the back of the villa to get his weapons and his horse. "I'll find that bastard if it's the last thing I ever do," he muttered to himself. "And then God help him and whoever is with him."

He led a party of ten men off towards the gates of the city. They clattered up on their horses just in time to see the gates closing. Asanes was not there, but some of his flunkies were standing about.

Gabros dismounted and walked over to the guards.

"Did any of you see a large man ride out today, in the last hour or so?" he asked pleasantly enough. "He may have been in the company of one or more others."

"Who the hell are you?" demanded one of the gate sentries.

It was too much. "I'm the one who is going to tear your balls off with a set of tongs and then open your guts with a wooden spoon!" Gabros roared, drawing his sword at the same time. The frightened guard fell back among his comrades, who were as startled as he.

There was the ominous sound of swords leaving sheaths as his men behind Gabros drew their weapons in support. The guards hesitated. They were outnumbered by the horsemen two to one.

"It's all right, comrades," one of Asanes' men called out. "They are looking for the same man we are." It helped to defuse the situation, but everyone was tense and fingering their weapons.

"Well, did you see anyone like that?" Gabros demanded again.

The only riders we have seen went by about an hour ago. They were farmers with a cart full of horse shit," one of the sentries volunteered.

"Cart? Riders? How many?"

"Two, I think. No three, one was driving the cart."

"Was one of them a big man? Ugly?"

"No, don't remember, don't think so. They had a pack animal with them."

"Which way did they go?" Gabros demanded.

The man pointed towards the north. "That way."

"That's got to be them," Gabros muttered under his breath. "Open the gates. I have to go after them," he called over to the sentries.

No one moved. "Didn't you hear me? Open the gates, you pile of excrement."

The guard looked offended. "Can't do that, Sir. Orders are to keep them closed. There is a fugitive loose in the city."

Gabros took a deep breath. He thought he was going to burst a blood vessel. "Open the God damned gates, you rock heads!" he bellowed. His men waved their swords menacingly and advanced on the small group of sentries.

The man who led them said resolutely, "If the emperor said to keep them closed, I have to hear from an official in the palace before I open them."

Gabros had had enough. "Disarm these flea wits and open the gates," he said with a tired gesture to his men. It didn't take very long. The guards valued their lives more than their orders and allowed the beams to be lifted and the gates to be opened.

"Tell your *leader* that I shall be back with the prisoner, *shortly.*" Gabros called back over his shoulder, as he and his men spurred their horses into a gallop heading in the direction of the castle on the mountain.

Gall when it helps is good,
Even if it's bitter;
But sweetness when it starts
To harm will soon devour
—Yosef Ibn Zabara

Chapter 30
A Good Chase

Reza looked back the way they had come with relief that the pursuit which he deemed inevitable had not yet begun. He glanced forward at Guy, who was leaning over his horse's neck, his fists almost white with his death-grip on the neck strap. Maymun held the reins in his left hand while he rode his own horse hard. They would have to negotiate the foothills, and then, on tired horses, they had another severe hurdle to overcome on the last steep slope of the final ascent to the castle itself.

"Water!" Guy begged. Reza cantered up to ride alongside to pour some water into his open mouth and over his swollen face. "Be strong, Guy. Not long now," he said by way of encouragement. Guy nodded and went back to his somnolent state.

Another hour at least, Reza surmised. He hoped the battered and semi-conscious Guy could last the pace. The ship's captain didn't look at all good. His breathing was labored; the beating had probably broken several ribs and his face was very swollen. Guy was a big man, and although his horse was the largest of the three it would be hard for the animal when they arrived at the steeper slopes of the mountain.

Their pace was slower than Reza would have liked, and as they arrived at the steeper slopes they slowed even more. The horses were sweating with the effort and beginning to blow. However, they were already well into the foothills and had a good view of the road all the way back to the distant city of Famagusta. Another glance behind them and Reza stiffened. Far back along the narrow road on the flat plain, he could see a small dust cloud. It could not be anything other than a group of riders on their trail.

"They come!" he called to Maymun, who nodded without words and shouted more encouragement to the tired horses. The boy hauled hard on the reins of the horse behind him. "Guy," he shouted, "stay on the horse. We have to hurry!"

Guy lifted his head painfully and nodded. He flapped his heels bravely and his animal responded.

Reza's eyes searched for a good place for an ambush but rejected the idea. They had to keep moving as fast as they could and gain height, then perhaps lose themselves in the rugged mountain gullies. He stared beyond the next bend in the road, up towards the ridge upon which the castle rested. Perhaps if the people up there could see them, help might come in some form or another. He had no doubt at all that, should the alarm be raised, Talon would send men, even come himself, to fend off the pursuit.

With his mouth set in a grim line he judged the distance between them and their pursuers. It was slowly being eaten up by the racing mercenaries. It would not be long before he had the hounds snapping at his heels. He drove his horse onward and slapped the horse carrying Guy on its rump with his bow; their pace picked up a little. He remembered another time when he and Talon had delayed a group of Seljuk cavalry by shooting down at them from a superior height. He would find a good place to make a stand, and from there he would ensure that many died before he went down.

Now the castle came into view: perched high above them it seemed very small from this distance. He focussed on the horses, shouting encouragement as the tired animals struggled up the road. A cold wind was flowing along the mountain from the east, chilling the riders, but Reza was grateful for the cold. Had it been hot their work would have been much harder on the horses. They passed the flat space where the trebuchet had been and rode on. By now the men following them had gained much ground and were only half a league behind. Even at this distance Reza could hear their shouts.

"Maymun, go on! Don't stop! I shall be waiting for them up there," Reza pointed to a ledge just fifty paces above them. "Take Guy to the castle and deliver him to Talon," Reza ordered.

Maymun wanted to object, but Reza waved him on impatiently. "Do as I say! It is very important that Guy be brought to safety."

They had almost reached the former camp of the emperor by this time. Suddenly Maymun gave an excited shout and pointed. There were men on horseback and others on foot racing along the ledge high above them under the castle walls, while still other men were standing on the battlements. " Thank God! They have seen us,

Reza!" he yelled. Just at that moment they both heard a muffled thump from high above them.

A small dark object with smoke and sparks spewing out of it flew over the walls of the castle and soared into the sky above them.

"Yes, they certainly have seen us," Reza remarked with a laugh. "Go, Maymun, greet our brothers who are coming down the mountain. I shall hold these scum off."

He laid his bow across his lap and drew out an arrow which he knocked, then he halted his animal and waited.

Gabros could smell his quarry. He knew that they were slowed by the very man that they wanted to save, so he drove his men ruthlessly onward. By the time they had reached the foothills he could catch glimpses of them as they struggled up the steepening slopes. All he had to do was to prevent them from making that last steep climb to the ridge, where the people in the castle could protect them. He shouted his men on with promises of reward.

"You will have gold and horses. I personally will see to that if you capture them. Drive on!" he shouted, as they spurred their flagging, sweating and blowing horses up the slope. He knew they had only a narrow window of opportunity which was growing smaller with each pace their quarry advanced. They passed a patch of flat land and charged on. One of the fugitives had inexplicably stopped and turned to face them; he was about two hundred paces ahead, sitting very still. Gabros grinned to himself, the fool was about to die, but nonetheless there was something ominous about the motionless horseman.

Then one of his men shouted a warning and pointed into the sky. "What is that?" he cried. They all looked up just in time to see a dark object hurtling towards them, trailing sparks in its wake. To a man they cringed with anticipation. What happened next was truly terrifying.

The object landed about thirty paces ahead, then bounced into the air like some hissing creature from hell. It exploded with a bright yellow flash and an ear-deafening bang. Pieces of wood and iron flew through the air, striking the group, wounding horses and men. All that remained was an evil looking puff of yellowish smoke.

Dazed and bleeding the men froze with shock, but the horses reacted. Screaming with fear, some even bucking with terror, the animals fought their riders for an escape. Two horses managed to bolt back down the slope with their riders simply hanging on, while the remainder of the riders hauled their horses together into a milling group. These were the unfortunate ones.

Another hissing black object fell out of the sky towards them, but this one exploded in the air with another great flash and ear-deafening clap of thunder almost overhead. This time the pieces frained down on them. Large splinters of wood pierced the flesh of men and horses; some fell over, either dead or wounded and screaming in agony.

Only four riders were left mounted. One of them was Gabros. His mind refused to accept what he had just witnessed, or that he was in mortal danger, until he looked about him at his comrades lying groaning or still, with screaming, struggling animals bleeding copiously on the ground. He felt chilled, and it wasn't the light wind that was tugging at his sleeves. He felt something wet on his neck and reached up to find that he had lost a piece of his ear. The pain became intense for a few agonizing moments.

He stared in shock at the carnage, then glanced fearfully up at the castle whence this horror had originated. He crossed himself. Then he saw the solitary rider galloping towards them, and it seemed that this apparition was yet another manifestation of the evil that lurked all around. The rider had his reins in his teeth and held his bow drawn ready to shoot.

Gabros gave a yelp of fright; despite his long experience as a soldier his instinct for survival was stronger at this moment than his resolve. Dragging his shredded wits together with a huge effort he spun his horse about, and putting spurs to his mount he galloped down the slope, followed by two others. One rider was not so fortunate. As he hauled his animal around an arrow thudded into his back, and he fell with a cry to join his dead and dying companions on the ground, adding his blood to the puddles already there.

Reza watched the three men fleeing back down the slopes towards Famagusta. There was little purpose in chasing them, as they were already out of reach of Reza's bowshot. Besides, they would take back news of the horrifying powers encountered here, which would deter other enemies. He dismounted and checked on the men and animals strewn around. He marveled at the destruction even as he went about his gruesome task of relieving the horses and men of what was left of their lives. He spared only one man, whom he dragged out from under his dead horse and bound tight with his own belt. The rest would have their heads joining the others on poles along the border.

Just as he was finished, Maymun came galloping up to halt in a small cloud of dust in front of him. "Did any survive, Reza?" he demanded excitedly.

"Yes. Did you deliver Guy to Talon?" Reza countered.

"The men from the castle took him, Master. I left him in their care." Maymun sounded uncertain as he saw at the grim look on Reza's face. "I swear he was in good hands."

"In future you will do as I say!" Reza barked. The boy cringed visibly. "You must learn to obey orders to the letter. In this case you disobeyed me!"

A very subdued Maymun dismounted hurriedly and kneeled at Reza's feet. "Forgive me, Master Reza. I meant no harm nor to disobey you," he bowed his head in dismay.

Reza sounded somewhat mollified when he said, "Get back on your horse and take this prisoner up to the castle, and this time present him directly to Lord Talon. Here."

He handed off a length of leather that ended knotted around the neck of his prisoner, who looked utterly cowed. Maymun stood up, "Yes, Master Reza, I shall not disappoint you." He leapt back onto his mount and, dragging the stumbling prisoner along behind him, made off up the slope towards the castle. Some men, led by Palladius, met him on the road a quarter of a league up the slope. Barely pausing, Maymun turned and pointed back at Reza, then continued on his way. The men on foot hurried down to join Reza, and to survey the destruction with awe.

"Truly, Lord Talon can hurl thunderbolts at his enemies. Had I not seen this with my own eyes I do not think I could believe it," Palladius said as he crossed himself.

"Restoring the trebuchet was a good idea. They nearly had us," Reza told him. "I shall leave you to dispose of the mess, Sergeant. Use the villagers if you need to. I am going up to the castle."

Palladius touched his forehead with respect. "As you command, Master Reza."

He watched Reza leave; he was in awe of this man and his friend Lord Talon. He knew he had made the right decision to stay and serve. The surviving, fleeing followers of Lord Doukas been put to death by the emperor, whereas he and the others who'd remained were treated well, the only expectation being that they soldier to the best of their abilities. it was a trade Palladius was well acquainted with, but he also knew that under Max, the imperturbable former Templar knight, he would learn more.

Reza arrived at the castle, where he was greeted enthusiastically by the guards. Yosef and Dar'an were there to embrace him, and then Talon joined them and the two embraced. "That was... close, my Brother," Talon remarked, when they drew apart, still holding arms and looking at each other with deep affection.

"You and I have known closer encounters, my Brother. It was a good chase," Reza grinned. "Now we know we can hurl death and destruction vast distances, and no less importantly, so do the idiots in Famagusta. Another fearsome legend!" They both chuckled.

"Did the ship reach harbor safely?" Reza asked Talon.

"They arrived early this morning and sent a messenger up immediately. The pigeon confirmed their report. I want to hear all about it, and what happened this morning."

"You shall. Dimitri is doing very well, despite the setback."

'That's good to hear. Did any of your pursuers escape?" Talon asked.

"Yes. Three of them, I suspect one was their leader."

"How many died?"

"Six, and one prisoner."

"Maymun insisted upon delivering the prisoner to my hands," Talon said with a dry note to his voice. "He looked chastened."

Reza nodded. "He is a good boy but needs to understand that orders are orders."

Talon nodded agreement. "He turned Guy over to our men at the top of the hill and went back for you?"

"Precisely my point. How is Guy?" Reza asked.

"I think you and I can leave the boys to get on with their duties and go and find out from our physician. Besides, I dare say you would like to see Jannat. She has been asking for you."

Reza punched him on the shoulder and ran off ahead of him towards the bailey, to pause briefly as Rostam came charging out of the main entrance to embrace him and ask a dozen questions. Reza swung him up into the air, then placed him down.

"Later Rostam," he called over his shoulder. He left the boy looking bewildered and dived into the building.

Talon scooped up Rostam on his way to the mews. "Come along, my son. You need to spend more time with the hawks. How are you going to be able to hunt otherwise? Later we need to send a pigeon off to Dimitri. You can help me to compose the message."

Rostam forgot his initial hurt at being abandoned by his uncle and chased after his father with a yell of excitement. "You too, Irene," Talon called over to the girl, who was hovering on the steps.

Reza raced up the stairs past surprised servants, who curtsied or bowed at his departing back as he rushed by. He charged into the solarium to find Jannat and Rav'an seated by a small fire, the shutters half closed against the winter chill. With a small cry of relief Jannat tried to stand up as he strode into the room.

"My Reza!" she exclaimed. "You are safe! I think you are just in time! I waddle like a duck these days, I am so full of our child." She laughed as he held her gently in a long embrace. He winked at Rav'an, who had risen to stand holding a small bundle in her arms. "I am so glad you are safe with us, Reza. We have been worried," she said, and kissed him on the cheek.

"It was just a little bit tight at times, but we managed to extricate ourselves from a serious problem."

"Come, sit with us and tell us all about your adventure," Jannat invited him.

He squeezed her gently. "I must first see how Guy is doing. Where is he?"

"He is with Theo, and they are in the spare bedroom upstairs."

He kissed Jannat and went upstairs to see how Guy was being treated. He was sitting up in bed with his chest bandaged and some evil smelling grease on his battered face. He grunted a greeting when Reza appeared. Reza grinned at him and took the huge hand that was proffered.

"You saved my life, my friend," Guy said, through cracked and swollen lips. "Thank you, I shall not forget."

"I wouldn't have bothered, but we still need you to captain our ship," Reza laughed.

Guy rolled his eyes and tried to smile, then nodded over towards the window. "Our lady has much in the way of physician skills, thanks be to God."

Theo had been grinding something in a small stone bowl when Reza arrived. She beamed at him and walked over to join them, still holding the bowl. "We have all missed you!" she said, sounding very happy to see him.

Reza smiled at her, then turned to Guy. "You are with the best of physicians, my friend. Get well soon. We have a lot of questions for you."

"Questions later, Reza. What he needs is rest and peace," Theodora told him.

"Then I shall see you later. Thank you, Theo. I know he is in good hands." Reza pecked her on the cheek and left.

Gabros and his two men—he was relieved to see that one was Nestongus, his best man—brought their staggering, lathered mounts to a halt in front of the city walls and waited for the gates to be opened. The horses were blown and the men thoroughly shaken; no one spoke of the horror they had experienced on the slope of the mountain. Brave and ruthless men though they were, they simply couldn't comprehend what had happened.

"Open the damned gates!" Gabros croaked. He longed for a drink.

Finally the gates groaned apart and the three men rode their horses in at a walk. The sentries on the walls were smirking, pointing and snickering amongst themselves as they watched the beaten men enter. Waiting for them just inside were Malakis and Asanes. Neither man was smiling, and they had a contingent of palace guards behind them.

Gabros halted his horse and his dark eyes stared at the two men from the palace; there was no recognition in his eyes, however; he was staring past them. His blood-bespattered face and beard were streaked with dust and sweat, his chain hauberk was in a similar condition, and his horse looked ready to drop. The singular thing about all three of the men was their wide-open stare. They looked to Malakis and Asanes to be in a state of total shock.

"Well, where is the prisoner, or prisoners?" demanded Malakis without preamble.

Gabros didn't answer.

"I asked you, where is the prisoner? Did you not hear me?" Malakis shouted irritably.

Gabros shook his head and mumbled, "He is gone. The wizard on the hill hurled thunderbolts at us."

"What do you mean? Wizard? Thunderbolts? What in God's name are you babbling about?" Malakis demanded.

Gabros now looked directly at him; it was a very tired look and he shook his head. "Just what I said. He hurled thunderbolts at us. We three are all that are left. Now I have to go back to my house."

Malakis and Asanes looked at one another. "You lost the prisoner, and I hear that you also lost a ship? Is that true? Is that wizardry too?" Malakis sneered.

"Yes, that is quite possibly true, now let me pass."

"I should put you in the dungeons, you mercenary pig!" Malakis snarled. "But I shall wait until the emperor comes back, and he can deal with you. I expect you will hang, so yes, you can pass, and you may dwell upon your fate until you are summoned."

Gabros gave him a mocking smile and touched his helmet with his hand in sardonic salute. Malakis feared Pantoleon, that much was evident. Gabros nudged his horse past the frustrated group of soldiers and their scornful but puzzled leaders and rode back to the villa. He arrived to find the remainder of his men waiting for him with a great deal of apprehension.

"Those fools from the palace came here to find you, Master," one of them said. "We told them you were off hunting the prisoner." The man hesitated. Clearly Gabros did not have the prisoner with him, and more than half the men were missing. Gabros didn't enlighten him, he just tossed the reins to him and went into the house. The first thing he did was to check that the locks on the rooms containing the treasure were still intact, then he went to the kitchens to eat and to think.

"Send Nestos in to see me," he called out to a servant.

Not long after, Nestongus, whom Gabros called Nestos, arrived. Gabros, who trusted almost nobody, trusted this man implicitly. Gabros had found him in the back streets of Constantinople and had had little difficulty in persuading him to work for Pantoleon. The mercenary was slight but very wiry and gave the impression of steel cord under the dark, loose clothing he favored. His hooded eyes never stopped moving and his silent nature distinguished him from his fellow men at arms, who knew nothing of his past, other than he was Gabros's closest man.

He entered silently, as was his way, and Gabros, as soon as he spotted him, waved him over. Gabros grabbed a chicken leg and led the way outside and up the steps until they were quite alone on the walls of the villa, where no one could hear what they were saying.

"I still don't understand what happened on that mountain," Nestongus said, still dazed despite his rigid self control.

Gnawing on the roasted chicken leg and watching the people below, Gabros said, "I want to talk about something else, not that."

Nestongus nodded and waited.

Gabros had done some serious thinking while they had walked their horses along the streets of Famagusta between the gates and the villa. The very last thing he needed was for the emperor to be told lies by that toad Malakis.

"You've seen the palace, haven't you?" he asked.

"Yes, it's a rambling dump, built like a flour sieve." This was what Gabros wanted to hear; he nodded and tossed the chicken leg over the wall and watched dispassionately as a beggar scrambled for the bone.

"So now you've also seen this man Malakis," he said, still chewing and looking off into the distance.

Nestos nodded. "When?" he asked simply.

"Give it a day or so, but it's got to be before the emperor comes back. This is strictly between you and me. I shall reward you, have no fear."

Nestos nodded. "Let me know when it's time," he said.

Malakis stormed back into the palace, seething with frustration. He had desperately wanted to arrest that arrogant pig from Constantinople, but something had held him back. He was now so unsure of his own position with the fickle emperor that for once he considered the consequences of his possible actions. If Exazenos had managed to worm his way into the emperor's confidence, then he, Malakis, might be making a mistake by going after his men. He needed to prepare for his encounter with the upstart from Constantinople.

In the meantime, he was going to take care of something else. It was essential that he weaken the power base of the concubine Tamura, and he knew just how to do so.

Asanes was angry and frustrated with his chief. "Why did you not arrest that dog's turd when you had the opportunity?" he demanded, using the insult that had rankled.

"Because, you imbecile, there are things going on that you don't understand!" Malakis snapped.

"I would have arrested him and put him in the dungeons, and then I would have tortured him, and then I would have torn his arms and legs off one by one, and then—"

"Shut the hell up, you dense pile of shit!" Malakis screamed. In the brief silence that followed he said more calmly, "Go and fetch the slave of that slut, Tamura. I want to talk to him."

Asanes looked baleful, but he went. He came back with two men holding a very frightened Siranus. They tossed him at the feet of Malakis, who had ordered a meal and was enjoying roast quail and river trout that would normally have been served only to the emperor. Replete, he belched comfortably and picked at his teeth with a dirty fingernail while he looked down at the kneeling slave, who whimpered with fear.

"I hate it when a man pisses himself with fright, but oh yes, I forgot! You are not a man, are you?" Malakis remarked nastily to the frightened boy.

"N... No, Lord," he cried.

"It has come to my attention that you and your mistress are humping?" Malakis said in a kindly tone.

Siranus jerked upright and stared up at him in stupefied surprise. "My Lord, No! No. Never. I mean, how could I?"

"You probably use a splint to keep it up," Asanes guffawed.

Siranus shook his head with a hopeless, scared look on his face and then began to cry.

Asanes slapped him across his face, knocking the young man onto his back, where he continued to weep. He wiped at the blood on his mouth and gasped, "My Lord, who would accuse my Lady of this? It is not true!" he rolled over onto his knees and crawled up to Malakis, weeping copiously. "My Lord, these are lies! I am... I am not able to do anything, so it is not possible!" He was clutching at Malakis's ankles.

Malakis shoved him out of the way with his foot. "I shall spare you now, but when the emperor comes back there will be charges leveled, and he will deal with you and that slut, your mistress. Be warned," he said with some satisfaction.

"Get this insect out of my sight," he told Asanes, who hauled the boy up by one arm and tossed him over to the two guards, who allowed the boy to crash to the stone floor where he lay sobbing with fear. They dragged his limp form away.

Siranus was dropped off at the bottom of the stairs that led to the women's quarters, where he lay for a while catching his breath, quite ignoring the two sentries who looked down their noses at him. Finally he crawled to his knees and painfully climbed to his feet, after which he staggered up the stairs to face the curious people moving about in the corridor.

He was not so battered that he could not see who was glad of his condition and made a mental note that the Lady Gabriella looked smug. Others rushed to help him, and one kindly old eunuch dabbed ineffectually at the cut on his upper lip where Asanes had hit him. Eventually he felt able to go and see his mistress, who exclaimed in horror and anger at the sight of him.

"Who did this to you?" she demanded between her teeth, her eyes wide with anger and concern.

"It was Malakis, my Lady," Siranus mumbled. His mouth hurt when he spoke.

"Oh, you poor thing!" she exclaimed. "What did he want?"

"He has been told that we are, we are, um, er... " Siranus couldn't bring himself to say it.

"Who told him that?"

"That woman Gabriella told him, I am sure of it. She and that slimy snake, Farragiu."

Lady Gabriella was an attractive but slightly stocky brunette with gray eyes from Macedonia. Isaac had quickly tired of her, so now she was bored, jealous of Tamura, and working mischief.

"Do you think he's puddling her?" she asked him bluntly, her eyes narrowed. "Farragiu, I mean."

He nodded, mute. Everyone was being looked after by their eunuchs in this palace.

She clenched her fists with rage as she watched him tear up again. She was quite jealous of his ability to weep at the drop of a word. "You should not be afraid, Siranus. You must pull yourself together, and get a message to that shadowy friend of yours; this is vital. I shall deal with that woman, but your friend must help us or we are finished. Malakis must have an accident."

He nodded tearfully. He knew that if the slightest hint of impropriety came to the ears of the emperor they were doomed. They would disappear, and Isaac would go back to humping twelve-year-olds. His stomach heaved and he ran off to vomit into a corner. Fortunately this went unnoticed, for Diocles had laid on some entertainment for the women and children of the emperor's harem. He could hear the sound of music and shouts as the performers went through their acts.

Later, when Tamura had helped him calm down and behave more rationally, he left the palace and disappeared into the streets of the city. He had become skilled at the art of eluding his followers, and surely he was followed, but he left them behind easily enough, for this was his world.

He talked to one of Dimitri's beggars, who had him sit in the darkness of a hovel of a tavern while he went to fetch Dimitri. The stocky ex-sailor's instincts for trouble were on full alert as he arrived. The day had, after all, been a busy one. Siranus, crouched in a corner, was alone and almost invisible when he entered.

"What is it you want to talk to me about?" Dimitri asked without ceremony, after a careful look around. Some of Talon's coin had ensured he was left strictly alone whenever he came here. The once attractive woman who ran the place, with its not so good wine and whores, respected his needs and directed her people to leave him alone unless he summoned them. She also kept watch for any unwelcome visitors. She had offered her other wares, but it was too early for that just yet. She was well-paid to protect his privacy.

"We are in serious danger. Someone has denounced my Lady and myself. The man Malakis is threatening to tell the emperor. That would spell certain death for her and for me," Siranus whispered.

Dimitri sat back and stared at Siranus, who looked as though he had been beaten. This sounded bad. "What do you mean, he denounced you?"

"They have told Malakis that we are, um, humping."

"But... aren't you, er... ?" Dimitri waggled his fingers uncertainly in the general direction of Siranus's crotch.

"Yes, but... well, I can still get it up, and then well... she likes it."

Dimitri shook his head in disbelief. How insane could this be? This woman had everything that a lady could desire, but she was still fucking her slave who didn't have any balls! He was having difficulty understanding this. *What is the matter with these people?* he thought, rubbing his balding head furiously.

"What else does she say?" he finally asked.

"That she will meet anyone and tell them about what is going on at the palace: there is a man called Exazenos who is getting close to the emperor."

Dimitri's ears pricked up. "Where is this Exazenos now?" he asked, knowing full well that he was with the emperor and would probably return within a week. Isaac, as usual, was leaving a swathe of misery behind him, which had been reported by Boethius in Paphos to Talon, who passed along the news. Boethius was safe at least, and Henry had left just in time on his ship.

"He is with the emperor, who told my lady that he took Exazenos to keep an eye on him. The emperor doesn't trust that man at all. But I am sure that Malakis is preparing a case against my mistress to present it to the emperor when he comes back. He is a vindictive man. You have to understand me, even a hint of scandal will be enough to convict us. The emperor is half mad and insanely jealous. He will torture us, kill us, and then... forget us! There is very little time left." Siranus almost wailed. His huge brown eyes welled and tears began to slide down his cheeks.

Dimitri glanced nervously around the gloomy room. No one seemed to have noticed; most were already too drunk or more interested in the prostitutes to notice two men having an agitated conversation in the corner.

"All right, all right, calm down. Getting excited won't help. We have a little time, so go back to your mistress and tell her to meet me at the cathedral two days from now. I shall listen and see what I can do for her."

Siranus was less than reassured by this, but it was all Dimitri was prepared to give until he had heard from Talon. Siranus returned to the palace and slipped inside, then found his way to the chambers of his lady.

"So they will meet with me?" she asked him.

"Two days from now you are to be there, veiled and in the back near to the columns on the left of the entrance, my lady."

"Good, then I now have a social visit to make," she told him, and left the chambers to walk along the darkening corridors which she knew well, to another chamber which she entered quietly. This was the bed chamber of Lady Gabriella, who was currently being entertained by the antics of the jugglers ordered in by Diocles to entertain the bored women.

Later that night, the Lady Gabriella arrived with her eunuch, Farragiu, tipsy and belligerent. "Those performers were terrible!" she exclaimed with a petulant moue as she threw herself on the bed. "The hostages can dance better. Bring me wine," she ordered him. He obliged happily, handing her a silver cupful poured from the decorated jug on the table by the shutters. She sat up to drink and then crooked her finger at him. "Get over here. I want some real enjoyment," she purred.

Farragiu smirked and, having put the jug down, prepared to oblige his lady. To his horror, he saw she was clutching at her stomach and then her throat. She fell back on the bed and made mewling sounds as streams of saliva dribbled out of her mouth. The silver goblet lay on its side and the wine was soaking into the bedclothes. He rushed to her side and leaned over her shaking form, trying to help, but he knew with awful certainty that it was too late.

She was grunting now with a look of stark terror on her face, writhing with agony as the poison took effect and began to destroy her liver. It seemed to Farragiu as he held her that her death lasted for hours, but it was only for three long minutes. One last frantic gurgle and she was dead. He fell over her body weeping; he had loved his demanding and petulant mistress.

Yesterday this day's Madness did prepare,
Tomorrow's Silence, Triumph or Despair:
Drink! For know you not whence you came nor why:
Drink! For you know not why you go nor where.
—Omar Khayam

Chapter 31
Murder in a Palace.

Talon and Reza were standing on the eastern track that led up to the castle gates with some of their trainees. The boys, including Rostam, were practicing with their bows; a full sixty paces away were two stuffed shapes of men on sticks with black rings drawn crudely on the area where the chest would be. Maymun and Junayd were vying with each other to see who could out perform the other. Neither could best Talon or Reza, but it was not from lack of trying.

Rostam was struggling to keep up with the other boys, but was doing well. He had learned that when Reza and Talon instructed, they also talked about interesting things, and his ears were wide open as he tried to hear what they were saying. The walls above were lined with a few interested idlers, and of course the sentries.

It was Junayd's turn to shoot. Pretending to ignore him, the two men focussed on recent events and some that were anticipated.

"So there is trouble brewing in the palace now," Reza remarked, scratching his cheek thoughtfully.

"So Dimitri says. I need to go down there and see what can be done. You certainly cannot go," he smiled at his crestfallen brother. "You know perfectly well why, but under any other circumstances you would come with me."

"You mean to deal with this Malakis?" Reza asked, sounding mollified. "Junayd, that was terrible." Reza rounded on the luckless would-be assassin. "What are you doing? You are supposed to kill the target, not scare it to death!" Reza told the embarrassed boy, who almost cringed with shame.

"I'm sorry, Master. I'll do better." It was a harsh judgement because the arrow had landed well, within a half-hand of the center.

"Rostam, see if you can do better," Reza sighed, turning away from the crestfallen Junayd.

"Ignore everything and everyone and focus all your attention on the target, like staring down a tunnel," Talon said by way of encouragement. They watched as the boy concentrated all his attention on the process, and off-winged an arrow to land high on the chest of his target.

"That's better," Reza said grudgingly. "See if you can match that, Junayd!" he said over his shoulder and turned back to the discussion with Talon.

His students, including Rostam, knew what a perfectionist Reza was, so they gave all they had to the task at hand. Soon there was a dense groups of arrows clustered around the center markings.

"Yes, and before the emperor comes back. It puts Pantoleon right where he wants to be, but we need to keep our spies alive in the meantime," Talon remarked thoughtfully, continuing their discussion.

"What set Malakis against her?" Reza asked.

"From what little the message told me she has been humping her slave or some such thing."

Reza snorted with amusement. "So now you have to go down there and save her worthless hide."

"You have to admit that having a spy in the emperor's bed chamber is really quite a coup."

"I agree, but it's going to be harder to get into that place now that the ship has been compromised," Reza pointed out.

Their students stepped aside as Talon set an arrow to his bow and casually loosed the shaft, which described a shallow arc and landed right in the middle of the dark patch on the second target.

Reza followed suit and his target was soon sporting an arrow dead center. "Focus!" he said loudly and stepped away to let the awed boys get going.

"I'll go by horse and get over the walls," Talon said.

"Aren't you getting just a little old to be climbing walls,?" Reza teased.

"I'll have Maymun climb them and throw down a rope. I hope he is as well trained as you brag he is, or we will still be there in the morning trying to get in, what with me being too old and suchlike."

"You should take Junayd with you as well, just in case there is trouble. I'd feel better for it; he's a good lad and doing well. When do you leave?"

"I should leave tonight but I, we, are hosting a feast with the village elders. It would be very rude to not be there, so Famagusta will have to wait one more day."

Reza sighed. Events like this bored him. They tended to drag on and there was too much speech making for his liking.

"This is all about owning a castle, Brother," Talon remonstrated with him, knowing what he was thinking. "At least that is what Max keeps telling me. He says that there are numerous responsibilities attached to being Lord, and by God I am finding that out every day."

"I'd prefer to be out in the hills, hunting and checking the lay of the land. You seem to be spending half your life dealing with either the mine or their crops and... their woes," Reza remarked.

Talon gave a rueful nod. He knew it, and he wasn't getting much sleep either. His daughter Fariba seemed to be a restless child, crying and keeping everyone awake half the night, despite the help of Theodora, who gave her tiny drops of a calming fluid. Rav'an was tired and irritable, although she tried not to be. Jannat was due any day now, and the women were often in a tight little huddle which excluded their menfolk.

"On that note, you can't go hunting tomorrow, for the elders will expect one of us to go to their villages and be shown their improvements, paid for with our coin, and their readiness for winter. The new olive grind-stone arrived from Paphos the other day and is to be installed and demonstrated. The mine needs to be inspected as well. That, my Brother, is the duty of the Lord of the castle. Of which you are one!"

"Arrgg!" Reza exclaimed. "Can I take Rostam with me?" He winked at the boy, who grinned, but nearly missed the target with his next arrow. He sent a chagrined glance at his father, who merely said, "If I was relying upon you for dinner I suspect I would go hungry. As your uncle says all the time, focus, my son." Then he nodded. "Of course he needs to get out and meet those people. Take Palladius with you as a bodyguard." Reza shot him an incredulous look.

"He would scare a dragon half to death if he smiled at it, so pretend he is your bodyguard."

Reza snorted with laughter.

"Look, here comes Max." Talon pointed off to their right, to where Max had exited the gates of the castle and was strolling unhurriedly towards them.

"Hello Max," they both called. He waved, then joined them and stood for a moment watching the young men practicing. He breathed in the cool evening air with a sigh of contentment.

"Your cough seems to have gone away," Talon remarked.

"Hello, Talon, Reza. Yes, our physician is a marvel!"

Talon and Reza exchanged an amused look.

"Those two are really very good, and Rostam seems to have the knack of it too," Max said, indicating the eager young archers.

"Humph. They could all be better," Reza grumbled.

Max ignored the comment. "What plots are you two hatching this evening? It's going to rain soon," he added as an afterthought.

"Talon has to go to Famagusta tomorrow, trouble at the palace," Reza said. "Woman in trouble." he grinned at his brother.

"There seems to be a lot going on down there," Max remarked. "Why so soon after the last event? Isn't it risky?"

"The emperor's fellow, Malakis, is threatening one of our spies and it's become serious enough for Dimitri to call for help," Talon told him.

"Well, just be careful, Talon. That is a pit of trouble."

"How is Guy faring?" Talon asked to change the subject.

"I've just come from visiting him. That Theo is remarkable," Max stated, his stern expression softening. "Guy has his voice back and is letting everyone know about it. Wants to climb out of bed and go sailing again. Theodora told him that she's coming to see you about chaining him to the wall. But old Simon is sick. He's picked up a chill from somewhere and Theo has put him to bed in her infirmary."

"It's not serious, is it?" Everyone liked the old Templar Sergeant, but it was clear to all that old age was taking its toll.

"His last days in Acre didn't do him much good. Theo wants to keep him under her eye."

"We need to keep him in this winter; it's getting too cold for him to be pottering about in the garden," Talon said. "That goes for you too, Max."

Max nodded agreement. "I wanted to talk to you about another matter, Talon."

"I'll go," said Reza, shifting.

"No, stay please, Reza; it affects us all, one way or another."

Reza dismissed the boys, and the two men turned their attention to Max.

"What is it, Max?" Talon asked, concern in his voice.

"We have a castle, villages and people who seem to be more happy and contented than formerly, Talon. But... "

"But what, Max?" Reza asked him.

"Some of the soldiers and the villagers are pious people, Reza. Their lives revolve around their faith. They have been asking me about a priest. We don't have one, and they have been afraid to ask why.... "

Reza and Talon exchanged glances. They and their families still practiced prayers, but very discreetly. This had become habit over many years. Neither had given much thought to the subject of a Christian priest in their midst, even though there was a very small but beautifully constructed Greek chapel within the castle walls. Talon now found himself on the horns of a dilemma.

He hedged. "Why don't they just go to the chapel and pray there?"

"The chapel is a good place, but they were wondering if it would be possible for a priest to come from time to time and hold a service?"

"What did they do before, under that Doukas man?" Talon asked.

"According to Palladius, he flogged the man who had the temerity to ask."

Talon just shook his head. "They should not be afraid to ask."

"You are a Templar, Max, or were until they jailed you. Why would you not be able to give them a service?" Reza asked.

Max raised his bushy eyebrows in acknowledgement but said, "I am not of the Greek church, Reza. I am from the Roman church, and there are schisms that cannot be crossed for this kind of thing. I cannot hold a service for them."

Again Talon and Reza looked at one another; they knew only too well about schisms within religions: the Sunni, Shia and Ismaili to name but a few.

"What about the villagers themselves? Is there no one who could fill the role down there? They would be welcomed here at the chapel," Talon asked Max.

"I asked that very question, Talon. They said no, but that they knew of a priest in Kyrenia who might be persuaded to come if we sent an escort."

"And you think that would be a good idea?"

"It would also be a good idea if you two attended," Max murmured. "God is a part of these people's lives, he is all around them. Both of you are considered to be magicians, which is dangerous, but the villagers appreciate that you protect them from worse dangers. But to be thought of as Godless too would not be a good thing."

They nodded reluctantly. Although Max was not particularly pious, he held to the standards that the Templar society had instilled in him, and he was giving out good advice. It behooved them to pay attention.

"I am going to the cathedral on this visit. I shall enlist help from Dimitri," Talon told his friends. They talked for a while longer, then Talon left to find Rav'an and tell her of his impending departure.

The entry to the city was, if anything, easier than getting into Acre. Talon wondered to himself as he climbed the wall and slipped over the parapet how it was that no one had decided to take the city for themselves. The sentry nearest to him was fast asleep about ten paces away, sitting on the floor of the walkway and leaning back against the parapet.

He dropped the rope to his two escorts and they appeared on top of the wall soon after. They both noticed the sleeping sentry but Talon put a finger to his lips and they said not a word. Talon then indicated to Maymun to lead the way back down the inside of the walls towards Dimitri's villa. The only sentries they wanted to test that night were those of Dimitri, whom they found awake but unable to detect the three shadows that suddenly appeared at their elbows. Once they had overcome their fright, one of the men went off to wake Dimitri.

He arrived in the kitchen looking rumpled and tired. It had been a busy week with little sleep for him, but he greeted Talon with an embrace and a friendly nod to the others.

They got down to business quickly. The visit would have to take place the following night in the early hours when most sentries and guards were at their slowest. The cook, according to Dimitri, was very happy that he was finally able to provide some assistance and would leave the door unlocked that led from the outer garden to the inner gardens, hence into the palace itself. Once inside, they would follow his directions to the chambers belonging to Malakis.

"There is something else, Talon," Dimitri said. He sounded hesitant.

"What is it?"

"All day yesterday the palace was in an uproar. I think one of the ladies at the palace has been murdered."

"Murdered, you say?" Talon asked, surprised, "Do you know who it was and why?"

Dimitri could only say, "I suspect it was the one that denounced Tamura. She died under very suspicious circumstances: the rumors are saying poison."

"This complicates things," Talon mused. "Everyone will be jittery and wide awake. Not a good moment for a night visit. This Tamura must be a dangerous person to cross."

Dimitri shrugged. "You're right of course, Talon, but I heard that the emperor is likely to arrive the day after tomorrow. There is no time left."

Talon cursed himself for not having come a day earlier. "Then we have no choice. We must go in and take care of the problem."

"You mean to, er, deal with him?" Dimitri had known this was the objective, but still he was somewhat awed by the cool deliberate attitude Talon presented.

His leader nodded. "And I want a small group to be ready to create a diversion if needed at a certain time, so that we can leave without attracting any attention." He explained what he wanted.

In the early hours of the morning, a slim figure in loose dark clothing climbed the wall of one of the neighboring buildings with relative ease, then from his crouched position observed the walls of the palace only a few long paces away. Famagusta, by virtue of its defensive walls, was a cramped city, and although the palace was separated from the grubby citizenry by its own walls, the space between was not great. It was certainly not an obstacle to the man crouched on the edge of the tiled roof beneath the parapet of the palace wall. He was waiting to see when the sentries would pass by, then he would gain entrance.

The night was quiet except for the barking of a dog, which although distant seemed never to stop. It was finally quelled by a yell, followed by a yelp as a missile found its mark, and then silence. The humanity of the city was slumbering under a cold clear night that was ablaze with stars. The intruder glanced up at the offending sky with a shake of his head. Cloud covering and no light were his best friends at times like this, but there was a time constraint and he had no options; he had to get into the palace.

A sentry did eventually slouch by, yawning and grumbling he dragged his spear behind him while he munched on some bread. He left a smell of garlic behind as he disappeared into a doorway that led down to the inner courtyard. As he rose from his prone position the figure's nose twitched at the sharp smell drifting his way. He tossed a grapple carefully over the palace wall just above him. It landed with a clink of metal on stone; he tugged it hard to make sure it was secure. With no further hesitation he took the rope and allowed it to swing him down a short distance to land with both feet on the wall; agile as a monkey, he hauled himself up the rope and tipped himself over the wall to slide down onto his belly and listen.

No sounds from anywhere. He disengaged the grapple and wedged it in a much less obvious place for a quick retrieval, coiled the rope and placed it in deep shadow, then began to trot silently along the same walkway that the sentry had just followed.

The emperor's abode was old, consisting of a rambling set of tall and low buildings cobbled together whenever someone decided to add a new structure. Hence it was not clear to the intruder exactly where he should go to gain entrance. However, sounds and candle lights in guard houses were sufficient to bring him to some likely entrance points. He suddenly froze. A low, guttural sound below and to his right about twenty paces away alerted him to the presence of others that were wide awake in the night.

His eyes swiftly searched the gardens below him. He was perched on the ridge of a tiled roof, and however carefully he went, the tiles make small cracking sounds when weight was placed upon them. Some sound must have alerted whatever lived in the large compound below. His eyes widened as he made out the forms of not one but two large shadows that were prowling, tails lashing. Both animals were looking up directly at him.

Despite the fact that they were imprisoned within the compound and the iron gate was secure, he still felt their menace and a cold chill went down his spine. In the starlight he could clearly see their yellow eyes fixed upon him and their distinctive spots: these were the emperor's hunting leopards! But the animals did nothing beyond gaze at him balefully with that unnerving stare and pace about restlessly, so taking a deep breath he continued along the ridge of the roof until he came to a balcony overlooking the wider gardens and climbed down onto this more secure perch.

He checked his weapons: a light cross bow was strapped to his back, his long dagger was secured to his belt—all he needed for what he had in mind. Several shuttered windows opened onto the balcony, and in less time than the span of several breaths he was inside the palace. His search took him past the living quarters of the women and their eunuchs, who were fast asleep, down to the ground floor, where he stopped to listen.

There were noises coming from below, where kitchens, cellars and perhaps the dungeons would be located. The sounds coming from below were those of singing. He shook his head in the dark and began to look for a way down. It was not long before he was in the kitchens, replete with the smells of spices, roasted meats, and olive oil. All was quiet except for the snores of several people at the far end who lived and worked in the kitchen. None of them knew of his arrival nor departure.

The loud talk and the bellowed singing came from the top of a narrow stairway that led downstairs from the kitchens; the cooler storerooms would be there. Like a phantom he glided down the stairs with his cross bow held ready in his left hand for quick use.

Just ahead of him was a dim light, and now he could make out the clear sound of loud voices and the dull clink of metal drinking cups.

He peered around the doorway to see two large men seated on stools at a rough wooden table, on which were the remains of a lavish meal. Chicken bones, the remains of a ravaged leg of lamb, and breadcrumbs were visible on copper plates. One man had his back to the intruder, while the other was staring into his cup.

"Last time we do this for a while," the far one slurred. "The Emp... Emperor is back tomorrow and we've got to be'ave."

"Damn him and his whore! When I've finished with her and that arse from Constant... Constantinople I'll have him eating out of my hand again. Then we can deal with that other fella!" This came from the man with his back to the intruder.

There was no doubt in the intruder's mind: this was his target, Malakis. The other would have to go too. No witnesses. He began to raise his bow to shoot the man facing him, another quarrel held in his left hand that supported the cross bow. Just as he was taking aim the man facing him stood up and abruptly left. He walked off into the darkness and the intruder could hear him urinating. A cry of protest came from that direction as he did so.

"Shut your mouth or I'll come in there and piss in your mouth, you scum!" the man shouted in the darkness. The protests died down. Before the other man came back Malakis lurched to his feet. "Need to go to bed, Emperor's back tomorrow. Got to look fine, keep my wits about me. Hey, Skleros! I'm going to bed. Send Asanes to me in the morning, not before noon!"

Staggering, he turned towards the doorway where the assassin was standing. Malakis, despite his foggy head and almost crossed eyes, became aware of the figure in front of him just in time to croak a warning and to raise his arm. His eyes widened with realization just as his killer shot him at close range with a bolt. It took Malakis in mid chest, knocking him backwards to fall across the table with a loud crash that echoed around the chamber. His large frame threw food and drinking vessels in all directions to land with clanks and clatters, and one stool broke as he fell across it. Malakis was dead when his body finally slid to the floor with a thump, a surprised expression still fixed on his face.

Skleros was either too drunk to move, or he disliked the sounds he heard, for he stayed where he was and shouted, "Malakis! What's happening? Tell me!"

The assassin hurriedly hauled the string back on his cross bow and slipped his spare bolt in place ready to deal with Skleros. In the semi-darkness of guttering candlelight that threw flickering, moving shadows onto the walls, the assassin became aware that he was not alone. He shot a hurried glance behind him and thought he saw a more tangible shadow slip out of sight, but it was very difficult to see. Nonetheless, his instincts were screaming at him to leave now before he himself became a victim.

Casting one last look in the direction of Skleros, he turned away and slipped back along the corridor, glancing uneasily behind him, then headed for his escape route.

Talon and Maymun huddled in the darkness of the corridor. They had only arrived themselves, in time to hear the crash of Malakis falling over backwards onto the table. Talon saw the assassin just as the slim dark figure reloaded and prepared to take out someone else. At that moment the figure must have had the instinct to feel that he was not alone. He turned but Talon ducked out of sight. The assassin seemed to decide to depart abruptly, leaving his other victim unmolested.

Moments later, Skleros called out again, and in the ensuing silence he crept out of the darkness with his sword drawn. He gasped when he saw the wreckage and the body lying on the flagstones. "Malakis!" he called out, and stepped forward. "Murder! God help us, murder!" he roared to the world to large.

Before Talon or Maymun could react, he charged, bellowing at the top of his voice, right past them. He brushed by Talon, who was plastered to the wall with Maymun next to him, without heeding them. The temptation to kill him occurred to Talon, but this man had not been their target, and besides, the alarm was already raised. It was time to leave, but not by the way they had arrived.

"Come on, we'll follow that other man," Talon whispered as they listened to Skleros roaring out the alarm as he laboriously climbed the stairs to the palace ground floor. He stumbled once but never stopped yelling.

They ran as fast as they dared along the short corridor to the area where they found the storerooms. Talon could see in the dim light ahead a figure slipping out of sight up the wooden steps leading to the ground floor. "That way!" he whispered urgently.

By now the servants who slept in the storerooms had been wakened by the noise and were sitting up rubbing their eyes. As Talon and Maymun emerged from the cellars into the kitchen, they were confronted by a big bleary-eyed cook who recklessly decided to try and stop Talon. Reaching out to his right, Talon grabbed the handle of a large copper pot off the rack and swung it hard onto the man's head. The pot gave out a satisfying clang as it came into contact with his skull, and the man collapsed in a heap.

Leaping over the prostrate man they chased after their quarry, who by now had departed the cluttered kitchen. Another big man began to blunder into their path and reached for Maymun, even managing to grasp his sleeve, but Maymun snatched up a heavy copper ladle and chopped up and down rapidly on the clutching arm. The burly figure cried out at the pain then fell aside, clutching his arm. The two scuttled up the stairs. The figure was racing up yet another flight of steps, so they followed.

The chase took them right up to the top of the two-storied building and out onto the roof. Climbing out onto the tiles, Talon saw his quarry sprinting lightly along the ridge of the building, moving very rapidly, glancing back from time to time. Then he spun about and Talon could see he was pointing a crossbow at them.

"Down!" he exclaimed. Both he and Maymun jumped down and ducked below the level of the tiles as a quarrel rattled the tiles between them. Talon shook his head. There would not be another chance. He leapt to the roof, unslung his bow and knocked an arrow. He could just see the figure running away. Bracing his feet wide, Talon took aim. In the clear light of the stars his target stood out as a dark silhouette at twenty-five paces.

The bow twanged and an arrow sped to thump hard into the back of his victim. With a squawk, the figure threw its arms into the air, then stumbled and fell to its knees before slowly toppling over to its left side and sliding down the tiled roof, dislodging tiles as it rolled over and over. With one last cry the figure fell over the edge of the roof down into a compound below. What Talon saw then turned his blood cold. Two large cats leapt out of the dark shadows and pounced onto the man, who was still just alive when he landed. With snarls and fearsome growls the two cats set upon the body which ceased to twitch as they rent it. Because it no longer moved, and all the fun having gone out of the kill, the two cats sat back on their haunches and contemplated their uninvited supper.

Wide-eyed with surprise, Talon shook his head. What was it about tyrants that moved them to keep such deadly animals? This was not the first time he had encountered ferocious, oversized cats. Sounds of alarm jolted him back to the present. Guards were running along the walls to their front, many of them carrying torches; there was no escape there, even if the assassin had come in that way.

Then someone looked in their direction: in the starlit night they could be clearly seen.

"Over there!" he yelled, pointing, and another guard hurled a torch towards them. It arced through the night and fell with a thump and shower of sparks on the roof, then rolled away to sputter out before falling over the edge.

"What is it?" another demanded.

"I saw someone on that roof over there!" the first person called.

"Get up there with the archers! Take them down!" shouted someone in authority.

Arrows began to whisper past them, some clattering onto the tiles; clearly this was not a way out anymore. Talon glanced down at the garden. "Hurry! We have to get back into the gardens and out through that gate!" He pointed to the dark cave of shrubbery that led to the doorway. They made their descent using the thick vines of wisteria which covered the interior garden walls. Then they had to run across the lawns between the shrubs.

By now the entire palace was wide awake and men were swarming along the pathways carrying torches, their light flickering off the soldiers' armor and helmets. Lights were even showing in the windows above the garden, as the resident women woke up to the alarms and frightened eunuchs lit candles. All the attention for the moment was concentrated on the roofs, where several men were now unsteadily pacing, trying to keep their balance while holding torches high in the air.

"Nobody here!" one called back, and promptly slipped and fell, sliding to the very edge of the roof. "Oh God, protect me!" he wailed as he looked down saw the big cats, which stared up at him with their large yellow eyes. Things had become very interesting for the leopards this starry night. The terrified man hung onto the ridge for life itself.

"The cats have got something down there with them," another one said, peering downward. "Looks like a body!"

It would be only a very short time before someone decided to investigate the bushes and shrubs of the garden. Indeed, Talon noticed several servants appear at the doorway of the building that led out onto the terrace overlooking the gardens. They too carried torches with them. There was no time to lose.

A reckless idea occurred to him. "Stay here, Maymun, but be ready!" he said, and he darted out of his dark refuge and made for the gates to the cats' compound. With a sigh of relief he noticed that it was heavily barred but not locked. He shifted the heavy bars out of the way and pulled the gates wide open. The leopards were still too preoccupied with the tantalizing activity on the roof above them to notice what Talon had done, but he was sure they soon would.

He turned and raced past Maymun. "Come along, Maymun, unless you want to be their second course!" he called in a hoarse whisper as he charged past, his arms and legs pumping him towards the doorway set into the wall. Maymun needed no further persuasion. "Dear God help us!" he muttered to himself as he chased after his leader as though the devil himself was after him.

"There they go! They're getting away! Stop them!" a guard shouted. A couple of bolts from crossbows snapped into the grass behind the two fleeing figures. The shouts intensified from the grounds as servants noticed the running pair; they had not yet noticed the open gates of the compound.

They were pointing and calling when someone noticed the two cats cautiously leaving their home. With a shriek of alarm a servant woman pointed at them, initiating a stampeding panic as others noticed the cats. Both animals, being unable to resist a fleeing creature of any kind, promptly decided to enjoy themselves and galloped after the servants as they fled into the palace itself.

Unnoticed by the cats, Talon and Maymun fled in the opposite direction pursued by flying bolts, arrows and curses from frustrated archers on the distant walls. If they could just get past that gate they could easily evade the sentries on the other side. A spent bolt chipped the stone wall as they dived through the gate and drew it closed. As they leaned against the wall panting, they heard a satisfying scream from the direction of the palace buildings.

"I think the leopards must have decided to go and investigate the rest of the palace. I hope that lady Tamura has the wits to keep to her rooms tonight," Talon panted.

Maymun gave a huff of alarm as they turned to head for the outer walls. A squad of spearmen were running towards them. "Inside here," he whispered to Talon, and vanished into the dense shrubbery nearby. Talon wasted no time joining him; they crouched, waiting and holding their breath as the soldiers rushed up to halt at the door.

"Are you sure that you saw someone here?" one asked.

"Certain of it, Sergeant. They must have gone inside," said another.

"Check the door in case it's unlocked," came the command.

There was a rattle close by and a muttered curse. "Damn me! It's not locked. Whoever they are, they must have slipped inside."

"I'm sure I heard a scream, Sergeant," another said.

"We've got them trapped if they did go in. Check the bushes first, and then we'll go in."

Just at that moment they heard urgent shouting on the other side of the closed door. There were shouts of fear and alarm, then more screams.

"Come on, something's going on in there. We've got to help! You two stay here and guard the door in case they slip past us, the rest of you follow me." The door was slammed open and the squad rushed through the entrance.

Two men remained at the open doorway, but they were so distracted by the bedlam in the gardens that they didn't see the two shadows detach themselves from the bushes nearby and lope across the intervening space between the inner and outer walls. Neither did they see the figures slip over the parapet of the outer wall and disappear into the streets of the city.

Inside the palace its inhabitants woke to widespread panic. The distant shrieks and yells woke Asanes from a drunken stupor where he lay in a small windowless chamber near the kitchens. The first thing he knew was a banging on his door, then one of the kitchen servants rushed in, shouting that they were under attack.

He woke up properly then and seized his sword, swung it about, cursed his headache, and sallied forth to run into a frenzied crowd of palace servants and eunuchs rushing about in all directions.

"Assassins!" some screamed. "Bandits!" others took up the cry. "The Arabs are here!" "Leopards!" yelled other terror-stricken people as they scrambled away from one or the other of these fearsome threats. He shook his head and cursed again.

"Where?" he roared, and then caught himself. His head threatened to fall off if he did that again.

One of the eunuchs paused long enough to cry, "It's the leopards, they are here!"

Asanes seized him by the throat. "Where? Tell me, or by your severed manhood I'll wring your neck!" he croaked.

"Somewhere," the eunuch struggled free and fled after the crowd. Asanes wiped his face as he watched their retreating backs. The leopards? How by the saint's bollocks did they get free? He needed to find Malakis or Skleros; they had been drinking downstairs the last time he had heard from them.

He made his way down to the cellars and found the corpse of Malakis lying amid the wreckage of his last meal. A serpent of fear began to uncoil in his stomach and drops of greasy sweat started to roll down his face. Hastily he retreated back up the stairs.

Asanes was just about to charge into the main hallway when he saw one of the leopards stalking a trembling slave, who cowered in a corner, moaning and feebly waving it away.

"Oooer," Asanes exclaimed to himself as he hastily retreated out of sight. So the cats had escaped! How in hell had that happened? He would be talking to their keepers, who might find themselves being fed to their animals once the emperor had finished with them.

Asanes left the luckless slave to his fate and went in search of more men. He came across Skleros and a contingent of men coming into the back entrance of the women's wing from the gardens.

"What the hell is going on?" Asanes roared. His head didn't fall off, although he resisted the temptation to hold it in place.

"We had an assassin's visit and Malakis was killed," Skleros began.

"I know that!" Asanes croaked. "What are the leopards doing in the palace?"

"I don't Goddam well know, and if you would stop interrupting me perhaps I can tell you more about Malakis!" Skleros was obviously very upset.

The two men were large and almost the same height. By this time they were almost nose to beaky nose as they asserted themselves. Neither liked the other, but under Malakis they had just managed to get along. Now that he was dead it seemed the right time to settle scores. Oblivious of their own astonished men and the chaos going on around them, the two large half-wits faced off.

With angry snarls they reached for each other's windpipes at exactly the same time and then grappled, locked in mortal combat, each trying to throttle the other, their fingers twitching like huge hairy tarantulas fumbling for a better hold on their necks. They swayed slightly, their teeth bared in a rictus of rage, their eyes beginning to bulge as the pressure grew. They were just about to strangle one another when a high-pitched voice interrupted their deadly preoccupation.

"Stop this! What in God's name are you two doing? There are assassins killing everyone and leopards running loose eating people inside the palace! If you don't do something about it I shall report both of you to the emperor who will be here *today*!" Diocles shouted at the top of his voice. He turned to the squad leader, who was standing behind Skleros wearing a bewildered look on his face, and said in a calmer voice.

"Sergeant, round up all the men who are not currently on the walls. Find the keepers and get those leopards back in their damned cage. At once! Leave some men for our protection." The sergeant saluted and told his men to follow him, leaving two chastened giants behind.

As the antagonists drew reluctantly apart, glaring malevolently at one another, Diocles stated, "You two will settle down, and you, Skleros, will tell us all you know." He looked around the room apprehensively for any sign of a lurking cat.

The leopards were otherwise occupied. They had parted ways, the one to torment the poor slave who was nearly dead from a heart attack as the leopard played "hook the mouse" with him; the other had discovered the stairway. This lead to interesting places and it had gone upstairs, where he had wandered about the wide corridors terrorizing the occupants of the women's quarters. Most of the women at first sight of the pacing animal prudently dived back into their rooms, slamming and locking their doors. Then they sought out their deepest darkest cupboards, where they joined the cowering eunuchs who were already there. They all wept, clutching at one another in stark terror, waiting to be devoured.

Tamura had not been so lucky. Siranus had been in the corridor when the leopard appeared at the head of the stairs, and he came rushing in to find her already awake but still in bed. "The leopard!" he quavered.

"What about the leopard?" she asked, puzzled, giving him one of those looks that said, "Idiot".

"It's... it's here!" he said. His face was ashen and he was wringing his hands.

"Of course it's here, you fool. It belongs to the emperor. Oh my God!" she exclaimed as the door was nudged open by a large spotted head with big yellow eyes and huge teeth. The animal slid into the room and looked around as it sniffed the air, its mouth slightly open

421

displaying long white fangs, then it moved deeper into the room. Ignoring Siranus, who had shit himself as he fainted to the floor, the animal padded slowly and silently towards Tamura, who was on the bed watching it with wide open eyes.

"Dear God, I'm so very sorry for what I did to Gabriella. Please forgive me!" she pleaded in a whisper. "I'll *never* do it again, I swear on all that is holy, just... just don't let it hurt me!" she gave off a pitiful little wail.

She had pulled the bed clothes up to her chin as though that might somehow protect her. Frozen in place, she stared with wide fearful eyes at the animal as it came closer, its tail lashing from side to side, its yellow eyes fixed upon her with a glare that petrified her soul. Summoning all her will power, Tamura said in a cracked voice,

"Go! Get away. Go away!" Her heart was beating so fast she thought it would burst out of her chest. The great cat rumbled deep in its throat and continued to move closer. Again it sniffed the air with its mouth slightly open, as though it was assessing the scent it had traced to her bed. It didn't threaten her other than by its mere presence.

They observed one another from a distance of no more than three paces, the one warily, while the other seemed to be frowning in puzzlement, a snarl hovering on its muzzle. Then they both heard the noise of many men rushing up the stairs. The moment was gone and the animal, with a growl of anger, spun around and vanished out of the half-open door in a flash. It was as though it had never been in the room, but Tamura felt as though it left a presence nonetheless. Her heart in her mouth, she dived out of bed and ran to the door to slam it shut, just as armed men arrived led by Asanes. He paused to hold the door open and looked her over. His eyes roamed her from head to foot.

"Did you see the leopard?" he demanded. His men ogled her too, she was only dressed in her flimsy night robe, which did little to hide her charms.

"Yes, it went that way," she told him with a haughty look, holding her scanty robe tightly about her. She pointed down the corridor in the direction it had fled.

He leered at her. "Busy having it away with that floppy prick, were you?" he asked with a nasty leer, nodding towards the prone Siranus, but he was gone with his men before she could react.

Eyes blazing with rage she glared after their departing figures. Perhaps she would take care of *one* more person before she stopped doing bad things, she thought to herself. She would clear it with God later. She stepped back inside the room, slammed the door and slid the bar into place.

She went over to Siranus, who was slowly coming to and sitting up. She slapped him to get his attention. "Get up, you stinky thing, and get cleaned up," she told him. "I can't believe you fainted at the sight of a mere leopard, for God's sake!"

He groaned and wept, "I'm sorry my Lady. I, I was just so afraid!"

"Be quiet and listen carefully. I want a snake. A very special kind of snake."

Talon and Maymun arrived out of breath at the gates of Dimitri's small villa. They were admitted by a jittery follower and shown into the kitchen where Dimitri sat at the table. He had been drinking some powerful arak and looked very nervous.

He leapt to his feet when he saw them. "Thank God Almighty you are safe!. I have not slept a wink! This spy business is *killing* me!" he told them, and pushed two small cups towards them. "I've even been praying! Can you imagine that? How did it go?" he asked, as he poured the fierce liquid into their glasses and refilled his own.

"It didn't," Talon said, as he downed his drink in one go. He winced. "What *is* that stuff?"

Maymun followed suit, then spent the next minute trying to breathe as it burned its way down his throat and its vapors filled his lungs. Dimitri smacked the boy on his back to help him to get over the experience, even as he cast apprehensive looks at Talon.

"What happened, for God's sake?" he asked. Junayd was there, looking disappointed that he had not been part of the expedition.

"Someone was there before us and took care of him. Then all hell broke loose... everywhere! "

Maymun coughed, then laughed, and coughed again, "That's because Master Talon let the leopards out of their cage and they were rampaging all over the gardens as we escaped," he spluttered.

"Dear Jesus protect us!" Dimitri groaned. Junayd snorted with laughter, looking incredulous. "Why did you do a crazy thing like that?" Dimitri demanded.

"Because the other man left a witness behind who raised the alarm and we were unable to get away. Useful creatures, those. Perhaps I'll get a couple for our place."

They were guarded by the eunuchs of the Emperor's court
Who dallied with the concubines, until they were caught,
Then their heads were toppled by a sharp steel blade
And buried in the field where their sisters were laid.
—David Lewis Paget

Chapter 32
An Unlikely Alliance

The emperor and his extensive entourage arrived at the gates of Famagusta in the early afternoon. Trumpets announced his arrival to the city at large and he was met by Asanes and the captain of the guard, who presented a colorful honor guard.

Isaac, who was fond of pomp and ceremony, rode his favorite white horse bedecked in silver and gold trappings through the gates as though he had come back from a triumph, and acknowledged the guard with a casual wave of his scepter. The two young men leading his horse were dressed in green hunting tights, their athletic chests adorned with tight ornate doublets sewn with silver thread, and they sported green caps with long peacock feathers on their carefully coifed hair. The trumpets blared and the pipes shrieked and wailed as the warriors followed the emperor into the city. They were immaculate in polished armor that gleamed in the weak sunlight of mid-winter and rode beautiful horses that had been groomed to perfection.

While the parade was impressive, it was significant that few of the citizens of Famagusta were there to greet their lord and master. His departures and arrivals were no longer an event of any real interest to them. This did nothing to improve his mood when he surveyed the meagre crowd that gave half-hearted cheers and even some distant jeers when he rode through the gates.

Pantoleon, not to be outdone by a petty emperor, was also mounted on a striking horse, but his was gray—a beautiful animal, spirited and high-stepping. Pantoleon himself was clad in armor that matched the mercenaries in bronze shine. His bodyguard stayed close.

Neither man had had a very successful journey to Paphos and back.

Isaac had missed a chance to capture an elusive ship that kept coming and going, seemingly at will, from the Paphos. There was rumor that it belonged to Sir Talon, that cursed magician on the mountain, of whom people talked in hushed tones. Worse, the pickings had become less bountiful, because merchants now knew of his approaches. Their daughters and even their wives were conspicuous by their absence whenever he arrived in a town. He had regretted not taking Tamura with him from the day he arrived in Larnaca and had to make do with ugly wenches his servants had dug out of some midden.

His other discontent was his growing concern that Pantoleon was superior in every way to him in intelligence. After losing four games in a row of chess, the emperor had kicked the board over and they had not played again, even when Pantoleon had promised earnestly that he would lose every game thereafter. Isaac was beginning to wish that he had killed him the first day and then plundered his house for his treasure.

Pantoleon for his part was utterly disaffected with this troll of a petty tyrant and had watched with almost unconcealed disgust as he used every pretext to steal money from the very people he needed to further the wealth of his island. Knowing that his future and perhaps his life depended upon being at the emperor's command, he had tried to advise Isaac tactfully when his actions regarding some issue were idiotic and counter-productive.

Pantoleon felt that he had failed dismally and so was very angry. He contemplated leaving this pitiful island to its disagreeable ogre and finding somewhere else to live. The very first thing he resolved to do was to load his treasure onto his ship and make sure it was able to leave at a moment's notice. Pantoleon did not wish to lose his hard-won wealth. At least he could rely upon Gabros, who was visible among the cavalry drawn up to greet them.

Looking around his retinue and the honor guard, Isaac noticed something else. "Where is Malakis?" he demanded, his tone truculent. "He knows very well that he should be here to greet me," his voice was loud as he addressed the captain of the guard and Asanes, who both looked apprehensive. "I shall punish him!" he threatened, raising his voice, his eyes bulging with anger at this slight.

"Um, er, Your Highness he is... er, he is dead," Asanes finally stated in a very low tone to the emperor. Pantoleon heard him, however, and shot a look of enquiry at Gabros, who gave him a warning look. Pantoleon noted with surprise that Gabros was wearing a bandage over his left ear.

"What's that? Dead? How can he be?" Isaac demanded, looking unsettled.

"My Lord, Your Highness, may we please escort you to the palace, and there we will make a full report," the frightened captain of the guard begged him.

"Yes, yes, all right," Isaac said, sounding uncertain. He allowed himself to be led off. Commands were shouted and men were dismissed. Pantoleon decided he was not wanted by the emperor, and although he was consumed with curiosity, he sidled up to Gabros and together they rode off .

"I will tell all when we get to the villa, Lord. The streets are crawling with spies," Gabros said out of the corner of his mouth.

It was a relief to Pantoleon to return to his luxurious living chambers and divest himself of the heavy armor. After taking wine and food he demanded, "What in God's name is going on?"

When an exhausted and very nervous-looking Gabros had finished his unadorned version of events and Pantoleon had calmed down enough from wanting to kill him with his own hands, he thought about what had actually occurred.

"What is this about thunderbolts flying through the air? You made that up, didn't you?" he demanded.

"Master, you will notice that we are short of several men. I am not lying about the thunderbolts. One of their shards took off a portion of my ear!" Gabros touched the bandage.

Pantoleon's look said he was unconvinced.

"I swear to you and before God that they were killed by the thunderbolts from the castle. It is only because of God's mercy that I am alive right now to tell you of that awful event," Gabros insisted.

Pantoleon shook his head and muttered, "Impossible. You are sure it was not Greek Fire?'

"No, Master. Greek Fire does not explode like a thunderclap after flying through the air from a great distance."

Pantoleon changed the direction of the conversation. "So you have not heard from Nestos, but Malakis is dead?" This might mean an opportunity, he mused to himself.

"That pig Asanes didn't want to say so, but he couldn't lie to the emperor. I only found out when you did, Master. I waited for Nestos near the wall where he went over, but he never came back, and when the guards began swarming all over the place I left. I still don't know what happened, but I fear Nestos is dead or captured."

"If he is captured we have a problem," Pantoleon murmured, more to himself. He thought for a while, then he glared up at Gabros, who was shifting from one foot to the other.

"You have made an appalling mess, Gabros. I should have been able to trust you to hold things together while I was away with that idiot Isaac. But no! You lose a ship, then its captain, for God's sake, and now you don't know who killed Malakis or even if Nestos is dead! I should have you executed." His tone was soft, but there was no mistaking the menace. Gabros stayed silent and sweated.

"I don't trust this so-called emperor as far as I can toss him," Pantoleon continued. "His behavior on the trip was very revealing. Mad as a goat, thinks he is next to God in elevation, and would not hesitate to destroy us for a short term gain without thought of consequence. He issues decrees that make no sense and no one knows what to do with them. Not even his Chief minister!"

Gabros nodded. The storm was moving on and he was no longer in the center of it. He wondered how his master had fared with the emperor. He'd ask the men who'd ridden with Pantoleon later—if he still lived.

"I have no doubt that avaricious Komnenos prick will make a try for my treasure. I want it to go back onto the ship and be gone from this villa by morning. No one is to know, other than our men. Do you think you can manage that without messing up?" he asked with a curl of his lip.

Gabros nodded emphatically. "Yes, Lord, I can."

"You will stay with the treasure until I decide what to do about it and you. I hope I make myself clear?"

Gabros bowed his head again and said, "Yes, master, it shall be done; and I shall make sure that the captain will be ready to sail at all times, within a moment's notice."

Pantoleon dipped his head in agreement. Suddenly he felt uneasy in this city. Better to be safe than sorry.

At that moment there was a commotion at the main doors. One of the guards rushed in to stand at the entrance to his chamber.

"What is going on out there?" Pantoleon demanded.

"The Emperor wishes to see you, Master. The messenger from the palace said at once!" the soldier reported.

Pantoleon exchanged glances with Gabros. "Make sure that nothing goes wrong, and get started right away," he told him. "I have not even had time to bathe!" he complained. "Tell the messenger that I am on my way," he called to the soldier, who vanished thankfully back to his duties.

Pantoleon was met at the palace entrance by Diocles, who was dressed very much as a Byzantine Prime Minister should. His under-robes were of the finest blue silk, while his overcoat could match any of those of Pantoleon's, who had hurriedly changed out of his riding clothes into something more appropriate for an emperor's audience. Diocles also wore a furred turban-like hat over his graying locks to fend off the chill; he looked worn and tired from the disruptions of the night before.

They greeted one another civilly but without any warmth. Diocles was wary of Pantoleon, while Pantoleon understood that Diocles, although old, might still be useful to him because he knew every secret in the palace, and secrets were power.

"I heard that there were alarms last night?" Pantoleon probed.

"There was indeed some excitement, and as you know by now, our colleague and friend Malakis was assassinated by some diabolical killer," Diocles said, his tone noncommittal.

"Assassinated!" Pantoleon feigned astonishment. "God protect us!"

"The emperor is, has been a little indisposed this last hour. But he has recovered and is asking for you, Lord." Diocles had just witnessed another one of the infamous tantrums of his master, and while outwardly he seemed composed, he was still shaken by its intensity.

Without further words, he led the way. Pantoleon observed a large number of servants running about and much cleaning going on. There appeared to have been quite a disturbance the night before. He wondered how the emperor felt about the incident.

He was not long in finding out. Diocles ushered him past supplicants, petty nobles and merchants who had gathered like vultures to the smell of carrion. He marveled at how little time it had taken them to assemble. Their resentful looks followed him down the corridor. Soldiers admitted them to a small chamber where the emperor sat at a table, disheveled, glowering, and looking decidedly out of sorts.

The room looked as though it had been partially destroyed by a whirlwind. There were papers, food, and drink spilled on the floor, over which tearful and terrified servants still crouched with mops and rags, attempting to clean it up. Broken furniture was heaped in one corner, and the curtains were torn.

He was very careful to keep his features impassive as he bowed deeply to his new Master and waited in silence.

Isaac glanced around. "You, stop what you are doing and get out of here," he shouted. The servants scuttled out of sight, leaving Isaac, Pantoleon and Diocles alone.

"Have you any idea what has been going on here?" Isaac asked him. "I am sooo cross! It all happened last night, for God's sake!" he exclaimed in bemused wonder. "Just before we came back! My Lady Tamura is abed with the vapors. A leopard went into her room while she was there, you know."

"Er, no Sire, I didn't know. How on earth did this happen?"

Isaac continued as though he had not heard. "My Gatherer of Information was murdered in his own office by nameless assassins! Did you know that?" he demanded.

Pantoleon looked shocked. "No, Sire, I did no—"

"Stop interrupting me! There were at least three of them!" Isaac interrupted, and his voice climbed an octave. "Yes, three for sure. One was killed, so we have his body. The remains of it, at least. My pets ate a part of his face. Hah! But they tell me he was dead before then. Had an arrow in his back. The other two got away!"

"Three assassins you say, Sire?" Pantoleon was still registering this detail when the emperor spoke again. This time he sounded a little more calm.

"I have come back to my home to find bedlam. Leopards wandering all over the place eating people and assassins killing everyone else! It is disgraceful!"

"I absolutely agree, Sire. You have appointed someone to investigate this crime, I presume?"

The emperor gave him a scowl with his slightly bulging brown eyes and a turned-down mouth.

"You will be my Gatherer of Information henceforth, Exazenos, or whatever you want to call yourself. It will be you. I have no one with enough intelligence to fill the position vacated by Malakis. He was really quite bright, you know; a little impetuous, but he knew his stuff."

Pantoleon could not have disagreed more, but he held his tongue and sent a silent thank you to whomsoever had done the deed. He was now just where he wanted to be! He also sent a silent prayer of thanks to whatever deity was keeping watch over him. He dropped to one knee before the emperor.

"I would be deeply honored, Sire. I shall serve faithfully unto death. You shall not regret the honor you have bestowed upon me."

Isaac flapped his hand. "Very good. Now, I am hungry and in need of relaxation. You may leave. Take up your duties tomorrow. Diocles will help you get acquainted with our people and the staff."

Pantoleon and Diocles backed out of the chamber and walked slowly towards the palace entrance.

"I would like to be the first to congratulate you, Lord Exazenos," Diocles murmured, as they walked abreast past the still-waiting crowd. He took a gamble and continued softly, "Your predecessor was an incompetent man who really didn't understand the subtleties of his work."

"Thank you, Diocles. I must discover who committed this foul deed as one of my first priorities. Leopards and assassins running about in the palace! Not while I am in charge. I will need to talk to many people, including... " he paused delicately, "My Lady Tamura. Could that be arranged?"

Diocles nodded. "I think so, Lord. I shall clear it with His Majesty."

"Make sure that you do. I want to see her within a day or so."

"That depends upon the emperor, Lord."

Pantoleon turned on Diocles. "Do you remember what our emperor did to his former tutor when he arrived on this island?"

Diocles' throat went dry. "He cut off his feet at the ankles, Lord," he croaked.

"That's right, old man. Now if I ask you for something in the future, make sure it happens promptly, or the same thing could happen to you."

Pantoleon smiled at the ashen-faced Prime Minister and strode out of the palace.

Isaac was greeted by Tamura with enthusiasm, although there was some pouting. After they had made noisy love—with much shamming on her part—that left him gasping for air, he asked her, "Did you have a bad scare with the leopard, my Precious?"

"If you had not left me here alone in this wretched place my life would not have been in danger at all, my Lord." Her eyes were wide with innocently remembered fear as she leaned on one elbow, looking in his eyes and describing little circles on his hairy chest with her fingers.

Isaac took this to mean the visit by his leopard, but Tamura had in fact meant something else entirely. She was still getting over the incident with the leopard, but the scare that Malakis had given her had shaken her to her bones, and there was still another phase to be carried out before she would feel completely safe. Siranus had left the palace some time ago, but had not yet returned. He would be very discreet, she knew, but it would be an expensive purchase.

"I have decided to have that man Exazenos become my Chief of information," Isaac stated to change the subject.

Tamura gave a tiny sigh. Pillow talk from the emperor was where her power lay. In this instance she had guessed already; still it was reassuring to hear it firsthand.

"Oh how lovely, my King, my Lord," she cooed. She knew better than to add that she thought Pantoleon would be far superior to his dead predecessor. Isaac was so fickle that he would probably change his mind in reaction. She had a potential ally there, and she was going to use him. She went back to work on Isaac, and soon he was excited and rampant again. "I do hope the women you took to your bed were clean," she murmured from under him.

"Don't fret, my darling. They were all virgins."

She stayed with Isaac all night, but for one interval when she hastened back to her own chambers, where she found Siranus.

"Well? Did you do as I asked?" she demanded. He pointed to a basket lying on the floor near the window. She was sure that it moved slightly.

His voice trembled. "It is as you requested."

"Good. Do it tonight, while I am with the emperor," she said. "You know where it should go?"

"Yes, my Lady. I know where to put it."

Tamura almost rubbed her hands with anticipation of the demise of her final threat.

The next morning Pantoleon woke to find that yet another disturbance had occurred in the palace, and the emperor was demanding that Pantoleon present himself at the palace forthwith.

He sighed as he struggled into this clothes. "Did you carry out my orders last night?" he demanded of Gabros, who was looking haggard from lack of sleep.

"Yes, Lord. The entire treasure is now on the ship. Nigel is there and a heavy guard has been placed with him."

"Good. At least something is going the right way. I should be back before too long. It's probably yet another panic over nothing."

He arrived to find the guards and servants looking jittery and the emperor huddled in his private chambers looked rumpled and distracted.

431

"Ah, there you are, Exazenos. I should not have to keep sending for you all the time," he paused as though he was not sure what to say next.

Diocles prompted him. "The death of Skleros, your Majesty?"

"I was just about to tell him that!" Isaac said, with an impatient wave of his bejeweled hand.

"Death, Your Majesty?" Pantoleon looked his enquiry.

"Yes, Skleros died last night, most horribly. They are saying it was a snake!" Isaac even glanced around as though the creature might even be in the room with them.

"They found the snake, Sire, and killed it," Diocles murmured with a look at Pantoleon.

"Who, may I ask, is Skleros, Your Majesty?"

"He is, was, the assistant to your future assistant, Asanes, who was the assistant to Malakis, who, as you know, is now departed," Diocles said, crossing himself and glancing heavenwards.

"Ah, thank you." Pantoleon was not really the wiser for that. He had no intention of using any of the incompetents in this palace to help him along. Gabros, for all his recent mess-ups, was still his man.

Isaac's face was filling up with blood and his eyes were beginning to pop. "I want this to stop!" he shouted without warning. Diocles shifted nervously as Isaac began to work himself into one of his tantrums.

"Assassins! Leopards and snakes all over the place! People are dying everywhere. What is going on? A snake doesn't just wander into my palace; someone put it there!" he yelled. "*You*," he turned on Pantoleon, "will move into the palace. I don't want to have to keep sending messengers for you! Find out what is going on and be quick about it," his globular eyes glared at Pantoleon as though threatening him with untold horrors should he fail.

Given that people appeared to be dropping dead all over the palace, Pantoleon was not eager to take up residence, but on second thought he felt that this might suit his plan very well. Where better to gain access to the Lady Tamura and find out what was really going on in this rambling old pile of stones and tiles?

"Yes, at once, Your Majesty," he said with a smile and a low bow. "I shall see to it immediately."

"Good. We have two executions in the main square today. I want you in attendance."

"What was their crime, Sire?"

432

"Tell him, old man," Isaac said, almost as though he didn't know.

"Sacrilege. They were caught drunk and pissing against the wall of the cathedral," Diocles murmured, cocking an eye at Pantoleon.

"Perfect, Your Majesty!" Pantoleon stated with a smile. He was looking forward to some entertainment.

It had been all over the palace by dawn that one of the kitchen slaves had found Skleros dead in the grubby little chamber that had once belonged to Asanes. Apparently, the newly promoted Asanes had given his room to Skleros, who used to sleep in a cell down in the dungeons, while he moved into the chamber vacated by Malakis. The panic at this new death only abated after a particularly brave slave discovered the snake lurking in one of the darker passages below the kitchens and promptly killed it.

The snake had completed its task, but upon the wrong person. When Tamura heard the news she felt ill. She wondered how long it would take Asanes to put two and two together and come to finish her off. Even he was capable of getting that logic right.

She sat in her own chambers staring off into space, having berated Siranus savagely for the mistake. That hapless fellow was in the other room, weeping and hiding from the wrath of his mistress, alongside her maid Martina, who was on the edge of weeping with fright herself. She had never seen her mistress so angry before.

It was in the early afternoon when Asanes came knocking. He had waited until the emperor had gone off with his new Gatherer of Information, his new chief, Exazenos, to witness the flogging and beheading of the two prisoners. With the palace quiet, he decided that he would have a little chat with the lady whore.

Tamura, Siranus, and Martina looked at one another in wide-eyed fright when loud banging shook her door. A trembling Siranus opened the door a crack and was promptly shoved aside by the huge man who strode into the room as though he owned it. He stood there, dominating the chamber with his vastness, and gave Tamura an unpleasant grin.

She wished now that she had gone with the emperor, but knew that sooner or later she would have to deal with this new threat to her position. At least he hadn't had time to report any suspicions to Isaac yet. Even a dunce like Asanes could work out the facts, and sure enough here he was here to finish her off. Her courage almost failed her as she contemplated his size and determination.

She gave him her best smile, though she was trembling all over. Seated on the bed she looked ravishing, and this was not lost on Asanes. She was making eyes at him and there was a leg exposed that took his attention away from his objective for just a moment.

"I know why you are here, but I am sure we can come to some kind of arrangement, Sir," she cooed from the bed.

"You sent that snake to get me!"

"As God is my witness I did not. How horrible! How could you think of me like that?" she cried piteously, looking shocked. "I thought you came here because of what Malakis said to Siranus the other day. Didn't you?"

He looked confused. "You didn't send the snake?"

She gave a theatrical shudder. "Oh my God! I am terrified of snakes, and that... " she pointed derisively at Siranus, "he would *die* if he had to come near one. Was it really a snake, and not a burst spleen from overeating?" she asked innocently.

"It was a snake, and a damn big one too. So you don't know anything about that?" Asanes asked her. He looked more stupid than ever as he wrestled with the confusion in his mind.

Tamura could sense the big man was finding it hard to put things together. Perhaps she could turn this around.

"You know, Asanes, I have always liked you," she said in a low tone as seductively as she could, although her throat was dry.

"You do? Er, you have?" His face began to wreath itself into a huge grin of pleasure.

"Oh yes!" she cried. "You're not like that man Malakis, so crude and ill-mannered. You are so big and strong, and I am sure that... " she allowed her eyes to drift slowly to his crotch, and a few more inches of soft thigh appeared. Asanes stared as though mesmerized by this apparition half lying on the bed and felt a stirring in his groin. He blinked and stared some more, unable to say anything.

As if on impulse Tamura sat up. "I am desperately thirsty!" she exclaimed. "Martina, you wretched child, bring me a drink of wine and one for my guest, at once! Be sure to use the best wine for my special guest!" Tamura shot her maid a hard look full of meaning, then smiled seductively at Asanes. "You should perhaps make yourself more comfortable?" she asked him, still smiling. She patted the bed next to her.

Martina appeared like magic from the other room and presented her with a silver cup, then handed one to Asanes, who took it without glancing at the maid. She disappeared like a puff of smoke.

Asanes could now smell Tamura's scent and his heart was beating like a kettle drum in his huge chest. Was this for real? He didn't want to think about it, simply to react. This was the first time he had been anywhere near a woman of such beauty in his life, and here she was virtually begging him to take her on this magnificent bed with silk sheets. He glanced around the chamber. They were quite alone; the maid and that slimy eunuch had vanished.

She sipped her wine and her eyes regarded him with an open invitation. "Lets drink to our... friendship," she suggested.

He took a gulp of the wine, then finished it off with a leer, tossed the metal cup away with a clatter on the tiles and reached for her; his nether regions were clamoring for attention. Hurriedly he loosened his trousers, which dropped to the floor. Tamura didn't know how long the dose would take to have its effect, but was sure of one thing: he was not going to have her nor any part of her. She slithered off the silk bed, exposing even more thigh, and put a hand on his chest, gently but firmly pushing him back.

"You must be patient, my good Sir. I shall do all the work; just lie back and enjoy yourself," she whispered. Asanes lay half on the bed, his lower legs hanging off. He was beginning to feel slightly wooly, but all his attention was on the woman leaning over him, undoing the cords that held his greasy doublet in place. He tried to reach for her hand but she pushed him away with a smile. "Be comfortable, Asanes. It will happen soon," she soothed him.

He shook his head, which was now feeling decidedly dizzy, and his stomach was beginning to ache. Suddenly he felt ill and tried to sit up but felt so groggy that his head fell back. An awful realization dawned and he glared up at the apparition still leaning over him. Her face was beginning to swim in front of his eyes.

"Curse you, woman! You've... you've poisoned me!" he croaked.

With a smile of pure venom Tamura evaded the huge hand that was seeking to grasp her by her throat and stood up. "Siranus!" she called. "Get in here, now!"

Siranus appeared by her side and the two of them stared down at the struggling, moaning man on the bed. To their collective surprise Asanes gave a gargling roar and heaved himself off the bed onto his feet, where he stood swaying as though very drunk before he grunted and almost doubled over with pain. "You whore! I hope you burn in hell!" he exclaimed. "I'm not dead yet. They will hear about this."

He turned away and began to stagger towards the door. "Stop him!" Tamura exclaimed, but then an idea occurred to her. She snatched Asanes' dagger that hung off his belt and ran past him towards the door, where she turned to face him. He had fallen to his knees, having tripped over his leggings, and was frothing at the mouth, gasping and groaning with agony as the poison took full effect.

Tamura was amazed that he could still move at all. He sent her a baleful glare that was truly frightening, but she steeled herself. With a cry of her own she stabbed him in the chest with the knife. The blade skidded off his rib cage, however, and did nothing more than to tear through the doublet and made him flinch. He reached for her, his huge arms held wide as though to embrace her, but even in his agony she knew that should he catch her he would crush her to death as he died.

Still she had to risk it, so she dived in and stabbed again, this time lower, and the blade went in all the way. She ducked but couldn't quite evade one of the swinging hands that batted her off her feet to tumble in a heap against the wall. She scrambled up and returned with her back to the doorway, shaking as she watched the shock on his face begin to fade into a blank stare. He looked up at her with the beginnings of a hurt look on his face. "I only... " Asanes didn't finish. He fell forward onto his face and died.

For what seemed like long minutes Tamura stayed where she was, looking down on the huge body. It was absolutely still, with a pool of blood beginning to form on the floor where the knife was embedded.

Siranus crept trembling up to the body and tried to turn it over. After a huge effort he managed, and the body slumped with a thud onto its back with the arms splayed and the ankles crossed. The whole front of the corpse was bloody. "Oh, my Lady!" Siranus exclaimed. "Oh, my God protect us. What do we do now?"

She eased herself away from the door and made sure it was locked, then knelt next to the body. "He was going to ravish me and then denounce us, and we would have been executed," she replied in as calm a tone as she could. "I must think, Siranus. Clean up the mess on the floor while I *think*," she repeated. "Martina, get in here," she called.

"Did you hide the bottle?" she asked the trembling girl, who couldn't stop looking down on the corpse.

"Yes, my Lady. But there was nothing left of the contents."

"Then destroy it and hide the pieces," Tamura said. Incredibly, it had taken almost the entire bottle's worth to kill Asanes. Gabriella had died from a fraction of the poison. Now she had to think, and think hard. How was she to report this to the emperor?

Pantoleon arrived back from the execution exasperated. The executioners were inept and had messed up the beheadings badly. There was something elegant about a good clean execution, but this had been bungled by those shams who called themselves executioners. There were many aspects of this copper pot empire that needed changing, and he was now in a position to make them. Slowly, however; it wouldn't do to hurry things along. His ultimate objective was to take it all from Isaac at the right moment. For now he wanted to see the Lady Tamura. As though she had read his mind, the eunuch who served her, a pretty fellow, appeared at his side as he took his leave of the emperor and whispered that Lady Tamura was asking for him in her private chambers.

Knowing that he was stepping out of the bounds of protocol, Pantoleon nonetheless agreed with a nod and follow the man along the long back corridors and up stairs. As he strode along he pondered the request. He would have to take great care; Isaac would not see visitations of this kind in any good light.

The slave stopped in front of an ornate door and paused. "My Lady is *very* distressed, My Lord. She asked for you and only you because of the nature of this request." Were there sounds of weeping coming from the room? Silently the eunuch opened the door.

Pantoleon strode into the chamber. The sight that greeted him stopped him in his tracks. Lying on his back on the floor near to the bed, as though he had fallen off it, dragging bed-linen with him, was Asanes. His torso was covered in blood and there was a knife sticking out of his lower chest. His pants were down around his ankles, displaying sizeable genitals. Even Pantoleon was impressed.

On the bed was Lady Tamura huddled in a fetus ball, disheveled and weeping copiously. On hearing the door open she sat up, and he saw the front of her robe had been torn, exposing her breasts which she clumsily tried to cover. There was blood on her dress and even her hands. Her face was streaked and smeared with tears, her hair was unbound and in disarray. She cried out when she saw it was Pantoleon and scrambled off the bed to throw herself into his arms.

"Oh, Exazenos! Thank God you have come!" she cried. "I have been so frightened." She began to weep again into his shoulder, shuddering as she did so.

"What happened?" Pantoleon said staring down at the body and feeling the warmth of the woman clinging to him. It was very disconcerting.

"He... he charged into my chambers and he, he tried to.... Oh God, what am I to do?" Tamura wailed.

Pantoleon turned to the slave. "What in God's name happened? Tell me!" he commanded.

Siranus was also weeping, but in between chokes and sniffling he said, "He must have known the emperor would be away, and so would a lot of other people, you included, my Lord. I am sure he would never have attempted anything like this had you been here. He is... has been obsessed with my Lady. He came in, he knocked me over," Siranus showed Pantoleon a bruise forming on his upper cheek bone, "and, and then he attacked my mistress! God protect us all," he whimpered.

Pantoleon sensed the sobbing had eased on his shoulder as they spoke. He gently pushed Tamura away from him, still holding her by her upper arms. "Will you be all right?" he asked with concern. She nodded with her head down and her eyes half closed. "Yes, yes, I think so. I had no choice. He would not listen to me!" she sobbed and choked on her tears.

Pantoleon took her around the other side of the bed and made her sit. "There now. It's over. Sit here and get your breath," he advised her. "You," he pointed to the slave. "Get her some water to drink and help clean her up. Find her some clean clothes; she can't remain in these."

"I have to ask," he said as he crouched in front of Tamura, who was weeping silently with her hands in her lap, twisting her fingers together in an agitated manner. "Did he violate you?"

She shook her head and her hair flurried about her face, half hiding it from him. "Almost, he was nearly on top of me. He was so strong I could not stop him! He did not get beyond that but if the emperor ever hears of this he won't believe me, then I shall die!" She wailed and reached for his arms. "Oh, what am I to do? That monster came here to, to... " she didn't finish, but the tears began to flow copiously again.

Pantoleon had little time for tears and wails normally, but the girl's distress affected him enough to elicit some sympathy for her plight. He came to a decision.

"You need not worry, my Lady. I shall deal with this," he told her. "Now you must calm down and we must make sure that no one knows but us. I shall have my people dispose of the body, and no one will be the wiser."

He almost smiled. He could take care of the problem, the emperor need never know, and the woman was his now without any shadow of doubt. The best kind of ally, right in the emperor's bed chamber.

"Oh, Exazenos, my Lord. How can I ever thank you?" she snuffled.

"I am sure we can think of something," he smiled over her shoulder as she came back into his arms.

Seeing the narrow path before you
Without any room to the left or the right
Will you boast of what you are?
With death and destruction like a wall
On either side, will your heart hold out
And will you be strong?
—Hapenini

Chapter 33

1186

News from Jerusalem

Talon noticed that there was a newcomer in the population of the castle. He was a square looking man of about thirty years, with grey beginning to form at his temples, and oddly marred features. He also wore distinctive robes, and Talon realized that the priest had arrived. On a signal, Max brought the man to Talon's work chamber and left him at the door. Talon stood up and waved the man to a seat opposite him. The priest walked into the chamber, looking nervous, and introduced himself as Psellos. He accepted a cup of wine and drank it appreciatively.

"This vintage is coming along, Lord," he said respectfully. "The villagers told me that you had taken an interest in their crops and their wine. I thank you for your mercy, and may God bless you."

Talon smiled. "Bless me for making a better wine, or for encouraging the villagers, Psellos?"

Psellos chuckled. "Both, perhaps." There was a small silence, then Talon asked bluntly.

"What happened to you?" the man's nose was virtually destroyed, and he breathed sonorously through what was left of it.

Psellos's gray eyes regarded Talon without fear. "A Frank called Châtillon, a murderous Lord from the Kingdom of Jerusalem, once visited this island. When he did, he ordered that all the priests, of the Orthodox Church, mind you, should have their faces disfigured." He indicated his face. "This is what happened to me."

Talon leaned forward. "I know this man, and I heard that he came to this island and disgraced himself. Did Manuel pardon him? I think I heard that?"

440

"He did, and I forgive him for it, although it was without provocation and some died as a result."

"He is a very mean-minded man, that Châtillon," Talon said, his anger visible on his features. "I am sorry for what he did, and I do not forgive him. Perhaps God will one day, but he is loathsome."

"You clearly have met him."

"Oh yes, we have indeed met, and on that occasion we were lucky. We sent him back to his lair with his tail between his legs."

The priest's eyes flashed; did Talon detect that he was pleased?

"They say...," Psellos hesitated. "I do not wish to offend, Lord."

"You may speak to me freely."

Psellos continued. "They say that you are a... magician, and that many fear you and your close followers, Lord, but... they also say that you are a fair and just man."

"I hope that the villagers feel that way. But you should know this, Priest. I do not harm those who would befriend me, nor my retainers, nor those under my protection. I shall use my powers only to protect them, the villagers and the herders, and you."

"I will serve you as best I am able, Lord."

"Do not betray me, serve the villagers well, and I will ask nothing more," Talon responded. "If there are improvements needed to the chapel, let me know and we can make repairs. I wish to be informed when next you have a service, as I intend to be there."

Psellos looked pleased. "Thank you, Lord. This I shall do. May God bless you for your kindness."

Psellos rose to leave, and after a bow, departed.

A little later there was a light knock on the door and Theodora put her head in the entrance.

"Talon, may I come in?"

"Of course, Theo. You are always welcome here," he said rising. "I have just met the priest."

"Psellos? Yes. He was a little nervous, having heard all those lurid tales about you."

"I did what I could to reassure him."

"Give him time. He has only heard from the villagers, and they think you can fly, hurl thunderbolts when enraged, and work all sorts of magic." She smiled mischievously at him. "The rest of us will tell him about the real Talon over time."

"How have you been since I saw you last?" he enquired, leaning over the table with a smile.

"Very well. I am kept busy and that is good... given what is going on in Famagusta."

"Dimitri tells me that affairs are somewhat chaotic in the palace. Somehow the emperor's retainers are dying all over the place." He chuckled.

Theodora looked apprehensive. "Does that mean that Pantoleon is consolidating his hold?"

Talon rubbed his face with both hands. He was tired. "That might be the case, but we have a spy in the middle of it all, so we will be kept informed of anything that he or Isaac thinks of doing."

"He will bring terror to this country," she said, her tone bitter.

"I fear so, but the emperor had already done that. What we have to do is to anticipate their next moves and try to stop them where we can. You are safe here, Theo. Remember that."

"I know, Talon, and I am very grateful. I love Rav'an and Jannat, who have made us more than welcome. On that note... "

"What is it, Theo?"

"Jannat is going to have her baby soon, which is to be expected; but Simon is not doing well."

"How bad is it for him?" asked Talon. He felt guilty that he had not gone to see his old retainer since his return.

"I do not think he will last another month, Talon."

"Then let's go and see him now," he said, standing up.

The visit to Simon was short, as he was asleep, but it was clear to Talon that his old retainer was not going to see the winter through. His cheeks were sunken and his breathing labored.

"I have given him herbs to ease the difficulty with his breathing, but there is little else I can do," Theo whispered to him as they left.

He shook his head sadly. "So many are leaving, or have left. God be kind to their souls," he murmured.

She squeezed his arm. "You have provided a haven for those you trust and protect. Be proud of that, Talon," she said in a low voice.

Life began to settle into a comfortable routine. The main event was that Jannat gave birth to a healthy boy, a few days later than anticipated and after a long night. The two men were again excluded from the birthing chamber. It was almost dawn and streaks of light had already begun to show in the east when Rav'an came down the stairs and told Reza he could go up and see his wife. Without a word but a dazed look and a gulp, he scampered up the stairs.

"It is a boy, and Jannat wants to call him Firuz. I hope that Reza is in accord," she told Talon, as he came to sit next to her and took her in his arms. "You look tired, my Love," he said.

"Not as tired as Jannat, I dare say. Or Theo, who took care of matters. That woman is a wonder. The Byzantine Greeks seem to be far ahead of the Franks when it comes to medicine and care."

"You are correct; the Latins have nothing to match it. The Greeks are in the same league as the Persians and the Egyptians. The Doctor Habbib would have enjoyed a visit to Constantinople; their hospitals are similar to the ones he is used to." He sighed. "Or they were. From what Theo has told us, the hospitals have suffered from the political upheavals. Were there not so much conflict, I think everyone would be further along with their medicines."

At that moment Max wandered into the room, blinking like an owl. "Well, has she had the baby yet?" he demanded, with a smile at Rav'an.

"She has, and it is time we all went up and congratulated the proud parents," Rav'an told him.

They arrived just as Reza was picking up his newborn son with a look of wonder on his dark features. "We have a son!" he exclaimed with a huge grin.

"What is his name?" Talon asked, when he had finished admiring the bundle in Reza's arms.

"His name is Firuz, we have agreed," Reza stated with a fond look at Jannat, who gave him a tired smile, strands of her hair still wet with sweat. Talon glanced over at Theodora, who was cleaning up while watching them.

"Thank you, Theo, for looking after our sister," he said.

She smiled back. "It was not too difficult. Jannat is a very healthy girl," she stated. "Now all of you must leave her to rest. It has been a long night for all of us."

But Talon was awakened by Rostam, who tentatively spoke to his father from the doorway of the bedchamber only a few hours later. Talon got out of bed, trying not to disturb Rav'an, who murmured. "What is it?"

"Nothing, my Love," he told her. "Go back to sleep." he glanced back at her as he was leaving. Her hair was strewn about her in a tumble of tresses while she burrowed under the blankets and furs. He wished he was back there with her, for the morning was chilly.

"What is it, Rostam?" he asked his boy as they headed down the stairs to the kitchens for something warm to eat and drink.

443

"A message has come in from Dimitri and another from Boethius, Father."

"Did you read them?"

"Yes. Dimitri said that 'P' is now fully in charge of gathering information in the palace. All opposition gone. And Boethius said that Jacob is in Paphos and wants to see you. He said it is urgent and that he will bring Jacob here."

Talon digested this information as he munched on a piece of bread and sharp goat's cheese at a kitchen table, while the cooks and servants went about their business around the two of them.

So Pantoleon was now virtually in charge. Talon hoped he had not made a terrible mistake. On reflection, there had not been very much he could have done. This would mean hard times for the island, of that he was sure. He wondered what Boethius wanted. His daughter Irene seemed happy enough at present. Talon doubted she should go back, however. It was precisely young girls that Isaac targeted on his regular rounds of his "empire". She was safe here.

A week later Boethius appeared at the castle, accompanied by Jacob from Acre. They had been ferried to the harbor by Henry, who was doing some trading with the eastern coast, often going to Tripoli to buy and sell, since he no longer sell in Famagusta. He also stayed well away from Acre. The crops and olive products were coming along, and so was the production of copper ore. In exchange they brought back Gaza fabric and silk which Rav'an and Jannat, with the help of some of the more adept village womenfolk, turned into clothes. Much else found its way back—including news.

Talon and his extended family welcomed the the Greek and the Jewish merchants, and over a good feast of venison, new-baked bread and vegetables hoarded for the winter, they heard tell of the general events going on in Palestine. Talon knew he could wait for Jacob to pass along the more important information later in the privacy of his work chamber.

When they were seated before a blazing fire and Boethius had been given a cup of wine, which Jacob declined, Talon asked the question. Max and Reza were with him, and all were eager to hear what Jacob had to say.

"Tell me, Jacob. Why would you risk the dangers of a winter sea just to come all this way to see me?" Talon asked with a smile at his agent.

Jacob smiled back and warmed his hands at the fire before answering. He looked older than Talon remembered: careworn.

"I shall be glad to talk about that in due course, Sir Talon, but first, perhaps, some news which will I hope substantiate what comes next."

"Tell me what you know," Talon prompted him.

"The first thing is that the King has died. But you knew that," he said with a sharp look at Talon, who nodded. "Yes, I knew," he responded. "March of last year," he said, his tone curt. He had mourned the King, whom he had respected enormously, and dreaded the future now that he was gone.

"Now the boy King, Baldwin, the late King's nephew, is very sick. The nobles are bickering endlessly over the succession, even before he is dead! The loudest voice belongs to one Raynald de Châtillon; do you know of him?"

"Oh yes, we do indeed. If ever there was a man who should not be allowed to dictate events, it is he."

Jacob nodded his head sagely. "You know your man, Sir Talon. Alas, it is indeed unfortunate. The young King is not expected to live beyond this year."

Talon was startled. "Is not Count Raymond of Tripoli still regent? Is he not in control of events in Jerusalem?" he demanded.

"That is his appointment, but alas, in name only. Lord Joscelin, Count of Edessa, Raynald de Châtillon and Gérard de Ridefort have all but usurped power for themselves and have accused My Lord Raymond of Tripoli of conspiring with Salah Ed Din. Châtillon in particular is most vitriolic about this, saying that he has become more of a Saracen than the infidels themselves."

Talon snorted with contempt and poured a cup of water, which he handed to Jacob.

"What is to become of the kingdom if young Baldwin dies?" he asked.

"Now therein lies the problem, Sir Talon. We talk about it endlessly, trying to see into the future, and we see much trouble ahead for our kind."

"Go on."

"To answer your question, Sir Talon, it is very likely that the three lords in question will choose Sibylla, the late King's sister. Raymond of Tripoli favors her half-sister Isabella, but he lacks support."

There was a long silence at this point. Talon explained what was happening to Reza, who had not followed the intricacies of the discussion, while the rest of the men in the room were silent. Then

Talon said, "So this brings us to what is going on in the camp of Salah Ed Din."

Jacob looked up from his musings. "Yes, that is right, Sir Talon. I personally do not think it will be long before he makes another attempt upon Jerusalem. His spies must be telling him the time is ripe."

"If I am not mistaken he has his own problems with his tribes," Max remarked.

"Although that is true, he is in a very strong position now. He holds Damascus and Aleppo, which are the two most strategic cities in Syria. From there he threatens Antioch and the kingdom of Armenia. The Christians of the Kingdom cannot protect them. So they, like Tripoli, have made separate treaties with him. Which, being the man he is, Salah Ed Din will honor, and that is more than can be said of men like Joscelin and de Châtillon," Jacob responded. "For Salah Ed Din it is a question of timing. His tribal leaders cannot war all year around. They have to supervise their harvests and be present for tribal meetings. Without them he cannot threaten the Christians."

"Should we then be so concerned?" Reza asked. He had followed that part.

"I feel that we should be, Reza. I do not think it will be this year; however, next summer is another matter," Jacob said. "Salah Ed Din has made the commitment that he and he alone can take Jerusalem back from the Christians, but he is very dependent upon his tribes and their quarrelsome leaders." Jacob gave them all a wry smile. "I sometimes wonder who is the most quarrelsome of either side," he said.

"Now that we know this much, what is your concern, and that of your people?" Talon asked.

Jacob was silent for a long moment before answering. "Acre is no longer a safe haven for Jews. When princes quarrel and fight, they want treasure, and they will take it from whomsoever is most vulnerable. We Jews are the most vulnerable, and the Bishop of Acre would not stop someone like Joscelin from coming in and taking what he wants from us."

Talon thought about this. "Where would you go?"

"That is a difficult question, Sir Talon. One which we are still pondering."

"One thing is certain. You cannot come here," Talon told him. He held up his hand to forestall a reply from the surprised Jacob. "Hear me out," he said.

"The emperor is an avaricious, greedy and stupid man. The moment you arrived he would plunder your possessions and leave you destitute, or worse. He now has a man who works for him who is, if anything, even more vicious and dangerous, who would hear of you no matter how hard we tried to hide the fact of your presence."

"Boethius has informed me of that," Jacob said sadly, "But still I dared hope. So we must discuss our holdings of your wealth, Sir Talon. That is the reason I am here."

"Most of it is still in the care of the Jews in Muscat, is it not?"

"That is so, and it could stay there as long as you wanted, in their care, as I do not think the Caliph wants to plunder the Jews. The treasure that is in Acre, however, must be transferred somehow. It will be difficult enough to get it out of the city as it is."

Jacob looked directly towards Talon. "I am truly sorry that I bring such bad news."

"You have told me what I need to hear, and I am deeply grateful; whether I like it or not is of no importance. Alas, I know of almost nowhere at present that is a haven of peace," Talon stated. "What news have you heard from Byzantium, Boethius?" he asked his merchant friend. "Would there be safety there?"

"Unlikely, Sir Talon," Boethius replied. "Outsiders of any sort are unwelcome now. The Normans from Sicily were driven out of Thessalonica after a big battle. They were also driven out of Durazzo and Corfu, but they keep the islands of Cephalonia. The spreaders of gossip say that Byzantium has seen a miraculous deliverance and has entered a gentler time. I hear from merchants, who now arrive in great numbers at Paphos, that there is a feeling of spring after a bitter winter. However, it is reported in quiet voices that Isaac Angelus is even more corrupt than Manuel and is selling government offices like vegetables in a common market."

"So other than that the monster is gone and we have his shade here, little has changed in Constantinople," Talon remarked with a grimace.

"Nothing changes very much, Sir Talon," Boethius agreed.

"I wonder what Theo will make of this," Talon mused.

"You don't think she is happy here, Talon?" Max asked.

Talon looked puzzled. "Why no, Max. She appears to be content, do you not think so?'

Max scowled. "Why should she not be content here? Is she not safe from the terror she endured while in that terrible city?" his tone was sharp.

Talon looked at his friend, who seemed to be upset. "I shall be at pains to ask her how she feels, Max," he said.

Again there was silence in the room, other than the crackle of the fire. Finally Talon said, "Reza, you could go back with Jacob and help with that matter, could you not? Henry will be your captain. Bring the treasure back here to Cyprus."

"Should he not take both ships, one to carry and the other to protect?" Max asked. Talon looked at his old friend and nodded. "Yes, that would be wise. I think we can manage here without them for a short while at least. How is Guy doing?"

"The last time I checked he was complaining about his inactivity. Theo—Theodora has had quite enough of him," Max said.

Reza shot a grin at Talon, who was clearly wondering what was going on with Max.

To change the subject, Reza said. "I can go and collect the treasure. We'll make arrangements. Famagusta can stew for a while and Paphos is quiet for the moment, is it not?" he asked Boethius.

"It is for the time being, Reza. No one knows what will happen when this Pantoleon gets moving."

"He is very dangerous, Boethius. Your child can stay here for as long as she needs to.

Boethius was clearly unhappy about the separation but saw the good sense of that. Talon insisted that he and Jacob stay for at least a week and then leave with Henry when the weather improved. Storms were sweeping in from the West and it had become quite cold and damp.

Much later in the day Talon found Reza and drew him aside to discuss something that was on his mind.

"What is going on with Max?" he asked.

Reza chuckled. "Jannat, my all-seeing and wise one, says that he is in love, Brother."

Talon closed his eyes. "Ah," he shook his head. "But... Max! The old wolf! I was wondering what was going on. Does Theodora feel the same?"

Reza responded with a laugh. "How should I know, Brother? You should ask the girls, they know everything."

"I had an odd message from Dimitri today," he told Reza, who looked interested.

"Dimitri keeps an eye on the villa belonging to Pantoleon. The night after the emperor arrived back in the city, there was a lot of activity. Furtive stuff, you know? They moved many small boxes out of the villa, and these found their way to the docks, where they were loaded onto the ship that is captained by Nigel."

"I wonder what he is up to?" Reza said. He was referring to Pantoleon. "Is he moving out?"

"I don't know. But why would he do that when he is now the man in charge? No. But... if I had any treasure, I most certainly would not take it with me to the palace. I might never be able to get it back. It could be that he is making sure that he has options if things do go badly for him. Remember, Isaac is not stable and could turn on him in a minute."

Reza nodded. "I say we should investigate."

Talon agreed. "But not just yet. Did Boethius not say that at one time the emperor was a friend of Salah Ed Din?" Talon asked, changing the subject to the one he most wanted to discuss.

"I heard that too," Reza responded.

"Then here is what I would ask of you, if you think it possible," Talon said. "It is dangerous, and only you can carry this off, but it is very important. And you can take anyone you want with you to accomplish this."

Talon finally found time to go hunting with Rostam and initiate his son into the pleasures of falconry.

To Rostam's delight, Talon ordered his hawkers to take the boy in hand and teach him what they could, and took every opportunity to join them when they went off into the hills. Small game, including deer, were plentiful. Despite the light powder of snow on the top of the ridge, they would ride down to the north side into the forests and bring back game for the table. Rostam took care of the hawks and was speechless when Talon presented him with one that was to be his.

"Make sure you listen carefully to our master Hawker, Rostam. He can teach you much," his father told him.

Rostam was growing into a strong youth and applied himself willingly to the grueling training Reza set him and his companions. Talon noted with approval how his son and the other trainees were forming bonds that would stand them in good stead later on in life.

His own work kept him out of the castle for many hours, even in winter. The villagers of the valley and the harbor, once they understood that he was concerned with their welfare, tripped over themselves to please him; but made many demands on his time.

"How goes the life of a Lord these days?" Reza asked him one evening, when he arrived back late, cold and hungry, to stand in front of the fire rubbing his hands to get some warmth back into his fingers.

"I am the provider of tools, the person they come to when they cannot decide whether to dig in this direction or that in the mine. Should we breed this or that sheep with that flock, and which of these cows should we slaughter for winter meat?" he grumbled to the room at large.

Theodora laughed. She had put Damian to bed and was now seated with Jannat and Rav'an. "Have you only just found out, Talon, that being a Lord entails responsibilities? They will be asking you to act as their judge next," she said with a smile at Rav'an.

"I have already been imposed upon in that direction, Theo. Palladius came to me and asked me to adjudicate for the villagers. Max handles the soldiers, thank God for that, with Palladius as his Second. How is the man doing, Max?" he asked.

"Well, he is a bit clumsy, but eager to please, and his men are terrified of him—especially when he smiles at them. That is just as it should be for a Sergeant." Max chuckled.

"The villagers set upon me the moment I arrive and give me no peace! Today they wanted me to declare against a young girl who has become pregnant. I think they wanted to have her whipped," Talon exclaimed.

"What did you say to them?" Rav'an asked. All three women were now alert and staring at him.

"I demanded to know who was the father. After some time a youth was pushed forward, a decidedly callow youth, I might add. He clearly wanted none of it, but I ordered that he marry her right then and there. Psellos approved, and he took care of the ceremony. He told me later it was the shortest marriage he had ever performed but good for the protection of the girl. I left the villagers with the instructions to provide them with a hut and that the girl was not to be harmed in any way. Psellos said that he would keep an eye on things."

"I am glad you told us about that, Talon," Rav'an said after calling on the maid to bring some food and drink for Talon. "I shall go and see them in the morning. You will come Jannat, Theo?"

"I shall come," Theodora stated. "After I have seen to Simon. I have not visited the villagers yet."

"They are in need of your services as a physician," Jannat said.

"Take Palladius with you, and some men at arms. Max, can you assist?" Talon asked.

"I shall accompany them," Max said firmly, and Talon smiled to himself.

"I shall not come, I need a break from their woes," he stated. "When I told Julian and John, the village leaders, that I needed some building and reinforcements done on the castle they looked very worried!"

"Why? Have you not treated them well?" asked Jannat, sounding amused.

Talon made a face. "You know very well I treat them fairly. When I asked why they looked upset, John said, "You will not throw our masons off the walls when we are done?"

Reza almost choked and Jannat giggled. Max gave a bark of laughter, which elicited a fond smile from Theodora. *So that was the way it was?* Talon thought to himself, then continued, while his audience looked on amused.

"To reassure them I said I would pay half in advance and the other half later. He seemed relieved."

"Did they really think that you might, Talon?" Theo asked.

"I fail to understand them most of the time, but I hope that with the arrival of Psellos they will cease to come to me with every single problem they have," Talon huffed.

"He finessed this castle, two villages and a harbor out from under a rogue, and now he complains," Rav'an sighed. "You, my Talon, are now Lord of a large region, in spite of the emperor, and your people need you."

"It is clear I have no friends in this room," Talon said, pretending to look glum. He fondled the ears of one of the hounds that were ever at his heels. They had pride of place by the fire, and gradually everyone else had become used to their presence. The hounds in return behaved respectfully enough. Somehow, he could not think how, the black cat had survived and was unafraid of the two huge hounds, which regarded it warily but did nothing to harm it. Irene kept a close eye on the cat, now curled up in her lap.

"I forgot to mention," Talon said to the assembled group. "I was down at the harbor village the other day with Palladius, looking forward to seeing Henry and Guy, when we were diverted by the sound of drums and pipes."

"Well, go on. What was that all about?" Reza demanded.

"Let him continue, my Reza!" Jannat said.

"Yes, well, we were curious, although the villagers were not very keen on us investigating. However, I insisted upon finding out, and we made our way along a very narrow street to a little opening wide enough for two carts to pass each other. There was a small crowd which parted as we arrived..." Talon could see he had the full attention of his audience.

"You will never imagine what I saw there."

"Don't keep us in suspense, Talon!" Rav'an insisted.

Talon glanced uneasily at Irene.

"Er, there was a woman, quite a young woman, lying on a blanket writhing, yes that was it, she was writhing about, as though in pain."

He regarded the startled looks of everyone in the chamber. "The music, there was even a plucking sound from a stringed instrument, never stopped, and the pipes were shrill. She was crying, and her skirts were um, up around her waist!" He was still somewhat shocked by what he had seen.

Rav'an shot a look at Irene who was listening with keen interest, but then so was everyone else. She frowned. "What was it all about, Talon?"

"I had to ask and the village head man. He told me that she had been bitten by a Tarantula on her 'you know what' and was having a fit because of it."

There was a collective gasp from everyone and an amused snort from Jannat. Even Max couldn't help himself, he gave a bark of incredulous laughter.

Rav'an looked over at Irene and said firmly, "Irene, my dear, it's time for bed. Go along now."

Irene looked upset. "But Aunty Rav'an, I want to hear."

"Yes, I'm sure you do; but, my little one, this is not for your ears right now. Off you go, and Rostam, you can go too." Her tone brooked no argument.

"The damage is done, Rav'an," Jannat said with a giggle. They might as well stay now." But Rav'an was adamant and the two youngsters were herded out of the door by a nurse who had been called.

"So what was this really all about, Talon? It's not one of your terrible jokes, is it?" Reza chuckled. Talon looked hurt and shrugged. "It's what they told me," he said defensively. "Palladius couldn't take his eyes off her."

"I'm sure he couldn't," Rav'an said dryly.

"I know exactly what it is all about," Theodora stated with confidence. All eyes swiveled to her.

"You do?" Talon asked.

"Yes, I do," she stated again. "You see, women have no way to release their pent up emotions. Especially," she paused with a dark look at the menfolk, "If they are not getting enough attention in the bed! There, I've said it." Her face aflame with embarrassment, she turned as though for support to Max, who had his mouth open, as did everyone else in the room. "She wasn't really bitten. It's how men explain away the odd behavior of their womenfolk."

"You know of this kind of thing?" Talon demanded, unable to hide his surprise.

"Yes, it is quite common in the islands. I have heard that it is not unusual on the mainland too, although I never heard of it in Constantinople. The shaking is a release from the constraints of their wretched lives where men tell them what to do all the time. On occasion they have to throw a fit. Rather than admit there may be a problem that has anything to do with how they treat their wives and daughters, the men say that she has been bitten by a tarantula. It's the kind of nonsense they would come up with," she finished, her face still burning bright red.

Jannat snickered, then said, "Beware then, my Reza, of when the tarantula bites me!"

"By the way," she added. "you did kill that one we found in the back rooms, didn't you? I cannot believe the screaming and fright from all the serving girls. You did, didn't you?" she repeated, staring at him accusingly.

"Well, er... not exactly," Reza mumbled, looking guilty.

"Reza!" both Rav'an and Jannat said together. "It was huge! What did you do with it?"

"I am keeping it in a box, as a present perhaps, for the emperor, when next one of us has to pay him a visit," Reza said, with a sly glance at Talon, who shook his head with amusement.

"It's all right for you men. You wear trews, but us women have to walk about in long skirts and it is not nice to see a mouse or a tarantula creeping about. They can get up a skirt and, and well, bite us in those places," Rav'an stated with a straight face. The room dissolved into howls of laughter.

"Lucky mice!" Reza stated, slapping his thighs and receiving glares from the women.

The next evening, Talon cast an eye over at Boethius, who was playing chess with Rostam while Irene sat nearby, happy that her father was with her. Jacob had pleaded fatigue and retired to bed and Henry had gone back to his ship. Talon wondered how long they would be able to continue this peaceful existence. Everything was so fragile; he knew that, especially life. A visit to the chapel might make him feel more sanguine about the future, which appeared bleak no matter which direction he looked. One thing that was very certain in his mind: unless Pantoleon was out of the way permanently, they would always be looking over their shoulders.

"I should become a pirate and live a carefree life on the sea," Talon stated.

"A pirate!" Irene squealed excitedly. "Lord Talon, you can't be a pirate. You are a knight!"

"Yes well, sometimes even knights change course, young lady," Talon said with a grin. "And it's Uncle or Talon to you."

"I know for a fact that although you have ships and are a great navigator, my Lord, you have an uneasy relationship with the sea," Rav'an said with a sly glance at him from under her brows.

"But he seems so comfortable with the sea. Didn't he bring us home from that perilous voyage all the way from China?" Jannat teased.

Rav'an snorted, "He hides it well, my Sister."

"Let's not forget that my son helped greatly with the navigation," Talon stated loud enough for Rostam to hear.

"Indeed," said Reza from his place opposite Jannat where they had been playing their favorite game of Chinese dominos. "The boy earned his keep then. I doubt if we would be here if Talon had been navigating alone!"

"Reza, that was unkind!" Jannat scolded him and leaned forward to give him a light slap on the knee.

"Ouch!" Reza pretended to be sorely wounded.

Talon laughed. "He is right, you know. Be thankful to God that he guided us all home."

"Are you so uncomfortable with the sea?" Theodora asked Talon with a glance at Max.

"Max and I were shipwrecked once and spent some time on a deserted beach. I lost my best horse because of it, and since then I have not, shall we say, loved the sea, although it has and still does provide us with wealth," Talon stated with a shrug.

"What's this? You never told us about this adventure!" Theodora demanded of Max, who looked uncomfortable.

"Tell us about it, Max, because Talon surely will not," Jannat urged him.

Rostam, hearing that a tale was about to be told, abandoned the game of chess, which he was losing, and eagerly came over, followed by Boethius and his daughter. "Tell us Max!" they all chorused.

So Max told them all about the shipwreck and the time he and Talon had spent in Egypt. By the time he had finished it was late, but there was little doubt that they had been enthralled.

"That explains the mystery of the ship that was stolen from Salah Ed Din and how Henry and Guy were freed," Reza said. "We heard a rumor all the way east in Isfahan. In Alamut they were laughing behind their hands at the discomfort of Rashid Ed Din, whom you tweaked, Talon. Both Rav'an and I did wonder even then if it had been you."

"You should tell more about these tales, you men. It passes the long nights away, and we all want to hear of them," Theodora said.

"Are we then as the wild warriors from the North who tell stories to while away the long winter nights, their tales becoming wilder and longer with the length of the season?" It was Talon's turn to tease.

"No, but we want to hear the real ones, and you men should entertain us," Jannat sided with Theodora. "It's music that we need too, I miss that."

Rav'an smiled at her. "We can ask Boethius to find us some instruments and make our own music," she said, then yawned. "It is time for all of us to go to bed. I shall lead the way. I hope that the maid has made a fire in our bed chamber, for I am cold. Those dogs of yours can stay in this chamber tonight, my Talon," she stated firmly.

Later that night, as they were preparing for bed she asked him, "Are we safe here, my Talon?"

His reply was thoughtful. "I do not wish to deceive you, Rav'an, but I cannot be sure. I had thought that Acre would be a safe haven and look how that turned out. From the report given by Jacob, I doubt if anywhere in Palestine will be 'safe' before very long. The nobles who do not understand the compromises needed to survive there will tear it apart, and then Salah Ed Din will strike."

"So where then?" she asked, with concern in her huge gray eyes. He stroked her thick hair absently, enjoying its silky feel under his hand.

"From what Boethius told us today, Byzantium is uncertain too. There is hope he says, but only time will tell. Even so, Theodora might want to go back home."

Rav'an snorted. "I suspect not."

"Why? What do you know that Reza and I do not?" he queried with a surprised chuckle.

"I suspect that she and Max are becoming close."

"Are you serious?" he asked, with a look of feigned surprise.

"You men are quite blind sometimes. Jannat and I have been watching them. It is very possible. Her boy adores Max."

"Isn't Max...?"

"You were going to say that he is a little old for her? Love has no boundaries, my husband. Let's see where it goes. Jannat and I only wish them happiness."

"Hmm, so that is indeed the lay of the land," Talon said, almost to himself. "But... as I was saying. There are few places that can provide the ideal haven, which is why I worked so hard to take this castle. Max gave me the idea, and it seems to have worked."

"I cannot fault you for that, my Warrior!" she laughed. " I can still see Doukas's face when you told him he had lost it! What a pig!"

"A castle perched on a peak like this is safer than, say, living in a port town like Paphos, despite the advantages of a town and market. There we would be at the mercy of anyone, including pirates. This emperor is as mad as his late uncle and just as dangerous."

"And does he not now have this monster, whom you know called... the one Theo fears so much?"

"Pantoleon, yes. I might have miscalculated there. Reza and I talk about how to deal with him almost every day. He brings an evil dimension to the situation on the island. But I don't think he will attempt to harm us. Not yet anyway," Talon told her, rubbing his bearded face thoughtfully. "One day there will be a reckoning, however. He will not die an old man."

She looked at him with her head slightly to one side in the flickering light of the candles and reached out to touch his face gently. "I don't doubt that," she whispered. "But I know that you carry a great responsibility on your shoulders. For that I love you."

Abruptly she smiled and said, "You do look like a pirate, you know: it's that small scar under your right eye. Are you sure that you don't want to stay at sea, pillaging and... what is the other thing pirates do?"

He reached for her and forced her gently back onto the bed. "Pirates are terrible people, but if you insist, I can show you?" he growled.

She laughed and kissed him, a long deep kiss, then reached over and snuffed out the candle.

The wrecks are all thy deed, nor doth remain
A shadow of man's ravage, save his own,
When for a moment, like a drop of rain,
He sinks into thy depths with bubbling groan,
Without a grave, unknell'd, uncoffin'd, and unknown.
—Lord Byron

Chapter 34

1187

The Terror

The Terror had begun, and the island, already cowed by the avaricious behavior of the emperor, groaned in anguish. Tales reached Talon from Dimitri of the tortures that took place in the dungeons of the emperor's palace, where it was said the new man in charge of procuring information did his awful work. Pantoleon was in his element, and he began with the nobility.

The first victims were the hostages, who were readily available for his sadistic practices. He started on the youths, who were the sons of the notables of the island. His pretext was that he wanted information. Pantoleon had his men visit every city and bring back in chains anyone who even looked like they were contemplating sedition. Inevitably, there were those among the population who were happy to denounce others against whom they had a grudge.

This suited him very well because he was not so interested in the intelligence as in the act of torture. Before long, revolution was being whispered about in dark hallways as grieving families lost relatives to the bloody maw of the dungeons of Famagusta. Their screams could be heard around the palace, and even the emperor began to find it distasteful.

Tamura was horrified and stunned. Pantoleon had initiated a clandestine affair with her which had been a disaster. Her shock at discovering his disfigurement had been impossible to conceal from a man who was hyper-sensitive about the subject. She had recovered her composure very quickly and continued to encourage him. His malaise, however, was too deep for even a seductress like her to overcome. He had become almost violent, then had left her with barely a word. She had lain there looking up at the ceiling, a cold block of ice within her belly.

Thereafter he kept his distance, and she gradually came to realize that, in fact, he didn't really need her at all. Rashly she accosted him one day and demanded that he come and visit her.

"Why, my Lord, do you not visit me? I yearn for the chance to be in your arms. Surely you need me as much as I do you?" she whispered enticingly.

He turned on her with a savage snarl, made all the more terrifying by his disfigured face, and said, "I am not interested in the emperor's seconds, my Lady. You would do well to remember that it is not I who need you, but the other way around!"

This had left her shocked and subdued. One thing was certain: she no longer had a powerful ally to whom she could turn. There was no telling when this sadistic monster would tear at her. She realized that there was no one to turn to and again felt quite alone. A tear slid down her cheek.

One day, a lookout on the walls of the castle called to Palladius that he could see horsemen coming up the track towards the castle. They halted at the level space, designated Trebuchet Flat, and paused. The warning signs were clear. Skulls were placed on poles either side of the road and a large notice told visitors to stay where they were and not continue on pain of death. So they waited.

Inside the castle, Talon and Reza were alerted. They had been down in the dungeons mixing more of their Chinese powder when the news came.

"How many are there?" Talon asked Palladius.

"I see six of them, Sir Talon. It's difficult to tell, but they seem to be more than just soldiers."

"Come on, Reza: let's take a look at these people and see what they want."

Leaving Max in charge of the fort and taking four of the companions, they rode out of the castle and down the track to stop in front of the nervous-looking travelers.

As Palladius had observed, they were not of the common cut normally associated with soldiers. They looked more like travel-worn men of means. These men in turn regarded with real apprehension the heavily armed men on horseback from the castle who had their heads and faces covered up to their eyes. This mask alone lent a menacing aspect to the visitors.

"We come in peace," a man who appeared to be their spokesman said, looking very nervous. "We wish to talk to Sir... Lord Talon."

"Who are you and what is your business here?" Reza demanded. "We will talk here."

"We are nobles from Kyrenia, Larnaca and Limassol."

Their spokesman rattled off a the names of his companions, then said, "We have come to see Lord Talon, to plead for his help against the emperor, who is destroying our children and our people."

"What help would that be?"

"You people defeated the army of the emperor once. You can do it again using your... magic," another interjected. "We have had enough!"

"Isaac does not disturb us up here."

"He issues decrees that no one can understand, not even his own damned eunuchs; his mercenaries enforce what they think they understand..." the man waved his hands about in utter frustration.

"It is creating a terrible confusion. No one knows what is going on nor what is going to happen next. It is very very bad for trade." His companions murmured their agreement.

Another interjected, "His mercenaries murder our people, and we know that monster of his, Exazenos, is behind it all," he said, raising his voice. "He kills for pleasure. He kills our sons, who the emperor took as hostages! The emperor is a monster, but this man is the devil himself."

Talon and Reza were silent. "I want to leave them some hope, but I shall not agree to anything," Talon said to Reza in Farsi.

"Perhaps it is time we did something," Reza replied in kind.

The visitors had begun to talk amongst themselves; the discussion was animated and sounded to Talon as though they despaired. Talon raised his hand off the pommel of his saddle to get their attention.

"We will take this message back to our leader, who will decide what should be done."

"Is that all you can offer?" one of the men almost shouted. "Then I, for one, will take matters into my own hands and raise an army!"

The man's tone was one of defiance borne of despair, but Talon was not going to provide them with an excuse for rash and dangerous action.

"So you expect to defeat the man who landed on this island a year ago and took every single one of your cities with a few hundred mercenaries, do you?"

The riders exchanged glances.

459

"Well, do you?" he demanded loudly. His words were met with embarrassed silence. These men were all too aware that they lacked fighting men of similar caliber to those of the emperor.

"We'll bring in mercenaries," the same man muttered.

"With what? You are all broke. He has stolen all your gold."

"We are desperate people. Tell Sir Talon that!" shouted the agitated man. "Even if it means death, it is better than what the foul emperor has made of this island."

"I shall tell him, have no fear of that. But I want you to go home and stay there. Be patient a little longer. We will see what can be done, but only on Sir Talon's terms. Do I make myself clear?" Talon barked at the cowed men facing him. They nodded in silence, turned their horses and walked off down the path.

"I have rarely seen such a dejected group of people," Reza remarked as they watched them leave.

Talon nodded. "It took a great deal of courage for them to come here. If word got out, their hostages would be tortured to death and they themselves hunted down. I gave them scant comfort."

"Come, let's go back and discuss this with our family."

As they rode back to the castle, Palladius rode alongside Reza and Talon. "Is there nothing we can do for them, Sir Talon? They sound desperate."

"They are desperate, Sergeant. But we cannot just charge down the hill and try to take the palace. There has to be a way to take Pantoleon out separately. That has to be carefully considered."

"I understand, Sir Talon." Palladius sounded chastened.

"Your concern is commendable Sergeant. Max tells me good things about you," Talon told him, which cheered him up considerably.

That evening, when the castle had quieted and Damian was in bed, they talked about the visit. Present were Max, now seated close to Theodora, Rav'an and Jannat and Rostam as well as Boethius and Jacob, who were still with them because of the winter storms that had swept in. Then there were Yosef and Dar'an. Talon had closed the door and posted a guard outside to ensure that no one could eavesdrop on their conversation.

Talon described the meeting with the visitors and what they had asked of him. "In all our dealings with them, we must at all times have our faces covered. That achieves two things. One, they do not recognize us whenever we are among them, which will be necessary from time to time, but also it puts them in fear of us."

"I had wondered how long it would take them to come to you, Talon," said Boethius. "This emperor is a despot, and he now has a monster working for him who is never so gleeful as when he is inflicting pain."

"That is why we must find a way to destroy him," Talon said to the room at large.

"Could you not go into the palace and kill him while he slept?" Rav'an said.

She received shocked looks from Boethius and Jacob; even Theodora gave Talon a sharp look. None of them really knew the full range of skills that Reza and Talon possessed.

Talon nodded. "That would be the preferred method, I agree," he responded. "But... I have the feeling that the palace will be a very difficult place to access since that incident with the leopards. I would not like to risk it. No, Pantoleon will not be easy to get to."

"Then what does that leave us with?" Reza demanded.

"I council patience for the time being," Talon said. "I received an interesting note from Dimitri some time ago, telling me that many chests of a small kind were loaded onto Pantoleon's ship."

"What does it have to do with us?" Max asked.

"I think it is his treasure, so it means that he does not trust the emperor any more than I do. Dimitri also told me that, according to his source inside the palace, Pantoleon travels from city to city. Using the vessel as a kind of moving base, he is spreading terror all over and then sailing on. He feels very secure on his ship, it seems."

"You mean that he is moving about too much to be surprised by anyone?" Theodora interjected.

"You should always be on my councils, Theo!" Talon smiled. "Yes, and furthermore, very difficult to visit in the dead of night."

"So how... ?"

"As I said, patience. We will not be dancing to the tune of those nobles but our own. We have two ships, Pantoleon has one. One day we will know where he is going and there we will meet him."

"How will you know?" Jacob asked him.

Talon smiled. "That is why we have people like Boethius and Dimitri working with us."

"This could take a while," said Reza. "But I, for one, am looking forward to concluding our business with the man."

"May God further your mission," said Theodora with feeling. It did not go unnoticed by all that she reached out and gripped Max by his wrist when she said that.

There was another surprise to come two days later. Again the alert sentry on the wall noticed and called down to Palladius, who was busy loudly berating one of his young soldiers for some sin or other. "One rider stopped at the Trebuchet Flat, Sergeant!" he shouted.

Palladius immediately notified Talon, who came and joined him on the wall. Looking down, he saw a lone horseman who had dismounted on the flat.

"Send two men down and bring him into the barbican," Talon ordered.

The rider turned out to be an old man dressed in rich traveling clothes. He looked decidedly nervous but grimly determined. Talon greeted him, with Reza, Max and Palladius in attendance. All the men had their faces covered. Boethius had been told to make himself scarce, in case he was recognized.

"Please be seated." Talon gestured to a chair next to a table laden with food. "You must be tired and hungry after your journey."

The man staggered to the chair and almost fell into it, mopping his brow as he did so. "I thank you for your hospitality, Sir," he said, as he helped himself to some water. "Your greeting down the hill is a little less welcoming." He was referring to the skulls of men and horses that lined the road.

"The display helps to keep the curious away. When you have quenched your thirst, perhaps you would like some wine?" Talon offered, as he took a seat opposite the old man.

His companions stood by, watching in silence. Their visitor looked bewildered for a moment, but then he relaxed; even in this menacing presence the people were behaving in a civilized manner. His hopes went up a notch.

"I thank you for your courtesy, Sir, and indeed I would welcome a glass," he said. He took a cautious sip of the wine, looked startled, and then beamed. "Yes, it is quite good!" He looked across at the covered face in front of him and noticed the green eyes studying him.

"Tell me, where have you come from?" the figure asked him pleasantly enough.

"I, er, I am the First Minister for the emperor and um, my name is Diocles," he responded. He heard a collective intake of breath from the men gathered around them.

There was a long silence after that, then Talon said, "My name is Sir Talon de Gilles, and I am at your service. What can we do for you, Lord Diocles?"

"It... it is difficult to say," Diocles stammered. "You see, Sir Talon, I am here in a very unofficial capacity."

"You mean... the emperor does not know you are here?"

Diocles nodded and ran a nervous hand through what remained of his white hair. He had taken his hat off when he sat down. Then he noticed the trebuchet and his eyes widened.

Talon noticed the direction of his glance and said, "No, we can't give it back; it won't fit through the gates."

"The last time I saw that it was in bits," Diocles murmured, with a twitch of his lips.

"Why are you here?" Talon asked gently.

Diocles coughed and then cleared his throat. "You see, there is a man called Exazenos who is now the emperor's Gatherer of Information. He has replaced the previous man, who came to an untimely end and, well, he is, he is a butcher!" Diocles exclaimed, then put his hand to his mouth as though he were appalled at what he had just said. "I'm so sorry," he said. "It just came out. But, but it must be said, this man is a monster!"

"We know about this man you know as Exazenos, Lord Diocles," Talon said. "More than you." His tone was dry.

Diocles's eyes widened. "You do? Then you know I am not talking nonsense."

"No, indeed. But why are you here? Just to tell me about this fellow?"

"N... No, not just that, Sir Talon. I am here to ask for your help. You, Sir Talon, are known as The Magician. Your followers are called the Assassins of Kantara. All over the island people talk about your powers. Mothers even discipline their children with the threat that you will come and make them disappear in a puff of smoke, or your killers will kidnap them to work for the devils who live inside your mountain!"

There were low chuckles at this from the men gathered about them, and the green eyes smiled, but Diocles went on. "Can you not do something to help us, Sir? Exazenos must be stopped before he destroys everything, everyone!" Diocles finished with a vague wave of his bony hand.

"What do you mean, everyone?" Talon asked.

"I am sure now that he is going to usurp the emperor's place, and then he will take us all to hell. The Emperor is bad, and I say

463

this who should not, but Exazenos is far worse!" Diocles exclaimed. His hands were beginning to fly about and his deeply lined face took on a haunted look.

"Sooo... he is not content to serve the emperor, he wants to be the emperor instead. Is that what you are telling me?"

"Yes, that's it! He wants to take Isaac down. Can you imagine that? He would be impossible. He is impossible right now! Even the emperor is afraid of him. I can tell; it's one of the reasons I am here."

"It couldn't happen to a nicer man," one of the masked men commented.

Talon raised his hand. "I see what you mean. It's bad enough with the Devil we have without adding to the island's problems with one who is even more insane?"

"Well, I wouldn't have put it quite like that, but yes, that is what is at stake," Diocles huffed.

"So because you are so faithful to the monster you work for, you have come to me to take out the monster you don't like so much?"

"I, er, um.... Isaac is somewhat controllable, when he is not signing idiotic decrees, but this Exazenos will not be. I fear for everyone, and even you should be concerned, because he will not honor any agreement you have with Isaac."

"What agreement?" There was a hard edge to Talon's reply.

"Sir, I might be an old man half way to my dotage, but I can read and am quite able to come to conclusions. I know you told him something on that stormy night, and there was a strange dagger sticking out of his pillow. He was scared out of his wits when I came to see him the next morning. Then when he gets home to the palace there is a chest of gold sitting waiting for him and a document which I happen to have seen."

The green eyes were smiling behind their cover again. "Lord Diocles, you are a remarkable man. It took courage to come here and talk to me. I appreciate that."

"You have no idea, Sir Talon." Diocles tapped his chest. "I didn't think my heart would survive it. May I have some more of that very good wine? Where did you get it? Alanya perhaps?"

"From here, right off my lands, Lord Diocles. I'm glad you like it. Would you like me to supply you with some in Famagusta?"

"I would be delighted! You will have many customers for a wine such as this. I shall recommend it," said the old man, who had by now relaxed visibly. Then he frowned, trying to bring them back to the reason for his visit. "Do you think you can do anything about this terrible situation, Sir Talon?"

"Perhaps," said Talon. "I might need your help to obtain information, however; news does not travel very fast."

"Yes," Diocles mused. "Anything to establish some calm in these choppy waters. Would message pigeons be of some help?"

"You took the words right out of my mouth, Sir." The green eyes smiled again. "I shall provide an escort back to the city gates for you. There are often dangers on the road, and I would not have you come to grief for your pains. You may take some pigeons. I just happen to have some here in the castle. Quite a coincidence! You must also take a bottle or two of wine with you."

Several weeks later, two pigeons arrived at the castle. The one from Dimitri informed Talon that Pantoleon was departing for Limassol by ship, as did the message from Diocles, but this one added that he might be going on to Paphos somewhat later in the month.

The weather was clear and storms were an unlikely occurrence for a while, so Talon decided that the two ships should sail for Paphos and then for Tyre leaving, him and Boethius in the city. Reza and his cutthroats were keyed up for the mission to Syria, while Rostam could hardly wait to be part of the venture. He was going to sail with Henry and be under his command. Irene went on the ship with her father, as it looked for the time being at least that Pantoleon was not venturing very far afield. Jacob was very relieved that finally he was going home, although none of them knew if the situation had changed since his arrival on the island.

Guy dropped Talon and Boethius, with his daughter, at Paphos, and then the two ships set sail for Tyre, which was set in a south-easterly direction. Reza was now in charge and his mission was to pick up the remains of Talon's treasure from the Jews of Acre before it was plundered by Lord Joscelin.

Within a few days they were in sight of land, and Acre was visible on the horizon. Now it became important to be careful, as people who lived on the coastline were alert for pirates and might sound the alarm. The last thing Henry wanted was to be chased by military galleys. Instead they sought out a quiet inlet where they could drop Jacob off.

Jacob was put ashore just north of Acre on a lonely beach and disappeared into the night. His task was to gather up as much of

Talon's wealth still held by his Jewish compatriots as he could and bring it to the south of Tyre in two weeks, where there would be much less scrutiny. They had arranged a series of agreed signals to decide on where exactly the transfer was to be made.

Henry's ship then put off from shore and rejoined Guy, whereupon the two vessels set sail for the area of land belonging to the principality of Antioch just north of Lattakieh: a small harbor tucked into a large cove. They arrived several days later, and once again a single ship nosed into the sheltered waters of the harbor and discharged a cargo. These men were led by Reza and they had a dangerous mission to perform, the kind that Reza exulted in, which was precisely why Talon had set him the task.

It took several days of discreet enquiry in the small town to discover where Salah Ed Din might be. Most people along the coastline in these parts paid attention to the rumors of his whereabouts, because they sensed danger. Then Reza took his four men and set out on horseback towards Aleppo, where Salah Ed Din had last been heard of by the Christian communities and the caravaners who hovered about the walls.

Two days later they were passing the ancient city of Apames and then headed Northeast in a straight line for Aleppo.

"Now is the time to be careful," Reza told his men. "Do not speak unless you have to, as we have a distinct accent and that might cause suspicion."

They were moving into a kind of no man's land between Antioch and the tribal states nominally controlled by Salah Ed Din's army. They were all dressed very much like tribal warriors and had no trouble with passing merchants and their camel trains; they simply appeared to be warriors on their way towards the prince's army. It was easy enough to ask directions and keep moving into an area which became increasingly crowded and busy.

By now they were passing encampments all along the sides of the old Roman road. Groups of armed men appeared and disappeared, seemingly at random, with larger caravans moving along the road in both directions. Before very long Reza and his men were covered with a fine layer of dust on their clothing and horses, surrounded by the noisy bleating of goats and sheep and the roaring of disgruntled camels.

Within a couple of days they came in sight of the main army encampment, and they paused on the rise of a hill to take it all in. The army spread out on the plain as far as the eye could see. In the distance was the great fortress of Aleppo that dominated the plains

all around. Ten miles west of Aleppo was the grand army of Salah
Ed Din. Here were tents of every description. For the most part they
were the dark black or tanned coverings of the Beduin, but among
these were many tents of a far richer kind that denoted wealthy and
powerful princes. There were innumerable herds of animals: from
goats and sheep to camels and horses in great numbers. Men on
horseback dashed about, creating small clouds of dust with their
passing that rose into the evening sky and created a light brown
haze. The setting sun to the West was a dark red color as a result.

"We must find a space for ourselves and then begin our search,"
Reza told his men. They had barely said a word to one another for
the last two days, but now they had to pretend to be a part of this
seething mass of warriors and tribesmen.

Their needs were simple but water was of concern, so they
searched for a well and camped not too far from it, near a group of
tents. Having seen to their mounts, the five men settled down to eat
and prepare for the night. The calls for prayers resonated across the
plain and everyone took out a small mat and faced south by
southeast. A low murmur came from the massed population as the
prayers were said. No one remarked the newcomers. Men were
coming in on a daily basis to be absorbed by the army of the Sultan.

There was one incident that evening when someone approached
them from the nearest camp out of curiosity. The man appeared out
of the darkness suddenly enough for Reza and his men to reach for
their weapons. Junayd even stood up from his position near the fire.

The man flinched at this display of martial alertness and said a
nervous, "As Salaam Alaikum."

Reza stood up and replied, "Wa Alaikum Salaam to you, Hadj."

The visitor was indeed a Hadj and was pleased at this show of
respect.

"Have you eaten? We have enough to spare," he offered.

"We have eaten, but God bless you for your kindness," Reza
replied.

"You have just arrived?"

"Yes, from a long way away to the southeast. We are of the Bani
Khalid tribe."

The old man started. "You have come a long way," he said,
pulling on his beard. Reza had chosen the name of a tribe feared all
over the southern deserts of Mesopotamia. The Bani Khalid were
notorious raiders and thieves. They would come out of the desert
and pillage an encampment, taking the herds, killing all the menfolk
and stealing the women and children.

"The cause has brought us all the way here. Will you join us for Khaffee?" Reza was well aware that the old man wanted to talk, so this was an offer that he would be unlikely to refuse. The others made way for him to sit amongst them. None spoke, leaving it to Reza to converse with the old man. They exchanged pleasantries and the usual grumbling about too many people, too much dust and not enough fighting with the God dammed Frans.

"There will be a shortage of water before long," the old man, whose name was Al Bara, told them.

"Will the army move then?" Reza asked.

"In about a week, as I understand it, we will all move nearer to Aleppo. The Great Sultan, may God bless his faithfulness forever, has ordered that we move before the rains come."

Reza nodded. That made sense. Should the rains come prematurely the plains would be transformed into a sea of mud. The area around Aleppo was more undulating and people could camp on the hills surrounding the city.

"Does the Prince reside in the city?"

The old man shook his head. "No, he is here with us. Whenever the army is on the move he is present."

"I have seen little of this camp, as we have only just arrived, but one thing is very curious," Reza said, as Junayd poured some more of the sweet black liquid into a tiny cup for the old man.

He took it gratefully and sipped, then he opened his mouth and smacked his lips. "What are you so curious about?" he asked.

"I see a tower, or what looks like a tower, in the distance. It stands quite alone, which is why I was curious. Is it some kind of siege engine? Those I recognize, but this is unusual."

Al Bara laughed. He had only two teeth left on his lower jaw and huge gaps in the upper jaw. "Ha. Ha! No! That is where our Great Leader Salah Ed Din sleeps at night."

Reza looked astonished and then skeptical. "Does he not like living in a tent?"

Again the Hadj chuckled. "The word is that he is fearful of those devils incarnate from the Hashashini who live in the mountains to the West. One Rashid Ed Din, you know of him?" Reza shook his head, although he knew of Rashid Ed Din very well indeed. Al Bara continued to lecture him. "No? He is also known as the School Teacher and has sworn to kill Salah Ed Din one day. Those evil people have tried several times in the past to kill our Great Leader and failed, so he is taking no chances. God damn the Killers."

"So he locks himself in there at night?" Reza asked with an incredulous smile.

"Indeed, and the guards are awake all night around him. No one can enter while he sleeps."

"Is that so... " Reza said quietly.

Two nights later, while the huge camp slept, Reza gained entrance to the tower. His men were now guarding the wooden building; the regular guards were unconscious, gagged and tied up in the darkness at the base the tower. One of them had had a large ornate key in his possession, which allowed Reza to gain silent entry.

Salah Ed Din woke with a start to find a dark figure who had only his eyes visible seated on the edge of the bed. "Who are you and how did you get in here?" he demanded.

"It was easy enough, Lord," Reza replied.

"Guards!" Salah Ed Din called. Two guards from outside promptly ran into the room, but they, too, were covered up to their eyes. Reza calmly lit a lantern and sat back. Salah Ed Din stared in alarm. "These are your men?"

"Yes, Lord."

Salah Ed Din had a sense of deja vu. This had happened once before. "Are you here to kill me?" He braced himself. He was a brave man and did not fear death, but masked men who penetrated his best defenses unnerved him.

"No, my Lord. I am here at the request of my Brother. You might know him. His name is Talon."

Salah Ed Din cast his mind back and nodded his head slowly, once. "I remember a Talon from Egypt. A Frankish slave; I watched him play Chogan once. Good player. What does he want from me?"

"A letter, My Lord. Just a letter."

"Is that all?"

"Yes, but it has to come from you. I shall explain... " At a gesture from Reza the two guards retreated, and Reza spent the next ten minutes explaining the reason for his visit to Salah Ed Din. "So you see, Lord, Talon is asking that you remember the favor he did for you a long time ago when you were in Egypt."

"He stole one of my ships! I'd have thought that was enough of a favor," Salah Ed Din rasped.

"He saved your life from those people who belonged to Rashid Ed Din, Sire. Worth a ship, and also perhaps a letter, don't you think?"

For the first time Salah Ed Din smiled. "This is brazen! *You* are brazen! You have risked much for a letter! Incredible! How does this Talon, this former slave, find people like you to assist him?"

"Because he is one of us and was trained with me. He is my Brother, and at present he is working hard to protect our families from an acquaintance of yours, Emperor Komnenos of Cyprus. Talon would have come himself otherwise. He does, however, send his most sincere greetings and wishes you well."

"Not a very likable man, that Isaac; none of those Greek tyrants are, but he keeps away from my affairs so I don't mind. So Isaac calls us 'friends', does he?"

"That is Talon's understanding. A letter from you would help to lock in place a truce between them. Otherwise he would have to resort to other plans, and you know what that means."

"Yes," Salah Ed Din said, with a hard look at Reza, "I do. Very well. I have parchment and ink on that table over there. May I rise and write what is needed?"

"Thank you, Lord. I think a simple message would be best. Easier to remember, if you know what I mean?"

Within a few minutes the letter was written and sealed with Salah Ed Din's own great seal.

As he handed the parchment over to Reza, Salah Ed Din said, "I did not know such people as you existed outside the ranks of that murderous gang of Batinistas. I still do not approve, but if you are a companion to Talon I can respect that. He did much to save a family in Egypt who are dear to me, and I did receive a message from him after a certain er, battle. He made sure a distant relative was buried properly. That meant a great deal to me." Almost as an afterthought he asked, "Have you killed all my guards?"

Reza chuckled. "If you will be kind enough to give us an hour, then you have my word you will find that they are alive and unharmed, Lord."

Salah Ed Din shook his head, an amused look on his lean features. "Pah! Let them stew until the morning. If they cannot defend me they should learn the penalty by having an uncomfortable night. Go now. Give my salutations to your... Brother."

"I will, Sire. God protect you, my Lord." Reza disappeared, and Salah Ed Din went back to bed to lie wondering about what had just happened, and remembering the green-eyed Frank who had ridden and played so well on the field of Chogan. He left the lamp burning; it would be many, many nights before he slept deeply again.

Reza and his companions arrived back at the port of Lattakieh late one afternoon, four days after they had vanished from the army encampment of Salah Ed Din. They then turned south, and on a cape jutting out into the sea, they lit a small fire and waited.

Two hours later, a boat crunched onto the beach below and they were helped aboard.

A relieved Guy greeted them. "Thank God you made it back!" he said as he gripped Reza by the hand and hauled him onto the deck. Reza had given him the gist of what he was going to attempt to do before leaving. Guy had said then that he thought Talon and Reza were both mad.

"I didn't expect to ever see you again, my friend," he growled after they had embraced. "Were you successful?"

Reza showed him the sealed parchment down in the cabin, after they set sail to join Henry for the voyage south towards Tyre. Guy was astonished to hear how it had been done. "That was incredibly dangerous, Reza," he said. "Was it that important?"

"Talon seems to think so, and I believe him. Salah Ed Din had no problem recalling his name. Even called him a ship thief. Ha Ha! Was it this ship he stole?"

"No, it is the one that Henry sails!" Guy gave a bark of laughter. "By God, but you are quite insane, Master Reza. All the same I am very glad that you are back with us."

"As am I! Now we have to meet up with Jacob, and then it is home for us all. I am missing my wife and little boy."

They joined Henry's ship, and after an exchange of greetings they turned south. Four days later they were anchored off the coast of the Kingdom of Jerusalem, south of Tyre, waiting for the caravan to arrive. The signal from shore came two nights later and boats were launched to start the process of loading.

Jacob met them on the beach and explained the delay.

"The situation in Acre has deteriorated, Reza," he told him. "I have left with everything I have. My family is up on the cliff waiting for us to complete this task, and then I am heading north."

"What is going on in the city?" Reza asked him with concern, "Are all of you leaving?" he meant the Jews.

It was hard to see his expression in the darkness, but Reza could see that Jacob was distraught. "Most of us. There are some die hards who think this will pass, but I don't think so. Not this time. We will be safer in the county of Tripoli. At least the Duke respects the customs in this part of the world and will give us what refuge he can. Bad times are coming, Reza."

"If you and your family wish to come with us, we will welcome you," Reza told him. "I know that Talon would say as much."

"I thank you for your kind offer, Reza. You have been good to me. Who knows? One day, perhaps, but we have relatives in Tripoli, so that is where we are going."

"Will you be safe on the road?"

"We are traveling at night to avoid marauding Franks. Salah Ed Din has decreed that our people should not be harmed by his people. They will honor that command, I think."

"What has been going on in the city?" Reza asked.

"Joscelin of Antioch paid us a visit, which was not a pleasant one. The Bishop is helping him with his quest for funds. They made a start on our community before Joscelin had to suddenly depart for Jerusalem. Something has come up. But all the indications are that he will be back, and then our people will be robbed of all we have."

"Then we should load and depart to allow you to continue with your journey," Reza stated.

Two hours later they embraced and Jacob said, "Go with God, Reza, and please give my respects to Sir Talon. I shall miss you all."

Reza watched him climb the narrow pathway towards the top of the cliff. He sensed that the world in this Kingdom was going to change. He was remembering the vast army of Salah Ed Din.

Swift of foot to avenge are we!
He whose hands are clean and pure,
Naught our wrath to dread hath he;
Calm his cloudless days endure.
—Aeschylus

Chapter 35

1187

Capture and Revenge

Talon and Boethius were careful to keep a very low profile when they arrived back in Paphos, for a new kind of person was to be seen lurking about on the streets. Their presence was brought to his attention by Nasuh and Khuzaymah, the two men he had assigned to protect Boethius. Talon guessed that these watchful people belonged to Pantoleon.

"How long have you been aware of them?" he asked, while they were eating late one evening at the villa.

Nasuh glanced at Khuzaymah. "Not very long, Master, only since a ship came here a few weeks ago that people said belonged to the Emperor, but he was not on board. There was instead a man with a very scarred face called Lord Exazenos. He came ashore and stayed at the castle. And there do not seem to be many of his men on the streets; by our count, about four."

Talon was digesting this information when Khuzaymah mentioned something else. "The rumor is Exazenos has turfed out the original people who lived in the castle and it belongs to him."

"Four, you say? Do they look competent?" he asked. He didn't ask how his men knew; they had been trained by him and Reza to be observant, and now their instincts were hard at work.

"We need to stay out of their sight, Master. Even though we do not stand out and are careful not to be seen armed, they might notice us, and then there could be a problem."

"You are right to do so," Talon agreed.

"This man Exazenos, Pantoleon or whomsoever he is has got other spies everywhere," Boethius murmured with a look at the door. "Some of my acquaintances have been arrested for sedition." He looked very nervous.

"So Pantoleon has really penetrated this city. He intends to make it his own, and all of its citizens bound to him through fear," Talon remarked thoughtfully. He, too, glanced at the door. He searched his memory for anything untoward that might have occurred here in Boethius's house. The only person who could possibly be suspect was the steward, but when he mentioned him to Boethius the merchant shook his head dismissively. "He has been with us for a generation, Talon. I don't think he could possibly be a traitor."

Talon let it rest at that for the time being, but resolved to have one of his men keep an eye open for any untoward behavior by the steward henceforth.

Talon and his men set about discovering the whereabouts of the newcomers and learning their habits. It turned out that the men were indeed watchful and appeared to be keeping an eye on the local population, but they were fond of their comforts.

In the evenings they could be found in one of the harbor wine houses and rarely left before midnight, when they appeared to be comfortably full. Having tracked them back to their villa, which was on the south side of the harbor, Talon felt satisfied that he and his men could deal with these newcomers should the need arise. In the meantime, he and his men would keep their own presence to a minimum.

They settled down to a routine whereby Talon assisted Boethius to find the right people to add to his tiny cell of spies in the city. It was not easy, because Boethius needed to keep his own presence a secret, while recruiting disaffected people around him. Famagusta had been easy by comparison, as Dimitri had brought men with him he could use and trust. Eventually Boethius declared that he had two men who were former servants of his who were in need of work and had been badly abused on former visits by Isaac and his army of thugs. They agreed willingly to work with him, and the slow process of training them began.

Two weeks later a pigeon arrived that changed all that. Jannat and Irene were working with the birds, now that Talon and Rostam were away. Boethius brought the message.

"Pantoleon is sailing, first to Limassol and then on to Paphos! Our contact says that he wants to consolidate his hold on this city. Beware!" Boethius informed Talon, who stared at the missive. The source was very likely Diocles, so the message was probably accurate. He mulled over the pending situation.

"We cannot leave, not by sea anyway," Boethius said, looking pale and very uneasy. His first instinct was to flee, and with good reason.

"We could leave by land, but it would be a long ride; and besides, I would like to see what he does when he gets here," Talon said. "We'll just keep ourselves out of sight and see what happens."

Boethius reluctantly agreed but was clearly unhappy.

A week later a ship nosed into the harbor and docked alongside the quay. Passengers, in the form of smart-looking soldiers and crew, came and went, then the ship was pushed to anchor in the harbor pool. Talon noticed Nigel prominent among the crew. Pantoleon's arrival was much earlier than they had anticipated, which worried Talon.

At least the arrival of the chief spy for the emperor was less obtrusive than those visits of the emperor, who came and went with much fanfare, and usually left at least one merchant destitute.

Standing on the quayside as close to the harbor pool as he could without been obvious, Talon studied the ship anchored inside the storm wall. Another week had passed, and the ship captained by Nigel had been in harbor for all this time without incident.

Nasuh, who had been posing as a fisherman, was able to get much closer to the ships and had told him of a small contingent of men who had left the ship and ridden off to the castle, where they'd remained. One matched the description of Pantoleon.

Dimitri had thought that Pantoleon might have his treasure on board, so Boethius's men were watching carefully to see any unloading took place.

There was not much activity on board. Talon gave up and walked back to the villa.

However, later that night one of the men that Boethius had posted to watch the ship came hurrying to the villa and told them the ship was being moved. Dropping everything, Talon and Nasuh raced over to the harbor and settled down to watch. The vessel was once again tied up at the wharf, and by the light of a few torches men were unloading heavy-looking boxes, which were loaded onto donkeys and led off into the darkness under heavy guard. Talon imagined he knew where they were going. It looked to him as though Pantoleon was taking up residence in the city of Paphos. Surprisingly, the work only went on for about an hour, then the men returned to the ship. It hardly seemed enough time to account for the sort of wealth that created an empire—or usurped one.

Back in the villa, Talon said to Boethius, "I am sure the emperor does not know anything about Pantoleon's movements to establish himself here. I wonder if we can cause some disaffection?"

"You mean... send a message to our friends in Famagusta?" Boethius asked. "Oh yes, I like the sound of that!"

The next morning a pigeon winged its way towards the castle on the ridge.

In Paphos the townspeople reacted with apprehension to the presence of the emperor's senior spy, especially as arrests grew in number. Hence there were fewer people on the streets, and the wine shops were empty at dusk, a sure sign of unease. Still, Pantoleon stayed in the castle for the most part, and Talon didn't get a glimpse of him for several days.

Then a note came via one of the gardeners, who seemed nervous as he delivered it, that there was more activity going on down at the harbor. Talon didn't think to ask the man where he had obtained the information, he simply reacted. Deeming it safe to move about, because as far as he knew Pantoleon had not left the castle, he decided to investigate and made his way towards the harbor dressed as a fisherman. He carried a basket on his shoulder and wore a filthy sack over his shoulders with a hood of the same material, looking as though he was on his way home from a hard day on the water. He went with Nasuh, separated by about fifty paces, which was their usual precaution. Nasuh was watching his back.

Talon had more than one reason to check on Pantoleon's ship. There was something on the foredeck of the ship that he wanted to investigate. He shuffled the length of the quay until he was almost opposite the still tied-up vessel, and there his suspicions were confirmed. From the ship at the quayside came a smell that was all too familiar to Talon. Pantoleon possessed Greek Fire! He stared at the covered devices on either side of the ship forward of the main mast, then scrutinized the rest of the deck. There were heavily armed men standing about.

Perhaps they were waiting until nightfall to continue with the unloading, he thought, as he slouched by. Talon turned away, then noticed something out to sea, a sail. As it turned out, it was two sails. He wondered if it might be Reza coming back to Paphos and hoped the journey had been successful. However, should it be his ships, there was going to be a problem with Pantoleon being in the city at the same time. Two ships arriving would not go unnoticed, and that was the last thing he needed right now. He also noticed a group of soldiers walking along the quay. It was time to leave; he could slip by the patrol easily enough, he assumed.

Someone must have thought he was paying too much attention to the ship as he walked back towards Nasuh, because a man looked up from giving orders on its deck, pointed at him and then shouted something. A group of armed sailors hurriedly left the ship and began to row towards the quayside. He was considering whether to make a run for it or continue acting inconspicuous when the patrol began to run towards him, their spears at the ready, and blocked his path. The men from the ship came up from behind, and he was surrounded.

The guards rounded up three other men who had been loitering on the pathway gawking at the galley. All three loudly declared their innocence and indignation at being accosted in this manner. Alongside them Talon whined, "Sirs, I am just a fisherman going home. Let me be, I beg of you."

"We'll see about that," growled one of the men from the boat. "We need workers this night, and you look strong enough." His men seized Talon and the others and held them, and the man off the boat snatched back Talon's hood.

"Why, what have we here?" he exclaimed, as he saw Talon's light hair and green eyes. Then he realized Talon carried a sword. "Hold him!" he cried, reaching for Talon's belt. "By God, he's armed!"

Talon spun within the grip of the two men and kicked out. One staggered back and fell, clutching his knee with a howl, while the other was tossed onto the ground to lie gasping on his back. Talon's sword flashed and he was on guard, facing the sailors. They were startled enough by his sudden and violent move—most of their victims were defenseless—to give him time to put his back to the low stone wall behind him, searching desperately for a means of escape. He was too far form the quay's edge to leap for the water.

The soldiers were quick to recover. Within moments he was surrounded by a row of men pointing long sharp spears at him. The man who had accosted him stared at him from behind the hedge of spears. "So you are a 'poor fisherman', eh? Drop the sword and give yourself up."

Cursing himself for his stupidity and carelessness, Talon looked around and saw there was no way out; he would never make it over the wall without getting a spear in the back, and there were far too many of them to fight. He stared hard at the man for a long moment before he laid his sword on the ground.

477

"Tell me your name!" the man shouted, but Talon was not looking at him. He had seen Nasuh, sliding into cover behind a pile of lobster baskets. The boy had the good sense not to come to Talon's aid, as that would have meant a useless death. Talon was seized and marched, not into town, as he'd expected, but onto the ship, where his arms were wrenched behind him and tightly tied. Then he was forced into the waist of the vessel while the man who had shouted at him went below.

Before very long, to Talon's great surprise Pantoleon stepped up onto the deck and stood in front of him. For a long moment the scarred face assessed him, and then recognition began slowly to dawn. "It is you!" He breathed in a low tone, almost to himself, staring hard at his prisoner. "You are Talon, the Templar. By God, I have you!" he smiled then, and Talon went cold.

Pantoleon stepped forward and smashed his fist into Talon's face. "My spies informed me that you were here in Paphos. Did you really think that I didn't have my finger on the very life pulse of this town? This miserable town is a village compared to what I used to control! But I intend to make it mine. The island will be docile enough for what comes next. This is just a taste of what I have in mind for what you did to my family," he snarled. "First, however, I shall present you to the Emperor. I have been looking for a coup of this kind."

Talon remained silent. He had a sick feeling in his gut. He shook his head and felt dizzy, wondering if his cheek bone had been broken. The place where Pantoleon had struck was beginning to swell rapidly.

"What? Nothing to say?" Pantoleon snarled.

"You are a fiend, and your father was a traitor. What else is there to say?" Talon replied.

This earned him a blow to the stomach that doubled him over with a gasp. But Talon, out of the corner of his good eye, had noticed the tops of two masts beyond the harbor entrance, between the horns of the sea breakers protecting the inner harbor. He wondered again who it might be and hoped fervently that it was his people coming back from Tyre.

"So you are the much vaunted *Magician* they are all talking about," Pantoleon sneered, and struck him again across the mouth with the back of his hand.

"Look, you!" he called out to his men. "You in particular, Gabros. This is the man who can throw thunderbolts at people?

Show us what you can do, *Sir* Talon," he jeered. Gabros looked nervous, but when nothing happened he grinned.

"You are right, Master," he said to Pantoleon. "This is no magician." He spat at Talon and turned his back.

"Your timing is impeccable, Sir Talon. We were just about to leave for Famagusta, and now we have a cargo that will please the Emperor, I have no doubt about that. The rat walked right into the trap!"

Talon wondered if his threat was still fresh in the emperor's mind. Isaac would be subjected to a horrible revenge if Pantoleon had his way, Reza would see to that.

"By the way, it was not hard to intimidate the steward of that pitiful merchant friend of yours. They are all the same: gold talks, and so does fear." Pantoleon chuckled. "It won't be long before every one of them is either working for me, or... is dead. The merchant will be taken care of when I get back from Famagusta. His daughter, I hear, is young and ripe. She will of course go to the emperor, once I am done with her father."

Feeling a freezing sensation down his back for Boethius, Talon glared at Pantoleon. "I hope I see you in hell."

This earned him another blow to the face with the flat of Pantoleon's hand that sent him stumbling backwards. The guards caught him and held him upright.

"Then hell it is, but I intend to make sure you proceed me, and that it is a very long and painful journey for you!" Pantoleon smirked. It came out as a ghastly grimace. Talon found himself staring into the insane eyes of a gargoyle. "I'll keep your odd looking sword to remind me of you." He tossed it to one of the men. "Take it below," he ordered.

"You did well, Gabros," he told his lieutenant. "Go ashore and guard the castle with your men, while I take a short voyage to present my prize to the emperor. I shall be back within a week. Nigel, we are leaving now! We have what we came for. Take the ship out to sea."

Only then did Talon become aware of Nigel, who had been standing on the afterdeck watching the events taking place in the waist. Talon glanced up at his erstwhile ship's captain, locked eyes with him and shook his head in disgust. Nigel turned away and began to issue orders for the ship to cast off.

Gabros jumped ashore and strode down the pier with four of his men, while the crew of the ship scurried about preparing for sea. No one seemed to have remarked the two sails just a league from shore, heading for the harbor entrance.

On deck there was much activity. Nigel called for the sails to be dropped on both masts, and soon they bellied and caught the rising wind. The ship surged forward and he gave orders for the rowers to stand down. It was then that he and Pantoleon noticed the two ships heading almost directly towards them. They were going to pass one another very closely, so Nigel stood next to the steersmen to make sure that there was no mistake. He didn't want a collision.

They were about a quarter of a league out from the harbor horns when the lead ship passed them on their port side. Then it was that Nigel saw Guy standing on the vessel with another man. Almost at the same time, Guy saw Nigel and pointed. He seized the arm of his companion, pointed again and bellowed something.

Pantoleon, who was standing next to Nigel, stared over the water. "That'sss that captain who got away, issn't it?" he demanded.

"Yes, Lord. His name is Guy, and—" he turned to scrutinize the other ship—"by God Almighty, that other ship is captained by Henry, another man belonging to Sir Talon! What are they doing coming into this harbor as bold as you please?"

"They are coming to pick up their leader, I don't doubt," Pantoleon laughed, struck by the absurdity of the timing. "Well, they are too late!"

Pantoleon reached out and hauled Talon, whose arms were now bound, and shoved him towards the side nearest to the approaching galleys.

"Your leader isss my prisoner!" he shouted across the space between the ships. "You will attack our ship at hisss peril!" He braced Talon up, so that there was no mistaking him.

He was answered by a roar from Guy that carried across the water. "Talon! Dear God, how? We see you! Harm him and you will pay a dreadful price, you bastard! Nigel! You will answer for your crimes, as will that piece of offal standing next to you!"

"Follow us and sink him!" Talon yelled at the top of his voice. "Sink us!" Talon shouted again, before Pantoleon knocked him to the deck.

"Get to work, you oaf!" Pantoleon snarled at Nigel. "Lay on more sail!" The forward ship was already beginning to turn, even as he watched. "They are going to give chase!" Nigel exclaimed, sounding worried.

"Then do as I ssay and put on more sail!" Pantoleon roared.

He looked down at Talon, who was lying on the deck bleeding from yet another cut to his face.

"Take him below and put him in the hold," Pantoleon ordered his men, who checked that Talon's arms and wrists were tight behind him. They then hustled Talon down the companionway at the aft of the vessel, along a short corridor and down another ladder to the lower deck, where he was thrust roughly into a dark hold which stank of old wood and filthy water.

He fell onto his knees in a half-hand of brackish water and took a deep breath of foul air that set him coughing. The ship rocked on a stronger wave and, losing his balance, he felt to his side, striking his shoulder hard against something with as sharp edge. The sudden pain was briefly agonizing, even after all the blows he had taken already. It was hard to move about in the rocking dark with his hands bound behind him, but he braced his knees wide apart and turned to grope at the low shape behind him, to find that he was kneeling next to a small chest of wood with a padlock. Moving cautiously through the sloshing bilge water, he discovered that there were about ten of these small boxes in the hold with him. So that was what Pantoleon had been unloading. Little good the knowledge would do him now, he thought ruefully.

Above him he heard the shouted orders and thump of bare feet, and then knocks and thumps as the rowers on the deck just above his head continued increased the pace of their work. The rhythmic beat of a drum hammered above his head. Talon's eyes gradually became accustomed to the gloom and he stared around him seeking something, anything that would help him to cut his bonds. He had to get off the ship before it was too far out to sea.

On Guy's ship there was pandemonium. "Is it really Talon on that ship!" Guy shouted sounding dazed.

Reza had seen and his heart had sunk. How in God's name had Talon managed to be captured? At the back of his mind he suspected some form of treachery but when he heard Talon he knew what he had to do. "Turn this ship now! Turn it now!" he yelled at Guy who had hastened to comply, but he asked, "What about Talon?"

"Do as I ask! Talon will understand, of that I am sure. You heard him. We have to stop that man no matter what. Talon is putting his trust in us although I do not know how we will accomplish this."

Reza thought of Rav'an and how she would react to the dreadful news if they failed. "We cannot fail!" he told himself with his teeth clenched. He slapped Guy on the arm. 'Wake up Guy!" he shouted.

Guys looked dazed and shaken. He kept muttering "God damn, God damn!"

"We must not fail, Guy! This is not an opportunity that comes around more than once and Talon knows it. We can take that ship and bring him back and I pray to God that we can save him, but we must first catch that ship. Can we do it?" Reza demanded.

"I will certainly try. We cannot let that man take Talon back to his blood soaked dungeons with him. And I owe Nigel for the last time," Guy growled regaining his self control. He had been badly shaken to see his leader in the hands of that monster. He shouted orders to his men to hurry. Many had already seen Talon on the deck of the other ship so they needed no persuasion. They ran to tighten the sails and lend help to the rowers.

The ship almost spun on its keel as his rowers and the crew brought it about in a welter of foam and agitated water. Then the oarsmen labored to drive it forward from a standstill, the water all around them churned into a froth by the long oars.

They had just gone about when Henry's ship came by. "Are you going after him?" Henry shouted over to them, as his own ship began the same complicated maneuver.

"Yes! Henry they have Talon as a prisoner! Follow us as fast as you can. It could take two of us to stop him," Guy shouted back.

"What! Jesu!" Henry swore. "Are you sure of that?" he called back. He had not seen the exchange between the ships.

"Yes, we are sure. We saw him, but he has ordered us to take that ship." Guy bellowed back.

Henry nodded unhappily. Then he shouted "Beware, my men tell me he has Greek Fire. "

"We have the Scorpions!" Reza shouted. "If we keep our distance he can't touch us and we can sink him."

"Hurry!" was all Henry called back. He then focussed on the difficult task of bringing his heavily laden ship about. Guy was captaining the lighter galley, so it was not long before they were racing after Pantoleon's ship, leaving Henry to gather speed as fast as he could.

"What are we doing?" Rostam asked him. Henry turned to the boy and paused, looking down at him before he reluctantly told him the news.

"You must be brave, young lad. Your father is a prisoner on that ship, and we must try our utmost to save him."

He reached out a hand to steady Rostam. The boy's face had gone white. "Be strong, lad. We and your uncle will not let that scum get away, and we will do all we can with God's help to get your father back. On that ship over there is your father's and my lady Theodora's mortal enemy, and we are going after him. If we succeed, we will be doing this island a huge favor!" Henry tried not to show his own distress.

Rostam nodded, his head down. "Yes, I will be strong, but we must catch them," he said. His tone was cold, and Henry looked at the boy. *God help his enemies if he grows to be a man*, he thought to himself.

With oars rising and falling at a frantic pace, Guy and his leading men shouted encouragement. The burly oarsmen lifted, pushed forward and dropped the oars, then strained back, repeating the process as fast as they were physically able. Crewmen squirted water into their gaping mouths from skins and doused them with seawater as they sweated and gasped within the confines of the lower deck.

"Tell the men below that I shall intercede with Talon to double their wages if we succeed in catching up with him," Reza said to Guy.

"You have no need to encourage them, Reza. It is Lord Talon whom they are after. But Nigel is not going to make it easy, Reza. Look!" Guy pointed, and Reza saw another small sail belly and fill on the vessel ahead of them. Guy turned and shouted a command, and men ran to do his bidding. A large flat sail was hauled up on the main mast; it took the wind and they all felt the answering surge from their own ship.

"We're gaining!" Reza called, barely controlling the excitement in his voice.

He ran down to the lower deck, below the rowers, and began to make certain preparations. In a short while he came back up on deck and hastened to the prow of their ship, carrying a wax paper bundle.

"You! Help him," Guy shouted to some sailors clustered in the waist. They ran to help, although with trepidation. They had seen these Scorpions in operation and were afraid of them. Reza had tested them at sea on their way to Tyre.

With Reza showing them what to do they removed the canvas coverings of the large wooden cross bows. Checked the thick ropes that were the strings for the bow, then the trigger mechanism for smooth operation.

Then they moved the Scorpion so that its front end protruded out of an opening that had been specially cut in the bows. The huge bow was drawn back with the aid of a small ratchet and the string locked onto the trigger mechanism. The men stood back to allow Reza room. They now had both Scorpions prepared for action.

The sea spray was beginning to fly into the air, sending drops over them as the bows ploughed into the waves, and he fretted. "Bring me some oil cloth covering, and be quick about it!" he ordered one of the sailors. "And tell Guy to stand off sixty paces. We must not get too close, or they will destroy us with that damned Greek Fire!"

Almost as though he had heard them, they noticed some activity at the bows of the other ship. Men stripped the covers off the Greek Fire apparatus on the port side of the ship they were following. They all watched with fascinated dread as the men on Nigel's vessel made preparations for using the deadly equipment. All knew of its reputation, and a few who had sailed with Talon when he himself had used the fearful stuff against pirates made the sign of the cross. A wisp of smoke came from a fire under the tank, heating the contents.

Even though he was in an agony of worry about Talon, Guy grunted with satisfaction as he noticed that despite his best efforts Nigel could not get as much out of his ship as could he. Then Reza signaled that he was ready, so Guy held his course and looked back to where Henry was coming up behind. Henry had all sails on and his oars were rising and falling with great speed. Despite that, it was clear to Guy that Henry could not help at this point. He waved to Reza. "Go ahead!" he called.

A small curl of smoke from the Scorpion in the bows on the starboard side was followed by a loud twang, and a huge arrow streaked away from the ship and sped in a low curve towards the Nigel's ship. It left behind it a thin trail of smoke. The arrow was well centered, but too high. It hissed between the two masts of the fleeing ship and plunged into the sea, almost a quarter of a league beyond.

"That must have at least scared the shit out of them," Guy muttered to himself, as he watched Reza and his crew hastily prepare another arrow. Pantoleon appeared to want to intimidate his pursuers, because a jet of flame shot out from the bows of his ship; but the fire, dripping flames as it arced out, only traveled about thirty paces before falling into the water. Flames spread across the waves as the terrible stuff burned with a ferocity that not even water could extinguish. There was a moan of fear from the crew on Guy's ship, men crossed themselves and threw frightened looks back at him.

"They did not reach us and cannot!" he roared at them, trying to reassure them. "We are out of their range." He sincerely hoped that he was right. He had no idea what the range of Greek fire apparatus was.

They all flinched as another long jet of flame soared out of the tube, this time it reached further than the last but was still only managed about forty paces. He glanced forward to where Reza was crouched over the scorpion. "Dear God, Reza, hurry up! What is taking so long?" he asked the world at large.

On Nigel's ship Pantoleon was staring back at the closing ship with a scowl of worry. They were still too far out of range. "Go and get the prisoner!" he screamed at his nervous men. "We'll see if they are prepared to shoot at us when they see their leader having his throat cut in front of them. Go!"

Guy's crew, feeling more confident once they were past the conflagration on the water, jeered and hooted, then watched with intense interest as Reza concentrated on re-arming his weapon. Once again they hauled the 'bow string' back and locked it in place. Then he crouched over the scorpion and sighted at his target. He forced himself to take a deep breath. Talon was depending upon his accuracy with a notoriously inaccurate device.

It took well over five minutes of concentration as he sighted on the bows of the other ship, but finally Reza raised his arm to indicate to Guy that he was ready.

"Hold her steady!" Guy roared at his steering men, and Reza turned back to his work. He knocked a tiny wedge from beneath the body of the Scorpion, thus tilting its point slightly downwards. Then he peered along the crude sight, one last check, taking in the motions of both boats, and lit the fuse. He stood back and pulled the release cord.

There was a loud twang and the apparatus jerked violently. A long dark arrow sped over the bows and arced towards the deck of Nigel's ship. This time the result was spectacular. The arrow struck with a thump that was even heard by Guy and his crew. It struck just above the water line, below and behind the Greek Fire apparatus.

There it stuck, hissing and sparking, and there was a blinding flash and a sharp report. The front of the enemy ship was enveloped in a cloud of yellowish smoke that hid the impact area. When the smoke began to clear, revealing the extent of the damage, the men on Guy's ship cheered. There was a gaping hole in the port side of the other vessel that was already taking water. Jagged splinters of the timber, some of them longer than spears, were raining from the sky, many landing close to Guy's ship, raising hundreds of small spouts of water as they pierced the water.

On the stricken ship men were staggering about, looking dazed.

"Brother, I hope you were nowhere near that hole," Reza said out loud. "Bring us closer, Guy!" Reza called. "Where is Talon? I want to see that man Pantoleon! He is mine when we board!"

Guy wanted to stand off far enough to make sure that the wind didn't bring sparks towards them. Reluctantly he gave the order to close with the other ship. He knew they had to get to Talon before their enemy dispatched him as they surely would if their ship went down.

Talon scrambled over barrels and chests as he hunted desperately for something to cut his bonds. He fell about in the darkness, barking his shins and knees and almost knocking himself senseless when he fell into a gap between the small chests and knocked his head on one. It was becoming increasingly difficult to keep his balance as the ship heaved up and down and his feet caught on invisible obstructions in the dark. Eventually he fell across a large barrel with a rusty iron hoop that he could use.

The noise of rowers above him working furiously to the drumbeat of the time-keeper took care of any sounds he might have made. There was an air of urgency coming from above, with frantic shouts and increasing speed of the rowers. His own desperation was driving him. Desperately he rubbed the hemp ropes agains the sharp edge of the barrel's hoop, bracing his legs to exert as much force and friction as he could. Gradually the bonds weakened and the fibers parted; finally the last strand fell off and he was free. Rubbing his wrists and upper arms to get the circulation going again, he paused to think. He drew his small knife from his boot and headed for the locked doorway.

Suddenly it was flung open. One of the men who had shoved him into the hold was now standing at the entrance, grumbling. "'Go and get him,' he says. Who is this fellow, anyway? Exazenos seems to want him on deck in a hurry. Why'd we stow him in the first place if he was needed above?"

The man peered into the darkness of the hold. "Where's he gone?" he exclaimed.

He got no further. Talon reached out of the dark and dragged him into the room, and his knife buried itself in the man's abdomen. While the first man lay groaning on the floor, Talon leapt out and faced the other. A short but vicious knife fight ensued, but the crew man was no match for the piston-like fist and the striking feet that seemed to come at him from all directions. Well used to brawls, he fended off the strikes, lashing out with his own blade. But he was a landsman, not a sailor, and momentarily lost his balance. And instant later he choked as Talon's blade was driven into his throat.

Talon peered up the narrow stairway leading to the rowing deck and began to climb. A man appeared at the top just as Talon was gliding up the final steps. Before the sailor could yell the alarm, a hand seized his jerkin and he was hauled off his feet and hurled head first down the stairs to crash into a heap at the bottom.

Without even looking to see how he had fared, Talon leapt up the last of the steps and found himself looking along a wide deck with men laboring at the oars. Their mouths were wide open to take gasping breaths and their faces contorted with the effort as they worked. No one noticed him until he was right behind the time keeper, who was beating out out the rhythm; then one of the rowers saw Talon poised to climb the stairs. The rower shouted and raised his arm to point. The time keeper whirled about, but it was too late. One slash of the razor-sharp blade and he fell, clutching his throat, desperately trying to stop himself from bleeding to death on the dirty wooden floor.

At just this moment the ship staggered and they were all flung sideways. The port side of the vessel exploded inwards and a thousand splinters of wood obliterated the rowers in that area.

Talon knew then exactly what had happened: Reza was somewhere out there and he had just fired a Scorpion. Mentally congratulating his brother on his aim, he knew Reza could have aimed at the middle of the ship, with devastating effect, but had taken the added risk to try and protect his brother. Talon knew it was imperative to get off the ship quickly, but there was one item he was not going to leave behind. He sped up the stairs, looking for the cabins. The screams and cries from above gave him added impetus.

He had only just reached the cabin deck when he felt and heard the splintering crash of another vessel hammering into the ship's side. The shock threw him to his knees as the entire vessel shuddered. Then he heard fierce yells of men boarding Pantoleon's ship.

Grimly deciding that speed would serve best, Guy had managed to bring his ship almost alongside Pantoleon's ship before the operators could get the Greek fire apparatus going again. The shock of the explosion had killed or maimed the men nearest to it, then the impact of the ships' collision rendered most of the other men incapacitated for those critical seconds necessary to aid Reza's boarding party.

In the mad rush over the side, Reza tapped aside a spear and lunged with his sword, spitting a large man with red hair who choked and fell under the feet of Reza's screaming followers. Another wielding an ax charged at Reza, the weapon held over his head to bring it down in a killing blow. Reza danced aside and ripped his keen-edged Japanese weapon across the man's exposed belly. Without even checking on his latest victim, Reza allowed himself to be propelled along the crowded deck towards the after part of the ship. All the while he searched for any sign of Talon and the one man he wanted to take prisoner, and finally discerned Pantoleon on the after part of the main deck, just below the steering deck. The fighting was savage, as every man on the deck knew there was to be no quarter, but Reza and his men had the advantage. But where was Talon?

Many of the men on the main deck forward were still dazed from the explosion and didn't put up much of a fight, but others rallied and fought hard. Men on both sides fell. Battle yells became screams of agony and the deck became slippery with men's blood. The clash of swords on swords and shields became a crazily irregular beat, but slowly the mercenaries of Pantoleon were driven back. Reza could see their commander fighting with skill and determination some way off, but because of the crush of men around him and the need to watch out for his own safety Reza was frustrated in his attempts to get anywhere near to engage his adversary.

Then something occurred that distracted everyone. The Greek Fire apparatus, shaken loose by the explosion and the tilting deck, fell over and ignited. Screams of alarm and fear filled the air as the flaming liquid spread along the wooden deck. The cordage on deck nearby caught and flared, while flames began to lick at the stays and rigging. The stricken vessel came slowly to a wallowing halt as the rowers abandoned their oars and tried to escape while the vessel began to settle in the water by the bows.

"Get off this ship, now!" Reza screamed fearfully at his men, and frantically pulled at those who were to engaged by fighting to hear. Reza then shouted, "Talon! Talon! Where are you?"

There was no answer from among the yells of dismay and fear all around him. There was no option but to leave the ship or go down with it. Reza tried desperately to break through the mob of men to get to the after end of the ship but could not break through. His men dragged at him shouting at him to leave with them. As he was forcibly dragged away by his men he cast a despairing look behind him. Where could Talon be?

Once they saw what had happened the rest of his men needed no further persuasion. They began to break off the fight and in a mad rush scrambled to get over the side onto their own ship, which Guy was already directing his men to push away from the stricken vessel. Some of his men fell into the sea and ropes were tossed to them, but most managed to get back onto the other ship; some of the mercenaries also tried to get to safety, but were speared as they tried, pleading to be rescued from their flaming ship. A thick column of stinking black smoke was rising into the sky.

Guy bellowed orders at his men to throw water onto everything exposed to the flames, working furiously to get his ship poled to safety well out of the danger area, as the rapidly flowing Greek fire began to pour over the side of Pantoleon's vessel into the sea to threaten his own ship anew.

Men on Pantoleon's ship began to jump overboard on the side away from the fire, while others tried to get a boat launched, struggling with it against the falling tackle and flames that threatening to engulf them. From the safety of his ship, Reza stared bleakly over at the other vessel with its dead and wounded, wondering where in all the destruction taking place Talon might be, and where Pantoleon might have disappeared to. There was no sign of either.

In the gloom and chaos of the cabin decks, littered with fallen lanterns and other debris, Talon stumbled about. He thought he heard someone calling his name but could not be sure. He could not go up on deck without a weapon, and the panicked rush of rowers scrambling for their lives prevented him from going forward. He was aware that the ship might be sinking, so there was only a short time left to find his weapon before the ship went down.

He was also chillingly aware that Pantoleon would almost certainly be coming to finish him off personally. The yells and sounds of fighting above him increased in volume, but he desperately needed a weapon, his own preferably. He flung one door open: it was full of stores. Another had bedding lying on the floor. His eyes flitted around the room but could not find what he was looking for. He had to kick the last door open, then looked into a sumptuously appointed cabin with wide windows that were shuttered. He cast about, urgently; he could feel the ship lurching in its death throws, also he could smell the stench of fire and a characteristic odor he remembered all too well.

He guessed that the Greek Fire apparatus might have gone up in flames, in which case not only was the vessel doomed but everyone on it, himself among them, unless he could find an escape path without going up on deck. Then he saw his sword lying on the bed near the shutters, where someone had tossed it carelessly. He had almost reached the weapon when he became aware of a presence at the entrance to the cabin.

He ducked and whirled, just in time to avoid having his neck severed by a blade that slashed so closely that he felt the wind. Pantoleon was facing him with a long sword held in both hands.

"Were you thinking of leaving, *Sir* Talon? I think not. You must be good; those men I sent would not normally fall so easily."

He stepped forward and went through a series of rapid stabs and slashes at Talon, who had grabbed a solid wooden stool and now tried to parry the savage blows. He took a grudging step back, and the sword chopped the stool away from his hands in moments. He sensed that he was very close to the back wall of the cabin by now; there was no escape. Pantoleon grimaced.

"I wasss always good with swords, almosst as good as being a charioteer. Ssome other time I would have liked to match skills with you, but my time has run out, and so has yourss. I will take your head with me to the emperor one way or the other," he ground out, as he raised his sword point to chest height again. Talon hurled his knife directly at his midriff, which Pantoleon only just managed to parry. The blade was flicked aside to clatter to the floor, and Pantoleon laughed as Talon stood, empty-handed and defenseless, before him. "Pathetic!" he gloated.

Just then the stricken ship gave a sickening lurch and the deck beneath them tilted sharply down towards the bows. The crackle of the fire and the screams of its victims became more clear, carrying with it the stench of burning flesh and smoke as the evil liquid engulfed its victims.

Both men were thrown against the walls and fell to their knees. Talon stopped himself from sliding down to join Pantoleon, who had come up against the doorway. Talon was still without his weapon, while Pantoleon held onto his sword with his right hand. With a shout Pantoleon lunged at him, trying for a blow to his shoulder. He wasn't as balanced as he might have been and slipped onto one knee, which provided Talon with an opportunity. He dived inside Pantoleon's guard and seized his sword arm at the wrist with his left hand.

He realized very quickly that his opponent was exceedingly strong and knew he didn't have much time to hold him. Talon smashed the flat of his right palm into Pantoleon's nose. It was enough to make Pantoleon shout with anger and pain as he jerked backwards, his nose broken. While beating Pantoleon's sword arm against the wall of the cabin, Talon kept battering his face at the same time with his right fist. His enemy had never before been in a fight of this nature, so his reaction was one of surprise more than training. He didn't have the skill to parry the blows and flailed back at Talon, who with one huge effort slammed Pantoleon's sword hand against the corner of the table one last time.

The sword fell with a clatter and an angry grunt from Pantoleon, who staggered forward and tried to wrap his arms around Talon in an attempt to crush him to death in the manner of the Greek wrestlers. Talon was having none of this. He seized Pantoleon by his jerkin with both hands and kneed him viciously in the groin, then hammered his forehead into Pantoleon's face. He felt the crunch of bone and cartilage as his forehead flattened what was left of Pantoleon's once aquiline nose. But then the ship gave another lurch, and they both tumbled down the sharply sloping floor of the cabin to land in a bruised heap near the doorway. Talon was not done with his enemy; as they struggled to get up, he coldly stabbed him in his eye with his bunched fingers, as he had been taught in the Dojo in Guangzhou. With a roar of pain his opponent fell backwards, doubled over and with his hands covering his ruined eye.

"Cursse you, Talon!" he screamed in agony. "I'll cut you into pieces for that!"

They were both laboring for breath; the room was full of smoke and the floor was tilting at a very dangerous angle. It was past time to leave. His sword had fallen from the bed; Talon dodged pantoleon, dived under the table, found his weapon, and slipped it into his sash. Pantoleon would have to wait for another time. He scrambled up the sloping deck on all fours, hauled himself over the bed to reach the windows, wrenched the shutters open, then clambered out onto the narrow balcony at the back of the ship.

He cast a glance around the side of the balcony and could see that the sea towards the front of the ship was on fire, but back here there was still clear water, although it was strewn with debris and some survivors, clinging to whatever they could. He balanced briefly on the rail of the balcony, then launched himself as far out as he could into the sea below, pushing off hard with his booted feet. The leap carried him about ten paces in all, but he landed badly. The breath slammed out of him and he went deep into the cold water, feeling the drag of his sodden clothes and weapon.

Perhaps that is what saved his life, because while he was struggling to come up to the surface he noticed that the sea where he had just entered appeared to be on fire. There was nothing to do but to swim as far away as he could under water. With his lungs about to burst he surfaced, gasping for air a good thirty paces away from the doomed vessel. The ship was canted at a steep angle, air was hissing out of its windows, and rumblings were coming from deep inside. As he gasped for breath he wondered what had happened to Pantoleon.

He was not long in finding out. Pantoleon clawed his way out through the window of the cabin onto the sloping balcony. He began to scream incoherently.

"No! No more Fire! I cannot... God protect me!" he wailed as he saw below him a sea that was on fire, the flames seeming to beckon to him. He hesitated, but was then driven further out onto the railings because a long flame reached out of the cabin as though it sought to draw him back inside.

With a shriek of pure terror he threw himself as far out as he could, but it wasn't far enough. The flames on the water seemed to embrace him as he fell screaming into them. Talon watched in horror as Pantoleon surfaced once, his mouth open in a silent scream and his arm lifted to the heavens as though imploring them for help. His wig was gone and his scarred face and head were alight with clinging fire as he sank beneath the waves for the last time.

Shocked, Talon turned away to swim for a broken spar that was rising and falling in the sea nearby. He reached it and with one last enormous effort he heaved himself up. Someone was already there and he objected to Talon joining him.

"Get off! There's room for only one here, bugger off!" he shouted, and flailed at Talon. He received an elbow in his face for his trouble. He clutched his nose and lost his grip. "Ouch! Save me!" he cried and was about to sink when Talon grabbed him by his collar and dragged him back to hang onto the spar. "Be nice, or I'll let you drown!" Talon snarled at the spluttering sailor. He heaved himself up higher to see where his ships were located. A boat was picking up survivors not far away, and he recognized his brother.

"Reza ! Reza !" he croaked. "Help me!" He was already shivering in the cold water.

Reza jerked upright up in surprise and looked around. "Did you hear that?" he asked the men with him. "I could swear I heard Talon just now."

"Over here!" Talon called, and waved his arm. His sword, while a treasure with which he was loath to part, was threatening to drag him down into the deep.

Reza saw him then, and his jaw dropped open. He thumped the man nearest him on the shoulder several times. "Over there! Now!" he roared, pointing, and the rowers bent to their task with a will.

Within moments Talon was being dragged out of the water, gasping and choking, by his very surprised but pleased men.

"How in God's name did you come to be here, Brother? I was almost sure you had perished in the ship. We didn't see you after he knocked you down and the ship left the harbor." Reza babbled happily as he embraced his brother fiercely.

"Pantoleon sent me below," Talon gasped, trying to catch his breath. "You'll break a rib if you keep this up," he told Reza with a huge grin. "That might actually have saved my life but now he is dead; I watched it happen. Don't forget that sailor who was with me."

"Should really let the bastard drown," one of his own crew muttered. They all snickered, but they hauled the frightened man onto the boat to join three other bedraggled men. Reza showed them a knife and told them to behave.

Let us cast off the haze
Of the mists from our band,
Till with far-seeing gaze
We may look upon the land
And say, "See. It is ours."
—Aristophanes

Chapter 36
The Tribute and a Warning

Talon was welcomed with astonishment and delight by Guy and the crew. They were shocked that he had been taken prisoner, but he reassured them that he was fine, even with his black eye and split lip. They all looked over at the still flaming waters and the floating debris on the oily waves where Pantoleon's ship had gone down, and waited for Henry's ship to catch up with them. Talon told Guy to have Henry come over because he wanted to discuss something of importance with all of them.

Talon stood by the rail, thoughtfully watching the prisoners bound and herded into a huddle. "Keep them below for the time being, and make damned sure that not one of them can escape," he told Guy, who relayed his orders and then rejoined Talon and Reza.

"Where is that rogue Nigel? I still want to repay him for his treachery," Guy growled.

"I didn't see him. We only recovered about five prisoners," Reza told him. "Shall we execute them?" he asked.

"We will deal with them later," Talon stated. "You are very sure you picked up all the survivors?" he asked.

"We sent out two boats and rowed all around, even after the ship had gone. Couldn't get near the fire, but it's very unlikely that anyone could have survived that," Guy told him. "We were looking for you Talon, damn the rest of them!"

Talon agreed. He had watched it consume Pantoleon.

"But what about you? What happened? How in the Devil's name did you come to be captured?" the questions were hurled at him as he discarded his vest and shirt and began to dry off.

"When Henry and Rostam arrive, bring them below. I want to talk to them and you two. I'll answer all your questions when they get here," he told them. "Guy, I need a change of clothes."

494

It was about half an hour later that he heard his companions stamping down the stairs, all talking at once. They barged into the main cabin and Henry shouted.

"Talon! God be praised, you are safe. Guy and Reza told us what happened. How by the Saint's bollocks did you get caught like that! You could have been killed!"

"Calm down, Henry. As you can see, I am fine, except for a few bruises." He was embraced by them all, with an especially hard and emotional embrace from Rostam, who looked white and shaken by the garbled news he had heard from Reza and Guy. Talon grinned at him and patted him on the shoulder. "I am fine, son. Don't worry."

The boy nodded, with tears of emotion in his eyes. "I am glad you are safe, Father. We ...we all are."

"Just don't tell your mother. Right, now settle down and listen to me, all of you. Guy, where is the wine? We have things to discuss," Talon ordered.

"I think the occasion demands stronger than wine!" Guy exclaimed. He rummaged in one of his cupboards and produced a rough-looking gray stone bottle. He wrestled the cork free with a pop, then proceeded to pour some clear liquid into small glazed cups. They all drank, including Rostam, who nearly choked. Henry thumped him on the back.

"This is what real sailors drink, my lad," he said. "He can really navigate, that boy of yours, Talon," he stated, with a fond laugh at the spluttering boy.

After answering their many questions about how he had been captured, Talon raised his hand and called for silence.

"I was betrayed back there in Paphos," he told the shocked group.

After a long silence Reza spoke. "I suspected as much. Boethius?" he demanded sharply, his eyes narrowing.

"No, his secretary, or steward, as he is known. Pantoleon is clever. He had set about intimidating people like that with a view to subverting their masters much more rapidly than I had imagined. I suppose he had a lot of practice at this kind of thing. His network of spies is larger than I had imagined too. We will have to be very careful with our next moves."

He took a sip of the fiery liquid and then pretended to look very glum. He said, "The ship which you have just sunk in all your wild enthusiasms was half-full of treasure," he stated.

They gaped at him.

"Oh no!" Reza muttered. "Now *that* I call a disaster. Saving you and killing Nigel and Pantoleon was one thing, all in a day's work. "

He exchanged grins with Talon. "But losing a shipload of his treasure is quite another thing. Guy, if you please," he held out his little cup which Guy dutifully filled.

"This is a God-*dammed* disaster!" Henry muttered out loud, and Guy filled his cup. "My God, we could have all been rich!" he sighed, as he too swigged down another gulp. Guy followed suit. "Bugger me! But we didn't know, Talon!" he almost pleaded.

Talon looked amused. "I did say that it was *half* full of treasure," he reminded them. "So one more drink and then we have work to do, as I know where the other half is, and we are going to take it. So listen carefully."

On the island, Gabros was called to the walls by one of his men. "Come up here, quickly, Master!" he shouted. The call sounded urgent.

Gabros ran all the way up the stone stairs to join his guard. "Look over there, out to sea!" the man pointed in a southwesterly direction. Gabros peered in the direction shown and could see in the distance, at least five leagues away, maybe more, a tall thin column of black smoke rising into the evening air. It was too far to make out anything else, but he was sure of one thing: that was the direction the ship had sailed a few hours before.

He wondered if it had anything to do with his master. An uncomfortable sense of foreboding settled over him. Perhaps the magician had managed to escape and this was the result. He shook his head. It could not be! His master was well able to deal with anyone at sea. After all, didn't he have the Greek Fire?

Late in the night, with the aid of a thin crescent moon, two ships anchored about one hundred paces off shore to the south of the city of Paphos. They lowered their sails, but many of the oarsmen remained on standby. Other volunteers were taken to the beach in the ship's boats, the heavily armed men were ordered to absolute silence. The boats dropped them into thigh-deep water, which they waded through very quietly to join the scouts, led by Talon and Reza.

Rostam had been allowed to come, but he had been given strict orders by his father to stay close to either himself or Reza at all times. "This is not a game, Rostam. How will I explain to your mother if anything should happen? Stay close and be alert at all times," he had admonished his son.

Once the men had all landed, thirty in all, the scouts, Yosef and Dar'an, with Junayd and Khuzaymah, led the way around the outskirts of the city in the direction of the castle. This fort stood back from the city, just outside the walls, at the beginnings of the foothills to the great mountain of Trudos. It would be no easy task to take it by any means. Talon had advocated stealth, naturally, but even that was a fraught process and could very easily go wrong, in which case they would have to make a very undignified and hasty retreat to the ships. He didn't want that, but he and his companions were equally determined that the emperor would not get a free run at the treasure.

They moved quickly and silently to arrive at the base of the hill on which the castle stood. It was not a large structure but was in good condition. Its towers were well placed to allow the sentries an unobstructed view, not only of the ground below but also of the city and any shipping that came and went in the harbor.

The task that Talon and Reza set their young warriors was to climb the walls and then lower ropes. Talon sent the three men, Yosef and Dar'an in the lead and Junayd close behind. Reza was going to be there to take out any sentries on the parapet, lest an alarm be raised.

His bow at the ready, Reza watched critically as Yosef and Dar'an began the vertical climb. The walls were not smooth, which was useful to the young men, and they climbed without too much difficulty. Reaching the top they stopped to listen carefully for any sound coming from behind the parapet. Yosef went over first, followed quickly by Dar'an, and then Junayd disappeared from view, leaving Reza hoping that all was well.

He glanced up at the moon, trying to estimate the time. Talon should have managed to position himself and his men in a good place near the gates, waiting for them to be opened.

Then a figure leaned over the parapet and dropped a cord. It landed nearby and Reza hastily attached a good thick rope to it, gave a tug, and the rope was dragged up the wall.

It paused for a long minute and Reza was left wondering what might have happened. Quite suddenly a figure was pushed over the parapet. It didn't scream, just fell in a limp bundle. Reza had to dive out of the way as it landed almost on top of him with a soggy thump on the dried grass. He stared at the body of one of the luckless guards, then he looked up, and another figure leaned out and waved. The rope began to move again, and finally it was jerked, which meant that it was secure.

Reza waved to the other small group of men, all burly oarsmen, who rushed silently up to the base of the wall.The first man began to clamber up the wall, using the rope. He carried a coil of rope with him and upon reaching the top he dropped the length to the waiting men below. Men swarmed up the two ropes, and before very long there were eight men crouching on the walkway. Yosef and Dar'an had gone ahead and were watching for any other sentries. Reza joined them, and Yosef pointed to one walking slowly along the walkway farther along the wall.

"Go and do it," Reza tapped him on the shoulder. Yosef sped off, and within a minute the sentry was dead and thrown off the wall. The sound of a body thumping onto the ground below came to Reza. "Time to go!" he whispered urgently to his men. They scampered along the wall and down the stone steps towards the gates. They had just made it to the gates when an alert soldier noticed the activity. He gave a shout of alarm and began to run towards the scene, but Reza drew his bow on the running man. In one swift motion an arrow was on its way and the sentry died, choking on his own blood from his pierced throat. Reza signaled to the men to open the doors.

The bars were lifted and the gates pushed open by the sailors, and Talon's men began to move across the threshold.

Some guard must have silently raised an alarm, for men began to pour out of the main bailey to defend the castle. They were met in the court by dark figures who attacked ferociously. The battle was brief but savage, with casualties on both sides. Men fell in silent struggle to the ground, stabbing or hacking at each other with their swords. Talon and Reza, after shooting some arrows into the enemy at the onset, joined in the fight, Talon calling to Rostam to stay close.

It wasn't long before he came up against Gabros. There was a small space around him that he had cleared. In the moonlight he stood at bay with a dripping sword and several of Talon's men lying wounded around him.

He saw Talon pushing his way towards him through the struggling fighters and shouted a challenge. "I knew it must be you! Come here, Magician, where I can cut you down! I'm not afraid of you!" he yelled, and jumped forward swinging a vicious blow at Rostam who ducked just in time and leapt to the side.

"Not today, Rostam." Reza hauled the boy to the side by his shield arm. "This is between your father and that man. Watch and learn."

The noise of fighting died down. Almost all of Gabros's mercenaries were dead or badly wounded. Reza quietly told his men to finish them off, which left Gabros standing and a couple of his best warriors with their backs to the bailey wall.

"So, no prisoners, eh!" Gabros grunted.

"No prisoners," Talon agreed.

"What did you do with my master?" Gabros asked, as he went into a crouch, his sword leveled at Talon. It glittered in the moonlight.

"He is in hell, and his ship is at the bottom of the sea, his treasure with it."

"So you have come for the rest." Gabros didn't wait for a reply. He leapt forward and swung his sword in a short arc, his shield held across his chest.

Talon stood his ground in the stance he had learned on the dojo in China, and his blade flicked the other's away, then flashed forward. Gabros only just had time to step sideways, but the tip of the blade still managed to slice a shallow cut into his sword arm. There was a sigh from the men gathered around, watching.

He blinked and took a pace back; his eyes betrayed the fact that he was startled. He was a good swordsman by any standard, but this menacing calm and speed unnerved him.

Gabros was not short of courage, so he lunged again and then followed up with several strikes and swings that were either parried or avoided. Then he made a bid to get in close where he could use his skill with the pommel and shield. It was a mistake; he took a sharp blow on his shield which made him lift it just enough to allow Talon to strike like a cobra.

His blade slid past the edge of the Gabros's shield and buried itself deep in his upper chest. Before he could react, other than to gasp with the pain and surprise, his opponent was back on guard, the tip of his blade level with Gabros's eyes, which now showed pain but also fear. Gabros knew he was mortally wounded.

Holding his head high he staggered towards Talon with the aim of one last bid to kill him, but his legs gave way and he went down on one knee. Before the astonished men, Talon's blade flashed one more time and Gabros's head was taken off to fall into the dust, before his body followed it with a dull thud.

There was complete silence for a long moment. All of Talon's had been sworn to silence, and Reza with his men had emphasized this need. There had been cries from the dying and wounded, but for the most part the entire battle had been fought in silence. Now it was profound.

Reza was the first to move and speak. "All of you. Spread out and find out if there are any other men hiding. No one is to be spared. Go!" he called out. His men rushed to obey. The two men who had remained with Gabros were despatched without ceremony. Talon didn't want news of any kind to get out until he was well done with what he had come to do.

By dawn they had full control of the castle and were looking down on the harbor. There were few ships in the pool, but Talon wanted to make sure of the spies. He sent Yosef with Junayd to the house of Boethius, to reassure the merchant that he was no longer a prisoner. Talon didn't doubt that Boethius would be keeping a low profile until he knew more.

"You are to tell Boethius that his steward is a traitor and he should be dealt with appropriately. Tell him to find an opportunity to come up to the castle as discretely as he can," Talon told Yosef. "You and the other boys are to deal with the spies tonight." Yosef grinned and left, looking happy. Talon looked at Reza for confirmation.

"They are very good, Brother. Not as good as you or I," he grinned, "but still, they are good. I agree, cleanse the city and let it have some peace."

Another messenger was sent to the ships to order them into the harbor that evening, when the loading would take place.

In all, they discovered twelve small chests full of gold ingots or gold coins, stacked down in the dungeons. "This is a king's fortune!" Reza exclaimed when they had opened a couple to verify the contents.

"I suspect that it really was an Emperor's fortune, Brother. I think Pantoleon stole this from the palace in Constantinople." He thought for a moment, then said, "Two for Boethius, which will make him very rich and allow him to buy a ship, perhaps. His business should prosper from here on."

"Dimitri?" Reza asked.

"Two for him. He will use it well, of that I am sure. Dimitri is very, very discrete." Talon laughed with Reza over that. Their former oarsman had come up in the world.

"We will take seven of them with us tonight, along with the ones for Dimitri."

"What about the other one?" Reza asked, looking puzzled.

"I shall explain later. Do you have the letter from Salah Ed Din?"

"Yes, of course. It is on Guy's ship."

"I want to hear all about the visit, but meanwhile we need to be ready by tonight, and Boethius must find us some donkeys."

Reza remarked later, while standing on the walls watching the city waking up, that the castle appeared to have had gained a sinister reputation because of Pantoleon.

"I went below and what I found was terrible. He didn't waste any time in bringing victims to the fort for his pleasure," he said to Talon. They went down together to look at the dreadful scene. Talon, hardened as he was to bloodshed, shuddered. The sickening evidence was there to be seen in the blood-bespattered cell where Pantoleon had worked. He imagined the horror in store for Boethius and his daughter, had they not been saved.

"The world is well rid of that monster. I shall take great pleasure in telling Theo," Talon said. "Ah, here comes a small party of visitors. I believe it is Boethius."

It was indeed Boethius, who was both shocked and delighted that Talon had survived. "Nasuh came back very agitated and told me that you had been captured by none other than Exazenos!" he told them. "I was worried sick, and since then we have been staying close to the villa, wondering what to do next. Then Yosef arrived told me of my steward." He paused and collected his emotions. "I could not let him off, Talon. I did as you told me. Yosef dealt with it. We will have to sniff out the others in this sad town, if we are not to live in fear all the time. If I had a ship I would have left, that's for sure," he said.

"Well, now you can afford a ship, but I don't want you to leave." Talon said, and showed the merchant the two chests that he had put aside for him. Boethius's eyes popped at the sight of the gold.

"Spend it very carefully, as the spies will switch allegiance to the emperor soon enough. However, I expect our men to deal with the ones that Pantoleon left behind before I leave."

He then went on to explain to Boethius who Exazenos had really been. Boethius gave a dazed shake of his head at the information.

"When Exazenos arrived in Paphos, rumors spread of a maniac who swam in blood and was close to Andronicus," he said. "People fear this place so much they dared not investigate, but those of us who remembered what happened in Constantinople began to put it all together. I am relieved to hear that he is in hell."

"I have need of your help this evening, and then there is one more task I ask of you before I leave," Talon said.

"Anything. Ah Talon," Boethius said, his voice full of emotion. "I had such a very bad night. I don't know what we would have done without you." He wiped a tear from his eyes.

Later Reza asked Talon, "Are the Greeks always this emotional?"

"Some are. I really think he would have missed me," Talon said, pretending to be thoughtful about it.

Reza gave a derisive snort and dodged a cuff that was aimed at him. "Look out, here comes Rostam. We'll have to behave like grown ups, as Max would put it," he laughed.

That evening, just before dusk had settled upon the city of Paphos, two ships sailed into the harbor. They tied up alongside the quay and gave the appearance of settling down for the night.

Much later a convoy of donkeys made its way onto the quay, where they were greeted by men from the ships who unloaded their bulky loads, after which the donkeys made their way off into the darkness and disappeared. To anyone watching, this might have been unusual and worth reporting.

As it happened no one was watching, since the former spies were lying dead in alleyways, to be discovered the next day by fishermen leaving for their work. No one had heard a thing. Two ships left at first light and disappeared out to sea, with no one the wiser as to why they had come and gone so quickly.

It became evident that the strange man form the castle, Exazenos, had departed, rumor saying that he'd taken an important prisoner with him and left his men to guard the castle, waiting upon his return. The citizens discussed the situation with apprehension. Stories abounded of what he had done in the dungeons of Famagusta, and no one wanted him to take up residence here.

Meanwhile, a pigeon had winged its way to the castle on the ridge with a message. Another had then been sent to Famagusta and arrived late the following day. Dimitri read the message tied to its leg and smiled.

A week later, Siranus delivered a message to Tamura from the spy who worked for the "man on the mountain". It caused her some confusion.

"Are you sure?" she demanded, wondering how she was going to pass along this kind of information to the suspicious and paranoid

Isaac, who had begun looking even at her with suspicion. Despite his erratic behavior he was not a complete fool, especially where his own survival was concerned, and he'd sensed that her behavior towards him had changed after the arrival of Exazenos, despite every effort on her part not to make it obvious.

"They are saying that the emperor should go to Paphos and take back the castle before it is too late," she said with a puzzled expression on her face. "How am I going to tell him that without giving myself away?" she wondered out loud. "Besides, isn't Exazenos there? Who has taken the castle?"

It had gradually dawned upon her that Exazenos was a monster who loved to destroy people in the most painful manner he could devise. Despite this, she had held onto the thought that the new devil was better than the one she hated most, until he had turned on her and threatened her with exposure. Now she felt alone and terribly vulnerable.

"I want to see this man and ask him directly," she stated to Siranus. "This doesn't make sense. Exazenos is in Paphos. He told me and the emperor that was where he was going."

Siranus agreed reluctantly to set a meeting up. A day later, he told her that it was all prepared. She could go to the cathedral, where she would be met.

Tamura excused herself to go to the Cathedral and pray. Isaac didn't monitor her activities that closely. She set out for the cathedral, making it obvious where she was going, and reached the cool gloomy building with its beautiful rounded archways in the afternoon, when a service was in process.

The priest was preoccupied, as were his acolytes, so it was not a problem for her to genuflect respectfully towards the altar and move slowly towards the dark shadows of the building, near to a thick pillar of stone. She watched her surroundings, careful of spies whom she was sure were everywhere, now that Exazenos was in charge of that department. At a fluted pillar she stood very still and waited.

A voice spoke to her from nearby that made her jump, she was so nervous. She shot a glance in the direction of Siranus, who had followed her in to watch her back, and he nodded.

"Madame, you wanted to know more about Paphos?"

"Yes, what is happening there?" she demanded, peering into the gloom. There was the figure of a stocky-looking man, but he was covered up, including his face, and his head was covered by a hood. As though anticipating her the figure said, "Please do not look at me, my Lady. Just listen." She turned away and stared up at the arches above.

"You must not disclose what I am about to tell you. Not yet."

"Very well, I am listening."

"The emperor will find out in due course that the man he knows as Exazenos is dead."

She gasped. "Dead?" she almost shrilled. Her voice was raised enough for him to lift a hand. "Please keep your voice down, my Lady," he admonished her.

"But how?" she whispered fiercely, her mind working with furious speed.

"That is not your concern, my Lady. Suffice it to say you need to keep this information to yourself for the time being and persuade the emperor to go to Paphos, and urgently, before it is too late. Tell him that Exazenos left some information behind inadvertently and one of the servants 'discovered' it."

Tamura was stunned. It had been over two weeks now since Pantoleon had departed and no word had come back to her, confirming her fears. She had hoped for something. Had they not declared for each other and had she not intimated that she was a willing agent against the emperor? Now in the blink of an eye all that had changed. "I... I need to think about this," she stammered.

"Yes, you should do that, my Lady. It has not escaped our attention that you were taking sides, and as you well know the wrong side can mean disaster," the figure said. His tone was dry. "Yes, we have other spies in the palace, my Lady, but... we value you."

Tamura felt cold. The words carried a threat she could not ignore, but at the same time some encouragement, so she lifted her pretty chin and said, "I shall tell the emperor and keep quiet about the other news."

"This should make it easier for you," the figure said, and thrust a package towards her.

"What is it?" she demanded.

"The letter you will show the emperor. This will convince him that Exazenos was going to betray him."

"He was?" she asked shocked.

"Read the letter, my Lady."

Tamura took the package and looked down at it. It was not sealed. When she looked up again the messenger had vanished. Again she felt a cold sensation trickle down her back. These people were truly frightening.

Collecting Siranus she hastened back to the palace, and in the privacy of her chamber discussed the situation with him. They opened the package and found a letter from a merchant in Tyre addressed to Pantoleon. They looked at one another and nodded their heads in agreement. This was damning, even if it was a forgery, which Tamura was sure it was.

Tamura and the emperor were seated in the gardens of the palace, enjoying the spring air. The garden was coming alive with buds and flowers, the fountain bubbled and gurgled to itself, and the leopards were safely caged, while some of the youthful hostages were practicing an elaborate dance on the lawn a few dozen paces away.

The food on the table was basic. Isaac liked his olives with bread and oil. The second course of wild game was due in a few minutes, and he was enjoying some new wine that his Chief minister had recommended. He appeared to have relaxed since his new chief spy had gone off to attend to business. Exazenos had frightened more than just the servants. Wherever he went in the palace he left a sense of darkness behind him. Tamura waited until Isaac had drunk another cup of wine before she asked him, as casually as possible, "Do you know what our chief spy is doing, my Lord?"

"Gone to Paphos to terrify the locals, I dare say. He has been gone for longer than I expected." Isaac chuckled, but it was a nervous laugh. "He even scares me, that one. He's done a good job with the other cities," Isaac replied more comfortably. His chief spy had cowed the nobles in their castles to the point where he, Isaac, didn't worry so much about an insurrection from that direction any more. He left unsaid how very uncertain he had become of his lieutenant, whose attitude had changed in subtle ways; before he'd left he had begun to behave less respectfully.

"Anyway, why do you ask?" he demanded, as he spat out an olive stone and took another swig of wine. "Good wine, this; a little new but it has potential," Isaac said savoring the ruby liquid.

"I think you should see this then, my Lord. It came to me, er, quite by accident. A nosey servant brought it to me from his room. I had him whipped but then I saw what it said and feel it my duty to bring it to you."

Isaac opened the folded sheet and began to read. Slowly his face turned purple and his eyes bulged as his mouth pouted. He gripped the paper and shook it with so much force that it tore in his hand.

"This, this scum of a merchant in Tyre is saying that once Exazenos has claimed Paphos he will provide more ships and men!" he exclaimed, drumming his heels. "The traitor! The filthy traitor!" he bellowed. All his good mood evaporated in an instant and he began to look for things to kick and throw about in the garden. A monster tantrum was on its way. The dancers vanished from the lawn.

"My Lord! My Lord! I beg of you be calm," Tamura implored him. "You must be calm, my Lord!" she cried again, clutching at his forearm. "To be enraged just now will only blur your vision; there is real danger here! You must be clear-headed about this issue or you, we, *all* of us will be in jeopardy. Remember, you yourself said that he is very cunning and dangerous!"

Isaac's blood pressure slowly subsided and he settled back into his chair in a slump. He took a deep breath and looked at her. Then he patted her hand.

"Of course, my Dear. You are perfectly right. Where would I be without you, my lovely angel?" he murmured. "I sensed that he was considering treachery before he left. Now we know for sure. The *baastaard!*" He shouted, savoring the word. "By God but he shall pay and pay again for that!" He straightened his back and shouted for his servants, who had been cowering in anticipation of a tantrum.

"Get me Diocles this instant!"

Diocles appeared like a genie from nowhere and stood trembling in front of the still heated emperor. "Your Highness?" he enquired, wringing his hands.

"Stop shaking, you dithering old fart, and tell the horse guards we are leaving within the hour."

"Where, where might we be going, Your Highness?"

"To Paphos, you fool, where else? You will stay here and mind the palace. I want all the people who work for Exazenos arrested and in prison by the time I get back."

The guards on the castle walls overlooking the city of Paphos were bored. Their job was to guard the locked chest down in the dungeon and to keep a lookout for any royal soldiers that might be coming to Paphos. Talon had assured them that they would sooner or later. One of them noticed a donkey with a man walking alongside coming up the wide path towards the gates. The rider halted the donkey, which seemed glad to do so as its load looked heavy.

"What do you want?" called down one of the men on the wall.

"I brought the wine that was ordered," the man called back up squinting in the sunlight.

"Wine you say? Wine? Never ordered any."

"Yes, you did, about a week ago. You owe me for this! You people ordered it and now you should pay!" the driver retorted. He sounded very cross.

"Get lost and don't come back," the man on the wall shouted.

"Damn you! I went to a lot of trouble to bring this up to this God-forsaken pile of stones!"

"If you don't go away I'll show you what you will look like with my spear rammed up your arse! Go away, and do it now!"

Grumbling and swearing, the man hauled his donkey around and walked slowly out of sight back towards the town.

Then one of the lookouts on the walls called the leader over, saying, "Nasuh, come and look at this. I see cavalry."

Nasuh trotted over to where his companion stood staring down towards the eastern walls of Paphos.

"They've arrived," he grunted. "We'll let them get close enough to see us moving about, then we'll leave. Put the figures up along the wall, then our task is done."

They clustered together, ready to depart via the back entrance, and watched as the horsemen clattered through the city, then turned onto the dirt track that led up to the castle. When the cavalry unit was within two hundred paces of the castle, they looked up and saw what they took to be men on the walls.

Shouting and gesticulating, they milled about on the ground in front of the gates, which were locked and barred. Calling up to one of the more exposed figures, the leader of the cavalry shouted, "Open up, in the name of the emperor!"

No one responded. "Get his attention!" Isaac ordered. With a glance at his leader, who nodded, one of the more enterprising of the horsemen loosed off a bolt at the figure standing silently thirty feet above them. The bolt struck the stone, chipping it very close by the sentry, but the man did not even flinch, nor look their way. None of the other sentries on the walls moved either, which was also very odd. A second bolt flew and struck the wall nearby again, but still no movement.

"My Lord, they are dummies!" exclaimed the leader of the riders to Isaac, who was seated next to him. "There is no one there!"

Isaac began to get angry. "Either get over the walls or break down the gates. I don't care how you do this!" he roared. He was tired from the long, three day ride and wanted nothing more than a good rest.

An hour later the gates had been battered open, and Isaac and his men entered a deserted castle courtyard.

"Where is that traitor?" Isaac roared. "Search the entire place for him! For anyone!"

His men spread out in small groups, weapons at the ready. Later, a soldier came up to Isaac, who was standing impatiently in the yard, tapping his boot with his whip. "My Lord," he said respectfully, "there is nobody here but we have found something. It was down in the dungeons, we are bringing it up now."

A few minutes later, the emperor's commander led the way out with two men struggling along behind him carrying a small but clearly very heavy chest. They placed it thankfully down on the ground in front of Isaac and stood back.

"Open it."

The cavalry officer beat the lock off the chest with a borrowed axe, then opened the chest. The men around gasped at the sight. It was identical to the first chest of gold that Exazenos had brought to the emperor when he had first come to him. Then the cavalry officer handed Isaac a note. It ran:

"This is the tribute for the next few years. Use it well."

Isaac studied the letter for a long moment. "So where is this traitor, Exazenos?" he demanded, "Where has he gone?" He knew well enough from where the note had come and he was afraid; but where was his chief spy?

"Your Highness?"

"What is it?"

"There is another letter in the chest. The leader handed over to Isaac a ribbon-bound roll of paper with an unmistakeable seal on it. He stared, recognition dawning on his face. Then, with a shaking hand that belied his confidence in the bragged about "friendship", he broke the seal and unrolled the missive.

The letter was from Sultan Salah Ed Din and contained all the flowery greetings that would come from one as exalted as he; there was no mistaking the seal nor the flourish if his own handwriting. It greeted him with great respect and affection, but the contents of the letter burned itself into Isaac's mind.

"Leave Sir Talon undisturbed. He is my friend."

"Take this chest back with us," the emperor said in a hoarse voice, his face flushed. "We leave for Famagusta tonight. Garrison the castle and secure it," he said shortly, and mounted his horse, only too eager to be out of this gloomy and now ominous fortress. He had an uneasy feeling, tinged with a whisper of relief, that he might never see Exazenos again.

A month passed, and another, but there was still no sign of Exazenos. It was as though he and the men who had been with him in Paphos had vanished into thin air. The emperor sent men to all his cities to make enquiries, but no one could help. There were a few in Paphos who thought he had left on a ship, but none were sure.

The mystery remained why he should have left when he had so much going for him. The chest full of gold presented its own puzzle, but Isaac was richer now and there was less need to plunder. He remained in his palace in Famagusta and took up his life with Tamura, who was by now firmly ensconced as his wife in all but name.

With her newly established position she settled scores with a few of her rivals; her power was such that she could banish whomsoever she liked from the palace. Several of the women in Isaac's harem were turfed out to survive as best they could on the streets and a couple of slaves turned up drowned in the harbor.

Isaac hung all the men who had been followers of Exazenos, and some who had not. What were a few innocent lives compared to his own security? Isaac didn't venture back to Paphos for a long time, thus enabling the city to recover from his depredations and reestablish some of its once flourishing maritime trade.

The one person who thought he might know what had happened to Exazenos, although not exactly how, was not talking. Diocles, who continued to act as the First Minister, kept his thoughts to himself.

A disconcerting moment came for him one sunny day months later, when Tamura accosted him in the gardens and asked him.

"Where did you go on that winter's day, Diocles? Was it to the Man on the Mountain? My slave saw you leave and head in that direction."

He nodded, guardedly and afraid, but she smiled and said, "I think I know why. That was courageous. Perhaps we should be thanking you?"

His respect for Tamura went up several notches. This young and quite beautiful woman was maturing into a queen. Perhaps between them they could contain Isaac's brutal excesses.

He followed her gaze towards the far distant enigmatic castle, perched on the knife edged mountain. It was now known to one and all as the home of the Assassins of Kantara. Perhaps its Lord, Sir Talon, might assist in that exacting task.

The End

Author's note.

I try hard to keep the 'Historical' aspect of my stories accurate. No tomatoes with their lettuce at that time! There's no point in changing the rich and extraordinary tapestry of history for the sake of a story. It misleads. However a story can be woven into that same tapestry and this is where Talon comes in.

Kantara castle, as some of you might know, actually exists. You can google it. The castle is located exactly as I have described on the long arm of Cyprus. In Turkish lands at present.

It was originally built by the Byzantines, once they had ousted the Arabs to help keep watch for their possible return and for pirates of course.

The view from the castle is truly magnificent! It was built in the 10th century but not very much at all has been recorded about it's history. Which is why it was too tempting to ignore and Talon and his people took the opportunity to steal it! What was he to do? You can't storm a place like that, but guile and skill can be used to good effect as has been proved time and again. Remember where he came from?

Isaac Komnenos was a horrible man as was his great uncle, Andronicus Komnenos, who ruled in Constantinople and who met the deserved death I have described. It is hard to imagine what life must have been like under these awful tyrants but people managed somehow. More on that perhaps later. For now Talon and family have a place to call their own. Who knows what might happen next?

James Boschert

About The Author

James Boschert

James Boschert grew up in the then colony of Malaya in the early fifties. He learned first-hand about terrorism while there as the Communist insurgency was in full swing. His school was burnt down and the family, while traveling, narrowly survived an ambush, saved by a Gurkha patrol, which drove off the insurgents.

He went on to join the British army serving in remote places like Borneo and Oman. Later he spent five years in Iran before the revolution, where he played polo with the Iranian Army, developed a passion for the remote Assassin castles found in the high mountains to the North, and learned to understand and speak the Farsi language.

Escaping Iran during the revolution, he went on to become an engineer and now lives in Arizona on a small ranch with his family and animals.

If You Enjoyed This Book

Please write a review.

This is important to the author and helps to get the word out to others.
Visit

PENMORE PRESS

www.penmorepress.com

All Penmore Press books are available directly through our website, amazon.com, Barnes and Noble and Nook, Sony Reader, Apple iTunes, Kobo books and via leading bookshops across the United States, Canada, the UK, Australia and Europe.

OTHER TALON BOOKS BY JAMES BOSCHERT

ASSASSINS OF ALAMUT
BY
JAMES BOSCHERT

An Epic Novel of Persia and Palestine in the Time of the Crusades

Knight Assassin
The second book of Talon

by

James Boschert

Assassination

in

Al Qahira
James Boschert

GREEK FIRE
BY
JAMES BOSCHERT

A Falcon Flies
by
James Boschert
The fifth book of Talon

Force 12 in
German Bight
by
James Boschert

Considering that oil and gas have been flowing from under the North Sea for the best part of half a century, it is perhaps surprising that more writers have not taken the uncompromising conditions that are experienced in this area – which extends from the north of Scotland to the coasts of Norway and Germany – for the setting of a novel. James Boschert's latest redresses the balance.

The book takes its title from the name of an area regularly referred to in the legendary BBC Shipping Forecast, one which experiences some of the worst weather conditions around the British Isles. It is a fast-paced story which smacks of authenticity in every line. A world of hard men, hard liquor, hard drugs and cold-blooded murder. The reality of the setting and the characters, ex-military men from both sides of the Atlantic, crooked wheeler-dealers, and Danish detectives, male and female, are all in on the action.

This is not story telling akin to a latter day Bulldog Drummond, nor a James Bond, but simply a snortingly good yarn which will jangle the nerve ends, fill your nose with the smell of salt and diesel oil, your ears with the deafening sound of machinery aboard a monster pipe-dredging ship and, above all, make you remember never to underestimate the power of the sea.

–Roger Paine, former Commander, Royal Navy .

PENMORE PRESS
www.penmorepress.com

When the Jungle Is Silent

by
James Boschert

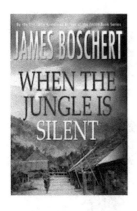

Set in Borneo during a little known war known as "the Confrontation," this story tells of the British soldiers who fought in one of the densest jungles in the world.

Jason, a young soldier of the Light Infantry who is good with guns, is stationed in Penang, an idyllic island off the coast of Malaysia. He is living aimlessly in paradise until he meets Megan, a bright and intelligent young American from the Peace Corps. Megan challenges his complacent existence and a romance develops, but then the regiment is sent off to Borneo.

After a dismal shipping upriver, the regiment arrives in Kuching, the capital of Sarawak. Jason is moved up to Padawan, close to local populations of Ibans and Dyak headhunters, and right in the path of the Indonesian offensive. Fighting erupts along the border of Sarawak and a small fort is turned into a muddy hell from which Jason is an unlikely survivor.

An SAS Sergeant and his trackers have been drawn to the vicinity by the battle, but who will find Jason first: rescuers or hostiles? Jason is forced to wake up to the cruel harshness of real soldiering while he endeavors stay one step ahead of the Indonesians who are combing the Jungle. And the jungle itself, although neutral, is deadly enough.

PENMORE PRESS
www.penmorepress.com

Penmore Press

Challenging, Intriguing, Adventurous, Historical and Imaginative

www.penmorepress.com